Miami Blu

Ex-con Freddy 'Junior' Frenger lands in Miami with stolen credit cards and plans for a new life of crime, and disappears with a snatched suitcase, leaving the corpse of a Hare Krishna devotee behind him. Homicide detective Hoke Moseley is soon on his case, chasing Junior and his hooker girlfriend through the Cuban ghettos, luxury hotels and seedy suburbs of Miami in a perilous game of hide and seek.

New Hope for the Dead

Sergeant Hoke Moseley is called to investigate the death of a young junkie in upscale Miami. But what seems like a routine OD gives Moseley cause to doubt – particularly when he meets the kid's stunning stepmother. With his two teenage daughters dumped on him by his ex-wife, a new beat partner struggling with an unplanned pregnancy and cold cases to solve, a dead junkie and his beautiful stepmother feel like the answer to Hoke's prayers . . .

Sideswipe

Sergeant Hoke Moseley's life is going to hell: his ex-wife just remarried, his teenage daughters want to quit school and his heavily pregnant beat partner is living in his house. A break seems long overdue, so Hoke decides to bail and watch the ocean roll. Then a handsome, cowboy-hatted psychopath plans another armed robbery, drawing a retiree into a life of crime and leaving half-a-dozen bystanders dead. A case right up Hoke's alley: weird, personal and twisted enough to make Hoke forget he no longer wants to be a cop.

The Way We Die Now

Hoke Moseley is stressed: his chief is making ominous plans for him, a man he sent down for murder has moved into his street and he's stuck on a tough cold case. The last thing he needs is an undercover job, just as he's beginning to make headway with his work. South of Miami he is taken as a migrant worker to a farm where rumours of murder and slavery are rife. With only a Filipino prostitute and his wits to protect him, Hoke faces vicious rednecks and his own scheming boss in this vibrant masterpiece of hard-boiled fiction.

Charles Willeford was a professional horse trainer, boxer, radio announcer and painter. He was also a highly decorated tank commander (Silver Star, Bronze Star, Purple Heart, Luxembourg Croix de Guerre) with the Third Army in the Second World War. Willeford is the author of twenty novels, and created the Miami detective series featuring Hoke Moseley.

HOKE MOSELEY OMNIBUS

Miami Blues
New Hope for the Dead
Sideswipe
The Way We Die Now

CHARLES WILLEFORD

An Orion paperback

Miami Blues first published in the USA in 1984
by St Martin's Press
New Hope for the Dead first published in the USA in 1985
by St Martin's Press
Sideswipe first published in the USA in 1987
by St Martin's Press
The Way We Die Now first published in the USA in 1988
by Random House
This omnibus edition published in 2015
by Orion Books,
an imprint of The Orion Publishing Group Ltd,
Carmelite House, 50 Victoria Embankment,
London EC4Y 0DZ

An Hachette UK company

3 5 7 9 10 8 6 4 2

A CIP catalogue record for this book
is available from the British Library.

ISBN 978-1-4091-6062-5

Printed and bound in Great Britain by
CPI Group (UK) Ltd Croydon, CR0 4YY
Typeset by Born Group within Book Cloud

The Orion Publishing Group's policy is to use papers that
are natural, renewable and recyclable products and
made from wood grown in sustainable forests. The logging
and manufacturing processes are expected to conform to
the environmental regulations of the country of origin.

www.orionbooks.co.uk

Contents

BOOK 1

Miami Blues

Haiku
Morning sun stripes cell.
Five fingers feel my hard heart.
It hurts, hurts, like hell.

F. J. Frenger, Jr

For Betsy

Chapter One

Frederick J. Frenger, Jr, a blithe psychopath from California, asked the flight attendant in first class for another glass of champagne and some writing materials. She brought him a cold half-bottle, uncorked it and left it with him, and returned a few moments later with some Pan Am writing paper and a white ball point pen. For the next hour, as he sipped champagne, Freddy practiced writing the signatures of Claude L. Bytell, Ramon Mendez, and Herman T. Gotlieb.

The signatures on his collection of credit cards, driver's licenses, and other ID cards were difficult to imitate, but by the end of the hour and the champagne, when it was time for lunch – martini, small steak, baked potato, salad, chocolate cake, and two glasses of red wine – Freddy decided that he was close enough to the originals to get by.

The best way to forge a signature, he knew, was to turn it upside down and draw it instead of trying to imitate the handwriting. That was the foolproof way, if a man had the time and the privacy and was forging a document or a check. But to use stolen credit cards, he knew he had to sign charge slips casually, in front of clerks and store managers who might be alert for irregularities.

Still, close enough was usually good enough for Freddy. He was not a careful person, and a full hour was a long time for him to engage in any activity without his mind turning to something else. As he looked through the three wallets he found himself wondering about their owners. One wallet was eelskin, another was imitation ostrich, and the third was a plain cowhide billfold filled with color snapshots of very plain children. Why would any man want to carry around photographs of ugly children in his wallet? And why would anyone buy imitation ostrich, when you could get an authentic ostrich-skin wallet for only two or three hundred dollars more? Eelskin he could understand; it was soft and durable, and the longer you carried it in your hip pocket the softer it got. He decided to keep the eelskin one. He crammed all of the credit cards and IDs into it, along with the photos of the ugly children, and shoved the two emptied wallets into the pocket of the seat in front of him, behind the in-flight magazine.

Comfortably full, and a trifle dizzy from the martini and the wine, Freddy stretched out in the wide reclining seat, hugging the tiny airline pillow. He slept soundly until the attendant awakened him gently and asked him to fasten his seat belt for the descent into Miami International Airport.

Freddy had no baggage, so he wandered through the mammoth airport listening to the announcements that boomed from multiple speakers, first in Spanish and then, half as long, in English. He was eager to get a cab and to find a hotel, but he also wanted some nice-looking luggage. Two pieces would be better than one, but he would settle for a Vuitton one-suiter if he could find one. He paused for a moment to light a Winston and reconnoiter a long line of American tourists and diminutive Indian men and women going to the Yucatán Peninsula. The vacationers kept very close to their baggage, and the Indians pushed along large boxes held together with strips of gray duct tape. Nothing for him there.

A Hare Krishna, badly disguised in jeans, a sports shirt, and a powder-blue sports jacket, his head covered with an ill-fitting brown wig, stepped up to Freddy and pinned a red-and-white-striped piece of stick candy to Freddy's gray suede sports jacket. As the pin went into the lapel of the $287 jacket, charged the day before to a Claude L. Bytell at Macy's in San Francisco, Freddy was seized with a sudden rage. He could take the pin out, of course, but he knew that the tiny pinhole would be there forever because of this asshole's carelessness.

'I want to be your friend,' the Hare Krishna said, 'and –'

Freddy grasped the Hare Krishna's middle finger and bent it back sharply. The Krishna yelped. Freddy applied sharper pressure and jerked the finger backward, breaking it. The Krishna screamed, a high-pitched gargling sound, and collapsed onto his knees. Freddy let go of the dangling finger, and as the Krishna bent over, screaming, his wig fell off, exposing his shaved head.

Two men, obviously related, who had watched the whole encounter, broke into applause and laughed. When a middle-aged woman wearing a Colombian poncho heard one of the tourists say 'Hare Krishna,' she took a Krishna Kricket out of her purse and began to click the metal noisemaker in the pain-racked Krishna's face. The injured Krishna's partner, dressed similarly but wearing a black wig, came over from the line he was working at Aeroméxico and began to berate the woman for snapping the Kricket. The elder of the two laughing men came up behind him, snatched off his wig, and threw it over the heads of the gathering crowd.

Freddy, who had slipped away from the scene, went into the men's room next to the bar on Concourse D and took the stick of candy out of his lapel. In a mirror he examined the pinhole and smoothed it out. A stranger would never notice it, he decided, but the flaw was there, even though it wasn't as bad as he had thought it would be. Freddy dropped the stick of candy into his jacket pocket, took a quick leak, washed his hands, and walked out.

A young woman slept soundly in a row of hard-plastic airport chairs. A two-year-old boy sat beside her quietly, hugging a toy panda. The wide-eyed child, drooling slightly, had his feet resting on a one-suiter with the Cardin logo repeated on its light blue fabric. Freddy stopped in front of the boy, unwrapped the stick of candy, and offered it to him with a smile. The boy smiled back, took the candy shyly, and put one end in his mouth. As the boy sucked it, Freddy took the suitcase and walked away. He took the Down escalator to the outside ramp and hailed a Yellow cab. The Cuban driver, who spoke little English, finally smiled and nodded when Freddy said simply, 'Hotel. Miami.'

The cabbie lit a cigarette with his right hand and swung into the heavy traffic with his left, narrowly missing an old lady and her granddaughter. He cut in front of a Toyota, making the driver stall his engine, and headed for the Dolphin Expressway. By this route he managed to get Freddy into downtown Miami and to the front of the International Hotel in twenty-two minutes. The meter read $8.37. Freddy gave the driver a ten, handed his suitcase to the doorman, and registered at the desk as Herman T. Gotlieb, San Jose, California, using Gotlieb's credit card. He took a

$135-a-day suite and signed the charge slip in advance, then followed the fat Latin bellman to the elevator. Just before the elevator reached the seventh floor, the bellman spoke up:

'If there's anything you want, Mr Gotlieb, please let me know.'

'I can't think of anything right now.'

'What I mean …' the bellman cleared his throat.

'I understand what you're saying, but I don't want a girl right now.'

The bedroom was small, but the sitting room was furnished pleasantly with a comfortable couch and an easy chair in matching blue-and-white stripes, a desk with a glass top, and a small bar with two stools. The refrigerator behind the bar held vodka, gin, Scotch, and bourbon, several rows of mixers, and a split of champagne. There was a price list taped to the door. Freddy looked at the list and thought that the per-drink prices were outrageous. He gave the bellman $2.

'Thank you, sir. And if you need me for anything at all, just call down to the bell captain and ask for Pablo.'

'Pablo. Fine. Where's the beach, Pablo? I might want to go for a swim later.'

'The beach? We're on Biscayne Bay, sir, not the ocean. The ocean's over there in Miami Beach. But we have a nice pool on the roof, and a sauna. And if you want a massage –'

'No, that's okay. I just thought that Miami was on the ocean.'

'No, sir. That's Miami Beach. They're separate cities, sir, connected by causeways. You wouldn't like it over there anyway, sir – it's nothing but crime on the Beach.'

'You mean Miami isn't?'

'Not here, not on Brickell Avenue, anyway. This is the fattest part of Fat City.'

'I noticed some shops off the lobby. Can I buy some trunks there?'

'I'll get you a pair, sir. What size?'

'Never mind. I'll do some shopping later.'

The bellman left, and Freddy opened the draperies. He could see the towering AmeriFirst building, a part of the bay, the bridge across the Miami River, and the skyscrapers on Flagler Street. The street he was on, Brickell, was lined with mirrored, shimmering buildings. The air conditioning hummed quietly.

He had at least a week before the credit card numbers would be traced, but he didn't intend to stay in the International Hotel for more than one day. From now on he was going to play things a little safer, unless, of course, he wanted something. If he wanted something right away, that was a different matter altogether. But what he wanted this time, before he was caught, was to have some fun and to do some of the things he had wanted to do during his three years in San Quentin.

So far, he liked the clean white look of Miami, but he was astonished to learn that the city was not on the ocean.

Chapter Two

The VIP Room – or Golden Lounge, as it was sometimes called, after the gold plastic cards issued to first-class passengers by the three airlines that maintained it – was unusually crowded. The dead man lying on the blue carpet was not the only one who was there without a gold card.

Sergeant Hoke Moseley, Homicide, Miami Police Department, filled a Styrofoam cup with free coffee – his third – picked up a glazed doughnut from the assortment on the clear plastic tray and put it back, then doctored his coffee with Sweet 'N Low and N-Rich Coffee Creamer. Sergeant Bill Henderson, Hoke's hefty partner, sat on a royal-blue couch and read John Keasler's humor column in the *Miami News*. Two middle-aged airport security men in electric-blue sports jackets stood by the door, looking as if they were ready to take orders from anybody.

A black airport public relations man, wearing a hundred-dollar brown silk sports shirt and yellow linen golf slacks, was making notes with a gold pencil in a leather notebook. He put the notebook into his hip pocket and crossed the blue-carpeted room to talk to two men who said they were from Waycross, Georgia, John and Irwin Peeples. They glowered at him.

'Don't worry,' the PR man said. 'As soon as the state attorney gets here, and I've had a chance to talk to him, you'll be on the next flight out for Atlanta. And a plane of some kind leaves for Atlanta every half-hour.'

'We don't want no plane of *some* kind,' John Peeples said. 'Me and Irwin fly Delta or nothing.'

'No problem. If we have to, we'll bump a couple and get you on Delta inside of an hour.'

'If I was you,' Bill Henderson butted in, taking off his black-rimmed reading glasses, 'I wouldn't promise these crackers anything. What we may be dealing with here is a Murder Two. For all I know, this whole thing might be a religious plot to murder that Krishna, with the two crackers in on it from the beginning. Ain't that right, Hoke?'

'I don't know yet,' Hoke said. 'Let's wait and see what the medical examiner and the state attorney have to say. At the least, Mr and Mr Peeples, you've got a long session ahead of you. We'll be wanting to talk to you downtown, and there'll be depositions to make out. As material witnesses to the' – he pointed to the body on the floor – 'demise of this Krishna here, the state attorney might decide to keep you in Miami under protective custody for several months.'

The brothers groaned. Hoke winked at Bill Henderson as he joined him on the couch.

The other Hare Krishna, the partner of the dead man, started to cry again. Someone had given him back his wig and he had stuffed it into his jacket pocket. He was at least twenty-five, but he looked much younger as he stifled his sobs and wiped his eyes with his fingertips. His freshly shaved head glistened with perspiration. He had never seen a dead person before, and here was his 'brother,' a man he had prayed with and eaten brown rice with, as dead as anyone could ever be, stretched out on the blue carpet of the VIP Room, and covered – except for feet in white cotton socks and scuffed Hush Puppies – with a cream-colored Aeroméxico blanket.

Dr Merle Evans, the medical examiner, arrived with Violet Nygren, a blond and rather plain young assistant prosecutor from the state attorney's office. Hoke nodded to the security men at the door, and the two were let through. Hoke and Bill Henderson shook hands with Doc Evans, and the four of them moved to the back of the lounge, out of earshot of the Peeples, the PR man, and the weepy Krishna.

'I'm new on the beat,' Violet Nygren said, as she introduced herself. 'I've only been in the state attorney's office since I finished up at the UM Law School last June. But I'm willing to learn, Sergeant Moseley.'

Hoke grinned. 'Fair enough. This is my partner, Sergeant Henderson. If you're an attorney, Miss Nygren, where's your briefcase?'

13

'I've got a tape recorder in my purse,' she said, holding up her leather drawstring bag.

'I was kidding. I've got a lot of respect for lady lawyers. My ex-wife had one, and I've been paying half my salary for alimony and child support for the last ten years.'

'I haven't been on a homicide up to now,' she said. 'My caseloads so far have been mostly muggings and holdups. But, as I said, I'm here to learn, Sergeant.'

'This may not *be* a homicide. That's why we wanted someone from the state attorney's office to come down with Doc Evans. We hope it isn't. We've had enough this year as it is. But that'll be up to you and Doc Evans to decide.'

'That's awfully deferential, for you, Hoke,' Doc Evans said. 'What's bothering you?'

'Here's what happened. The body under the blanket's a Hare Krishna.' Hoke looked at his opened notebook. 'His name's Martin Waggoner, and his parents, according to that other Krishna over there, live in Okeechobee. He came down to Miami nine or ten months ago, joined the Krishnas, and they both reside in the new Krishna ashram out on Krome Avenue in the East 'Glades. These two have been working the airport for about six months, their regular assignment. The airport security people know them, and they've been warned a couple of times about bothering the passengers. The dead man had more than two hundred dollars in his wallet, and the other Krishna's got about one-fifty. That's how much they've begged out here since seven A.M.' Hoke looked at his wristwatch. 'It's only twelve-forty-five now, and the Krishna over there said they usually take in about five hundred a day between them.'

'Pretty good money.' Violet Nygren raised her pale eyebrows. 'I wouldn't have guessed they collected so much.'

'The security people said there're two more Krishna teams working the airport besides this one. We haven't notified the commune, and we haven't called the Krishna's parents up in Okeechobee, yet.'

'You haven't told us a hell of a lot, either,' Doc Evans said.

'Our problem, doc, is witnesses. There were maybe thirty witnesses, all in line at Aeroméxico, but they took the flight to Mérida. We managed to snag these two boys over there' – Hoke pointed to the Georgians, who looked to be in their forties – 'but only because the uglier one on the right stole the victim's wig. The airline employees behind the counter said they didn't see anything. They were too busy, they said, and at check-in time I suppose they were. I got their names, and we can talk to them again later.'

'Too bad,' Henderson said, 'that we couldn't find the lady with the Krishna Kricket.'

'What's a Krishna Kricket?' Violet Nygren asked.

'They sell 'em out here in the bookshops and drugstores. It's just a metal cricket with a piece of spring steel inside. You click it at the Krishnas when they start bugging you. The noise usually drives them away. There used to be a Krishna-hater out here who gave them away free, but he ran out of crickets or money or ardor – I don't know. Anyway, the two brothers over there said she was closest to the action, and she kept clicking her Kricket at the Krishna until he stopped screaming.'

'How was he killed?' Doc Evans said. 'Or do you want me to look at him now and tell you? I've got to get back to the morgue.'

'That's the point,' Hoke said. 'He wasn't actually killed. He bothered some guy wearing a leather coat. The guy bent his finger back and broke it. Then the guy walked away and disappeared. The Krishna went down on his knees, started screaming, and then, maybe five or six minutes later, he's dead. The security men brought his body in here, and the PR man over there called Homicide. So there it is – the Krishna died from a broken finger. How about it, Miss Nygren? Is that a homicide or not?'

'I never heard of anybody dying from a broken finger,' she said.

'He must have died from shock,' Doc Evans said. 'I'll tell you for sure after I've had a look at him. How old is he, Hoke?'

'Twenty-one – according to his driver's license.'

'That's what I mean,' Doc Evans said, compressing his lips. 'Young people today just can't stand up to pain the way we could when we were younger. This one was probably malnourished and in lousy shape. The pain was unexpected and just too much for him. It hurts like hell to have your finger bent back.'

'You're telling me,' Violet Nygren said. 'My brother used to do it to me when I was a kid.'

15

'And if you bend it back all the way,' Doc Evans said, 'until it breaks, it hurts like a son of a bitch. So he probably went into shock. Nobody gave him hot tea or covered him up with a blanket, and that was it. It doesn't take very long to die from shock.'

'About five or six minutes, the Peeples brothers say.'

'That's pretty fast.' Doc Evans shook his head. 'Shock usually takes fifteen or twenty minutes. But I'm not making any guesses. For all I know, without examining the body, there could be a bullet hole in him.'

'I don't think so,' Bill Henderson said. 'All I saw was the broken finger, and it's broken clean off – just hanging there.'

'If it was an accident,' Violet Nygren said, 'it could still be simple assault. On the other hand, if the man in the leather jacket intended to kill him this way, knowing that there was a history of people dying from shock in the Krishna's background, this could very well be Murder One.'

'That's really reaching for it,' Hoke said. 'You'll have to settle for manslaughter I think.'

'I'm not so sure,' she continued. 'If you shoot a man and he dies later on from complications caused by the bullet, even though he was barely wounded when shot, we change the charge to either Murder One or Murder Two. I'll have to research this case, that's all. We can't do anything about it anyway until you catch the man in the leather jacket.'

'That's all we've got to go on,' Hoke said. 'Leather jacket. We don't even know the *color* of the jacket. One guy said he had heard it was tan; another guy said he'd heard gray. Unless the man comes forward by himself, we haven't got a chance in hell of finding him. He could be on a plane for England or someplace at this minute.' Hoke took a Kool out of a crumpled package, lit it, took one drag, and then butted it out in a standing ashtray. 'The body's all yours, doc. We've got all of the stuff out of his pockets.'

Violet Nygren opened her purse and turned off her tape recorder. 'I should tell my mom about this case,' she said. 'When my brother used to bend my fingers back, she never did anything to him.' She laughed nervously. 'Now I can tell her he was just trying to kill me.'

Chapter Three

Frederick J. Frenger, Jr, who preferred to be called Junior instead of Freddy, was twenty-eight years old. He looked older because his life had been a hard one; the lines at the corners of his mouth seemed too deep for a man in his late twenties. His eyes were a dark shade of blue, and his untrimmed blond eyebrows were almost white. His nose had been broken and reset poorly, but some women considered him attractive. His skin was unblemished and deeply tanned from long afternoons spent in the yard at San Quentin. At five-nine, he should have had a slighter build, but prolonged sessions with weights, pumping iron in the yard, as well as playing handball, had built up his chest, shoulders, and arms to almost grotesque proportions. He had developed his stomach muscles to the point that he could stand arms akimbo, and roll them in waves.

Freddy had been given a sentence of five-to-life for armed robbery. The California Adult Authority had reduced the sentence to four years, fixing an earlier parole date for two years. After serving the two years, Freddy had been offered a parole, but he turned it down, preferring to do two more years and then get out of prison without any strings attached. He accepted the label in his jacket – the file folder that held his records in the warden's office – which had him down as a career criminal. He knew that he would commit another crime as soon as he was released, and if he was on parole when he was caught, he would be returned to prison as a parole violator. Violating a parole could mean eight or even ten more years of prison before beginning the new sentence for whatever it was that he was caught doing after he got out.

San Quentin is overcrowded, so there are not enough jobs for everyone and a man must earn a job. Freddy liked to work (when he worked), and he was efficient. Assigned, after several months of idleness, to kitchen duty, he had observed the operation closely.

17

He had then written a ten-page memorandum to the warden, explaining in detail how the staff could be cut and the service improved if certain correction officers and prison chefs were removed and replaced. To Freddy's surprise, he found himself back in the yard.

His report, which would have earned a management major in college a B+, earned Freddy the enmity of several kitchen screws. These officers, with their solid links to the prisoner power structure, directed that Freddy be taught a lesson for his temerity. Two black prisoners cornered Freddy in the yard one afternoon and worked him over. At the yard captain's hearing, they claimed that Freddy had jumped them for no reason and that they were merely attempting to defend themselves from his psychopathic, racist attack. Inasmuch as Freddy had tested out as a psychopath and sociopath (so had the two other prisoners), he was sent to the hole for six days for his unprovoked attack on these innocent inmates. The black yard captain also gave him a short lecture on racism.

During the six dismal days in the hole, which included revocation of Freddy's smoking privileges and reduction to bread and water with a plate of kidney beans every third day, Freddy reviewed his life and realized that altruism had been his major fault.

Back when he had been a juvenile offender, he had been sent to the reform school at Whittier, where he had organized a sit-down strike in the dining hall in an effort to get seconds on Sunday desserts (rice pudding with raisins, of which Freddy was very fond). The campaign failed, and Freddy had stayed at Whittier for the full three years of his sentence.

Again, at Ione, California, in the Preston Institute for Youthful Offenders, Freddy had extended himself, planning the escape of a boy named Enoch Sawyers. Enoch's father, who had caught his son masturbating, had castrated the boy. Mr Sawyers was a very religious man and considered masturbation a grievous offense to God. Mr Sawyers was arrested, but because of his religious connections and the laudatory testimony of his minister, he had been sentenced to two years' probation. But when young Enoch, only fifteen years old at the time, had recovered from his unelected surgery, he had become a neighborhood terror. Deprived of his testicles and taunted by his schoolmates, he had demonstrated his manhood almost daily by beating one or more of his tormentors half to death. He was fearless and could take incredible amounts of punishment without, apparently, noticing or caring how badly he was hurt.

Finally, at seventeen, Enoch had been sentenced to Preston as an incorrigible menace to the peace of Fresno, California. At Preston, among some very hardened young prisoners, Enoch again felt compelled to prove his manhood by beating up on people. His technique was to walk up to someone – anyone – and slam a hard right to his fellow prisoner's belly or jaw. He would continue to pummel his victim until the person either fought back or ran away from him.

Enoch's presence in the dormitory was unsettling to the other prisoners. Freddy, to solve the problem, had befriended him and worked out an escape plan, telling Enoch that he could prove his manhood to the authorities once and for all by escaping. Escaping from Preston was not so difficult, and Enoch, with Freddy's help, got away easily. He was caught in Oakland four days later when he tried to beat up three Chicago beet-pullers and steal their truck. They overpowered him, kicked out his remaining front teeth, and turned him over to the police. Enoch told the officials at Preston that Freddy had planned his escape, so Freddy's good time was revoked. Instead of eighteen months, Freddy spent three years there. Moreover, Freddy had also taken a severe beating as soon as Enoch was returned to Preston.

In the hole at San Quentin, which was not altogether dark – a pale slice of light indicated the bottom of the door – Freddy thought hard about his life. His desire for the good of others had been at the root of his problems, making his own life worse instead of better. And he hadn't really helped anyone else. He decided then to look out only for himself.

He quit smoking. If your smoking privileges are revoked but you don't smoke, the punishment is meaningless. Back in the yard, Freddy had quietly joined the jocks in the daily pumping of iron and had worked on his mind as well as his body. He read *Time* magazine every week and took out a subscription to the *Reader's*

Digest. He also gave up sex, trading his pudgy punk, a golden brown Chicano from East Los Angeles, for eight cartons of Chesterfields and 200 Milky Way candy bars. He then traded the Chesterfields (the favorite brand among black prisoners) and 150 of the Milky Ways for a single cell. He also made his peace with the prisoner power structure. He had turned selflessness to self-interest, learning the lesson that everyone must come to eventually: what a man gives up voluntarily cannot be taken away from him.

Now Freddy was out. Because of his good behavior they had let him out after three years instead of making him serve the full four. They needed the space at San Quentin, and inasmuch as some two-thirds of the prisoners were classified as psychopaths, that could not really be held against him. On the day Freddy was released, the assistant warden had advised him not to return to Santa Barbara, but to leave California and find a new state.

'That way,' the assistant warden said, 'when they catch you again, which they will, it will at least be a first offense in that particular state. And bear in mind, Frenger, you were never very happy here.'

The advice had been sound. After three successful muggings in San Francisco – with his powerful muscles, it was a simple matter to twist a man's arm behind his back and ram his head into a wall – Freddy had put three thousand miles between himself and California.

Freddy turned on the water in the tub and adjusted it for temperature. He undressed and read the information on the placard beside the corridor door. Checkout time was noon, which gave him twenty-four hours. He studied the escape diagram and what to do in case of fire, then took the room service menus into the bathroom. When the tub was filled, he turned off the faucet. He went back to the bar, filled a tall glass with ice and ginger ale, and got into the tub to read the menus.

He glanced at the room service menu, and then studied the wine list. He didn't know one wine from another. Vintage years meant nothing to him, but he was amazed at the prices. The idea of paying a hundred dollars for a bottle of wine, even with a stolen credit card, struck him as outrageous. The thought also made him cautious. He knew that as long as he did not buy anything that cost more than fifty dollars, most clerks would not call the 800 number to check on the status of the credit card. At least this was the usual policy. And in hotels, they usually didn't get around to checking the card until the day you checked out. But he had taken a $135-a-day suite. Well, he wouldn't worry about it, and as he thought about the mugging of Herman T. Gotlieb in the alley, he felt a little more secure. That was the safe thing about mugging gays; the police didn't worry much about what happened to them. At the very least, Mr Gotlieb had a bad concussion, and he would be a very confused man for some time.

Freddy got out of the tub, dried himself with a gold bath sheet, and wrapped it around his waist. He needed a shave but had nothing to shave with; his face was clean but felt dirty with its blond stubble. He went through his stuffed eelskin wallet again. He had $79 in bills and some loose change. The San Franciscans he had mugged had carried very little folding money. He had seven credit cards, but he was going to need some more cash.

He put the stolen Cardin suitcase on the coffee table. It was locked. If there was a razor in the case he could shave. He didn't have a knife – perhaps there were bar implements. Yes, a corkscrew. It took five minutes to jimmy the two locks. He opened the suitcase and licked his lips. This was always an exciting moment, like opening a surprise package or a grab bag. One never knew what one would find.

It was all women's stuff: nightgowns, skirts, blouses, slippers, and size 6½ shoes in knitted covers. There was a black silk cocktail dress, size seven, a soft blue cashmere sweater, size seven–eight, and a pair of fold-up Cardin sunglasses in a lizard case. The items were all expensive, but there was no razor; apparently, the young mother who had owned the suitcase didn't shave her legs.

Freddy dialed the bell captain and asked to speak with Pablo.

'Pablo', he said, when he got the bellman on the line, 'this is Mr Gotlieb up in seven-seventeen.'

'Yes, sir.'

'I'd like a girl sent up. A fairly small one, size seven or eight.'

'How tall?'

'I'm not sure. How tall are sevens and eights?'

'They can run pretty tall, from five feet on up to maybe five-six or more.'

'That doesn't make any sense. How could one dress fit a woman five feet tall or five feet, six inches tall?'

'I don't know, Mr Gotlieb, but women's sizes run funny. My wife wears a size twenty-two hat. I wear a seven and a quarter, and my head's a lot bigger than hers.'

'All right. Just send me up a small one.'

'For how long.'

'I don't know. What difference does it make.'

'You're still on nooner rates. I've got one small one for you now, but she gets off at five. That's all I got now. Tonight, I can get you another one, even smaller.'

'No. That's okay. I won't even need her till five.'

'In about twenty minutes, then?'

'Tell her to bring me up a club sandwich, with some dill pickle slices on the side.'

'She can't do that, sir, but I'll send the room service waiter up with the club sandwich.'

'Good. And I'll take care of you later.'

'Yes, sir.'

The club sandwich, a nice one with white turkey meat, bacon, American cheese, lettuce, and tomato slices on white toast, was $12, plus a $1 service charge. Freddy signed for it and gave the waiter a $1 tip. Even though there were pickles, potato chips, cole slaw, and extra paper cups of mayonnaise and mustard on the side, Freddy was appalled by the price of the club sandwich. What in the hell had happened to the economy while he was in prison?

Freddy ate half the sandwich and all of the pickle slices, then put the other half into the refrigerator. The other half, he thought, is worth six bucks – Jesus!

There was a light knock on the door. Freddy unfastened the chain and opened the door, and a young girl with small and very even teeth came in. She was a small one, all right, standing about five-three in her high heels. Her well-defined widow's peak and smallish chin made her face heart-shaped. She wore tight jeans with ROLLS-ROYCE embroidered on the left leg in three-inch white block letters; a U-neck purple T-shirt, and dangling gold earrings. Her soft kangaroo leather drawstring bag was big enough to hold schoolbooks. Freddy estimated her age at fifteen – maybe sixteen.

'Mr Gotlieb?' she said, smiling. 'Pablo said you wanted to talk to me.'

'Yeah,' Freddy said. 'How old are you, anyway?'

'Nineteen. My name is Pepper.'

'Yeah. Sure it is. You got any ID?'

'My driver's license. I just look young because I don't wear makeup, that's all.'

'Let's see the license.'

'I don't have to show it to you.'

'That's right. You don't. You can leave.'

'But if I show it to you, you'll know my right name.'

'But I'll still call you Pepper.'

She took her wallet out of the bag and showed Freddy her Florida license. The name on the license was Susan Waggoner, and she was twenty years old – not nineteen.

'This says you're twenty.'

She shrugged. 'I like being a teenager.'

'What're the rates?'

'For nooners – half-hour limit – fifty dollars until five o'clock. Then it goes up to seventy-five. I get off at five, so for you it's only fifty, unless you want extras.'

'Okay. Let's go into the bedroom.'

Pepper pulled down the spread on the queen-size bed, then the sheets, and smoothed them out. She slipped off her shoes, her T-shirt, and her jeans. She was not wearing a bra, nor did she need one. She rolled off her panties, lay down on the bed, and put her hands behind her head as she spread her skinny legs. As she locked her fingers behind her head, her small breasts almost disappeared, except for the taut strawberry nipples. Her long auburn hair, in a ponytail fastened with a rubber band, made a curling question mark on the right side of the pillow. Her well-greased pubic hair was a kinky brownish yellow.

Freddy unwrapped the bath sheet and dropped it on the floor. He probed her pregreased vagina with the first three fingers of his right hand. He shook his head and frowned.

'Not enough friction there for me,' he said. 'I'm used to boys, you see. Do you take it in the ass?'

'No, sir. I should, I know, but I tried it once and it hurt too much. I just can't do it. I can give you a blow job if you like.'

'That's okay, but I'm not all that interested anyway. You really should learn to take it in the ass. You'll make more money, and if you learn how to relax –'

'That's what Pablo said, but I just can't.'

'What size dress do you wear?'

'It depends. I can wear a five sometimes, but usually I'm either a six or a seven. It depends on who makes it. They all have different sizes.'

'Try this on.' Freddy brought her the black silk dress from the sitting room. 'Put your shoes on first, and then look at the mirror. There's a full-length mirror on the back of the bathroom door.'

Pepper slipped into the dress, turned sideways as she looked into the mirror, and smiled. 'It looks nice on me, doesn't it? I'd have to take it in some at the waist though.'

'You can have it for fifty bucks.'

'All I've got with me's a twenty. I'll give you a free blow job for it.'

'That's no offer! A man can get a free blow job anywhere. The hell with it. I'm not a salesman. Keep the dress. And while you're here, take this suitcase full of stuff. There're some skirts and other things in it, and a nice cashmere sweater. Take the suitcase too.'

'Where d'you get all these nice clothes?'

'They belong to my wife. When I left my wife I took the stuff with me. I paid for it, so it was mine to take.'

'You left your wife?'

'Yeah. We're getting a divorce.'

'Because of the boys?'

'What boys?'

'You said you were used to boys, and I just assumed that –'

'Jesus Christ. How long've you been working for Pablo?'

24

'Since the beginning of the semester. I go to Miami-Dade Community College, Downtown. I need the money for school.'

'Well, one of the first things you should learn is not to ask clients personal questions.'

'I'm sorry. I didn't mean to pry.' She started to cry.

'Why're you crying, for Christ's sake?'

'I don't know. I just do sometimes. I'm not doing very good at this, not even nooners, and when I go back to Pablo without any money, he'll –'

'There's a plastic laundry bag in the closet. Put the clothes in it, and give Pablo the empty suitcase. He can get the locks fixed, and he'll have a two-hundred-dollar suitcase. I'll square you with Pablo later. Okay?'

Pepper stopped crying, wiped her eyes, and got back into her own clothes. She packed the clothing neatly into the plastic laundry bag.

'What do you do when you get off duty at five?'

'I usually walk downtown, have some dinner, and then go to class. Tonight's my English class at six-fifteen, and it runs until seven-forty, unless Mr Turner lets us out early. Sometimes, when we've got a paper to write, he lets us go home to write it.'

Why, Freddy wondered, is she lying to me? No college would ever accept this incredibly stupid young woman as a student. On the other hand, he had known a few college men in San Quentin. Although they usually got the best jobs there, they didn't appear to be any smarter than the majority of the cons. Maybe the girl wasn't lying. He didn't know anything about college requirements, but maybe they would be much lower for women than for men. It would be a good idea to have a woman with a car show him the city. So far it was all white buildings and a blur of greenery.

'I'll tell you what, Pepper. I'll buy you dinner and then wait for you to get out of class. Then you can drive me around some. You've got a license, so I suppose you've got a car?'

'My brother's car. I get to keep it all the time, but I've got to meet him at the airport at eight-thirty tonight to collect some money from him. He works out there, and gives me his pay every day to deposit in the bank. Where he works, he isn't allowed to have a car.'

'You don't live together?'

'Not anymore. We did at first, when we first came down to Miami from Okeechobee, but now I've got the apartment to myself.'

'That's all right. I don't mind riding out to the airport again. I just want to get familiar with the city. I'll give you a decent tip, or buy you a drink, or maybe take you to a movie. What do you say?'

She smiled. 'I'd like that. I haven't had a *date* date since I came down here, Mr Gotlieb –'

'You can call me Junior.'

'Junior? All right, and you can call me Susie. Pablo told me to call myself Pepper so that customers would think I was hot. Pablo's my manager, like, and he knows all about these things. Most men, I've noticed, just laugh when I tell them my name is Pepper. You didn't – Junior – and I think you're awfully nice.'

'I am nice, Susie, and I like you a lot. I'll tell you what. Just leave the bag of clothes with me and take the suitcase down to Pablo. That way he won't know you got the stuff, and I can take it with me when we meet.'

'I usually eat dinner at Granny's. It's a health food restaurant right near the campus, about eight blocks from here. I walk because I leave the car in the parking garage near the school, but you can take a cab there. The cabbies all know where it is, even the ones who don't speak English.'

She handed him the bag of clothing.

'I'll see you at Granny's at five, then.'

'It'll be closer to five-fifteen, but I'll get there as soon as I can.'

'Good. And have a prosperous afternoon.'

'Thank you. But whatever you do, don't tell Pablo. We aren't supposed to go out with the johns – that's why I want you to meet me at Granny's.'

'Pablo, in my opinion, is an asshole. I'll just tell him I had jet lag and that kept me from performing. I'll slip him ten bucks and he'll be so happy he won't say a word to you. But I won't tell him about our date. Don't worry.'

Susan blushed, and looked shyly at the floor. 'You can kiss me on the cheek and sorta seal our date. That way I know you'll really come to Granny's. I know you men don't like to kiss us on the mouth …'

'I don't mind kissing you on the mouth.'

'You don't?'

Freddy kissed her chastely, almost tenderly, on the lips, and then led her to the door. She waggled her fingers and smiled; then he closed the door after her and chain-locked it. She had forgotten the empty suitcase, and he still had the bag of clothes. He would give the suitcase to Pablo instead of the ten bucks he had intended to give him. As long as he had the clothes, he knew she would come to Granny's.

He still had plenty of time to do some shopping.

Chapter Four

Bill Henderson and Hoke Moseley worked on their reports for the rest of the afternoon at the double desk they shared in a glass-walled cubbyhole at the new Miami Police Station. As sergeants they were entitled to the tiny office, which had a door that could be closed and locked, but it was much more crowded and uncomfortable than the space the other plainclothes detectives had in the large, outer bullpen. The room was undecorated, except for a twenty-two-by-thirty-inch poster on the one unglassed wall. A hand holding a pistol, with the pistol aimed at the viewer, was in the center of the wall. The message, in bold black letters beneath the pointing pistol, read MIAMI – SEE IT LIKE A NATIVE.

When they took the depositions of the brothers Peeples, only one man at a time could be accommodated in the tiny room. Irritated by the Georgians' uncooperative attitudes, they let the two men find their own way back to the airport by taxi instead of returning them to the PR man in a police car.

Hoke flipped a quarter. Henderson lost, which meant that Henderson had to call Martin Waggoner's father in Okeechobee and break the sad news. While Henderson called, Hoke went downstairs to the station cafeteria and got two cups of coffee in Styrofoam cups. He drank his in the cafeteria and brought the other cup, now barely warm, back upstairs to Henderson. Henderson took one sip of the lukewarm coffee, replaced the lid, and dropped the cup into the wastebasket.

'Mr Waggoner said his son had a sister living with him here in Miami, and he wouldn't accept the truth of his son's death until she identified the body. His son was a deeply religious boy, he claimed, and was not the kind to fight anyone. I told him there wasn't any fight, and about how it happened and all, and he said that there had to be more to it than that. I know how he feels,

28

the poor bastard. When I told him his son died from a broken finger I felt like I was lying myself.'

'He didn't die from a broken finger. He died from shock.'

Henderson shrugged. 'I know. And I told him what Doc Evans said about shock. Anyway, I made the call to Mr Waggoner, so you can take the sister down to identify the body.'

'You lost the coin toss –'

'And I called Mr Waggoner. The sister's a new development, and my wife expects me home for dinner. We're having company over. You're single –'

'Divorced.'

'But single, with no responsibilities or obligations.'

'I pay alimony and child support for two teenage daughters.'

'Sometimes you break my heart. Your evenings are bleak and empty. You have no friends –'

'I thought you and I were friends?'

'We are. That's why you can get a hold of the sister while I go home to my assertive wife, my gawky teenager son, and my daughter with acne. I can then entertain for drinks and dinner a couple my wife likes and I can't stand.'

'Okay, since you point out the joys I'm missing, I'll go. Got her address?'

'I wrote it all down, and I've made some calls. She lives in Kendall Pines Terrace out on One-fifty-seventh Avenue. Building Six East, apartment four-one-eight.'

'Kendall? That's a helluva ways out.' Hoke transferred the information from the yellow pad to his notebook.

'Luckily for you she isn't home. Susan Waggoner goes to Miami-Dade, to the New World Campus downtown. She'll be in class at six-fifteen. I already called the registrar, so if you stop by the office, they'll send a student assistant up to the classroom with you and get the girl out of class. You've even got time to get a drink first. Two drinks.'

'And so everything works out for the best, doesn't it? You can go home to dinner, and I can escort a hysterical young girl to the morgue to see her dead brother. I can, then, in all probability, drive her to hell and gone out to Kendall and get her calmed down. Then I have to drive her all the way back to Miami Beach. Maybe, if I'm lucky, I'll be home in time to watch the eleven o'clock news.'

'What the hell, Hoke, it's all overtime pay.'

'Compensatory time. I've used up my overtime pay this month.'

'What's the difference?'

'Twenty-five bucks. Haven't we had this conversation before?'

'Last month. Only last month it was me who had to sit in the hardware store until four A.M. while you went home to bed.'

'But you were on overtime pay.'

'Compensatory time.'

'What's the difference?'

'Twenty-five bucks.'

They both laughed, but laughing didn't mask Hoke's uneasiness. He didn't know which was worse – telling a father that his son was dead or telling a sister that her brother was dead, but he was glad he didn't have to tell both of them.

Chapter Five

In his new clothes Freddy looked like a native Miamian. He wore a pale blue *guayabera*, white linen slacks with tiny golden tennis rackets embroidered at irregular intervals on both pants legs, white patent-leather loafers with tassels, a chromium dolphin-shaped belt buckle, and pale blue socks that matched his *guayabera*. He had had a $20 haircut and an $8 shave in the hotel barber shop, charging both to his room, together with a generous tip for the barber. He could have passed as a local, or as a tourist down from Pennsylvania to spend the full season.

Freddy arrived at Granny's a little before five and ordered a pot of ginseng tea, telling the heavy-hipped Cuban waitress that he was waiting for a friend. He had never tasted ginseng tea before, but he managed to kill some of the bitterness by adding three spoons of raw brown sugar to his cup. The menu didn't make much sense to Freddy. After looking it over, he decided he would order whatever Susan ordered and hope for the best. The ginseng tea was foul, but it had seemed like a better choice than the gunpowder tea the waitress had recommended. He had run out of cigarettes, his first pack smoked since leaving prison. But when he asked the waitress to bring him a fresh package of Winston 100s, she told him that no smoking was allowed at Granny's, and that 'cigarettes are poison to the body.'

Actually, Freddy realized, he didn't truly want a cigarette. Kicking the habit in prison had been difficult. Six days in the hole without a cigarette had given him a good start, helping his body get rid of the stored nicotine, but it hadn't helped his psychological dependence on smoking. There were very few things that a man could do alone in prison. Smoking was one of them. Smoking not only helped to pass the time, it gave a man something to do with his hands. Until he started pumping iron in earnest, those long days of wandering around in the yard without a cigarette had been his worst days in stir. And yet the first thing he had done when he got into the San Francisco bus terminal was to buy a package of Winston 100s. He had picked them because of the deep red package. He had somehow associated smoking with freedom, even though smoking was a form of slavery. That settled it. He would give it up before he got back into the habit. Otherwise, when he got back to prison, he would have to go through all of that painful withdrawal business again.

Susan, still in her work clothes, arrived a few minutes after five. She waved from the door and then joined him at the table-for-two against the wall. She ducked her head and sat under an ominous hanging basket containing a drooping mass of ferns. She was obviously pleased to see Freddy.

'You forgot the suitcase,' Freddy said, 'but I gave it to Pablo. The clothes are in the bag under the table.'

'I didn't really forget. I just thought better of it. A lot of employees know what I do in the hotel, and they don't like me. They don't like any of us girls, because of the money we make. So if a maid saw me with a suitcase, she'd call the security office and say that I stole it from a guest or something. Then, when I told the security officer the truth, he'd still check with you, and he'd find out that you didn't have any other luggage. That could make some trouble for you. What I think, when you left your wife, is that you took the wrong suitcase. You took hers instead of your own. Isn't that right?'

'Something like that. That's interesting, Susan. I didn't think you could figure out something that complicated.'

'I wasn't always a thoughtful person. When I was in high school in Okeechobee, all I thought about was having a good time. But at Miami-Dade, the teachers want us to use our minds.'

'Where's Okeechobee?'

'It's up by the lake, when you drive north to Disney World.'

'What lake?'

'Lake Okeechobee!' Susan laughed. 'It's the biggest lake in the whole South. Everybody gets their water down here from Lake Okeechobee.'

'I'm from California. I don't know shit about Florida.'

'I don't know shit about California, either. So I guess we're even.'

'Lake Tahoe's a pretty good-size lake in California. Have you heard of Tahoe?'

'I've heard of it, but I don't know where it is.'

'Part of it's in Nevada, and the rest is in California. On the Nevada side, you can gamble in the casinos.'

'You can't gamble in Florida, except on horses, race track and trotters, on dogs, and jai alai. Oh, yes, you can gamble on cock-fighting and dogfighting, too, if you know where to go. But all other forms of gambling, the governor says, are immoral.'

'Is the governor a Jesuit?'

'That's a Catholic, isn't it?'

'An educated Catholic, the way it was explained to me.'

'No, he's a Protestant. It would be a waste of money for a Catholic to run for office down here.'

'Tell me about Okeechobee, and tell me why you came to Miami.'

'It's a lot hotter up there than it is here, for one thing. And it rains more, too, because of the lake. It's a little town, not big like Miami, but there's lots to do, like bowling and going juking, or fishing and swimming. If you don't like country, you wouldn't like Okeechobee. If a girl doesn't get married, there isn't much future there, and nobody ever asked me to get married. I did the cooking for my daddy and my brother, but that didn't stop me from getting pregnant. That's why I came to Miami, really, to get me an abortion. My father said it was a disgrace to get pregnant that way, and he told me not to come back –'

'The *Reader's Digest* said about forty percent of the girls who get pregnant aren't married. What's he so uptight about?'

'My brother, Marty, had a big fight with him about that. He told Daddy it's the Lord's fight to punish people, and that Daddy didn't have any right to sit in judgment on me. So the upshot of all that was that Marty had to go with me, and he was told not to come back either. Daddy doesn't believe in much of anything, and Marty's really religious, you see.'

'So you both came down to Miami?'

She nodded. 'On the bus. Marty and me are really close. We were born only ten months apart, and he's always taken my side against Daddy.'

The waitress interrupted. 'You want more tea, or d'you want to order now?'

'I'll have the Circe Salad,' Susan said. 'I always get that.'

'Me, too,' Freddy said.

'You'll like the Circe Salad. Daddy gets mad, but he always gets over it. I think we could go back now, and he wouldn't say a word. But we've done so well down here, we're going to stay a long time. We're saving our money, and when we've got enough saved Marty wants to go back to Okeechobee and get us a Burger King franchise. He'll be the day manager, and I'll manage nights. We'll build a house on the lake, get us a speedboat, and everything.'

'Marty has it all figured out.'

Susan nodded. 'That's why I'm going to Miami-Dade. When I finish English and social science, I'm going to take business and management courses.'

'What about your mother? What does she think about you two leaving?'

'I don't know where she is, and neither does Daddy. She was working the counter at the truck stop, and then one night, when I was only five, she ran off with a truck driver. Daddy traced her as far as New Orleans, paying a private detective, and then the trail got cold.

'But Marty and me are doing real good here. He's got a job collecting money for the Hare Krishnas, and he gives at least a hundred dollars of it every day to me to put in the bank. It's a hard life for Marty, compared to mine, because he's restricted to camp at night, and he has to get up at four A.M. every morning to pray. But he doesn't mind working seven days a week at the airport, not when he makes a hundred dollars a day for us to save.'

'I think I saw one out at the airport today. I don't understand this Hare Krishna business. What are they, anyway? It doesn't sound American.'

'They are now. It's some kind of religious cult from India, a professional beggars' group, and now they're all over the United States. They must be in California, too.'

'Maybe so. I never heard of them before, that's all.'

'Well, Marty saw the advantages right away, because it's a way to beg legally.'

Susan leaned forward and lowered her voice.

'What he does, you see, is put a dollar in one pocket for the Krishnas, and a dollar in another pocket for us. The Krishnas, being a religious organization, can beg at airports, whereas if you were to go out there and beg, they'd put you in jail.'

'In other words, your brother's stealing the Krishnas blind.'

'I guess you can put it that way. He said they'd kick him out if they ever found out. But they aren't going to catch on. I meet Marty every night by the mailbox outside the Airport Hotel, which is right inside the airport. While I pretend to mail a letter, he slips the money into my purse. He's got a partner who's supposed to be watching him, but Marty can always get away for a minute to go to the men's room. What I can't understand is why those passengers out there hand him fives and tens, and sometimes a twenty, just because he asks for it. He says they're afraid not to, that they're all guilty about something they've done bad. But he sure collects a lot of money on a twelve-hour shift out there.'

The waitress brought their Circe Salads: large chunks of romaine lettuce, orange slices, bean and wheat sprouts, shredded coconut, a blob of vanilla yogurt, and a topping of grated sugar-cane sawdust soaked in ginseng. The salad was served in a porcelain bowl in the shape of a giant clam shell.

'I've never eaten in a health food restaurant before.'

'Me neither, till I came to Miami. You don't have to eat it if you don't like it.'

'I don't like the ginseng root. Do they put it in everything here?'

'Just about. It's supposed to make you feel sexy, so they use ginseng because they don't serve meat here. That's the reason, I think.'

'I'd rather have meat. This would be all right without the ginseng taste. How'd you do this afternoon?'

'Fifty dollars. One Colombian, and an old man from Dayton, Ohio. Counting all those clothes you gave me, it was a good day for me. Besides, I got to meet you. You're the nicest man I've ever met.'

'I think you're nice, too.'

'Your hands are just beautiful.'

'Nobody ever told me that before. Here – take the rest of my salad.'

'You didn't even try the yogurt.'

'Yogurt? I thought it was soured ice cream.'

'No, it's yogurt. It's supposed to taste a little sour.'

'I don't like it.'

'I'm sorry, Junior. I guess I should've had you meet me at the Burger King. It's right across from the school.'

'I'm not hungry. I had a club sandwich in my room, before I bought these new clothes.'

'Your blue shirt matches your eyes. Did you buy it because it matched your eyes?'

'No. I liked the extra pockets. It's too hot to wear a jacket, and I need the pockets. Is it always this hot?'

'It's only about eighty-five. That's normal for October. In the summer it gets really hot, especially up in Okeechobee. And then there's mosquitoes, too. It gets so hot you can't do anything even if you wanted to. When you go out to a drive-in movie at night, all you do is sweat and drink beer and spray Cutter's.'

'Cutter's?'

'That's mosquito spray, and it really works, too. Oh, they'll still buzz around your ears, but they won't land on you – not if you spray on enough Cutter's. There's another brand, when you spray too much on, you get a rash. But you don't care about the rash, because you've already got a rash from prickly heat. We better pay and go to class.'

'I'll pay. Give me the ticket.'

'No, it's my treat. If you want to, you can go to class with me. It's air-conditioned, and Professor Turner won't mind. He'll think you're a member of the class anyway. He told us he doesn't learn our names. He finds out the names of the A and F students soon enough, he says, and the rest of us don't matter. I'm only a C student in English, so he's never even called on me yet.'

There were thirty-five students in the class; thirty-six, counting Freddy, who took the last seat in the row by the back wall, behind

Susan. There were no windows, and the walls, except for the green blackboard, were covered with cork. The city noises were shut out completely. The students, mostly Latinos and blacks, were silent as they watched the teacher write *Haiku* on the green board with a piece of orange chalk. The teacher, a heavy-set and bearded man in his late forties, did not take roll; he had just waited for silence before writing on the board.

'Haiku,' he said, in a well-trained voice, 'is a seventeen-syllable poem that the Japanese have been writing for several centuries. I don't speak Japanese, but as I understand haiku, pronounced *ha – ee – koo*, much of the beauty is lost in the translation from Japanese to English.

'English isn't a good language for rhymes. Three-quarters of the poetry written in English is unrhymed because of the paucity of rhyming words. Unhappily for you Spanish-speaking students, you have so many words ending in vowels, you have the difficulty in reverse.

'At any rate, here is a haiku in English.'

He wrote on the board:

The Miami sun,
Rising in the Everglades –
Burger in a bun.

'This haiku,' he continued, 'which I made up in Johnny Raffa's bar before I came to class, is a truly rotten poem. But I assure you I had no help with it. Basho, the great Japanese poet, if he knew English and if he were still alive, would positively detest it. But he would recognize it as a haiku because it has five syllables in the first line, seven in the second, and five in the third. Add them up and you have seventeen syllables, all you need for a haiku, and all of them concentrating on a penetrating idea.

'You're probably thinking, those of you who wonder about things like this, why am I talking about Japanese poetry? I'll tell you. I want you to write simple sentences – subject, verb, object. I want you to use concrete words that convey exact meanings.

'I know you Spanish-speaking students don't know many Anglo-Saxon words, but that's because you persist in speaking Spanish to one another outside of class instead of practicing English. Except for giving you Fs on your papers, I can't help you much there. But when you write your papers, pore – *p-o-r-e* – over your dictionaries for concrete words. When you write in English, force your reader to reach for something.'

There was a snicker at the back of the room.

'Basho wrote haikus in the seventeenth century, and they're still being read and talked about in Japan today. There are a couple of hundred haiku magazines in Japan, and every month articles are still being written about Basho's most famous haiku. I'll give you the literal translation instead of a seventeen-syllable translation.'

He wrote on the blackboard:

Old pond.

Frog jumps in.

Water sound.

'There you have it,' Mr Turner said, scratching his beard with the piece of chalk. 'Old pond. Frog jumps in. Water sound. What's missing, of course, is the onomatopoeia of the water sound. But the meaning is clear enough. What does it mean?'

He looked around the room but was unsuccessful in catching anyone's eye. The students, with sullen mouths and lowered lids, studied books and papers on their armrest desk tops.

'I can wait,' Mr Turner said. 'You know me well enough by now to know that I can wait for a volunteer for about fifteen minutes before my patience runs out. I wish I could wait longer, because while I'm waiting for volunteers I don't have to teach.' He folded his arms.

A young man wearing cut-off jeans, a faded blue tank top, and scuffed running shoes without socks, lifted his right hand two inches above his desk top.

'You, then,' the teacher said, pointing with his chalk.

'What it means, I think,' the student began, 'is that there's an old pond of water. This frog, wanting to get into the water, comes along and jumps in. When he plops into the water he makes a sound, like splash.'

'Very good! That's about as literal an interpretation as you can get. But if that's all there is to the poem, why would serious young men in Japan write papers about this poem every month in their

38

haiku magazines? But, thank you. At least we have the literal translation out of the way.

'Now, let's say that Miami represents the old pond. You, or most of you, anyway, came here from somewhere else. You come to Miami, that is, and you jump into this old pond. We've got a million and a half people here already, so the splash you make isn't going to make a very large sound. Or is it? It surely depends upon the frog. Some of you, I'm afraid, will make a very large splash, and we'll all hear it. Some will make a splash so faint that it won't be heard by your next-door neighbor. But at least we're all in the same pond, and –'

There was a knock on the door. Annoyed, Mr Turner crossed to the door and opened it. Freddy leaned forward and whispered to Susan. 'That's some pretty heavy shit he's laying down. D'you know what he's talking about?'

Susan shook her head.

'Us! You, your brother, and me. What's the other word mean he keeps talking about – *onomatopoeia*?'

'It's the word for the actual sound. Like *splash*, when the frog jumps in.'

'Right! See what I mean?' Freddy's eyes glittered. 'You and me, Susan. We're going to make us a big splash in this town.'

Chapter Six

Professor Turner stepped back into the room and cleared his throat. 'Is Susan Waggoner here today?'

She raised her hand.

'Come out into the hallway, please. Bring your things with you.'

Susan put her books into her oversize bag. Freddy followed her into the corridor, carrying the laundry bag. The teacher frowned at Freddy and shook his head.

'This doesn't concern you, son. Go back to your seat.'

'If it concerns Susan it concerns me,' Freddy said. 'We're engaged.'

Sergeant Hoke Moseley, looking at the floor, lifted his head and nodded when the student assistant asked him if she could leave.

'Susan,' Mr Turner said, 'do what you've got to do, and stay out of school as long as it takes. When you return to class, see me in my office and I'll let you make up any assignments you missed.' He looked sternly at Freddy for a long moment. 'You've already missed several classes, but the same goes for you.' He returned to his classroom and closed the door.

Hoke showed the pair his shield. 'Sergeant Moseley. Homicide. Isn't there a lounge somewhere where we can sit down and talk?' Hoke hadn't expected to see such a young girl. She looked more like a high school kid than a college student. But if she was engaged to this hard-looking jock, she was probably older than she looked. It was a help to have the fiance present; maybe he wouldn't have to drive her out to hell-and-gone Kendall after all. Her boyfriend could take her home.

'There's a student lounge down on the second floor,' Susan said. 'We can go there. I haven't done anything bad. Have I, Junior?'

Hoke smiled. 'Of course you haven't.' Hoke started toward the elevator. 'Let's go down to the lounge.'

They sat at a glass-topped table on three unstable wire Eames chairs in the study area near the Down escalator to the main floor. Hoke lit a cigarette and held out the package. When they shook their heads, he took one drag and dropped the cigarette into an empty Coke can on the table.

'I've got some bad news for you, Miss Waggoner. That's why I wanted you to be seated. Your brother, Martin, in a freaky accident at the airport, died today. And your father, when we called him in Okeechobee, asked us to have you identify the body. We've got an ID already from the other man who was working with your brother at the airport, so there's no mistake. It's just that we need a relative for a positive identification. After the autopsy we can turn the body over to either you or your father. You are eighteen, aren't you?'

'Nineteen,' Susan said.

'Twenty,' Freddy amended.

'Just barely twenty. This is hard to believe. How did it happen?'

'An unidentified assailant broke your brother's finger, and Martin went into immediate shock and died from this unexpected trauma to his middle digit.' Hoke pursed his lips. 'It happens sometimes.'

'I've changed my mind, officer,' Freddy said. 'Can I borrow one of your cigarettes?'

'Sure.' Hoke offered the pack, and held a match for Freddy to light the cigarette.

Susan shook her head, looking bewildered. 'The airport's a dangerous place to work. My brother's been attacked out there before, you know. A man in the men's room gave him a black eye once, and a lady from Cincinnati kneed him in the balls one morning. He walked bowlegged for almost three days. He reported both cases to the security people out there and they just laughed.'

'I'm not surprised,' Hoke said. 'Your brother was a Krishna, and the airport lost its case in court when they tried to get them barred from begging out there. So I can see how security would turn their heads the other way when Krishnas are attacked. On the other hand, the Krishnas annoy a lot of people with their aggressive tactics.'

'What do you think, Junior?' Susan turned her head.

Freddy dropped his cigarette into the Coke can. 'I think we should go and take a look at the body right now. It may not be Marty after all, and I'm pretty sure the sergeant here would like to get it over with and go home to his dinner.'

'My car's down in the patio.' Hoke started for the escalator, and they followed him.

Hoke's well-battered 1974 Le Mans was indeed parked on the school patio. He had been unable to find a parking place on the street, so he had jumped the curb and driven over the flagstones to within a few yards of the escalator. There were winos lounging on the patio benches. Two old men, by the wall outside the bookstore, slept noisily on flattened cardboard boxes. Two other derelicts on a nearby concrete bench jeered and gave Hoke the finger as he unlocked the alarm in the left front fender and then unlocked the door and took his police placard off the dashboard. He shoved the placard under the front seat before unlocking the door to the passenger side of the car.

'We'd better all sit in front,' Hoke suggested. 'A man was sick on the back seat yesterday, and I haven't had a chance to get it cleaned up yet.'

Susan sat in the middle. Freddy, on the outside, unrolled his window. 'Why does the college let these winos hang around the school?' Freddy said.

'They suspended the old vagrancy laws a few years back. We can't arrest 'em anymore, and if we could, where would we put 'em? On top of the normal eight thousand vags who come down here for the winter, we've got another twenty thousand Nicaraguans, ten thousand Haitian refugees, and another twenty-five thousand Marielitos running around town.'

'What's a Marielito?' Freddy said.

'Where have you been?' Hoke said, not unkindly. 'Our wimpy ex-president, Jimmy Carter, opened his arms to one hundred and twenty-five thousand Cubans back in 1980. Most of them were legitimate, with families already here in Miami, but Castro also opened his prisons and insane asylums and sent along another twenty-five thousand hardcore criminals, gays, and maniacs. They sailed here from Mariel, in Cuba, so they call them Marielitos.'

As Hoke reached forward and switched off the police calls on his radio, a ragged Latin man came up to his window and pounded on it with his fists, shouting:

'Gimme money! Gimme money!'

'See what I mean?' Hoke said. 'When you drive around Miami, Susan, always keep your windows rolled up. Otherwise, they'll reach in and steal your purse.'

'I know,' Susan said, 'my brother told me.'

Hoke backed expertly into the street, honking his horn until the traffic gave way.

As Hoke drove north on Biscayne Boulevard toward the city morgue, Freddy said, 'This old boat rides pretty smooth. You wouldn't think so, just from looking at it.'

'I had a new engine put in it. It's my own car, not a police vehicle. The radio belongs to the department, and the red light, but they give us detectives mileage if we use our own personal vehicles. Fifteen cents a mile, which doesn't begin to cover it, and nothing for amortization. But the convenience is worth it. If you order a vehicle from the motor pool you have to wait for a half-hour or more, and then it may be low on gas or have a bad tire or something. So I usually drive my own car. I should do something about the dents, but I'd have them back again the next day. Twenty percent of the drivers in Miami can't qualify for a license, so they drive without one.'

The morgue was a low one-story building. Its limited storage space had been supplemented by two leased air-conditioned trailers to keep up with the flow of bodies that were delivered every day. Hoke parked, and they followed him into the office. Dr Evans had left for the day, but Dr Ramirez, an assistant pathologist, took them to a gurney in the hallway and showed them the body.

'That's Martin, all right,' Susan said quietly.

'I never met Martin, sergeant, but he looks like a nice guy,' Freddy said. 'He doesn't look anything like you, Susan.'

'Not now he doesn't, but back when we were little and almost the same size, people used to take us for fraternal twins.' She looked up at Hoke. 'We were born only ten months apart, although Marty looks older than me now.' Tears welled from Susan's eyes, and she brushed them away impatiently.

'Is it true,' Freddy asked Hoke, 'that a man's hair and fingernails keep growing after he's dead? I notice some stubble there on Marty's chin.'

'I don't know, although I've heard that myself. Is it true, Dr Ramirez?'

'No, it isn't true. That's just normal stubble on his face. He probably shaved this morning, and that's just his growth for today. One thing for sure, the nail on his middle finger won't grow any longer. The finger was broke clean off. We haven't done the autopsy yet, but Pussgut took a cursory look when he first came in, and there were no other wounds.'

'"Pussgut,"' Hoke explained to Freddy and Susan, 'is what the people around here call Dr Evans when he isn't around to hear them say it. They call him that because of his paunch.'

'I'm sorry,' Dr Ramirez said. 'I meant to say "Dr Evans." Is the sister here going to sign the papers?'

'I'll sign something to say he's my brother, but I won't sign anything else. Anything else, funeral arrangements or anything, you'll have to notify my father. It's his responsibility, not mine.'

In the office, Susan signed the form Dr Ramirez made out. He Xeroxed a copy on the office machine and gave it to Hoke. Hoke folded the Xeroxed form into a square and tucked it into his notebook. They shook hands with Dr Ramirez and then went out to the car. When they were seated, Hoke suggested that they stop for a drink.

'Fine with me,' Freddy said. 'But make it some place where I can get a sandwich.'

'We'll stop at a Brazilian steak house on Biscayne. They've got the best steak sandwiches in town.'

They were shown to a table right away. Hoke ordered a rum and Coke, Freddy a glass of red wine, and Susan asked for a Shirley Temple, claiming she never drank anything stronger than beer and that she didn't feel like having a beer on top of the yogurt she had eaten for dinner. The waiter, a Salvadoran with very little English, had difficulty with the Shirley Temple. Hoke had to cross over to the bar and explain to the Costa Rican bartender how to make it.

Hoke waved away the menu, which was printed in Portuguese, and ordered two steak sandwiches and three flans. The steak sandwiches arrived, redolent of garlic, along with the desserts.

Freddy dug into the custard immediately, and finished it before he covered his sandwich with A-1 Sauce.

'Where'd you do your time?' Hoke asked Freddy. 'Marianna or Raiford?'

'Time? What time? What makes you think I did time?'

Hoke shrugged. 'The way you tucked into that flan, and because you ate it first, before tackling your sandwich. How long were you in Marianna?'

'I don't even know where Marianna is.'

'It's our state juvenile reform school. Where're you from?'

'California. Santa Barbara. I came here to Miami to study management at Miami-Dade. When we graduate, me and Susan're going to get us a Burger King franchise somewhere. So she's studying business and management, too. I think I see what you mean, though, about eating my dessert first. But that's because I was an orphan and raised in a foster home. There were three other guys there, all of us about the same age, and you more or less had to eat your dessert first or somebody else would snatch it.'

'The same ritual, you'll discover, is practiced at Raiford. So at least if you ever get into trouble down here you've got a good habit going for you. I didn't get your name, except for the "Junior."'

'Ramon Mendez.'

'You don't have a Spanish accent. Have you got your green card?'

'I'm not a Chicano, I'm an American citizen. And I've got ID if you want to see it. Just because a man's got a Spanish name, that doesn't make him a refugee or something. It just so happens that Mendez was my father's name, but my mother was as big a WASP as you are. Besides, I already told you I was brought up with all white guys in a foster home!'

'Don't get excited, Ramon. We're just having a little pleasant conversation here. Do you speak Spanish?'

'A little, sure. I went to school in Santa Barbara, and we had our share of Chicanos out there. You pick it up a little playing softball. You know, shouting "Arriba, arriba!" when a guy's trying to reach second base on a steal.'

'You pump a little iron, too, right?'

'A little. I can jerk three-twenty-five, but I don't like to do it. I'm not really into heavy lifting. I just like to work out, that's all.'

'What's your bicep?'

Freddy shrugged. 'I haven't measured in a while. It used to be twenty-one inches. I doubt if it's that much now.'

'I'm impressed.'

'Well, I'm not one of your body lovers. As I said, I just like to work out for the exercise, that's all.'

Hoke turned to Susan. 'How's your Shirley Temple, Miss Waggoner? Would you rather have some coffee? Some espresso?'

'No, no, this is fine. I was supposed to meet my brother at the airport tonight at eight-thirty. And he was gonna give me two hundred dollars to make the car payment. D'you have his wallet and money for me?'

'If you phone your father and ask him to call me and okay it, I can hand over the effects. There's a little more than two hundred in the wallet. I've got it locked in my office drawer.'

'Do I have to call my father? Can't you just give it to me?'

'No. He's the one who should decide on the disposition of the effects, money included.'

'He'll just say no, and I need the money for the car payment. He'll probably take the car, too, won't he?'

'Is the car in your brother's name?'

She nodded and began to cry. 'It just isn't fair! We both worked hard to buy that car, to make the down payment and all, and now my father'll get it!'

'Maybe your brother left a will?'

'Why would he have a will? He was only twenty-one years old. He didn't expect to die from a broken finger! I still don't see how anybody can die from a broken finger.'

'Let me explain,' Hoke said. He finished the last bite of his sandwich and wiped his mouth with his napkin. 'Dr Evans is the best pathologist in America, and he's the best doctor and dentist, too. He said it wasn't the finger, but the shock that set in because of the broken finger. And if he says that, it's gospel. Let me tell you about Dr Evans. 'Bout a year ago, I had some abscessed teeth, and the only way I could chew was to hold my head over to one side and chew like a dog on the side that didn't hurt. I was having lunch with Dr Evans, and after lunch, he took me back to the morgue, shot me up with Novocaine, and pulled all my teeth. Every one of them. Then he made an impression and had these teeth made for me by the same technician who makes all of the Miami Dolphins' false teeth.'

Hoke took out his dentures, put them on a napkin, and handed them to Susan.

'I didn't even know you had false teeth,' Susan said. 'Did you, Junior?'

'No, I didn't,' Freddy said. 'Let me take a look at those.'

Susan passed the teeth to Freddy, and he examined them closely before giving them back to Hoke. 'Nice,' he said.

'I call 'em my Dolphin choppers,' Hoke said. He sprinkled some water from his glass on his dentures, then slipped the dentures back into his mouth and adjusted them. 'That's the kind of doctor Dr Evans is – and he didn't charge me a dime. He just did it for the experience, he said. I went home after he pulled my teeth, drank a half of a fifth of bourbon, and didn't feel a thing.

'But to get back to the will, if your brother was a sworn-in Krishna, they might've had him make out a will for them. As I understand it, when you join the group, you're supposed to sign over everything you own to them. I'd better check that out.'

'In that case, the Krishnas'll get the two hundred dollars and the car. Either way, I'll be shit out of luck, won't I?'

'Perhaps. His partner's notified them at the ashram by now, so if he does have a will on file, they'll probably come down to the station tomorrow to see me. They may not know about the car, but his partner will know he collected some money out at the airport today. Just in case, I won't mention the car to them. As a Krishna, I know he isn't supposed to own a private vehicle. Does your father know about the car?'

'I don't know. But I don't think so.'

'Don't worry about it, then. Just keep quiet, and make the payments. After a few months, or when it's paid for, you can get a lawyer to have it changed over to your name.'

Hoke took out his wallet, shuffled through his card case, and handed Susan a business card. 'When you need a lawyer, try this guy, Izzy Steinmetz. He costs a little more, just like the breath mints, but he's worth it.' Hoke smiled at Freddy. 'He's a good criminal lawyer, too, in case you ever get into trouble.'

'Hang on to the card,' Freddy said to Susan. 'Maybe Mr Steinmetz can help us when we get our Burger King franchise.'

The waiter brought the check. Hoke took it, and left a $3 tip on the table. They walked over to the cashier by the double doors. Hoke put the check and his credit card on the counter. The manager smiled, tore the check in half, and pushed the card back.

'Your credit's no good here, Sergeant Moseley. Why don't we see you in here more often? It's been quite a while now.'

'I'm working days now, and living over at the Beach. I'll try to get by more often. Thanks, Aquilar.'

'That was nice of him,' Freddy said, after they were outside, 'to tear up the check that way.'

'But you noticed,' Hoke said, 'that I offered to pay. Aquilar's a nice guy. We go back a long way, and I did a favor for him once.'

'What kind of a favor?'

'I called him on the phone. Where do you want me to drop you, Susan?'

'Second and Biscayne'll be fine.'

Hoke dropped them off at the corner of Second and Biscayne. He started to make an illegal U-turn to get back to the MacArthur Causeway and then changed his mind. He didn't want to go home; he never wanted to go home. He continued down the boulevard and headed for the Dupont Plaza Hotel.

The pair had puzzled him. He had tried to jar them into some kind of reaction by showing them his Dolphin choppers, but they hadn't even risen above the level of mild curiosity. Cold fish. The jock was obviously an ex-con. There was no way that Mendez could be his real name. With that bronze tan, he looked like an Afrika Corps Nazi, and it was definitely a tan, not dark skin.

Besides, the world was too fresh and new to him, as though he had been out of circulation for some time. The way he had crooked that Charles Atlas arm around the tiny cup of flan – who did he think would try to take it away from him, anyway? It wasn't enough that Carter had destroyed the city by sending in all the refugees, Reagan was importing ex-cons from California. Even if immigration was stopped altogether, it would be another twenty years before Miami got back to normal again.

And the girl. She had looked at her dead brother as if he were a piece of meat. True, she had cried at the morgue, but she had cried much harder about the possible loss of her car and the $200. How could a girl as simple-minded as Susan Waggoner get into college?

Hoke drove into the Dupont Plaza garage and parked on the ramp by the wall. As he locked the car, a Cuban attendant came running over. He had a parking stub in one hand, and a one-ounce hit of café Cubano in the other.

'I'll take those keys,' he said, holding out the parking stub.

Hoke showed him his shield and ignored the stub. 'Police business. I'll leave the car right where it is. When more cars come in, drive around it.'

Hoke went into the bar lounge, filled a paper plate with chicken wings, hot meatballs, and green olives, then went to the bar. He ordered a beer reluctantly because a beer in the Dupont Plaza bar cost as much as a six-pack in the supermarket, but the free hors d'oeuvres just about made up for it. Hoke liked the Dupont Plaza, the quiet Mickey Mouse music that came over the speakers, and the tables beside the windows where he could watch the traffic on the Miami River. There was an older, dressed-up crowd here, and although his blue poplin leisure suit was out of place, he had once picked up a forty-year-old widow from Cincinnati, and she had taken him up to her room.

Hoke showed the bartender his shield and asked for the telephone. The bartender reached under the bar and placed a white telephone in front of Hoke. As a matter of principle, Hoke never gave Ma Bell a quarter to use a pay telephone. He dialed Red Farris's number from memory.

'Red,' Hoke said, when Farris answered, 'let's go out and do something.'

'Hoke! I'm glad you called. I tried to get you twice today, once at the station, and once at your hotel. The hotel didn't even answer.'

'You've got to let it ring. Sometimes the clerk's a way from the desk.'

'I let it ring ten times.'

'Try twenty next time. I was out at the airport most of the afternoon, on a homicide.'

'How come they called you instead of Metro?'

'I'll tell you when I see you. It's an interesting case.'

'That's why I tried to call you, Hoke, to tell you my good news. Are you ready? I resigned today.'

'Resigned from the department? You're shitting me.'

'Not this time, Hoke. I told you before I've been writing letters around the state. Well, the chief of police in Sebring offered me a job as desk sergeant, and I took it.'

'That means going back into uniform, doesn't it?'

'So what? I'll be out of Miami. When I typed up my resignation, I never felt better.'

'What kind of salary goes with it?'

'Not much.'

'How much? Sebring can't pay Miami's union scale.'

'I know. It's only fourteen thousand, Hoke. I'm making thirty-one in Robbery, but the chief said there'd probably be another two thousand a year when the new Sebring budget comes out.'

'Christ, Red, that's less than half of what you're making now.'

'I know, and I don't give a shit. It doesn't cost as much to live in Sebring, and the chances are that I'll live a hell of a lot longer up there.'

'There's nothing going on in Sebring. They have the race once a year, and that's it.'

'I know. That's why I took the job. Last week, a kid in Overtown threw a brick through my window.'

'You shouldn't drive your car in Overtown. You know that.'

'It was a squad car, Hoke. I was down there with Nelson to pick up a fence. We never found him, either. But that brick was it. I'd been wavering, because of the money and all, but the next morning I called the chief in Sebring. He's a nice guy, too, Hoke. You'd like him. He's a retired detective from Newark. That's in New Jersey.'

'I know where Newark is, for God's sake.'

'Don't get pissed off, Hoke.'

'I'm not pissed off, I'm just surprised, that's all. I know damned well you aren't going to like living in a little town like that. Why don't we meet some place and talk about it?'

'I can't, Hoke. I've got a lot of things to do and then I've got to meet Louise later when she gets off work.'

'When are you leaving, Red? I'll see you before you go, won't I?'

'Oh, sure. I'll be in town for another week at least. If I can't sell my condo, I'll have to rent it out. But we'll get together. We'll tie one on to celebrate.'

'Right. I'm here at the Dupont bar, if you can get away for a while before you pick up Louise.'

'I can't, Hoke. Not tonight.'

'Call me, then.'

'I'll call you.'

'I'm real happy for you, Red, if you think that's what you want.'

'Thanks, Hoke. It's what I want.'

'Call me.'

'I will.'

Hoke racked the phone, and the bartender put it beneath the bar again. 'Another beer, sir?'

'Yeah. And a double shot of Early Times. I don't want any more of the stuff on this plate either. Can you dump it for me?'

Hoke took his shot of whiskey and fresh bottle of beer over to a table by the window. He really hated to see Red Farris leave the department. He was one of the few bachelor friends Hoke had left. Red was almost always available to go out for a few drinks, or a little bottle pool, or to bowl a few lines. And Red Farris had saved his life, too. They had gone to pick up a wife-beater who was out on bail. The man's wife had died, and that upgraded the charge from assault to second degree murder. It was a simple pickup; the man didn't put up any fight or argument. He had been too shocked by the news of his wife's death. And then, just as Hoke had started to put the handcuffs on him, the man's twelve-year-old son had come out of the bedroom and shot Hoke in the chest with a .22 rifle. Farris got the rifle out of the kid's hands before he could get off another shot, and Hoke spent six weeks in the hospital with a nicked left lung. It still hurt if he took a very deep breath. But if Red Farris hadn't twisted that rifle out of the kid's hands – Well, the kid was in a foster home somewhere, the kid's father was up in Raiford, and the boy's mother was dead. In Miami, a family could break up in a hurry.

It used to be a lot different when Hoke was still married. Four or five couples would get together for a barbecue and some beer. Then, after they ate, the women would all sit in the living room and talk about how difficult their deliveries had been, and the men would sit in the kitchen and play poker. The big kids would watch TV, and the smaller kids would be put to sleep in the bedroom. That had been real Florida living, but now all the white families were moving away. There were six different detectives Hoke had known who had left Miami in the last year alone. And now Farris – that was seven. Of course, Henderson could get out for a night once in a while, but Bill Henderson was married, and he always worried about staying out too late.

Hoke looked out at the river, never the same river. He wanted another double shot of Early Times, but not at these prices. Hoke left the bar and got his car from the parking ramp. As he checked the window locks, the smell of the vomit on the back seat was almost overpowering. When he got to the Eldorado Hotel, he'd get one of the Marielitos who lived there to clean it out.

Chapter Seven

The one-way street was narrow after they left the well-lighted area of the Columbus Hotel on Biscayne. The sidewalk was cracked and broken from recent roadwork, and there were few pedestrians.

'Where's the parking garage?' Freddy took Susan's thin arm as they skirted a Bob's Barricade horse and a flaming kerosene pot.

'Up about four blocks. I didn't want the detective to see my car. I'm sorry now I even mentioned it to him. If he lets it slip out to Daddy that I've got it, he'll take it.'

'That prick detective's pretty sharp. Unless he does it on purpose, he won't let anything slip out. He sure picked up on me in a hurry. I think I had him fooled on the dessert business, because I really was in a foster home in Santa Barbara. But he knows that a man can't hold down a regular job and still work out six hours a day building up muscles like mine.'

'Why'd you tell him your name was Ramon Mendez? You don't look nothing like these Cubans.' She pointed to four ragged Mariclitos across the street. They were unwrapping a large bundle of clothes between two parked cars.

'I told him Mendez because I checked into the hotel under the name of Gotlieb with a stolen credit card. Wait. Let's go over there and see what they've got in that bundle.'

'Let's don't! You don't want to have nothing to do with these people, Junior. It's just something they stole, anyway.' She tugged at his arm.

'Okay. But it's always interesting to look into a bundle. You never know what you'll find.'

'You mess with these Cubans and they'll pull a knife on you.' At the next corner, they waited for the light to change. 'If your name isn't Gotlieb, and it isn't Mendez, what is it?'

'Junior, like I told you. My last name's Frenger. I'm really German, I suppose, but I don't remember my parents. I was in four different foster homes, but no one ever told me anything about my parents. They said I was an orphan, but they could've been lying about that. They lied about everything else, so it's possible my parents are still alive somewhere. I've always thought my father must've been an important man, though, or he wouldn't've named me Junior. At least that proves I'm not a bastard. You don't name a kid after yourself if you aren't married. What d'you think?'

'I'm too upset to think right now. On top of everything else, I think Mr Turner's going to make us write a haiku, and I don't think I can do it.'

'It seems simple enough to me. There're only seventeen syllables. Five, seven, and five. I'll write some for you, and you can keep 'em in your purse. Then, if he gives you a makeup paper in his office, you can copy them in your own handwriting.'

'Suppose I have to explain what they mean?'

'I'll tell you what they mean after I write them.'

'Would you?'

'Sure. We're engaged, aren't we?'

'Did you really mean that? When you told Mr Turner we were engaged?'

'Why not? I've never even gone steady before.'

They reached the six-story parking garage. Susan showed her parking pass to the attendant behind the bulletproof window. He took her keys from the board, raised the grate an inch, and slid them across the Formica countertop.

'I pay eighty dollars a month to park here. And that's the student rate. Some of these downtown lots charge three dollars an hour, and they make so much money they won't give you a monthly rate.' They took the elevator to the fifth floor. 'But they're nasty about it here. If I don't get here early enough in the morning to get a space, the garage fills up and they put out a full sign. So even though I've paid in advance, I still can't park. It isn't fair.'

'You use that word a lot.'

'What word?'

'*Fair*. Now that you're twenty years old –'

'Only by one month –'

'– you'd better forget about things like *fair* and *unfair*. Even when people talk about the weather, *fair* doesn't mean anything.'

'But there's such a thing as –'

'No, there isn't. Jesus, is this your car?'

Susan unlocked the driver's door to a white 1982 TransAm. There was a flaming red bird decal on the hood and flowing red flames painted on all four of the fenders.

'It's mine now, if they don't take it away from me. It was the first thing we bought when we had enough saved for the down payment. Marty was crazy about it. But he only got to drive it two or three times. What he wanted was a car that would impress his friends when we went back to Okeechobee. That's why I'm pretty sure he never told Daddy about the car. He wanted to surprise everybody. There are real leather seats, you know. Black glove leather. D'you want to drive, Junior?'

'No. I can drive, but I'm not a very good driver. And even though I've got three California licenses on me, I don't fit the descriptions. Besides, you'd have to tell me where to turn and all.'

Freddy got into the passenger's soft bucket seat. He felt as though he were sitting in a deep pit, even though the visibility was excellent through the tinted front window. The side and back windows had been layered with chocolate film; they were almost black.

Susan started the engine. 'I'll turn the air conditioning down in just a second. It'll really freeze your ass off if you leave it on high very long.'

'Do you need gas? I've got Ramon Mendez's Seventy-six card.'

'This thing always needs gas. It only gets about nine miles to a gallon. Something's wrong with the carburetor, I think.'

'Well, don't worry about gas. I can get all of the gas credit cards we'll need.'

Susan roared down the spiraling driveway and into the street. She drove through the streets aggressively, taking the Eighth Street ramp to the overhead freeway to South Dixie. But once on South Dixie, in three lanes, the traffic was heavy, and it was stop-and-go driving until they reached South Miami and Sunset Drive. The heavy traffic thinned out slightly when she turned west on Sunset.

'People can't see in at all, can they?' Freddy said.

'Not very well. To see inside you have to put your face right up against the glass.'

'I haven't seen much of the city, either.'

'You can't see much at night. I'll take you around tomorrow, anywhere you want to go.'

They had the car filled at a Shell station. Freddy paid for the gas with Gotlieb's credit card. As the attendant wrote down the license number on the sales slip, Freddy shook his head. 'I forgot they did that. Tomorrow we're going to either get some new license plates or a new car. We should've stopped along the way so I could've picked up some new license plates. I could've changed them before we got the gas.'

Susan opened the door, jumped out, and dashed after the attendant. She got the credit slip back, and paid the man cash for the fuel. She got back into the driver's seat and tore up the credit slip.

'I'll probably lose the car, but we might as well keep it as long as we can.'

'That was quick thinking, Susie. I'm so used to using credit cards, I never thought about paying cash.'

'I always pay cash. Still, I try not to carry more'n fifty dollars on me at a time.'

'Tomorrow I'll get us some out-of-state plates we can switch. And tomorrow night I'd better get some Miami credit cards. I'll get some for you, too, some ladies' cards, so you can buy things when I'm not around.'

There were thirty four-story condominium apartment buildings in the complex that made up Kendall Pines Terrace, but only six of the buildings had been completed and occupied. The other buildings were unpainted, windowless, concrete shells. Construction had been suspended for more than a year. Almost all of the apartments in the occupied buildings were empty. For the most part, their owners had purchased them at preconstruction prices during the real estate boom in 1979. But now, in fall 1982, construction prices had risen, and very few people could qualify for loans at 17 percent interest.

'There's been some vandalism out here,' Susan said, when she parked in her numbered space in the vast and almost empty parking lot. 'So they built a cyclone fence and hired a Cuban to drive around at night in a Jeep. That's stopped it. But sometimes, late at night, it's a little scary out here.'

There was a tropical courtyard in the hollow square of Building Six-East. Broad-leaved plants had been packed in thickly around the five-globed light in the center of the patio, and cedar bark had been scattered generously around the plants. There was a pleasant tingle of cedar and night-blooming jasmine in the air.

Susan had a corner two-bedroom, two-bath apartment with a screened porch facing the Everglades. There was eggshell wall-to-wall carpet throughout the apartment, except for the kitchen, which had a linoleum floor in a white brick pattern. Both bathrooms had been tiled in blue and pink. The furniture in the living room was rattan, with blue-and-green striped cushions. There was a large brass bed in the master bedroom. In the smaller bedroom, Susan's, there was a Bahama bed and a rattan desk. There were antique white Levolors in all of the windows, but no curtains or draperies.

While Freddy looked around the apartment, Susan got two San Miguel beers out of the refrigerator. She took Freddy out to the screened porch and pointed toward the dark Everglades.

'In the daytime you can see them, but not now. For the next four miles or so those are all tomato and cucumber fields. Then you get to Krome Avenue, and beyond that it's the East Everglades – nothing but water and alligators. It gets too drowned with water to build on the other side of Krome, and Kendall Pines Terrace is the last complex in Kendall. Eventually, the rest of those fields will all be condos, because Kendall is the chicest neighborhood in Miami. But they won't be able to build anymore in the 'Glades unless they drain them.'

'This apartment looks expensive.'

'It is, for the girl that owns it. She put every cent she had into it, and then found out she couldn't afford to live here. She's just a legal secretary, so she had to rent it out, furniture and all. We only pay her four hundred a month rent, but she was glad to get it. She tried to sell or rent it for four months before we came along. Even with our four hundred, she still has to come up with another four-fifty every month.'

'Where does she live now?'

'She had to move back with her parents in Hallandale, and she's twenty-five years old. I know how bad she feels. I'd never move back in with Daddy. I'd rather die first.'

'This is good beer.'

'San Miguel dark. It's the best, and it comes all the way from the Philippine Islands. The man at Crown gets it for me. Of course, in addition to the four hundred a month, the electric bill comes to another two hundred.'

'No shit?'

Susan nodded. 'On account of the air conditioning. And it'll be going up again soon. The anchorette on Channel Ten said so last night. Without the money from Marty coming in, I don't think I can handle it. I'm worried.'

'Don't be. We're engaged, so I'll take care of it.'

Freddy put his fingers on the screen. The dead man in the morgue was sure as hell the same guy at the airport. He hadn't meant to kill him; all he had wanted to do was break the guy's finger. Just because of the jacket, and now he didn't even have the leather jacket with him. What he did have was the simple-minded younger sister. He could feel the damp jets of air coming through the screen. There were only six cars parked in the ten-acre parking lot. The white TransAm, in its numbered slot, seemed to glow in the sixth row. Every other parking light in the lot had been turned off, to save energy, perhaps, and the other lights had been dimmed. The moon wasn't up yet, and beyond the cyclone fence was blackness. Looking out and down into the dark land mass, Freddy felt as if he were on the edge of an abyss. Perspiration from his armpits trickled down his sides.

'Let's go back inside,' Freddy said. 'Doesn't it even cool off at night?'

'A little. Around four in the morning it'll drop down to seventy-seven or so, but then the humidity'll go up.'

Freddy took off his shoes and his shirt. Susan sat on the couch in the living room. 'D'you want to watch some TV, Junior?'

'Not now. I've got to make a phone call. Where's the telephone book?'

'There's two books over there, under the breakfast table. The phone's on the –'

'I can see the phone.'

Freddy looked up the number of the International Hotel. He called the desk, checked out, and told the clerk to charge everything, including his barber bill, to his Gotlieb credit card. 'Yes,' he finished, 'I did have a pleasant stay.'

Freddy joined Susan on the couch and told her to bring him a pair of scissors. He cut up the Gotlieb credit and identification cards, and put the cut pieces into the ashtray.

'Now,' he said, 'Mr Gotlieb's no longer in Miami.'

Freddy patted the lounge, and Susan sat beside him. 'I liked the way you handled yourself at the morgue, Susan. What were you thinking about, anyway, when you saw your dead brother?'

'I was thinking about the times when he used to bend my fingers back when he wanted me to do something. It really hurt, and after a while he didn't have to bend them back. All he had to do was threaten to do it, and I'd do whatever he wanted. He was religious, I guess, but he was awfully mean. He said he wanted to go to heaven, and now he's got what he wanted.' She was lost in thought for a moment, then she looked up.

'What I want to do, first thing tomorrow, is go down to the bank and take out the CD. Then I can start another one some place else. We've got a ten-thousand-dollar CD saved, plus another four thousand in our joint NOW account. And I sure don't want Daddy or the Krishnas to get it.'

'Good. We'll do that first thing. Now that we're engaged, we're going to start our platonic marriage. D'you know what that is?'

Susan nodded. 'Beth had one, on *The Days of Our Lives*, when she moved in with the lawyer. And I want one too. I've been really lonely out here at night. I didn't like Marty, but even so, I missed him when he moved out to the camp.'

'Why didn't you like him? He was your brother.'

'Remember, before, when I told you I never went steady? Marty's why, that's why. He's the one that got me pregnant, and I think Daddy suspicioned it, too. And then when we came down to Miami and I got the abortion, Marty couldn't find any work. He met Pablo when he was looking for work at the hotel. So then he made me go to work for Pablo. I don't like working at the hotel, Junior, I really don't. That old man from Dayton, Ohio, today was disgusting.'

'You've turned your last trick for Pablo. You're living with me now.'

'You really don't know Pablo. He smiles and bows and all that, but he's mean. And he knows where I – where we live, Junior.'

'Don't worry about Pablo. I'll take care of him. Do you remember that Bob Dylan song about the lady lying across a brass bed?'

'I don't remember. Maybe I did. They don't play much Dylan on the radio anymore.'

'Well, here's what you do. Go into the bedroom, take off your clothes, put two pillows under your stomach, and lay face down on the big brass bed. I'm gonna have another beer, and then I'll be right in.'

'You're gonna do it to me the back way whether I want to or not, aren't you?'

'Yeah.'

'In that case, I'd better get another San Miguel for you, and some Crisco for me.'

Later, bars of moonlight came through the slanted vertical Levolors and made yellow bars across Freddy's hairless chest. Susan, in a shorty nightgown, snuggled close to him and used his extended right arm as a pillow. Freddy chuckled deep in his throat and then snorted.

'Remember that haiku the teacher wrote?'

'Not exactly,' Susan said.

The Miami sun/Rising in the Everglades/Burger in a bun. That's what I was laughing at. Now I know what it means.'

Chapter Eight

There was a middle-aged man sitting in the glass-walled office with Sergeant Bill Henderson when Hoke arrived in the squad room. Hoke checked his mailbox and then signaled his presence to Henderson with a wave of his arm. Henderson beckoned for him to come over. Henderson got to his feet and smiled as Hoke crossed the crowded squad room. Most of Henderson's front teeth were reinforced with silver inlays, and his smile was a sinister grimace. Hoke and Bill had been working together for almost four years, and Hoke knew that when Henderson smiled, something horrible about human nature had been reconfirmed for his partner.

Hoke cracked open the door. 'I'm going down for coffee, Bill. I'll be right back.'

'I already got you coffee.' Henderson pointed to the capped Styrofoam cup on Hoke's side of the double desk. 'I want you to meet Mr Waggoner. We've been having an interesting little chat here, and I know you'll want to hear what he's got to say.'

Hoke shook hands and sat in his chair. 'Sergeant Moseley. I'm Sergeant Henderson's partner.'

'Clyde Waggoner. I'm Martin's father.' The man from Okeechobee was wearing a white rayon tie with a blue chambray work shirt, and khaki trousers. There was a thin nylon Sears windbreaker folded over his left arm. He had short brown hair with shaved temples, the kind of haircut they call white sidewalls in the armed forces. His skin was sallow, but it was blotchy in places from long exposure to the Florida sun, and there were scars on his nose and cheeks from debrided skin cancers.

'I suppose you came for your son's effects,' Hoke said, unlocking his desk drawer. 'Sorry I'm a little late this morning, but I had to drop off some dry cleaning.'

Mr Waggoner looked down at his scuffed engineer boots, made a goatlike sound in his throat, and began to cry. The sound was softly muffled, but the tears that came down his blotchy cheeks were genuine. Hoke directed a puzzled look at Henderson, and his partner broadened his brutal smile.

'Just tell Sergeant Moseley the same story you told me, Mr Waggoner. I could summarize it, but I might leave something out.'

Mr Waggoner blew his nose on a blue bandanna and stuffed the handkerchief into his left hip pocket. He wiped his cheeks with his fingers.

'I can't prove nothing, sergeant, as I told Sergeant Henderson here. All I can tell you is what I think happened. I hope I'm wrong, I surely do hope so. My business is bad enough already, and a scandal like this could make it worse. Okeechobee's a small town, and our moral standards are a lot different up there than they are down here in Miami. You know what they call Miami up in Okeechobee?'

'No, but I don't suppose it's complimentary.'

'It ain't. They call it Sin City, Sergeant Moseley.'

'Are you, perhaps, a man of the cloth?'

'No, sir. Software. I got me a software store in Okeechobee. I sell video games, computers, and rent out TV sets and movies.'

'My father owns a hardware store in Riviera Beach,' Hoke said.

'He's smarter than me, then. What I had in mind when I opened the store was a computer business for the commercial fishing on the lake. The government sets quotas, you see, and I figured if the fish houses had computers they could always prove exactly how much fish they caught and all that. Plus they'd know when they was falling behind, and so on. Then last year, when the lake went down to nine feet, the government stopped commercial fishing almost altogether. No nets allowed, you see, so all the fish houses're just about out of business now. Besides, nobody's buying computers up there because there ain't no programs written up for lake fishing anyway.'

'So you're just about out of business, right?'

'Oh, no – I'm doing all right. But I borrowed money to expand, and the interest is hurting me. My movie rental club alone pays my rent each month, but I'm in pretty heavy to the bank, you see. But I ain't here to talk business. What I was telling Sergeant Henderson here is that I suspect foul play.'

'What kind of foul play?'

'That was no accident that killed Martin. That was murder.'

'If so, it's the first of a kind.'

'Let him finish,' Henderson said. 'There's more.'

'That's the best kind,' Mr Waggoner continued, 'the kind that looks like an accident but really ain't. I've seen it on *The Rockford Files* more'n once, and if it wasn't for Jim Rockford, a lot of people'd get away with it, too.'

'What makes you think your son's death wasn't an accident?'

'I'd really rather not talk about it because it's so painful to me, as a father, you see. But I'm also a good citizen, and justice, no matter how harsh, must be done. Even to kith and kin ...' He started to cry again, softer this time, and reached for his handkerchief.

Hoke took the plastic lid off his coffee and sipped it. It was cold. 'When did you get this coffee?'

'I got in a little early today,' Henderson said. 'But I didn't know you'd be a half-hour late.'

Hoke replaced the plastic lid and dropped the cup of coffee into the wastebasket. He lit a cigarette, took a long drag, and butted the cigarette in the ashtray as he allowed the smoke to trickle out through his nose.

'So you think, Mr Waggoner,' Hoke said, 'that this unidentified assailant who broke your son's middle finger killed him on purpose? Is that right?'

'That's about the size of it.' Mr Waggoner blew his nose, examined his handkerchief, and then put it back into his pocket. 'I think the man, whosoever he was, was hired to do it. That's what I think.'

'The chances of killing a man that way are pretty remote, Mr Waggoner. I doubt if more than one man in a thousand – I don't know the actual statistics – would die from a trauma to his finger. It would be pretty stupid to hire someone to kill anybody in that manner.'

'You might be right about that. But if a man was hired to injure somebody on purpose, and then that person died because of the injury, wouldn't that be a murder for hire?'

'A case could be made for that, I suppose. Except for a thousand unidentified passengers a day who don't like Hare Krishnas, who hated your son enough to hire someone to break his middle finger?'

'That's what's so painful to me.' Mr Waggoner sighed. 'I think my daughter hired him.'

Hoke took the morgue identification form out of his notebook, unfolded it, and placed it on the desk. 'Susan, the daughter who identified the body? Or do you have another daughter in mind?'

'No. Susan's the only daughter I got. And Martin was my only son. None of us got along too good, I'll admit that, and I sent her packing when she got pregnant. But Martin, even though he's the one that done it to her, was my only son, and she shouldn't've had him killed. Susan's just like her mother, who was no good either, so I know she talked Martin into doing it to her in the first place.' Mr Waggoner lowered his voice and his head. 'Men are weak. I know that because I'm weak when it comes to women myself. We all are, even you two gentlemen, if you don't mind my saying so. A woman can make you do anything she wants you to do with that there little hair-pie they've got between their legs. I know it, and you know it, too.'

'Let me get this straight,' Hoke said. 'Your own son impregnated his sister, your daughter, Susan, and then Susan hired someone to kill him for revenge. Is that right?'

'That's right. Yes, sir.'

'And where's the baby?'

'Susan had her an abortion here in Miami. I gave her eight hundred dollars when I sent her down here to get it. You can check that out easy enough, and Martin went with her, telling me he'd come back. He never did, though.'

'Are you positive Martin was the father?'

'No doubt about that. They was alone in the house all the time, and Martin, he never let her go out with no one else. I didn't see what was going on at first. I just thought he was protecting her from those other boys up there, the way a big brother'll look after his little sister. But after they left, I looked around the house some, and I found things. Martin, pretending to be so religious and all – butter beans wouldn't melt in his mouth – had two French ticklers hid in his old high school Blue Horse notebook way back in the closet. And they was other things, too ...' He looked at the toes of his boots and whispered. 'Noises in the night ... you know the kind. Down deep, I guess I must've known what they was up to all along, but I didn't want to believe it, so I pretended it was something else.

'I don't fear God or no man. What I fear is that little hair-pie, that's what I fear. And knowing what I know, and knowing what kind of girl Susie is, a sneaky little girl, I just know she got her revenge on Martin. But as I said, I can't prove nothing. I had to tell you what I think. The rest is up to you. I just hope you prove I'm wrong.'

'If I type up a statement about your suspicions,' Henderson said, 'will you sign it?'

'Well, no. I told you, and that should be enough. I'll sign for Martin's effects, though. I know I've got to do that.'

'I'm sorry,' Hoke said, 'but in view of what you've told us, we're going to hang on to them for a while. At least until we complete the investigation.'

'Including the money? Sergeant Henderson said Martin had more'n two hundred dollars in his wallet.'

'That's right. The money, too. He might've left a will, and in that case the money'll go into probate.'

'I understand. I guess that's the price a man pays for doing his duty. How do I get the body?'

'It depends upon when they finish the post-mortem. But you can notify any funeral director to take care of it for you. If you want a cremation, the Neptune Society will do it for you and scatter his ashes at sea.'

'Can't I get the ashes myself? I'd like to scatter 'em on the lake. Martin always loved the lake as a boy, so that's where he'd like to be scattered.'

'You can do whatever you like. You don't, by law, have to have the body embalmed, so don't let anybody talk you into that, Mr

Waggoner. Thank you for coming in.' Hoke stood up, and so did Mr Waggoner.

'You'll let me know, then, how the investigation comes out?'

'No. All our inquiries will be confidential. If the investigation's negative, it would be foolish to let anyone know we made one in the first place. So you don't have to worry about any publicity.'

'I may not look it,' Mr Waggoner said, 'but I'm ashamed. I'm deeply ashamed of what I had to tell you. Thank you both for being so patient.'

'I'll take you to the elevator,' Henderson said. 'It's easy to get turned around in this building.'

Henderson took a glazed doughnut out of his desk drawer, broke it in half, and offered the smaller half to Hoke. Hoke shook his head, and Henderson began to eat the doughnut.

'How'd you like Mr Waggoner's little story, Hoke?'

'I found the bit about the hair-pie instructive.'

'Me, too. Although I knew already that I was weak in that regard. You ever been in Okeechobee?'

'Years ago. But not since I left Riviera Beach. My dad and I went fishing for catfish on the lake a few times, but we only went into the town a couple of times. There's nothing much there, or there wasn't ten years ago. It's just an elbow bend on the highway north. I wouldn't think the town could support a software store, even if Waggoner rents out film for TV. But for all I know, Okeechobee's probably tripled in size by now, just like every other town in Florida the last few years. If a man likes to fish, it wouldn't be a bad place to retire.'

'Apparently, there's a shortage of women. Otherwise, a brother wouldn't have to screw his own sister.'

'You know I spent some time with the girl, Susan, last night, and there might be some truth to what Waggoner told us.'

'Bullshit. If you hire somebody in Miami to do a beating for you, you get a professional job with bicycle chains. You don't pay anyone fifty bucks to break a lousy finger.'

'But wouldn't a girl be chicken-hearted and not want her big brother hurt too badly?'

'Anything's possible. You want to check it out? We've got better things to do, you know.'

'Susan's boyfriend was with her when I took her down to the morgue. He's an ex-con, I'm positive, and strong enough to break someone's *arm*. He gave me a phony name, Ramon Mendez, and for no good reason that I could see – unless he's on the run.'

'Did you run a make on the name?'

'On Mendez? We've got hundreds of them. Remember when we tried to get a make on José Perez? Twenty-seven with records popped up. These Latins all have four last names and a half-dozen first names, including at least one saint on the list. And they use the ones they want at the time. But this boyfriend isn't a Latin in the first place. Remember the intelligence seminar we went to last year, the one the agent from Georgia gave? He was with the GBI.'

'I remember that sonofabitch all right. He learned my name in the first class and called on me at every session.'

'Well, Susan's boyfriend had blue eyes just like his – flat and staring. And he never looked away. I'd planned to lean on him a little, but after we talked for a while I knew I'd be wasting my time. Now, if Susan asked him to, this guy would break her brother's finger or neck without even thinking about it. He's done time, I'm sure, and he might even be a fugitive. He says he's from California, here to study management at Miami-Dade.'

'That's possible. People come from all over the world to study at Miami-Dade.'

'Not from California. In California, you can go to college free. So why would a man come three thousand miles to pay out-of-state fees at Miami-Dade?'

'You can go to college free in California?'

'That's right, right on through a bachelor's.'

'Why don't you check him out, then, at Miami-Dade?'

'I will. But I'll have to find out what his right name is first.'
Hoke got up, and pushed his chair into the desk kneehole.

'Is that where you're going now?'

'No. I'm going down to the cafeteria for some coffee and a doughnut.'

Chapter Nine

Susan made scrambled eggs with green peppers, buttered rye toast, and fried baloney slices for Freddy's breakfast. After he finished eating, he took his cup of coffee out to the screened porch. The brown, cultivated fields stretched out for several miles, and there were bands of dusty green that faded into a misty, darker green toward the horizon. The country was so incredibly flat he couldn't get over it. There wasn't a single mound or a dip or a gully for as far as he could see. And, from the fourth floor, the horizon had to be at least twenty or twenty-five miles away. Susie's apartment was on the western side of the building and shaded in the morning, but he knew that the sun would bake this side all afternoon.

Inside, with the air conditioning set on seventy-five, the apartment was nice and cool. Out on the porch, where the humid heat was at least eighty-five, the sudden change brought a shock to his skin. But he decided he liked the heat. Freddy didn't wear any underwear, and his linen slacks stuck to the backs of his legs as he sat in the plastic-webbed porch rocker. Susan, wearing white shorts and a light blue bikini halter, brought out the coffeepot and refilled his cup. Her bare feet were long and narrow, and she looked about thirteen years old.

'Explain about the bank business again,' Freddy said.

'It isn't a bank, it's a savings and loan, but it works just like a bank. I don't know the exact difference except that the S and L pays a higher interest rate. Marty and me got a CD for ten thousand in both our names, and a NOW checking account. The interest from the CD goes into our checking account automatically at the end of each month. There's more'n four thousand in it. So I'm going to draw it all out and start another CD and another NOW account in some other S and L. That way they won't be able to get none of it because it'll all be in my name.'

'That's no good,' Freddy said, shaking his head. 'They can still sue you, those Krishnas with their lawyers, and then they'll tie up all the money until the judge decides who gets it. What you do, when you go down there, is take out all the money and bring it to me. I'll take care of it.'

'That's too much money to keep around in cash. In Miami, somebody'll steal it from you.'

'I'll rent a safe-deposit box, except for some walking around money. I don't want you to worry about it. What you don't have, they can't take away from you.' He finished his coffee, handed her the cup. 'Now that we've got our platonic marriage going, I'll take care of you. Don't you worry about interest or anything else. If you want something, anything – and I don't mean just because you *need* something, I mean *want* something – tell me, and I'll get it for you. Who's that guy down there?' Freddy pointed to a man wearing a dark blue suit, complete with vest, getting into a new Buick Skylark in the parking lot.

'I don't know his name. He lives down in two-fourteen, and he carried some groceries up here for me once. He's a prephase real estate salesman, he told me. That's why he has to wear a suit and tie all the time.'

'What's a prephase salesman?'

'I don't know, but that's what he said he was. He seemed very nice and said he had a daughter about my age in junior high back in Ohio. I didn't tell him how old I was or proposition him. I don't think it's a good idea to fuck people where you have to live.'

'You'd better get going to the S and L. So go ahead and get dressed.'

'I am dressed. You don't have to get all dressed up out here in Kendall. All the women out here wear shorts and halters.'

'Except you. I don't want my wife running around like some little kid. Put on a dress and shoes and stockings. Do something about your hair, too. It's all tangled.'

'Aren't you going with me?'

'No. I'm going to study the street map of Miami. We'll go out when you come back.'

Freddy watched Susan drive out of the parking lot. He put on his shirt, but not his shoes, and took the fire stairs down to the second floor. He twisted the knob of the front door to 214 as far as it would go, and then forced the door open with his shoulder. It sprung open easily.

He found two $100 bills in the Bible on the bedside table and a loaded .38-caliber pistol in its leather holster in the drawer of the same table. There was a locked drawer in the metal home desk in the living room, but he found the key in the middle pencil drawer. He opened the locked drawer and found a cowhide case containing fifty silver dollars, each mounted in a round numbered slot. This was a collection, and much more valuable, he knew, than the $50 face value. When he rented the safe-deposit box, it might be a good idea to keep the collection to use as getaway bread. He took two pairs of black silk socks from the dresser and put his stolen items into a brown paper grocery sack he got from a stack under the kitchen sink. He added a package of six frozen pork chops from the freezer compartment to the sack, then returned to his own apartment.

The clothes in the salesman's closet, unhappily, had been at least two sizes too large for Freddy, but he was satisfied with his haul, especially with the pistol. He put the pork chops on the kitchen table so they would thaw for dinner. Then he shaved with a disposable lady's shaver Susan had unwrapped for him, and took a long tub bath.

Soaking in the tub, Freddy examined the Miami city map, section by section, from Perrine to North Bay Village. The greater Miami area was five times longer than it was wide, a long narrow urban strip hugging the coast and the bay, with no way to expand unless the buildings were built higher and higher. There was no way the city could expand any farther into the Everglades until they were drained, and the coastline was completely filled. If a man had to escape from the cops, he could only drive north or south. Only two roads crossed the Everglades to Naples, and both of these could be blocked. If a man drove south he would be caught, eventually, in Key West, and the cops could easily bottle up a man on the highways if he headed north, especially if he tried to take the Sunshine Parkway.

The only way to escape from anyone, in case he had to, would be to have three or four hidey-holes. One downtown, one in North

Miami, and perhaps a place over in Miami Beach. There would be no other safe method to get away except by going to ground until whatever it was that he'd have done was more or less forgotten about. Then, when the search was over, he could drive or take a cab to the airport and get a ticket to anywhere he wanted to go.

Well, Freddy thought, I've already got me a nice little hidey-hole out here in Kendall.

Susan returned before noon with two bags of groceries and $4,280 in fifties and twenties. Freddy sat at the uncleared breakfast table and counted the money while Susan began to put away the groceries.

'It's ten thousand dollars short,' he said.

'That's because I took out another CD at the S and L in Miller Square. There's plenty of money right there to spend or to lock away in a safe-deposit box, without losing interest on the other ten thousand every month. There was already a penalty of almost four hundred dollars I had to pay for cashing in the CD early. I had to pay the penalty, but it's stupid not to have the interest coming in every month. I was getting one-thirty-two a month before, but the new S and L's only paying ninety-two.' Susan picked up the package of frozen pork chops and frowned. 'That's funny, I don't remember getting –'

Without rising, Freddy slapped Susan a sharp blow across the face. She fell down, dropping the pork chops, and the package slid across the linoleum floor. She began to cry and to rub her reddened cheek, which began to swell immediately.

'Part of being married,' Freddy explained, 'is learning to do exactly what your platonic husband tells you to do. I'm not some daddy you can defy, and I'm not a dumb brother you can manipulate. Do you know what "manipulate" means?'

Susan nodded through her tears. 'Uh-huh. I saw a program on it once, on *Donahue*.'

'I'm not unreasonable. You're probably right about the interest rate and all. I don't know much about things like that. But the main thing here is that you didn't do what I told you to do. And you weren't really concerned about the interest rate, either. You kept the other ten thousand because you didn't trust me. Don't

71

say anything. Not a word. I don't want to hear any lies. What I'm going to do, I'm going to let you keep the other ten thousand in the S and L. I don't need it right now, and you don't need it, and I realize you're insecure and need the money for your peace of mind. Now, put the pork chops back on the table and leave them there so they'll thaw out. I'll want them for dinner tonight, with whatever else you fix that'll go good with the pork chops.'

'Will baked sweet potatoes be all right?'

'That's your department. Now, aren't you going to ask me where I got the pork chops?'

'I figure that's none of my business.'

'That's right. Now you're learning.'

Freddy looked through Susan's purse and took out the car keys. 'I'm going down to the hotel to fix things up with Pablo for you. Then I'm going to get oriented around town. I should be back around six – that is, if I don't get lost. But I've checked out the map, and I don't think I will as long as I keep the avenues and the streets straight.'

'I'm supposed to go to social science tonight. English on Monday and Wednesday, and social science on Tuesday and Thursday nights.'

'No, I don't think so. I don't want you in school right now. Call up and tell your science teacher there's been a death in the family. Professor Turner already knows. I'll decide whether I want you to go back at all.'

Freddy counted off a thousand dollars and pushed the rest of the money across the table. 'Here.' He folded the bills in half and put the roll into his right front pocket. 'Take the rest of the money and stash it in a safe place somewhere in the apartment.'

Freddy turned at the door. 'One other thing. Call a locksmith and have him come out and put a deadbolt lock on the door. These push-button locks are engraved invitations for burglars.'

'I already checked on deadlocks, and they cost more than sixty dollars. Is that all right? To pay that much, I mean?'

Freddy pointed to the stack of money on the table. 'What would you rather lose? Sixty dollars, or all of that?' He pushed in the button on the doorknob, and closed the door gently behind him as he left.

Susan, slightly dazed, opened the refrigerator, stared into its depths for a moment, closed the door, took a roll of toilet paper out of the grocery sack, looked at it, dropped it back inside, started toward the bathroom, changed her mind, and then ran swiftly to the South Miami telephone book and turned to the Yellow Pages.

Chapter Ten

Hoke Moseley and Bill Henderson sat close together on a pink silk loveseat in the living room of 11K, a townhouse in the Tahitian Village. Two-bedroom townhouses in the Tahitian Village started at $189,000, and the owners of this three-bedroom townhouse had also put out a good deal of money for the Latin Baroque furnishings. There were twisted, ornate bars on all of the downstairs windows. The interior color scheme was predominantly purple and rose. The wall-to-wall carpeting was richly purple, and the color was echoed without subtlety in the violet velvet draperies. The thick draperies hung in deep folds from two-headed iron spears in the living and dining rooms.

In the purple living room, two men, definitely Latins, with their hands and feet bound with copper wire, were face down on the floor. They had both been shot in the back of the head, and their faces were unrecognizable. A dark-haired young woman wearing a black-and-white maid's uniform, complete with a white frilly cap, had been shot in the hallway that led to the kitchen. Her hands and feet were also bound with copper wire. A small boy, two, or possibly three years old, had been shot in the head, but the child did not have his hands and feet bound. He was in the sunken bathtub in the rose-tiled bathroom on the second floor.

There was considerable activity in the townhouse. The forensic crew was busy. Two technicians were dusting for fingerprints, and another man was taking flash photographs from various angles. The ME, Dr Merle Evans, was sitting at the glass-topped wrought-iron table in the dining room and writing notes on his clipboard.

The lady of the house, who had been out shopping at the Kendall Lakes Mall, said that she had returned to find her husband, her brother, the boy, and her maid dead. A Colombian with only rudimentary English, she had become hysterical. When he arrived,

Doc Evans had given her a shot and sent her in an ambulance to the American Hospital emergency room.

After a quick initial look at the scene, Hoke Moseley and Bill Henderson had knocked on the nearby doors in the Tahitian Village, dividing up the townhouses, asking questions, and now they were comparing notes.

'No one I talked to,' Henderson said, 'heard or saw anything.'

'I didn't do any better. These people here apparently kept to themselves, and I couldn't find anyone who knew or talked to them. They spoke Spanish and nothing else. Sometimes, in the morning, the maid took the little boy to the pool, but the adults never used the pool. And that's where the people of this complex get acquainted. A Colombian corporation, the manager told me, owns this townhouse, pays all the bills and maintenance, and people just come and go. When they come, they've got a letter in Spanish authorizing their stay, and he hands over the keys. When they leave, one of them returns the keys. He's never had any trouble with any of the tenants, he claims. They're always nice, quiet tenants, or so he says.'

'Did he have their names?'

'No. The letter he showed me just said to admit the bearers for an extended stay. I don't read Spanish, but he does, and that's what the letter said.'

'He wouldn't lie about something like that,' Henderson said, 'but we can check it out, anyway. There had to be at least four shots, but no one heard even one. I can't get over that.'

'Maybe it's a good thing they didn't hear the shots and come running out. Chances are, they'd be dead, too.'

'Somebody had to hear something. They just don't want to get involved, that's all.'

Doc Evans joined them. 'They've been dead about two hours. That may not be exact, but from the body temperatures, I'm not far off.'

Hoke nodded. 'That coincides with what the woman said. She was gone for about two hours, and they were all alive when she left. I hope you can find some evidence of heroin when you open 'em up, doc. There's no dope in the apartment. Without some indication of dope, we can't say positively that the killings are drug-related. We can say that we think they are, but that isn't the same. If they're dope-related, nobody gives a shit, but if this was a murder-robbery, all these folks living out here'll get panicky.'

'It's obviously a professional job,' Doc said. 'Too bad about the kid, though. At his age, he couldn't've identified anybody anyway.'

'Colombian drug families are like that, doc,' Henderson said. 'They kill everyone in the family. They have to do it. If they hadn't killed the boy, someday, as a man, he'd kill them. When can I talk to the woman at the hospital?'

'Any time. She'll be a little dopey, but she can talk now. Why?'

'I've got a theory. I think she knew the killers. I also think they killed these people here, and then she drove them to the airport to catch a plane. Then she drove back here to report the bodies. As soon as she knew they were safely away, she called the department.'

'Jesus, Bill,' Hoke said, 'you don't seriously believe that a mother would help the killers of her own child get away, do you?'

'Well, how do we know it's her child? Life is cheap for those fuckers in Colombia. They might've brought the kid along with that plan in mind all along. Anyway, that's what I think, and I've got another reason besides. I'll take Martinez along to use as an interpreter.'

'Why not? I'll wait here. I asked Kossowski from Narcotics to get a warrant so we can search her Caddy. She went shopping, she said, but I didn't see any packages in the car. If there's nothing in the trunk, your theory might be better than I think right now. Anyway,' Hoke finished, 'after we search the car, I'll call you at American.'

'I'm going to lean on her.' Henderson got to his feet. 'Maybe their passports are in the trunk, too. There's not a scrap of ID in the house.'

'The killers probably took the passports. But go ahead. You're bound to find out more than we know now.'

Kossowski, together with an assistant state attorney, arrived a few minutes later with a search warrant for the purple Cadillac. Kossowski and Hoke searched the car. The car was leased, not owned, and was very clean. There was nothing in the trunk except for a set of tools. There was a neatly folded map of Miami in the glove compartment and a well-chewed cigar in the ashtray. There were no pen or pencil markings on the map.

'This kind of search doesn't mean much, Hoke,' Kossowski said. 'When I get it downtown and take it apart, if there's a single grain of horse I'll find it.'

'Take it, then. I think Henderson's on to something.'

Hoke called the American Hospital and had Henderson paged. He was in the emergency room.

'Bill,' Hoke said, 'the car, on a perfunctory search here, was clean. I told Kossowski to take it downtown for a vacuum job. There were no packages in the trunk. It might be a good idea for you to twist the woman's arm.'

'I've been trying, but all I get is *nunca*, like it was the only word she knows.'

'Find out what her husband and her brother were doing in Miami.'

'They were on vacation, she said.'

'That isn't good enough.'

'Martinez told me we should threaten to take her out to Krome to the alien detention camp and turn her over to the INS. She has no papers, and as an illegal alien, a few days living with those Haitian women out there might get her to talking.'

'Don't just threaten her. If she won't say anything, take her out there and let the INS have her. Tell them she might harm herself, and they can slap her in solitary for a couple of days.'

'As soon as we can get her out of emergency and into a private room, I'll be able to get tougher. There's no problem getting her a room – she's got nine hundred dollars in her purse. The hospital'll be glad to give her a private room until her money runs out.'

'Whatever you decide, Bill, it's okay by me. Evans is taking the bodies now, and the forensic crew's almost finished. I'll wait around and seal up the townhouse, and check with the morgue later. Then I'll call you.'

Two hours later, Hoke stopped at a restaurant in Kendall Lakes. He had eaten his usual diet breakfast (one poached egg, one slice of dry toast, and coffee) but nothing since. It was almost four-thirty when he looked over the menu of Roseate Spoon Bill of Fare, a popular short-order restaurant in the rambling shopping center. When it came to eating, Hoke had a major problem. He had lost weight the year before, dropping from 205 to 185 pounds, and he wanted to keep it off, but at the same time he was always hungry. He could stick to his diet for two days at most, and then he went overboard on meat and mashed potatoes. With his new teeth, he could chew almost anything.

After a prolonged study of the wide-ranging menu, he decided to compromise. He ordered a Spanish omelet with cottage cheese instead of french fries, a dish of apple sauce, and told the waitress to hold the toast.

While he waited, Hoke leafed through his notebook and tried to organize his thoughts. He crossed out the name of Ronald I. France. He could do nothing to help him; the grand jury had decided to prosecute this old man for shooting and killing a twelve-year-old boy who had ripped up his flower bed. The old man was seventy-two years old, and he had cried when Hoke had taken him in for booking. According to the neighbors, he had been a nice old man, but killing a kid for ripping up a flower bed had been too drastic. It didn't help that Mr France had claimed he only wanted to wound the kid a little with his twelve-gauge shotgun. If that had been the case, why had he loaded the gun with double-aught shells? But Hoke didn't cross out the *address* of Mr France. Sides had been taken in the neighborhood, and Mrs France, also seventy-two, was going to get some harassment.

Marshall Fisher – a DOA – suicide. That was cut-and-dried, but there was going to be an inquest, and he'd have to appear. He made a check mark to watch his in-box for a notice on Fisher.

There were three convenience-store killings under investigation, but no leads. Signs were posted in English and Spanish in all the convenience stores, stating that the managers were only allowed to have $35 in the cash register. But the Cuban managers were killed by Cuban gunmen for the $35. American prisons didn't frighten Marielito criminals; after Castro's, American prisons were country clubs. And when a witness to a killing was found, which was seldom, he was too scared to point out the killer.

When Hoke ran across the address, 'K.P.T. – 157 Ave. – 6–418E,' he was puzzled for a few moments. Not only was he hungry but he had a lot on his mind. There was no name, and he didn't know anyone who lived out this far in Kendall. Then he recalled that this was Susan Waggoner's address. Inasmuch as 157th Avenue was Dade County, and not Miami Police Department territory, Hoke rarely got this far west. All of West Kendall came under Metro Police jurisdiction.

Hoke was curious about this peculiar couple, and especially the jock, although he didn't believe for a second that Susan had ordered 'Junior Mendez' to break her brother's finger. She had seemed too dimwitted even to entertain the idea, but still, it wouldn't hurt anything to talk to her while he was out this way. He might pick up some information on the boyfriend. If they were college students studying for degrees in management, maybe he and Henderson should enroll in a seminary and work on doctor of divinity degrees.

The tall unfinished buildings in Kendall Pines Terrace reminded Hoke of the Roman apartment houses he had seen in Italian neorealist movies. The Salvadoran guard on the gate explained how to get to Building Six, and Hoke took the winding road to the last parking lot, avoiding the speed bumps by going around them on the grass. He parked in a visitors' slot to avoid being towed away – as advised by the gatekeeper – and rode the elevator to the fourth floor.

Susan opened the door on the first knock, having a little difficulty with the new deadbolt lock, which was still stiff.

'I don't have much to tell you, Miss Waggoner,' Hoke said. 'But I was out this way, so I thought I'd drop by for a few minutes and talk to you.'

Susan was wearing a black dress with hose and black pumps. She had also applied some rouge to her cheeks and wore pink lipstick. There was a string of imitation pearls around her thin neck. The dress was too big for her, and she reminded Hoke of a little girl playing dress-up in her mother's clothes.

'Would you like a beer, sergeant? Coffee?'

'No, no. Thanks, but I just had lunch.'

'Lunch? It's almost five-thirty.'

'An early dinner, then. I missed lunch, actually, so I had something just now at the Roseate Spoon Bill.'

'I go there a lot. I like the Mexican pizza.'

'I've never tried that.'

'It's really good. Lots of cheese.'

'I'll try it some time. Your father came in this morning, Miss Waggoner, and he claimed the two hundred dollars.'

'He would.'

'But we're going to hold on to the effects for a while. I was going to call the Krishnas today, but I've been busy with other things. Has your father contacted you today?'

Susan shook her head. 'He won't, either. But I don't plan on going to the funeral, anyway.'

'He said he was going to cremate your brother and scatter the ashes on Lake Okeechobee.'

'Martin would like that. He always liked the lake.'

'Your father's staying at the Royalton, downtown, if you want to call him.'

'I don't.'

'Where's Mendez?'

'Who?'

'Ramon. Your fiancé?'

'Oh, Junior, you mean. His name is Ramon Mendez, Junior, but he always goes by Junior. He hates to be called Ramon.'

'How'd you happen to meet him?'

'We met in English class at Dade. He helped me write my haikus. I was having trouble with them.'

'Haikus? What are they?'

'It's some kind of Japanese poem.'

'I see. So you met at school and got engaged.'

'That's right. But now we have what's called a platonic marriage.'

'He lives here with you, then?'

'He should be home soon. If you want to ask questions about Junior, you should talk to him.'

'What smells so good?'

'That's dinner. I'm cooking stuffed pork chops. I use Stove-Top dressing, shallots, and mushrooms, all smothered in brown gravy.

Also, baked sweet potatoes, peas, and a tomato and cucumber and onion salad. Do you think I should make hot biscuits?'

'Does Junior like biscuits?'

'I really don't know. I've got white bread, but I think I'll fix some. Most men like hot biscuits. Would you like to stay for dinner?'

'I've already eaten. I told you. You've got a lovely apartment here, Miss Waggoner.'

'Oh, I don't own it. I rent it, furnished.'

'It must be rough on you, working and going to school, too.'

'It isn't so bad. The work at the International Hotel isn't hard, and I don't have to work at night.'

'What are you – a maid?'

'Oh, no!' Susan laughed. 'Maids only get minimum wage. I get fifty dollars a trick, and split it down the middle with Pablo. I'm one of Pablo Lhosa's girls. That is, I was, but I quit. Now that we've got a platonic marriage, Junior doesn't want me to work for Pablo anymore.'

'You're a hooker, then?'

'I thought you knew. You aren't going to arrest me, are you?'

'No, that isn't my department. I just work homicides. I guess I've been lucky so far. I was with the Riviera Police Department for three years, and I've been in Miami for twelve, and I've never had to work Vice. When d'you expect Junior home?'

'When he gets here. It doesn't make any nevermind to me. The pork chops are in the Crockpot, and the other stuff won't take long. The potatoes are already done. He said he'd be home at six, but he might be late.'

Hoke handed her one of his cards. 'Have Junior call me when he gets home tonight. It says the Eldorado Hotel in Miami Beach, but I'm reachable there. If the phone isn't answered right away, tell him to let it ring. There's only one man on the desk at night, and if he's away from the desk it takes a little time to get an answer. Somebody'll answer eventually.'

'All right. I'll tell him, but that doesn't mean he'll call you.'

'Just tell him I've been looking through some mug books.'

'Mug books?'

'He'll know what I mean.' Hoke went to the door.

'Sergeant Moseley? You didn't tell Daddy about the car, did you?'

Hoke shook his head. 'No. He didn't ask, and I didn't volunteer.'

The traffic was heavy on North Kendall and heavier on Dixie, when Hoke turned toward downtown. It was after seven by the time Hoke reached Lejeune Road. He stopped for gas and made a phone call to the duty officer in Homicide, leaving a message for Sergeant Henderson to call him at home. He made another call to the morgue and learned that they did not plan to start the post-mortems on the Colombians until the next day, probably late in the afternoon. He paid for the gas, put the receipt in his notebook, and decided to go home. He could work on his report in the morning. Perhaps by then Henderson would have something from the woman's testimony.

Hoke took the MacArthur Causeway to South Beach but decided to stop for a boilermaker at Irish Mike's before going home. Mike brought him the shot of Early Times and a Miller's draft, then waited until Hoke downed the shot and took a sip of beer.

'I suppose you'll be wanting this on the tab, sergeant?'

'Yeah, and one more shot besides. I've still got enough beer.'

'D'you know what your tab is?'

'No, you tell me.'

'It was eighty-five bucks.' Mike poured another shot into Hoke's glass. 'Not countin' these two.'

'I didn't know it was that much.'

'That's what it is, sergeant. When it hits a hundred I'm gonna eighty-six you till you pay the whole tab. I wouldn't object to something on account right now.'

'I wouldn't mind giving you something on account, Mike, but I'm a little short right now. I'll bring in fifty on payday, but don't let it run up so high again.'

'I'm not the one that runs it up – you are.'

Mike went into the back, and Hoke quickly downed the second shot, finished the beer, and left the bar. He was depressed enough already without being hit for an $85 bar tab. Hoke didn't drink all that much, but when he wanted a drink he hated to drink alone in his room. Fortunately, he had a bottle of El Presidente at home. This was one time he would have to keep himself company.

Hoke got into his car and drove to the Eldorado Hotel.

Chapter Eleven

Before leaving Kendall Pines Terrace, Freddy had locked the pistol in the glove compartment and spread the city map of Miami out on the passenger's seat. He turned east on Kendall and took the Homestead Extension Freeway north toward the city. The traffic didn't get heavy until he turned east again on Dolphin Expressway toward the airport. By watching the overhead signs carefully, he avoided the lane that would have taken him across the causeway to Miami Beach and managed to bluff his way into the left lane that took him down to Biscayne Boulevard. He was astonished by the erratic driving on the freeway. If they drove this way in Los Angeles, he thought, most of these people would have been killed within minutes. Freddy didn't consider himself a good driver, but compared to these Miami drivers he was a professional.

On impulse, he turned into the Omni Mall and took the ramp to the third level before finding a parking space. The parking garage was color-coded as well as numbered, and he wrote *Purple 3* on his parking ticket before putting it into his hip pocket.

Using the Mendez Visa card, he bought two short-sleeve sports shirts in the County Seat, and then paid cash for a featherweight poplin suit in an Italian men's store. The suit was on sale for $350. To make the sale, however, the salesman had to get a pair of pants with a twenty-nine-inch waist from another suit to go with the size forty-two jacket. He bought two $25 neckties in another men's shop, using the Mendez card, and then a pair of cordovan tasseled loafers for $150 cash at Bally's. He returned to the TransAm and locked his purchases in the trunk. He went back into the mall and bought a stuffed baked potato at One Potato, Two – asking for the Mexican Idaho, which included butter, chili con carne, jack cheese, and tortilla chips. The chili was hot, and he drank a large Tab with lots of ice.

All he had to buy now was a box of white shirts and a present for Susan. She was not the kind of girl who had been given many presents, and she would be happy with anything he got her. She was so passive in bed that he doubted that she had ever had any tips from her clients.

In addition to its three shopping levels, the air-conditioned mall was anchored at each end with a Penny's and a Jordan Marsh department store. There was also an involved egress to the Omni Hotel. A man could get lost quickly in the Omni Mall, but not for very long because of the color-coded exits and numbers.

A portly man in a blue-and-white seersucker suit was standing in front of the store window and looking intently at the merchandise. As Freddy glanced at him, wondering what it was in the window that held his attention, a small dark man with a bushy head of curly hair bumped against the portly man, apologized, and walked on. Freddy saw the small man slip the wallet out of the heavy man's hip pocket, but the man hadn't felt a thing. Freddy trailed behind the small man, who was wearing a blue serge suit and a blue wool tie, to the escalator and watched him drop the wallet into another man's folded newspaper, *El Diario*. The pickpocket continued through the mall, and the one with the newspaper, a tall dark man with black sideburns down to and even with his mouth, took the Down escalator.

Freddy got on the escalator behind him. He followed him past Treasure Island and the carousel, and into the lowest level of the mall. The man strolled past the Unicorn Store, a T-shirt store, skirted a French sidewalk café, and then went into the men's room. Freddy waited outside the door counting to thirty, then went in. The tall man with the sideburns had the wallet in his hands. He looked up at Freddy for a moment and then back down at the wallet. Freddy grabbed his left wrist, twisted it behind his back with one motion, and then ran the man into the white-tiled wall, face first. The man screamed something in Spanish and tried to get his right hand into his trousers pocket. Freddy jerked the left arm higher and it broke at the elbow. As the arm cracked, the man vomited and fell to his knees. Freddy kicked him behind the ear, and the man went unconscious.

Freddy picked up the wallet from the floor and stuffed it into his pocket. He searched the man on the floor. There was a pearl-handled switchblade knife in his right front pocket and a roll of bills held together with a rubber band in the left hip pocket. He found another wallet in an inside jacket pocket. Freddy stuffed these into his pockets and washed his hands. A teenager, wearing a red-billed Red Man cap, jeans, and a CLASH T-shirt, walked in and saw the man on the floor, bubbling blood from his mouth and ears, then went to the urinal.

'What's the matter with that guy?'

'Ask him,' Freddy said, blotting his hands dry on a brown paper towel.

'I don't want to get involved,' the teenager said, unzipping his fly.

Freddy left the men's room and took the stairwell up to Level Two. He bought a box of three white-on-white Excello shirts at Baron's. He bought a pedestal coffee cup that had *Susie* printed on the side in Old English script, and a half-pound bag of Colombian coffee. He asked the girl at the coffee shop to gift-wrap the two items together, which cost him an extra $1.50. He returned to his car and locked his new purchases into the trunk before getting into the front seat and turning on the engine and the air conditioning.

Freddy counted $322 from the portly man's stolen wallet, $809 from the tall man's wallet, and $1,200 from the tight roll of bills. In the middle of the tight roll of American money, there was an even tighter roll of 10,000 Mexican pesos. So, not counting the pesos, which he might be able to exchange later, he was $2,331 richer than when he had arrived at the Omni – minus the cash he had put out for his shopping, of course. This was absolutely the best haul Freddy had ever made in a single day. He had also picked up two new credit cards – the fat man's – a Visa and a MasterCard. The tall man with sideburns, apparently the other half of a Mexico City pickpocket team, had a green card in the name of Jaime Figueras in his wallet. This meant that he could work in Miami, but it didn't authorize him to work as a pickpocket; he would be unlikely to report his mugging to the police. If that damned kid hadn't come into the men's room, Freddy could have waited for a few minutes and made another nice haul after the short partner came down for his cut. But probably it was just as well. He had gotten in trouble before by staying too long in a men's room. Vice Squad cops pretending to be gay, and some who didn't have to pretend, hit public rest rooms all the time to top off their daily arrest quotas.

Freddy paid the parking fee to the Cuban girl at the exit and drove south on Biscayne Boulevard, planning what he would say to Pablo Lhosa at the International Hotel.

By the time he had crawled through the heavy traffic to Dupont Plaza, Freddy decided that it might be best not to see Pablo at all. Pablo knew him as Gotlieb, and by now, or at least in another day or two, the hotel would find out that it had been stiffed by a stolen credit card. Of course, the hotel would get its money, in all probability, but Pablo would have some leverage to use against him. Perhaps for the moment it would be best to do nothing. He would tell Susan not to answer her phone, and when Pablo came out to see her he could take care of him. By that time, some kind of solution would occur to him.

Freddy circled the Dupont Plaza and drove back down Biscayne to the Omni. This time he pulled into the hotel entrance. He turned over the ignition key, but not the trunk key, to the valet. He registered at the desk as Mr and Mrs Junior Waggoner and pocketed the room key. He counted out $1,000 in cash for a $120-a-day room and told the clerk he would return with his baggage later when he came back from the airport with his wife.

No, he told the clerk, he didn't know how long he would be staying, but to remind him when his bill got up to $900, and he would either check out then or put down some more cash as an advance. Freddy waved off the bellman and took the elevator up to his room.

He stashed the extra wallets and the pesos in the bedside table next to the king-size bed and went back down to the lobby entrance for his car. He paid for the valet parking, gave the valet a quarter, and turned off the salsa that was blaring full blast from his radio. If the valet hadn't turned on the radio he would have gotten a dollar instead of a quarter, Freddy reflected. He headed south on Biscayne again. He crossed the Miami River and drove down

Brickell. He now had two nice hidey-holes, one in Kendall and another downtown in Omni. To avoid the sun and the heat, he could work the Omni Mall; the way the Omni was laid out, it was a thief's paradise. If he only robbed pickpockets, he could work for weeks without any fear of detection. Of course, there would be competition; there was bound to be in a perfect setup like that. Freddy didn't mind a little competition. As the fly said, crossing the mirror, 'That's just another way of looking at it.'

Freddy parked on the roof of the bus company's parking garage and spent two hours exploring the Miracle Mile in Coral Gables. The stores were owned by Americans, but they catered to Latin tastes. Women's clothing was on the garish side, with lots of ruffles and flounces. Primary colors were predominant, with very few pastels in evidence. Men's suits were gray or blue, with thin stripes in rust or coral, and the shirts and ties were like those Freddy remembered from Santa Anita, when he used to spend his afternoons at the track. Except for the incredible cleanliness, the Coral Gables shopping street reminded Freddy of East Los Angeles, although East LA had never been this prosperous.

In a sporting goods store, Freddy bought three All-American Official Frisbees, charging them to the Mendez credit card. He went back to the roof of the parking garage, took the Frisbees out of the paper sack, and ripped off their plastic wrappings. He then sailed them, one at a time, across the street, and over a lower roof, watching them land and skitter in the heavy traffic on LeJeune Road. Two cellmates at San Quentin had owned a Frisbee, and Freddy had often watched them throw it back and forth to each other in the yard. They would laugh when they caught it, and they would laugh even harder when one of them failed to catch it. Freddy had always wanted to toss it himself, but the two cons never let anyone else into their game, and of course, no one ever asked them for a turn. But throwing the three Frisbees hadn't been much fun; perhaps you needed a partner to aim at.

Freddy got lost trying to get through the complex of the University of Miami, gave up, and finally drove around the school before he could find Miller Road. He got back to Kendall Pines Terrace at six-thirty.

Freddy dumped his packages on the couch, handed Susan her gift-wrapped present, and checked the new deadbolt lock on the front door. He accepted the girlish kiss she planted on his cheek for the gift and told her to buy some 3-in-One Oil the next time she went to the store. She told Freddy about Sergeant Moseley's visit and handed him the detective's card. Freddy made her repeat word for word everything that had been said.

'Did he say "local" mug shots, or "wanted" mug shots?'

'He just said mug books. He said you'd know what he meant.'

'You shouldn't've told him you worked for Pablo. That wasn't too bright.'

'I thought he knew.'

'The best thing to say to a cop is nothing. Remember that. Did Pablo call you?'

'No. Well, he might have. There were two phone calls, but I didn't answer the phone. If it was Pablo, I knew I wouldn't know what to say, and if it was you, you would've said you'd call and you didn't.'

'At least you did something right. Get your purse. I'm going over to Miami Beach and see the cop.'

'What about dinner? Everything's ready.'

'We'll take it with us.'

In the closet there was a large cardboard box filled with Martin's fishing gear. Freddy dumped it out, and Susan packed the box with the Crockpot and the rest of the items on her menu. Working hurriedly, she was soon ready to go, and she had to wait for Freddy to shower and change into his new suit and Bally loafers. The .38 made a bulge in Freddy's jacket pocket, but he didn't like to carry a pistol in his waistband because of an accident a friend of his had once in San Diego.

As the blacks used to say in the yard at Quentin when they wanted to get even with a bully, Freddy was 'going to pull that fucker's teeth, man!'

Chapter Twelve

When Hoke walked into the lobby of the Eldorado Hotel, Old Man Zuckerman jumped up from his faded brocade chair by the entrance and handed him a neatly folded paper napkin. Hoke thanked the old man and put the napkin in his pocket. Mr Zuckerman smiled toothlessly and sat back down in his chair. Mr Zuckerman was well into his eighties, and his 'job' was to give every person who entered the hotel a paper napkin, and he forced it on visitors and residents alike, including Mr Howard Bennett, the owner-manager, every time they came in. Hoke figured that this job that Mr Zuckerman had invented for himself helped to keep the old fellow alive. And Old Man Zuckerman had an endless supply of paper napkins, because he helped himself to all he would need when he ate his meals at Gold's Deli down the street.

The Eldorado Hotel was a deteriorating art deco hotel that was on the verge of being condemned. It was scheduled to be torn down if Redevelopment came to South Miami Beach. But Redevelopment had been in the planning stage for almost ten years now, and nothing was ever done. Because of the building moratorium on South Beach the owners weren't repairing anything they didn't positively have to take care of, except for meeting the most minimal requirements for fire and safety. By acting as an unpaid hotel security officer when he was off duty, Hoke got a free room, but he had been considering moving out for several months.

His problem was money. Every other paycheck went to his ex-wife in Vero Beach, and he had to live on the other half. After term life insurance payments, car insurance, retirement payments, and union dues, he had to live on less than $12,000 a year. With a free room and with his battered Le Mans paid for, that should have been enough – or more than enough – but there had been his own hospital bills, plus a new and enormous bill for his two

daughters' orthodontist. He had ripped up the bill from the orthodontist, but then Patsy, his ex-wife, had threatened to take him
to court. Part of the divorce settlement was that he would pay for
the girls' medical expenses. Straightening teeth, in Hoke's opinion,
came under beautification, and was not a necessary medical
expense. But to avoid going to court, he had finally sent the orthodontist a check for $50 and told him he would try to make some
regular payments on the $1,800 bill.

The shabby lobby was depressing. Eight old ladies, all members
of the Eldorado Hotel TV Club, sat in a silent half-circle, watching
a television set that was bolted and locked to the wall. When Hoke
looked across the room, four Marielitos, playing dominoes at a
corner table, got respectfully to their feet, nodded shyly at him,
and sat down again when he acknowledged their greeting with a
wave of his right arm. On his way to the desk Hoke took a look
at the TV screen and saw a green snake eat a red frog. Education
Night. He checked his mailbox (Eddie Cohen wasn't at the desk)
and decided that tonight he would only make perfunctory rounds.

On the way to his room on the eighth floor, he stopped the
elevator at each floor, looked up and down the halls without getting
out, and then went on. On the fifth floor, however, he saw Mrs
Friedman wandering around in her nightgown. He locked the
elevator and led the old lady back to her room before going up to
six. She often got confused, and when she happened to leave her
room she could never remember her room number. Rumor had it
that the meals-on-wheels program was either going to be reduced
or cut out altogether, and when that happened, he didn't know
what Mrs Friedman would do for sustenance. Even when her social
security check came in, she wouldn't be able to find her way down
to Gold's Deli and back.

It was depressing to think about Mrs Friedman, but it had been
even more depressing to find out that Susan Waggoner was a whore.
Even Hoke wouldn't have figured that in a hundred years. Bill
Henderson, who had worked Vice for three years, probably could
have taken one look at Susan and known, but Hoke hadn't suspected
it. Hell, Hoke's fourteen-year-old daughter was built better and
sexier-looking than Susan.

And then there had been that dead baby – and the maid. The kid probably couldn't talk in sentences yet, and the maid couldn't have been more than nineteen or twenty. He didn't mourn the two Colombians. They were men in their early thirties, and whatever it was that they had done to be killed for, they had done it in their maturity. The maid, if she had been hired locally, might be a lead, but he suspected that she had been brought along from Colombia to take care of the baby.

Any way he looked at it, it was a rotten business.

Instead of going to his room, Hoke took the stairs from the eighth floor to the roof. The only good thing about the Eldorado Hotel was the view from the roof. He lit a cigarette and looked across Biscayne Bay at Miami. The white uneven buildings looked like teeth, but at this distance it was a white smile. There was even a gum-colored sunset above the skyline, and in the northwest above the Everglades there was a stack-up of black clouds that looked like thousand-dollar poker chips. It was raining in the 'Glades, and perhaps enough rain would be left to reach the city and cool it off a little during the night. Hoke finished his cigarette and tossed it off the parapet into the swimming pool behind the hotel. The pool, a small one, had been filled with sand. Without water, no one could use it, but Mr Bennett saved money on maintenance costs with a pool full of sand. There was a lot of trash scattered over the surface. Hoke decided to put in his report that the trash was a fire hazard so that Mr Bennett would have to have it cleaned up.

Hoke unlocked the door to his room and switched on the light by the door. The small room was stifling and smelled of dirty sheets, unwashed socks and underwear, bay rum, and stale tobacco smoke. Howard Bennett, the cheapskate owner-manager, had invaded Hoke's room during his absence and pulled the plug on Hoke's window air conditioner to save energy costs. Hoke plugged in the air conditioner and turned it up to High.

He took off his leisure suit jacket, his gun, his handcuffs, and sap, and tossed the equipment on the top of his cluttered dresser. He switched on his small black-and-white Sony and poured two inches of El Presidente brandy into his tooth glass. *Family Feud* was on the tube, and for the hundredth time Hoke wondered about the definition of *family* in America. There were five family members on both teams, but no mothers or fathers. Instead, there were various uncles and cousins and spouses of the cousins, plus one teenage kid who bore no resemblance to either family and had probably been borrowed from neighbors for the program.

There was a knock on the door. Hoke sighed and hid the glass of brandy behind a photograph of his two daughters on the dresser. The last time he had had a visitor knocking on his door it had been Mrs Goldberg, from 409. Her ex-husband, she told him, had sneaked into her room while she was watching television in the lobby and had stolen her pearl-handled hairbrush, the hairbrush that had belonged to her mother. Hoke had gone down to 409 with her and found the hairbrush in the bottom drawer of Mrs Goldberg's dresser.

'He must've hidden it there,' she said.

Later on, when Hoke had mentioned the incident to Mr Bennett, the manager had laughed and told Hoke that Mrs Goldberg had been a widow for fifteen years.

Hoke reached for the doorknob.

Chapter Thirteen

Susan drove. The traffic was all coming their way, so she made good time as she drove east on Killian to Old Cutler, then turned north to drive through Coconut Grove. The tropical foliage was thick and green on Old Cutler, and after they passed Fairchild Gardens, the air roots from the overhanging tree branches frequently whipped the roof of the car.

Susan rejoined South Dixie beyond Vizcaya, then took Brickell Avenue to Biscayne Boulevard. She took the toll-free MacArthur Causeway to South Beach. The Eldorado Hotel was near Joe's Stone Crab Restaurant, and because Susan knew where the restaurant was she had no trouble finding the old hotel on the bay.

'Wait in the car,' Freddy told her, after she parked in the small lot beside the hotel.

'How long?'

'For as long as it takes me. If he's home, it won't take long. If he isn't home, I'll have to wait in his room till he gets there. So just sit here and wait.'

'Can I play the radio?'

'No. It might attract attention. Stop asking dumb questions.'

Freddy went into the lobby, and Old Man Zuckerman tottered over to him and handed him a napkin. Freddy nodded his thanks, and the old man went back to his chair and fell into a half-doze. There were four men playing dominoes in the corner of the lobby and some old ladies watching TV at the other end. The battered card table, where the Latins were playing, was lighted by a 1930s wrought-iron bridge lamp with a rose shade and tarnished gold tassels. The men all wore T-shirts and jeans, none of them clean. One man had a machete scar running from the top of his head down his left cheek, ending beneath his chin. All four men had blackish homemade tattoos on the backs of their hands and arms.

Freddy walked to the table, and the conversation stopped.

'Sergeant Moseley's room?' Freddy handed $10 to the man with the scar.

'Top floor.' He pointed his finger at the ceiling. 'Eight-Oh-Nine. *Gracias.*'

'A *casa?*'

The man ignored the question, pursed his lips, and studied his dominoes. Freddy grabbed the man's wrist, squeezed it, and took the $10 bill out of his paralyzed fingers.

'*Si, señor,*' the man said. 'A *casa.*'

'*Un hombre duro,*' Freddy said. He wadded the ten into the man's palm and closed his fingers on it.

'*¡Despotico!*' The scar-faced man nodded, and the other three Cubans laughed. Freddy crossed the dim lobby to the elevators.

Outside 809, Freddy took out his pistol, knocked on the door, and pressed his back against the wall. Hoke Moseley opened the door, saw no one, and took a step forward. Freddy, with a sweeping motion of the gun, caught Hoke on the side of the jaw. As Hoke fell sideways, Freddy had time for another backhand blow, and Hoke's false teeth flew out of his mouth and bounced on the dusty hall carpet. Freddy put the teeth into his jacket pocket and dragged the unconscious body inside the room. After closing the door, he kicked the supine man in the jaw with the point of his shoe. The jaw cracked audibly, and blood poured from Hoke's nose and mouth.

After taking off his jacket, Freddy sat on the edge of the unmade bed. He needed to cool off for a minute or so. His shirt was already drenched with sweat, and he didn't want it to darken his new suit jacket. The air conditioner in the window labored away, but it produced more noise than cold air. In the humidity, the slightest exercise provoked a good deal of perspiration. In California, Freddy would have had to work out for at least a half-hour to build up such a sweat. It was like breathing through a wet bath towel.

The room was grungy. Here was a pig, Freddy thought, who actually lived like a pig. Aluminum foil covered the sliding glass door that opened on to the tiny balcony. The foil was there to reflect the heat away from the room in the afternoons, but it hadn't helped much. The dirty beige carpet was ringed and spotted with coffee and other food spills. The sheets on the three-quarter-size bed were dirty, and there was a pile of unwashed laundry in the corner next to an overflowing wastebasket.

There were two police uniforms in heavy plastic garment bags in the closet, along with a black suit and two poplin leisure suits. There were a half-dozen clean short-sleeve sports shirts on hangers, one white dress shirt, and three neckties.

In the bottom drawer of the dresser there was a one-ring hot plate, a small saucepan, a tablespoon, a knife, a fork, three cans of Chunky Turkey Soup with noodles, and a box of Krispy saltines. There was a half-loaf of rye bread, four eggs in a brown carton, a jar of instant coffee, and a bottle of Tabasco sauce. The other dresser drawers contained papers neatly filed away in cardboard folders, Fruit of the Loom underwear, and black lisle socks. There were several T-shirts, two pairs of ragged khaki gym shorts, and a pair of blue-and-red running shoes. The cop didn't have another pair of black dress shoes, except for the pair he was wearing. Of course, Freddy thought, he might have more shoes and clothes in his locker at the police station.

The detective, in any event, was living incredibly cheap, and Freddy couldn't understand it. On top of the man's dresser was a ticket to a lot of money: a badge and an ID in a worn leather holder, a holstered .38 police special, a sap, and handcuffs. Freddy searched Hoke's pockets. He found keys, a wallet, a package of Kools, Dupont Plaza Hotel paper matches, and eighty cents in change. There were $18 in the wallet, several business cards with notes on them, and one MasterCard. There were also two small photos in the wallet, older versions of the two young girls in the framed photo on the dresser. The detective's notebook was in his leisure jacket. Freddy flipped through it idly but could make out nothing intelligible from the shorthand Hoke used in the notebook.

Freddy sat on the edge of the bed again and tapped the black leather sap gently into the palm of his other hand. The light blow stung. The tapered sap, eight inches long, with a wrist loop at one end, was filled with buckshot. Once, in Santa Barbara, a cop had slapped Freddy on the leg with one almost like this one. There had been no reason to hit Freddy with the blackjack; Freddy had been handcuffed at the time and was sitting quietly in a straight-backed chair. The cop had tapped him because he had wanted to tap him. The pain had been excruciating. His entire leg had gone numb, and unbidden tears had burned his eyes.

Still seated, Freddy reached out, and slapped the sap sharply against the top of Hoke's right leg. Hoke groaned, and made scrabbling motions with his fingers on the frayed carpet. Freddy shrugged. Hitting the unconscious man had given him no pleasure; he still didn't know why the cop in Santa Barbara had tapped him with the sap. Policemen undoubtedly had some kind of inborn perverted streak that normal men like himself didn't have.

Freddy got a brown paper sack from the closet and dropped the holstered .38, the badge, and ID holder into it, along with the sap. He now possessed a cop's license to steal, and the equipment to go with it. He added the handcuffs to the sack and put Hoke's $18 on top of the dresser. He then put five $20 bills on top of the $18; it would help to confuse the pig even more when he woke up.

Freddy closed the door, which locked behind him, took the elevator down, and left the lobby by the side terrace French windows to avoid being seen by the domino players and the old ladies. The players could identify him, he knew, but four Latins with homemade prison tattoos wouldn't volunteer any information about an injured cop. Not unless, Freddy grinned, someone slipped them ten bucks or so – and investigating officers didn't give out any free money for information.

Freddy told Susan to take the Venetian Causeway back to the Omni Hotel in Miami. When they reached DiLido Island, he told her to stop on the other side of the island by the bridge. When she stopped the car, he got out and threw the teeth in the bay. He climbed into the front seat again.

'What did you throw away?' Susan said.

'None of your business. If you need to know, I would've told you. How many times do I have to tell you not to ask questions?'

'I'm sorry,' Susan said. 'I forgot.'

They turned the car over to valet parking, and when Freddy showed his room key to the doorman, a bellman came out with a cart and brought Susan's prepared dinner up to their room. Freddy dialed room service and ordered a bottle of champagne, a pot of coffee, and table service for two. They ate the stuffed pork chops and still-warm sweet potatoes by candlelight in the handsomely appointed room, with a magnificent view of Biscayne Bay and the Miami Beach skyline.

Freddy complimented Susan on the pork chops and biscuits, even though they were cold.

If Susan was still curious, she kept her questions to herself.

Chapter Fourteen

When Hoke moved his right leg it hurt more than his jaw, but at least he could move it. The top of his head seemed to rise and fall eerily with each breath. His head was immobilized by two pillows so that he could not move it more than an inch or two to either side. His wrists were tied loosely to the bedrails with gauze, which prevented him from feeling his face or poking at the bandages. There were tubs and racks with bottles in each side of his bed, and clear fluids dripped into both arms. Perhaps that was why his arms were restrained.

Hoke's lower face was completely numb. From his position on the bed, with his head raised slightly, all he could see was a gray steel contraption on the wall. He wondered vaguely what it was, but it was two more days before he found out that the steel frame was a bracket for the television set, and that if he signed a piece of paper he could have a TV set brought in so he could watch the tube instead of the bracket.

By the end of the first week, when Hoke could sit up and go to the bathroom without help, he considered ordering the TV set, but he never did. As he recalled, there were too many commercials about food, in color, on TV, and he knew that the commercials would make him hungrier than he was already. Sometimes, when he closed his eyes, he could visualize the Burger King double cheeseburger with the bacon sizzling on top. He was hungry all the time.

There were four beds in the ward, but Hoke was the only occupant. This was a special oral surgeon's ward in St Mary's Hospital in Miami Shores, and it was used exclusively by dentists and oral surgeons who had patients with special problems. Except for a fourteen-year-old Jewish American Prince whose mother had him checked in overnight to have a back tooth extracted, Hoke had the small ward to himself throughout his stay. Hoke disliked the room, hated the hospital, and detested the gay male nurse, a Canary Islander who took an unseemly pleasure in giving Hoke an enema.

Hoke had been operated on by an oral surgeon named Murray Goldstein, and by his own dentist of several years standing, Dr David Rubin. Dr Rubin professed sympathy for Hoke, but he had never forgiven him for having Doc Evans pull his teeth out in the morgue. Still, he seemed elated by the fact that Hoke's damaged jaw would be able to support a new set of false teeth. But the new teeth had to be held off until Hoke's jaw had healed and all of the bone splinters came out. Meanwhile, his mandible was immobilized, wired here and there, and he drank his meals through a glass straw. The bruise on top of his right leg was the size and shape of a football, and he limped for several days after he was up and into his bedside chair.

While he was still punchy from the drugs and unable to talk, Red Farris visited him and brought Louise along. He could remember Red's droopy red mustache hanging over him, and Louise's white face and rain-dark hair hovering ghostily in the doorway. He couldn't remember what Red Farris had said, but Red had left a note with his presents, all of which Hoke found later in his bedside table. There was a bottle of Smirnoff vodka and a one-pound package of fudge wrapped in gold paper with the note:

Use the vodka for mouthwash. It's breathless. Louise made
you some fudge. When I get settled in Sebring, you can come
up for recuperation and we'll go dove hunting.
Take care.
'Red'

When Farris didn't come back later, after Hoke could have visitors, Hoke assumed that he had left for Sebring. But Hoke knew that he would never go dove hunting with Red Farris; once a man left Miami, that was the end of it, and Red knew it as well as he did.

Although his jaw was still wired and he could talk only with difficulty, Hoke was glad to see Bill Henderson. Bill told Hoke that the case of the four dead Colombians had been solved.

Henderson had borrowed a skycap's uniform and cap, put them on one of his black detectives, and had him falsely finger the Colombian woman as the person in a purple Cadillac who had dropped off two men at the Miami International Airport. Confronted by this direct, if false, identification, she had broken down. The child, as it turned out, was the maid's, not her own, and the child was not supposed to be killed. She was upset about that, which helped to make up her mind, too. The killers were back safely in Cartagena and would never be extradited. But at least their names were known now, so it was unlikely that the same pair would be used in Miami for more assassinations.

'I knew she was in on it for sure, Hoke, when you told me there were no packages in the trunk. The woman had nine hundred bucks in her purse, and there is no way that a woman could shop for two hours with that kind of money and not buy something.'

Henderson shrugged. 'But she hasn't been arraigned yet. I've got a hunch that they'll set bail for a hundred thousand and let her skip back to Colombia. That's what usually happens.'

Hoke nodded, and made a circle with his thumb and forefinger. Henderson pulled his chair closer to the bed.

'You got any idea who did this to you, Hoke?'

'Uh-uh.' Hoke rolled his head back and forth on the pillow.

'Got *any* ideas?'

Hoke nodded and then shrugged. He was tired, and he wanted Henderson to leave.

'I talked some to Eddie Cohen, the old fart on the desk, and he says he didn't see any strangers in the hotel. The manager questioned some of the old ladies who sit around the TV set in the lobby, and they didn't notice anyone either.'

Henderson got up, and walked to the window. He looked down into the parking lot. 'I – ah – I checked your room, Hoke, and I really don't think you should be living in a crummy place like that. All those social security types and Marielitos – it's depressing as shit, Hoke. When you get out of here, you'll have to recuperate for a couple of weeks. I can put you up at my house. We can put a cot out in the Florida room, and Marie'll look after you.'

'No dice, Bill.' Hoke closed his eyes. After a few seconds, Henderson tapped him on the shoulder.

'Well, think about it anyway, old sport. I'd better get outta here and let you get some rest. If you need anything, let me know.'

After Henderson left, Hoke found the carton of Kools and the new Bic lighter his partner had left in a paper sack on the floor beside his bed. Hoke had lost his desire to smoke; if he was lucky, maybe the desire wouldn't return.

Captain Willie Brownley was Hoke's third visitor. The captain had been there to look in on him a couple of times before. Brownley was black, and it was the first time Hoke had seen the Homicide chief in civilian clothes. He always wore his uniform in the office, complete with buttoned-up jacket. Now he wore a pink Golden Bear knitted shirt, mauve corduroy jeans, a white belt, and white shoes. With his gold-rimmed glasses, Brownley looked more like a Liberty City dentist than a police captain. Hoke had known Brownley for ten years, and at one time had worked for Brownley when he commanded the Traffic Division. Although Brownley had little aptitude for Homicide work, he had been placed in charge of that division so that he could eventually be promoted to major. The black caucus in the union had been demanding a black major for several years, and Brownley was being groomed.

Brownley opened his briefcase on the bed and handed Hoke a one-pound box of fudge that had been wrapped in gold paper and tied with a flexible gold string.

'My wife made some fudge for you, Hoke,' he said. 'And if you can't eat it now, you'll be able to later. And the boys asked me to bring you this card.' He handed Hoke a Hallmark get-well card that had been signed by forty of the forty-seven members of the Homicide division, including Captain Brownley.

Without thinking, Hoke had counted the signatures and was wondering why the other seven hadn't signed. Then he felt ashamed of himself. There were a hundred reasons – sickness, leave, shift changes – why they all couldn't sign the card.

'For a while there,' Captain Brownley said, 'we were worried about you, but Dr Goldstein said you're going to be fine. The only immediate problem is to take care of the paperwork on your lost gun and shield. I hate to lay it on you, Hoke, but we've got to protect you.

'I've brought the forms along and a legal pad, and you can take care of the paperwork now. It's been about six years since a Homicide cop lost his shield and gun, but the big question to answer in your case is why you were living in Miami Beach instead of Miami in the first place. I knew you were living in the Eldorado, and I okayed it as a temporary residence. But you've been there for almost a year now, and that puts both of us in a spot. As you know, all Miami cops are supposed to live in Miami –'

'I know at least a dozen who don't –'

'I know more than that, Hoke, including a city commissioner who commutes down here from Boca Raton. But he has an official address in Miami to beat the system, and we can do the same. Henderson told me your official address is his house, so put that down on the forms.'

'There's no way I can live with Henderson and his wife.'

'I'm not asking you to; all I want you to do is use his address on the forms so we can cover our ass. First, fill out the Victim's Report so I can get a cop from Robbery to begin an investigation. Next, you've got to send me a red-liner memo explaining the circumstances, and third, you need to fill in this Lost and Damaged Equipment form. As soon as you've done this, I'll get the badge and gun numbers into the computer. Just write the info on the yellow pad and sign the forms. I can have them typed at the station. It's a legitimate loss, so the city'll replace your gun and badge at no cost to you, and that's about it. I'll do everything I can to prevent an investigation of why you were living in the Eldorado instead of Miami.'

'That rule's never enforced,' Hoke said. 'There're guys with condos in Hialeah and Kendall, captain.'

'Nothing is enforced until something happens. Then it's a different story. A black division chief isn't allowed to make any mistakes. I gave you temporary permission to live on the Beach, and you stayed for a year. It's my mistake for not following up on you, because now there's a thief running around Dade County with your gun and buzzer. If he ever realizes the kind of power that represents, the department'll be in a lot of trouble.'

102

Hoke shrugged and reached for the ball point pen. 'When do you want all this info?'

'Why don't you do it now? I'll go down to the cafeteria downstairs and get a sandwich and some coffee. I want to get that info into the computer.' Brownley turned in the doorway. 'You want anything? Coffee?'

Hoke shook his head, and pulled his wheeled tray closer to the bed.

'Okay, then, Hoke, I'll be back in an hour. Don't let the nurse or no one else touch my briefcase.'

Hoke filled in the forms, and wrote the red-liner memo. Although it was possible for a cop to be suspended with pay for not living in Miami, the rule was never enforced, and he thought Brownley was a little paranoid about it. But then, Brownley wanted that promotion, and Hoke didn't want to jeopardize it. Perhaps he would, after all, have to move away from the Eldorado – but he sure as hell wouldn't move in with Henderson. Hoke didn't like Marie Henderson, and he liked Henderson's kids even less.

When Captain Brownley returned for the forms, Hoke told him to thank his wife for the fudge.

'I'll tell her. D'you want any visitors, Hoke?'

'I'd rather not, captain. I look like hell, and it hurts me to talk.'

'Okay, I'll pass the word, but I'll be back ex officio. One other thing, Hoke, you'll have a new partner when you come back to duty. I let Henderson stay with you when he was promoted to sergeant because you guys work well together, but things've changed lately. I'm getting five new investigators, all Cubans, all bilingual, and neither you nor Henderson speak Spanish. I've put Lopez with Henderson, and you'll have a bilingual partner when you get back. Even if you and Henderson were bilingual, I'd have to break you up. I'm too short on experienced people to let two sergeants work together any longer.'

'I'm not surprised,' Hoke said. 'Did you know that Red Farris resigned?'

'In Robbery?'

'Yeah, and he had ten years in. He was in Homicide before you came in as chief.'

'I knew Red. I didn't know him well, but I knew him enough to talk to him. He was a good man. We're losing too many good people, Hoke.'

With his memory refreshed by the reports he had just written, Hoke went over again in his mind what had happened. There had been a knock on the door. Was it timid or imperious? Was it three raps or two? He couldn't remember. Masculine or feminine – he felt, somehow, that it was feminine, but he wasn't sure. His response had been so automatic, it was as if he had known the caller. He had hidden his drink behind the photograph of his two daughters. Why? He was entitled, for Christ's sake, to have a drink in his own room and to answer his door with a drink in his hand. It wasn't the Dominican maid, he knew her timid, tentative knock; and it wasn't Mr Bennett. If that bastard Bennett had wanted to clobber him, he would have gypped the assailant on the fee, and the job wouldn't have been so thorough.

That left the Marielitos, but Hoke felt that the resident Cubans could be eliminated. When Hoke had first moved into the Eldorado, the refugees had been a continual problem. There had been twenty of them all in one room, and Mr Bennett had charged them three bucks a night to sleep on mattresses on the floor. They got drunk, they fought, they were loud, and they brought women in, terrifying the Jewish retirees who lived there on social security. Hoke had shaken down their room a couple of times and picked up a .32 pistol (no one had claimed it or knew how it got there) and three knives. Finally, when Reagan took away their $115-a-month government checks, the refugees without jobs had moved out, unable to pay the three bucks a night. Hoke had then persuaded Mr Bennett to get rid of the worst offenders, so now there were only five or six Marielitos left, and they all had jobs of some kind. Hoke figured they all liked him. He would pass out a dollar now and then – to wash his car or to bring him a sandwich from Gold's Deli. So if his attacker was a Marielito, it had to be one that he had evicted. But the attack wasn't in the Latin manner. When a Latin wanted revenge, he also wanted you to know all about it, and he would tell you at great length precisely what he was going to do to you and why before he got around to doing it.

Hoke knew that he had his share of enemies. What policeman hasn't? He had put his quota of people away, and the parole board released them faster than they were incarcerated. There were bound to be a few who might keep their promise to get him when they were released. On the other hand, a stretch in prison had a way of cooling people off. There was ample time for reflection in prison, and time, if it didn't eliminate animosity, at least ameliorated it. Hoke, like most men, considered himself a good guy. He couldn't conceive how anyone who knew him could attack him in such a cruel, impersonal way.

Hoke came to the conclusion that he had been mistaken for someone else, and the incident was some kind of crazy mixup.

He also thought it was peculiar that both boxes of fudge, the one from Louise and the one from Captain Brownley, had been wrapped in the same gold paper and tied with the same kind of flexible gold string. A few days later, when he was limping around the hospital corridors, just to get out of his room, he went into the hospital gift shop. There was a pyramid of fudge on the counter, each pound wrapped in gold paper. Hoke looked at a box and saw the sticker on the bottom: *Gray Lady Fudge – $4.95.*

Chapter Fifteen

Freddy had always been a light sleeper, but noise had seldom interrupted his sleep. In prison, he could sleep soundly while two men in the same cell argued at the top of their voices, and with bars clanging throughout the block. But if there was a change in the pattern of the usual noises he would awake immediately, as alert as an animal, until he discovered what had disturbed the pattern. He could then drop back to sleep as easily as he had awakened.

He awoke now, at four-thirty A.M., but heard nothing except the gentle hissing of the cold air from the wall ducts. Susan, her left thumb in her mouth, slept soundlessly beside him, naked except for the sheet they had pulled waist-high over themselves. There was a gentle flurry in Freddy's stomach, as though mice were scrambling around inside. His mouth was dry, and despite the air conditioning, there was a light film of perspiration on his forehead. His right leg began to jerk involuntarily, and it took him a moment or two to control the tic. He threw off the sheet and sat on the edge of the bed. To his surprise, he was a little dizzy. He poured a glass of water from the bedside carafe and ate the piece of chocolate that the maid had left on his pillow when she had turned down the bedcovers.

Freddy was having an anxiety attack, but because it was his first, he didn't know what was happening. He picked up his watch and watched the second hand sweep around as he took his pulse. He found the rate of seventy disturbing; as a rule, his pulse was a steady fifty-five. He went to the dresser, picked up Hoke's .38 police special, cocked it, and checked both closets and the bathroom. No one. He lowered the hammer carefully and replaced the weapon in the holster. He wanted to smoke a cigarette. All he had to do was to pick up the phone and he could have a carton in the room within minutes, but he didn't reach for the telephone. People in hell, he thought, want piña coladas, too. Their problem is that they can't have them. My problem is that I can have everything and anything I want, but what do I want?

He didn't want anything, including the cigarette he had thought he wanted. What did he want? Nothing. In prison he had made mental lists of all kinds of things he would get when he was released, ranging from milk shakes to powder-blue Caddy convertibles. But he didn't like milk shakes because of the furry aftertaste, and a convertible in Florida would be too uncomfortably hot – unless he kept the top up and the air conditioning going full blast. So who would want a convertible?

What he needed was a purpose, and then, after he had the purpose, he would need a plan.

Freddy pulled Susan into a sitting position. 'Are you awake, Susie?'

'I think so.'

'Then open your eyes.'

'I'm sleepy.'

Freddy poured a glass of water and splashed some water into Susan's face. She rubbed her puffy eyes and blinked. 'I'm awake.'

'Tell me again,' he said, 'about the Burger King franchise.'

'What?'

'The Burger King franchise. You and your brother, remember? How does it work? How much money do you need, and why do you want one?'

'It wasn't my idea, it was Marty's. What you need, he said, is about fifty thousand dollars. Then you borrow another fifty thousand from the bank and go to the Burger King people. They tell you what's available, and you buy it or lease it and run it by their rules. Marty wanted to build one up in Okeechobee. He even had the location picked out.'

'But why did he want it? What was his purpose?'

'To make a living, that's all. You hire school kids real cheap, and you make a nice profit. All you have to do, as the manager, is hang around all the time, see that the place is clean, and count your money. When you pay back the bank loan, everything else you make from then on is gravy.'

107

'What was your part supposed to be in all this?'

'Well, he said we'd split up the work, so that one of us would be there at all times. Otherwise, these kids who work for next to nothing will steal you blind. So if he was there days and I was there nights, we could prevent that.'

'Is that what you wanted?'

'I don't know. It seemed like such a long way off, I didn't think much about it. Marty liked to talk about it, though. I guess I didn't care. It would be something to do, I guess. I don't know.'

'Well, I think it's stupid. I can't see any point to hanging around a Burger King all day, no matter how much money you make. Don't you know why it's stupid?'

'I never thought too much about it.'

'I'll tell you why. Your life would depend on the random desires of people who wanted a hamburger. So you can just forget about Burger King.'

'Okay. Can I go back to sleep now?'

'Yeah. I'm going out for a while. Don't let anyone in while I'm gone. Do you want anything while I'm out?'

'Uh-uh ...' She was asleep.

Freddy, carrying Hoke's sap and handcuffs in his jacket pocket and the holstered pistol clipped to his belt in the back, and with the badge and ID case in his right trousers pocket, left the deserted lobby. He walked down Biscayne toward Sammy's, which was open twenty-four hours. The predawn air was damp, cooler this time of morning, and there was a taste of salt in the air from the bay.

At the corner, a tall black whore at the curb clawed at his arm with long black fingers.

'Lookin' for some fun?' she said.

Freddy showed her his badge. 'Call it a night.'

'Yes, sir.' She crossed the street on the yellow light and walked swiftly away, her high heels clattering in the dark.

Freddy continued on to Sammy's, went into the clean, well-lighted restaurant, and took a corner booth. Power, he thought. Without the badge, he would have had an argument, and it would have been difficult to get rid of the whore unless he had decided to kick her in the ass. And that could have, might have, caused him some trouble. It was trouble he could handle but a hassle all the same. With the badge, it was so easy …

A rangy red-haired waitress came over to take his order.

'Coffee. Is that okay, or do I have to order something with it?'

'Most people do, but you don't have to.'

'Okay. And pie, then.'

'What kind?'

'I'm not going to eat it, so what difference does it make?'

'Yes, sir.'

Freddy didn't want the coffee, either. But the long walk in the cool air had allayed his anxiety somewhat, and he began to work out a plan that would lead to a purpose. What he needed to do, he decided, was to get organized and to start over. The haiku about the frog coming to Miami and making a splash of some kind made a lot of sense. Alone, with this new city and a new chance, he could do something or other if he could only figure out what it was he was meant to do. What he wanted to do was to dump Susan, but he realized that he was now stuck with her. He had, strictly by accident, caused the death of her stupid brother. The fact that it was her brother's fault and not his didn't make any difference. Without anyone else to look after her now, she had become Freddy's responsibility. She would get no help from her father, that was a certainty. So now it was up to him. His first idea, about buying her a Burger King franchise, was out. She had no real interest in the idea, and she wouldn't be capable of running a place like that if she had one. Her dumb brother, in all probability, wouldn't have been able to run one either.

Freddy sipped his black coffee and counted the pecan halves on top of the piece of pie the redhead had brought with the coffee. The pie was warm and smelled good, but he had eaten one hell of a dinner. He wasn't hungry …

A black man wearing a Raiders fedora walked into the restaurant carrying a knife. He grabbed the red-haired waitress's wrist and twisted her arm into a half-nelson. She squealed and he put the point of the knife into her neck a quarter of an inch, just far enough to draw a trickle of blood, and told her to open the register.

There were two patrons in the restaurant besides Freddy, and they sat paralyzed at the counter. They were middle-aged Canadian tourists, getting an early breakfast before a drive to the Keys. The robber apparently hadn't noticed Freddy in the corner booth, or else he wasn't concerned about him. His concentration was on the waitress and the money in the till when Freddy shot him in the left kneecap. The report of the .38 was loud, but the man's scream was piercing enough to make the Canadians shudder. He dropped the waitress's arm and his knife, then fell, still screaming, to the floor. Freddy stopped the screaming in mid-shrill when he tapped him behind his right ear with the heavy leather sap.

Freddy flashed his badge. 'It's okay, dear,' he said to the waitress. 'I'm a police officer.' He held up the badge so the middle-aged couple at the counter could see it. Freddy smiled. 'Police. Go ahead and finish your breakfast.'

The waitress sat at the counter, put her head down on her crossed arms, and began to cry. Freddy took the billfold from the unconscious man's hip pocket and dropped it into his own jacket pocket with the handcuffs. He took out the handcuffs, decided he didn't need to use them, and then told the middle-aged couple to stay where they were while he made a call for an ambulance from the radio in his police car. They both nodded, still too numb to reply.

Freddy put a dollar bill under his coffee cup at his booth, left the restaurant, and walked back to the Omni Hotel. As he entered the lobby, he heard the police siren as the panda car hurtled down Biscayne toward Sammy's. He sat in a red leather chair in the lobby and took out the robber's billfold. Eighty dollars. There were three driver's licenses in the billfold, all with different names but with the same picture. Freddy had no use for the licenses or the billfold, but he could always use another eighty dollars. He dropped the billfold into a potted plant and took the elevator up to his room. He had an idea now, on how to take care of Pablo Lhosa.

Freddy shook Susan awake, told her to take a shower and get dressed. He ordered coffee, orange juice, and sweet rolls from room service. The continental breakfast was at the door by the time Susan was dressed.

'The breakfast's for you, to wake you up,' he said. 'Go ahead and eat while I tell you what to do.'

'Want some?' she said, biting into a prune Danish.

'If I'd wanted something I would've ordered it.'

Freddy told Susan to drive back to the apartment and to pack up his purchases from the day before and to bring them to the hotel. He told her where he had hidden the coin collection in the leather case, and to bring that, too. Also, while she was home, she could pack a few things she might need herself for a few days' stay at the hotel. 'Don't think about it too much. If you forget something, we can always buy it here at Omni. The important thing is to pack my stuff and get the money, then come back here without running into Pablo. He won't be up this early in the morning. On your way back, make sure you aren't followed. If you pick up a tail, lose him before you drive back to the hotel.'

'Is somebody after us, Junior?'

'Not us, but me, yes. I'm not a likeable person, so someone is usually after me. And because you're with me now, that means somebody'll probably be after you, too.'

'I don't understand.'

'That isn't important. When there's something important you really need to understand, I'll explain it to you. Right now, when you finish your coffee, I want you to get moving. Here's the extra room key. Change clothes when you get home, too. Wear a skirt and blouse and some saddle shoes.'

'What saddle shoes? I don't have any shoes with saddles. I can wear my running shoes.'

'Okay. We'll get you some saddle shoes later, so you'll look like a college girl. But that'll be after I deal with Pablo.'

'Do I have to see Pablo again? I'm afraid of him.'

'Did Pablo fuck you when you first went to work for him?'

'No. I just sucked him off, is all. He wanted to see if I knew how to do it, and then he gave me some pointers, afterward. Pablo knows a lot.'

'No, you don't have to see Pablo again. Just beat it now, come back here, and if I'm not here, watch the TV until I get back. If you get hungry, call room service.'

After Susan left, Freddy drank what was left of the orange juice. His mouth was still dry. He found it exhausting to talk to Susan, and he was never certain whether she understood everything he told her. Apparently she did, because so far she had done everything right, and she had also picked up on his lies when he had talked to the cop in the Brazilian steak house. But she also had the bad habit of telling the truth when a lie would have done her more good. She shouldn't have told the detective that she was hooking at the hotel. The way she looked, no one would have ever guessed what she did for a living. Later on, when he had more time, he would talk to her about what to say and what not to say; otherwise, she would get herself – and him – into some bad situations.

Freddy called the desk, and found out that the barber shop didn't open until eight-thirty. He took a shower and glumly watched the *Today* show on television until eight A.M. Restless, he got dressed again, and took the elevator to the lobby, sharing the cage with a Latin family with four small children and an old lady with a hairy mole on her chin. The elevator reeked of musk and garlic, and because the rotten kids, on getting in, had pushed all the buttons, the elevator stopped at every floor on the way down.

The barber shop was open. Freddy got a shave. After the shave, the barber combed Freddy's hair and said:

'You have lovely hair, but you really should let it grow. It's much too short for today's stylings.'

'Your hair's too long,' Freddy said. 'You look like a fruit, and if I couldn't tell by your hair, that Swiss army earring you're wearing still gives you away.'

Freddy climbed into the first cab in line, and told the old woman who was driving to take him to the International Hotel.

'That's the one on Brickell, isn't it?'

'Are there two International Hotels?'

'Not that I know of –'

'Then it must be the one on Brickell, right?'

'That's what I meant.'

People were going to work, and the traffic was heavy. The cab's meter ticked away with the speed of light. When she pulled up at the entrance, Freddy said:

'I'm not going to be long. If you want to wait, you can take me over to Miami Beach.'

'That beats going to the airport. But you can pay me now, and I'll turn off the meter.'

'Don't you trust me?'

'As much as you trust me.'

'Keep the meter running.' Freddy counted out four twenties. 'If it gets up to this much and I'm not back, you can leave without me.'

'Yes, sir.'

Freddy made a casual tour of the enormous lobby. There were three restaurants and a coffeeshop, three bars, and a dozen specialty shops selling resort clothes and gifts. There was a small conference room next to the Zanzi Bar, with a black-lettered sign outside the door:

BEET SUGAR INSTITUTE
SEMINAR AT 11 A.M.
CASH BAR IN ZANZI BAR AT 10

The Zanzi Bar wasn't open yet, and no one was in the small conference room, although there was a lectern, a movie screen, and thirty or more folding chairs set up for the seminar. Freddy went to a house phone, asked for the bell captain, and waited for him to get on the line.

'Tell Pablo Lhosa,' he said to the captain, 'to come to the small conference room next to the Zanzi Bar.'

'Is anything wrong, sir?'

'Of course not. I'm running the seminar for the beet sugar people, and if anything was wrong I'd call the manager – not Pablo.'

'Right away, sir.'

The 240-pound Pablo arrived in three minutes, huffing slightly, the two bottom buttons of his monkey jacket unbuttoned because of his belly. Freddy closed the door to the conference room and hit Pablo in the stomach. Pablo gasped and staggered slightly, but he didn't fall. A knife appeared in his right hand. Freddy showed Pablo his badge.

'Put the knife away, Pablo.'

Pablo closed the knife and returned it to his pocket.

'My name isn't Gotlieb, Pablo. My name's Sergeant Moseley, Miami Police Department. And that little girl you sent to my room, Susan Waggoner, is only fourteen years old. Your fat ass is in trouble.'

'Her brother told me –'

'Her brother's dead, and he lied to you. He was killed at the airport, and it was on the news. You're one of the suspects. Did you have Martin Waggoner hit, Pablo?'

'Hell, no! I didn't – I don't know nothing about it!'

'I've got a signed deposition from Susan that you're her pimp, so your greasy ass is on fire.'

'Susie's lying to you, sergeant. She's nineteen, not fourteen. I checked on that. Sergeant Wilson knows I run a few girls here. There's no problem. Why don't you call Sergeant Wilson? I pay him every week. You guys ought to get together.'

'Wilson doesn't know you're hustling kids. Susie told me about the pointers you gave her.'

'Honest to God, sergeant!' Pablo raised his right arm. 'Her brother showed me her driver's license.'

'Her brother's dead, and licenses can be forged. Your Cuban ass has *had* it.'

'I'm not a Cuban, I'm a Nicaraguan. I was a major in the National Guard. Sergeant Wilson told me – you know Sergeant Wilson, don't you?'

'Fuck Wilson, and fuck you, Pablo. How much're you paying Wilson?'

'Who said I was paying him anything?'

Freddy took out his blackjack and started toward Pablo. Pablo held up his hands and backed away.

'Don't. Please. I give him five hundred a week.'

'All right.' Freddy put the blackjack away. 'I'll let you off the hook, Pablo. From now on, you give Wilson two-fifty a week, and you can send the other two-fifty to me. Just put it in an envelope and send it to me, Sergeant Hoke Moseley, at the Eldorado Hotel. By messenger – not by mail.'

Pablo shook his head. 'I'll have to talk to Sergeant Wilson first.'

'Don't worry about Wilson. I'm the man with Susie's signed deposition, not Wilson.'

'I guess you don't know Sergeant Wilson, then. He won't stand for any split like that.'

'In that case, it'll cost you seven-fifty a week instead of five hundred, won't it?'

'Give me a break, for Christ's sake!'

'I have. But I'd rather take you in and book you. There're plenty of girls in Miami over eighteen without putting young kids into the life.'

'I didn't know. That holy sonofabitch! I asked Marty first thing because she looked so fucking young, but he swore that –'

'Martin Waggoner's dead, Pablo, and there's no one to back you up. You can start paying today. Tonight, by ten P.M. An envelope to the Eldorado Hotel.'

'That's in South Beach?'

'That's right, on the bay side, three blocks from Joe's Stone Crabs. Just give it to the man on the desk tonight, and tell him to put it in the safe for me.'

'All right, but I'm going to talk to Wilson, and he'll have something to say to you about this.'

'I'm sure he will. Tell him if he wants to talk to me, we can meet in the Internal Affairs Office. Tell him that.'

'You didn't have to hit me, either.'

'I wanted to get your attention, and I thought you might have a knife. Good-bye, Pablo.'

Pablo looked as if he might have something more to say, but he turned and left the conference room. He didn't close the door behind him.

He'll send the $250 tonight, Freddy thought, but after his talk with Wilson, whoever that is, he'll probably discontinue the next payment. But maybe not. Sergeant Wilson would worry about those two magic words *Internal Affairs*. Even straight cops were frightened by the investigators in Internal Affairs. At any rate, a confused Pablo Lhosa wouldn't come looking for Susan. As time passed, old Pablo would try to forget that he had ever known her.

The old lady, smoking an aromatic Tijuana Small, was still waiting for Freddy when he came out of the hotel. The meter was ticking away.

'Turn off the meter now,' Freddy said, as he got into the back seat. 'It reminds me of the passage of time. I'll give you another hundred bucks, and you can give me a tourist's grand tour of Miami Beach. And then, when you get to Bal Harbour, you can drop me at a real estate office.'

'I've got nothing better to do,' the old lady said.

When Freddy handed her the money she lifted her Mercury Morris T-shirt, with the number 22 on the back, and stuffed the bills into her brassiere.

Chapter Sixteen

The work on Hoke's mouth, as planned by Doctors Rubin and Goldstein, did not pan out as well as they had hoped. Hoke's new teeth were almost fragile compared with his old Dolphin choppers; his jaw wouldn't hold a set of heavier teeth. After the jaw healed, and it healed remarkably fast, the restraints were removed and a pan holding evil-tasting pink plaster was jammed into Hoke's mouth. Impressions were made, and twenty-three days after the assault, Hoke had a full set of slightly yellow upper and lower dentures. Hoke had wanted whiter teeth, but Dr Rubin told him that whiter teeth would look false, and that the yellow ones were more natural for his age.

Nevertheless, when Hoke forced himself to take a long look at his new visage, the teeth looked phony, and he was alarmed by his overall appearance.

Hoke had lost weight on the liquid diet and was down to 158 pounds. The last time he had weighed 158 pounds he had been a junior in high school. He was only forty-two, but with his sunken cheeks and gray beard he thought he looked closer to sixty. The crinkly sun-wrinkles around his eyes were deeper, and the lines from the corners of his nose to the edge of his lips looked as if they had been etched there with a power tool. His habitually dour expression underwent a startling transformation when he smiled: the yellow teeth gave him a sinister appearance.

But Hoke had no reason to smile.

The departmental insurance had covered 80 percent of his hospitalization and a good portion of his dental and surgical fees, but Hoke still owed the hospital and the two doctors more than $10,000. Except for the one night when he had shared the four-bed ward with the teenager, he had had the ward to himself. As a consequence, the hospital had charged him for a private room, except for that one night. On that night, it was charged as a semi-private room. Hoke's insurance didn't cover a private room, so the 'private' room meant an extra $10 a day on his bill. Hoke protested the charge to no avail. When he left the hospital, the nurses packed his bedpan and enema equipment, telling him that he had paid for them and was entitled to take them along.

Before leaving the hospital with Bill Henderson, who had driven over to pick him up, Hoke had a talk with the priest-counselor who wanted to work out some kind of a reasonable monthly payment plan. The talk had ended with both of them angry because Hoke insisted that he couldn't possibly pay more than $25 a month on the enormous bill.

Henderson drove Hoke straight to the Eldorado so he could get his car. The police radio was missing, and so was the battery.

'The departmental put in a new radio, Hoke,' Henderson said, 'on the strength of a Lost and Damaged Report, but they sure as hell won't get you a new battery.'

'There goes another fifty bucks.'

'What the hell? You've got the hundred and eighteen bucks the guy didn't find, or didn't want, on top of your dresser, and two paychecks waiting for you in Captain Brownley's office.'

'One of those checks goes to my ex-wife,' Hoke reminded him. 'But what I can't figure out is that money you found in my room. I'll swear that I had less than twenty bucks when I got home. Otherwise I'd've given part of the hundred to Irish Mike to bring down my tab.'

'Maybe the guy felt sorry for you. He took your wallet, so he had to take the money out to leave it on your dresser.'

'Guys like that don't feel sorry for anyone. Let's go in and talk to Mr Bennett. And Bill, I really don't want to go home with you. I appreciate your offer, but I'm too much of a loner to put up with Marie and your kids. I want to be alone for the next couple of weeks.'

'I thought you might feel that way, so I talked to Mr Bennett myself. In fact, I won't go inside with you, because Bennett and me – well – we had some words. I got on his ass about the lousy room he had you in, so finally he agreed to give you a small suite on the second floor. Suite two-oh-seven. The old lady who had it for eleven years died.'

'Mrs Schultz died?'

'I think that was her name. Anyway, she had some nice things, and he's left them there and cleaned up the place. You were missed around here while you were in the hospital. The old people were scared shitless when you were attacked. So I guess your Mr Bennett finally realized that a free security officer was worth two rooms instead of one.'

'I guess you knew all along I wouldn't move in on you and Marie?'

'I had a hunch. The main thing was to give you a Miami address, so be sure to use my address on your correspondence. Anyway, I brought all your stuff with me in the trunk of the car, just in case you wanted to stay here.'

'Come on in, Bill. You don't have to be worried about Bennett.'

Eddie Cohen, the old man who was both night and day desk clerk when he wasn't doing something else, was happy to see Hoke. Eddie rubbed his stubbled chin and pointed to Hoke's gray beard.

'You look like Dr Freud, Sergeant Moseley.'

They shook hands. 'Before or after the prosthesis?'

'Before *and* after. You lost yourself a little weight.'

'Twenty-seven pounds.' Hoke smiled.

'Your new teeth are beautiful! Simply beautiful!'

'Thanks. You know Sergeant Henderson?'

'Oh, yes. We talked the other day. Mr Bennett said to say welcome back for him. He's up in Palm Beach for the weekend. D'you know about your new suite?'

'Sergeant Henderson just told me.'

Eddie shook his head. 'Mrs Schultz went quietly in her sleep. She watched *Magnum P. I.* in the lobby, went on up to bed, and Mrs Feeny found her the next morning.'

'She was the expert on *General Hospital* in the TV Club, wasn't she?'

'Right. And *Dallas*, too.'

'My stuff's out in Sergeant Henderson's car. Some sonofabitch stole my radio and battery while I was –'

'No.' Cohen shook his head. 'Just your radio. I saw the radio was missing on my morning check outside, so I had Gutierrez take out your battery and put it in Mr Bennett's office. So you've still got your battery. You see,' he turned to Henderson, 'When they built the Eldorado back in 'twenty-nine, people used to come down here by rail and ship. So there weren't enough cars around then to build parking garages the way they do now.

'Oh, yes, I've also got some money for you.'

Eddie Cohen went into the office and returned with two Manila envelopes. The flaps were sealed with Scotch tape.

'I opened these when they was delivered, and there was exactly two hundred and fifty dollars in each envelope. I told Mr Bennett, of course, and we kept the money locked up in the safe. Maybe I shouldn't've opened them' – Eddie shrugged – 'but I thought it might be something important.'

'That's okay, Eddie,' Hoke said. SGT. MOSLEY was printed in capitals with a black felt-tipped pen on each envelope. 'Who brought the envelopes?'

'Some Cuban kid on a mini-bike. Both times. He just said to put the envelopes in the safe for Sergeant Moseley. That's all I know. I didn't have to sign a receipt or nothing.'

Hoke counted the money on the desk. The bills were all used tens, fives, and singles.

'What's going on, Hoke?' Henderson asked.

'I haven't got a clue. Let's walk over to Irish Mike's and have a drink.'

'That's a lot of dough not to know anything about it –'

'I know. Let's talk about it at Irish Mike's. While we're gone, Eddie can get my stuff out of your car. Okay, Eddie?'

'Sure. Go ahead. Gutierrez is around here someplace. He'll take it up for you.'

'You said you felt a little weak before,' Henderson said. 'Can you walk two blocks in the sun?'

'I need to walk off a little adrenaline.'

They found seats at the bar in Irish Mike's. Mike shook hands with Hoke, and frowned. 'That beard looks terrible, sergeant.'

'The doc said to leave it on for a couple of weeks.'

Hoke took one of the Manila envelopes out of his leisure jacket pocket and counted out $100 on the bar. He pushed the money across to Irish Mike. 'Take care of my tab, and leave what's over as a credit.'

'Your credit's always good here, sergeant. You know that. I'll just check your tab and give you back the change.'

'No. Leave it. I want to see what it feels like to have a credit for a change. Early Times. Straight up. Water back.'

'Similar,' Henderson said.

Mike served their drinks and retreated to the other end of the bar to sell a twenty-five-cent punch on his punchboard to a white-bearded old man.

'D'you think it's a good idea to be paying off old debts with money you don't know where it came from, Hoke? Or do you?'

'Do I, what?'

'Know where the money came from. That's a lot of money. You aren't into something you haven't told me about, are you?'

'I don't know where it came from, and I don't care. Maybe you guys in the division took up a collection for me?'

'That'll be the fucking day. First you find an extra hundred on your dresser you don't know about, and then you get a couple of two-fifty payoffs in anonymous brown envelopes. It must've come from the guy who clobbered you.'

'I hope so. But it's no payoff, Bill. Maybe the bastard feels guilty. If so, it's because he assaulted the wrong man. I've gone over every case I could think of in the last ten years. Lying in the hospital, I've had plenty of time to think, and I couldn't think of anyone who'd lay for me like that. There're a couple of guys who might've been happy to kill me, but that's what they would've done. A beating like the one I got wouldn't've been enough.'

'Even so, Hoke, if it was me, I'd be damned leery of spending any of that dough till I found out where it came from.'

'Fuck where it came from. I need it, and I can use it. I'll be in Monday to pick up my paychecks, but Captain Brownley said to take two weeks' sick leave before coming back to duty. And that's what I'm going to do. How's your new partner Lopez working out?'

121

'Lopez is a Cuban, for Christ's sake. He saw *The French Connection*, so now he wears his gun in an ankle holster the way Popeye did in the movie.'

'No shit?' Hoke bared his yellow teeth in a smile.

'God's truth. Let's have the other half.' Henderson signaled to Irish Mike for two more, and took out his wallet.

'Put your money away,' Hoke said. 'I've got a credit going here.'

Gutierrez had put all of Hoke's clothing away neatly by the time Hoke returned to his new suite. It was a small suite, all right, even with the sitting room, and it looked even smaller because the late Mrs Schultz had crammed a great many purchases from garage sales into the sitting room during her eleven years of residence. There was a comfortable Victorian armchair stuffed with horsehair, where Hoke could sit and watch his little Sony, and there was a handsome rolltop desk with a matching swivel chair, flush against the wall. Hoke put his files and papers into the desk drawers, happy to have a desk in his room. In his tiny room on the eighth floor, he had had to unfold a bridge table that he kept under the bed, when he wanted to eat or to do some paperwork at home. The brass bed in the bedroom was full-size, too, which meant that he could bring a woman to his room and not be embarrassed.

Hoke took out his dentures, which irritated his gums, and put them to soak in a plastic glass with some Polident. Dr Rubin had said it would take a little time to get used to them and to note the rough spots, if any, and they could be adjusted on Hoke's next visit to the office. Hoke examined his face in the mirror and was appalled. Without his dentures, he looked even worse. His gray beard, almost an inch long, reminded him of Mr Geezil in the old 'Popeye' comic strip. His chances of ever getting a woman into his new brass bed seemed negligible, and he hadn't been laid for five months. With a sigh, Hoke left the bathroom.

There was a single window air conditioner in the bedroom, but very little cold air filtered into the sitting room. If he couldn't wangle another room air conditioner from Mr Bennett, he would have to buy an overhead fan. On the wall above the desk, there was a large painting of three white horses pulling a fire truck. The horses' nostrils flared, and their eyes rolled wildly. That was one hell of a painting, Hoke decided, and probably worth a lot of money. He was surprised that Mr Bennett had left it in the room instead of selling it –

There was a rapping on the door – three sharp peremptory knocks.

Hoke panicked. He pulled open drawers in the desk, ripping a fingernail in the process, forgetting for a frenzied moment or so that his gun had been stolen. What could he use as a weapon? There was a heavy glass paperweight on the desk, with a butterfly preserved in its interior. Hoke snatched it up and stood with his back against the wall beside the door.

'Who is it?' Hoke said.

'Sergeant Wilson,' a deep voice rumbled. 'Miami Police Department.'

'Slide your ID under the door.'

'Are you kidding?'

'Try me. The next thing you hear, if you hear anything, will be a bullet through the door!'

'Je-sus Christ!' The deep voice was disgusted.

A moment later, the ID card with Wilson's photograph on it was slipped beneath the door. Hoke picked it up. It showed that Wilson was black, six feet, two inches tall, 230 pounds, and a sergeant in the MPD, Vice Division. He was also ugly. His nose was almost as wide as his lips, and he had a boxer's cauliflower ears.

Hoke took off the chain lock and opened the door. The man reached for his ID card. He held his badge in his other hand. He took the ID card from Hoke's fingers and put it back in his card case; then he put his badge away.

'What's up, sergeant?' Wilson said. 'You got a guilty conscience?'

'I just came home from the hospital.'

'I know. I checked. You also got something that belongs to me. Let's have it.'

'I don't know what you're talking about. I've never seen you before.'

'I've seen you. I'm in Vice, and you've been moving into my territory. Let me have the envelopes, please.' He held out a huge hand.

Hoke was puzzled. If Hoke had been paid off by mistake, how could anybody take him for Sergeant Wilson? Whoever it was who mixed them up had to be colorblind or badly misinformed.

'The envelopes addressed to me?'

'The ones addressed to you.'

Hoke handed over the two brown envelopes. Sergeant Wilson counted the money. 'It's a hundred dollars short.'

Hoke cleared his throat. 'I spent a little.'

'Give me your wallet.'

'Fuck you.'

With the flat of his palm, Wilson pushed Hoke into the swivel chair by the desk and held him there with very little effort. Hoke struggled, realized how weak he was, and slumped back into the chair. Wilson took the wallet out of Hoke's hip pocket, counted out $100, and tossed the wallet on the desk. He put the bills into the brown envelope and then put both envelopes into the breast pocket of his beige silk sports jacket.

'Pablo wants the girl back, too, old-timer. Make sure she's back at the International Hotel by ten A.M. tomorrow, and all will be forgotten. Not forgiven, but forgotten. Otherwise ...' He looked around the room and shook his head. 'I guess you're desperate for dough, livin' in a dump like this, but you must've been crazy to fuck with me.'

Wilson checked the bedroom and then took a quick look into the bathroom. He noticed Hoke's false teeth in the plastic glass. He dumped the water into the sink, opened the window in the sitting room, pushed out the screen, and tossed the teeth out the window.

Hoke almost asked, what girl? But he knew that the girl was Susan Waggoner. And he knew now who had put him in the hospital. He didn't know why, and he didn't know why he'd been sent money, but he intended to find out.

Wilson closed the door softly behind him as he left the room.

It took Hoke twenty minutes to find his teeth, but they had landed in a cluster of screw-leaved crotons and weren't damaged. He put them into a fresh glass of water with another helping of Polident and wondered what in the hell he was going to do next.

Chapter Seventeen

After the cab tour of Collins Avenue in Miami Beach, Mrs Freeman made a brief stop so that Freddy could take a closer look at Lincoln Road, the once famous and now deteriorated shopping mall. Freddy suggested a late breakfast.

'You ever eat at Manny's?' Mrs Freeman said. 'You can get a crab-meat omelet, and they give you a basket of hot rolls with butter and honey. And it's the only place left on the Beach with free coffee refills.'

'Sounds good.' Freddy nodded. 'I used to eat crabmeat omelets a long time ago on Fisherman's Wharf, when I lived in San Francisco.'

Manny's was tucked away between a four-story kosher spa and a boarded-up two-story warehouse. Mrs Freeman parked her cab in the weedy warehouse lot and they went into Manny's. The fish odor inside was strong. Mrs Freeman ordered the crabmeat omelet, but Freddy shook his head.

'I've changed my mind. Give me a Denver omelet.'

'What's that?' the Pakistani waiter asked.

'It's eggs scrambled up with chopped ham, green peppers, and onions.'

'What he wants,' Mrs Freeman said, 'is a western omelet.'

'That we got,' the waiter said, and went off to the kitchen.

'In California, we call it a Denver omelet.'

'So you're from California?'

'What makes you say that?'

'You just said, "In California –"'

'Just because I said that I'd been in California doesn't have to mean that I'm *from* California. People are too quick to imply bad things about people before they've thought them out.'

'So you live in Miami, then?' Mrs Freeman shook her gray curls. Her gray dentures had a translucent quality. Her pale blue eyes were clear.

'Yeah. What I'm looking for is a nice little house, but what I've seen of Miami Beach so far doesn't appeal to me. What's up a little farther north?'

'Well, after we pass Bal Harbour, WASP territory, we start to hit Motel Row. The Thunderbird, The Aztec, theme places like that. They cater mostly to Canadian and British blue-collar vacationers in the summer, and American families down here on the cheap during the season. Mostly families from New York, Jersey, and Pennsylvania. But if you're looking for a little house to rent, we can go on past the row and over to Dania. There're some nice little houses there, and it's a quiet town, too, except for the jai alai fronton.'

'We'll take a look.'

'What they do in Dania, they sell antiques. There're dozens of little antique shops along US 1. Fakes mostly, but the furniture's a lot better made nowadays than the real thing used to be.'

'I like new furniture.'

'Well, that's what you buy in Dania. New antiques.'

Freddy liked the looks of Dania. The small stucco homes reminded him of southwest Los Angeles, down around Slauson and Figueroa. The main street was also US 1, which would give him a straight shot into Miami, where US 1 became Biscayne Boulevard. He told Mrs Freeman to cruise slowly up and down the tree-shaded streets so he could look for For Rent and For Sale signs. There were several, but Freddy told her to stop at a small white house surrounded by a white picket fence. There were two towering mango trees in the front yard, and the owner had planted a border of geraniums alongside the house on both sides of the front door. There was an attached garage as well.

Freddy knocked on the door and negotiated with the owner. She was a widow whose husband had died recently, and she wanted to sell the house and move back to Cincinnati to live with her daughter and son-in-law. Until she sold the house, she wouldn't have enough money to leave.

'I don't know whether I want to buy or not,' Freddy said, 'but I'll tell you what I'll do. I'll rent it for a couple of months, and then if I like it you can give me an option to buy it. If I don't buy, you'll still have two months' rent money to spend, and you can leave for Cincinnati right away. How much are you willing to rent it for?'

'I don't really know,' the widow said. 'Would two hundred and fifty be too much?'

'That's not nearly enough. I'll give you five hundred a month, in advance, and you can leave the furniture, pack up, and go on up to Cincinnati tonight.'

'I don't know that I can get ready that soon –'

Freddy counted out $1,000 on the fake cobbler's bench.

'But I guess I can make it all right,' she said quickly, scooping up the money. Freddy got a receipt, and after two phone calls the widow said she could be out of the house by ten that night, and that she would leave the keys next door when she left. Freddy returned to the cab and told Mrs Freeman he had rented the little house.

'Furnished or unfurnished?'

'Furnished.'

'How many bedrooms?'

'One, I think, but I didn't look. There's a big screened porch out back, too.'

'I'm not trying to pry into your business, mister, it's just that you're so innocent-like. How much is she charging you?'

'What's it to you? You're a nosy old bat, Mrs Freeman. Did anybody ever tell you that?'

'Lots of times. You should've let me negotiate for you. They call this town Dania because it was settled by Danes, and it takes a Jew to outsmart a Dane. That's all I'm saying.'

'I never question prices. Money's too easy to get in Miami. That's why the prices are so high down here.'

'In that case,' she said, shaking her curls, 'you can give me a ten-dollar tip when I drop you off at the Omni.'

When they reached the Omni, Freddy gave the old lady a $10 tip. 'You're not as sharp as you think you are, Mrs Freeman. I was going to give you a twenty.'

Her high, cackling laughter followed him into the lobby.

Susan, wearing white cut-offs and a Kiss T-shirt, was eating a tuna salad sandwich and drinking a Tab when Freddy unlocked the door and came into the room. The bed had been made, the curtains were drawn back, and the room was delightfully cool.

'Why aren't you watching TV?' Freddy said.

'I was. I did the exercises with Richard Simmons, switched over to cable, and then did aerobics for five minutes. And that was enough TV for me. I sent your pants with the little tennis rackets and your blue *guayabera* to the cleaners. They'll be back by three, the boy said.'

'Good. I like that. I've been out getting oriented and thinking about what to do, so I rented us a little house up in Dania.'

'By the fronton?'

'No, but it's only about eight blocks away. Maybe we can go some night. I've never seen any jai alai. They don't have it in California. Not that I know of, anyway.'

'The first game you see is exciting. But after the first game it's almost as boring as watching greyhounds.'

'We'll go anyway. But I don't want to talk about that right now. Let me have the rest of that Tab. It's hotter than a sonofabitch outside. What I wanted to ask you was this –' Freddy finished the Tab. 'You said your girl friends up in Okeechobee got married, right?'

'Most did, those who didn't leave for someplace else, or just stay home and mope around. There isn't much choice up in Okeechobee.'

'What do they do then, after they're married, I mean?'

'Take care of the house, shop, fix dinner. Sue Ellen, who was in the eleventh grade with me, has three babies already.'

'Is that what you want? Babies?'

'Not anymore. Once I did, but not since the abortion. I'm on the pill, and I use foam besides – unless the john says he wants to go down on me. But now that we're married, I guess I can go off the pill and quit using the foam, too.'

'No, stay on the pill. I don't want any babies either, but if you did, I thought I might try it that way some time. Right now, I like the way we're doing it.'

Susan blushed happily. 'Would you like the other half of this tuna sandwich?'

128

'No. I had a western omelet for a late breakfast. What else do the married girls do up in Okeechobee?'

'Not a lot, the girls I ran around with. They don't work because there isn't much work there to speak of, and their husbands wouldn't want them to, anyway. It makes a guy look bad if his wife has to work, unless they're in business together or something and she has to help him out, sort of. They visit their mothers, shop at the K-Mart, or go roller-skating at the rink sometimes over at Clewiston. On weekends there're barbecues and fish fries. I guess the married girls my age do the same things they did in high school, except they just go with one guy, and that's usually the same guy they were fucking all the way through high school anyway. The best thing, though, they get away from home and their parents. They can stay up late and sleep late, too. If it hadn't been for Marty, I probably would've been married now.'

'Okay, so let's say we're married, which we are, though it's a platonic marriage. Is that what you'd like to do? Keep a house, fix regular meals, go shopping? I know you're a good cook. I liked those stuffed pork chops a lot.'

Susan smiled and looked at her wriggling toes. 'I did all the cooking at home. You just wait till you taste my chuck roast, with sherry in the gravy! I make it in the Crockpot with little pearl onions, new potatoes, and chopped celery and parsley. I use just a tiny pinch of curry powder – that's the secret to Crockpot chuck roast.'

'It sounds okay.'

'It is good, too, let me tell you.'

'I've never been married before.' Freddy took off his jacket and kicked off his Ballys. 'I lived with a woman for about two months once. She never cooked anything or kept house or did much of anything a wife's supposed to do. But when I came home you see, she was someone to be there. I came back one night and found that she'd left, taking the five hundred bucks I had stashed under the carpet with her. I was going to look for her, and then I realized that I was damned lucky to get rid of her so easily. She was a junkie, so I didn't try to find her.

'I had a Filipino boy living with me once, too, in Oakland. But he was a jealous little bastard, and he questioned me all the time. I don't like to be questioned, you know.'

'I know.'

'What I'm getting at, Susie, or what I want, is a regular life. I want to go to work in the morning, or maybe at night, and come home to a clean house, a decent dinner, and a loving wife like you. I don't want any babies. The world's too mean to bring another kid into it, and I'm not that irresponsible. The niggers and the Catholics don't care, but somebody's got to – d'you know what I mean? Do you think you can handle it?'

Susan began to cry and nod her head. 'Yes, oh, yes, that's what I always wanted, too, Junior. And I'll be a good wife to you, too. You just wait and see!'

'All right, then. I'm going to take a shower. You can stop crying and pack everything, and then we can get moving. If you think you're happy now, wait'll you see the little house I've got for you in Dania.'

Susan wiped her eyes. 'But what about your shirt and pants I sent to the cleaners?'

'The bellboy'll hang 'em in the closet. I'm not giving up this nice room. It'll be an office for me, because most of my work'll be in the Omni shopping mall.'

But it wasn't that simple. The widow in Dania, as it turned out, couldn't leave for two more days. They spent those two days shopping for things they needed for the house, including a new microwave oven for Susan. Then, when they did get into the house, the water and electricity had been turned off, and it took Susan an entire morning to find the water company and Florida Power to put down deposits. There was also the gas company to contact, and they had to have a man come out to fill the propane tank outside the kitchen window.

Freddy also sent Susan to the bank to exchange the ten thousand pesos he had lifted from the Mexican pickpocket, but she brought the money back.

'The man at the bank told me they weren't changing pesos anymore,' Susan said. 'He said my best bet would be to go out to the airport and find someone who was going to Mexico and to make a deal with him. Should I?'

'I think not. The airport's too dangerous to be bothering the tourists out there. Remember what happened to your brother? Just put the pesos back in the Ritz cracker box with the rest of the money.'

When they got into the house, Freddy streamlined the house by moving everything he didn't like into the garage. Susan wanted a telephone, but Freddy didn't.

'If we had one,' he said, 'who would we call?'

'The repairman for the washer. The washer works okay, but there's a leak in it or something because there's always a big pool of water after every load. And you might get in trouble sometime and want to call me from jail or something.'

'Don't put a damned jinx on me.'

'I'm not, but a house isn't like an apartment where you can always call the manager to fix something. We've got a septic tank out front. Did you see the bright green grass in the big square patch under the mango tree outside the living room? That's where it is, and I'll bet you those roots are breaking through the tiles. If you treat 'em right, septic tanks work like magic, but if you don't, they'll back shit up through the john and fill the whole house.'

'Get a phone, then. But put it in your name, not mine.'

Susan wanted the car; so did Freddy. They compromised and Susan drove Freddy to the Omni every morning at nine. She picked him up at four P.M. and brought him back to Dania.

In the mornings, Freddy would go directly to his hotel room and change into slacks, running shoes, and a sports shirt with long square tails. The tails covered the holstered pistol he wore at his back, and the handcuffs on his belt were also hidden. He carried the sap in his right hip pocket, and his badge and ID in his right front pocket.

He got to know each shopping level well, and he had escape routes mentally mapped out for quick getaways from each floor. He was soon able to tell vacationing South Americans from permanent Miami Latin residents. He could spot the South American men by their dark suits; and the women did not, for the most part, have that little shelf above their buttocks that Cuban and Puerto Rican women had. If he was unsure, he could listen to them talk: the South Americans spoke Spanish softer and slower than the Cubans.

He came to realize how lucky he had been on that first day when he had mugged the Mexico City pickpocket.

There were a good many security people working the mall, some in uniform, and others in plain clothes. He could almost set his watch by the security officer in Penney's. The man wore a billed fisherman's cap, a flowered sports shirt, and jeans. He spent an average of fifteen minutes on each floor and took fifteen-minute breaks at 10:30 A.M. and 3:30 P.M. in the employees' lounge. Every day at lunchtime he ordered the special, whatever it happened to be, in the deli on Level Three.

There were others, Freddy was sure, who were not that regular and much harder to spot. If they didn't have uniforms, they could be damned near anybody. But Freddy felt protected with Sergeant Moseley's buzzer in his pocket. The lost badge was undoubtedly on the computer of the Miami Police Department, and any Miami cop might question it, but the MPD didn't pass on that kind of information to the private agencies that firms like Omni International and the department stores hired. So, if he got into any trouble, all he had to do was flash the buzzer, and he could get out of almost any situation.

During his first three days of work at the Omni, the only thing Freddy managed to steal was a package he took out of an unlocked station wagon on Rose Two. Later, when he opened the package in his hotel room, he found two pairs of kids' jeans, size eight, husky. He gave the jeans to one of the Jamaican maids.

His fourth day of work was also frustrating. That night after dinner he took the TransAm and drove around the city, then broke into an appliance store on Twenty-seventh Avenue. The alarm went off the moment he heaved a concrete block through the wire-mesh window of the back door. He reached in and opened the door, and grabbed an RCA color TV set and two electric digital clocks. Forty minutes later, when he cruised slowly by the store, driving in the opposite direction, the alarm bell was still ringing and the cops had still not investigated.

Susan hooked up the TV set to the aerial that was already on the house, and the set worked fine, except for a snowy Channel 2, but neither of the digital clocks kept accurate time.

The next day was better. Freddy caught two pot peddlers in the Jordan Marsh restroom on the second floor. They were arguing fiercely about money when he came in and didn't even look in his direction until he had them covered with his .38.

'Freeze. Police,' Freddy said.

They froze. He took their wallets and six ounces of marijuana in a plastic Baggie. He handcuffed both of them, left wrist and right wrist, around the pipe in the first toilet stall, and left the restroom. He would have left the keys to the handcuffs just out of their reach, but he didn't have them. They could explain their situation to whoever it was that rescued them, he supposed, but at least he had plenty of time to get back to his room in the Omni Hotel.

There were $300 in cash, four $50 unsigned traveler's checks, and a gold St Christopher's medal in the wallets. There were no credit cards, and only one driver's license – a license for Angel Salome. The wallets weren't worth keeping, and neither was the driver's license, but the small medal was a nice gift for Susan. The unsigned traveler's checks were good to have, and it was the first time he had ever seen completely blank checks like that, which a man could sign with any name he wanted.

Susan settled in very quickly to a domestic routine. She cooked ample breakfasts for Freddy, surprising him with Belgian walnut waffles, shirred eggs, and French toast made with sourdough bread. Then, after she dropped him off at the Omni, she shopped at the supermarkets, cleaned house, and planned her dinners. One day she was able to buy Okeechobee catfish, which she fried, together with hush puppies, and she served steak fries and collard greens on the side. Freddy didn't like the catfish because of the bones, but he enjoyed the other meals she prepared. She always topped off the dinners with tart desserts, too, like Granny Smith apple pie, bubbly with butter, brown sugar, and cinnamon. One night she baked a turkey breast and served it with all the trimmings, including a mince pie that she baked from scratch.

She washed and ironed the clothes and sheets, and started a small vegetable garden in the backyard, planting cucumbers, radishes, and a single row of tomato plants along the back fence. She made friends with Mrs Edna Damrosch, the widow next door, who worked as a saleslady in a Dania antique store on Wednesdays and Saturdays.

On the days Mrs Damrosch didn't work and when Freddy wasn't home, they visited each other's houses to watch soap operas and to discuss the lives of the characters.

One night Susan cooked fried chicken. She planned to serve cheese grits, Stove-Top dressing, canned peas, and milk gravy with the chicken but discovered she was out of milk. She grabbed her purse and asked Freddy for the car keys. Freddy was watching the news on television and, as usual when he was home, was wearing only jeans. There was a window air conditioner in the bedroom, but none in the living room where the TV had been set up, and the room was always warm and stuffy.

'Where do you want to go?'

'I just want to run down to the Seven-Eleven for some milk.'

'Fix iced tea instead.'

'I need milk for the gravy.'

'I'll go. You'd better stay here and watch what you're cooking.'

Freddy, without putting on a shirt or his shoes, picked up his wallet and the keys from the cobbler's bench and drove the six blocks to the nearest 7-Eleven. He went to the dairy case, deliberated for a moment on whether to buy a quart or a half-gallon of milk, and then slid back the glass door. A short stickup man entered the store, held a gun on the manager, and told him in Spanish to give him the money in the register. The stickup man, in his early twenties, was very nervous, and the gun danced in his shaking hand.

The frightened manager, without a word, gave the gunman the $36 in the till. The stickup man put the bills in his pocket and backed toward the glass double doors. He then stuck the pistol in his waistband and took four cartons of cigarettes from a counter display. He noticed Freddy for the first time. Startled, he dropped the cigarettes and reached for his pistol again. Freddy, reacting impulsively, picked up a can of Campbell's pork and beans and threw it at the gunman, who turned sideways, just in time. The can hit the window, narrowly missing the man's left shoulder.

The glass shattered and a triangular sliver of glass gashed the man's throat. It was a shallow cut, but it began to bleed. The man dropped his gun, clutched his neck, and rushed through the double doors. Freddy went after him, but as the man got into the passenger seat of a heavy Chevrolet Impala, the driver drove forward and up over the curb, heading for the doors. By the time Freddy skirted the stacked bread shelves and reached the doorway, so had the car bumper. Both doors crashed down on Freddy as the driver rammed them. The car then backed away and careened into the street. The falling doors slammed Freddy onto the floor and pinned him. The manager lifted off the doors, and Freddy got shakily to his feet. As the manager hurried to the phone, Freddy got into his car and drove home – without the milk.

When he got home, Freddy gave Susan the car keys and wrote out a list of supplies for her to get at Eckerd's drugstore. He turned off the gas under the food in the kitchen before going into the bathroom to check his injuries. His left wrist was sprained badly, but he didn't think it was broken. There might be a hairline fracture, but he didn't think it was any worse than that. There were a dozen cuts on his face, however, and more on his chest where his chest had been scraped by shards of glass. The worst thing was his right eyebrow. The eyebrow, skin and all, was one big flap hanging down over his eye. He would have to sew it back on and hope that it would grow together again. The other cuts in his face were not only deep, they were penetrating punctures, but they wouldn't require stitches. The cuts on his chest were ridged scrapes, but not as deep as the punctures on his face, so he figured they would scab over within a few days.

When Susan got back, he asked her to thread the smallest needle in the packet with black thread. He sewed the eyebrow flap on to his forehead with small stitches. Susan watched the first stitch and then vomited into the toilet bowl.

'That doesn't help me much, you know,' he said. 'Go into the bedroom and lie down.'

The flap, after he had put as many stitches into it as he thought it would hold, was more than a little crooked, and the eyebrow slanted up at a curious angle, but that was about the best he could do. He was in considerable pain, but he felt lucky that he hadn't lost the eye. By midnight, he knew that the entire eye area would be black and blue. His face was swelling already. He dabbed at his face cuts with balls of cotton soaked in peroxide, and when all of the cuts had stopped trickling blood, he plastered them with Band-Aids. Susan had bought the kind that were blue and red and dotted with white stars, and he ended up with fourteen patriotic Band-Aids on his face and neck. He washed his chest with a washrag, and then with peroxide, but decided not to bandage the scrapes.

His sprained wrist was now twice its normal size. He had Susan splint it with tongue depressors and bind it as tightly as she could with strips of adhesive tape. He could move his fingers, but it hurt. He sent her back to Eckerd's to get a canister of plaster of Paris and cut pieces of gauze into eight-inch strips while she was gone. When she returned, they mixed the plaster with water, soaked the strips of gauze, and he had her wrap them in overlapping strips around his wrist. The cast, when she finished, was thick and heavy, but when it dried it would immobilize his arm just in case there was a hairline fracture. Freddy took three Bufferin, then ate some fried chicken, although he had no appetite for it.

'Are you going to tell me about it, Junior?'

'About how dumb I was, d'you mean? Sure, I'll tell you about it. I forgot for a minute that Miami, like any other city, is a dangerous place. I didn't take my gun to the store, not even my sap. Not only that, I broke my own rule, and I tried to help someone else instead of looking after my own ass. This straight life we've been leading has given me a misplaced sense of security, that's all. For a moment there, I must've thought that I was some kind of solid citizen. That's all.'

'But what *happened* to you?'

'Two guys in a blue Impala ran over me.'

Susan nodded but looked thoughtful. 'I thought it must've been something like that.'

Chapter Eighteen

Marie Henderson was active in a Miami NOW chapter and had a subscription to *Ms* magazine. When Bill Henderson had first told Hoke that his wife was subscribing to *Ms*, Hoke didn't believe him, so Henderson brought one of her copies down to the office and showed him the printed address label. It was made out to Ms Marie Henderson.

'That's incredible,' Hoke had said, shaking his head morosely at the irrefutable evidence.

'Isn't it?' Henderson agreed. 'Now you've got some kind of idea of what I have to put up with ...'

Hoke parked at the curb in front of Henderson's ranch-style house. He didn't see Henderson's car in the carport. He walked reluctantly up the brick walk to knock on the door anyway. Perhaps, he thought, Bill wouldn't be gone very long.

Marie Henderson, a tall bony woman of thirty-eight with brown, frizzy hair, seemed happy enough to see Hoke. She invited him in, pointed toward Henderson's comfortable recliner, and asked him if he would like a drink.

'Sure.' Hoke nodded. 'Early Times, if you've got it.'

'We've got it.' She brought a bottle of Early Times and two shot glasses from the bar and put them on the coffee table in front of him. She went into the kitchen and returned with a pitcher of ice and water.

'That's the way Bill drinks it – straight with water back, so I suppose you do, too.'

'Yeah. It gives you a little lift this way.'

'I'm sure it does.' Marie smiled. 'You don't look too bad, Hoke. Bill said you looked like death warmed over. The beard could do with some trimming.'

'The doctor said to leave it on for a while.'

'He didn't tell you not to trim it, did he? You know who you remind me of with that beard? Ray Milland. Did you see that picture when he was sick and in a wheelchair? His daughter was a librarian, and he had her wait on him hand and foot. The way it turned out, he didn't need the wheelchair at all. He was faking it to make a slave out of his daughter. Finally, the girl pushed him over a cliff and got all the money he was hoarding in a cigar box under his bed, or something. Did you see it?'

'No, I didn't see it.'

'Well, you didn't miss much. It was on the cable a couple of months ago. If it comes back, I'll call you.'

'I don't have cable. I saw Ray Milland in *Love Story*, when he played the father, but I don't remember exactly how he looked.'

'He looked good then. That was several years ago. But you look a lot like him now, something about your smile, I think.'

'Thanks. When is Bill coming back?'

'He's out bowling. He's not on a regular team, but when Green Lakes Landscaping is short a man, they come by and get Henderson. He's only got a one-thirty average, so they don't come by for him often.'

'He did tell me that he was doing some bowling for the exercise.'

'Bowling for two hours once or twice a month isn't too much exercise, is it?'

'I guess not. When'll he be home? Maybe I'd better come back later?'

'Stick around. He'll be home soon. Pour yourself another drink.'

'How're the kids, Marie?'

'Out, I'm happy to say.'

Hoke had two more drinks before Henderson came home, but there was no more conversation because Hoke and Marie had run out of things to talk about.

When Henderson came in, carrying his bowling ball and bowling shoes in a blue nylon bag, Marie got up from her chair and went into the kitchen. Hoke rose quickly. He was a trifle dizzy and feeling the effects of three drinks.

'Did Captain Brownley get a hold of you?' Bill asked as he got a shot glass from the bar.

'No. I've been here for almost an hour.'

Bill poured a drink, and tossed it down. 'I tried to get you before I left. I let the phone ring about fifteen times, and no one answered. What kind of a hotel is that, anyway?'

'Sometimes Eddie's doing something else, and he isn't on the switchboard. I told Mr Bennett he needs someone on the desk all the time, but he says the old people don't get that many calls. The Eldorado's probably got the smallest staff of any hotel on the Beach. So what's up, Bill?'

'You're here, so that's why I thought Brownley had called you. Sit down a minute. I'll be right back.' Bill left the room and returned a few moments later with a large brown envelope, which he handed to Hoke. Hoke opened the envelope and took out a pair of handcuffs.

'Are those yours?' Bill asked. 'There's an *M* in red fingernail polish on the right cuff –'

'Yeah.' Hoke nodded. 'They're mine all right. Remember Bambi, the woman in the Grove I was sleeping with about two years back? We were playing a little game one night and – well, anyway, I used her nail polish to mark one cuff. Where'd you get them?'

'Robbery. They've had 'em for a few days. Two guys were cuffed together in the men's john in Jordan Marsh, in the Omni store. They claimed they were cuffed up by some crazy cop who took their money. The Robbery people just figured these two guys were into something kinky and let them go. Then, a couple of days later, one of the detectives in Robbery happened to notice the initial, and remembered the red-liner memo on your lost buzzer and pistol. He sent the cuffs over to Captain Brownley through interoffice mail. So that's that.'

'No, Bill, it's much worse than that.'

Hoke filled Henderson in on Sergeant Wilson's visit, and told him about the order to get the girl, Susan, back to the International Hotel in the morning. Still sensitive about his fragile, ill-fitting teeth, he omitted the part about Wilson throwing them out of the window.

'This guy's trying to get you into trouble, Hoke. It may be the girl's boyfriend, and maybe not. Why, though, is something else. One guy I really know is Wilson. He was in Vice when I was still in Vice, and he's a vicious sonofabitch. Mean, but I always thought he was straight. I haven't seen him in a couple of years, however, and a lot can happen to a man in two years.'

Hoke scratched his bearded jaw. 'In two seconds a lot can happen to a man.'

'What're you going to do about Wilson?'

'I don't know. I could go to Brownley with it, but how do I explain the five hundred bucks?'

'You just tell it like it happened, and you're covered. I was there, and I can back up your story. It links up with the way this guy – what's his name?'

'Mendez. Only that isn't his name.'

'Anyway, it links in with the way he used your cuffs to rob two bastards and leave 'em in the john. If you want me to, we can leave Brownley out of it, and I'll talk to Wilson.'

'If you could get across to him that he's after the wrong guy –'

'I will. But it won't be all that easy because you were spending his money.'

'I didn't know it was Wilson's. Besides, he got his five hundred back. I can't get the girl back and wouldn't if I could.'

'I'll talk to him. I know how to deal with a prick like that.'

'I appreciate that, Bill.'

'D'you have a gun?'

'I get my new gun and shield back Monday, when I see Captain Brownley.'

'I'll get you one. I've got a chrome Colt thirty-two automatic you can have. I used to carry it in Liberty City in case I needed a throw-down piece. It's not much good, but the magazine holds seven rounds.'

'I can give it back to you on Monday. It really feels funny as hell driving and walking around Miami without a weapon.'

'I can imagine.'

Henderson got the .32 out of the desk in the dining room and gave it to Hoke. Hoke removed the magazine, checked the chamber, and then slipped the magazine in again and loaded the pistol with a round in the chamber. He flipped up the safety with his thumb and put the weapon into his hip pocket.

'In case you're interested, Hoke, I gave Martin Waggoner's effects to his father when he took the body back to Okeechobee. I used my key to your desk.'

'That's okay, but what about the Krishnas?'

'They didn't have any claims.' Henderson smiled. 'I called the head honcho out there when I didn't hear from them, and I got the impression that Martin Waggoner was a novice, not a full member, and was about to be thrown out anyway.'

'Did he tell you that?'

'Not in so many words, but that's the impression the honcho gave me. He wasn't even interested in the funeral arrangements, even though I told him what Mr Waggoner had in mind.'

'Martin was probably ripping them off. That's some family, isn't it? Incest, prostitution, fanaticism, software ... I'd better go home, Bill. This is really only my first day to be traipsing around, and I'm bushed as hell.'

'Want me to drive you home?'

'Hell, no. I just mean that I'm tired. Otherwise I'm okay.'

'Be careful, Hoke. This guy, this Mendez, or whatever his name is, seems like a crazy bastard to me. And when he finds out that you're up and around, he might come after you again.'

'I'll watch myself all right, don't worry.'

Hoke was almost certain that the man from California was after him, but he couldn't figure out why. He didn't feel safe until he got home and had locked the door and bolted it behind him.

On Sunday, Hoke stayed in bed almost all day. He braved the heat at noon and walked to Gold's Deli for the Sunday chicken-in-the-pot special, but he napped again during the afternoon. At six, he made his regular rounds of the hotel and discovered that Mr Bennett had, during his absence in the hospital, put chains and a padlock around the quick-release handles to the back fire door exit. Hoke got the keys from the office, unlocked the chains, and put them into the storage room behind the unused kitchen. Later, when he made out his report and put it on Mr Bennett's desk, he reminded the manager that the fire marshal could close the hotel down for a serious violation like that.

For dinner, Hoke heated a can of Chunky Turkey Soup on the hot plate in his room, and then watched *Archie Bunker's Place* on television. After the show, he called Bill Henderson.

'Everything's okay, Hoke,' Henderson said. 'I talked to Wilson last night, explained things to him, and he'll be on the lookout for Mendez himself.'

'I don't think that's his real name.'

'All right, all right! What do we call him then?'

'I'm sorry. Mendez, I guess.'

'Anyway, Wilson wants to find him as much as we do now. Apparently the guy scared the hell out of Pablo, and Wilson told me that Pablo's talking about going back to Nicaragua. I also reassured Wilson that neither one of us is going to say anything to Internal Affairs. We've got enough to do in Homicide without worrying about what's going on in Vice. He also told me to tell you he's sorry about your teeth.'

'I'm sorry about them, too. I have to pour hot sauce on everything now in order to get any taste.'

'How you feeling otherwise?'

'Okay. I'll probably see you in the morning when I come in to get my gun and badge from Brownley.'

'I don't think so. I'll be out with Lopez. We're doing that investigation about the woman who sat on her kid, and I'm letting him handle it. But I'm watching him.'

'What case is that?'

'It was in the papers. This woman was punishing her kid, a six-year-old, and she sat on him. She weighs about two-forty, and she crushed in his chest. The kid died, and now she's up for manslaughter. It'll probably be reduced to child abuse, but we've got to knock on doors all morning to see what the neighbors've got to say about her and the kid.'

'Did she do it on purpose?'

'I think so. But Lopez, being Cuban, doesn't. Cubans, he says, don't punish their kids no matter what they do, so he thinks it was an accident. We'll find out after we've knocked on a few doors. Incidentally, I found out who your new partner's going to be. Ellita Sanchez. D'you know her?'

'The dispatcher? The girl with the big tits?'

'Girl? She's at least thirty, Hoke, and she's been on the force for six years.'

'Yeah, as a dispatcher. What does she know about Homicide? Shit, I'm sorry I called you.'

'No, you're not. I got Wilson off your ass. Besides, Sanchez really has got a nice pair of knockers. And she can write in English, too. Lopez can't. If it wasn't for being married, I'd trade you Lopez for Sanchez, but Marie would have a fit if I had myself a female partner.'

'I thought Marie was liberated.'

'She is, but I'm not.'

'I'll lock your little thirty-two in your desk drawer.'

'Keep it, old buddy. I'm not in any hurry for it.'

Captain Willie Brownley, wearing his navy-blue uniform, complete with heavy jacket, sat behind a huge pile of paperwork in his glass-walled office. He gave Hoke a short lecture about hanging on to his new badge and .38 pistol this time.

'In my report, Hoke, I stressed the severity of the attack, and there'll be no problems with your record. The only problem you might have is with Ellita Sanchez. She told me that she would rather work with someone else instead of you. I get the idea she doesn't think you're macho enough – losing your gun and all.'

'Jesus! Didn't you tell her the circumstances?'

'She knows, yes. But all the same, she wants to do well as a detective and asked me to put her with someone else. I think I straightened her out on that score, but I want you to know how she feels so you can win her over. She realizes that you're the sergeant, and she'll do whatever you tell her.'

'I'm still going to be out for my two weeks' leave.'

'I know. I'm moving Henderson and Lopez into the bullpen, and Sanchez into your office. Maybe she can catch up on some of your back paperwork.'

'In that case, I'll see you in two weeks.'

'Get rid of that beard before you come back. You look like that Puerto Rican actor, José Ferrer.'

Hoke drove to the Trail Gun Shop and bought a new holster and a pair of handcuffs, charging them to his MasterCard, one that he had obtained from a bank in Chicago that issued them without a thorough credit check. It was the only charge card he had left, and he never missed sending the bank in Chicago the monthly payment of $10.

He then drove to the International Hotel, parked in the yellow zone, and looked for Pablo Lhosa. He showed Pablo his badge and ID, and asked him where they could go to talk. Pablo took him downstairs to the employees' locker room and opened his locker, which was secured with two padlocks. He took out a leather sports jacket and handed it to the detective.

'He left this jacket in his room,' Pablo said. 'He checked out of the hotel by telephone, paying by credit card. He was registered under the name of Herman T. Gotlieb, San Jose, California. The card, it turned out, was stolen. That's all I know. This jacket's too small for me, but it's expensive, and brand new. I want you to find him, lieutenant –'

'Sergeant.'

'Yes, sir. This guy is scary. You should see his eyes –'

'I have.'

'What I think, I think he's a hitman of some kind, imported from California.'

'What gave you that idea?'

'Just the way he acts.' Pablo shrugged. 'I don't have no proof, but I know what a killer looks like. I served ten years in the National Guard in Nicaragua, and I've dealt with men who looked like him before.'

'I'll find him. If you see him again, or if you can think of anything else, call me at my home address.' Hoke gave Pablo one of his cards. 'Let the phone ring for a long time. Sometimes no one's at the switchboard. But don't call me at the department for the next two weeks. Call me at home.'

'Have you checked her apartment?' Pablo said. 'They might be out there. A friend of mine checked once, but they weren't there. That doesn't mean that they won't be back. If you want to go out there, here's the keys to her apartment.' Pablo took two keys off his ring and handed them to Hoke.

'How come you've got her apartment keys?'

'My friend gave 'em to me. He's got keys to everything in Miami. Here, why don't you keep the jacket, too? Except for the shoulders, you're both about the same size.'

'Don't you want it? It's an expensive jacket.'

'It won't fit me. I'm a forty-eight portly.'

'Thanks. I'll find him, Pablo.'

'It can't be too soon for me. I don't like violence of any kind.'

'Yeah ...' Hoke smiled. 'That's why you left the Nicaraguan National Guard after only ten years.'

Hoke used the pay phone in the lobby to call a friend of his in Records. He asked his friend to run a check on Herman T. Gotlieb in San Jose, California.

'How long will it take?' Hoke asked.

'It depends on a lot of things. Give me a couple of hours, okay?'

'I'll call you back, then. I don't know where I'll be two hours from now.'

Hoke drove out to Kendall. He drew his pistol before he knocked on the door. When no one answered, he used the keys to get in. He looked through the rooms, but he couldn't tell for certain whether the pair was still living there or not. There were no men's clothes, but there was plenty of food in the refrigerator. The air conditioning was on, set for seventy-five degrees, and the brass bed in the master bedroom was unmade. There was a small jar of Oil of Olay and a can of Crisco on the bedside table. Except for two six-packs of San Miguel beer in the refrigerator, there was no liquor in the apartment. Hoke knew he shouldn't be in the apartment without a warrant, but he was positive that a fingerprint check on the jock would turn up a record in California. But how could he get a warrant? He couldn't tell a state attorney that he was positive it was Mendez who had attacked him. He had no tangible proof.

Hoke ate a bowl of chili and two tacos at the Taco Bell before going home. The hell with his diet. He needed to get his strength back. He took a shower and opened a package of Kools. The mentholated smoke tasted wonderful. A man would be a fool to give up smoking altogether. One cigarette, one, just one, once in a while, couldn't hurt.

He called his friend in Records. Herman T. Gotlieb, a mugging victim in San Francisco, had been found unconscious on Van Ness Avenue. He had been DOA when his body arrived by ambulance at the San Francisco General Hospital.

Hoke was not surprised by the information. He looked in the telephone book, noted the page and a half of Mendezes, and laughed. There were five Ramons and one Ramona, but it would be useless to call any of them because he knew that the man's name was not Mendez. All he knew for certain was that the man was armed and dangerous and that he somehow had to find him.

Chapter Nineteen

For several days after the fiasco at the 7-Eleven, Freddy was moody and inactive. His aching wrist gave him a good deal of pain, and although he didn't admit it to Susan, the nagging nature of the hurt made it difficult for him to sleep at night. They didn't have cable television, but he watched a Bowery Boys film festival on Channel 51 night after night, scowling at the commercials. Toward four A.M., when a faint Atlantic breeze wafted in through the open windows, Freddy would turn off the TV and fall into a restless sleep. Susan would be awakened by the sudden silence as the set clicked off. She would then tiptoe into the living room and cover him with a sheet.

After his shower and breakfast in the morning, Freddy sat on the back porch and looked through the screen at the lizards scurrying for survival in the backyard. There was a picket fence around the backyard, and a Barbados cherry hedge had been planted against the fence. Susan had neglected her small garden, and the tomato plants had withered. A dead coconut palm – killed by lethal yellow – arched up obscenely in the center of the yard. The fronds were gone, and the top of the tree was a shredded stub. Two lizards, in particular, Freddy noted, made the palm their home base. One, a hustler, darted here and there in search of mosquitoes, but the other one, the fatter of the two, moved rarely, except to inflate and deflate its mottled purple throat. When a mosquito came within range – zip! it was gone. In addition to being skinnier than the fatter, immobile lizard, the hustler lizard had lost the tip of its tail. Freddy thought there might be a lesson of some kind here for him to learn.

Freddy was reminded of Miles Darrell, an old fence he had worked with in Los Angeles. Miles would sometimes plan and bankroll a robbery and take half the profits. If the perpetrators were caught, Miles wrote off his investment and let it go at that. On the other hand, Miles was never a participant, and his careful plans usually worked out successfully. If the hooligans he recruited for a job were picked up, they accepted the bust stoically, and none of them ever informed on Miles. To do so would have been foolish. Even when convicted, the average stay in the joint was only two years, and a man knew when he got out he could count on a stake from Miles until he got back on his feet again.

Freddy had learned early in his career that it was best to work alone. If two or three men were in on a job and one was caught, the others would almost invariably be picked up later. Either deals were made by the man who was apprehended, or they would be picked up as the apprehended man's friends or acquaintances.

On the other hand, Miles, who had never been arrested, only got half the haul when a job was successful. The best method, Freddy concluded, was to plan and execute your own job. That way, no one could inform on you, and if you were successful, everything you got was yours. What he would like now was one large haul. One well-planned job, where the take would be large enough for several years of semiretirement living. Semi, not full retirement, because a man would have to put his hand in from time to time to keep from getting bored, but with enough money stashed away so that he could wait and pick and choose – like Miles. Miles had been a careful planner, and 90 percent of his jobs had been successful.

Perhaps Freddy had been too pessimistic about his life. He had figured, for as long as he could remember, that someday he would end up in prison for life, wandering around the yard as an old lag, muttering into a white beard and sniping cigarette butts.

But that didn't have to be – not if he could plan and execute one big job. Just one big haul …

But nothing came to him. He had no concrete ideas except for the germ, and the germ was that he had Sergeant Hoke Moseley's badge and ID. The badge was an automatic pass to free food and public transportation; it could also be used to bluff someone out of a considerable sum of cash. But who?

After lunch and a Darvon, Freddy usually napped on the webbed recliner on the back porch. He would awaken after an hour or two, covered with perspiration. He would then do a dozen one-arm pushups with his good arm and take a shower. He couldn't shave because of the cuts on his face. After a few days these cuts began to fester. They filled with yellow pus, and he had to pull off the colorful Band-Aids. He awoke one afternoon from his nap with a fever, and it made him dizzy when he tried to sit up in the recliner. He asked Susan to bring him some Bufferin and a pitcher of lemonade.

Susan brought the Bufferin and lemonade, and then left the house. She returned a few minutes later with Mrs Damrosch, a short middle-aged woman who talked through a professional, meaningless, saleswoman's smile.

'Susan said you refused to see a doctor, and that you probably wouldn't let me take a look at you either. But you're wrong there, boy, I'm taking a look. I nursed my husband for three years before he died, and I can do the same for you – although you aren't going to die.' She stuck a thermometer under his tongue and told him to close his mouth.

'Not bad,' she said, when she removed the thermometer. 'It's only one-oh-two, and we can get that down with some antibiotics. I've got a medicine cabinet full of 'em.'

She slipped her glasses down her nose and peered into his face, still smiling and shaking her head. 'Some of those punctures've still got glass in 'em. I'll go home and be right back.'

'Go with her, Susie,' Freddy said, 'and make sure she doesn't call a doctor.'

Mrs Damrosch had no intention of calling a doctor. She returned with medicines, unguents, a razor blade, and tweezers. She crosscut each of the punctures in his face with the razor blade and removed bits of glass with her tweezers, telling Freddy in her cheerful voice that it would hurt. She also removed the crude stitches Freddy had taken to replace his eyebrow. She made some butterfly adhesive patches and replaced them on the gaping places that had not, as yet, grown back together. She used two more butterfly patches on the two deepest wounds on his face but said it would be best just to let the others drain.

She and Susan helped Freddy walk to the bedroom. Edna Damrosch poured Freddy a glass of gin, made him drink most of it, and then sponged his muscular body with a mixture of water and rubbing alcohol. When she removed Freddy's jeans, Susan took the sponge away from her and said:

'I'll take care of that part.'

Edna laughed. 'I would too if I were you!'

This drastic treatment, in addition to penicillin tablets every four hours, broke Freddy's fever. By noon the next day he was sitting up in bed and eating a roast beef sandwich. He remained in the air-conditioned bedroom for two more days at Edna's insistence, then felt strong enough to take a long, soaking bath.

When he looked at his face in the mirror, he could barely discern the scabbed crisscrosses beneath his beard. The thick stubble, a quarter of an inch long in some places, was a mixture of blond, brown, and jet-black whiskers – not matching his burnished yellow hair in the slightest. If he was careful he could probably shave, but he decided to keep the incipient beard. It would cover the scars somewhat, and it might be a way to change his appearance. By now the Miami police were looking for him, but they weren't looking for a man with a blond, brown, and blackish beard. The beard, together with the healing scabs, made his face itch, but he was determined not to scratch his neck or face. His refusal to scratch caused jerky tics to develop on both cheeks, but at least the tics relieved the itching. The following day he took a hammer to the cast on his arm. His wrist was stiff and slightly atrophied, so while he watched TV he squeezed a tennis ball to strengthen his wrist and fingers.

Three weeks after the accident at the 7-Eleven, Freddy put on his Italian suit, took the car keys, and drove into downtown Miami. He had studied the Yellow Pages and the ads in the *Miami Herald*, and he had a tentative plan. He cased three different coin dealers before picking a major one on Flagler Street. Flagler was Miami's main street, and the downtown stretch of Flagler was one-way, but just around the corner on Miami Avenue there was a yellow loading zone. If Susan pulled into the loading zone and sat in the car, a mere thirty yards around the corner from the coin dealer's, she could probably stay there for a half-hour or more before some cop came along and told her to move. The coin dealer, a man named Ruben Wulgemuth, had a reinforced steel door to his shop, and there was a circular, revolving bulletproof window in the wall beside the door. To transact business with the dealer, patrons outside on the sidewalk placed their coins or whatever into the drawer of the revolving window. Except for his regular customers, Wulgemuth didn't let anyone inside his shop. But Freddy knew how to get inside.

Over the asparagus that night, Freddy explained Susan's duties to her. Freddy had never eaten asparagus before, nor had he ever tried hollandaise sauce, but he liked it a lot, especially with the center-cut ham steak and scalloped potatoes au gratin. Susan, whose part in the plan was minimal but essential, was apprehensive because Freddy did not feel that it was necessary to tell her what he was going to do.

'I know you don't like questions, Junior,' she said, 'but I want to do it right.'

'I don't mind questions,' he said, appropriating Susan's uneaten asparagus. 'I just don't like dumb questions.'

'You haven't told me what's going down. If I knew what you were going to do, it would help me do what you want me to do.'

'No, it wouldn't. All you have to do is park in the yellow zone and keep the engine running. Nothing could be simpler. I'll get out of the car and do my business with the coin dealer. If a cop or a meter maid comes along, tell them that you're waiting for your husband to finish a transaction with the coin shop around the corner. The cops know Wulgemuth does business with people on the street, and that's a legitimate reason to park in a loading zone. They may make you move anyway, but then you just drive around the block as fast as you can without breaking the speed limit and park there again. If you're forced to move, lean on your horn with a long two-minute blast as you come by the shop. I'll be inside, but I'll hear you.'

'It'll only take a few seconds to pass the shop, so how can I blow the horn for two minutes?'

'Start blowing when you turn the corner onto Flagler, and keep the horn on all the way up the block after you pass the shop. That's what I mean by a two-minute blast. Think, Susan, think. If someone looks at you funny for holding down the horn, pretend like it's stuck.'

'Like this?' Susan dropped her jaw, made an O with her mouth, and opened her eyes wide.

'That's it!' Freddy laughed.

'You laughed! I don't remember you laughing before, not even at TV.'

'You never did anything funny before. I don't laugh at TV because it isn't real.'

'All right. So what I do is park there and keep the engine running. If nobody makes me move, I just wait for you. When you get back into the car I drive down to Biscayne, take the MacArthur Causeway, and pull into the parking lot on Watson Island.'

'The Japanese Garden parking lot. We'll stay parked in the lot until it gets dark, and then we'll drive back here to Dania by way of Miami Beach. The Japanese Garden has been vandalized, so they've closed it for repairs. No one parks in the Garden lot now, except for a few fishermen in the daytime and some lovers at night. So, if we aren't followed, it'll be easy to hide out there all afternoon until it gets dark. You'd better pack some kind of lunch and a thermos with iced tea.'

'Suppose we're followed – and why would anybody want to follow us?'

'Don't worry about it. If we're followed, I'll deal with it, but we won't be. When you ask why, you're asking another dumb question.'

'I'm sorry.'

'What's for dessert?'

'Sweet potato pie.'

'I've never had that before.'

'It tastes like punkin pie. If I didn't tell you, you'd probably think it was punkin pie, but sweet potato's better.'

'I'll try it. I like pumpkin pie.'

'You want whipped cream on it?'

'Of course.'

After dinner, Susan drove them to the Dania jai alai fronton. While she was buying the tickets, Freddy scouted the parking lot and unbolted a Kansas license plate from a Ford Escort. He locked the plate into his trunk to exchange for the TransAm plate when they got home. Freddy watched the first game and decided he didn't know enough about the game or the players to make an intelligent wager.

Susan, however, by betting on the Basque players who had the first name of Jesus – there were three that night – won $212.35.

Chapter Twenty

Hoke still had Bill Henderson's .32 automatic pistol when he left the police station. He had meant to lock it in Henderson's desk drawer, but when he had seen Ellita Sanchez sitting at the double desk in the little office, he changed his mind. He had got a good look at Sanchez, however, and noticed that she did indeed have large breasts, although they were disguised somewhat by her loose silk blouse and the large silk bow that was tied under her throat. Her black hair was bobbed the way they used to cut the hair of little Chinese girls. The back of her slender white neck looked as if it had been shaved. She wore blue-tinted glasses, and she was frowning, with tightly pursed lips, as she read through a file. She tapped the glass top of the desk absently with a yellow pencil. If he went into the office, she would surely ask him some questions about the paperwork. Sanchez was a formidable-looking woman, and Hoke did not relish the idea of working with her, or as Brownley had put it, 'winning her over.' So he had left the station without talking to her.

Hoke thought about Ellita Sanchez now, however, as he sat in his room, trying to figure out his next move. Whatever he did, he would have to be careful. He didn't want to involve Sergeant Wilson, the Vice cop, nor did he want to make a legal mistake of some kind that would result in bail or a quick release for Mendez. He had to get that man off the street forever.

There was no doubt in Hoke's mind that Mendez had mugged the unfortunate Gotlieb, whose credit card he had then stolen and used at the International Hotel, but he had no proof of the mugging, nor could he get a warrant on the strength of how he happened to feel about it. And there was always the possibility that Mendez had bought the stolen credit card from someone else. For fifty bucks apiece, a man could buy all the stolen cards he wanted at the downtown bus station.

Hoke went to the desk and poured an overflowing jigger of Early Times into his tooth glass. Too much. He poured part of it back into the bottle. His hands shook a little, and he spilled part of his drink. He could hear his heart beat. The more he thought about Mendez, the more afraid he was. This was not paranoia. When a man has beaten you badly and you know that he can do it to you again, a wholesome fear is a sign of intelligence.

There was only one thing to do, and that was to find Mendez and follow him. Then, if he could find his gun and badge on the bastard, he could bring him in for assault or attempted murder. At the very least, Mendez could be held for a few days without bail, long enough to run a fingerprint check out to California to see what they had on him. If the man had a record, and Hoke was certain he had one, the chances were good that he was wanted in California, too. If he wasn't on the run from California, why had he come to Miami?

Hoke had calmed down a little. The drink had helped so much he poured another one. His hands were steady now. Hoke lit a Kool and picked up the phone. After he listened to it buzz at the switchboard fifteen or sixteen times, he lost count. Finally Eddie Cohen answered the phone.

'Desk.'

'Eddie, this is Sergeant Moseley. Dial my number at the police station for me, will you, please?'

Ellita Sanchez picked up the phone before it could ring a second time. 'Homicide. Detective Sanchez.'

'Hello, Sanchez. This is your new partner, Sergeant Hoke Moseley. I was in earlier today to see Captain Brownley, but you looked so busy I didn't want to bother you. Anyway, Captain Brownley —'

'Who? You want Captain Brownley?'

'No.' Hoke hesitated. Sanchez didn't have much of an accent, but Hoke realized that he was talking too fast for her to follow him. 'This is Sergeant Moseley. I am your new partner.'

'Yes, sergeant.'

'We're going to be working together. You and me. Captain Brownley told me today. When I came to see him.'

'Yes.'

'I want you to do a couple of things for me.'

'What?'

'You can probably handle it all with a few phone calls. If not, take a car and visit Florida Power and Light, and the phone company. The water department, too. Perhaps you should check the water company first.'

'What case is this one? Should I not read the file first?'

'No, that won't be necessary. Just take down this information as I give it to you.'

'Captain Brownley told me you wouldn't be back to work for two weeks. If you're on sick leave, why are we working on a new case? And why are you withholding information from me when I'm your partner? I don't understand this at all. So, before I do anything for you, Sergeant Moseley, I'm going to check with Captain Brownley to see if it's all right. The way I –'

'Shut up.' Hoke's deep voice dropped an octave with anger.

'What?'

'I said shut up. Now listen, Sanchez, because I don't want to repeat myself. We are indeed new partners, but I am the senior partner, and a sergeant. You're the junior partner, and you're not a detective yet. So far you're a dispatcher with a Latin name. And because you have a Latin name, you've been given a chance to work with me as a detective.

'Luckily for you, you've been assigned to a patient, understanding Homicide detective who'll take the time to explain the facts of life to you. *If*, under any circumstances, I give you an order, or a request, or a suggestion, and you go over my head to check it out with Captain Brownley or go to anyone else who happens to be my superior, I guarantee you that you'll be lucky to become a dispatcher again.

'In fact, you'll never see the inside of a police station again. I'll see to it that you're assigned permanently to the night shift at the Orange Bowl, from midnight to eight A.M. So if you don't want to spend the rest of your police career checking the locks on vending machines, get a pencil and a piece of paper and follow my instructions. Do you understand, or do I have to run it by you again?'

'I understand, sergeant.'

'Good. Check with the water department, the F.P. and L., and Ma Bell. And see if anyone named Waggoner or Mendez – W-A-G-G-O-N-E-R, and you can spell Mendez – put down a new deposit in the last three weeks. Water, Florida Power, and phone company. Just during the last three weeks. If you don't get a list of names and addresses from these three, make another call to the Public Gas Company, just in case there's an outside tank. Any questions?'

'No. I got it.'

'Then call me back here at the Eldorado Hotel by five today on what you've found out. Let the phone ring at least twenty times before you hang up. The man at the desk is hard of hearing. If I don't hear from you by five, I'll call you at your desk by five-thirty. Got that?'

'Yes.'

'Till five, then.'

'Yes.'

Hoke got up from the rolltop desk and crossed to the side table by the Victorian armchair where he had left his bottle of Early Times.

That wasn't exactly what Captain Brownley had in mind, Hoke thought, when he said I would have to win Ellita Sanchez over. By the time I finish this drink, she'll be in Brownley's office. By the time I start to pour another, she'll be explaining to Willie Brownley how I have been discriminating against her for being a Latin, first, and for being a woman, second. She'll tell Brownley about my threat, and I'll have to make it good. Whether there are enough people left in the department who owe me enough favors to send Sanchez to the Orange Bowl is a moot question. But I can get her out of Homicide. That much I know I can do. Vice! Sergeant Wilson. Sergeant Wilson threw my teeth out the window. He owes me for that. I can get Wilson to ask for her in Vice. A few months of trapping johns on 79th Street will be good training for Sanchez, and after she works for a mean prick like Wilson for a couple of weeks she will surely wish to hell she had done what kindly old Hoke Moseley asked her to do ...

Hoke finished his drink. He lit another cigarette, smoked it down to the cork tip, and put it out in the ashtray with the Hotel Fontainebleau logo. There was no telephone call from Captain Brownley.

At four-thirty P.M. the phone woke Hoke from his nap. Sanchez had a list of names and addresses for him. There were two Mendezes, one Wagner, one Wegner, and one Susan Waggoner. Susan Waggoner, however, was not in Dade County. She had put down deposits for water, electricity, gas, and a telephone in Dania, which was right over the county line in Broward County.

Hoke hadn't told Sanchez to check in Broward County, but he had, apparently, frightened her into using initiative.

Chapter Twenty-One

The rain began to fall lightly at four-thirty A.M., but by six, when the lightning flashed and the thunder rumbled, passing over Dade County from the Everglades, the rain came down in torrents. Hoke cursed the rain and rolled up the window to avoid getting drenched. The windows steamed almost immediately, and he had to wipe the inside of the windshield with his handkerchief.

Hoke had been parked under a cluster of sea-grape trees since four A.M. The overhanging branches with their huge leaves concealed most of his car from Susan Waggoner's little house a hundred yards away on the other side of the street. The rain, as he thought about it, would make tailing easier. He didn't know whether Mendez was in the house with Susan or not, but he was certain that she would lead him to Mendez if he followed her long enough.

When the lights in the house went on at six-fifteen, Hoke was more than a little surprised. He hadn't expected the girl to get up so early. Hoke took a leak in the coffee can, replaced the lid, and placed the warm can on the floor in front of the passenger's seat. He wanted another cigarette, but he wouldn't light one now because the girl might see the glow. The girl was his only lead to Mendez, and he didn't intend to take any chances. The white TransAm, with its Kansas license plate, would be easy to follow, whereas his own beatup Pontiac blended right in with the thousands of dented cars on Miami's highways. No, the only thing that bothered Hoke was the actual apprehension of Ramon Mendez, but he would be able to handle that when the time came ...

Freddy awoke at six, went to the bathroom, showered, and then shook Susan awake. Freddy was pleased by the rain and asked Susan how long she thought it would last. Susan, who was bustling in the kitchen preparing a large breakfast, went to the window and looked out.

'This is the tail end of the hurricane season, and we always get a lot of rain. It could last three or four days, or it may pass over in two or three hours. From the looks of the sky, I'd say all day.'

Susan ladled chipped beef and peppery milk gravy over six buttered toast points. She set the plate in front of Freddy and stepped back as he forked a huge mouthful and chewed with his eyes closed.

'This is good SOS,' he said. 'But you should've fixed home fries to go with it. SOS tastes better over potatoes than it does on toast. That way, you can eat the toast separately with a little marmalade. This gravy's so thick I can hardly taste the butter on the toast.'

'It won't take a minute to fix some home fries, if that's what you want. There's a cold baked potato in the fridge, and I can slice it up –'

'No, this is okay. I meant for next time. I like a big breakfast when I go out on a job. Gives a man energy.'

'How's your wrist?'

Freddy got up from the table, dropped to the floor, and did a one-arm pushup with his bad arm. 'That's one,' he said, wincing as he sat at the table again. 'Tomorrow I'll try for two.'

'Does it still hurt, I mean?'

'A little, when I do pushups. But I don't think it was ever broken, or it wouldn't've healed by now. Probably just a bad sprain.'

'I guess this rain don't make no nevermind to your plans, does it?'

'It helps us, that's all, by cutting down the visibility. Did you fix the lunch yet?'

'Tuna fish sandwiches, what's left of the vinegar pie, some apples and bananas. And two bags of Doritos. There's tea in the thermos, and a six-pack of Dr Pepper. I already put the stuff in the car.'

Freddy nodded, and poured another cup of coffee. 'That's plenty. We probably won't be hungry anyway, after this big breakfast, but after you've been sitting in a car for a few hours, eating gives you something to do. You'd better put an empty coffee can in the car, too.'

160

'What for?'

'Sometime, Susie, before you ask a stupid question, why don't you think for a minute? Where d'you think the iced tea and those Dr Peppers are gonna go?'

'The can's to pee in?'

'See how easy it is?'

Susan frowned. The two little lines between her eyes deepened, and she compressed her lips.

'If something's bothering you,' Freddy said, 'spit it out. I don't like the way you're behaving this morning.'

'What you're making me do isn't fair.'

'How's that?'

'The man's the man, and the woman's a woman in a marriage. You're supposed to go out and bring in the money, and I stay home and keep house. It isn't fair to make me help you do whatever it is you're going to do, and I'm scared.'

'What're you afraid of? All you've got to do is park the car in the yellow zone and wait for me to come back.'

'I think you're going to do something illegal, and if I'm helping you, I could get into trouble, too. I gave up a promising college career to marry you and take care of the house and all, and I shouldn't have to –'

'Who's been filling your head with all this shit? Edna Damrosch, next door?'

'Nobody has to tell me when to be scared. I know enough to be scared when I'm doing something I'm not supposed to do.'

'So if I tell you what I'm going to do, you won't be scared, is that it?'

'That's right.'

'I'm going to rob this coin dealer, a guy named Wulgemuth. The coin collection I'm taking with me will help me get inside his shop. It's worth a couple of hundred bucks, or more, but I'll leave it there when I take the man's cash. He's got his own safe, and he deals in gold and big money, so his safe'll have a lot of cash in it. No telling how much. That's what I plan to get. So now you can relax.'

'Relax? I'm more scared than ever.'

'See what I mean? That's why I didn't tell you before. I knew you'd act this way. Just keep in mind how simple your part is. You park and drive the car. There's nothing to wet your pants about.'

'And I won't get into trouble?'

'Not a chance. This job is foolproof. I've checked it out from every angle. When it's all over we'll have so much money I'll take you on a Caribbean cruise.'

'Why can't you do it alone?'

'Because I can't take a chance and have the car towed away while I'm in the store. You've got to be in it.'

Susan nodded and started to gather the dishes.

'Leave the dishes. You can do them later tonight, after we come home.'

The heavy rain and several accidents on the highway had slowed traffic on the Dixie Highway to a crawl, and Hoke Moseley had no trouble following the TransAm.

Although it was after nine A.M., the bruised sky and the heavy rain made it seem like early dawn. Impatient drivers with their lights and wipers on inched along the flooded streets, crowding over toward the center line. Some honked their horns just to be honking their horns. When Susan sped up to race through a yellow light, Freddy told her to slow down.

'There's no hurry,' he said. 'It doesn't make any real difference when we get there. Even the noon hour would be okay. I've checked twice, and the man is alone in his shop and doesn't close up for lunch. Probably brings it with him.'

'I'm sorry. It's just that I'm still scared and a little nervous. Besides, if you stop for a yellow light in Miami you get rear-ended.'

'I can't understand why you're scared. All you've got to do is park in the yellow zone, and –'

'I know all that! I'm going to be all right.'

The yellow loading zone on Miami Avenue was vacant. It was long enough for three compact cars or for one car and a full-size truck. After Susan pulled into the loading zone, Freddy told her to back up to the end of the zone so she couldn't be blocked from behind. 'That still leaves room for a truck to park in front of you in case somebody needs to unload something for that *ropa* store.'

Next to the Cuban clothing store there was a narrow shop with a stuffed llama in the window. The store claimed to sell genuine Peruvian imports, but the floor beneath the llama was layered with Timex watches and zircon rings in black velvet boxes. On the corner was a small Cuban cafeteria with a Formica counter to serve customers on the sidewalk.

Freddy held the coin case in his lap. He took out his .38 pistol, checked it, and then put the pistol back in his right coat pocket.

'You – you aren't going to shoot Mr Wulgemuth, are you?' Susan said, licking her thin lips.

'Not unless I have to,' Freddy said. 'But sometimes,' Freddy shrugged, 'they make you do it.' Freddy smiled like a butcher's dog. 'Like the time I broke your brother's finger. He irritated me, and I had to break it.'

'You killed Martin?'

'I didn't kill anybody. I broke his fucking finger, that's all. And if you force me into it, by not doing exactly what I tell you, I'll break your skinny neck.'

Freddy got out of the car and ordered two café Cubanos at the counter. He downed his quickly and took the other one, in its one-ounce paper cup, back to the car. Susan rolled down the window, and he handed her the coffee. Her hand trembled so much she spilled most of the coffee on her jeans. There was a rim of white around her lips. Freddy shook his head impatiently.

'D'you want another cup?'

Susan shook her head. Her knuckles holding the wheel were white.

'All right, then. Stay awake, keep the engine running, and I should be back in about ten minutes.' Carrying the coin case in his left hand, Freddy walked away from the car.

Hoke was stopped by the red light. Susan, in the TransAm, had made it across just in time. Hoke watched her pull into the yellow loading zone on Miami Avenue and then back up to the end of the zone. Except for the spaces in front of her TransAm, there were no other vacant spaces on the street. A horn honked behind him. Hoke rolled down the window and waved the driver around. The man had to back up before he could pull forward again to get around Hoke's car. He cursed Hoke and shook his fist as he roared by.

Hoke watched Mendez get out of the car and buy coffee at the cafeteria. He took a cup back to the car. Hoke wondered if that was why they had stopped – to get a fucking cup of Cuban coffee? Another car pulled up behind Hoke and stopped. The light was green again, and the driver leaned on her horn. Hoke waved her around.

When Hoke looked back at the TransAm, he noticed Mendez turning the corner onto Flagler. As Mendez disappeared into the rain, the TransAm pulled away from the curb, with its tires squealing on the wet street, and raced down Miami Avenue. Hoke followed the TransAm, thinking, he's going to buy something on Flagler, and she's going to circle the block to pick him up so he won't get wet. But Hoke had guessed wrong. That's why a man needed a partner. If he had had Bill Henderson with him – or even Ellita Sanchez – she could have followed Susan, and he could have gone after Mendez on foot.

When Hoke realized that the TransAm had got into the lane leading to the I-95 overpass, he switched lanes, bluffed his way into the outside lane, and made a left turn at First Street. He drove down a block, made another left, and finally got back on Flagler. The cars were barely moving and Hoke was caught by two red lights, but he inched along Flagler, watching the pedestrians make short dashes from one overhanging awning to the next. There was a crowd of South Americans with shopping bags standing in the arcade that catered to Venezuelans and Colombians. Hoke stopped completely to look them over. Mendez, in his light suit, would stand out among all those foreigners in funereal black. Hoke took out his pistol and laid it on the seat beside him. He looked at the empty bracket from which his radio had been stolen, and swore. Horns honked behind him, and he moved forward again. His only chance was to spot Mendez in the street, and that seemed damned unlikely. Deep down, way down there in the pit of his stomach, he hoped he wouldn't find him.

Freddy's hair was wet and the shoulders of his gray silk suitcoat were soaked through by the time he rounded the corner to Flagler and reached the window of Wulgemuth's Coin Exchange. Freddy pressed the buzzer beside the window and smiled when he saw

Wulgemuth's alert face behind the glass. The coin expert was in his early fifties but looked older because of his bald head, which was encircled by a clipped wreath of stubby white hair above his ears. His bulbous nose and his sunken cheeks were pitted with old acne scars.

'I'm a police officer,' Freddy said into the recessed microphone. 'Turn the window.'

The bulletproof window revolved. Freddy placed the cowhide coin case in the drawer, and dropped his ID card and badge, still in its leather holder, on top of the case. The window revolved and Wulgemuth's face disappeared.

There were more people shopping on Flagler than Freddy had expected to see on such a miserable, rainy day, but most of them, Freddy supposed, were used to the rain. The rain was warm, and in places the sidewalk steamed. The temperature, despite the rain, was eighty-two degrees, as Freddy could see by the lighted digital clock on the bank tower a block away. The time was 10:04. The time and temperature flashed off, and were replaced by an aqueous message in dotted green lights:

THE AMERICAN WAY
IS OUR IRA

The message puzzled Freddy. What was an IRA? He heard the window revolve. The badge and the ID were in the drawer, but not the coin case. Wulgemuth's face was in the window again. 'What's your business, sergeant?'

'Police business,' Freddy said. 'I've been trying to get a line on these stolen coins, and I've got some other things to ask you about. Open the door.' Freddy took his badge out of the drawer.

The face disappeared. A buzzer on the door lock sounded, and Freddy turned the knob as the door lock was released. The buzzing stopped as he stepped inside.

'Shut the door!' Wulgemuth called from the back of the shop.

Freddy closed the door with his hip. Wulgemuth had the coin case open on the counter at the end of the narrow shop.

'These coins were stolen, you say?'

'Yeah. I brought them down from the property room. We picked them up on a fencing bust, and we figured if we could get a line on the owner we could find out something more on the burglars. Is this a valuable collection, or not?'

Wulgemuth shrugged. 'What you're talking about here, sergeant, is intrinsic value. That's what I deal in. It's worth what someone wants to pay for it, and that's probably a lot more than its face value. This is by no means a rare collection, even though a cursory look shows that all the coins are in pretty fair condition.'

'Did you ever see it before?'

'As a collection, no, but I've seen a lot like it. What happened to your eye, anyway?'

'Car accident.'

'You oughta sue the doctor who sewed you up. You could make a bundle.'

'He said it would look okay once it scarred over.'

'He lied. Anyway, this isn't my coin case, either.'

Freddy closed the lid on the case, and snapped the two hasp locks closed. 'I'll try another dealer. Can you show me one of your coin cases? I'd like to see how different yours are from this one.'

'I don't have any on hand, not right now.'

'Not even in your safe?'

'None for silver dollars.'

'Who else sells cowhide cases like this one, then?'

'You're on the wrong track, sergeant. All the trade magazines advertise cases like this. You can order coin cases by mail, from cheap canvas jobs to custom-made ostrich with your initials in gold.'

'I see.'

'How come a Homicide detective's so interested in tracing stolen property? Is there a murder involved in this collection?'

'That's confidential, Mr Wulgemuth. I'm also checking out your place here for security. We've had a tip, you see, and we're thinking about putting a stakeout in here. Someone – we don't know who – has been hitting coin dealers.'

'You're telling me! D'you know how many times I've been robbed? Before I put in that window, I was hit three times in one month! But I don't need any stakeouts now.'

'Why not?' Freddy smiled, and reached into his jacket pocket for his pistol. His fingers closed over the cross-hatched grip.

'Because of Pedro.' Wulgemuth turned his head. 'Pedro!'

The door in the back opened with a bang. A short, wide-shouldered, dark-haired man came through the doorway. His double-barreled shotgun was pointed at Freddy's chest. His dark, serious face was expressionless.

'He's been watching you all the time through the peephole in the door.' Wulgemuth laughed. 'It's okay, Pedro. This is Detective Sergeant Moseley. He's with the police department.'

Pedro lowered his shotgun and turned toward the back door. As he turned, Freddy pulled out his .38 and shot him in the back. Pedro fell, face down, through the open door to the back store-room. The shotgun clattered on the terrazzo floor but did not go off. Freddy was still looking down at Pedro, deciding whether to fire another shot, when Wulgemuth with a sweeping motion brought up a machete from beneath the counter. In a wide arc, he brought it down on Freddy's left hand, which was resting on the coin case. Freddy's little finger, the ring finger, and the middle finger were lopped off cleanly at their second joints. The force of the downward swing drove the blade into the leather of the case. Freddy shot Wulgemuth in the face. The bullet made a round hole just below his nose. He fell back with a gurgling sound, dead before his bald head hit the terrazzo floor.

For a long moment, Freddy looked without comprehension at the exposed and bloody bones of his left hand. The hand was numb at first, and then he felt a jolt that raced back and forth from his hand to his elbow. The stumps of his fingers were bleeding, but not as much as he would have expected them to bleed. He wrapped his handkerchief around his wounded hand, lifted the hinged Formica lid, and went behind the counter. He tried to open the six-foot wall safe, but the combination safe was closed and locked. He opened the cash drawer behind the counter. There were several bills in various denominations, as well as change in separate compartments. Freddy dropped his pistol back into his jacket pocket and scooped up the stack of tens and twenties. He turned over Wulgemuth's body with his good hand and took the coin dealer's wallet out of his hip pocket. Freddy stuffed the wallet and the bills into his inside jacket pocket and went to the front door.

He couldn't open it. He returned to the counter and stuck a paper clip into the door's buzzer release so he could get out. He shut the heavy door behind him as he left, and the door lock continued to buzz. Anyone could walk in now, and the first one to do so would discover the bodies. But he still had plenty of time. Freddy put his wounded hand into his trousers pocket and walked through the rain to the corner, fighting an urge to run.

There was a white Toyota half-ton truck in the yellow loading zone, but Susan and the white TransAm were gone.

Freddy made an abrupt about-face and started back toward Flagler. Perhaps it had been a mistake to tell Susie that he had broken Martin's finger. Anyone else might have questioned him about it; it was so unlikely to meet a brother and a sister in two different places on the same day in a strange town. But she had believed him because he had never lied to her before. He hadn't told her much of anything about himself, so there had been no need to lie. But her whining had pissed him off. Of course, she might have been forced to move by a meter maid. In that case she would be coming up Flagler by now and he could wave her down from the curb. In the pelting rain, he stared down the street at the crawling cars on Flagler. A battered Pontiac Le Mans stopped suddenly in the middle of the street.

Freddy and Hoke recognized each other at the same time. Hoke stuck his left arm through the open window and pointed his pistol at Freddy.

'Freeze! Police!' Hoke shouted.

There were three women with umbrellas on the sidewalk. Freddy stepped in among them, gave Hoke the finger, and ran. He knew that the cop wouldn't fire into the pedestrians. For a cop to use deadly force, his life had to be threatened. Freddy crossed the street against the red light, dodging the slowly moving cars, ignoring their horns, and trotted up Flagler toward Burdine's Department Store. He looked back once as he entered the store, but no one was following him. He walked briskly through the store, past the men's clothing section, and then took the back exit to First Street. There were more than a dozen people in a ragged half-formed line as the Hialeah Metro bus pulled up to the bus stop. Freddy pushed through the umbrellas to the head of the line, and as the door opened, entered the bus and flashed his badge in the driver's face.

'Police,' he said. 'I'm looking for a nigger with a radio.'

The bus driver jerked his thumb. 'There's three of 'em back there.'

The bus was crowded. Every seat was filled, and Freddy had to elbow his way through the standing passengers. There were three black men with radios in the long back seat, and they had spread out so no one else could sit down. But only one man, with a khaki knitted watch cap pulled low over his forehead, had his radio turned on. He was bobbing his head to a reggae beat. Freddy showed the man his badge and told him to turn off his radio. Sullenly, the man turned down the volume a fraction of an inch.

'I said, "Off!"'

The man apparently saw something in Freddy's eyes. The radio was clicked off, and several nearby passengers clapped their hands. After three blocks, Freddy pulled the cord, and the driver stopped at the corner. As Freddy pushed through the back doors, the radio started again.

Hoke got out of the car and watched Mendez dodge nimbly between the cars as he ran across the intersection and up the crowded sidewalk. Hoke lost sight of him when he slipped in front of two elderly women with shielding umbrellas. Hoke looked around for a uniformed policeman. There was usually a traffic officer on this corner, but there was no cop here today. He was probably inside somewhere, drinking coffee and staying out of the rain. The stalled traffic behind Hoke's car honked ominously. He couldn't leave the car in the middle of the intersection and run after his quarry. Hoke got back into his car, scanning the sidewalk as he picked up some speed, but he didn't have much hope. The man could have zipped into any one of thirty stores, including Woolworth's and Burdine's.

Susan, Hoke figured, was taking the I-95 Expressway back to Dania, which would get her home twice as fast as a trip back to Dania on South Dixie. Hoke would have to go back to Dania, question her, and then if she refused to tell him where Mendez was, could threaten to book her on a solicitation charge. He could threaten her, but he couldn't pick her up. Dania was in Broward County, and Hoke had no jurisdiction in Broward County.

At Sixth Street, Hoke turned right and found a parking space in front of a cigar store. He went inside, showed the man behind the counter his badge, and asked for the phone. The phone was on the wall behind the dealer's back, but the receiver was on a long cord. The dealer, a white-haired Latin with a hoarse voice, handed the receiver to Hoke.

'You tell me number. I dial. No one can come behind counter. I dial.'

Hoke gave the man his office number. Ellita Sanchez answered the phone.

'This is Sergeant Moseley, Sanchez. Is Bill Henderson around?'

'He was in earlier, but he's not here now. I think he went downstairs for coffee.'

'You don't happen to know any cops in Dania, do you?'

'No. I've never even been to Dania.'

'That's okay. I want you to get a message to Sergeant Henderson. Tell him that I need a cop from Broward County to meet me at two-four-six Poinciana, in Dania. You remember – the address of Susan Waggoner in Dania you got for me yesterday.'

'I've got a cousin on the force in Hollywood. I could call him, if you want.'

'He'll do, but I'd rather have a Dania cop. Talk to Henderson first. He'll know what to do. But if you can't find Henderson, call your cousin in Hollywood. Tell Henderson that I've got a good chance to pick up Mendez.'

'You can't arrest anybody in Broward County.'

'I know it, Sanchez. That's why I want a cop from Dania, and I don't know anyone there and it would all be too complicated to explain to anyone there over the phone. So just tell Henderson what I've told you. D'you understand?'

'I'll go down to the cafeteria right now and look for him.'

'Good girl.' Hoke handed the receiver back to the white-haired man. The man smiled and held up two fingers as he took the receiver. 'Last month at Dania I hit two trifectas.'

'Wonderful,' Hoke said. 'Thanks for the phone.'

There was a tiny cafeteria next to the cigar store. Hoke ordered a double espresso, drank it, and then bought two Jamaican hot meat patties to eat in the car on his way to Dania.

Chapter Twenty-Two

As the taillights of the Metrobus disappeared into the rain, Freddy walked through an A-1 Park-and-Lock lot and into an Eckerd's drugstore. He bought a roll of gauze and a roll of adhesive tape and left the store. He kept his injured hand in his trousers pocket, and flexed his thumb and forefinger. They responded in time with the shooting pains to his elbow. The hand was no longer numb, but the pain wasn't steady. It flashed and flickered off and on like a broken neon sign.

A bearded man in his early thirties wearing a dirty yellow T-shirt stood under a ragged awning in front of a boarded-up storefront. He was drinking from a bottle in a brown paper bag.

'Are you drunk?' Freddy asked him.

The man shook his head. 'Not yet.'

'I'll give you five bucks to do something for me.'

'Okay.'

'Bind up my hand.'

Freddy handed the bearded man the sack from Eckerd's, moved back into the recessed doorway, and took his wounded hand out of his pocket. He unwrapped the sticky handkerchief.

The derelict put down his bottle carefully by the wall and took the gauze and adhesive tape out of the sack. Freddy held out his hand and the man shook his head and clucked.

'Nasty,' he said.

He wrapped Freddy's hand tightly with the gauze, including the unimpaired forefinger, but left the thumb free. The man's fingers were shaky but functional.

'You can't do nothin' without your thumb,' he explained.

He used all the gauze and all the tape because he didn't have a knife to cut off the excess, but the wrapping was so tight it looked like a professional job.

'That'll do her till you get to a doctor.'

Freddy gave the man $10.

'This is a ten,' the man said.

Freddy shrugged. 'Five's for the bandage job, and the other five's for getting me a cab.'

'I'll be right back.' The man hesitated. 'Don't let anybody touch my bottle.' Limping slightly in his huaraches, the man hurried toward Flagler in the rain. The rain had a steady beat to it now, as though it would last forever.

Freddy picked up the bottle and took a long swig from it. Muscatel wine. Sweet and fruity, and devoid of subtlety. Freddy drank the rest of it anyway and put the bottle down by the wall again. The sweet wine didn't lessen the pain in his hand. He needed whiskey for that, but the Darvon he had back at the house in Dania would help more than whiskey. He regretted his hasty retreat from the coin exchange. He should have scooped up the stubs of his fingers he left behind. The cops would get his fingerprints from them. Shit. Murder One. The time had come to get the hell out of Miami. He would tell Susie to drive him to Okeechobee. She undoubtedly knew a doctor up there, and after he got his hand fixed up they could head north. They could hole up along the way in one of those Days Inns that dotted I-95 in every small Florida town. Then, when his hand had healed, he would decide what to do next. Maybe they could fly out to Vegas. There was a lot going on in Vegas.

A Veteran's Cab pulled up to the curb. The derelict got out, and Freddy handed him another $5. 'I finished off your bottle,' Freddy said. 'Buy yourself another.'

'That's all right. Thanks a lot. I didn't mean you, anyway. I meant if somebody else came along. Thanks!'

Freddy got into the cab. He began to sweat, and a wave of nausea swept over him as his stomach cramped. He leaned forward and vomited on the floor. It all came up, filling the cab with the aromas of chipped beef, milk gravy, and muscatel wine.

'That's gonna cost you, mister!' the driver said bitterly.

'Don't worry about it.' Freddy passed a twenty-dollar bill across the back of the seat, and the driver's fingers snatched it. 'Just drive north on Dixie until I tell you to stop.'

'Okay,' the driver said, 'but this twenty's for the cleanup, not for the fare on the meter.'

When they reached Dania, Freddy told the driver to stop at a closed Union service station on the highway. Freddy doubled the tab on the meter, but he got no thanks from the grim-faced driver. The cabbie made a U-turn and started back toward Miami without a word.

Freddy's house was twelve blocks from the gas station, a long walk in the rain, but now that he had a Murder One rap hanging over him he sure as hell didn't want the driver to know his address. Jesus, it had all happened so fast. He had gone by the place three or four times when he had cased out the coin dealer, but the man had always been alone in his shop. Who would have suspected that Wulgemuth had a dumb sonofabitch in the storeroom with a shotgun? Well, that was tough shit for Pedro, and tough shit for Wulgemuth – and tough shit for his fingers, too. Susan would be home now, unless she had misunderstood everything he had told her and had driven over to Watson Island and parked in the Japanese Garden parking lot. But she wasn't that dimwitted. Some traffic cop or meter maid had made her move, and she had either circled the block while he was still in the coin shop, or made a second tour of the block and perhaps a third. She might still be downtown, circling the block again and again, but she would give up eventually and drive home to Dania.

Wet all the way through his jacket and shirt, Freddy slogged through the rain with soggy trousers and wet feet. When he got home he would take a Darvon and drink some chocolate milk to settle his stomach. It might be a good idea to get Edna Damrosch to take a look at his injured hand. No, that would mean explanations, and this time she would call a doctor. He would just take some Darvon, some penicillin tablets, and wait till they got to Okeechobee. The pain wasn't all that bad. He could stand a little pain, but those missing fingers would certainly make him a marked man – and for life, too.

The TransAm wasn't parked in the driveway. The stupid little bitch. She was still downtown, circling the block and looking for him. He should have given her a time limit. He needed her right now, and she wasn't home.

He let himself into the house, surprised to see that the lights were still on in the kitchen. He thought he had turned them off when they left. He went into the bathroom, swallowed two Darvons, and sipped some water from the cup on the sink. The door to the closet was standing open. Susan's two suitcases were missing. Her black dress wasn't on the hanger in the closet. He ran into the kitchen, took down the Ritz Cracker box from the back shelf where the provisions were kept, and ripped open the top.

The money was gone. All of it, including the 10,000 Mexican pesos they hadn't been able to exchange. Freddy laughed. So Susan had skipped out on him, taken some of her clothes, the money, and gone home. He had known she was nervous – she told him so – but he hadn't taken into account how truly scared she must have been. Maybe she thought he was going to shoot the coin dealer. Well, as it turned out, she was right.

She must have bolted as soon as he had rounded the corner to Flagler. It was understandable, but unexpected. Now he would have to find his own way up to Okeechobee, track her down, get his money back, and find a way to dispose of her body. He couldn't let her live, not now, not after finding out what he had already known from the beginning – that he couldn't trust Susan; that, in the final analysis, a man couldn't trust anyone. But especially not a whore.

Freddy took Wulgemuth's wallet and the wad of bills from the till out of his jacket pocket. With his good hand, he counted out five twenties and eight tens on the kitchen table. He had another six or seven hundred in his own wallet. Even though he had left the coin case in the shop, he was still ahead in the operation. He wasn't broke, and he still had a shitload of credit cards –

Hoke Moseley stepped through the door to the kitchen from the screened back porch. He pointed his .38 at Freddy.

Freddy turned and stared at Moseley for a long moment, taking in the gray haggard face, the steady pistol, the wet, ill-fitting leisure jacket.

'Raise your hands,' Hoke said, 'level with your shoulders.'

'What'll you do if I don't, old man, shoot me? And what are you doing in my house? Where's your warrant?'

'I said to raise your hands.'

Freddy grinned and raised his hands slowly.

'Where's Susan?' Hoke said.

'You tell me, man.' Freddy lifted his chin. 'I had all my money in that Ritz Cracker box, and she cleaned me out and took off.'

'Why'd she take off that way, after she dropped you off downtown on Miami Avenue?'

'Look, my hand hurts, and I've got to get to a doctor. Can I drop my left hand? It hurts like a sonofabitch. You got some crazy people in this town, d'you know that? I go into Wulgemuth's to sell some coins, and the crazy bastard and his bodyguard try to kill me with a damned sugarcane knife. Is that why you're here? I was coming down to tell you about it as soon as I saw a doctor.'

Hoke was genuinely puzzled. 'What happened in Wulgemuth's?'

'I just told you.' Freddy rested his bandaged hand on his chest. 'I took some silver dollars down to Wulgemuth's Coin Exchange to get them appraised. If the price was right, I was going to sell 'em. Then him and his bodyguard, a crazy Cuban with a shotgun, tried to rob me. Old man Wulgemuth tried to hack off my hand with a damned machete, and he got most of it, too. I'm hurting, man, and you've got to get me to a doctor!'

'Then what happened?'

'When?'

'After this respectable businessman's unprovoked attack.'

'I took a cab home, because Susie wasn't waiting for me any longer, that's all.'

'Before that, before you left the store?'

'I got lucky. Before these two crazy people could kill me, I was able to get the gun out of Wulgemuth's drawer and defend myself with it.'

'And you shot them?'

'I have no idea. I just started shooting, and when they ducked for cover I ran out. I don't think I hit either one of them. I was just concerned with getting out and finding a doctor, that's all.'

Freddy moved his feet, inching toward Moseley. Hoke stepped back and extended his arm.

'Back up! Turn around slowly, lean against the wall, and spread your legs.'

Freddy shook his head. 'I can't do it. I'd pass out. Most of my fingers are gone, and I'm liable to go into shock any minute ...' Freddy's voice dropped to a theatrical whisper. 'Things are going black, all purple and black ...' His knees buckled, and as he dropped to the floor, he managed to break his fall with his right hand. He fell over on his left side, groaned piteously, and fished in his jacket pocket for his pistol. As the .38 cleared the pocket, Hoke shot him in the stomach. Freddy screamed and rolled over, trying to get to his feet and get the pistol out of his pocket at the same time. Hoke shot him in the spine, and Freddy stopped moving. Hoke bent down and fired another round into the back of Freddy's head.

Hoke slumped into a kitchen chair and put his pistol on the table. When Bill Henderson, Ellita Sanchez, and Sanchez's uniformed cop cousin from Hollywood came through the unlocked front door, Hoke was still sitting in the kitchen chair, smoking his third cigarette.

Chapter Twenty-Three

'You okay, Hoke?' Henderson asked.

'I'm not hurt, if that's what you mean.' Hoke dropped the cigarette on the floor and stepped on it as he got to his feet.

'Stay there,' Henderson said. 'Sit down.' Henderson told the uniformed officer to go out to the front porch, and to prevent anyone else from coming into the house. 'You don't have to stay out in the rain, Mendez. Just turn on the porch light, and stand inside the front door.'

'Mendez?' Hoke said, starting to get up again.

The officer left the kitchen. 'Yeah,' Henderson said, 'Mendez is Sanchez's cousin, a traffic officer from Hollywood. Why in the hell didn't you wait for us, for Christ's sake?'

Sanchez was on her knees beside Freddy's body. She took a Swiss army knife out of her handbag, opened the small scissors, and started to cut away the bandage on Freddy's left hand. Hoke watched her with keen interest.

'I was afraid he'd get away, Bill. It looked as if he was preparing to leave, and I didn't think I'd have any trouble. I didn't intend to shoot him, but when he went for his gun ... well ...'

'Did you know he killed Wulgemuth and his bodyguard at the coin exchange store?'

'He said he shot his pistol, but denied hitting anyone. According to him, he was attacked by the two men and he shot back in order to get away.'

'Bullshit. It was on the radio. Didn't you have the radio on when you drove after him to Dania?'

'I haven't got a radio. Remember? Somebody stole it when I was in the hospital.'

'But you did see him coming out of Wulgemuth's Coin Exchange, right?'

'With a gun in his hand,' Sanchez said, looking up with a smile. She raised Freddy's unbandaged left hand. 'See? Three fingers missing. When the ME matches them up, Sergeant Moseley'll be credited with a quick solution to a double murder.'

Hoke shook his head. 'I didn't see him come out of any coin exchange. I was tailing him, hoping to get some probable cause to shake him down. As an ex-felon, if he had a pistol on him, I was going to pick him up. I lost him, and then picked him up again on the corner of Flagler and Miami Avenue.'

'Listen carefully, Hoke.' Bill took a chair from the table and sat in front of Hoke, looking directly into his eyes. 'You're in some jurisdictional trouble if you don't get your story straight. And here's the way you tell it, and this is the way we'll write it up. You were tailing him, yes, and you lost him for a while, right? Then you saw him coming out of Wulgemuth's store and putting a gun into his pocket as he came out. Suspecting him of a robbery, you called Sanchez for backup from Broward County, and then drove here to his house after losing him downtown when he ran away. Isn't that what happened?'

'Something like that.'

'No, exactly like that.'

'All right. Exactly like that.'

'After you called Sanchez and she got a hold of me, we found out about the killing of the two men. Sanchez called her cousin, and he came here in his own car. We knew you were in danger, so we didn't have time to contact the Broward County sheriff's office, you see. You knew he had a gun because you saw it when he came out of the store. As an off-duty police officer, you went after him and contacted higher authority, through Sanchez.'

'I also suspected him of a California assault, and I had reasonable cause to pick him up on that.'

'Okay. That's your story. Don't change it. I'll call Captain Brownley and Doc Evans. Brownley'll call the Broward sheriff, and I imagine Doc Evans will contact the Broward County ME. The report's going to be a jurisdictional mess.'

'What about the girl?' Sanchez said, joining them at the table. 'What's her name?'

179

'Susan Waggoner,' Henderson said. 'We'll put out an APB on her. In this rain, she can't get too far away. I'll get out the all-points as soon as I call Brownley.'

'D'you want me to call?' Sanchez said.

'No, I'll call. Why don't you make some coffee? This is going to be a helluva long evening.'

'I'll make the coffee,' Hoke said, getting up.

Sanchez went to the sink, and turned on the tap. 'Find the pot,' she said. 'We'll make it together.'

Captain Brownley and the Broward County sheriff both made some compromises, and so did the Broward County medical examiner. It was more important to clear up the murders of the coin exchange proprietor and his bodyguard than it was to hold hearings in Broward County. A young lieutenant from the Dania Police Department, who was temporarily in charge while the Dania chief of police was hunting wolves in Canada, was awed by all of the brass from Dade and Broward counties and was willing to do almost anything to get Freddy's body out of town as quickly as possible. In a small town like Dania, shootings of any kind were bad for business.

Susan Waggoner was picked up by a Florida state trooper in Belle Glade. Her TransAm was impounded there, and she was brought to the Miami police station by the trooper. The trooper who picked her up also gave her a ticket for having tinted windows in the TransAm that were twice as dark as the law allowed.

Hoke, Henderson, and Sanchez were still working on their joint report when Susan was brought in. They took her down to an interrogation room, and Henderson read her her rights.

'D'you understand,' Hoke said, 'that you can have a lawyer present? You don't have to tell us anything if you don't want to, but we need to clear up a few things.'

'I don't know what this is all about,' Susan said. 'When we had the windows tinted on the car, the man said it was legal. You see a lot of people driving around Miami with tinted windows, and a lot of them are darker than mine.'

'Never mind the tinted windows,' Hoke said. 'I followed you in my car from Dania to downtown Miami, and I was across the street when you parked in the yellow loading zone on Miami Avenue. I saw your boyfriend get out of the car –'

'Junior?'

'Junior. And then you took off almost immediately. Did you know he was going to rob the coin store?'

'No. Why would he rob the store? He had some silver dollars to sell. That's what he told me, and he wanted me to go with him. I didn't want to go because of the rain, and when I said I'd stay in the car and wait for him he got mad at me. That's when he told me that he was the one who broke my brother's finger out at the airport. Remember that?'

'He told you that?'

'That's right. And I'll sign a statement to that, too. We'd had some arguments before, and he even hit me once, but I stayed with him because of his other good qualities. But when I found out that he was the one responsible for Martin's death, I got scared. I realized that I was in danger from him, and I got scared. Once he told me that, you see, he'd always know that I had something on him, and he could kill me, too. So I just took off, came home to Dania, got my money, and left. I was on my way back to Okeechobee when the state trooper pulled me over in Belle Glade.'

'What were Junior's good qualities?' Sanchez asked.

Susan frowned. She poked out her lips. 'Well, he was a good provider, and he liked everything I cooked for him. There were lots of good things about Junior I liked. But I'm not going to live with him anymore.'

'Junior's dead, Susan,' Henderson said. 'Didn't you know he had a gun?'

'Yes, but I didn't know he was going to rob anybody. He carried a gun for protection. He almost got killed a few weeks ago by a gunman in a Seven-Eleven store. So he needed the gun for protection, he told me. Junior's dead?'

'That's right,' Henderson said. 'He was killed.'

'I guess his gun didn't do him much good, then, did it? I'm sorry to hear that. I never wished him any harm. I wasn't going to tell on him, either, about Martin, I mean, but I don't want to get in no trouble on account of Junior. I didn't do anything. I just want to go back to Okeechobee. All I've had is trouble of some kind or other ever since I came down here for my abortion. What I'd say, if you asked me about Miami, I'd say it's not a good place for a single girl to be.'

'Jesus Christ,' Hoke said, 'let's get out of here a minute, Bill.'

Hoke and Henderson went out into the hallway.

'I'm afraid, Bill,' Hoke said, 'that I'd have to confirm her story. She did drop him off, and then leave immediately, and I followed her until she got on the ramp to I-Ninety-five. You can't charge her for dropping her common-law husband off downtown. If she claims she didn't know he was going to rob the store, we can't hold her as an accessory.'

'Is she really that dumb, or is it an act of some kind?'

'It's consistent, whatever it is. Why don't we just take her statement and put her on a bus for Belle Glade so she can get her damned car.'

'You mean just let her go?'

'I don't see what else we can do. Her statement will clear up the death of Martin Waggoner, and we can always find her if we need her later. Okeechobee's a small town. We'll tell her not to leave Okeechobee or come back to Miami again, and that's it.'

'That's just hearsay. We still can't prove that Junior killed Martin, or broke his finger.'

'We'll send his picture up to those two Georgia boys. Maybe they can identify him from the picture. At any rate, I'll call the assistant state attorney, and tell her about Susan's statement. She can decide whether to close the case or not. It's not up to us, anyway.'

Henderson and Sanchez stayed in the interrogation room to obtain a statement from Susan Waggoner, and Hoke went back to his office. He found Violet Mygren's phone number, and called the office.

'Thank you,' a female voice answered, and then, for five minutes, Hoke listened to muzak as he held the phone to his ear.

'Thank you for waiting,' a man's voice said. 'How may I help you?'

'Is this the state attorney's office?'

'Yes, it is. How may I help you?'

'This is Sergeant Moseley, Homicide. I want to talk to Miss Violet Nygren, one of your assistant state attorneys. This is the number she gave me.'

'I don't think we've got anybody here by that name.'

'Yes, you have. She was assigned to that case at the airport. A guy got his finger broke and died from shock. Martin Waggoner.'

'I don't know her. What's her name again?'

'Nygren. N-Y-G-R-E-N. She was young and had just joined the office. A UM Law School graduate.'

'Okay. Let me take a look at the roster. Can you hold the line a minute?'

'Yeah.'

'I'm sorry,' the man said, when he came back on the line, 'but we don't have any Nygrens on the roster. If you want me to, I'll check with a few people here and then call you back. I don't know half the people here myself. We've got one hundred and seventy-one assistant state attorneys, you know.'

'That many? I thought you only had about a hundred.'

'We got some more money last year. But they come and go, you know. Want me to check and call you back?'

'No. I'll hold the line while you check. I like listening to the muzak.'

'That's on the other line. I can't get you any muzak on this phone.'

'Never mind. Just find out what happened to Violet Nygren.'

Hoke lit a cigarette. He raised his shoulder to hold the phone against his head and examined his hands. They were shaking slightly, as the reaction finally settled in, but as long as he kept busy he wouldn't have to think about it. As he butted the cigarette in the desk ashtray, a woman's voice came on the line.

'Hello? Are you there?'

'I'm here,' Hoke said. 'Who are you?'

'Tim asked me to tell you about Violet. You are Sergeant Moseley, aren't you?'

'Yes.'

'Well, Violet Nygren resigned a few weeks back. She got married, but I don't know her married name. But I know she married a chiropractor out in Kendall, and I can get her married name for you tomorrow, if you like. I didn't know Violet very well, but I know she wasn't happy here as a state attorney. I don't think she'd've been with us much longer even if she hadn't got married and quit – if you know what I mean.'

'I think I do. But it's not important. Somebody must've taken over her caseload, so I'll just send a memo over to your office, and you people can take it from there.'

'I'm sorry I couldn't be more helpful.'

'You've helped a lot. Thanks.'

When Henderson and Sanchez went into Captain Brownley's office to go over the written report, Hoke was excluded from the meeting and told that his turn would be next.

Hoke could see the three of them through the smudged glass walls of Brownley's office, and he felt a little apprehensive at being left out. Brownley was a good reader, and if he spotted any discrepancies, Hoke knew that he could be in some deep trouble. Hoke went into the men's room to take a leak and two younger Homicide detectives congratulated him warmly, so warmly that he decided not to go down to the cafeteria for coffee and a sweet roll. As far as his fellow police officers were concerned, the department had won one for a change. The robbery-murder on Flagler and the killing of the suspect would only rate a three- or four-inch story in the local sections of the Miami newspapers, but it was big news within the department.

Hoke returned to his little office and waited, trying to sort out his feelings, and came to the conclusion that Freddy Frenger, Jr, AKA Ramon Mendez, had played out the game to the end and didn't really mind losing his life in a last-ditch attempt to win. Junior would have been good at checkers or chess, thought Hoke, where sometimes a poor player can beat a much better one if he is aggressive and stays boldly on the attack. That was Junior, all right, and if you turned your head away from the board for an instant, to light a cigarette or to take a sip of coffee, he would steal one of your pieces. Junior didn't have to play by the rules, but Hoke did. Nevertheless, Hoke decided to keep this checkers analogy to himself. No matter how he rationalized his actions, Hoke suspected that the real reason he had killed Freddy Frenger was that the man had invaded his room at the Eldorado Hotel and beat the shit out of him. And if he could do it once, he could do it a second time. On the other hand, to think that way was just another oversimplification. After all, Frenger had tried to pull his gun, so Hoke had shot in self-defense: the extra round he had put into the back of the man's head was merely insurance. But any way Hoke looked at it, the quality of life in Miami would be improved immeasurably now that Freddy Frenger was no longer out on the streets …

Henderson opened the door. Ellita Sanchez, smiling, was with him.

'Your turn, Hoke,' Henderson said.

'We'll wait for you down in the cafeteria,' Sanchez said.

Hoke shook his head. 'Not in the cafeteria. I don't want a bunch of people coming around.' Hoke looked at his wristwatch. 'Christ, it's after four A.M. Why don't you guys go home? You don't have to wait for me.'

'We'll wait for you in the parking lot,' Henderson said. 'Then we'll go get a beer.'

Henderson and Sanchez left before Hoke could say anything else.

Captain Brownley was on the phone. As Hoke hesitated outside the office, Brownley held up his left hand, signaling Hoke to wait. Hoke lit a cigarette, and tried not to look through the glass door at Brownley. At last, Brownley hung up the phone, stood, and beckoned for Hoke to come in.

'Sit down, Hoke. I see you started smoking again.' Brownley sat down, and put his elbows on the desk. Hoke pulled the ashtray toward him as he sat down, and stubbed out his cigarette.

'I never really quit, captain. I just abstained for a while, that's all.'

'How d'you feel?'

'Still a little shaky, but I'll be all right.'

'I know you will. But for an experienced police officer, that was just about the dumbest trick you ever pulled. Not only should you have waited for backup, but going after a man like Frenger called for a SWAT team.'

'I was afraid he was going to get away –'

'That's no excuse. You knew he was armed, even if you didn't know he'd killed Wulgemuth and his bodyguard.'

185

'Maybe I should've waited a little longer, but –'

'Shut up! How in the hell can I chew your ass if you keep interrupting me?' Brownley frowned, took a cigar out of the humidor on his desk, and began to unwrap it.

Brownley's face was creased with thousands of tiny wrinkles. His face reminded Hoke of a piece of black silk that has been wadded into a tiny ball and then smoothed out again. But the captain's cheeks were grayish with fatigue, and there were a few gray hairs in his mustache as well – gray hairs Hoke hadn't noticed before. How old was Brownley, anyway? Forty-five, forty-six? Certainly no more than forty-seven, but he looked much, much older.

Brownley, turning his cigar as he lighted it with a kitchen match, looked at Hoke with unreadable eyes. The whites of his eyes were slightly yellow, and Hoke had never noticed that before either.

'I just got through talking to the chief,' Brownley said, 'and we made a compromise. I'm going to write you a letter of reprimand, and it'll go into your permanent file.'

Hoke cleared his throat. 'I deserve it.'

'Damned right! The chief, on the other hand, is going to write you a letter of commendation. You might be puzzled by the ambiguity of his letter, but it'll be a commendation. That will also go into your permanent file. So one letter will, in a sense, cancel out the other.'

'I don't deserve a letter of commendation.'

'I know you don't, but this case'll give the chief something positive to talk about at the University Club next week, and besides, it'll help you out at the hearing. And in a way, maybe you do deserve a commendation from the chief. That was good police work, getting Sanchez to call Ramon Mendez –'

'Who?'

'Ramon Mendez. Sanchez's cop cousin in Hollywood.'

'I forgot for a minute. Mendez was one of Frenger's names –'

'I know. But the fact that we had at least one Broward County officer at the scene helped to get us off the hook when we entered Broward's jurisdiction. Because of the seriousness of the crime, we probably would've been okay anyway, but having a Broward officer present helped save a little face. This is politics, Hoke, not police work. I'm sending Officer Mendez a commendation, as well as one for Henderson and Sanchez. And your letter of reprimand will be fairly mild, because the chief just confirmed my majority.' Brownley puffed on his cigar. 'As of the first of the month, you can call me Major Brownley.'

'Congratulations, Willie.' Hoke grinned.

'Major Willie.' Brownley took a cigar out of the humidor and offered it to Hoke, but Hoke waved it away.

'I'll stick to cigarettes, major. What happens to me now?'

'As you know, there's no standard operating procedure. Usually, when a cop shoots a suspect, we just send him home to wait for the hearing or we give him a desk job while he waits. If the shooting's accidental or if it looks like a grand jury matter, the officer's usually suspended, with or without pay. In your case, as long as you're on sick leave anyway, you just go home and wait for the hearing.'

'There's a few things to clear up first. I want to call San Francisco, and –'

'You'll go home and stay there. Don't come into the station until the hearing. You can call Sanchez, and let her clear up any loose ends. Don't talk to the press or to anyone else about the case. You're not going to have any problems at the hearing. Deadly force was justified, and you'll be cleared.'

'All right. I'll call Sanchez. She can handle things all right.'

'She likes you, too. Of course, when I told you to win her over, I didn't mean for you to prove what a good shot you were, but at least she's not complaining about her supervisor.'

'It won't be the same as working with Bill Henderson, but then, Bill can't type eighty-five words a minute, and she can. So I guess it'll even out.'

'Get the hell out of here, Hoke. I've still got some calls to make.'

Hoke got to his feet. 'I'd like to go up to Riviera Beach to spend a few days with my father.'

'Okay. Just call in every day. As long's we can reach you by phone.'

They shook hands, and Hoke left the office.

When Hoke got to the station parking lot, Henderson and Sanchez were waiting for him. The morning air was moist and hot, and Hoke could feel his pores opening. The humid air felt good after the stale air conditioning of the station, and Hoke didn't really mind the little rivulets of perspiration that rolled down his sides.

Ellita Sanchez had removed her blue faille suit jacket, and her upper lip was beaded lightly with sweat. Henderson's heavy shoulders, slumped with fatigue, and his eyes were bloodshot. Hoke knew that neither one of them wanted a beer as much as they wanted a bed, but he also suspected that they were as reluctant as he was to break up a process they had shared, a certain sense of teamwork.

'How'd you make out, Hoke?' Henderson said.

'I'm still on sick leave, but I'm supposed to stay away from the station until the hearing. Brownley said I could go up to Riviera Beach, though, and stay with my father if I wanted to, and I think I will.'

'You haven't been up to Riviera for a while, have you?'

''Bout a year ago, when the old man got married again – remember?'

'Let's go to the Seven-Eleven,' Sanchez suggested. 'You guys can get a beer, and I'll get a grape Slurpee. My throat's dry, but it doesn't feel like a beer for breakfast.'

'Suits me,' Henderson said. 'We can take my car.'

'Let's walk,' Hoke said. 'It's only a block. We can stretch our legs.'

They walked to the 7-Eleven, down the narrow Overtown sidewalk, Hoke beside Sanchez, with Henderson lumbering a few feet ahead of them.

'You ever been to Riviera Beach, Ellita?'

'Never. I've been to Palm Beach, but not to Riviera.'

'Palm Beach is right across the inlet from Singer Island, and Singer's a part of the Riviera Beach municipality, with the best beach in Florida. So, if you went as far as the northern end of Palm Beach, you were looking across at Singer. I grew up in Riviera Beach, but I didn't know it was actually called Riviera until I was almost twenty years old. We always called it Rivera. *Rivera* – that's what everybody called it. Funny, isn't it?'

'I've noticed that a lot of Miamians call Miami Mi-amah. I guess it's what you grow up with.'

'In Riviera, that's how we can tell the natives from the tourists. Most of us still say Rivera.'

When they got to the 7-Eleven, Sanchez asked the manager to fix her a grape Slurpee. Hoke and Henderson went to the freezer. Henderson got a Bud, and Hoke reached deep into the box to get a cold Coors. Each paid for his own drink, and then they went outside to drink them. A few blocks away, in the nascent morning light, they could see the vultures circling above the county courthouse tower, preparing to fly to the city dump for their breakfast feeding.

'That yellow Nova,' Sanchez said, pointing to the dusty car parked by the Dempsey Dumpster, 'has been there for three days. I remember seeing it.'

'Probably the manager's car,' Henderson said. 'There's no one else around here.'

Sanchez walked down to the car. 'It's got Michigan plates.'

Henderson cracked open the glass door to the store. The manager had *The Star* open on the counter and was reading it. He looked up. 'You from Michigan?' Henderson said.

'What?'

'Are you from Michigan?'

'Michigan?' The manager shook his head. 'Ponce. In Puerto Rico.'

'That your car? The yellow Nova?'

The Puerto Rican shook his head. 'My wife's got my car. She drives me to work, and picks me up. That car's been parked there for three days.'

'You guys better come down here a minute!' Sanchez raised her voice. She threw her waxed cup, still half full, into the dumpster. Hoke and Henderson joined her at the back of the Nova. 'D'you smell anything funny?'

Henderson bent over and sniffed at the trunk. He smiled broadly at Hoke. 'Take a sniff, Hoke. Be my guest.'

Hoke took a deep sniff at the trunk lid, where it joined the body. The odor was unmistakable; it was the familiar odor of urine, feces, death. Hoke raised his head, returning Henderson's knowing metal-studded smile with a wry grin.

'You two stay here,' Hoke said, 'I'll walk back to the station and send down a squad car –'

'No you won't,' Henderson said. 'Go home, Hoke! Just get in your car and go home. We'll take care of the body. You're on sick leave and off duty. Remember?'

'He's right, Hoke,' Sanchez said. 'It'll be at least another hour before we can run a make and get a warrant to open the trunk. Go on home. Please.'

'But I'd like to see –'

'Beat it!' Henderson said, pushing Hoke's shoulder.

'All right. But call me tomorrow, Sanchez. There're a few things –'

'I'll call you,' Sanchez said. 'But right now you'd better get going.'

'You call me, too, Bill.'

'I will, I will. Good-*bye*, Hoke.'

Hoke returned to the police station parking lot and got into his car. As he drove out of the lot he could see Ellita Sanchez leaning back against the trunk of the yellow Nova. Henderson was probably still in the store, using the manager's phone.

Hoke drove down to Biscayne Boulevard and turned north, hugging the right lane so he could make the cut-off at the MacArthur Causeway for Miami Beach. Feeling slightly guilty about leaving Henderson and Sanchez stuck at the 7-Eleven, he pulled down the visor against the morning sun rising above South Beach and headed for the Eldorado Hotel, where Old Man Zuckerman was waiting for him in the lobby with a fresh, neatly folded paper napkin.

The following news item was published in *The Okeechobee Bi-Weekly News:*

VINEGAR PIE WINS

OCALA – Mrs Frank Mansfield, formerly Ms Susan Waggoner, of Okeechobee, won the Tri-County Bake-Off in Ocala yesterday with her vinegar pie entry. The recipe for her winning entry is as follows:

Pastry for a nine-inch crust
1 cup seedless raisins, all chopped up
¼ cup soft butter
2 cups sugar (granulated)
½ teaspoon cinnamon
¼ teaspoon cloves
½ teaspoon allspice
4 eggs, large, separated
3 tablespoons 5 percent vinegar
1 pinch of salt

Cream the butter well with sugar. Add spices and blend well. Beat in yolks with a beater till smooth and creamy. Stir in chopped raisins with a wooden spoon. Beat egg whites with a dash of salt until they are soft, then slide onto sugar mixture. Cut and fold lightly but well. Turn into pastry-lined pan. Bake fifteen minutes in preheated 425°F oven. Reduce heat to 300°F and bake for twenty minutes longer, or until top is beautifully browned and center of filling is jellylike. Cool on a rack for two or three hours before cutting.

When Mrs Mansfield was handed the prize by the judges (a $50 US Savings Bond), she said, 'I never met a man yet that didn't like my pie.'

BOOK 2

New Hope for the Dead

*'Man's unhappiness stems from his
inability to sit quietly in his room'*

PASCAL

To Betsy and the boys

Chapter One

'CRAP,' Sergeant Hoke Moseley told his partner, 'is the acronym for finding your way around Miami.' He glanced at Ellita Sanchez as he shifted down to second gear, and waited for her to nod.

She should know that much already, having been a police dispatcher for seven years, so there was no need to explain that C stood for courts, R for roads, A for avenues, and P for places. It didn't always hold true that courts, roads, avenues, and places all ran north and south. Sometimes they looped in semicircles and wild arabesques, especially the roads.

Hoke's major problem with Ellita was making conversation. He never knew exactly what to tell her or what to take for granted, even though he was the sergeant and she was the new partner. She seemed to know almost everything he told her already, and she had only been in the Homicide Division for four months. Some of the things Hoke knew from experience and had tried to explain to her – like the fact that junkies sometimes rubbed Preparation H on their track marks to reduce the swelling – she knew already. CRAP was one of those oddities that very few cops knew about, and he really hadn't expected her to say, 'I know.'

Perhaps, he thought, her two-year A.S. degree in police science at Miami-Dade Community College was actually worth the time and money she had invested in it. At any rate, she was getting more sensitive to his moods. She just nodded now, instead of saying 'I know,' and this had begun to irritate him visibly. And something else was bothering Sanchez. Her pretty golden face was more somber lately, and she no longer smiled as broadly in the mornings as she had at first. Her quiescent moodiness had been going on for more than a week now. At first, Hoke had attributed it to her period – if that's what it was – but a week was a long time. How long did a period last? Well, whatever it was that was bothering her, it hadn't affected her work. Yet.

One thing Hoke knew for sure: He hadn't done anything to offend her. If anything, he had bent over backward to make her an *equal* partner – subject to his directions, of course. He almost always explained why he was doing something. But Sanchez was, first of all, a woman, and she was also a Latin, so perhaps there were some sexual and cultural differences here and he would never really know what was on her mind.

Sometimes, though, when he wanted to make a humorous comment, the way he had with his old partner, Bill Henderson, and then took a look at her, with those huge tits looking voluptuous and maternal in the loose silk blouses she always wore, he held his tongue. Having a female partner in the car instead of Bill wasn't the same. Maybe he should let Sanchez drive the car once in a while. But that didn't seem right either. The man always drove, not the woman, although when he and Bill had been together, Bill had driven most of the time because he was a better driver than Hoke, and they both knew it. For all Hoke knew, Ellita Sanchez was a better driver than either Bill or himself.

Tomorrow, then, maybe he'd let her drive – see how it worked out …

'The next street,' Sanchez said, pointing to the green-and-white sign, 'is Poinciana Court.'

'Yeah.' Hoke laughed. 'And it's running east and west.'

They were looking for an address in Green Lakes, a Miami subdivision built during the housing boom of the mid-1950s when the developer was looking for young families with small children, for Korean war veterans with $500 saved for a down payment and jobs that paid them enough to afford a $68-a-month house payment. These had all been $10,000 houses then, with thirty-year fixed mortgages at 5½ percent interest. That wasn't expensive, even then, for a three-bedroom, one-bathroom house. Today, however, these same houses in Green Lakes, now thirty years old, were selling for $86,000 and more, and at 14 percent interest rates. Many similar housing areas in Miami, depending upon their locations, were slums now – but not Green Lakes. The wide curving streets and avenues, named as well as numbered, were lined with tall ficus trees and Australian pines. There were 'sleeping policemen,' painted yellow, every hundred yards or so, road bumps that didn't let a driver get into high gear. Many owners, as they prospered, had added bathrooms, 'Florida rooms' – glass-enclosed porches – garages, and carports, and most of the homes, if not all, had their backs and new Florida rooms facing man-made square lakes, with water the color of green milk. The lakes were originally rock and sand quarries, and much too dangerous for swimming (at least a dozen people had drowned before the Green Lakes Homeowners' Association had banned swimming altogether), but the lakes had Dade County pines and jogging paths around their borders, and in the evenings there would usually be a cooling breeze sweeping across the water.

As neighborhoods go, Green Lakes was a nice place to live.

The subdivision was close enough to Hialeah for most shopping purposes, but far enough away to avoid the Latin influx, and still much too expensive for a lot of black families. These conditions would all change with time, of course, but when they did the houses would probably appreciate to $100,000, and variable interest rates would be sitting in the low twenties. The residents who lived in Green Lakes now were lucky, and they knew it. The crime rate was low because of an effective Crime Watch program; there hadn't been a homicide in this subdivision for more than two years.

Hoke spotted the blue and white squad car parked in front of the house. The hatless harness officer was leaning against a ficus tree at the curb, smoking a cigarette and talking to two teenage girls. The girls, wearing tank tops, jeans and running shoes, kept their ten-speed bikes between themselves and the cop. As Hoke pulled to a stop behind the police car, the radio in the blue-and-white crackled. Aggressive birds sang back from the trees, and sprinklers whirred on a nearby lawn. A few houses down, a dog barked from behind closed doors.

As Hoke and Sanchez got out of the car, the officer, a Latin with square-cut sideburns down to and even with his dark eyes, moved away from the tree and told the two girls to get moving. They rode away for about a hundred yards, stopped and looked back.

'Sergeant Moseley,' Hoke said. 'Homicide.' He glanced at the officer's nameplate. 'Where's your hat, Garcia?'

'In the car.'

'Put it on. You're under arms, you're supposed to be covered.'

Garcia got his hat from the car and put it on. The hat looked two sizes too small resting on his abundance of black curly hair. He looked ridiculous in the small cap with its scuffed visor, and Hoke could see why the man didn't want to wear it. On the other hand, he could also get a decent haircut.

'Where's the decedent?' Hoke asked.

'In the house. Officer Hannigan's inside.'

Sanchez started toward the house. Hoke indicated the two girls who were inching back, pushing their bikes. 'Don't let a crowd gather. Before long, gapers'll show up, so keep 'em across the street.'

Officer Hannigan, a rangy blonde in her early twenties with purple eye makeup and coral lipstick, opened the door before Hoke and Sanchez reached the front porch. She had licked or gnawed most of the lipstick from her long lower lip.

'Don't you have a hat either?' Hoke said.

'It's in the car.' She flushed. 'Besides, Sergeant Roberts said it was optional whether we wore hats or not.'

'No,' Hoke said, 'it's not an option. Any time you're wearing a sidearm, you'll keep your head covered. If you want me to, I'll explain the reasons why to Sergeant Roberts.'

'I'd rather you didn't.'

'Where's the decedent?'

'Down the hall, in the small bedroom across from the master bedroom. We didn't go into the room, but I looked at it – the boy, I mean – from the door. He's an OD all right, and was DOA as reported.'

'That's very helpful, Hannigan. Let's go into the dining area, and we'll see what else you can tell us.'

The living room, except for two squashy, lemon-colored beanbag seats, was furnished with antique-white rattan furniture, with yellow Haitian cotton cushions on the couch, the armchair, and the ottoman. There were vases of freshly cut daisies on three low, white Formica-topped tables. The beige burlap draperies were closed, and three circular throw rugs, the same color as the draperies, were spaced precisely on the waxed terrazzo floor. The dining area, which held a round Eames pedestal table and four matching chairs, was curtainless. The open vertical Levolors filled the room with bright morning sunlight. A blue bowl in the center of the table held a half-dozen Key limes.

'All right,' Hoke said, as he sat at the table, 'report.'

'Report?'

'Report.' Hoke took a limp package of his specially cut-short Kools out of his jacket pocket, looked at it for a moment and then put it back. Sanchez, unsmiling, stared at the young woman but did not sit down. Hannigan clutched her handbag with both hands and cleared her throat.

'Well, we received the call on the DOA at oh-seven-thirty. I was driving, and we started right over. There was a mix-up, I guess, and at Flagler we got another call to abort. But just a few minutes later, before I could find a turnaround, we were told to continue.'

'Do you know why?'

'No. They didn't say.'

'There was a boundary dispute, that's why. A block away, on Ficus Avenue, the Hialeah boundary begins. So at first they thought the DOA should go to Hialeah instead of Miami. But after they rechecked the map, Miami won the body. We would have preferred, naturally, to give it to Hialeah.' Hoke took out his notebook and ballpoint. 'Who discovered the decedent?'

'The boy's mother, Mrs Hickey. That's Loretta B. Hickey. She's divorced, and lives here alone with her son.'

'What's the dead child's name?'

'He isn't a child. He's a young man, nineteen or twenty, I'd say, offhand.'

'You said "boy" before. How old are you, Hannigan?'

'Twenty-four.'

'How long you been a police officer?'

'Since I graduated from Miami-Dade.'

'Don't be evasive.'

'Two years. Almost two years.'

'Where's the mother?'

'Now?'

'If you keep twisting the strap on your handbag, you'll break it.'

'Sorry.'

'Don't be sorry; it's your purse. The boy's mother.'

'Oh. She's next door with a neighbor. Mrs Koontz. The young man's name is ... was Jerry Hickey. Gerald, with a G.'

Hoke wrote the information in his notebook. 'Has the father been notified?'

'I don't know. Joey, Officer Garcia, didn't notify anyone, and neither did I. Mrs Koontz might've called him. But we were just told to –'

'Okay. Unlatch that death grip on your purse and dump the contents on the table.'

'I don't have to do that!' She looked at Sanchez for support, but Sanchez's disinterested expression didn't change. 'You have no right to –'

'That's an order, Hannigan.'

Hannigan hesitated for a moment, chewing some more on her lower lip. With a shrug, she emptied the handbag on the table. Hoke poked through the contents with his ballpoint, separating items that ranged from a half-empty package of Velamints to three wadded balls of used tissues. He picked up the ostrich-skin wallet. Tucked between a MasterCard plate and Hannigan's voter's registration card, in a plasticene card case, were two tightly folded one-hundred-dollar bills.

'That's my money,' she said. 'I won it at jai alai last night.'

'Did Garcia win, too?'

'Yes! Yes, he did. We went together.'

'Sit down.' Hoke indicated the chair across the table as he got to his feet. 'Put your stuff back in your purse.'

Hoke opened the front door and beckoned to Garcia. As Garcia ambled toward him, Hoke fanned the two bills in his left hand, and extended his right. 'Let me see your share, Garcia.'

Garcia hesitated, his brown face mantling with anger.

'He wants to see our jai alai winnings!' Hannigan called shrilly from the dining area.

Garcia handed over his wallet. Hoke found eight one-hundred-dollar bills, folded and refolded into a tight square, behind the driver's license.

'That what you call an even split, Garcia? Eight for you, and only two for Hannigan?'

'Well – I found it, not Hannigan.'

'Where?'

'In plain sight, on top of the dresser. I – I didn't touch nothing else.'

'You and Hannigan are assholes. Stealing a ten-dollar bill is one thing, but don't you think Mrs Hickey would miss a thousand bucks and scream to the department?'

Garcia looked away. 'We – we figured the two of us could just deny it.'

'Sure. The way you did with me. Ever been interrogated by an Internal Affairs investigator?'

'No.'

'You're lucky then you didn't try to lie to me. Now hustle your ass next door and get Mrs Hickey. Bring her back over here.'

'What – what about the money?'

'The money's evidence.'

'What I mean, what about me and –?'

'Forget about it. Try and learn a lesson. That's all.'

Hoke returned to the dining area. 'Hannigan, we're going to examine the body. While we're in the bedroom we can't watch the silverware and you, too, so go back to your car and listen to the radio.'

The concrete-block-and-stucco house had three bedrooms and one bathroom. Two of the bedrooms were half the size of the master bedroom. The bathroom could be entered from the hallway, and also from the master bedroom. At the back of the house there was also a Florida room that could serve as a second living room, with glass jalousies on three sides. The back lawn sloped gently to the square milky lake. A sliding glass door led from the master bedroom to the Florida room, and across the hall from the larger bedroom was the spartan room occupied by the dead Gerald Hickey.

Mrs Hickey's bedroom held a round, unmade king-sized bed, with a half-dozen pillows and an array of long-legged nineteenth-century dolls. There was a pink silk chaise longue, a maple highboy with a matching dresser and vanity table, and a backless settee. The vanity table, with three mirrors, was littered with unguents, cold creams, and other cosmetics. The round bed was a tangle of crumpled Laura Ashley sheets in a floral pattern not observed in nature, with a wadded lavender nightgown-and-peignoir combination at the foot of the bed.

Sanchez picked up one of the long-legged dolls. Hoke sniffed the anima of the owner – Patou's Joy, perspiration, cold cream, bath powder, soap, and stale cigarette smoke.

'You ever notice,' he said, 'how a woman's room always smells like the inside of her purse?'

'Nope.' Sanchez dropped the doll on the bed. 'But I've noticed that a man's bedroom smells like a YMCA locker room.'

'When were you' – Hoke started to say 'inside a man's bedroom' but caught himself – 'inside the Y locker room?'

'When I was on patrol, a long time ago. Some kid claimed he'd been raped in the shower.' She shrugged. 'But nothing ever came of the investigation. No doubt someone cornholed him, but we figured he claimed rape because the other kid wouldn't pay him. It became a juvenile matter, and I was never called to court.'

'How long were you on the street?'

'Just a little over three months. Then I spent a year guarding manholes all day so Southern Bell could hook up wires under the street. Then, because I was bilingual, they made me a dispatcher. Seven years listening to problems and doing nothing about them.'

'Okay ... let's take a look at the body. You can tell me what to do about *it*.' Hoke closed the door to the master bedroom and they crossed the hallway.

Jerry Hickey, with his teeth bared in a frozen grin, was supine on a narrow cot. Except for his urine-stained blue-and-white shorts, he was naked. His arms hugged his sides, with the fingers extended, like the hands of a skinny soldier lying at attention. His feet were dirty, and his toenails hadn't been clipped in months. His eyes were closed. Hoke rolled back the left eyelid with a thumb. The iris was blue.

On a round Samsonite bridge table next to the bed there were three sealed plasticene bags of white powder and shooting paraphernalia – a Bic lighter, a silver spoon, and an empty hypodermic needle with the plunger closed. There was the butt of a hand-rolled cigarette in an ashtray, and three tightly rolled balls of blue tinfoil. Hoke put the butt, the tinfoil balls, and the square packets of powder into a Baggie, which he stuffed into the left-hand pocket of his poplin leisure-suit jacket. The right-hand pocket was lined with glove leather and already held several loose rounds of .38 tracer ammunition, his pack of short Kools, three packages of book matches, and two hard-boiled eggs in Reynolds wrap.

Hoke stepped back a pace and nodded to Ellita Sanchez. There was a knotted bandanna tied around the dead man's upper left arm. She examined the arm without loosening the crude tourniquet and looked at the scabs on his arm. 'Here's a large hole,' she said, 'but the other track marks look older.'

'Sometimes they shoot up in the balls.'

'You mean the scrotum, not in the balls.' Sanchez, with some difficulty, pulled down the stained boxer shorts and lifted the man's testicles. There were a half-dozen scabs on the scrotum.

'This malnourished male,' she said, 'about eighteen or nineteen, is definitely a habitual user.' She pointed to a row of splotchy red marks on the dead man's neck. 'I don't know what these are. They could be thumb marks or love bites.'

'When I was in school,' Hoke said, smiling, 'we called 'em hickeys. That's what we used to do in junior high in Riviera Beach. Two of us guys would grab a girl in the hall between classes, usually some stuck-up girl. While one guy held her, the other guy would suck a couple of splotches onto her neck. Then' – Hoke laughed – 'when the girl went home, it was her problem to explain to her parents how she got 'em.'

'I don't get it.' Sanchez appeared to be genuinely puzzled. 'Why would you do something like that?'

'For fun.' Hoke shrugged. 'We were young, and it seemed like a fun thing to do to some stuck-up girl.'

'Nothing like that ever happened at Shenandoah Junior High here in Miami. Not that I know of, anyway. I saw girls with hickeys at Southwest High, but I don't think any of them were put there by force.'

'You Latin girls lead a sheltered life. But the point I'm trying to make is, these marks look like hickeys to me.'

'Maybe so. From the smile on his face, he died happy.'

'That's not a smile, that's a rictus. A lot of people who aren't happy to die grin like that.'

'I know, Sergeant, I know. Sorry, I guess I shouldn't joke about it.'

'Don't apologize, for Christ's sake. I don't know how to talk to you sometimes.'

'Why not try talking to me like I'm your partner,' Ellita said, compressing her lips. 'And I didn't like that crack about my sheltered life, either. Growing up in Miami and eight years in the department, I don't even know what sheltered means. I realize I'm still inexperienced in homicide work but I've been a cop for a long time.'

'Okay, partner.' Hoke grinned. 'What's this look like to you?'

'This is just an overdose, isn't it?'

'It looks that way.' Hoke closed his fingers and made tight fists, reaching for something that wasn't there. He crossed to the closet. A pair of faded jeans and a white, not very clean, short-sleeved *guayabera* were draped over the closet door. Hoke went through the pockets of the shirt and pants and found three pennies, a wallet, and a folder of Holiday Inn matches. He added these items to the Baggie and then looked at the top of the dresser against the wall. There was no suicide note in the room, either on the card table or on the dresser, but there were two twenties and a ten on the dresser top.

Hoke pointed at the money without touching it. 'See this? Amateurs. Our two fellow police officers left fifty bucks. A professional thief would've taken all of it. But an amateur, for some reason, hardly ever takes it all. It's like the last cookie in the jar. If there'd been twenty-two bucks on the dresser, they'd have left two.'

Hoke added the bills to the stack of hundreds and handed the money to Sanchez. 'Later on, when you write the report, lock all this dough in my desk. I'll get it back to Mrs Hickey later.'

The top dresser drawer contained some clean shorts and T-shirts, and a half-dozen pairs of socks. The other drawers were empty except for dust. The narrow closet held a dark blue polyester suit, still in its plastic bag from the cleaners, two blue work shirts, and one white button-down shirt on hangers. There were no neckties. There were no letters or other personal possessions. The only clue to the dead man's activities was the book of matches from the Holiday Inn – but there were two dozen Holiday Inns in the Greater Miami area, with two more under construction.

Hoke was puzzled. If there had been a suicide note, Mrs Hickey could have found it and flushed it down the john. That happened frequently. A family almost always thought there was a stigma of some kind to a suicide, as if they, in some way, would be blamed. But this didn't look like a suicide. This kid, with a thousand bucks and more heroin to shoot up with when he awoke, should have been a very happy junkie. It was, in all probability, an accidental overdose, perhaps from stronger heroin than Jerry was used to taking. One less junkie, that was all.

But Hoke still wasn't satisfied.

'Take a look in the bathroom,' Hoke said to Sanchez. 'I'll call the forensic crew.'

Hoke called Homicide from a white wall phone in the kitchen. The OIC of the forensic crew would inform the medical examiner, who would either come out or wait at the morgue. In either case, there would be an autopsy.

Hoke lit a Kool, being careful not to inhale, and went outside. The two girls with the bicycles had disappeared. Hannigan, wearing her cap, sat in the front seat of the police car with the door open. Hoke wondered what was holding up Garcia and Mrs Hickey. He cut across the lawn. As he stepped through a break in the Barbados cherry hedge between the two yards, the front door opened and Garcia came out, hanging on to a strug-gling, giggling woman. The woman's face was reddened and blotchy and streaked with tears. She had a fine slim figure and was taller than Garcia. Her wide-set cornflower-blue eyes were rolling wildly. She was, Hoke estimated, in her late thirties. She wore a pair of green cotton hip-huggers, a yellow terrycloth halter – exposing a white midriff and a deepset belly button – and a pair of tennis shoes without socks. Her long, honey-colored hair was tangled. She stopped giggling suddenly, raised her arms above her head, and slid through Garcia's encircling arms to the grass. With her legs spread, she sat there stubbornly, sobbing with determination.

'Where's your hat, Garcia?' Hoke said.

'I left it in the house. It fell off.'

'Get it and put it on. When you wear a sidearm with a uniform, you're supposed to be covered at all times.'

A short, matronly-looking woman with steel-gray hair edged shyly out of the doorway, making room for Garcia to re-enter the house. She was wringing her hands, smiling, and her face was slightly flushed. She wore red shorts and a T-shirt. She was at least forty-five pounds overweight.

'It's all my fault, Lieutenant,' she said. 'But I didn't mean it.'

'Sergeant, not lieutenant. Sergeant Moseley. Homicide. What's all your fault? Mrs Koontz, isn't it?'

She nodded. 'Mrs Robert Koontz. Ellen.'

'What's all your fault, Mrs Koontz?'

'Lorrie – Mrs Hickey – was very upset when she found Jerry dead. She came over here, so I thought it would be a good idea to give her a drink. To calm her down a little, you know. So before I called nine-eleven, I poured her a glass of Wild Turkey.'

'How big a glass?'

'A water glass, I'm afraid.'

'Did you put any water in it?'

'No. I didn't think she'd drink all of it, and she didn't. But she drank most of it, and then it hit her pretty hard. I don't think I've ever seen anyone ever get so smashed so quick.' Mrs Koontz giggled, and then put her fingers to her mouth. 'I'm sorry, Sergeant, I really am.'

'You should've put some water in with it.'

Sanchez knelt on the grass beside Mrs Hickey, and handed her a wadded tissue to wipe her face.

'Perhaps you and Officer Sanchez can get Mrs Hickey back into your house?' Hoke said. 'I can't talk to her that way. Put her to bed, and tell her I'll be back this evening. It'll be best to have her out of the way when the lab group gets here anyway.'

'I'm really sorry about her condition –'

'Don't be. The world would look better if everybody drank a glassful of Wild Turkey in the morning.'

Hoke signaled to Garcia, who had retrieved his hat from the house. They walked to the police car, and Mrs Koontz and Sanchez helped the sobbing Loretta Hickey into Mrs Koontz's house.

There were a dozen area residents standing across the street on the sidewalk. The neighbors, muttering to one another, stared at the two houses.

'Keep those people over there, Garcia,' Hoke said. 'I'll lock the back door, and you, Hannigan, can stay in the backyard to keep people from coming around to peep in the windows. You stay out front, Garcia, and don't answer any questions.'

Hoke returned to the Hickey house and opened the refrigerator. There was no beer, but he settled for a glass of Gatorade, which he topped off with a generous shot of vodka from an opened bottle he found in the cabinet above the sink. He sat at the Eames table in the dining area, put his feet on another chair, and drank the Gatorade-and-vodka like medicine.

Sanchez returned to the house, sat across from Hoke, and made some notations in her notebook. 'Except for some Dexedrine, and it was in a prescription bottle for Mrs Hickey, there's nothing of interest in the bathroom. Hickey obviously hasn't taken a bath in some time, and Mrs Hickey hasn't had time, I suppose, to take a shower this morning.'

'We'll see how the P.M. goes, but it's probably a routine OD. I'll talk to Mrs Hickey tonight, and we can work on the report tomorrow.'

'You didn't have the right to make Hannigan dump her purse, Sergeant.'

'That's right. I didn't.'

'How'd you know she and Garcia took the money from the dresser?'

'I didn't. How could I know?'

'The way you acted. You seemed so positive.'

'I just had a hunch, that's all.'

'If she reports you, you'll be in trouble. I'm your partner, but I'm also a witness. It puts me –'

'Do you think she will?'

'No. It's just that …'

'Just that what?'

'If you hadn't found the money, you could've been in a jam. Or if they'd stuck to their phony story that they'd won the money at jai alai, you –'

'In that case, I'd've turned it over to Internal Affairs. Then, when Mrs Hickey reported the money missing, Garcia and Hannigan would've been suspended for an investigation. Sometimes a hunch pays off, and sometimes it doesn't. Pour yourself a Gatorade-and-vodka and relax.'

'I don't drink,' Sanchez said. 'On duty.'

'Neither do I. I'm taking the rest of the day off to look for a place to live. I'll take my car, and you can wait for forensic. Garcia can give you a ride back to the station in their car.'

'We've got a meeting with Major Brownley at four-thirty.'

Hoke finished his drink and grinned. 'I know.' He washed his glass at the kitchen sink and put the wet glass on the wooden dryer rack. 'I'll see you then. But until then, I'm on comp time.'

Chapter Two

Although Miami is the largest of the twenty-seven municipalities that make up the Greater Miami area, it does not have the desirable, middle-class residential areas or the affordable neighborhoods that the smaller municipalities have. There are several expensive, up-scale neighborhoods, but very few policemen, even those with working wives, can afford these affluent enclaves. There are slum areas and black neighborhoods with affordable housing, but WASP policemen with families avoid them, as they avoid the housing in Little Havana.

When a neighborhood becomes black or Latin, Anglo policemen move out with their families. Latin cops prefer Little Havana and have no problem in finding decent housing for their extended families, but the middle-income housing where married WASP cops prefer to live is in short supply, now that Miami's population is more than 55 percent Latin. As a consequence, the Anglo family men in the department had moved out of the city to the burgeoning Kendall area, to suburban South Miami, to the giant condo complexes in North Miami, and to the new and affordable subdivisions in West Miami.

The city's policemen were required to carry their badges and weapons at all times, to be ready to make an off-hours arrest or assist an officer in trouble. But with so many men living out of town, few were actually available. It seemed logical to the new chief of police that if all thousand Miami police officers were living within the city limits, there would be a marked drop in the crime rate. There had in fact always been an official rule to this effect, that a cop had to reside within the city, but until the new chief had taken over it had never been enforced. Now, uncompromising deadlines had been established for all of the Miami police officers living in the other municipalities to move back to the city. To most cops, the rule was unreasonable and unfair, because many of them had purchased homes in the other communities. Many resigned rather than move back, and had little difficulty in finding new police jobs in their adopted municipalities, although most took a pay cut. Others, with too much time in the department to resign, left their families in the other cities and rented small, cramped apartments or moved in with their Miami relatives. Still others, after desperate searches, of course, found suitable housing.

The strict enforcement of the rule had resulted in the loss of more than a hundred officers, many of them highly competent veterans. Because of city budget problems, the department was already short more than 150 people, so the force was reduced to approximately 850 full-time policemen. With this personnel shortage, plus the difficulty in recruiting new minority policemen, who had a priority under the Affirmative Action plan, it now seemed imperative for the new chief to maintain the rule. The damage had been done, but at least most of the remaining cops now lived within the city limits and were available during their off-duty hours.

Hoke Moseley, however, had a special problem. As a sergeant, his annual salary was $34,000. For a single, divorced man, this should have been enough to live on fairly well in Miami. But because of the terms of his divorce settlement, Hoke had to send half of his salary – every other paycheck – to his ex-wife, who lived in Vero Beach, Florida. Ten years earlier, when Hoke had signed the agreement – which also gave his ex-wife, Patsy, the full-time custody of their two daughters – he had been willing to sign almost anything to get out of his untenable marriage. At the time of their separation, he had been living rent-free with a young advertising woman named Bambi in her two-bedroom condo in Coconut Grove, a desirable neighborhood within the city limits. But later on, after the divorce, and after he had broken up with Bambi, he realized how foolish he had been to agree to the pre-divorce settlement. He still had to pay the income tax on $34,000 out of the $17,000 he had left, plus paying out money for the pension plan, PBA dues, Social Security, and everything else. The everything else included medical expenses for his two daughters, and these bills had been costly over the years, especially dentists' and orthodontists' bills. Patsy also sent him the bills for the girls' new Easter and Christmas outfits, school clothes, and for the summer camp the girls liked to go to in Sebring, Florida, which included horseback riding – an extra fee. If Hoke had only had his own lawyer, instead of sharing Patsy's, and had opted for alimony instead of a pre-divorce settlement, he could have at least taken alimony payments off his income tax. But Patsy had hired a sharp woman lawyer who had persuaded Hoke to sign the financial agreement.

After Bambi, he had been forced to live in cheap efficiency apartments, and he had even tried living in private homes with kitchen privileges. But he had gone deeper into debt as the years passed. He ran up large dental bills himself as his dentist tried vainly to save his teeth, but at last they were all extracted, and he was fitted with a complete set of grayish-blue dentures. These fragile-looking teeth were so patently false that they were the first thing people noticed about Hoke when they met him.

Two years earlier, before the department had been taken over by the new chief, Hoke had found a solution that had solved some of his financial problems. Howard Bennett, the owner-manager of the Eldorado Hotel, a seedy art deco establishment in South Miami Beach, had taken Hoke on as security officer. Hoke was given a rent-free two-room suite, and all he had to do was to spend his nights in the hotel, and most weekends. He had a view of Biscayne Bay and the Miami skyline from his window, and he could take the MacArthur Causeway into Miami and reach the downtown police station in fifteen minutes. Or less, depending upon the traffic. On the other hand, Miami Beach was not Miami, and Major Willie Brownley, the Homicide Division chief, had told Hoke to move back inside the city.

'It's imperative that you get out of the Eldorado as soon as possible,' Major Brownley had told him. 'Next to Coral Gables, South Beach probably has the highest crime rate in Dade County. And sooner or later, in that crummy neighborhood, you're going to get mixed up in a shooting or something and have to make an arrest. Then, when it comes out that you're a Miami cop, and not a Miami Beach cop, I'll be blamed because you aren't supposed to be living there in the first place.'

'It's a quiet place, the Eldorado,' Hoke had said. 'Mostly retired Jewish ladies on Social Security.'

'And Mariel refugees.'

'Only five left now, Willie. I got rid of the troublemakers. But I'll get out. I just want to know how much time I've got, that's all.'

'Two weeks. You've got comp days coming. Take a few days off, find a place to live, and get the hell out of there. You're the only man left in my division who hasn't got a Miami address.'

'I've got a Miami address. Officially, my mail goes to Bill Henderson's house.'

'But I know you're still living in the Eldorado.'

'I'll be out in two weeks, Willie. Don't worry about it.'

'I'm not worried. Two weeks, or you'll be suspended without pay till you're back in the city.'

A week had gone by already, and Hoke still hadn't found a rent-free place to live. He had contacted several downtown hotels about the sort of arrangement he had with the Eldorado, but he had been turned down flat. The fleabag transient hotels downtown weren't suitable for Hoke. The better hotels wanted full-time security officers only and weren't willing to provide a free room to a part-time security officer with irregular hours – not when they could rent out the same room for seventy-eight dollars a night or more.

Maybe, Hoke thought, the Safe 'n' Sure Home-Sitting Service in Coconut Grove would be the solution. It was worth a try, and if it didn't work, he would have to find a room in a private house again, with kitchen privileges – some place with a private entrance. The way rents had increased in the last few years, he could no longer afford a cheap efficiency apartment: There were no *cheap* efficiencies. Once again, Hoke marveled at the brilliance of Patsy's lawyer. No specific sum of money had been mentioned in the divorce agreement. It stated merely that Hoke would send every other paycheck, properly endorsed to Ms Patsy Mayhew (his wife had resumed her maiden name), including any and all cost-of-living increments and raises. Ten years ago Hoke had been a patrolman earning $8,500 a year. He had lived much better, with Bambi, on half of that sum than he was living on now at $17,000. But ten years ago he had never dreamed, nor had any other police officer, that he – or even sergeants – would ever be paid $34,000 a year.

Who could have predicted it? On the other hand, his oldest daughter would be sixteen now, and his youngest fourteen. In two more years, his new lawyer told him, when his oldest daughter became eighteen, he would petition the court and see if he could change the arrangement. Patsy's salary (she had an executive job of some kind with a time-sharing hotel chain in Vero Beach) would also be taken into consideration by the judge – when the time came. But right now, his lawyer advised him, nothing could be done. Hoke would just have to live with the agreement he had so unwisely signed.

'Too bad,' the lawyer had said, shaking his head. 'I wish I'd been your attorney at the time. When a couple getting a divorce decides to share the same lawyer, he has two fools for his clients, but one of them is more foolish than the other. I would never have allowed you to sign such a dumb and binding agreement.'

Hoke had more than an hour to kill before his appointment in Coconut Grove with the house-sitting service. It was too early for lunch, but he was starving. He stopped at a 7-Eleven, bought a grape Slurpee, and then ate his two hard-boiled eggs and slurped the Slurpee in his car in front of the store. This was his usual diet lunch, and it was as unsatisfactory as his diet breakfast, which called for two poached eggs and half of a grapefruit. He could get by on this diet fare all day, but could rarely stick to it by nightfall. By the end of the day he was always too hungry to settle for the three ounces of roast beef and can of boiled spinach his diet called for, so he usually ate something that tasted good instead – like the Colonel's extra-crispy, with a couple of biscuits and gravy. But even so, Hoke had lost weight and was down to 182 pounds. He had given up a daily six-pack habit, and that had helped, but he felt deprived and resentful. He was also trying to quit smoking, in an effort to lower his blood pressure and save some money, but that was harder to do than it was to diet. Although, now that cigarettes cost $1.30 a pack, it made a man think twice before lighting up a cigarette worth six and a half cents. Hoke stubbed out his short Kool, put the butt in his shirt pocket for later, and drove to Coconut Grove.

Hoke parked on Virginia Street, not far from the Mayfair shopping complex, and put his police placard on top of the dashboard in lieu of dropping a quarter in the meter. The Safe 'n' Sure Home-Sitting Service, the outfit Hoke was looking for, was only a short distance away from the Mayfair's parking garage. Hoke had selected this agency from one of six display ads in the Yellow Pages. Not only was Coconut Grove a desirable place to live, but out here he might be lucky enough to get a residence with a swimming pool.

Ms Beverly Westphal, the woman Hoke had talked with on the telephone, was on the phone again when Hoke came into her office. He was fifteen minutes early. A tinkly tocsin above the door announced his entrance. The small room – the front room of what was undoubtedly Ms Westphal's private residence – looked more like a living room than an office. The first impression was reinforced by the round oak table that served as her desk. The desk held a metal tray and the remains of a pizza, as well as her telephone, nameplate, and a potted philodendron.

Ms Westphal was about thirty, and she wore Gloria Vanderbilt jeans, a black U-necked T-shirt with the word MACHO across the middle in white block letters, and green-and-red jogging shoes. A small pocket watch dangled from the T-shirt. She didn't wear a brassiere beneath the T-shirt, and her breasts had prolapsed. Her brown eyes were popped slightly, Hoke noticed as she hung up the phone. She was the kind of woman with whom Hoke would avoid eye contact if he happened to see one like her in a shopping center.

Ms Westphal told Hoke to pull a chair up to the table.

'At least you're a WASP, Sergeant Moseley.'

'Yes, and I'm not bilingual.'

'That isn't important. I've got more Latin house sitters now than I can use, but there's a shortage of WASP sitters at present. There's a thousand-dollar security bond, and if you don't have a thousand dollars –'

'I don't have a thousand dollars.'

'– I can get you a bond for a hundred in cash.'

'I can raise that much.'

Ms Westphal summarized the situation for Hoke. Three years before, when white flight had begun in earnest, it was easy to move away from Miami. A house could still be sold for a handsome profit then, and the happy seller moved to Fort Lauderdale or Orlando or far enough north to avoid hearing any Spanish. But white flight had increased as the crime rate increased, especially after the influx of Castro's 125,000 Marielitos, and the newer and higher interest rates kept young couples from buying used homes. Nevertheless, the inflated prices were holding steady. A used home sold eventually, but instead of a quick turnover, sellers often had to wait for a year or more to find a buyer. But people who wanted to move away still moved, and if they couldn't sell their house or rent it, they needed someone to watch the empty residence to discourage burglary and vandalism.

Ms Westphal had separate lists of homeowners. One was a group that had moved and didn't want their houses to remain unoccupied while their agents were trying to sell them; the other was a shorter list of homeowners who wanted to take vacations of from two weeks to two months in North Carolina, and didn't want their houses left unoccupied. Homeowners on both lists paid her fifteen dollars a day for the service. Out of this amount, the sitter received five dollars a day At the end of each two-week period, she gave the sitter seventy dollars in cash.

'If there's anything I hate,' she said, 'it's fooling around with all of that withholding tax and minimum-wage bullshit paperwork.'

'I understand,' Hoke said. 'Using cash eases your paperwork burden, and the government's.'

'Exactly. What d'you know about house plants?'

'I've never owned one.'

'That's an important duty. You have to take care of the house plants. But the owners usually leave detailed instructions, so all you have to do is follow them.'

'I can do that.'

'What about dogs and cats?'

'Cats are okay. I lived with one once, but I've never owned a dog.'

'Well, this place I'm sending you to has a dog that goes with it. You'll have to feed and water the dog as well as the house plants. The last five people I've sent out there have turned the place down. I don't understand what the problem is. None of them would say why they backed out. It may be the dog. But you, being a cop and all, should be able to handle a dog.'

'As I told you on the phone, Ms Westphal, I'll be coming and going at odd hours, so it's probably a good idea to have a dog on the place. I don't mind the dog.'

'That's about it, then.' Ms Westphal handed Hoke her business card, with the address of the house scribbled on the back. 'But if you tell me no, too, you'll have to give me a reason. Otherwise, I'm going to ask Mr Ferguson to try another agency.'

'What is it? A house or an apartment?'

'It's a small house, but it's quite lovely. Two bedrooms, one bath, with a kidney-shaped pool in back. There are some orange trees, too, but you won't have to worry about the yard. Mr Ferguson's got a gardener for that. You'll have to spend your nights there, but the fact that you come and go at different times is a plus. The house has a TV and air conditioning, but there are no nearby stores. You've got a car, haven't you?'

'A 1973 Le Mans, but it's got a new engine.'

'Good. I'm going out now myself, but I'll be back by two or two-thirty. Talk to Mr Ferguson. Then come back here and we'll work out the bond arrangement and the contract.'

The mailbox on Main Highway had the number and Mr Ferguson's name stenciled on it. There was a gravel driveway in a sigmoid loop, and the house was hidden completely from the road by palmettos and a thick stand of loblolly pines. As Hoke parked in front of the house, Mr Ferguson, together with his dog, a bushy black-and-burnt-orange Airedale, came out of the house. The moment Hoke got out of the car, the dog, slavering, gripped Hoke's right leg tightly with his forelegs, dug his wet jowls into Hoke's crotch, and began to dry-hump Hoke's leg in a practiced, determined rhythm. Mr Ferguson, a red-faced, red-haired man in his early forties, wearing a gray, heavy cardigan sweater despite the eighty-five-degree temperature, lit his pipe with a kitchen match.

Hoke tried to shake the dog loose. 'Ms Westphal sent me out about the house-sitting job.'

'I know,' Mr Ferguson said after he got his pipe going, 'she called me. Come on inside.' Mr Ferguson started toward the door, and Hoke managed to kick the amorous Airedale viciously enough to dislodge him when Mr Ferguson turned his back. But the dog darted ahead through the door before Hoke could close it. The moment Hoke closed the door, the dog was on him again, his forelegs clamped like a vise around Hoke's right thigh. Hoke took out his pistol.

'If you don't get this animal off me, I'm going to kill him.'

'No need to do that,' Mr Ferguson said. 'Rex! On the table, boy!'

The dog released Hoke's leg at once and jumped to a chair, then onto the kitchen table, which still held the dirty dishes from Mr Ferguson's lunch. Mr Ferguson reached between the dog's legs, above the red, pencil-sized penis. 'Old Rex gets horny living here without a mate, but if you jack him off once or twice a day, he stays mighty quiet.' The dog climaxed, and Ferguson wiped the table with a paper napkin. Rex jumped to the chair, then to the floor, and crossed to a corduroy cushion under the stove.

'What I want to do,' Mr Ferguson said, 'is go up to stay with my mama in Fitzgerald, Georgia. She's dyin' of cancer, you see, and the doctors only give her six or seven months to live. I don't think it'll be that long, but however long it takes, I'm gonna stay with her. She's all alone up there, with no friends, so I have to go up whether I want to or not. A man only has one mama, you know.'

'Why not bring her down here? Wouldn't that be better than leaving your job and your house?' Hoke shivered. The air conditioning was set for sixty or lower; no wonder Mr Ferguson was wearing a sweater.

'No, I can't do that. She's too old, and she don't want to leave her friends up there.'

'You just told me she didn't have any friends.'

'She has friends, all right, but they're all dead and in the cemetery. Mama's eighty-six years old. But she's got her own little house, and sick as she is, she wouldn't want to come down here to Miami. And I can't take Rex up there with me. Mama don't like dogs, and she never did. And I know she wouldn't 'low Rex in the house. I hate to leave Rex down here, but I don't see no other way out of the situation. Do you?'

'You could hire somebody to stay with her.'

'No, I couldn't do that. Jesus Christ Himself couldn't get along with that old woman. Nobody'd stay with her for more'n a day or two. No, I have to go. A man's only got one mama. Want to see the rest of the house? I got a pool out back. Rex likes to dive for rocks. You can throw a rock in the deepest part, and he'll dive right in and bring it to you. Labrador retrievers do that, but not many Airedales.'

'I've got another appointment, Mr Ferguson. Ms Westphal will call you later.'

'You gonna sit my house for me?'

'I don't think so. I've still got a couple of other options.'

'That's too bad. Rex liked you a lot. I could tell.'

Hoke drove back into the Grove, parked behind the Hammock Bar, and drank two draft beers before returning to the Safe 'n' Sure office. After his experience with the frigging dog, Hoke felt entitled to the drinks. Except for Rex, the house would have been ideal.

Ms Westphal unlocked the front door, and they went into the office together. 'Sorry you had to wait,' she said. 'What I need is a secretary. I was going to buy an answering machine, but most people won't talk to them anyway.'

'I don't want to sit Mr Ferguson's house.'

'You, too? What's the problem out there, anyway?'

'Well, part of the deal is that you have to jerk the dog off every day. I don't know why he didn't tell you about that in the first place. But Mr Ferguson owns a concupiscent Airedale.'

'What kind of Airedale?'

'Sex-crazed. He humps your leg, and he won't let go till you jack him off.'

'How long does it take?'

'Less than a minute. Closer to thirty seconds than a minute.'

'What's the big deal then, Sergeant? I used to jerk guys off in junior high. Oh, don't look so surprised. If you didn't, you never got a second date. It seems to me that getting a lovely home to live in free, and five dollars a day besides, should be worth a minute of your time every day.'

'Not to me it isn't. If it ever got out in the division that I – look, I'm just not interested.'

'Let's talk a minute. I'll tell you what. It'll only take me ten minutes to get over there. Why don't you take the house, and then when the dog jumps your leg you can call me. I'll drive over and handle it for you.'

'Why don't you sit the house yourself? Then you could get a secretary and let her live here. You'd have someone here to answer your phone when you were out, and you'd have a nice house with a pool for a few months.'

'That isn't a bad idea, you know.'

'I know. What else do you have?'

'I've got a duplex in Hialeah.'

'No, it's got to be in Miami. Not necessarily in the Grove, but within the city limits.'

'All I've got in the Grove right now is a week at Grove Isle. A two-hundred-and-fifty-thousand-dollar condo, complete with sauna.'

'A week isn't enough. I need a place for at least a month or two.'

'I'll call you. But you should've told me you didn't like dogs. It would've saved a trip out to Mr Ferguson's house.'

'Until I met Rex, I didn't know I didn't like dogs. But please call me soon, because I need a place before the end of the week.'

'I'll see what I can do.'

But from the cool tone of her voice, Hoke had a hunch, as he headed downtown on Dixie Highway, that it would be a damned cold day in Miami before she called him again.

Chapter Three

Hoke shared a small office at the Homicide Division with Ellita Sanchez. The upper half of the wall that faced the squad room was glass, and there were several wanted posters affixed to the glass with Scotch tape. Most of the space in the little office was taken up by a large double desk, the kind favored by small real-estate firms. There was a D-ring bolted to the desk so that suspects could be handcuffed to it. A glass top covered the desk, and lists of telephone numbers and various business cards were scattered beneath the glass for easy reference. As a consequence, even when the desk was cleared, it looked messy. The desk was rarely cleared, however. There was a two-drawer filing cabinet, two metal swivel chairs, and one customer's straight chair that was usually piled high with copies of the two daily Miami newspapers. The IBM Selectric typewriter was, of course, on Ellita's side of the desk.

On the wall facing Hoke's side was an unframed poster of a masked man pointing a pistol. Beneath the picture, in large boldface, was the current Greater Miami Chamber of Commerce slogan: MIAMI'S FOR ME! Technically, this small office, the only enclosed office in the division other than Major Willie Brownley's much larger glass-walled office, belonged to Lieutenant Fred Slater, the executive officer and number-two man for Major Brownley. But Lieutenant Slater, who preferred a desk in one corner of the bullpen, where it was easier to keep an eye on everybody, had given the small office to Hoke Moseley and Bill Henderson to use. A few weeks earlier, when Major Brownley had broken up their partnership, Hoke had been assigned Ellita Sanchez as his new partner, and Sergeant Bill Henderson had been moved to the bullpen. Sergeant Henderson's new partner, Teodoro 'Teddy' Gonzalez, was the newest investigator in the division, and Henderson was supposed to break him in to homicide work, as Hoke was supposed to break in Ellita Sanchez. Bill and Hoke had worked together as partners, even after Henderson had been promoted to sergeant, for more than three years. They had worked well together, but because neither of them spoke Spanish, and both refused to learn the language, Major Brownley had broken them up and assigned them bilingual partners. Hoke, being senior to Henderson, had kept the little office, and Henderson and Gonzalez now occupied two beat-up metal desks next to the men's room. There was no women's room; Ellita had to take the elevator down to the second floor.

With more than half of Miami's population a mixture of various Latins, but mostly Cubans, and with more Salvadoran and Nicaraguan refugees coming in daily, the change in partners had been inevitable. Bill and Hoke hadn't been happy about the switch, but they had accepted it without complaint because there was nothing they could do about it. Altogether, there were forty-seven detectives in Homicide, and, thanks to Affirmative Action, the balance was about even between Anglo and Latin officers. Not counting Major Brownley, who was black, there were three black detectives, and one of these was a Haitian. The Haitian detective, a Sorbonne graduate, spoke French fluently, as well as Creole and English, but he had less work to do than any of the others. The Miami Haitian population, about 25,000, was the most peaceful ethnic group in town. The occasional homicides in Little Haiti usually involved somebody from outside their district shooting one of them for fun from a passing car.

When Hoke came into the office, Ellita Sanchez, with the help of a small hand mirror, was applying a coat of American Dream to her lips. Except for this vividly red and wet-looking lipstick, Ellita used no other makeup. Because the corners of her mouth turned down slightly, unless she was smiling the two tiny red lines that tugged at the corners of her lips sometimes made it seem, at first glance, as though her mouth were dribbling blood. Hoke wondered if anyone had ever told her about this effect.

'How'd it go?' Hoke said.

'We'll know more later. The assistant M.E. said he thought it was an OD, not a suicide, but not for the record. I sent for Hickey's file. According to the computer, he's got a record, so I asked for a printout.'

Hoke handed her the Baggie with the items he had picked up

in Hickey's room. 'Send the tinfoil balls and the bags of powder to the lab to be checked out. Send the roach, too, if you want – or take it home and smoke it.'

'I don't smoke pot, Sergeant.' Ellita put the roach into her purse.

Hoke went through Hickey's wallet, a well-worn cowhide fold-over type, and removed a driver's license, expired; a slip of paper with a telephone number, written in pencil; a cracked black-and-white snapshot of a mongrel with a ball in its mouth; a folded gift coupon for a McDonald's quarter-pounder, expired; a Visa credit card in Gerald Hickey's name, expired; and a tightly folded twenty-dollar bill that had been hidden behind the lining of the wallet.

'Not much here.' Hoke passed the twenty across the desk. 'Put this bill with the others.'

'I've already sealed the money in an envelope.'

'In that case, you'll have to unseal it, won't you?'

Ellita cut the flap of the brown envelope with the small blade of her Swiss army knife, took out the money, flattened the twenty, and added it to the other bills. She placed the money in a new brown envelope, threw the mutilated envelope into the wastepaper basket, and then sealed the money inside. She wrote 'Gerald Hickey' and '$1,070' on the outside of the envelope before passing it to Hoke across the desk. Hoke put the envelope in the side pocket of his leisure jacket, and shook his head.

'I didn't mean to snap at you. But I had a weird experience this afternoon, and I still haven't found a new place to live. Why do you think, Sanchez, that Hickey would carry a picture of a mongrel dog in his wallet?'

Ellita stood up, leaned over the desk, and frowned at the items on the desk. 'Everything else is expired, so I'd say the dog is probably dead, too. Maybe it was once his dog, and it died, so he wanted to keep the picture as a *memento mori*.'

'A *memento mori* is a human skull, not a picture of a dog. But you may be right. There was no indication of a dog living at the Hickey house. Pass me the phone.'

Hoke dialed the number on the slip of paper.

'Hello.'

'I'd like to speak to Jerry Hickey,' Hoke said.

'Who?'

'Jerry Hickey.'

'He don't live here no mo'.' It was a black woman's voice.

'Who is this, please?'

'Who is you?'

'I want to buy Jerry's dog. When he left, did he leave his dog with you?'

'He didn't have no dog. I don't 'low no dogs here. Who is this?'

'When did Jerry move?'

The woman hung up the phone.

'You're probably right about the dog, Sanchez.' Hoke handed her the slip of paper. 'Get the address of this number from the phone company. It doesn't mean anything to us, but I can pass it on to Narcotics. It might be a lead for them. Jerry had to get the heroin somewhere. He hadn't been living at home long. I'll find out how long this evening when I talk to his mother.'

Ellita nodded. 'You want some coffee, Sergeant?'

'Do you?'

'We've got a half-hour before we meet with Major Brownley.'

'I know that. I asked if you wanted some coffee.'

Ellita nodded.

'In that case,' Hoke said, 'I'll go. You've gone the last three times, and it isn't supposed to work that way. Bill and I always took turns. I've been taking advantage of you. How many sugars?' Hoke got to his feet.

'None. I keep Sweet 'N Low here in my desk.'

Hoke took the elevator downstairs to the basement cafeteria. For some reason, he thought, Ellita seemed to be afraid of him. Several times lately he had noticed her staring at him, and she looked frightened. He couldn't understand it, because he had been leaning over backward to be friendly with her. Maybe it was the meeting coming up with Major Brownley. Most of the detectives in the division were afraid of the major. As a rule, Brownley kept his distance, either by communicating with his detectives through Lieutenant Slater or by sending out memos. It was unusual for Brownley to call a special meeting this way. As he filled two Styrofoam cups with coffee, Hoke wondered vaguely what the old fart wanted.

Chapter Four

Major Willie Brownley, the first black ever to be appointed to that rank in the department, leaned back in his padded leather chair and got his cigar drawing well before he said anything. His face, the color of an eggplant, but not as shiny, was lined with tiny wrinkles. His cropped hair was gray at the temples, but his well-trimmed mustache was still black. The whites of his eyes were the color of a legal pad. He looked of indeterminate age, but Hoke knew that Willie Brownley was fifty-five, because Hoke had worked for the major when he had been a captain in charge of Traffic. The major wore his navy-blue gabardine uniform even on the hottest days, with the jacket always buttoned, and his trim military appearance made him look younger than his age.

The three detectives sat facing Brownley's desk, with Henderson on the right. Henderson was a large, paunchy man who almost always wore a striped seersucker jacket with poplin wash pants. Although he was officially six feet, two inches tall, he appeared six-four because he wore Adler's elevator shoes. Henderson thought the extra two inches made him look slimmer. They didn't, really, but the extra height did make him look more formidable. Henderson was an affable man, but his front teeth, both uppers and lowers, were laced with a tangle of silver wire and gold caps. When he smiled, these brutal metal-studded teeth were more than a little frightening, particularly when he questioned a suspect. But his smile rarely changed, whether he was interrogating someone or eating a bowl of chili.

Hoke and Ellita sat closer together on the left of the desk, facing the major. Ellita had a yellow legal pad and a ballpoint pen. Before they went to Brownley's office, Hoke told her it might be a good idea to take a few notes.

Brownley dropped the burnt match into an ashtray made from a motorcycle piston, looked at Hoke, shook his head, and smiled.

'Hoke, you must be the last man in Miami wearing a leisure suit. Where'd you find it, anyway?'

'There was a close-out in the fashion district. I got this blue poplin and a yellow one just like it for only fifty bucks in a two-for-one sale. I like the extra pockets, and with a leisure suit you don't have to wear a tie.'

'You don't wear a leisure suit to court, do you?'

'No. I've got an old blue serge suit I wear to court. Is that what this meeting's about, Willie? My taste in plain clothes?'

'In a way. What I'm doing is what they suggested in the Dale Carnegie course I took last year. I'm putting you all at ease by developing a relaxed atmosphere. You all relaxed now?'

Hoke shook his head, Henderson smiled, and Ellita said, 'Yes, sir.' Hoke took the butt of the Kool from his shirt pocket, lit it, and dropped the match into Brownley's piston ashtray. He took two drags and then put out the butt.

'Until I tell you different,' Brownley said, 'consider this meeting as confidential. It'll probably get out in a few days, about what you're doing, simply because of what you're doing, but I don't want the press to get wind of it. If anyone in the department asks you what you're doing, just say you're on a special assignment and let it go at that. Until we see where we're going, I think we can get away with that much, anyway.'

Brownley puffed on his cigar before he continued. 'You've all heard the rumors about the new colonelcies the chief's passing out, haven't you?'

Henderson shook his head. 'Colonelcies? There aren't any colonels in the department. Except for assistant chief – and we got three already – major's as high as we go.'

'I heard something about it the other day,' Hoke said, 'but I didn't pay any attention to it.'

'It isn't official yet, but it's no longer a rumor. The chief's found a sneaky way around the no-raise budget this year. He's creating a new rank of colonel, and there'll be eight of them passed out. The new rank'll mean an extra eighteen hundred bucks a year for those promoted. It'll also mean eight major and captain vacancies. So although there's no money in the new budget for raises, a good many deserving officers will be getting more money when these promotions are okayed by the city manager.'

'What about the cop on the street?' Henderson said. 'What'll he get?'

'He'll get zip. On the other hand, with more supervisors, it'll mean more vacancies for him, too, if he passes his exams high enough.'

'It stinks,' Henderson said. 'I was in the infantry, and we only had one colonel, the regimental commander, for a fifteen-hundred-man regiment. We've got way less than a thousand cops, and we've already got a highly paid chief, three overpaid assistant chiefs, and now he wants eight new colonels. What we're gonna look like is a damned Mexican army, all generals and no privates.'

'A police department's not a rifle regiment, Bill,' Brownley said. 'You can't equate a professional police officer with a grunt private. Most of our officers have got at least a junior college degree of some kind.'

'I know, I know.' Henderson scowled. 'But what we need's more men on the street, not more brass sitting on their ass.'

'You and Hoke both should take the exam for lieutenant. I've told you that before. Promotions are going to break wide open for qualified people. But that's your problem. What I want is one of the colonelcies. And I've come up with a way for you two' – he looked at Ellita, and smiled – 'and you, too, Sanchez, to get it for me.'

There were four stacks of rust-colored accordion files on the table against the wall. The major pointed at them. 'I've been going through the old files. These are fifty old unsolved homicides. All of them go back a few years, some much longer than others. Some of these, I know, could've been solved at the time. But they weren't solved, or resolved in some way, because there wasn't enough time. There's never enough time. Most breaks, as you know, come in the first twenty-four hours. After three or four days, something else comes up, and after two weeks, unless you get a break accidentally, you're on a new case, or even three new cases. After six months, the homicide's so far back in pending, it's colder than the victim.

'I'm not telling you something you don't know already. I didn't become the Homicide chief because I was a detective. I'm an administrator, and I was promoted for my administrative ability. It didn't hurt that I was black, either, but I wouldn't have kept my rank if I couldn't do the work. It seems to me, if we can solve some of these cold cases, it'll make our division and the entire department look even better than it is. And if that happens, they'll have to make at least one of those new colonels a black man. What I want is one of those silver eagles and another gold stripe on my sleeve.'

'Time's always been the problem, Willie,' Hoke said. 'When we get a chance we work on old cases, but a new dead body is found damned near every day in a car trunk, a tomato field, an apartment –'

'I'm not finished, Hoke. Time is what I'm going to give you. You rank Bill, so you're in charge. But the three of you are going to get two full months to do nothing else but work on these fifty cold cases I picked out.'

'What about the cases we're on now?' Henderson said. 'We've got, me and Gonzalez, a triple murder in Liberty City, and no leads at all. Tomorrow we're supposed to –'

'Gonzalez will have to handle that one by himself. Hoke, you can give your current cases to Gonzalez, too. I know he lacks experience, but he'll report directly to Lieutenant Slater, and he'll get all the help from Slater he needs. I can't spare four men for this assignment, but the three of you, in two months' time, should get some positive results.'

'Three months,' Henderson said, 'would be better.'

'I know.' Brownley smiled. 'And six months would be better than three months, but you've got two. I've already gone through the old files and picked out these fifty. Take them with you, go through 'em again, and decide which cases to work first. You know more about the possibilities than I do. Any questions?'

'That office we've got,' Hoke said. 'It's too small for the three of us. Can we have one of the interrogation rooms to work in on a permanent basis?'

'Take Room Three. There's a table and some folding chairs in there already. It's yours for as long's you need it. I'll inform Lieutenant Slater. Anything else?'

'When Hoke and I turn all our cases over to Gonzalez, he'll shit his pants,' Henderson said.

'He'll be all right with Slater. Just fill Slater in on what's been done so far. Slater knows what you all will be doing, but Gonzalez doesn't. Just tell him you're on a special assignment, Bill, and to do the best he can. You have any questions, Sanchez?'

'No, sir. I think it's a good idea, that's all.'

'It would be a better idea if we had three months,' Henderson said.

'Solve at least ten of these cases in two months, and I'll give you the extra month,' Brownley said.

'Fair enough.' Henderson picked up an armload of files and left the office.

After the cold cases were stacked in piles on Hoke's desk, he looked at them and shook his head. 'It's five-thirty. We'll start going through them tomorrow morning in the interrogation room.'

'If you want me to, I can take a couple home with me tonight to read,' Ellita said. 'I haven't got anything else planned.'

'No. I want to think about how best to work things out. You guys go home.'

Henderson broadened his smile slightly. 'I think I'd better take Teddy out and buy him a drink before I give him the news. Did you notice Gonzalez through the window when we were in Willie's office? The poor bastard went to the can three times. He probably thought the meeting was all about him. But you can't blame him. If I'd been left out there, I'd've thought the same thing.'

After Henderson and Ellita left, Hoke locked the office, got his Pontiac from the lot, and drove out to Green Lakes to pay another visit to Mrs Hickey's house.

Chapter Five

The rush-hour traffic on Flagler Street was heavier than usual because of the rain. In July, during the rainy season, showers and thunderstorms begin at four or four-thirty every day and continue into the early evening hours. Hoke didn't mind the rain or the traffic, or the fact that he was working overtime without compensation. He appreciated doing anything that would delay his getting home to the Hotel Eldorado in Miami Beach – any delay, that is, that didn't cost money. The long nights at the Eldorado were dull, so he was always glad when he had an excuse to postpone going home.

The pile of old cases on his desk troubled him a little, but not very much. Brownley had had a good idea there, despite his selfish motivation, and Hoke looked forward to the two-month assignment. He didn't think they would be able to solve ten cases, but even if they could solve three or four, it would be better than none. He just wished that he had been the one to select the fifty cases to work on, instead of Willie Brownley. If he and Henderson had gone through all the cold cases, and there must be several hundred, they could have done a much better job of winnowing them than Brownley. On the other hand, the fact that Brownley had selected these particular files out of all the other unsolved cases gave Hoke at least a weak excuse for failure if they didn't resolve any of them at all.

The best way to work it, he decided, was to have each of them read all of the cases first. Each reader could then select the ten most likely cases to work on. If they all came up with the same three or four homicides on their lists, these would be the cases to work on first. If they all had the same half-dozen, it would be even better.

Hoke didn't know why Brownley had assigned Sanchez instead of Gonzalez to his team, but it was probably because he didn't think Slater could work well with a woman. Slater had a very short fuse, and Brownley undoubtedly felt that Slater would feel more comfortable chewing on Gonzalez's ass every day than he would Sanchez's. Regardless of the reason, Hoke was happy to have Sanchez instead of Gonzalez. She could spell, as well as type, so he would have her keep the daily notes and write the weekly progress reports that Major Brownley wanted. Sanchez didn't have much of a sense of humor, but he would be working with Henderson again, who did, and that was a big plus.

Loretta Hickey was no longer the distraught youthful mother Hoke had last seen sobbing on the lawn that morning. When she opened the door, she was rested, clean and sweet-smelling, and wearing a black-and-white silk djellabah. Sober, Mrs Hickey was a handsome woman. Her long hair, freshly shampooed, still had damp ends, and she had brushed it straight back. Her high white forehead was shiny and without makeup, but there was a pink trace of lipstick on her full lips.

She asked Hoke for identification. He had to tell her his name and show her his shield before she would unlock the screen door. She stared at Hoke with bold blue eyes and without apparent recognition.

'Are you always this cautious?' Hoke said, stepping into the living room.

'No, not always.' Her face relaxed a little. 'But I thought it might be those two men coming back.'

'What men?'

'They said they were friends of Jerry's, but I'd never seen them before. Neighbors have been coming by all afternoon, bringing food, but these two came at about three-thirty, when no one else was here. They got upset when I told them that Jerry was dead. Then they started looking in his room.'

'That room is sealed.'

'I told them that, but they broke the strip of paper and looked around in there anyway. They asked me if Jerry had left a package for them, and I told them no. Then one of them asked if the police had found twenty-five thousand dollars in the room! I told them that Jerry had a thousand, but not twenty-five thousand.

234

But the thousand wasn't there either. That's when they started dumping the drawers out on the floor.'

'What did they look like, these men? Did you ask them for ID?'

Mrs Hickey shook her head. 'No. I'd thought at first they might just be more neighbors. I didn't know half the people who brought food over this afternoon. And they didn't look like friends of Jerry's, either. They looked more like Yuppies, well dressed with blow-dry hair – like Brickell Avenue or Kendall types. One of them was wearing a silk suit, and the other had on a linen jacket. They were in their mid-twenties, I'd say. The one in the suit had black loafers, the other man wore brown-and-white shoes.'

Hoke grinned. 'The man with the black shoes did all the talking, right?'

Loretta Hickey nodded. 'How'd you know that?'

'I didn't. But guys who wear two-tone shoes have an ambivalent personality, and are indecisive.' Hoke studied the drape of the silk djellabah and wondered if she was wearing a bra. 'What else did they say about the twenty-five thousand?'

'Jerry was supposed to deliver the money to them yesterday, but he didn't show up, and they'd been looking for him. I told them that Jerry had a thousand dollars, and I knew that, because he showed it to me when I came home from work yesterday evening. If he had more, he didn't tell me anything about it. The thousand was on the dresser when I found him this morning. I had assumed it was still there, because I didn't go back into the room again. But it was gone when we went into the room, so –'

'I have it in my pocket,' Hoke said. 'Tell me, did you let Jerry in yesterday?'

'No, I wasn't here. I'd already gone to work, but he came to the house in the morning, he told me.'

'How'd he get in? There was no key with his effects.'

'He used the key I keep hidden in a fake rock. If you live all alone and happen to lock yourself out – and I've done it – you've got a problem. I'll show you.'

She opened the screen door and led Hoke outside. She picked up a gray stone about four inches long and handed it to Hoke. It weighed four or five ounces and had a flat bottom. Hoke opened the flat part by sliding it to one side and found the key concealed in the recess. He hefted the stone in his hand. 'This is the phoniest fake stone I've ever seen. Where'd you get it?'

'I ordered it from a catalog. It's supposed to be granite. It looks real to me.'

'Yeah, but we don't have any granite in south Florida. We've got gravel, and we've got oolite, but not any granite. A burglar who spotted this in your yard next to the house would know that it was a fake. What you should do is leave the key with a neighbor instead.'

'I've done that. Mrs Koontz, next door, has a key, and I've got a key to her house.'

'In that case, I'd advise you to keep this phony stone inside the house. What else did these men say?' Hoke opened the screen door, and they went back into the living room.

'Nothing else. Mrs Ames, from across the street, came over with a Key lime pie, and while I was around the back letting her in, they slipped out the front door and left.'

'Did you see their car?'

'It was a convertible. The top was down. It was light green, an apple green.'

'You didn't take down the license number?'

'No, I was talking to Mrs Ames, telling her what had happened. It wouldn't have occurred to me anyway.' She looked away. 'Would you like a drink, Sergeant?'

'A beer would be okay.'

'I've got vodka, and a six-pack of Cokes, but no beer.'

'Make it a Coke, then. I usually drink beer or bourbon, but I can drink almost anything, except for Mr Pibb.'

Hoke followed Mrs Hickey into the dining area and sat at the Eames table while she went into the kitchen. The table was loaded with food. There was a baked ham, studded with cloves; two cheesecakes; two Key lime pies; and a large brown ceramic casserole dish filled with Boston baked beans, topped with parboiled strips of fatty bacon.

'You ever see so much food?' Mrs Hickey said, coming back from the kitchen. She handed Hoke a tall glass of Coca-Cola over

236

ice cubes. 'On top of all this' – she made a sweeping gesture over the table – 'there's a big tuna salad in the fridge and a half a watermelon.' She blushed. 'I've had two ham sandwiches already, and both with mayonnaise.'

'That's natural. Death makes a person hungry. Those beans look good to me.'

'Would you like some? I'll never be able to eat all this food by myself.'

'I'm on a kind of diet. I'd rather have the beans, but I'll settle for some tuna salad.'

'I'll fix you a plate.'

Hoke didn't want the tuna salad either, but he thought it might help if he gave Mrs Hickey something to do with her hands. She had to be embarrassed about her morning's performance, but she was covering it well. He needed to know more about Jerry Hickey. If Jerry had ripped off twenty-five thousand dollars, where was it? Of course, he might not have ripped off anything. The two guys could have been looking for him for something else, and told Mrs Hickey that as a cover story. On the other hand, it was plausible. Drug people stiffed each other all the time, and a junkie like Hickey might not have considered the consequences of taking down a dealer. If these two dealers, or whoever they were, had been dumb enough to trust that kind of money to a junkie, they deserved to be ripped off. The kid, if he took the money, had hidden it somewhere, stashed it away, figuring that he would hide out here for a few days, then pick it up and take off. He had kept out a thousand, probably, as an emergency fund ...

The tuna salad was attractively presented: a heaped portion on a lettuce bed, garnished with two deviled egg halves, green and black olives, and celery sticks. To keep Hoke company, Mrs Hickey had a slice of Key lime pie. She took two bites, then got up and started the percolator in the kitchen.

'This is good tuna salad,' Hoke said, 'but I never put hard-boiled eggs in mine. I prefer the classic recipe. One pound of tuna, one pound of chopped onions, and one pound of mayonnaise.'

Loretta Hickey laughed. 'Oh! All that mayonnaise! I'm sorry. I guess I shouldn't laugh, but I couldn't help it.'

'Don't ever apologize for laughing, Mrs Hickey. Life goes on, you know, no matter what. That's what your neighbors were trying to tell you when they brought this food over.'

'I know. And I don't want to seem callous. I should feel sorry about Jerry's death, but I always knew that something would happen to him sooner or later. So in a way, I'm just as glad it's over. I don't mean I'm happy about his death – don't get me wrong – but his father and I gave up on Jerry a long time ago.'

'I understand, I think. What I'd like from you now is a little background information on your son –'

'Jerry isn't my son. That is, I wasn't responsible for him the way I would've been if he'd been my own son. Or even my legal stepson.'

'That isn't quite clear. Gerald Hickey isn't your son?'

'No. I'm divorced. Jerry's my ex-husband's son. Only Jerry wasn't his natural son either. He was my ex-husband's adopted son. That is, Jerry was my ex-husband's ex-wife's son by her first husband. Harold, my ex-husband, adopted Jerry when he married Marcella, his first wife, because she had custody of Jerry from her first marriage. You see, when he married Marcella, she talked Harold into adopting Jerry. Then, after they were divorced, Marcella left town, and he had to keep Jerry because Jerry was now his legal responsibility. Harold didn't know where Marcella went, and he's never heard from her again. Jerry was fifteen when they were divorced, and then Harold married me about a year later, when Jerry turned sixteen. But I never adopted Jerry, so I wasn't his legal stepmother or anything like that. He just came with Harold and the house. This house.'

'You may not believe me,' Hoke said, pushing his plate to one side, 'but I can follow you. I run into a lot more complicated families than yours in Miami. Then you divorced Harold, right?'

'That's right. I never got along too well with Harold, but I always got along with Jerry because I didn't try to play the mother act with him. Jerry was too old for me to try that anyway, when Harold and I got married, and I'm not the maternal type. I got along with Jerry much better than Harold ever did, but then Harold was responsible for him legally.

'At any rate, when I got my divorce I also got the house – this one – as part of the settlement. Harold wanted a bachelor pad, so he asked me to keep Jerry, too. He gave me an extra two hundred a month in the agreement, so I let Jerry stay on. By that time Jerry and I were pretty good friends. He did pretty much as he wanted to do, and I didn't care. After he got his car, I didn't see him much. He got into a little trouble with the police, but his father always got him out of it. After he dropped out of school, he was sometimes away from the house for two or three weeks at a time. He ran around with a bunch in Coconut Grove, but he never brought any of them here. So to tell you the truth, Sergeant, I don't know all that much about what he was doing, or where he spent his time. But I wasn't legally responsible for him. I do know, or feel, that this place was a kind of a sanctuary for him. I never bugged him, and there was always food to eat here if he wanted to come home and eat it. Harold still sent me the two hundred every month, whether Jerry was here or not, even after Jerry turned eighteen.'

'Did you know that Jerry was on drugs?'

'I suspected it, but I wasn't positive. As I said, I wasn't legally responsible for –'

'Yes, you did mention that. Where did Jerry get his money to live on? Did he have a job?'

'Not lately. He used to get odd jobs now and then, at the Green Lakes Car Wash, and as a bag boy. He offered to help me once in the flower shop, but I turned him down. He wasn't a dependable boy, so I knew he wouldn't stay for more than a few days, and I didn't want to add another failure to his list. Harold mailed him a check once in a while, but that was after he quit school. While he was in school I gave him an allowance, but when he dropped out of school I stopped it. After his driver's license was suspended, he sold his car. He made about two thousand on the sale. But that was several months ago.' She ate the last bite of her pie. 'Anyway, it's all over with now, isn't it? Including my extra two hundred a month from Harold. That's what I wanted to ask you about.'

'What?'

'A favor. Somebody has to tell Harold about Jerry. And I just can't make myself do it. Would you call and tell him for me? I think he ought to be told soon, because it wouldn't be very pleasant for him to read about it in the papers or hear it on the radio.'

'Jerry's name won't be released to the papers until they've checked with us that his next of kin's been notified. The press is pretty decent about things like that. But I'll call him if you want me to.' Hoke got to his feet. 'Where does he live?'

'At the Mercury Club, in Hallandale. I'll get his number for you.'

Harold Hickey, Hoke thought, must have a bundle. The Mercury Club was right on the ocean, with tight security, and had its own small marina. The Mercury Club was still restricted, too: no Jews, blacks, or Latins. When all of the civil rights legislation was considered, it cost a great deal of money to keep a private club restricted nowadays.

Hoke dialed the number Mrs Hickey gave him. After two rings, a voice came on the line. The voice was deep and husky; each word was enunciated self-consciously.

'This is a recording. I am Harold Hickey, attorney at law. I am temporarily unable to answer the phone in person. In a moment or so, when I finish speaking, you will hear a tone. At that time, if you are so inclined, you may leave your name, phone number, and message. I will return your call at my earliest convenience.'

Hoke waited for the tone, and said: 'This is Detective-Sergeant Hoke Moseley, Homicide, Miami Police Department. Your son Gerald died this morning under peculiar circumstances. For additional information, call me after ten P.M. at my residence, the Eldorado Hotel, Miami Beach. Don't give up too quickly.' Hoke gave the number, then added, 'If you don't call me at the hotel, you can reach me at Homicide, Miami police station, tomorrow after seven-thirty A.M.'

Hoke racked the phone and turned away. Loretta had an expression of dismay. 'What was that all about? Were you talking to a recording?'

'He wasn't there, so I gave the machine the information.'

'Jesus! You told the recording Jerry was dead? I could've done that myself. Except that I'd never tell a recording anyone was

240

dead. That'll be a shock to Harold when he plays it back. The reason I asked you to call him in the first place was I thought you could do it gently.'

'There isn't any gentle way to tell someone that a member of his family's dead. The direct method's as good as any. Besides, if Mr Hickey was sensitive, he wouldn't have a recording answer his telephone for him. By the time he calls me back, he'll have had time to digest the news.'

'You don't know Harold.' She looked away, toward the bedrooms. 'But at least he didn't have to discover the body, the way I did.'

'I think the coffee may be ready.'

'Just a sec. I'll see.'

When Loretta returned with the coffee and cups on a tray, Hoke handed her the envelope containing $1,070 and asked her to count it. He then asked her to sign a receipt.

'This money's yours, or your ex-husband's. Or you two can split it. But you'd better tell him about it.'

Loretta Hickey nodded. 'Suppose those two men come back? They might say it's theirs.'

'If they come back, call me.' Hoke put his card on the table. 'Let me have your home and office number too.'

She gave him the numbers, and Hoke wrote them down in his notebook.

'Is this money evidence, Sergeant?'

'No. I've got a list of the serial numbers, and that's all I'll need. If I were you, I'd put the money into your night deposit at the bank.'

'I don't think I want to leave the house tonight. Can't you keep the money for now, and give it to me tomorrow at the shop?'

'I suppose.' Hoke put the receipt into the envelope with the money, and returned the envelope to his jacket pocket. 'Where do you work?'

'I have my own shop, the Bouquetique, a flower and gift shop in the Gables, on Miracle Mile. Do you know where it is?'

'I can find it, but I don't know exactly when I can get there. Did you make that name up all by yourself, or did you inherit it?'

'I made it up. It's a combination of bouquet and boutique.'

'I suspected that. What do you sell besides flowers?'

'Smart things. Gifts. Vases, ceramics, turquoise jewelry from New Mexico. Little things like that.'

'All right. I might have some more questions for you. Try and make a list of Jerry's friends – men and women – and I'll see you then. If I can't make it tomorrow, I'll call you. When was the last time you saw Jerry?'

'This morning – but you mean before that, don't you?'

Hoke nodded.

'About a month ago. He came by one night and got two shirts, but he only stayed for a few minutes. He was living in the Grove, but he didn't tell me where, and I didn't ask. Somebody drove him over and waited for him outside. He was only here a few minutes. He just got the shirts and left.'

'Who brought him – a man or a woman?'

'I don't know. I was working on some accounts here at the dining table, and didn't go outside with him when he left.'

'It doesn't matter. If you're pressed for money, I can leave you some of this thousand.'

'I'm not pressed for money, Sergeant. What makes you think that?'

'I didn't say I thought so.' Hoke smiled. 'I'm always pressed for money, so I guess I usually assume everybody else is, too. Meanwhile, if you think of anything else about your conversation with those two men, or if they pester you again, call me at the Eldorado Hotel in Miami Beach. I wrote the number on the back of my card.'

'The Eldorado? That's in South Beach, isn't it?'

'Right. Just off Alton Road, next to the condemned Vizcaya Hotel, on the bay side.'

'How can you possibly live in such a terrible place? If you don't mind my asking.'

'When I got my divorce, my wife got the house, the car, the furniture, the children, the weed-eater, my tankful of guppies – the same old story.'

'You're not married now, then?'

'No.' And you've got a very nice house, Hoke thought.

'Perhaps you can come over for dinner one night? I've still got all this food.'

242

'Why not?' Hoke finished his coffee and got to his feet. 'There'll be a post-mortem on Jerry, but we'll let you know when you can recover the body.'

'That's all right. Harold'll take care of all that. So tell him, not me. I don't think he'll want a funeral, but he'll probably call me about that.' She walked Hoke to the front door. 'How come, Sergeant Moseley, you live in Miami Beach, anyway? I thought it said in the paper that all the Miami police had to live in the city.'

'That's a long story, Mrs Hickey. I'll save it for another time. I don't think those men will come back, but keep the bolt on the door anyway, and if they do come back, don't let them in. Just call me instead. All right?'

'I will. Good night, and I'll see you tomorrow.'

'Tomorrow. And thanks for the tuna salad.'

The rain had stopped, and the dark clouds had moved west over the Everglades. Hoke drove cautiously on the still-slick streets. At eight-thirty there was enough light left to drive by without his headlights, because of Daylight Saving Time. But when he reached the MacArthur Causeway, Hoke turned on his lights anyway. Some people drove like maniacs across this narrow link to Miami Beach.

Hoke hadn't been laid in four months, and Loretta Hickey, all fresh and sweet-smelling from her shower, had made him horny. If he had stayed much longer, he might have made a move on her. But the timing wasn't right. Her emotions had been drained that morning. She had discussed Jerry as if he were a stranger. She had been coming on to him toward the end of their conversation, though. She knew how sexy she was in that thin floor-length robe. It was funny how some women were sexy and others were not. Ellita Sanchez, despite her ample bosom and good legs, didn't do it for him. But underneath, she probably smouldered. She was thirty-two, and still lived with her mother and father. He doubted if she had ever been laid. On the other hand, her bed was Cuba: The right man could fry an egg on her G-spot. Living at home that way, and saving her money, she would have one hell of a dowry for some macho Cuban to squander on a sexy mistress some day. At thirty-two, however, her chances of getting married in the Cuban community were negligible. Most of those Cuban girls were married by the time they were eighteen or nineteen. Ellita was no longer an old maid of twenty-five; officially, after thirty, she was a spinster.

Hoke parked in his marked slot in front of the hotel and glanced up at the electric sign. The neon spluttered, but it still spelled ELDORADO in misty rose letters. The shabby lobby was occupied by a half-circle of old ladies watching the flickering television, bolted and chained to the wall, and by four male Cuban residents playing dominoes at an old card table. By tacit consent, the live-in residents of the hotel kept to their own sides of the lobby. The only time the Cubans watched TV was when President Reagan, their hero, was on the tube. The noise at the card table stopped when Hoke crossed the lobby to the desk to check his mail. Eddie Cohen, the ancient desk clerk, was not behind the desk, and there was no mail in Hoke's box.

Hoke's thoughts kept returning to Loretta Hickey as he made his routine, if perfunctory, security check on each floor on his way up to his suite. After he made out his report for Mr Bennett, which he would leave on the manager's desk in the morning, Hoke undressed and took a tepid shower in his tiny bathroom. Thinking of Loretta Hickey again, and about how she must look under her robe, Hoke masturbated gloomily in the shower. Christ, he thought unhappily, I'm getting too old to jerk off this way. I've got to get out of this hole and find a place where I won't be ashamed to bring a woman.

Chapter Six

As usual, Hoke awoke without the aid of a ringing alarm at 6 A.M. It was a habit held over from his three years in the army. He invariably awakened at six, regardless of the hour he went to bed.

After his one year of junior college in Palm Beach, Hoke had enlisted for three years as a Regular rather than wait to be drafted. An R.A. man had an advantage over the draftees, and the Vietnam War had had little effect on Hoke, except that he probably wouldn't have enlisted in the army if it hadn't been for the war. He had spent three uneventful, but not unpleasant, years as an M.P. at Fort Hood, Texas. Most of that time had been spent at the front gate, saluting and waving cars on and off post. He had also pulled his share of guard duty, wandering around unlighted warehouses, but on the whole his had been a safe war. He had gone home twice to Riviera Beach, Florida, on leave, but spent his other furloughs in El Paso and Juarez, where he had some great times with his bunky, Burnley Johnson.

Hoke had never attended any of the army's special schools, which could have led to a promotion, nor had he applied for any. He made PFC when he completed basic training, and he was discharged as a PFC. He then went home to Riviera Beach, worked in his father's hardware and chandlery store for two years, and married Patsy, a girl he had dated at Palm Beach High School.

He finally quit at the hardware store when he realized that his father would never relinquish the management to him for as long as he lived. Hoke's salary was no larger than any of the other clerks', and Hoke's father, who had become wealthy from his real-estate investments on Singer Island (having bought up island property during the 1930s), refused to give Hoke a larger salary because he said it would smack of favoritism. The old man was tight, there was no question about that, but he had married an attractive well-to-do widow after Hoke's mother had died, and the two of them lived very well in a large house on the inland waterway.

Frank Moseley was seventy now, and he still went to the store every day. He had never given Hoke a share of the profits, nor did Hoke expect to get anything when he died. Hoke suspected that the bulk of the estate would go to the widow and to Hoke's two daughters, Sue Ellen and Aileen. The old man doted on his granddaughters, and Patsy was wise enough to drive down from Vero Beach often enough to maintain the old man's interest, yet not often enough to become a nuisance. Hoke had not seen his girls since Patsy divorced him and moved to Vero Beach. Patsy thought it would be better that way. The most recent photographs he had of the girls were from four years ago. He had never paid much attention to the children when they had lived together, Patsy said, and she didn't want their new lives upset by occasional, so-called duty visits.

Patsy was unfair in this regard, Hoke felt, but there was enough truth in what she said to discourage him from pursuing the matter legally.

Thanks to Hoke's M.P. background, limited though it was, he had no trouble getting into the Riviera Beach Police Department, and he and Patsy were happy enough during the three years he spent on the force as a patrolman. As a hometown boy – and a 'Conch' – Hoke got along well with people, and Riviera Beach, before the 1970s boom and the unforeseen development of condominiums on Singer Island, was relatively crime-free. Patsy kept busy with the children all day, and Hoke drove a patrol car, alternating between day and night shifts. During his off-duty time, he either fished or went to the beach at Singer Island, the widest and nicest beach on Florida's east coast.

One night Hoke stopped a speeding Caddy. The driver dismounted with a gun in his hand when Hoke approached the car, and Hoke shot the man without even thinking about it. There were three kilos of cocaine in the trunk of the Caddy. The driver had been killed instantly; Hoke was cleared almost immediately and received a commendation from the chief. The rest of his police work at Riviera Beach was routine.

A few months later, after three years on the Riviera Beach force, Hoke applied for and was accepted by the Miami Police Department. It had been pleasant living in Riviera Beach, and Patsy had some family there, too, but with the girls growing up, Hoke needed the larger salary he could earn as a Miami policeman.

It was difficult at first. Hoke made more money, but it cost more to live in Miami. To earn extra money, Hoke volunteered for overtime, and he always worked the football games on Saturdays and Sundays in the Orange Bowl during his off-duty time. He neglected Patsy and the girls, but after she started to nag him and make his life unpleasant at home, he spent even fewer hours there. He met Bambi, began an intense affair, and studied for the sergeant's exam in the downtown public library. The girls were noisy at home, and he couldn't concentrate. Then Patsy joined a neighborhood 'consciousness-raising' group, found out about Bambi, and their marriage was over.

Without any family obligations, except for endorsing and mailing every other check to Patsy, Hoke had prospered in the department. He had enjoyed his earlier work in Traffic and liked being a detective even better, especially after he was promoted to sergeant. But the life had taken a toll on his face.

Without his false teeth, Hoke looked much older than forty-two, and this morning, when he looked into the mirror, still thinking about Loretta Hickey, he wondered if she would ever be interested in him as a lover. She could hardly be interested, he thought, if she saw him without his teeth. His eyes were his best feature. They were chocolate brown, a brown so richly dark it was difficult to see his pupils. During his years in the Miami Police Department, this genetic gift had been useful to him on many occasions. Hoke could stare at people for a long time before they realized he was looking at them. By any aesthetic standard, Hoke's eyes were beautiful. But the rest of his face, if not ordinary, was unremarkable. He had lost most of his sandy hair in front, and his high balding dome gave his longish face a mournful expression. His tanned cheeks were sunken and striated, and there were dark, deep lines from the wings of his prominent nose to the corners of his mouth.

Hoke took his dentures out of the plastic glass where they had been soaking overnight in Polident, rinsed them under the faucet, and set them in place with a few dabs of Stik-Gum. He looked a little better, he thought, with the blue-gray teeth, and he always put his dentures in before shaving. One thing he knew for certain, he looked much trimmer and felt much better at 182 pounds than he had at 205.

The window air conditioner labored away while he dressed (today he wore the yellow leisure suit), and then he made a final check of the room to see if he had forgotten anything. Today was Friday, and his sheets wouldn't be changed until Saturday morning. The sitting room was a mess, and there was a pile of dirty laundry in the corner of the bedroom. The Peruvian maid would pick up his laundry when she changed the sheets and bring it back on Saturday evening. There was a sour, locker-room smell in both rooms.

Hoke checked his .38 Chief's Special, slipped it into his holster, and clipped the holster into his belt at the back. He would be reading most of the day, so he left his handcuffs and leather sap on the dresser before going down to the lobby.

As Hoke took his daily report into Mr Bennett's office, Eddie Cohen, the desk clerk, called to him from the desk.

'Sergeant Moseley,' the old man said, 'you had a call about three A.M., but I told the lady I couldn't wake you up unless it was an emergency. She said it wasn't an emergency, and she didn't give her name. But I wouldn't wake nobody at three o'clock in the morning for nothing.'

'Thanks, Eddie. What did she sound like? The caller, I mean?'

'Like a woman. It was a woman's voice, that's all.'

'Okay. If she happens to call back today, try and get her name and number. The plug on my air conditioner was pulled out again when I got to my room last night. I've told you before not to pull it out. The room was like a damned oven with the burners on high when I came home.'

'Mr Bennett sends me around to pull out the plugs when nobody's home. If no one's in the room, it just wastes energy, he said.'

'I understand your position, Eddie, but that rule doesn't apply to me. It takes about two hours for that beat-up air conditioner to cool off the suite. Also, tell Emilio to set some rat traps around the dumpster again. I spotted two Norways in the back corridor last night.'

'It ain't the dumpster they're after.' Eddie shook his head. 'These old ladies put their garbage in the hallways instead of taking it down to the dumpster.'

'Never mind. Have Emilio set the traps. I put it in my report to Mr Bennett. He can pay off the inspectors, but if one of these old ladies ever gets bitten by a Norway, they'll come down on us again.'

Hoke got into his car, wondering why he should be concerned. Within a week, he'd have to get out of the hotel anyway. He didn't know where he would be, but he would be somewhere else. With all of the money he owed, a suspension without pay would be a disaster. And any time his check to Patsy was more than a day late, he got a threatening call from her bitchy lawyer.

When Hoke got to the station at seven-thirty, he learned that Ellita was already there and had moved all of the cold case files down to the interrogation room. He sent her down to the cafeteria to get coffee and a jelly doughnut. He hadn't felt like poaching eggs, and boiling two more, on his hot plate this morning; now his stomach rumbled with hunger. He divided the huge pile into three more or less even stacks without counting them. He also got some legal pads and Bic ballpoints from his office. Sanchez returned with three coffees and Hoke's doughnut.

'Sergeant Henderson's still out there in the bullpen talking to Lieutenant Slater and Teddy Gonzalez,' she said, 'but I brought coffee for him, too. Are you going to brief Teddy on what we've been doing?'

'Gonzalez'll be busy enough as it is. For now, we'll hang on to our own cases. There's only the one child-abuse case and a suicide. We can complete them and handle the cold cases, too.'

'But Major Brownley said —'

'I know what he said. But there's no hurry on our pending cases. After we get the P.M., we can close out the Hickey overdose case, too. I talked to Mrs Hickey last night and found out that the kid was in over his head. Two guys came around yesterday afternoon and told her that Hickey had ripped them off for twenty-five thousand bucks.'

'There was only a thousand in his room.'

'I know. I'm giving it to her today. What I figure, Hickey stashed the money somewhere, and then was so excited by the idea that he gave himself a stronger fix than he thought he was getting.'

Ellita nodded. 'It could've happened that way. But Mrs Hickey could've also taken the extra twenty-four thousand and left the thousand on top of the dresser.'

'No.' Hoke shook his head. 'She wouldn't do that.'

'You told me yesterday that an amateur never takes it all, and that only pros take everything.'

'That's true as a general rule, but it doesn't apply to Mrs Hickey. I talked to her for a long time, and she isn't the kind of woman who'd steal from her stepson.'

'Jerry isn't her son?'

'No, she inherited him from her ex-husband, along with the house, when they got divorced.'

'It's a possibility, just the same.'

'No way. She's a successful businesswoman, with her own flower shop in the Gables. Forget about it. We've got a lot of work to do.'

Sanchez watched him and sipped her coffee.

Hoke took off his jacket and draped it over the back of the folding chair. He had been wearing the same short-sleeved flowered sports shirt for three days, and there were three concentric white rings of dried sweat under the armpits. He wouldn't have a clean shirt until Saturday evening. The windowless room was cool enough, with plenty of cold air coming through the ducts, but he realized that if he could smell the dried perspiration on his shirt, Ellita could, too. So what? He could smell her overdose of Shalimar perfume, with an extra overlay of added musk. Like most Cuban women, she used too much perfume.

'Just take a stack,' Hoke said, 'and read them all. When I get through my stack we'll exchange. After we've read all the cases, we'll each vote on the three most likely cases to work on. Then we'll see what we've got. Take your time, Ellita. My idea's to discover the ten most likely cases. If we all come up with the same ten, we'll have a consensus. But we won't look at each other's choices till we've each gone through all fifty of them. I don't want to prejudice you or Bill by telling you my choices as we go along.'

'You won't. But we won't get through all these cases today.'

Hoke shrugged. 'We've got two months. But the ones we do agree on, even if it takes us a week, will save us a lot of useless running around later.'

They went to work, not speaking, and taking occasional notes. Bill Henderson joined them at nine-thirty. Hoke briefed him on the plan, and Henderson moved his stack down to the far end of the table.

'That extra cup of coffee's yours, Bill,' Hoke said.

'Thanks, Ellita,' Henderson said, removing the plastic lid. He sipped the coffee and made a face. 'Christ, it's stone cold. I'll go down for some more. Anybody else ready for more coffee?'

'I'll get it,' Ellita said, getting up. 'I didn't think you'd be out there so long with Slater and Gonzalez.'

When she was gone, Henderson got up and sat on the table next to Hoke. 'I was already late this morning in the first place, and then I had to argue with Slater. He wanted me to go over tomorrow afternoon to Miami Beach and guard wedding gifts at a reception There's fifty bucks in it, less Slater's ten percent for giving you the job, but you have to wear your uniform. That isn't bad, Hoke, fifty bucks for drinking champagne for three hours while you just stand around. But I couldn't take it because I promised Marie I'd take her and the kids to the Metrozoo. Now, if you can use fifty bucks, Hoke, you could get the job if you asked Slater.'

'My uniform's too loose on me now, Bill. But I wouldn't take it anyway. When I made sergeant, I promised myself I wouldn't do any more moonlighting. I'm not uptight about it, and I could use the dough, but I resent Slater's ten percent rake-off. I've told him so, and that's why he never asks me to take any moonlighting jobs. So if I asked him for this one, he'd think I'd changed my mind.'

251

'I know what you mean. I was just passing along the suggestion. The other reason I'm late, I had to talk to my son this morning. I had a note from his P.E. coach that Jimmy won't take a shower after P.E.'

'How old is Jimmy now?'

'Fourteen. I asked him about it, and he said he doesn't want the other boys looking at his thing.'

'Is it too big or too small?'

'I don't know. He won't show it to me either. But he was stubborn about it, so I gave him a note to take to the coach, telling him that Jimmy has scabies. I said he couldn't take showers until he got through using sulfur ointment to get rid of it.'

'He'll have to take a shower sooner or later.'

'I know. But Jimmy's sensitive, Hoke. Daphne's a year younger, and she's tougher than he is. If they'd let her, she'd take a shower with the boys in Jimmy's place.'

'That's because your wife's in NOW. Does Marie let Daphne read her *Ms* magazines?'

'Daphne doesn't read anything. And she hasn't learned a fucking thing in school. Last week, she asked me when we were going to have the next Bicentennial celebration. She still reads at the third-grade level. But she isn't dumb. She can watch a mystery on the tube, and tell you who the guilty person is before the first commercial. I thought she might have dyslexia, but I had her tested and her eyes are okay. She just doesn't like to read. But Jimmy's read my entire Doc Savage collection already, and most of my Edgar Rice Burroughs Mars books.'

'I don't know whether my daughters can read or not.'

'Do you ever miss 'em, Hoke? The girls?'

'No. I mean, I do once in a while ... but I don't. They were real little when they left, and I didn't know them that well. I'm just not a family man.'

The three of them worked until eleven-thirty, and then Hoke checked his in-box in the office. There were two phone messages to call Harold Hickey, in addition to the regular distribution. The second telephone message from Hickey said he would be at home all day. There were no lab reports, and nothing pressing to answer in the mail.

252

Hoke told Henderson and Ellita that he was going out for a few hours, and suggested that the two of them break for lunch.

'I should be back before four o'clock, but I've got some house-hunting to do.'

'Don't rush into anything, Hoke,' Henderson said. 'If push comes to shove, I can always put you up on a cot in my Florida room for a few days.'

'Thanks, Bill, but I don't get along too well with Marie, as you know. She's always accusing me of making a sexist remark, and I never know what she's talking about.'

'I didn't mean on a permanent basis. But it would be better to sleep in my Florida room for a few days than to get a suspension without pay.'

'Thanks, Bill. If I have to take you up on it, I will. Anyway, if I'm not back by four-thirty, lock the files up in my office and we'll start on 'em again Monday. Until we start work on an actual case or two, we'll just put in a normal eight-hour day.'

'I might come in tomorrow for a couple of hours,' Ellita said.

'That's up to you. But you don't have to – anyway, I should be back before four.'

Hoke left the office and drove to Hallandale, but he took U.S. 1 instead of the I-95 Expressway. About once a month, when Hoke had to be in the north part of town, he stopped at Sam's Sandwich Shoppe for a tongue on rye. Hoke didn't abuse the privilege (once a month was just about right), but he liked to stop at Sam's because Sam always tore up his lunch check. Not only was the sandwich free, but except for Wolfie's in Miami Beach, Sam made the best tongue sandwiches in Dade County.

Chapter Seven

The guard at the sentry box outside the Hallandale Mercury Club wore a powder-blue uniform, a gold cap with a black bill, and a shiny black-patent-leather Sam Browne belt, complete with holster. There was no weapon in the holster. The man held a Lucite clipboard in his left hand and a one-ounce paper cup of Cuban coffee in his right. Droplets of coffee from the guard's thick mustache had dribbled onto the light blue jacket.

Hoke stopped at the lowered black-and-yellow-striped semaphore arm. The guard looked at his clipboard, and at his coffee, then put the cup down, realizing that he would need his right hand to write on the pad in the clipboard.

'Ramon Novarro,' Hoke said, 'to see Mr Harold Hickey.'

The guard looked at his mimeographed sheet, found Hickey's name and apartment number, and wrote 'R. Novarro' opposite Hickey's name. He checked Hoke's auto tag number, added that to the clipboard, and pushed a button that raised the arm.

'Apartment 406,' the guard said.

Hoke drove through the gate, parked on the grassy verge, and walked back to the gatehouse. The compact complex of clubhouse and three separate low-rise apartment buildings was enclosed by a buff-colored ten-foot wall. The wall was topped with three strands of barbed wire. Two locked gates on the ocean side, opening to the marina and the beach, were marked 'Members.' Hoke assumed that members held keys to both gates.

'How do you know,' Hoke asked the guard, 'that my name's Ramon Novarro?'

'What?'

'I said, "How do you know my name's Ramon Novarro?" You didn't ask me for any ID. You didn't look very hard to see if I was armed, either.' Hoke took his .38 out of the belt holster, showed it to the guard, and returned it.

'In fact,' Hoke continued, 'you don't know who I am, or who I'm going to see. All you know is that Harold Hickey has an apartment here, and you knew that much before I drove up to the gate. Why didn't you call Mr Hickey and tell him that a Mr Ramon Novarro was here to see him? He might've told you that Novarro is dead, and has been dead, for several years.'

Hoke showed the guard his shield and ID folder. 'I'm a police officer. How much they pay you, three sixty-five an hour?'

'No, sir. Four dollars.'

'For what you aren't doing, that's a good sum.'

Hoke got back into his car, drove to the guest parking area in front of the clubhouse, and made a guess. If the three buildings were each three stories, and they were, Apartment 406 should be in Building Two on the first floor. He was right. He lifted and dropped the brass knocker on Hickey's front door three times. The door was opened by a Filipino houseboy, actually a wizened man of about sixty wearing pink linen trousers, a gray silk house jacket and a white shirt with a black bow tie. He led Hoke down the hallway, past the living room, and into Hickey's den-office. The living room and the den were furnished with black leather and chrome armchairs and glass-topped tables. Hickey was seated in a black leather, deeply cushioned armchair. As Hoke came in, he got to his feet and switched off the television. Hickey wore a purple velour running suit and a pair of white rabbit-fur slippers. The air conditioning hissed quietly, and Hoke figured it was well below 65 degrees.

Hickey smiled, revealing expensively capped teeth, and the smile made him almost handsome. His black hair was worn long, in a modified Prince Valiant cut, but the youthful effect was spoiled by a baseball-size bald spot at the crown. Hickey was tall and lean. His nails had been buffed and polished, and there was a gold University of Miami ring on his left hand.

'I just got a strange call from the gate guard.' Hickey smiled. 'Words to the effect that a dead policeman was on the way to see me.'

'Did he tell you his name?'

'Ramon Novarro. Wasn't he the actor who was killed by a hustler a few years ago?'

'He's dead, but I don't remember the circumstances. I remember seeing some of his films, from when I was a kid, but none of the titles. He was always running someone through with a sword.'

'No matter. Sit down, Mr Moseley. Would you like a drink?'

'A Tab.'

'Two Tabs,' Hickey said to the doorway. 'You are Mr Moseley, aren't you?'

Hoke nodded. 'I was testing your gate guard. You people pay for security, but you don't get very much.'

'I know. But a gate guard is a deterrent, if nothing else. We used to pay more for armed guards, and then one night a Nicaraguan guard at the gate shot a hole in the manager's car. The manager thought all the guards knew him, but he didn't take the turnover into account. So when he drove through the gate without stopping, a new guard took a shot at him. After that, we decided it would be best to have unarmed guards.'

Hoke sat in a leather chair that faced the sliding glass doors to a bare travertine-marble patio. There were two potted spider palms on the patio, but no chairs. Hoke pointed toward the patio with his chin.

Hickey smiled. 'I never use my patio. If I feel the need of some sun, I go over to the pool by the clubhouse. That's why there's no furniture out there.'

'No. I was just thinking you don't have much of a view from here, with the wall only twenty feet away.'

'I didn't buy this place for the view. I bought it because I could finally afford to live in a place like this. I tried to call you last night, twice, but I didn't get an answer. You said on the phone that –'

'I'm sorry about that. There's only one desk man at the Eldorado, and when he's not at the desk there's no one on the switchboard. I'm sorry you couldn't get through. It's been inconvenient for me, too, at times. At any rate, when I called you from Mrs Hickey's house, I didn't know at the time who you were. Later on, I remembered that you were one of the drug lawyers profiled in the paper a few months back.'

'An inaccurate portrait. I handle drug cases once in a while, just like any other lawyer, but I specialize in taxes. Lately, I've been turning down drug cases. The dealers can afford my fees, but they think they can get off simply because they've paid a large fee. I always tell them in advance that I can get a few delays, or get them out on bond, but if they're guilty, they're going to do a little time. Things have changed a lot down here, you know, with the Vice President's task force on drugs.'

The houseboy brought in two cans of Tab; each can was wrapped neatly in a brown paper towel, with the towel secured by a rubber band. The houseboy left, and Hoke removed the straw. He noticed a crude black-and-white drawing on the wall above Hickey's computer table.

'Is that an original Matisse?' Hoke asked, lifting his Tab.

'James Thurber. It's a woman. That thing in her hand is either a martini glass or a dog collar, I've never been able to decide which.'

'Looks more like a bracelet to me.'

'Yes, it could very well be a bracelet.'

Hoke sipped from the Tab. 'I suppose you phoned Mrs Hickey last night?'

'When I couldn't get you, yes.'

'You know that Jerry died from an overdose of heroin?'

Hickey nodded. 'That's what she said.'

'What I'd like to know is the kind of relationship you had with your son, Mr Hickey. How close you were to him, for example; whether you were the stern father, or what?'

'Why? What's that got to do with Jerry's death?'

'I don't know. It occurred to me last night that he might've met some of your clients, your drug dealers. If so, he could've made a connection through them, or one of them. He'd been on drugs for a long time.'

'Jerry never met any of my clients. He never came to my office because it was off limits to him. To be frank, we didn't have any relationship, not of the sort you mean. In the first place, Jerry wasn't my real son. I suppose you know that already.'

'Your wife told me.'

'Ex-wife. Did Loretta also tell you how she happened to become my ex-wife?'

'No. But I didn't ask.'

'I found out she was fucking Jerry, that's how. He was seventeen at the time. I don't know how long it had been going on, but as soon as I found out about it I moved out. I didn't really care. In fact, it was a good excuse to get a divorce. She couldn't fight me about something like that in court, so we obtained a simple no-fault divorce. I made some concessions I didn't have to make, but a man always has to do that if he doesn't want to be distracted. I was just getting into making some big bucks, so I wasn't hurt financially. She got the house, of course, and one of the cars.

'Legally, you see, I got stuck with Jerry when my first wife divorced me. Jerry was her son, and I was asshole enough when we first got married to adopt him. So not only did I get rid of Loretta, I got rid of Jerry at the same time when my divorce came through. It was a good deal all the way around.'

'Except, perhaps, for Jerry.'

'Jerry had no complaints. He had a place to live, and no one ever hassled him. Loretta didn't want to keep him, but she couldn't very well get out of it. What happened between them wasn't any love affair, or anything close to it. She'd been drinking one day, and I suppose she got a little horny. Jerry, who was seventeen, happened to be available. It happened a few more times, I suppose. You know how it is, once you get it, you can always get it again. But it was all over by the time I found out about it, I'm pretty sure.'

'How'd you find out? It's none of my business, but I'm curious.'

'Mrs Koontz, the next-door neighbor, told me. I didn't believe her at first, but then when I questioned Jerry he admitted it right away. "I didn't think you'd mind, Mr Hickey," he said. And of course I didn't mind, because then I had an excuse to get out of a bad marriage.'

'Your son called you "Mr Hickey"?'

'Most of the time, yes. I didn't want him to call me "Dad" because he wasn't my real son. I don't see anything wrong with that. After all, I supported him, so I was entitled to a little respect.'

'Yours wasn't exactly a loving relationship then?'

'He got some love from Loretta.' Hickey smiled. 'He admitted it, and so did Loretta after I confronted her with his confession. I made him put it in writing, in case she wanted to fight the divorce.'

'How'd Jerry get on the spike without you finding out about it?'

'I did know about it. I recognized the signs right away. I advised Jerry to get off drugs at once. I also told him I'd pay for drug counseling. But he claimed he could handle it, and that was that. A lot of young people are into dope down here, you know.'

'I know.'

'I don't even smoke pot. But Jerry could get drugs anywhere in the city in five minutes, so long as he had the money.'

'But you gave him the money.'

'I gave him a small allowance after he quit school, but I advised him to finish high school. And I told him I'd put him through college. But when he dropped out of high school, I lowered his allowance. In this state, a father's no longer responsible for a child after he reaches eighteen. But I would've sent him to college. No one ever helped me.' He leaned forward in his chair. 'I put myself through the University of Miami by washing trays at night in the old Holsum Bakery in South Miami. And I did maintenance work to get a free efficiency apartment. No one ever gave me a fucking penny. Miami offers a young man more opportunities than any other city in the United States. If you want to get ahead down here, you take advantage of them. Jerry fell by the wayside. It's not society's fault, and it's not Reagan's, and it's not mine.' Hickey, sitting back, started to yawn; he put a hand to his mouth. 'Excuse me. But this is a sore point with me. Every day, if you look at the women's section of the paper, you'll see articles blaming the parents for the way their kids turn out. It's all bullshit.'

'It isn't easy to always know the right thing to do, I suppose. But then, I'm not a family man.'

'When can I get the body? I'd like to send somebody over to get Jerry cremated.'

'After the autopsy. I can recommend Minrow's Funeral Home, if you don't have anyone else in mind.'

'What do you get? A ten percent commission?'

Hoke didn't mind the question, not from a Miami lawyer. As it happened, Hoke didn't get any commission, but he usually recommended Minrow when someone asked, because he and Minrow had been neighbors when Hoke first moved to Miami. If he denied getting anything, Hoke knew that Hickey would merely consider him a fool.

'No,' Hoke said. 'I just get a flat fifty bucks for each referral.'

'Okay. I'll call Minrow's and mention that you recommended him. It makes no difference to me.'

'At one time,' Hoke said, getting to his feet, and placing the empty Tab can on the glass-topped desk, 'there was a number you could call in Miami, and a man would come by in a taxi cab. You paid him five bucks and he took the body away and you never heard of it again. But I don't think that number's in service any longer.'

'Is that the truth, Mr Moseley, or are you trying to be funny?'

'Sergeant Moseley.' Hoke pointed to a framed blue-and-green oleograph on the opposite wall. A blue man playing a violin floated upside down above a white house in a green sky. 'Is that one of Jerry's crayon drawings, from when he was a kid?'

Hickey shook his head. 'No, it's a Marc Chagall.' He leaned forward and switched on the television. A commercial touting the new aviary at the Metrozoo appeared on the screen, and Hickey turned off the sound.

'I like the picture anyway,' Hoke said, turning in the doorway. 'Just one more question, Mr Hickey, and I'll be on my way. Did Jerry ever carry any large sums of money for you?'

Hickey got to his feet. He shook his head. 'No. I never wrote Jerry a check for more than a hundred dollars at a time. The most money he ever had was when he sold his car. I paid four thousand for his Escort, and he sold it for only two. He should've gotten a lot more than that.'

'That almost always happens. You always pay more for a car than you sell it for.'

'I know that. But I should've kept the title so he couldn't've sold it at all.'

'We all make mistakes sooner or later, Mr Hickey. Thanks for the Tab.'

The Filipino appeared and escorted Hoke to the front door.

Chapter Eight

As Hoke drove back toward the city after cutting over to I-95, he wondered why he had wasted time talking to Harold Hickey. Hoke wasn't fond of lawyers, especially lawyers like Hickey who managed to get low bonds for their drug clients and then advised them to skip the country to avoid prison. On the other hand, someone had been furnishing Jerry with money. Jerry's father gave him an allowance, but he wouldn't have given the kid a thousand dollars. A thousand bucks for a drug dealer, on the other hand, was small change. And now that he was dead, the missing $24,000 was gone forever. It was possible that Jerry had been a small-time pusher in the Grove to help him support his own habit. But it still bothered Hoke that an experienced user, with a large sum of money and more drugs available, would take a deliberate overdose, or even OD accidentally. It just didn't fit the pattern.

Hoke returned to U.S.1, and then stopped at an Eckerd's drugstore to buy a package of Kools. After he paid for the ciga-rettes, he showed the clerk his shield and asked if he could use the telephone. Since the pay phone rates had jumped from a dime to a quarter a few years back, Hoke, as a matter of principle, had never paid to use a phone again. He called Ms Westphal at the house-sitting service. When she answered after the first ring, Hoke identified himself and asked if she had found any more prospects for him.

'I'm now willing,' he said, 'to take a short-time sitter's job, even if it's only a couple of weeks. How about that apartment on Grove Isle?'

'That's gone. I've got a garage apartment on Tangerine Lane in the black Grove. It'll be available next Friday for twenty-one days. It's owned by a Barbadian sculptor who's going up to New York for a one-man show. He uses the garage under his apartment as his studio, and he doesn't want his tools and things left unguarded.'

'That's right in the middle of the black Grove, isn't it?'

'Not exactly in the middle. It's off Douglas a few blocks. But you're a policeman, and you've got a gun, so it shouldn't bother you to live in a black neighborhood.'

'I told you I couldn't be there much in the daytime, except for weekends.'

'Daytime doesn't bother Mr Noseworthy. The man who lives in the house in front'll be home during the day.'

'That's a pretty funky neighborhood, Ms Westphal.'

'Listen, Sergeant, I think you're a little too finicky for this kind of work. Perhaps you should look for another agency –'

'No, no, I'll take the garage apartment. Of course, I'd like to look at it first.'

'There's nothing to see. It's got a bed, a sink, a hot plate and a refrigerator, and you use the bathroom in the house in front of the garage. There's no dog, if that's what's bothering you. If you don't want it, I can easily get a black house-sitter for a furnished apartment like this one.'

'Okay, I'll take it. I'll drop by one day next week for the key.'

Ms Westphal gave Hoke the address and reminded him to bring a hundred dollars for the bond when he came by for the key.

'If you could give me my hundred-and-five-dollar salary in advance,' Hoke suggested, 'you could just hang onto the hundred for the bond and pay me five dollars.'

'You're very droll, Sergeant.' Ms Westphal laughed and hung up the phone.

Hoke returned to his car. Major Brownley, he knew, would recognize the address in the black Grove and would wonder why in the hell he had moved there. He didn't want the major to know that he would be living rent-free as a house-sitter. He wondered if the Bajan sculptor had a phone. If not, he would have to make some kind of arrangement with the neighbors to take his phone calls. The problem was, in that neighborhood, not many people could afford a phone. He'd just have to wait and see. Moving, at least, was no problem. Except for a cardboard box full of his files and old papers, all he had to move were his clothes and his little Sony TV. And his hot plate; he'd better take his hot plate. Even if Noseworthy had one, Hoke would probably need his own for the next move, although he could hardly move down any lower than a garage apartment in the Coconut Grove ghetto. Yes, he could; the Overtown ghetto was worse.

When Hoke returned to the station, he stopped for a moment to say hello to Bill and Ellita and then he checked his mail. There was a printout on Gerald Hickey. Hoke sat in his office and read the rap sheet, which went back to Jerry's junior-high-school days.

In the eighth grade Jerry had gotten into a fight with a black student, claiming that his lunch money had been taken. A knife had been confiscated, but neither boy had been cut. No charges filed, but the officer who had been called by the principal had made a written report of the incident.

There were two separate arrests for 'joyriding' in stolen cars. Jerry was merely a passenger each time, and stated he didn't know the car – in each incident – was stolen. No charges filed.

There was another arrest when a woman claimed Jerry had exposed himself to her while standing on her front lawn. The misdemeanor was reduced to committing a public nuisance when Jerry claimed he had merely stopped to urinate on the woman's lawn. Although the incident happened at 3 P.M., Jerry said he didn't see the woman sitting on her front porch ten feet away. Charge dismissed. Counsel for Jerry had been Harold Hickey.

Arrested for smoking marijuana, with two other juveniles, in Peacock Park, Coconut Grove. Charge reduced to loitering. No charges filed. Released to father's custody.

Two more pickups for 'loitering' in Coconut Grove. No charges filed. Released at station.

Picked up in a Coral Gables parking lot. A glasscutter confiscated. Jerry claimed he found the glasscutter in the street, and that he didn't know what the tool was used for. No charges filed.

Picked up in the parking lot, Sears, Coral Gables store, for shoplifting. Subject's father paid for the item – a brass standing lamp, complete with parchment shade, with a blue eagle painted on it. Released to father's custody. No charges filed.

There was also a brief report from an interview with a psychiatric social worker:

Hickey, Gerald. Age: 16 – 4 mos. 68 inches tall. Wt. 147 lbs. Adopted. I.Q. (Stanford/B) 123. Intelligent, but rambles when asked direct questions. Sociopathic personality. Schizoid tendencies; unrealistic goals, i.e., wants to be 'Russian interpreter at U.N.' or a 'marine biologist.' Suppressed sexual anxieties. Admits to hustling gays for money, but not always 'successful.' Smokes pot daily. Mixes codeine with pot, but doesn't use PCP. Cooperative. Despite sociopathic attitude and quick temper, Jerry would probably thrive in a disciplined environment, e.g., live-in military school. Father can afford it. Therapy recommended.

s/t M. Sneider, MSW

Not much. Hoke wished now he had read the file before he talked to Harold Hickey. He could have asked him why he hadn't sent Jerry to a military school. Of course, at a military academy, a weak kid like Jerry would have been cornholed by the upper classmen, but they would have kept him off the spike. On the other hand, this was about the time of Hickey's marriage to Loretta, so Harold might have thought that she would be a stabilizing factor for Jerry. But that was speculation. Not a single overnight stay in Youth Hall or jail. In a legal sense, Jerry wasn't a juvenile delinquent officially. To become a bona fide juvenile delinquent, a kid had to be charged, found guilty, and the case adjudicated. If Jerry had been pushing dope, he had managed to avoid ever being apprehended for it.

Hoke phoned the lab and asked if they had completed the report on the contents of the Baggie that Sanchez had sent for analysis. He was promised a report for Monday, Tuesday at the latest.

'Make it Monday,' Hoke said and hung up.

It was only three o'clock, and he should take the money to Loretta Hickey. But there were all those files to be read. Henderson and Sanchez would have made a dent in them by now, and he would have to catch up. Hoke looked up the number of the Bouquetique in Coral Gables, then wrote it in his notebook before dialing.

A childish, incredibly high voice answered. 'Bouquetique. How may I help you?'

'Mrs Hickey, please.'

'She's designing in the back. May I help you?'

'Just take a message. Tell her that Sergeant Moseley will be in to see her tomorrow.'

'Sergeant Moseley?' the tiny voice chirped.

'That's right. You are open on Saturday, aren't you?'

'Oh, yes! Saturday's our busiest day.'

'Okay. I don't know what time, but it'll be some time tomorrow.'

Hoke hung up the phone. The voice sounded like a little girl around six or seven years old, he thought. Why would Loretta Hickey employ a child to answer the telephone? Hoke went to join Bill and Ellita in the interrogation room.

Bill and Ellita were sitting close together at Bill's end of the table. Both were studying material from the same accordion file. Hoke lighted a Kool, but before he could sit down, Bill held up an eight-by-ten black-and-white glossy photograph.

'Remember this guy, Hoke?'

Hoke looked at the photo and grinned. It was a picture of an unsmiling middle-aged man – a head-and-shoulders shot – wearing an open-collared polo shirt.

'Captain Midnight.'

'That's right,' Bill said. 'Captain Morrow. I was telling Ellita about him. He was the pilot we called Captain Midnight. We must've talked to him a half-dozen times three years ago.'

'He was clean.'

'He wasn't clean. He was eliminated as a suspect because we couldn't prove anything. Anyway, I'd been looking at his file just before Ellita and I went over to have lunch at the Omni. Otherwise, I don't think I'd have recognized him. The fucker was sitting on the bus bench at the southwest corner of Biscayne when we went in, and he was still sitting in the same place when we came back to get the car. But if I hadn't just been looking at his photo here, I wouldn't've recognized him. He's a bum now, Hoke. On a hunch, I sent Ellita over to talk to him because I figured he might recognize me. She asked him if he'd missed his bus, and he told her he was waiting for his wife.'

'His wife's dead,' Hoke said. 'Her head was smashed in by a four-pound sledgehammer. He was our only suspect, Ellita, but we finally suspended the case.'

'He did it, Hoke, I know he did,' Bill said.

'We think he did it. We couldn't ever prove it, Bill. He passed the polygraph without a tremor. I know the machine can be beat, but in his case, if he did kill her, the indications were that he didn't know he'd killed her. After he passed the test, we had to drop it altogether.'

'According to your notes,' Ellita said, 'he didn't have any reason to kill his wife. They'd only been married a year, and the neighbors claimed they were a happy couple. He didn't need money – not as a pilot earning fifty thousand a year.'

Hoke sat down and flipped through the papers in the file. 'We should be reading the other cases. We can vote on this one later if you want, if you want to put it on your list. But right now we should follow my plan.'

'Tell him, Ellita,' Henderson said.

'He was very confused, Sergeant Moseley,' Ellita said. 'I tried to talk to him, ask him a few more questions like "Are you sure your wife's bus stops here?" and he just repeated what he said the first time. Finally, he got angry. He said, "You aren't my wife," and walked away.'

'I signaled Ellita to go get the car,' Bill said, 'and I tailed him. He lives over on Second Avenue, down from the old Sears store, in Grogan's Halfway House, or what used to be the halfway house. It's just a rooming house now. Grogan lost his license and his city funds when the bag lady starved to death on the front porch. Do you remember that, Hoke?'

'Yeah. It was a legal problem. There was no law to cover it, although the paper wrote an editorial on the case. What happened, Ellita, was weird. There were about ten guys staying at the halfway house at the time. All of them were on parole, but some had jobs and others were on a methadone program and just lived there. Do you remember the bag lady case at all?'

'No. How long ago was it?'

'Seven or eight years. I don't remember exactly. Anyway, this old lady climbed onto the porch when it was raining. She was run down, physically, like most bag ladies, and she just lay there for four days. The guys in the halfway house, including Grogan, had to step over her for the first day or so, and then she managed to crawl over to the wall. The point is, no one helped her or gave her any food or water. She was too weak to move, so she just died there. Finally, after she died, someone told Grogan the woman was dead, and he called the rescue squad to pick up her body. When he was asked why he didn't call them the first day she showed up on the porch, he said he didn't mind her lying there. She didn't bother anybody, he said, but he would've called the police if she'd tried to come inside the house. When they were questioned, the parolees in the halfway house all claimed that they didn't see anything wrong with a woman lying out there, moaning, on the porch.'

'And so Grogan lost his license for the halfway house?'

'Yeah, but not for that. If someone comes up on your front porch to get out of the rain, you can let him do it out of the goodness of your heart. That person isn't your personal responsibility. But a lot of people in town were pissed off because the old lady died. Four days is a long time. So housing inspectors were sent out, and they yanked Grogan's license for faulty wiring and drainage problems.'

'But Grogan's house is still there, Hoke,' Henderson said. 'Only now his place is a rooming house, and that's where Captain Morrow lives. Ellita picked me up in the car, and we came back here. I went over his file and I think we should talk to Captain Midnight again. The man owned a hundred-thousand-dollar home, he had money in the bank, and he was an airline pilot. Where did all of that go in only three years? He looks like he's been on the street for months. And he looks at least twenty years older than he did the last time we talked to him. If he's sitting around on a bus bench waiting for his dead wife, he's confused and disoriented. Maybe he'll admit now that he killed her if we lean on him a little. The time to kick a man, Hoke, is when he's down. You know that.'

'Maybe he was waiting for a new wife. He could have gotten married again, you know.'

'Tell him, Ellita,' Henderson said. 'Did he look like a married man to you?'

'No one would marry a bum like that. He's a sick man, not a drunk, not talking to himself or anything like that, more like a man lost somewhere in his own thoughts.'

'Let's go talk to him, Hoke,' Henderson said. 'You know he's guilty and so do I. If we can crack a case on our first day, Willie Brownley'll shit his pants.'

'Okay. But let me look at the file for a minute.'

Everything in the file led to Captain Robert Morrow as a prime suspect. After dinner he had left his house, he said, to get a package of cigarettes. While he was at the 7-Eleven, he drank a cup of coffee, a large one, and talked to the Cuban manager. His house was only two blocks away, and he was gone for only twenty minutes – twenty-two minutes at most. When he returned home, he found his wife in the kitchen. Someone had taken his four-pound sledgehammer from the garage and hit his wife over the head with it while she was washing pots and pans at the sink. Death was instantaneous, with a hole in her skull big enough to hold an orange. From the way it looked, she hadn't known what hit her. The sledgehammer, without prints, was on the floor beside her body. When he discovered her body, Captain Morrow had telephoned 911 and waited outside on the front lawn until the police arrived, smoking two of the cigarettes from the package of Pall Malls he had bought at the 7-Eleven.

He had shown little or no emotion about his wife's death, but he had explained that to Hoke and Henderson. 'After two years in 'Nam, I don't find the sight of a dead body particularly upsetting,' he had said.

He had understood his Miranda rights, but he talked freely anyway, without a lawyer present. 'I didn't do it,' he claimed. 'If you charge me, I'll get a lawyer, but I can't see paying a lawyer who'll just tell me to remain silent. I haven't done anything to remain silent about.'

Hoke and Bill had talked to the neighbors, to the Morrows' friends – they didn't have many acquaintances – and Mrs Morrow did not, apparently, have any enemies. Nothing had been stolen from the house, not even the three-thousand-dollar diamond ring that Mrs Morrow had taken off her finger before washing the pots and pans. The ring was still on the counter right next to the sink.

What had bothered Hoke and Bill most, however, was why Captain Morrow had gone to the 7-Eleven to buy cigarettes. He had a carton of Pall Malls, with only two packs missing, in his dresser drawer. Also, there was a pot of coffee in the Mr Coffee machine in the kitchen. The pot was half full, and the red light on the base of the coffee maker showed that it was still warm enough to drink. He had, for some reason, lingered in the convenience store, establishing an alibi with the manager before returning home. Two witnesses had seen him on his walk to the store and back, but that merely confirmed that he had been in the store.

The case had been frustrating. Hoke and Bill had talked to Morrow several times. At one point, Hoke had advised him to confess and to plead 'post-Vietnam stress syndrome,' which would mean, in all probability, a lighter sentence or a commitment of a year or two to a psychiatric hospital.

'I didn't do it,' Captain Morrow said. 'And I don't have any stress problems. If I did, they wouldn't have me flying a 707 back and forth to Rio.'

After the pilot passed the lie detector test, they had put the case away, pulling it out occasionally only to take another look at it. But there were no more leads, and it looked as though Captain Morrow had managed to get away with murder.

'Why not?' Hoke said. 'It won't hurt to talk to him again. Bill and I will do the talking, Ellita. But you check out a micro-cassette recorder from Supply and keep it in your purse. Just record everything that's said, and don't get too close to him. You got handcuffs, Bill?'

Bill nodded.

'I didn't bring mine today. I didn't think I'd need 'em.'

Chapter Nine

From the looks of Grogan's rooming house, an ocher concrete-block-and-stucco two-story structure on Second Avenue, very few repairs, if any, had been made since Grogan had lost his city contract to run a halfway house. The unpainted concrete porch, almost flush with the cracked sidewalk, held two rusty metal chairs. They were occupied by two aging winos. There was no rail, and as soon as Hoke, Henderson, and Ellita stepped onto the porch, the winos stepped off the other end of the porch and started briskly down the street. Hoke wore high-topped, lace-up, double-soled black shoes, which gave him away as a cop if his face did not. Henderson usually reminded people of a high-school football coach. Ellita, of course, although she wore sensible low-heeled black pumps, was not so obviously a police officer. Today she wore a red-and-white vertical-striped ballerina-length skirt with her cream-colored silk blouse.

A black-and-white TV crackled in the living room, but although the set was on, no one was in the room to watch it. There were some battered chairs of wicker, and a low coffee table piled high with old *Sports Illustrated* and *Gourmet* magazines. There was a sign on the wall saying 'Thank you for not smoking,' and there were no ashtrays in the room; nevertheless, there were more than a dozen cigarette butts ground into the scuffed linoleum floor.

The landlord was in the kitchen. He was sitting at a table by the window, overlooking a backyard that contained a wheelless 1967 Buick on concrete blocks, a discarded and cracked toilet, and a pile of tin cans. The backyard was enclosed by a wooden fence, but only the top third of the fence was visible because of the jungly growth of tall grass and clumps of wild bamboo. The proprietor, a gray-haired man in his mid-sixties, was eating a bacon-and-fried-egg sandwich.

Hoke showed the man his badge. 'Are you Mr Grogan?'

'You're looking at him. Reginald B. Grogan. What can I do for you, Officer?'

'We'd like to talk to Captain Morrow.'

'No Captain Morrow here. People come and go, but I haven't had a boat captain here since I lost the methadone people.'

'He's an airplane captain. A pilot.'

'No pilots either. Never had one of them. People here now are mostly day laborers, although a couple are on Social Security. But no Morrow.'

Henderson showed Grogan the photograph of Captain Morrow but pulled it back when Grogan reached for it. 'Your fingers are greasy. Just look at it.'

'You can't eat a bacon-and-egg sandwich without getting a little grease on your fingers.' Grogan peered at the photo, squinting. 'That looks something like Mr Smith, but Mr Smith's a lot older than that.'

'Smith?' Hoke said.

'John Smith. Lives upstairs, last door on your right down the hall. Right across from the john.' Grogan bit into the sandwich, and a trickle of undercooked yolk ran onto his chin.

'Mind if we talk to him?' Hoke said. 'We don't have a warrant. We just want to talk to him.'

'Sure. Go ahead. I'm eating my second breakfast now, or I'd show you up. Besides, my fingers are greasy. But you can't miss his room. It's right across from the john. He's paid up through Sunday, but I don't know if he's in or not.'

Upstairs, the house had been modified by plywood partitions to make ten small bedrooms out of four larger ones, but the bathroom at the end of the corridor had not been altered. Two dangling unshaded light bulbs, one of them lighted, illuminated the narrow corridor. The door to the room across from the bathroom was closed. Hoke tapped on the door. No answer. He tried the knob, then opened the unlocked door.

John Smith, *né* Robert Morrow, was sitting on the edge of a narrow cot. He was using a metal TV table as a desk, and was writing with a ballpoint in a Blue Horse notebook. He looked up when the three detectives entered the room, but there was no curiosity in his face or eyes. His disheveled gray hair needed cutting, and he hadn't shaved in several days, but he wasn't dirty. His khaki work pants and his blue work shirt were both patched, but they were clean. He tapped his right foot, and as he did so the upper part of the shoe moved but the sole did not, because it was detached from the upper. The room was about eight feet by four, and a four-drawer metal dresser, painted to look like wood, completed the furnishings. Because the room was at the end of the building it had a window, and the jalousies were open. The tiny room was filled with light from the afternoon sun. With four people in the room, it was very crowded. Bill stood in the open doorway. Ellita moved to the dresser and leaned against it. Hoke smiled as he bent over and put out his right hand to shake Morrow's. Morrow shook hands reluctantly.

'It's good to see you again, Captain,' Hoke said. 'Do you remember my partner, Sergeant Henderson? That's Ms Sanchez over there. She was talking to you earlier –'

'She was harassing me, and I had to leave my bench. But I've got no complaints against her. A man can't just sit in his room all the time. But it's quiet here in the daytime, so I usually work here anyway. If you don't mind, I'd rather you'd all go away.'

'What kind of work are you doing?' Hoke said.

'You can remain silent if you want to,' Bill added. 'What you say could even be held against you.'

'That's right,' Hoke said. 'You don't have to tell me anything.'

'That's a fact,' Bill said, loud enough for Ellita to get it on tape.

Hoke rubbed his chin. 'If you've got enough money, you could have a lawyer present.'

'He doesn't need any money, Hoke,' Bill said. 'If he can't pay, we can get him a lawyer free.'

'This is a benevolent state.' Hoke smiled. 'The government will pay for a lawyer if you're broke. Do you understand?'

'Why do I need a lawyer?' Morrow frowned. 'I haven't done anything illegal.'

'It's just that we don't know what you're working on,' Hoke said. 'Maybe it's legal and maybe it isn't.'

'My system,' Morrow said, compressing his lips, 'isn't for sale!' He closed his notebook and slid it under the slipless pillow. He crossed his arms in front of his chest.

'It looks to me,' Hoke said, glancing around the room, 'like your system, whatever it is, isn't working. You seem to be living under – what's the term? – reduced circumstances, Captain. The last time we talked to you, about three years ago, you were living in a nice neighborhood with a swimming pool in your backyard.'

'That's because they changed the wheels on me. My system is foolproof, but they got onto me and rigged the wheels.'

'When did you invent your system?' Bill asked from the doorway. 'Before or after you killed your wife?'

'Before. Frances just didn't understand, that's all. I told her we could become millionaires within a year or so, but she wanted me to keep flying. She didn't have faith in me. She wouldn't let me resign from the airline, or even take an extended leave of absence. And she refused to sign the papers so I could sell the house.'

'We always wondered why you killed her, but could never come up with a motive,' Hoke said. 'Let me take a look at your notebook for a moment. I promise not to use your system.'

'You can believe Sergeant Moseley, Captain Morrow,' Henderson said. 'He's got his own system.'

'He couldn't understand mine anyway.' Morrow shrugged. 'Even if I explained it, you still wouldn't understand it. Look at the note-book all you like.' He handed Hoke the Blue Horse notebook.

Hoke paged through it. There were long columns of figures on each page, with the arabic numbers written as small as possible with a ballpoint pen. The numbers 36, 8, 4, and 0 were circled on each page.

'You're right, Captain,' Hoke said, passing the notebook to Henderson. 'It's too complicated for me.' Henderson riffled through the pages, shook his head, and returned the notebook to Morrow.

'If we promise not to use it, will you explain some of it to us?' Hoke said.

'Do you promise?' Morrow narrowed his eyes.

Henderson raised his right hand, and so did Hoke.

'I promise,' Hoke said.

'Me, too,' Bill said.

Morrow pointed to Ellita. 'What about her?'

'I won't tell anyone either,' Ellita said, raising her right hand. 'I promise.'

Morrow wet his lips. 'It's too complicated for a woman to understand anyway. Frances couldn't understand it, and I tried my best to explain it to her.'

'Is that why you killed Frances?' Bill asked. 'Because she was too dumb?'

'Frances wasn't dumb!' Captain Morrow raised his voice. 'She was a receptionist for a lawyer when I met her, and she had a high-school diploma. But mathematics are beyond a woman's comprehension. They're too emotional to understand arithmetic, let alone logarithms. Here, let me show you.' Morrow opened his notebook and pointed to the vertical columns of figures. 'It's not that hard to understand, not if you have the patience. Even you two men should be able to grasp the basics. You bet the eight and the four three times, then you bet thirty-six five times. Meanwhile, you watch the Oh, the house number. The Oh and the double-Oh are both house numbers, but the single Oh is the one you watch. If the Oh doesn't come up during your first eight bets on the three numbers, then you start to play the Oh only, and double up until it hits. Four, eight, and thirty-six come up more often than any of the other numbers, and I can prove it by my notebook. So you'll break even, or pull ahead a little while you wait for the Oh to miss eight times. After eight times, the Oh's odds change, and it only takes a few turns of the wheel, doubling up, before it hits. Then, what you've done, you've made a nice profit for the day. If you play my system every day, betting with fifty-cent chips, you'll earn about five hundred dollars a day. No one understands roulette any better than I do.'

'Where'd you play roulette?' Hoke said. 'Nassau?'

'Aruba. After I sold my house I moved to Aruba and rented a little beach house. I just rented it. I could've bought it, but I didn't. Sometimes, when the wheel wasn't right – it's dry in Aruba, but there's more humidity some days than others, and humidity affects the wheel, you see – I'd fly over to Curaçao. I'd play the casinos there. But I liked Aruba best. I had a housekeeper, and learned enough *Papiamento* to tell her what I wanted for lunch and what to get at the store. I got up late, swam some, ate lunch, took a nap, and then had another swim. Then I would eat dinner at one of the hotels, and play in the casino till midnight. I put in a six-hour working day, and my system worked fine. When I won five hundred, I quit for the day. Otherwise, on slow days, when I only won two or three hundred, I still quit after putting in six hours of play. After six hours, it's hard to maintain your concentration, you see.'

'You must've made a lot of money,' Bill said.

'I did. But then something happened. What I think is, they got onto me and changed the wheels or something. I started to lose, but it wasn't my system's fault. My system's foolproof. All you need is concentration and patience. One mistake, one bet on the wrong number out of sequence, and it won't work. And that's what I don't understand. I never varied from it. Before I took my leave of absence from the airline, I'd already tested the system in Nassau, in San Juan, and in Aruba, you see. I'd fly deadhead down there and spend a weekend in the casinos. It never failed me, and that's what I tried to explain to Frances. I *hated* flying. Flying a plane's the most boring job in the world, and roulette was our ticket out. But Frances just couldn't understand.'

'But your wife was two months pregnant,' Hoke said. 'Maybe she wanted the security your job offered her?'

Morrow snorted. '"There is no security," General Douglas MacArthur once said, "there's only opportunity." Besides, I told her there'd be no problem in Aruba with the baby. It would be just as easy to get an abortion in Aruba as it was in Miami. Or, if she wanted to, I told her, she could have her abortion in Miami, and then join me later in Aruba.'

Ellita started to cry. She didn't make a sound, but tears rolled down her cheeks. Hoke and Bill looked at her, and then at each other.

'Excuse me,' Ellita said, breaking in sharply. 'But I've got to go to the bathroom across the hall. Would you guys mind waiting till I get back before you go on? I don't want to miss any of this conversation, and I ... I think your system's brilliant, Captain Morrow.'

Captain Morrow smiled, and got to his feet. 'Not at all.' He sat down again as Ellita left the room and closed the door behind her.

'Did you lose it all, Captain?' Hoke asked.

Morrow nodded. 'I think we'd better wait for the little lady. She said she didn't want to miss anything.'

'Sure.' Hoke nodded. Henderson broadened his metal-studded smile, and then offered Morrow a cigarette.

'No thanks. I don't smoke.'

Ellita opened the door, and took her place against the dresser. 'Thanks for waiting,' she said.

Morrow nodded and pursed his lips. He looked blankly at Hoke.

'Did you lose all the money?' Hoke said.

Morrow nodded. 'Except for a thousand dollars I left here in Miami. I've been living on that. They wouldn't extend my leave of absence, so next week I've got to find another flying job somewhere and get requalified. Then, when I get another stake together, I'm going to Europe. But this time I won't stay so long in one place. I'll go to Monte Carlo for a few days, and then to Biarritz. The system works on any roulette table, so long as they don't change the wheel.'

'You won't have to go back to flying again, Captain,' Henderson said, unhooking his handcuffs from his belt. 'We're going over to the station now, and then, after we get your confession typed and you sign it, about eight years from now – it takes about eight years for all the appeals, right, Hoke?'

'About eight years.' Hoke nodded.

'About eight years from now,' Bill went on, 'they'll burn your gambler's ass in the electric chair.'

Bill handcuffed Morrow's hands and pushed him toward the doorway. Ellita snapped her purse closed.

'Can I have my notebook?' Morrow asked.

'Sure.' Hoke picked up the notebook, unbuttoned the top button of the pilot's shirt, and dropped the notebook in.

Then, while Henderson and Sanchez escorted Morrow to the car, Hoke got six dollars back from an unhappy Grogan (for the two nights' rent Morrow had paid in advance), gave the landlord a receipt, and added the six dollars to the thirty-seven dollars left in Morrow's wallet.

Chapter Ten

Bill Henderson had Captain Morrow handcuffed to the desk in Hoke's office. While Ellita typed a condensed confession for Morrow to sign, Hoke telephoned Major Brownley at home.

'It isn't necessary for you to come down, Willie,' Hoke explained. 'I'll get an assistant state attorney over here and get Morrow booked for first degree.'

'Is he dangerous? I mean, dangerous to himself? If he is, you'd better have him locked up in the psycho cell at Jackson.'

'He's disoriented, but not suicidal. Altogether he lost more than two hundred thousand bucks, including the insurance money he collected on his wife. Losing the money's just about all he can think about. Everything else seems irrelevant to him now, and the confession's just a minor annoyance. If we put him in a psycho cell, it might weaken the case. I think the best thing to do is just book him and then let the judge decide whether he wants a psychiatric evaluation or not. Morrow didn't ask for a lawyer, but I called the public defender's office anyway, and they're going to send someone over. But the confession'll be signed before anyone gets here. Sanchez has just about got it typed now. Besides, we still have his confession on tape.'

'You read him his rights?'

'It's on the tape.'

'You did a good job, Hoke.'

'Henderson spotted him, not me. It was just a fluke, Willie, a lucky accident. We didn't even know Morrow was back in the city. So I don't think it's a good idea to put out any PR about our special assignment yet. Hell, we haven't finished reading through the cases you picked out.'

'The papers'll pick up on it soon, Hoke. Morrow's wife was pregnant when he killed her, and reporters love stuff like that.'

'But we can still release this first one as just another routine case for the division. Later on, if we get lucky again, we can fill them in on the cold-case business. So why not just say we've been working on this case for a long time, which we have, and let it go at that?'

'Okay. If the public defender gives you any flak, have him call me. I'll be home all evening.'

Hoke went down to the cafeteria and got four cups of coffee. By the time Hoke got back to the office, Morrow's confession was signed, all five copies, and had been notarized by the division secretary. Ellita and Henderson had signed it as witnesses.

The assistant state attorney was a happy man, but the public defender, a young woman who had passed the bar recently, was not. If they had called her in time, she complained, she would have advised Captain Morrow not to sign the confession.

'Why not?' Hoke said. 'We had it on tape anyway, and this makes it easier to follow.'

'Are you going to ask Captain Morrow any more questions?'

'No. All we need to know's in your copy of the confession. But if we do, we'll call you first, now that you've advised him to remain silent.'

'You guys think you've got away with something, don't you?'

'The important thing is that Morrow didn't. He killed a young woman of twenty-five who was carrying his child. She never did any harm to anyone, and she didn't deserve having her head crushed by a sledgehammer just so this sonofabitch could gamble away their savings.'

'He's unbalanced now, and he had to be insane at the time of –'

'Maybe so, but if you plead him not guilty by reason of insanity, he'll fry for sure. I'd advise you to plead guilty to second degree and let him take a mandatory twenty-five years. But I don't care what you do. Right now, unless you want to talk to him some more, we're taking him over to the jail.'

Hoke told Ellita to lock up the cold cases in the office and go home. He and Henderson would take Morrow to the lockup.

Henderson took Morrow's arm and guided him out of the office. Ellita got to her feet, blocking Hoke from the door. 'Did you people say anything while I was out of the room at Grogan's?'

'No, but I didn't think it was very professional for you to take a side trip to the can in the middle of an interrogation.'

'It was all I could think of to do,' Ellita said. 'The battery in the recorder went dead, so I had to get out of the room to change it, that's all.'

'Did you have an extra battery?'

'Of course.'

'Okay, then. That's professional. Did you get it all on tape?'

'Everything, if you didn't talk while I was out of the room.'

Hoke patted her awkwardly on the shoulder. 'You did the right thing, Ellita. Go on home.'

On the way to the Dade County Jail in the car, Morrow cleared his throat. 'I signed the confession, the way you wanted and all, so I'd like to ask you guys a favor.'

'Sure, Captain,' Henderson said. 'What can we do for you?'

'Well.' Morrow licked his lips. 'I'd appreciate it if you guys didn't tell the airline about this matter. If they found out I was a gambler, they'd put the word out on me, and I'd never get another crack at flying again. Airlines are like that. They consider gambling as obsessive behavior, you know, and if it ever gets on your record, they won't rehire you as a pilot.'

'I won't tell the airline,' Bill said. 'How about you, Hoke?'

'I won't tell 'em either.'

'Thanks,' Morrow said, 'thanks a lot.' Relieved, he sat back and studied his notebook until they got to the jail.

It was after 11 P.M. when Hoke got back to his suite at the Eldorado. He was exhausted from the long day, and he was hungry. He heated a can of chunky turkey-noodle soup on his hot plate and sat at his small Victorian desk to eat it out of the pot.

Above the desk there was a painting of three charging white horses pulling a fire wagon. There was a brass chimney on the back of the wagon, spewing white smoke. The nostrils of the horses flared wildly, and the crazed eyes of the horses showed whites all around. Hoke liked the picture and never tired of looking at it when he sat at the small desk. The little sitting room was busy. The previous tenant, an old lady who had lived in the suite for twelve years before her death, had furnished the room with small items she had picked up over the years at garage sales. There was a mid-Victorian armchair stuffed with horsehair, and a Mexican tile-topped table holding Hoke's black-and-white Sony TV. There were several small tables on long spindly legs (tables that are called either wine or cigarette tables), and each table held a potted cluster of African violets. There was a patterned, rose-colored oriental rug on the floor (a Bokhara, and quite a good one), but it had faded over the years and was spotted here and there with coffee and soup stains. On flat surfaces, including the built-in bookcases, there were abalone ashtrays, stuffed and clothed baby alligators, seashells, and a black, lacquered shadow box on the wall contained several intricately intaglioed mezzusahs, including one that had been made from a cartridge used in Israel's Six Day War with Egypt. There was more than enough room on the bookshelves for Hoke's books: Except for a copy of *Heidi* (overlooked by Patsy when she left him), Harold Robbins's *A Stone for Danny Fisher*, and a *Webster's New Collegiate Dictionary*, Hoke didn't keep any more books in his collection. When he bought and read an occasional paperback novel, he dropped it off in the lobby so that one of the guests could read it.

There were purple velvet draperies for the single window, but they were pulled back and secured by a golden cord so they wouldn't interfere with the efforts of the laboring window air conditioner. The walls were crowded with pictures, watercolors of palms and seaside scenes for the most part, but Hoke's second-favorite picture was a copy of *Blue Boy*, with the boy's costume fashioned of real parrot feathers. Each fluffy blue feather had been painstakingly glued in place by someone, and when a breeze from the air conditioner reached the picture and ruffled the feathers, the figure shivered. The face, however, was not the boy in the original picture, but a photograph of Modest Moussorgsky's head, scissored from an encyclopedia, complete with the composer's magnificent mustache. The walls were papered with pink wallpaper, and dotted with tiny white *fleurs de lis*.

The bathroom was also small, but the sitz-bath tub had a shower as well. There was also the little windowless bedroom. Most of the bedroom was taken up by a three-quarter-sized brass bed, but there was still room enough for an eight-drawer walnut dresser. The closet was roomy enough for Hoke's old uniforms and blue serge suit, and he kept a cardboard box of his papers in the closet as well.

This small suite was Hoke's sanctuary, and he was reluctant to leave it. Not only was it rent-free, it was home. He wondered if Mr Bennett would let him take the *Blue Boy* and the fire horses when he left, and decided that he would not. If the pictures were removed, they would leave lighter-colored square spaces on the wallpaper, and would have to be replaced with others.

After washing the small boiler pan and the spoon in the bathroom basin, and putting the utensils back in the high-boy drawer, Hoke bundled up his laundry, wrapping it all in his yellow leisure suit jacket. The Peruvian girl, a maid with no English, would pick up his laundry in the morning, including his gray sheets, and have it all back to him by Saturday night. She would wash and iron his two poplin leisure suits, put them on hangers, and by Monday morning he would be all set for another week's work.

Hoke took a long shower, put on his last clean pair of boxer shorts, and decided to watch *The Cowboys*, an old John Wayne movie he had seen before and enjoyed. He poured the last two ounces of his Early Times into a glass, added water from the basin tap, and put the empty liter bottle into the wicker wastebasket under the desk. He drank half the drink and turned on his Sony before sitting in the Victorian armchair. The telephone on the desk buzzed.

It was Eddie Cohen. 'I hope I didn't wake you …'

'I wasn't asleep. Who's calling?'

'No one's calling. It's these two girls. There're two girls down here, and they say you're their father.'

'What?'

'I thought they was kidding me at first, and I told them you wasn't married. Then one showed me your picture, and it's you all right, wearing a police uniform.'

'Two girls?'

'Teenage girls. They don't look nothin' like you, Sergeant. But they say they're your daughters. You want me to bring 'em up, or do you want to come down?'

'I'll be right down.'

Hoke put on a pair of khaki Bermudas, a gray gym T-shirt, and slipped into his shoes without putting on any socks. There were no clean black socks left in the drawer. He put his wallet and ID case and badge into his pockets, and slipped the holstered .38 into the belt at his back. His keys were on the desk, and he dropped them into his right front pocket. He went into the bathroom, put his dentures in, and quickly combed back his thinning hair.

In the elevator down, he recalled the 3 A.M. phone call from the woman Eddie had told him about. That must have been Patsy, he thought, but she had claimed it wasn't an emergency. If sending his daughters down to Miami in the middle of the night wasn't an emergency, what would Patsy consider an emergency? But then, maybe the caller hadn't been Patsy. Something was up.

The desk was well lighted by overhead fluorescent tubes, but most of the lamps in the lobby had been switched off. The TV set was dark, and there were no Cubans playing dominoes. On Friday nights, the resident Cubans went out to nearby bars to spend their weekly paychecks. Sometimes, when they got drunk and brought women back, Eddie Cohen had to call Hoke to quiet them down, since the resident pensioners were usually in bed by nine or nine-thirty.

The two girls, both wearing shorts, T-shirts, and tennis shoes, were standing by the desk. Hoke wouldn't have recognized either of the girls on the street, but he figured that the taller girl was Sue Ellen, and the smaller was Aileen. Despite Cohen's observations, the girls bore a greater resemblance to Hoke than they did to their mother, now that Hoke had a look at them. They both had Hoke's sandy hair – an abundance of it – and Sue Ellen had an overbite. With her mouth closed, her two upper teeth rested on her lower lip, where the teeth had left permanent tiny dents. Both girls were slim, but Sue Ellen was well rounded at the hips, and she needed the brassiere she was wearing under her 'Ft. 'Luderdale' T-shirt. Aileen was more gangly, with a boyish figure, and there were no adolescent chest bumps yet beneath the thin cotton of her T-shirt. They weren't pretty girls, Hoke thought, but they weren't plain either.

Aileen's generous mouth was filled with gold wire and tiny golden nuts and bolts. Her teeth were hardly visible, because the places that weren't covered by gold wires were concealed by stretched rubber bands. She wore a black elastic retainer, with the cords stretched across her cheeks, and headphones, with a cord leading down to a Sony Walkman on her red webbed belt. Both girls appeared a little anxious. Sue Ellen looked down at the photo in her hand, and then looked back at Hoke again before she favored him with a tentative smile.

'Daddy?'

'You're Sue Ellen, right?' Hoke said, shaking her hand. 'And this is Sister.' Hoke smiled at the younger girl.

'We don't call her that anymore,' Sue Ellen said.

'Aileen,' the younger girl said. She shook hands with Hoke, and then backed away from him. But Hoke didn't let her get away. He hugged Aileen, and then hugged Sue Ellen.

Hoke turned to Eddie Cohen, who was grinning behind the desk. 'These are my daughters, Eddie, Sue Ellen and Aileen. Girls, this is Mr Cohen, the day man and the night man on the desk, and the assistant manager.'

'How do you do,' Sue Ellen said. Aileen nodded and smiled, but didn't say anything. She took off the earphones and switched off the radio.

'Where's your mother?' Hoke said.

'She should be in L.A. by now,' Sue Ellen said. 'She tried to call you, she said, but couldn't get ahold of you. But I've got this letter …' Sue Ellen took a sealed envelope from her banana-shaped leather purse and handed it to her father.

Hoke unsealed the envelope, but before he could remove the letter, a Latin man of about thirty-five or -six pushed through the lobby doors, shouting as he approached the desk. 'What about my fare? I can't wait around here all night! I gotta get back to the terminal.'

'Did you girls fly down from Vero Beach?' Hoke said.

Sue Ellen shook her head. Her curls, down to her shoulders, swirled as she looked toward the cab driver. 'We came down on the Greyhound. We got into Miami about seven, and we tried to call here a couple of times' – she looked at Eddie Cohen – 'but no one answered the phone. We had a pizza, and then we went to a movie. Then, after the movie, we decided to take a cab over here.'

'You girls shouldn't be wandering around downtown Miami at night. Don't ever do that again.'

'We were all right. We checked our suitcases in a locker at the bus station before we went to the movie.'

The suitcases were next to the desk: two large Samsonites and two khaki-colored overnighters.

'What about my fare?' the cab driver said. He was wearing a white dress shirt, with the sleeves rolled up to his elbows, and tattered blue jeans. There were blue homemade tattoos on the backs of his dark hairy hands. He put his hands on his hips and pushed his chin out.

'How much is it?' Hoke said.

'I'll have to take another look, now. The meter's still runnin'.'

'I'll go with you. Eddie, wake up Emilio and have him take a folding cot up to my room – and the girls' suitcases.'

'I've got some empty rooms on your floor,' Eddie said.

'I'm aware of that.' Hoke shook his head. 'But Mr Bennett would charge me for them. The girls'll stay in my suite.'

Hoke followed the driver outside, reached through the window, and punched the button to stop the meter. The charge on the meter was $26.50.

'How long you been waiting?' Hoke asked.

The driver shrugged.

Hoke looked into his wallet. He had a ten and six ones. Hoke showed the driver his shield and ID. 'I'm Sergeant Moseley, Miami Police Department. I'm going to inspect your cab.'

Hoke opened the back door and looked inside. The back seat had a small rip on the left side, and there were three cigarette butts on the floor. All of the cab's windows were rolled down.

'Did you turn on the air conditioning when the girls got into the cab?'

'No, but they didn't ask.'

'That's a Dade County violation. You're supposed to turn it on when passengers get in, whether they ask for it or not. The floor's dirty in back, and the seat's ripped. Let me see your license.'

After exploring his wallet, the driver reluctantly handed Hoke his chauffeur's license. It was expired.

Hoke, holding the license, jerked his head toward the lobby. 'Let's go inside. Your license has expired.'

At the desk, Hoke got a piece of hotel stationery, a ballpoint, and took down the man's name, José Rizal, and license number, and the number of his cab. 'If you came across the MacArthur Causeway, José,' Hoke said, 'a trip from the bus terminal wouldn't have been more than ten or eleven dollars. So you must have come over to Miami Beach by way of the Seventy-ninth Street Causeway to run up a tab of twenty-six bucks.'

'There was too much traffic on Biscayne, and I couldn't get on the MacArthur.'

'Bullshit.' Hoke returned the driver's license and handed him six one-dollar bills. 'I don't have my ticket book with me right now, but if you'll come by the Miami police station on Monday morning, I'll pay you the rest of your fare and write out your ticket for the county violations and your expired license.'

For a long moment the driver stared at the bills in his hand, and then he wadded them into a ball and put them in his pocket. He turned abruptly and walked to the double doors. At the doorway the cabbie turned and shouted:

'Lechon!'

He ran out the door, got into his cab, and spun the wheels in the gravel as he raced out of the driveway. Hoke knew that he would never see the driver again.

'Did he cheat us, Daddy?' Sue Ellen asked.

'Not if you enjoyed your unguided tour of Miami Beach.'

Hoke then opened and read the letter from Patsy:

Dear Hoke,
I've had the girls for ten wonderful years, and now it's your turn. I'm going out to California to join Curly Peterson. We're going to get married at the end of the season. The girls were given a choice, and they said they'd rather live with you instead of with me and Curly. Perhaps they'll feel differently later, and can spend the Xmas season with us in California.

Anyway, you can take them for the next few months, and if they don't come out to Glendale at Xmas-time, I'll see them when spring training begins again in Vero Beach. It's about time you took some responsibility for your girls, anyway, and even though I'll miss them and love them, they want me to have my share of happiness and I know you do, too.

I'm pretty rushed right now, getting ready to leave, but I'll send down their shot records and school records and the rest of their things before I catch my plane. Whatever else you were, you were always responsible, and I know that our girls will be happy and safe with you.

Sincerely yours,
Patsy

Sue Ellen took a package of Lucky Strikes out of her purse, then searched in the clutter for her Bic disposable lighter.

'Let me have one of your Luckies,' Hoke said. 'I left my pack upstairs.'

Sue Ellen handed him the pack, lit her cigarette, and then Hoke's. He returned her package.

'Who's Curly Peterson?' Hoke said.

'That's the man Mom's been living with – you know, the pinch hitter for the Dodgers. Sometimes he plays center field. She met him two years ago when the Dodgers came to Vero for spring training. He just renegotiated his contract, and he'll get three hundred and twenty-five thousand dollars a year for the next five years.'

'How much?'

'Three hundred and twenty-five thousand a year.'

'That's what I thought you said. I remember the name vaguely, but I can't picture anyone named Curly Peterson. I don't follow baseball much anymore. There're too many teams anyway.'

Aileen looked at the floor and made a circle on the carpet with her right foot. 'He's a black man.'

'He isn't *real* black though,' Sue Ellen said. 'He's lighter than a basketball.'

'Just the same,' Aileen said, 'he's a black man.'

'He isn't as dark as Reggie Jackson. They both gave me auto-graphed pictures, so I can prove it.'

'He's mean, too,' Aileen said, still looking at the floor.

'Curly isn't really mean, he's just inconsiderate,' Sue Ellen argued, 'as Mom said. He's had a lot on his mind, renegotiating his contract and all.'

Hoke's mind was frozen. For a moment, he had difficulty in getting his thoughts together.

'What's his batting average?' Hoke said, clearing his throat.

'Two-ninety, and he's got a lot of RBI's.'

'That's pretty good for a pinch hitter. He took you to all the games, did he?'

'We had passes to all the spring-training games in Vero.'

'Do you like baseball?'

'Not particularly. And we didn't like Curly either. But Mom's gonna marry him, not me.'

'Why don't you like him?'

'Well, one time he was having his lawyer and his agent over to dinner, and he told Mom he wanted everything just so. Me and Aileen helped, cleaning the house and all, and Curly came over early to check everything over. We vacuumed, dusted, and even washed the fingermarks off the doors. Then Curly took out his Zippo lighter, got up on a chair, and flicked his lighter in the corner of the ceiling. When he did that, the spiderwebs in the corner turned black and you could see them. You couldn't see 'em before, but the smoke from the lighter turned 'em black, you see. He didn't say nothing about how nice the rest of the house looked. He just showed us the cobwebs, and said, "You call that clean?" Then he went off with Mom in the kitchen.'

'It was a mean thing to do,' Aileen said.

'That wasn't the only awful thing he did, Daddy,' Sue Ellen said. 'That's just a sample. But I didn't mind too much because, if you didn't take it personally, it was kinda funny. I guess I didn't like Curly because he didn't like us – me and Aileen, I mean. We were in his way. He was there to see Mom, not us, but there we were, always hanging around. We were just a big nuisance to Curly.'

'Do you girls know what's in this letter?'

287

Sue Ellen shook her head. 'No, but I don't want to read it. On the bus coming down, me and Aileen agreed that we weren't going to be played off between you two.'

Hoke put the letter back into the envelope. 'What did she say to you when you left?'

'Not much. Just that we were to come down here, and not to talk to anyone. That she'd send the rest of our things down later. She was so excited that Curly actually sent for her, she didn't say much of anything. Mom wouldn't admit it, but I don't think she thought Curly'd ever ask her to marry him. But when he did, she couldn't get out of Vero fast enough.'

Eddie came down the hall from the dining room, which had been closed for years and served now as a catchall storage room. He was carrying a folding canvas cot by its webbed handle.

'Emilio's not in his room,' Eddie said. 'I'll get you some sheets and towels.'

'That's okay,' Hoke said. 'I'll get the sheets, and put the cot together when I get upstairs. You'd better stay down here with the switchboard.'

Hoke got the sheets and a thin cotton blanket from the linen room, as well as bath and face towels. Hoke and the girls took the suitcases, the cot, and the linen upstairs in the elevator.

'This is an awful big hotel to only have one old man like Mr Cohen working,' Aileen said.

'It's only half full now, but even so, the Eldorado's got the smallest staff on the beach,' Hoke said. 'But the dining room's closed, and so's the kitchen. Only permanent residents live here, and if they want any maid service, they have to pay extra. Not many of them can afford to pay extra, so we only have two maids during the daytime. Emilio does all the maintenance, like cleaning the corridors and taking care of the yard. He's a Cuban, a Marielito, so Mr Bennett gives him a free room for the work he does, but no salary.'

'How can he eat with no salary?' Sue Ellen asked.

'Tips. And he also has some kind of a government refugee allowance, too.'

Hoke made up the brass bed with clean sheets and gave the bed and the cotton blanket to the girls. He had to move the Victorian chair and two spindly tables in the sitting room to make room for the cot. The girls, who were used to having their own beds, didn't like the idea of sleeping together. They argued about who would sleep on the outside; neither girl wanted to sleep next to the wall. Hoke realized that they were tired and irritable, as well as excited, but he finally told them to shut up and go to sleep.

But Hoke couldn't sleep. There was no mattress, and the canvas cot was stiff and uncomfortable. He was also too worried to sleep. When he moved to that small garage apartment in the Grove ghetto, could he take the girls there, too? He wanted a drink, and considered walking over to Irish Mike's, where he could drink on his tab, but he decided against it because the girls might wake up, wonder where he was, and get frightened.

It was a rotten trick for Patsy to send the girls down to him without any warning. If Curly Peterson – Hoke's mind froze again momentarily – was making $325,000 a year and didn't want the girls around, why couldn't the ballplayer cough up enough money to put them into a private school somewhere?

Unable to sleep, Hoke slipped on his khaki shorts again and took the elevator to the roof. There was a duckboard patio on the roof, and at one time there had been a bar as well, but very few residents came up to the roof now. Hoke looked across the bay at the Miami night skyline, which was beautiful at this distance. A warm wet breeze came from the ocean, and it felt good on his bare back. To his right, Hoke saw the lights on the four small islands that made up the connecting links for the Venetian Causeway. Straight ahead was the dotted yellow line of light bulbs of the MacArthur Causeway. On his left, farther south, Hoke could see the lights of Virginia Key and Key Biscayne. He lit a Kool, and remembered the old joke that had circulated after Nixon sold his house on Key Biscayne.

'What's the difference between syphilis, gonorrhea, and a condominium on Key Biscayne?'

'You can get rid of syphilis and gonorrhea.'

But more to the point, how could he get rid of these two darling but unwanted girls – at least until he got straightened out? In the morning, he would call his father. Frank had four bedrooms in his big house on the inland waterway in Riviera Beach. Maybe the old man would take them for the summer, or even for a month or two until he could work something out. Even two weeks would help a lot. By that time, maybe he would have a decent place to live in Miami. But now, with the two girls, he would need at least a two-bedroom apartment, or maybe a small house in a safe, quiet neighborhood. Next Friday was payday, and his next paycheck was supposed to go to Patsy – then he felt a little better, a swift surge of relief. Now that Patsy had sent him the girls, the agreement was canceled. Finished.

Feeling a little better, but not much, Hoke butted his cigarette for later, went back to his canvas cot, and fell asleep.

Chapter Eleven

Hoke took the girls to Gold's Deli for breakfast. It was only two blocks away, so they walked. On their way over to Washington Avenue, Hoke pointed out the dilapidated condition of the old apartment houses and small hotels, and explained that there had been a moratorium on new construction for several years because there was supposed to be a master plan for complete redevelopment. But no redevelopment funds came through, so the owners of the buildings made only enough repairs to satisfy the fire marshal. He also told them to notice the population mix; young Latins and old Jews predominated.

'South Beach is now a slum, and it's a high-crime area, so I don't want you girls to leave the hotel by yourselves. If you had a doll, and you left it out overnight on the front porch of the hotel, it would probably be raped when you found it in the morning.'

Both girls giggled.

'Maybe that's stretching it a little, but between First and Fourteenth Street, South Beach is not the real Miami Beach you see in the movies. If you were looking out the window of the cab last night, and paying attention, you'd've noticed the difference. North of Sixteenth there are tourists out on the streets, lights, open stores and restaurants, and so on. But as soon as you reach Fifteenth, heading down this way, there are no people anywhere at night. On the corners, you'll see two or three Latin males, maybe, but none of the old people leave their rooms after the sun goes down. And I don't want you girls to go out alone at night either.'

'Why do you live here, then?' Sue Ellen said.

'We're moving next Friday. The owner of the hotel had a security problem with Marielitos, so I was just helping him out temporarily, that's all.'

In Gold's, the girls ordered Cokes and toasted bagels with cream cheese. Hoke ordered two soft-boiled eggs and a slice of rye toast.

'Did your mother give you any money?' Hoke said, while they were waiting to be served.

'Fifty dollars apiece,' Sue Ellen said, 'after she bought our bus tickets.'

Hoke held out his hand. 'Let me have it.'

Sue Ellen had forty-two dollars, and Aileen had thirty-nine and some change. They handed over the money reluctantly.

Hoke counted it. 'Where's the rest of it?'

'We spent some coming down,' Sue Ellen said. 'Then we had a pizza and went to a movie.'

'I played Donkey Kong in the bus station,' Aileen said.

Hoke gave each girl a dollar bill. 'Until you get jobs, and I'll help you find work when we get back to Miami, I'll give you both a dollar a week as an allowance. But for a while, money'll be rather tight.'

'You can't do much of anything with a dollar,' Aileen said.

'I don't want you doing much of anything. I've got to go over to the station after breakfast. You can either go with me, or stay in the hotel, where Mr Cohen or Emilio can keep an eye on you.'

'Can we swim in the pool?' Sue Ellen asked. 'I noticed the sign in the corridor pointing to the pool.'

'There's a pool out back, on the bay side, but Mr Bennett had it filled with sand. If you have a pool, you see, you have to have maintenance and insurance. The bay's too polluted for swimming, and I don't want you girls going over to the ocean by yourselves.'

'At home, we had our own pool,' Aileen said.

'Did you girls really choose to live with me, or did your mother send you down here against your will?'

'We said we'd rather live with you, Daddy,' Sue Ellen said.

'All right, then. Just remember that I don't make three hundred and twenty-five thousand a year. But my job's got other compensations.'

'Like what?' Sue Ellen said.

'Well, for one thing' – Hoke smiled – 'I've got my two daughters back.'

Apparently it was the right thing to say. Sue Ellen smiled. Aileen covered her golden mouth with her hand, so Hoke knew that she was smiling, too.

The girls decided to go with Hoke instead of hanging around the hotel. But Hoke made them change from their shorts into dresses before driving across the MacArthur Causeway.

'Tomorrow afternoon we'll go up on the roof, and you can watch the cruise ships come in through Government Cut. We've got more cruises out of Miami than any other place in the world.'

'I've never been on a cruise,' Sue Ellen said.

'Me neither,' Aileen said.

'I went once, for a weekend in Nassau. It isn't worth the money. A weekend in Nassau's like a weekend in Liberty City.'

'Where's Liberty City?' Aileen asked.

'It's just a black ghetto in Miami – one of the biggest.'

When they got to the station, Hoke took the girls into the interrogation room, and then got them some typing paper and pens from his office.

'I'll be working in my office, doing some paperwork, but you girls can draw pictures to pass the time. I know you like to draw.'

Sue Ellen laughed. 'I'm sixteen years old, Daddy.'

'You used to like to draw.'

'That was a long time ago. I remember. I also remember the time you handcuffed me to the table in the patio.'

'I never did that.'

'Yes you did, too. I remember. And I cried.'

'You were only six when you left Miami. My handcuffs wouldn't close around your little wrists. They were only about this big around.' Hoke made a circle with his thumb and forefinger.

'That's why you put the cuff around my ankle instead. I remember lots of things. You'd be surprised.'

'All right, then, if you don't want to draw, write letters to your mother. I'll get some envelopes later.'

Hoke returned to his office and telephoned his father in Riviera Beach. On Saturdays, the hardware store was only open until noon, but Frank Moseley rarely went in until ten, so Hoke knew he could still catch the old man at home.

'It's Hoke, Dad,' he said, when Frank answered.

'How are you, son? Did the girls get there all right?'

'Sure. They're with me now, I'm at the police station. Did Patsy tell you she was sending them down to me?'

'Yes, she called me, and she said she'd call you.'

'She didn't. The girls arrived last night, and I didn't have a clue.'

'That's funny. She told me she'd call you and explain.'

'Well, she didn't. Things are a little awkward for me right now, Dad, and I was wondering if you and Helen could take the girls for a couple of weeks.'

'We aren't going to be here, son. If you hadn't called me, I would've called you on Monday. But in ten days, Helen and me are taking a round-the-world cruise on the Q.E. II. Twelve thousand dollars apiece for an inside stateroom, but the boat goes everywhere. I've never had a real vacation, except for the week of our honeymoon, when Helen and I went to St Thomas. And Helen wanted to go on the Q.E. II, so that's that.'

'I think that's great, Dad. In ten days, you say.'

'That's right. The boat leaves from New York, but it stops in Fort Lauderdale. You can bring the girls up to Port Everglades to see us off, and we'll have a little going-away party in the stateroom. They say it's quite a ship, and I know the girls would like to see it. My tickets are in the mail, and when I get them I'll leave boarding passes for you, with the stateroom number and so on. You can meet us on the ship.'

'If I can make it, I'd like to see it. How's Helen, by the way?'

'Excited. She's got a wardrobe trunk and two suitcases packed already, more than enough stuff for three months. She made me buy a tuxedo. On the ship, you wear a tux every night.'

'Not on the first night, Dad. The first night out, as I understand it, is informal.'

'I know that much from watching Love Boat. But Helen says it won't be the first night out for us because the first night out will be from New York, so I'll have to wear mine. But I don't mind. I look pretty good in it for an old man. Something like that DeLorean fellow, only I'm a lot better-looking.' The old man laughed.

'I'd like to see you in it.'

294

'I'll show it to you on the boat. I don't like the suspenders though. They hurt my shoulders.'

'Don't wear 'em then. With the jacket on, nobody'll know.'

'Helen will. She said if you don't wear suspenders, the pants don't hang right. But I'll be okay. You give the girls love from Grandpa, and I'll see you all on the boat.'

'If I can't make it, I'll let you know.'

'Try and make it. I think you'd like to see the boat, but I also know how busy you are. If you send me your size, Hoke, I'll get a suit made for you in Hong Kong.'

'I don't need a suit, Dad.'

'Send me your measurements. I'll get you one anyway. A man can always use a new suit, and in Hong Kong they're dirt cheap. Helen'll get presents for the girls.'

'It was nice talking to you, Dad. Give Helen my best regards.'

'I'll tell Helen you called ... I'm awful sorry –' Frank started to cough, and then he gasped for a moment before catching his breath. 'Excuse me. I'm – I'm really sorry about Patsy and that colored ballplayer.'

'I don't want to talk about it, Dad.'

'Right. Me neither. Well, you give the girls my love, you hear?'

'I will, Dad. And have a *bon voyage*.'

'Thanks. I've got to get down to the store. There's a lot to do before I leave.'

'Sure. And if you send postcards, mail 'em here to the station. I'm moving, but I don't have my new address yet.'

'I can call you from the boat. There'll be a phone in the state-room, so I can call the store every day. So we'll be in touch, son.'

'Sure, Dad. I've got to get to work myself.'

Hoke hung up the phone, wondering how Helen had managed to talk the old man into a round-the-world cruise. It was probably the phone in the stateroom that did it, he concluded. The fact that Frank could call every day and pass on some unneeded advice to his manager had been the clincher. Nevertheless, even though Frank wouldn't be able to take the girls, Hoke was happy for the old man. Christ, Frank had all the money in the world from his real-estate deals. It was about time he spent some of it.

295

Hoke rechecked the paperwork on the Captain Morrow case, wrote a short covering memo to Major Brownley, and then took the file case into Brownley's empty office and left it on the chief's desk.

Hoke took the next case from his unread stack of files and opened it. There had been an argument in a bowling alley, and a man named Rodney DeMaris, an ex-Green Beret captain, had gone out to his car, returned to the bowling alley with a .357 magnum, and shot a bowler named Mark Demarest five times in the chest. The five holes in Demarest's chest, fired at close range, could be covered by a playing card. Hoke looked at the Polaroid shot of Demarest's chest, taken at the P.M. by the pathologist, and marveled at the tight pattern. DeMaris had then driven away and disappeared. Hoke wondered why Brownley had selected this old case, dating back five years, and then he found a Xeroxed page from a detective's notebook stating that a man who looked something like DeMaris had been seen in town two weeks ago, driving a green 1982 Plymouth. The officer had tried to stop the driver, but the suspect had evaded him on I-95. That wasn't much of a lead; the detective didn't even get the license number of the Plymouth. The detective wasn't positive that the man had been DeMaris, but the fact that the suspect refused to stop had reinforced the possible identification. Hoke decided not to waste any time on that one. What was he supposed to do – drive around town looking for a green Plymouth? Hoke put the file to one side, and reached for the next one.

The phone rang. It was Ellita Sanchez, and she was crying.

'I'm so glad you answered, Sergeant Moseley,' she sobbed. 'I've been trying to call your hotel ...' Ellita was crying so hard Hoke had difficulty understanding her. She was also talking over band music – some kind of frantic salsa. He could hear horns honking and street noises in the background.

'Where're you calling from? I can hardly hear you.'

'Just a second – don't hang up!'

'I'm not going to hang up. Try and calm down a little.'

As Hoke listened, trying to pick Ellita's voice out of the background noises, Lieutenant Slater came into his office. His white, pockmarked face loomed above the desk like a dead planet. He wore a blue shirt with a white collar and white barrel cuffs, and the vest and black raw-silk trousers of his five-hundred-dollar suit.

'What're those girls doing down in Number Three?'

'Just a minute, Slater, I'm talking to my partner.'

'I'm at the little cafeteria outside the La Compañía Supermarket at Ninth Avenue and Eighth Street,' Ellita was saying. 'Can you come right away?' She had stopped crying and her voice was calm.

'I guess so. What's the matter?'

'I'll tell you when you get here. It's an emergency, of my own, and I don't know what to do. Do you have any money?'

'A little. How much do you need?'

'A dollar. I've had three coffees, and I want to give the cafeteria lady a quarter for using her phone.'

'I've got that much. I'll be there as soon as I can.'

'Please hurry.'

'I'll be right there. Everything will be all right.'

Hoke put the phone down. Slater was still glaring down at him.

'Those girls are my daughters, Lieutenant. Why? What's the matter?'

'You should've checked them in with me, that's what's the matter.'

'You weren't at your desk when we came in.'

'I was at my desk when you sneaked that file into Major Brownley's office.'

'I didn't sneak it in, I took it in.'

'Everything's supposed to go through me. Otherwise, I won't know what's going on around here.'

'Take a look at it if you like. It's the Morrow file.'

'I'm not allowed in Brownley's office when he's not there, and neither are you.'

'For Christ's sake, Slater. I'm on a special assignment with Henderson and Sanchez. You know that, because Brownley filled you in when he assigned Gonzalez to work with you. What do you want from me?'

'I want you to follow the chain of command, Sergeant. You're no better than anyone else around here.'

Hoke nodded, realizing suddenly why Slater was so angry. He had not been asked by Brownley to attend the meeting about the cold cases, nor had Brownley, in all probability, consulted him about their selection.

'Okay, Lieutenant,' Hoke said. 'I'm supposed to send Brownley a weekly progress report. I'll see that you get a Xerox of it next week. Okay?'

'See that you do. And don't go into the major's office again when he's not there.'

Hoke got up and smiled. 'Come on, Slater. I'll introduce you to my girls.'

Hoke took him to the interrogation room, introduced the girls, and then handed his daughters two dollars apiece. 'Lieutenant Slater'll show you where the cafeteria is downstairs, and vouch for you so you can eat there. I've got to leave the station for a while, so you girls can have lunch down there. Try the special. On Saturday it's usually macaroni and cheese. Isn't that right, Lieutenant?'

'I don't know. I don't eat in the cafeteria. I've got an ulcer.'

'Anyway, girls, go with the lieutenant. I appreciate you taking the girls down, Slater.'

'That's okay. I'll just go and get my jacket first.'

'When'll you be back, Daddy?' Sue Ellen asked.

'As soon as I can. It's a little emergency. Nothing for you to worry about.'

Eighth Street was only one-way at Ninth Avenue, so Hoke drove west on Seventh Street, turned south on Ninth Avenue, and took the first empty parking space he could find. He put his police placard on the dashboard and walked to the corner. Ellita was on the sidewalk, outside the pass-through counter of the tiny supermarket cafeteria. Music blared from a radio on a shelf behind the counter. Ellita was wearing tight Jordache jeans with a U-necked white muscle shirt. Her bare golden arms were devoid of the bracelets and gold watch she habitually wore. Her gold circle earrings dangled from her ears, however. It was a common Miami joke that doctors could always tell Cuban baby girls when they were delivered at the hospital: They were born with their ears already pierced. Hoke had never seen Ellita in tight jeans before, but she looked good in them, he thought. The full skirts she wore on duty had disguised her voluptuous figure. Ellita smiled when she saw Hoke, and he noticed that she wasn't wearing lipstick.

'We can't talk here,' she said. 'Where's your car?'

'Around the corner –'

Ellita took his arm and started toward the corner. She stopped abruptly. 'Just a second. Let me borrow that dollar.'

Hoke gave her a dollar bill. Ellita passed it through the window to the old lady behind the counter, said something in rapid Spanish, and rejoined Hoke by the supermarket entrance. They walked to the car.

'Where's your purse?' Hoke said. 'Did you leave it back there on the counter?'

Ellita shook her head, bit her lower lip, and began to cry.

Hoke unlocked the door and Ellita got into the front seat. Hoke got behind the wheel and took the placard off the dashboard.

'There should be some Kleenex in the glove compartment,' he said. He slid the placard under the front seat.

'I'll be all right.' Ellita wiped her eyes with the backs of her fingers. 'I called you, Sergeant, because ... because I didn't know what else to do.'

'You can call me Hoke, Ellita. After all, we're partners, and this isn't an on-duty situation – or is it?'

'You know how much I respect you, Sergeant –'

'Even so, I'm only ten years older than you. I'm not your father, for God's sake.'

Ellita started to cry again. Hoke opened the glove compartment and found a purse-sized package of Kleenex.

'Here.'

Ellita wiped her eyes with a tissue. Her familiar perfume and moschate odor was overwhelming within the confines of the car, especially with the windows rolled up. Hoke started the engine and switched on the air conditioning. As Ellita raised her arms to blow her nose, Hoke noticed the damp tufts of jet-black hair beneath her arms. Ellita didn't shave her armpits; that was something else he hadn't known about his partner. It had been a long time since Hoke had spent any time in the front seat of a car with a weeping woman. He found Ellita's underarm hair a little exciting, and remembered again that he hadn't been laid in more than four months. After Ellita's problem was straightened out, there might still be time to drive over to Coral Gables and give Loretta Hickey her money, and maybe set up something ...

'All right,' Ellita said calmly. She sat back and looked straight ahead, staring at a red Camaro parked in front of them. The bumper had a strip on the right side reading DIE YOU BASTARD. On the other side of the bumper was the logo for the Cuban Camaro Club. 'My father threw me out of the house, Hoke.'

Hoke grinned. 'How could he do that? You pay the rent on the whole house, you told me.'

'You don't understand. In a Cuban family, he's the father, and it's always his house, his rules.'

'What did you do? Did you have an argument, or what?'

'This is embarrassing. But if I can't tell you, I guess I can't tell anyone. The trouble is, I told my mother, and I should've known better. She told my father and he threw me out of the house. I don't have my purse, my pistol, my checkbook, my car keys – nothing! All of a sudden, there I was, outside of the house on the porch. He locked the door, and I couldn't get back in. I waited awhile, then I knocked on the door because I could hear my mother crying inside. I said, "I'm your daughter, and I've got to get my things." He said, "I have no daughter." Then he wouldn't say another word. He gets like that sometimes. He's very stubborn and unreasonable. Last year, when he flew up to Newark to visit my aunt – his sister – he got into trouble with the airline because he wouldn't fasten his seat belt.'

'Why not?'

'He thought if he fastened the belt, people would think he was afraid. He finally fastened it when the stewardess told him the captain used his, too. But for a while there, they were radioing for clearance to taxi back to the terminal.'

Hoke smiled, shook his head, and took out his cigarettes.

'But he's my father, Hoke. He's made up his mind, you see, and now he won't change it. Maybe, eventually, when he gets used to the idea, he might change it, but right now he's angry and bitter. He thinks I've betrayed and disgraced him, which I guess I have, but right now I need my checkbook, weapon, badge, and car.'

'He knows, doesn't he, that a cop's supposed to have his – her weapon with her at all times?'

'Of course he knows that, but at the moment he isn't thinking rationally. Later on, after my mother works on him, he'll calm down a little, but it'll never be the same between us again.' She shook her head. 'Don't worry. I'm not going to cry again.'

'What did you do to him? You don't have to tell me, of course.'

'I'm pregnant, Hoke. Seven weeks. I've known for a week now, and this morning I told my mother. I *told* her not to say anything to him, but I should've known better. She tells him everything.'

Hoke nodded and lit a Kool. 'That explains why you started crying when I was talking to Captain Morrow in his room. You didn't know his wife was pregnant when he killed her –'

'Of course I knew!' Ellita widened her eyes. 'I read the file. I'm not that unprofessional, Hoke. I was crying out of frustration because of the damned battery on the tape recorder ...'

Hoke saw that he had touched a nerve. He decided to try to make Ellita feel better about having told her mother.

'You couldn't hide a pregnancy from your father, Ellita. He'd've found out sooner or later, unless you got an abortion. But you've still got plenty of time for that.'

'I can't get an abortion, Hoke. A baby's got a living soul.'

'Soul or no soul, a lot of women do. What's the father got to say about it?'

'The father doesn't know about the baby. He doesn't even know my last name. I don't know his last name either, but I can find out easily enough. His first name's Bruce. That's all I know right now.'

Hoke smoked his Kool and sat back. He didn't have to ask any more questions. She was going to tell him about it now anyway, whether he wanted to hear it or not.

'I didn't date Bruce, Hoke. It was just one of those things that happens. All I ever do, it seems, is work, go home, sleep, and then pull my shift again. I should've moved out and got my own apartment years ago. But Cuban girls don't do things like that, because we can't give our parents a valid reason. How come, your parents want to know, you want to rent an apartment and be lonely, and

301

go to all that expense, when you can live comfortably at home? It makes no sense to them for an unmarried girl to leave home. With a son it's a little different, but even then they don't like it. But it didn't make any sense to me either, economically. I'm very comfortable at home. I pay the rent on the house, but my parents pay for everything else – utilities and food. I've got my own bedroom, my own TV set and stereo. My mother works part-time in Hialeah, at the Golden Thread garment factory. My father's with Triple-A Security. He's not just a security guard, either. He's in personnel and hires all the Latin guards because he's more or less bilingual.'

'He has a little English, you mean.'

'Enough. Much more than my mother. We speak Spanish at home. What I'm trying to say, I guess, is that I somehow got into a rut, a comfortable rut. But for the last two years, ever since my thirtieth birthday, I felt that life was passing me by. It was ridiculous to be a thirty-year-old virgin, and yet I never met anyone I liked, or who liked me well enough to – well, to pressure me. And it didn't help that I had to be home by ten-thirty when I did go out.'

'You're kidding. Ten-thirty?'

'You don't know Cuban fathers. It's his house and his rules, I'm telling you.'

'But you pay the rent –'

'That doesn't matter. What else would I do with my money – living at home? With three incomes, even though my mother just does piecework, there's plenty of money for whatever we need. My mother cooks and cleans the house, and I don't do much of anything. I studied hard at Miami-Dade. Except for the one F I got in philosophy, I had straight As.'

'I know. I checked your records. And so, one night, you went out, and –'

'That's right. On a Friday night, which is the big night in Coconut Grove, not Saturday –'

'I know, Ellita. If you don't get something lined up on Friday night, you don't have anyone for the weekend.'

'I went to the Taurus, and it was jammed. I met Bruce in the bar. He bought me a drink, and then I bought him one. He was nice-looking. Blue eyes. He wore a suit and tie. A detail man for a pharmaceutical firm, he said. We went to his apartment instead of getting a third drink. This wasn't any Silhouette romance, Hoke. We went straight at it, Bruce because that's what he does on Friday nights, and me because I wanted to have the experience. It was a little exciting, I guess, but not what I expected.'

'And because you were drunk you didn't take any precautions.'

'I wasn't drunk, Hoke. I wasn't even high. Bruce had a vasectomy, he told me. I didn't believe him at first, and then he showed me the two little scars on his balls.'

'On his scrotum, you mean.'

'On his scrotum, right.' She managed a little laugh. 'We did it twice. Then I took a shower in his apartment, got dressed, and I was still home before ten-thirty. Bruce was very nice, a lot younger than me, about twenty-five, I'd say.'

'But a liar.'

'I guess so. Now. But he did have those two little scars. Maybe he had the operation and it didn't take.'

'More likely, he didn't want to wear a raincoat. I can find out for you. Remember where he lives?'

She nodded. 'I know where he lives, but I don't want to see him again. I don't want him to know I'm pregnant. I'll just go ahead and have my baby and take care of it. But right now I'm scared. I've never been away from home overnight before by myself, can you believe that? And I don't have my gun, my badge, my checkbook, or my car. I'll need my clothes, too.'

Hoke sat for a moment, thinking. Then he put the car in gear.

'All right, let's go, Ellita. I'll get your stuff for you.'

Chapter Twelve

Ellita didn't want her parents or neighbors to see her, so Hoke parked a block away from the Sanchez residence and walked the rest of the way to the house. It was much bigger than Hoke had expected, a three-bedroom concrete-block-and-stucco house with a flat, white gravel roof and an attached garage. The front lawn was freshly mown, and there were beds of blue delphiniums on both sides of the front porch. Ellita's brown Honda Civic was parked in the driveway. Old man Sanchez probably kept his own car in the garage. His house; his rules.

Hoke opened the gate in the white picket fence and glanced curiously at the shrine to Santa Barbara in the yard. The shrine was fashioned of oolite boulders and mortar; in the recess there was a blue vase of daisies and ferns at the feet of the not quite life-sized plaster statue of Santa Barbara.

The front door opened before Hoke could ring the bell. Mrs Sanchez waited in the doorway. If she had been crying, as Ellita claimed, she didn't look like it. She was a handsome woman, about two inches shorter than Ellita, and her black hair was streaked with gray. Her features were delicate, and she had brown luminous eyes.

'I'm Sergeant Moseley, Mrs Sanchez. I've come to pick up some of Ellita's things.'

'Come in, Sergeant.' Mrs Sanchez stepped back. 'Ellita's told us a lot about you.'

Hoke entered the living room. There was a bright yellow velvet couch against the wall; a matching easy chair was in one corner, and there was an abundance of black wooden furniture, carved with pear and leaf patterns, in both the living room and dining room. The wall-to-wall carpeting was pale blue. Dominating the living room, however, was a life-size plaster statue of St Lazarus in front of the fireplace. A fireplace in Miami was rarely if ever used, so the Sanchezes had probably decided that St Lazarus was a better decorating solution than a pot of tropical plants. On the carpeting surrounding the statue, and beneath the saint's outstretched, imploring hand, there were dozens of coins, most of them quarters. It took eight quarters to park and four more quarters to ride the Metrorail, so St Lazarus would be a good candidate as the patron saint of Metrorail, Hoke thought.

'Is Mr Sanchez at home? I'd like to talk with him.'

Mrs Sanchez pursed her lips and shook her head. 'He's in his room. This is not a good time, Sergeant. This is a very *bad* time.'

'I understand. But tell him I'd like to talk to him later. Ellita's my partner, you know, and we think a lot of her in the department. And in the division. You should be very proud of your daughter, Mrs Sanchez. I've got two daughters of my own, and I'd be happy if they turned out as well as Ellita.'

'Thank you.' She touched his arm. 'I'll show you Ellita's room.'

Ellita's room was the master bedroom at the back of the house, and on the right of the corridor. She had her own bathroom, too. Her parents, being so old, probably wanted their own separate, if smaller, bedrooms, and wouldn't mind sharing a bathroom. There were three sets of curtains on the bedroom windows. In addition to the layered curtains, there were heavy crimson draperies. The unmade double bed was layered with pink sheets, a blanket, a comforter, and a rose bedspread spaced with embroidered dark red roses. There were four pillows on the bed, and a reading lamp was clamped to an ornately carved black walnut headboard. The color TV was on a wheeled cart, so Ellita could watch it from the bed, or from the red velvet upholstered La-Z-Boy. There was an oil painting of the Virgin in a gilt frame above the vanity table, with a lighted votive candle on a shelf below the painting. There was a framed color poster of Julio Iglesias on the opposite wall. The stereo, in a blond wooden cabinet, was directly beneath Julio's poster.

Mrs Sanchez slid back the louvered doors to the walk-in closet. 'Her clothes are here.'

'I'll need her purse, too. It's important that she has her ID, badge, and weapon. And her checkbook.'

Mrs Sanchez brought Ellita's purse from the dresser. The .38 and ID with the badge were in the purse, and so were Ellita's keys, checkbook, and wallet. There was a corner desk, and Hoke looked through the drawers. Ellita had a NOW checking account, as well as a regular checking account, so he added this checkbook to the purse. He also found two white passbooks; they were two $10,000 Certificates of Deposit. She would need them, too. He picked up Ellita's gold wristwatch from the bedside table, and dropped it into his jacket pocket.

'Does she have a suitcase?' Hoke asked. 'Maybe you can help me pick out some clothes?'

'There's a box in the garage.' Mrs Sanchez hurried out of the room.

Hoke took two cream-colored silk blouses from the closet, the kind with long sleeves, and tossed them on the bed. He removed a black skirt and a red skirt from the closet, and added them to the blouses. That's all Ellita would need for a couple of days. In midsummer, she wouldn't need any jackets or sweaters. He went through her dresser, however, and picked out a purple silk nightgown, two pairs of black silk panties, and two brassieres. He took a peek at the size, 38-C. He added a jar of Eucerin, a toothbrush, and a tube of Colgate to the pile, but he did not include the atomizer of Shalimar or Ellita's bottle of musk. She was wearing enough perfume already, he thought, to last her for a week. Stockings, she would need stockings. There was a pair of pantyhose drying in the bathroom. He tossed the pantyhose on the pile, and then couldn't think of anything else.

Mrs Sanchez returned with a cardboard box that had once held a dozen boxes of Tide.

'Ellita has a train case,' she said. While Hoke packed the clothing into the cardboard box, Mrs Sanchez got the train case, a red-and-blue plaid one, down from the closet shelf and packed it with cosmetics and vials from the vanity table, including the Shalimar and the musk and a plastic tree that held a dozen pairs of earrings.

'I guess this'll do for a few days,' Hoke said, 'but if you would pack the rest of Ellita's stuff, she can come by for it one day when Mr Sanchez isn't home.'

Mrs Sanchez started to cry. She ran into Ellita's bathroom and closed the door.

Hoke decided not to wait for her to come out. He put the box under his left arm and carried the train case in his right hand as he walked down the corridor to the living room.

Mr Sanchez, a short, stocky man with black hair and a gray mustache, wearing green poplin wash pants and a white long-sleeved *guayabera*, was standing in front of St Lazarus. His short arms were folded across his chest, and he stared at Hoke without expression.

'Mr Sanchez? I'm Sergeant Moseley, your daughter's partner.'

'I have no daughter.' Keeping his arms crossed, Mr Sanchez turned his back on Hoke and faced the statue.

'In that case, we have nothing to talk about.'

Hoke left the house, put the box and the train case down beside the Honda Civic, dug the keys out of the purse, and unlocked the car. He put the box, purse, and case on the back seat, then shoved the front seat back as far as it would go before maneuvering himself into the driver's seat.

He drove down the block and parked behind his Pontiac. Ellita was standing on the curb. Hoke handed her the keys and her wristwatch after he got out of the car.

'What do you want to do now?'

'I don't know,' she said. 'I guess I should find a motel or something, and then look around for an apartment.'

'Don't you have a girl friend or a cousin or someone who can put you up for a few days?'

'I've got some girl friends, but they live at home too. Because of the situation, their parents wouldn't want them to get involved. The same for relatives – even more – because of my father, you see.'

'Your father's a fucking asshole.'

'Please, don't say that, Sergeant Moseley. You just don't understand him, that's all.'

'I don't want to understand him. He wouldn't even talk to me, for Christ's sake. What's more natural than a woman getting pregnant? That's what women *do*!'

'My mother'll have the priest talk to him. That might help some. But I doubt it.'

'Jesus!' Hoke said, laughing. 'I forgot all about the girls. They're still down at the station, and I was going to suggest that we have lunch and discuss what you should do!'

Hoke told Ellita about his daughters, about how they had arrived in the middle of the night.

'Why not stay at the Eldorado with us over the weekend?' he said finally. 'By Monday you can phone your mother and see how your father feels about things. Maybe by Monday he'll want you back, once he realizes that he'll be stuck for the house rent.'

'No, he won't. He knows I'll continue to pay the rent.'

'Even after he threw you out?'

Ellita nodded. 'My mother lives there, too, you know.'

'How much do you pay?'

'Five-fifty a month.'

'You can rent a damned nice one-bedroom apartment for that much – already furnished.'

She shook her head. 'Does the Eldorado have any empty rooms?'

'Plenty. You know where it is. Drive on over, and I'll meet you in the lobby after I pick up the girls. But don't sign in – I'll negotiate a deal for you.'

Hoke got into his car and let Ellita drive away first before he switched on the engine and the air conditioner.

He didn't understand women at all, he decided. He had considered Ellita Sanchez a mature, responsible woman, and he had discovered in her a young, frightened child, in some things no more grown-up emotionally than his own teenage daughters. But she was his partner, so he would have to look after her until she decided what she wanted to do.

And Hoke had other things on his mind. He wanted to see Loretta Hickey sometime this afternoon. There were only a couple of loose ends to tie up on Jerry Hickey's OD, and then he was almost certain he could get something on with Loretta. He could tell when a woman was coming on to him, and it wouldn't take much effort on his part to get Loretta bedded.

Hoke drove back downtown to the station. He drove cautiously, as a man had to do to survive in Miami traffic, but when the way was obviously clear, he drove through red lights and only paused at stop signs to shift.

Chapter Thirteen

Slater and the two girls were at the lieutenant's desk. The executive officer was showing them slides of homicide victims on a viewer he had set up. Some of the slides were in color and others were in black and white, but the photos were graphically clear on the lighted, eight-by-ten-inch glass screen.

'I've been showing the girls some pictures, Hoke,' Slater said. 'Explaining some cases. You worked on the Merkle shotgun case, didn't you? The one we called the "Laura" case because her face was unrecognizable?'

'That was Quevedo's case,' Hoke said, 'but I did some legwork for him. I think we all did. They caught the perp when he tried to sell the gold chain. It was a driveway killing, girls. This guy followed Mrs Merkle home from the supermarket because she was wearing a heavy gold chain around her neck. He shot her for the chain and about forty bucks' worth of groceries. Any woman who wears a gold chain is asking for it in Miami. And if she wears it every day, she can count on somebody snatching it eventually. But this guy was a crazy. He didn't have to kill her. You girls don't wear neck chains, do you?'

Sue Ellen and Aileen, still staring wide-eyed at the gory face on the screen, shook their heads.

'Don't do it, girls,' Slater said. 'They usually work in pairs, driving around town till they spot someone. Then one guy jumps out, snatches the purse and chain, gets back in the car, and they drive off. They're hard to catch because the woman usually gets hysterical and can't remember, half the time, whether the perps were black or white. Our problem with Mrs Merkle was that even though we knew who she was, we couldn't prove it for a while. There were no fingerprints of hers on file either, so we couldn't get an ID. She was unrecognizable, as you can plainly see, and we were trying to identify her from an oil painting – a portrait – instead of a photo. But the people who knew her said the painting didn't look like her, and they wouldn't give us a positive ID. That's why we called it the "Laura" case, from the old movie with Clifton Webb. It was a pretty good movie, too. If it comes back on late TV some night, you girls oughta see it.'

Hoke laughed. 'We kidded Quevedo about falling in love with the oil painting. Eventually he got so pissed we had to stop. What made it so funny was that Quevedo had never heard of the movie, so he didn't even know what we were kidding him about. Besides, no one could've loved that face in the painting.'

Slater laughed. 'I remember now. I'd forgotten about that part of it.'

'I appreciate you looking after the girls, Lieutenant. But I'll take 'em off your hands now.'

'Your partner okay, Hoke? No trouble?'

'No, no, she's fine. She just wanted me to take a look at a guy she thought she recognized at the supermarket. But he was gone before I got there. Thank the lieutenant, girls.'

'Thank you, Lieutenant Slater,' Sue Ellen said. 'Especially for the dessert.'

'Thank you,' Aileen said.

They went back to Hoke's office as Slater began to put his slides away.

'We got the special,' Sue Ellen said. 'Macaroni and cheese, but didn't have enough money left over for dessert. So Lieutenant Slater bought us apple pie.'

'That was nice of him, but don't ever let him get you anything else. Slater's not into altruism, so –'

'What?'

'Never mind.' Hoke sat down behind his desk and looked at Sue Ellen. 'I'll just say that Slater likes to have everybody under some kind of obligation to him ... but don't worry about it. Did you finish the letters to your mother?'

'I couldn't think of anything to write,' Sue Ellen said.

'Me neither,' said Aileen.

'Bring the paper and pens with you. You might be able to think of something later. We've got to get back to the Eldorado now, and then you can meet my partner. She's going to be staying at the hotel with us for a few days.'

'You've got a lady detective partner?' Aileen said.

'That's right, and she's a good one, too.'

'Think I could be a detective? When I grow up?'

'No. The best career for a girl is marriage. Even my partner, who's a very good detective, probably wishes she was married now. But don't mention that to her.'

Hoke unlocked his desk drawer, retrieved the envelope of money for Mrs Hickey, and then drove the girls back to the Eldorado Hotel.

Ellita Sanchez was waiting for them in the lobby, and Hoke introduced her to Eddie Cohen as his partner. There was an empty room two doors down from Hoke's suite, and Hoke told Eddie to give Ellita the professional rate – or 10 percent off the ten-dollar daily room charge.

'I don't think Mr Bennett'll go for that,' Eddie said.

'If he doesn't,' Hoke said, 'tell him to talk to me.'

After Ellita registered, they went upstairs. Hoke carried Ellita's cardboard box, and Sue Ellen carried the train case. The small room was hot and musty, but the window air conditioner worked after Hoke switched it on and kicked it a couple of times. Hoke registered the expression on Ellita's usually impassive face; he detected depression beneath her attempt to smile. The scarred linoleum floor had sections missing, and the furnishings, a metal cot with a thin mattress and patched sheets, a straight ladder-backed chair, and a dented three-drawer metal dresser – all painted dead-white – completed the inventory. The cracked gray walls had been painted with a cheap water-based paint, and the walls were powdery to the touch. The faucets in the bathtub and sink dripped. The washbasin, with most of the enamel missing, was rusty. There was no toilet paper in the bathroom, and there was only one face towel.

'I'll go down and get you some more towels and toilet paper,' Hoke said, 'but until this room cools off, you'd better come down to our suite.'

Hoke left them in his suite to get acquainted, took the elevator downstairs again, and returned with two bath towels, two rolls of toilet paper, and a dozen small bars of soap. He dropped these off in Ellita's room and returned to his suite. Ellita was showing the girls her .38 pistol – although she had taken the precaution of removing the rounds before letting them handle it.

'Look,' Hoke said, 'I've got to go out this afternoon. There's not much to do around the hotel, so why don't you take the girls over to the Fifth Street Gym, Ellita, and watch the boxers work out? Tony Otero, the Puerto Rican lightweight, is preparing for a fight later this month, and he's a pretty good boy. You can walk over there and kill the rest of the afternoon. Then this evening, when I come back, I'll take you all out to dinner.'

'I thought you said we're not supposed to go out alone,' Aileen said.

Hoke pointed to Ellita, who was sitting in the Victorian chair and reloading her pistol. 'You won't be alone. Ellita's with you, and she's armed. You'll be safe with her, and besides, nobody'll bother you in the daytime. I was going to suggest going to the beach, but I know Ellita hasn't got her suit with her. It'll rain later this afternoon anyway.'

'The sun's out now,' Sue Ellen said. 'How can you tell?'

'Because in July it always rains in the afternoon.'

'Don't worry about us, Hoke,' Ellita said. 'We'll find something to do. If you have somewhere to go, go ahead.'

'I'm out of cigarettes,' Sue Ellen said, 'and the machine in the lobby takes six quarters for a pack. Can I have some change for cigarettes?'

'No.' Hoke took two Kools out of his pack and handed them to her. 'Better make these two last. If you can't support your habit on the allowance I gave you, you'll just have to stop smoking till I can find you a job somewhere.'

Sue Ellen poked out her lower lip. 'I don't like the menthol kind.'

Hoke snatched the two Kools back from her and returned them to his pack.

'When will you be back?' Ellita asked.

'I don't know exactly, but I'll be back before dark. I've got to go to Coral Gables, and then, if Bill's back from the Metrozoo, I want to talk to him about something.'

Ellita nodded and started for the bathroom. As Hoke was on his way out, to his surprise the two girls each kissed him on the cheek.

Hoke parked on the second level of the bus station in Coral Gables, put his police placard in place instead of feeding the meter, and walked over to Miracle Mile, a block away. The Bouquetique was a narrow shop between a luggage store and a Cuban *joyería*. The flower arrangements in the window were artificial for the most part, and there was no FTD logo, but there were signs for Visa and MasterCard on the glass door. If Loretta Hickey wasn't a member of FTD, Hoke thought, and had to depend on walk-in customers only, she would be hard-pressed to pay the high rents charged on Miracle Mile. During the last two years the street had been upgraded and tile sidewalks had been added. The Mile merchants had all been assessed accordingly for the beautification.

A short Oriental woman was behind the counter. Behind her a tall, lighted refrigerator held flower arrangements and a huge vase of red roses. It was cool in the shop, and there was a pleasant odor of freshly cut flowers and ferns. In a glass-topped case beside the counter were the so-called smart things Loretta Hickey sold as well as flowers. There were silver bracelets, turquoise rings, earrings and necklaces, and a half-dozen glass paperweights.

'Yes, sir?' the Asian woman said, in a high tiny voice. She was the woman Hoke had talked to on the phone and had thought was a child. She stepped back two paces as Hoke moved to the counter, and Hoke wondered why Mrs Hickey would hire such a shy woman as a salesperson. He decided it was because Loretta could probably get her for the minimum wage.

'Tell Mrs Hickey I want to see her.'

'She's designing in the back. I can help you?'

'No. Just tell her Sergeant Moseley is here.'

The woman pushed through the bamboo curtains that separated the front from the back workroom. It was almost three minutes before Loretta Hickey came through the curtains. Her lipstick was freshly applied, and Hoke figured she had redone the rest of her makeup as well.

'I meant to come earlier,' he said, 'but I was delayed.' He opened the envelope and removed the receipt Loretta had already signed. 'You'd better count it.'

'I trust you.' She smiled.

'But cut the cards.'

Loretta counted the money, replaced it in the envelope, and then put the envelope into the wide front pocket of her blue cotton smock. Her honey-colored hair was in two braids down her back, and her face was flushed slightly.

'I was going to ask you out to dinner tonight,' Hoke said, 'but a few other things have come up.'

'I thought you were coming to my place for dinner. I've still got all that ham, and –'

'Ham'll keep. But I won't be free till Monday night. And I'd prefer to take you out to dinner. Then, if we don't get enough to eat, we can always go back to your house and snack on the ham.'

'All right. But most restaurants in the Gables are closed Monday nights.'

'We don't have to eat in the Gables. I know a nice place on Calle Ocho. You like Spanish food? I don't mean Cuban, I mean Spanish.'

'They use so much garlic ...'

'Okay. Seafood it is, then.'

'I'm not picky. It's just that even when you tell them no garlic they put it in anyway.'

'I know a good seafood place. Incidentally, I talked to Mr Hickey, your ex, and he's going to have Jerry cremated.'

'Oh? Have they released the body?'

'Not yet. On Thursday, as I recall, there were about twenty-five P.M.s ahead of him. They only do six or seven a day, unless there's an emergency, and then they hire extra help. As you know, if you looked at the paper, there was a fire at the Descanso Hotel last week, and they've got about six charred bodies to identify, too, so –'

'I'm sure Harold'll call me when the cremation takes place. Did he say anything to you about me?'

'What do you mean?'

314

'About Jerry and me. Harold had this ridiculous idea that Jerry and I – well, it was just crazy. There's no way in the world I could ever get interested in a kid like Jerry.'

'No, he didn't say anything to me. But I went through a divorce myself, Loretta, and it always changes people. In fact, my wife accused me of having an affair with a young woman in the Grove. At the time of our divorce I was putting in fourteen-hour days, so I wouldn't've had time for anything like that. Even if I'd had the money it takes for motel rooms.'

'I often work twelve-hour days myself. Right now, I'm making a funeral wreath. I wish I could get more funerals.' She blushed. 'I didn't mean what you think.'

'I know what you meant, and I hope you get more funerals, too. Anyway, Minrow's Funeral Home will be taking care of Jerry's cremation. So if you want to add anything to the announcement in the papers, or if you want to invite some of Jerry's friends, you should call Minrow.'

'Jerry didn't have any friends that I know of. I tried to make a list for you, and couldn't think of anyone. But I'll call Mr Minrow. There should be some flowers, even at a cremation.'

'Okay, then, Loretta. I'll pick you up at your house Monday night about eight-thirty, depending on the traffic.'

'All right.' Loretta reached across the counter to shake hands. Hoke held her hand with both of his, pulled her toward him, and kissed her on the lips before he released her hand.

He turned toward the door when he heard the high-pitched girlish giggle from behind the bamboo curtain.

Hoke stopped at a Greek restaurant on his way back to his car and ate a Greek salad for a late lunch. It wasn't enough, and he was still hungry, but he decided to let it do until dinner. He showed the cashier his badge and asked her if he could use the phone. He dialed Henderson at home, and Bill answered.

'I'm glad I caught you. I didn't think you'd be back from the zoo yet, and just took a chance.'

'We didn't go. Marie took the kids to Bloomingdale's instead. They hadn't seen the new store yet, and she just got her Bloomie's card in the mail.'

'You should've intercepted it, Bill, and cut it into little pieces.'

Bill laughed. 'It's in her name, not mine. And Marie's flush right now. She just sold the same house she sold three months ago, and picked up an identical four thousand in commissions. The same house, at the same price.'

'I don't get it. How'd she sell the same house twice?'

'Marie says the house sells itself. The entire interior, every damned room, is paneled in cypress, and the wood's waxed and polished. People flip when they see the paneling. Then when they buy it and move in, the wood's so damned dark they have to keep the lights on all the time, even at high noon. If they painted the paneling, the house would be ordinary, so they can't do that, you see. But a woman, spending her days in a dark house like that every day, gets depressed after a couple of weeks. So they sell it again, and move. Marie says she'll probably sell the house again before the end of the year.'

'At any rate, you won't get stuck for her Bloomie's bills.'

'No way. So what's up, Hoke?'

'I'd like to talk to you. Can you meet me at the Shamrock for a beer?'

'I guess so. But I want to look at some Toros this afternoon.'

'Toros?'

'The mowers. I've been thinking about buying me a riding mower, and Toro's supposed to be the best. If I had a Toro riding mower, I could probably get my son to mow the lawn. Kids love to ride these things. In fact, if I had a mower, I wouldn't mind doing the lawn myself.'

'Why not tell Jimmy that he can't use the Toro until he takes a shower after P.E.?'

Henderson laughed. 'Because that would probably work, and then I'd never get to ride it.'

'I need to talk to you for a while, Bill, but I don't want to interfere with your afternoon.'

'I'll meet you at the Shamrock in a half-hour, Hoke. There's no hurry about the Toro. It was just something I was going to do, that's all.'

'Thanks, Bill. In a half-hour then.'

316

Hoke hung up the phone, thanked the cashier, and walked back to the bus station to retrieve his car.

Hoke was pleased with himself, by his boldness. He hadn't known in advance that he was going to kiss Loretta, but she had leaned right into it. If that fucking Asian woman hadn't been there, the kiss would have lasted a lot longer. For a moment, he had forgotten all about Ellita and the girls; he had almost changed the date from Monday to tonight. He drove to the Shamrock, parked in the dirt lot in the back, and went into the bar.

Chapter Fourteen

The lighted clock in the Shamrock said two-thirty. Henderson was already there, sitting at the bar with a light Coors draft in front of him. Two men in three-piece suits were at the end of the bar talking about cars. They looked like used-car salesmen, but Hoke knew that they were both detectives with the Metro Police Department. Prince was on the jukebox, singing 'Head.' The two elderly men who had played the song – one was an investigator for the D.E.A.; Hoke didn't know the other one – were listening to the lyrics, frowning with concentration.

Hoke ordered a draft Michelob for himself, and then he and Henderson moved to a table in the corner by the front window.

Hoke told Henderson about the arrival of his daughters, and then told him about Ellita's pregnancy and about checking her into the Eldorado. Henderson's fixed smile didn't change, but he listened attentively, and he didn't touch his beer while Hoke was explaining.

'Right now,' Hoke finished, 'they're over at the Fifth Street Gym watching Tony Otero work out. So far, I haven't had enough time to think everything out, and I don't know what to do about Ellita. That's why I wanted to talk to you about it.'

'The situation's newer to me than it is to you, Hoke.' Henderson sipped his beer. 'Ellita'll be okay, I think. In the long run she'll be in a healthier situation. No one in her thirties should still be living at home. A few years back, she'd've been fired for getting pregnant, but not now. She can work till she starts showing, and then she can get an authorized maternity leave, married or not. Then, once the baby's born, she can be back to work within a month or two.'

'I don't know what to tell Willie Brownley, or whether I should tell him or not.'

'It's not your problem, Hoke. Our new assignment's only for two months, and if Ellita's only seven weeks pregnant, she's not going to show anything for another two or three months. Besides, it's up to her to talk to Willie, not you. Her being pregnant sure as hell won't interfere with our assignment. There's no danger involved, and if it ever looks like there might be, we can always leave her in the office. Or something.'

'Ellita won't ask for any favors, Bill. She may not be a libber like your wife, but we can't patronize her just because she's knocked up. She wouldn't stand for it.'

'In that case' – Henderson widened his metal-studded smile – 'we'll have to be subtle.'

'You're about as subtle as a hurricane.'

'What about you? You've already given her the weekly reports to do, and you had her type Morrow's confession. I could've done that, you know.'

'Ellita types without looking, and you and I both have to look. There's another thing she told me. The battery went dead on the tape recorder when we were talking to Morrow, and she saved our ass by getting the battery changed out in the hall.'

'Jesus, I didn't know that. I just thought it was a bad time to take a piss.'

'I didn't know either, till she told me last night.'

'Don't tell Brownley anything about the pregnancy. We've got to hang onto Ellita, Hoke.' Henderson shook his head. 'Do you really think she was a virgin, and got knocked up her first time out?'

'I'd like to believe it, Bill, but I can't. She's thirty-two years old. I don't see how she could live in Miami for twenty years and stay a virgin. I don't doubt that this Bruce guy she picked up was a one-night stand, but she must've experimented at least a few times before she met him. Hell, she went to Shenandoah Junior High, Southwest High, and Miami-Dade.'

'Think about what you just said for a minute, Hoke.'

'What do you mean?'

'You've got two teenage girls now, that's what I mean. Fourteen and sixteen, right? Have you talked to them about sex yet? If you don't talk to them soon and get them on the pill, you could have three pregnant girls on your hands before school starts.'

'I hate to think about anything like that.'

'You have to, Hoke. You're a father now, and you don't know what Patsy told them, or if she told them anything. Over on Miami Beach there's teenage boys running around with perpetual hard-ons, and they can talk a couple of provincial girls from Vero Beach into doing damned near anything.'

'Okay, I'll talk to them. You want another brew?'

'I'll get 'em.'

Henderson went over to the bar to order. Hoke had wanted some advice, but not the kind he was getting. Henderson came back with two frosted mugs of beer.

'You ever talked to your kids about sex, Bill?'

'That's Marie's department. I might talk to Jimmy a little later and give him the standard lecture. I've warned them about drugs. Cripes, even the kids in elementary school are smoking pot already.'

'I've got to find a decent place to live, Bill. That's my first priority.'

'Why don't you borrow some money from the credit union?'

'I owe 'em too much already. I'm still paying for last year's vacation and for the new engine in my car. But I'll be a little better off now, because I won't have to send Patsy any more paychecks.'

'Do you want to bring Ellita and the girls over to the house for dinner tomorrow? I can barbecue some burgers in the back-yard, and we can drink a few beers. It'll get Ellita's mind off her troubles.'

'I'll take a raincheck, Bill. I'm gonna spend the day looking for a house, or maybe a two-bedroom apartment.'

The afternoon rain began, and the temperature in the air-conditioned bar dropped immediately. The bartender switched off the overhead fans. Hoke looked through the window. The rain came down so hard and the sky was so dark, it was difficult to see across Red Road.

'I haven't been much help, have I?' Bill said.

'Sure you have, Bill. Sometimes just talking about things is enough. The problem is I've got girls instead of boys. If they were boys, I could give 'em ten bucks apiece, tell 'em to hitchhike out to the West Coast for the rest of the summer. Then, by the time they came back, I'd have everything straightened out.'

'Would you do that?'

'Why not? That's what my old man did for me when I was sixteen. When I got out to Santa Monica, I worked on a live-bait boat and saved enough money to ride the Greyhound back to Riviera Beach. I had a great summer out there in California, even though the ocean was too damned cold to swim in. But you can't do something like that with girls. I'll get them jobs next week, though. If they're working all day, they won't get into any trouble.'

'I might be able to help you there, Hoke. Marie knows a lot of people. Sue Ellen can get a work permit. But Aileen, all you can get for her is maybe a baby-sitting job. You have to be sixteen to get a work permit.'

'I'll worry about that next week. But if you can find something for Sue Ellen, I'd appreciate it.'

'I'll talk to Marie.'

'You want another beer, Bill?'

'I don't think so. To tell you the truth, I feel a little guilty about taking the day off. Teddy Gonzalez called me at home last night. He's stuck on the triple murder in Liberty City, and Slater's no help at all. These three guys – all of them black – were tied hand and foot with copper wire, and then machine-gunned from the doorway. We know the killer was in the doorway because of the way the empty cartridges were scattered, and because there were no powder burns on the victims. Two were dead when the patrol car got there, and the third guy died before the ambulance arrived.'

'It sounds like a professional hit.'

'More like a semi-professional hit, Hoke. The guy said "Leroy" before he died. A pro would've made sure they were all dead before leaving.'

'Just "Leroy"? Nothing else?'

'That's all. There was no evidence of drugs in the house. The neighbors said these three guys had been living there about a week. We got an ID on all of them, but none of them was a Leroy.'

'Christ, Bill, there must be ten thousand men named Leroy in Liberty City.'

'It could've been worse. He could've said "Tyrone." Anyway, Slater told Teddy Gonzalez to check out everyone in the neighborhood named Leroy. In the first place, no one wants to talk to a white cop down there, especially a Latin cop, and Teddy's been running into problems without a partner. That's why he called me, and I didn't know what to tell him.'

'What about Leroy's floating crap game?' Hoke said, taking a sip of beer. 'I don't know if it's still in business, but Leroy's game used to move around the neighborhood in the vicinity of Northside, and that might be what the guy was talking about, or trying to say. Tell Teddy to check out the game. If it's still around, that might be a lead.'

'I never worked in Liberty City. Where was the game?'

'Tell Teddy to check the files. Leroy's game was busted a few times, and he moved it around a lot, but the game was always in the vicinity of the Northside Shopping Center, because that was where the gamblers had to park. They had to walk to the game from there. Tell him to check with some of the patrol cars in the area.'

'I don't know, Hoke. But it's a better lead than trying to check ten thousand Leroys who won't open the door. I'll give Teddy a ring when I get home.'

'Sure you don't want another beer?'

'I don't think so. I didn't really want this one. It's still early; I think I'll drive over and look at the Toros.' Henderson got up, slapped Hoke on the shoulder, and pushed through the swinging doors into the rain.

The Clash was playing 'London Calling' on the jukebox. Hoke strained to listen, trying to make out the lyrics, but could only understand every third or fourth word. The whole song made no sense to him. He finished his beer and the rest of Henderson's.

Hoke drove back to Miami Beach in the pelting rain. He drove slowly. He was in no hurry to get back to the hotel. His little suite was no longer a sanctuary; it was full of females with un-resolved problems.

Chapter Fifteen

After Hoke parked in his space at the Eldorado, he circled the hotel to check the bay side. Some of the residents had been dumping their trash into the sand of the filled-in swimming pool again, and the garbage pickup people had left a lot of litter scattered around the dumpster. Hoke entered the hotel from the rear entrance and wrote out his report at the manager's desk, reminding Mr Bennett to call the exterminators again. Hoke wondered sometimes whether Mr Bennett ever read his reports. The conditions rarely changed, but that was the manager's problem, not his – although Hoke hadn't considered the Norway rat invasion as one of his reporting duties when he had agreed to take on the unpaid security position at the hotel.

The girls were in Ellita's room. The three of them had been shopping, and Ellita had made curtains from red crepe paper and tacked them above the window with thumbtacks. The girls had arranged two large crepe paper bows, and these bows had been thumbtacked to the gray walls. Ellita had bought takeout food from a Cuban restaurant, together with red plastic plates and tableware. The girls had brought up one of the card tables from the lobby. There was enough red crepe paper left over for a tablecloth, and the table was set for four. A small pot of African violets had been brought from Hoke's suite as a centerpiece. A Styrofoam cooler filled with iced Cokes and beer was next to the card table.

'What's all this?' Hoke said. 'A party?'

'I hope you don't mind, Hoke,' Ellita said, 'but we decided to eat in instead of going out tonight. The girls said they never had any Cuban food before, and we wanted to surprise you.'

'I'm surprised. But there's only one chair. If you move the table by the bed, I can sit on the bed. I'll get a couple more chairs.'

Hoke walked down the hall, opened an empty room with his master key, and brought back two straight chairs.

'Where'd you get all this stuff, anyway?' Hoke said, arranging the chairs around the table.

'The food's from El Gaitero's, but the rest of the stuff's from Eckerd's and the 7-Eleven.'

'We met Tony Otero, Daddy,' Aileen said, smiling behind her hand, 'and Sue Ellen asked him if she could feel his muscle.'

'Shut up, Aileen,' Sue Ellen said, punching her sister on the arm.

'Did he let you feel it?' Hoke asked.

Sue Ellen nodded and blushed. 'Aileen felt it too.'

'How about you, Ellita?' Hoke said. 'Did you feel Tony's muscle, too?'

Ellita laughed, showing her white teeth. 'He's just a little fellow, Hoke. He only weighs a hundred and thirty-four pounds.'

'I didn't ask you how much he weighed.' Hoke grinned. 'I asked you if you felt his muscle.'

'Of course.' Ellita laughed again and began to open the cartons.

There were fried pork chunks, black beans and rice, yucca, and fried plantains, all packed in separate cartons with tight foil-topped cardboard lids. There were two loaves of buttered Cuban bread, sliced lengthwise.

The girls didn't like the yucca and refused to eat it. Aileen pushed the chunks of pork around on her plate, and Hoke asked her why she wasn't eating the best part of the dinner.

'They hurt my teeth and gums, Daddy. My teeth hurt all the time anyway, and I can't chew anything hard. I was supposed to see the orthodontist last Wednesday, but Mom was too busy to take me and said you'd make an appointment with someone down here.'

'Do you like those ugly braces?' Hoke said. 'They look like hell, to tell the truth.'

'They're too tight. I told Dr Osmond that, but he said they're supposed to feel too tight.'

'I'll take 'em off for you when we finish eating. You got any Valium in your purse, Ellita?'

'I should have,' Ellita said. She got up from the table and looked into her purse for her pillbox. 'I've got Valium, Tylenol-3, and some Midol.'

'Give her a half Valium now, and one T-3. By the time we're through eating, they should be working a little.'

Aileen took the Tylenol-3 and the half Valium with a sip of Coke.

'Do you know how to take off braces, Daddy?' Aileen asked.

'Sure. I was a dental assistant for a while when I was in the army. I learned how to do everything, including extractions. They never taught me how to make false teeth though. If they had, I'd make a better set than the ones I've got now.'

'I think I feel a little dizzy already,' Aileen said, putting the back of her hand to her forehead dramatically.

'Are you all through eating?'

Aileen nodded. 'I'm not hungry.'

'There's flan for dessert,' Ellita said, 'but I'll save yours for you.'

'Flan?'

'It's a caramelized custard. You can eat it without chewing.'

'I don't think I want it. Not now, anyway.'

'In that case,' Hoke said, 'go back to the suite and sit in the armchair. I'll be down in a few minutes.'

Holding the back of her hand to her forehead, and staggering slightly, Aileen left the room, closing the door behind her.

Hoke grinned. 'She's pretty good, isn't she?'

'I never knew you studied dentistry, Hoke,' Ellita said.

'Neither did I. But you want the girl to have a little confidence in me, don't you?'

Sue Ellen giggled. Hoke poked Sue Ellen in the ribs with a forefinger, and she giggled again.

'And don't *you* tell her any different.' Hoke finished the rest of his dinner. He then ate the pork chunks on Aileen's plate, and opened another can of beer.

'Are you ready for your flan?' Ellita said, opening another carton.

'I'll skip dessert. I'm trying to cut down on sweets. What I'll do, Ellita, I'll clip those braces off with my toenail cutters. I've got a good pair, made in Germany, and they'll cut damned near anything. You can hold her head still. Here, go down to the suite now and give her the other half Valium, and take her Coke along.'

It took Hoke more than a half-hour to clip off the rubber bands and the tiny bolts that held Aileen's braces together. The tight rubber bands were more difficult to snip away than the tiny bolts. There was a narrow gold strip glued to her lower teeth, however, and he couldn't get it off. There was no way that he could get a purchase on it with the clippers.

'I think,' Ellita said, 'you'll need some kind of solvent to remove that.'

'Does the lower band hurt, Aileen?' Hoke said.

'I don't know. My whole mouth hurts now, so I can't tell.'

'I'll leave the lower band on, then. I've got to go to the morgue on Monday or Tuesday, and I'll ask Doc Evans about it. He's probably got some kind of solvent he can lend me. But right now, you'd better lie down. Give her another T-3, Ellita.'

Ellita took the girl into the bedroom. Hoke told Sue Ellen to gather up all the garbage in Ellita's room and take it downstairs to the dumpster. 'But don't throw away the plastic silverware or plates. Wash that in Ellita's bathroom, and put it away in her dresser.'

Hoke lit a cigarette and turned on the TV. Ellita came out of the bedroom and closed the door just as the phone rang. She picked it up.

'Put him on,' she said into the phone. 'Yes, sir, he's here. Me? We were just going over our plans for Monday, that's all. Yes, sir. Just a second.'

She covered the mouthpiece. 'It's Major Brownley.'

'Shit,' Hoke said. 'You shouldn't've answered the phone.' He took the phone from her.

'Sergeant Moseley.'

'What's Ellita doing in your room, Hoke?' Brownley was pissed.

'We're trying to get a handle on what to do Monday, that's all. In fact, I met with Bill Henderson earlier this afternoon. We're all enthusiastic about the assignment, Willie, but there's so much to do it's hard to tell what to do first.'

'That shouldn't be a problem if you saw my flag.'

'What flag?'

'The red flag I attached to the Mary Rollins file. I put the Rollins file on the top of the stack so you'd get to it first.'

'I didn't see it. What I did, you see, was to divide the piles into three batches. So either Bill or Ellita must've got that one. Hold on a minute.' Hoke put his hand over the mouthpiece. 'Did you look at the Mary Rollins file? Do you remember?'

Ellita nodded. 'I had it, and then put it into my reject pile. It isn't even a definite homicide, it's a missing person.'

'Ellita saw it, Major Brownley,' Hoke said into the phone, 'but I didn't. I told them we'd read all the cases first before we decided which case to work on.'

'Consider that number one, then,' Brownley said. 'I just had another irate call from Mrs Rollins, Mary's mother. I've had one or two calls a month from this woman for the last three years. I want this woman off my back. Anyway, I told Mrs Rollins that you were working on this case personally, so from now on you'll get all her angry phone calls. Then you'll see what I mean.'

'I'll look at it first thing Monday, Willie.'

'That's all I had to tell you, Hoke. That, and that it was an unpleasant surprise to have Sanchez answer the phone in your hotel room on a Saturday evening. You know how I feel about things like that.'

'I explained that. We were just –'

But Brownley had hung up.

Hoke hung up, turned, and grinned at Ellita. 'Willie suspects a little hanky-panky. When you get up enough nerve to tell him you're pregnant, he'll put two and two together, come up with five, and tell you that Bruce, your detail man, is another Coconut Grove myth.'

'I didn't plan to tell him about Bruce. The major's entitled to know I'm pregnant, but there's no hurry about telling him. But you're right, Hoke, I shouldn't have answered your phone.'

'Fuck him.' Hoke shrugged. 'Let Willie think what he likes. He will anyway. Tell me something about this Rollins case.'

'It goes back about three years. Mary Rollins disappeared, but they found her car. They also found her shorts – they called 'em hot pants then – in a pole-bean field off Kendall Drive. Her bloody T-shirt was with the hot pants. They both had Type-O bloodstains, and Mary had Type-O blood. That's about it. There was no body. Her friends at work were interviewed, but no one saw her after she left work to go home on a Friday afternoon. She didn't have any boyfriends, apparently. Because of the bloody clothing, it was listed at first as a possible homicide, but was changed later to a missing person case. I remember it from yesterday because I had to look up a word in MacGellicot's notebook. He talked to a woman in Boca Raton, and then he wrote in his notes, "Hostile to males. Nugatory results. Maybe female investigator should talk to her."'

'You mean "negatory."'

'No. "Nugatory." I looked it up. It means having no worth or meaning. It's about the same as negatory, but what MacGellicot meant, I think, was that the woman was stalling him because he was a man, and she didn't like men.'

'Why didn't he say "lying" then? Why use a dumb word like "nugatory"?'

'We could ask him.'

'He left the department two years ago. Mac had a degree in sociology from the University of Chicago, and he got a police chief's job in some small town in Ohio. We lose a lot of good detectives that way. These little towns that advertise for a chief in the journal always flip when a Miami homicide cop applies for the job. But they usually want a new chief to have a degree besides. It's not a bad life compared with the things we have to do. Six cops, one patrol car, and a sign hidden behind a tree to make a little speed-trap money. The only crime you have to worry about is teenage drinkers pissing on the gravel in front of the town's only gas station.'

'We can call MacGellicot on Monday, can't we?'

'No, we'll just look at the file. See what else it says. Maybe you can drive up to Boca and talk to the woman, if she's still there. We'll have to do something, now that Willie called. Funny you didn't notice the red flag.'

'A bunch of the files are flagged, Hoke. You haven't got to yours yet, maybe.'

'That's what pisses me off. I don't mind doing the job, but I hate to be told how to do it. I don't like being called at home either, just to get some woman off Brownley's back.'

Hoke finished his beer.

'Tomorrow I'm going to see Ms Westphal at the house-sitting service again. She's got an efficiency available for three weeks in the black Grove, starting next Friday. She also pays the sitter five bucks a day for living in it. If you don't mind living in the ghetto, Ellita, I can talk her into letting you have it. Three weeks'll give you a base, and you can then look around for a decent place to live. Or maybe, after three weeks, you can move back home.'

'I'm not going back home again, Hoke. If I did, I'd get the silent treatment from my father. It's time I left anyway. I would like to get a place in the same neighborhood though. That way, my mother could come over and help me with the baby.'

'You've got months to go before you have to worry about a baby-sitter.'

'I know, but I've thought about it.'

'How do you feel? Physically?'

'I feel fine. I like your girls, Hoke. Not only are they well behaved, they adore you.'

'How could they? They don't even know me, for Christ's sake. And I don't know what to do with them either. You've helped me a lot.'

'Did you call their mother yet? To let her know that they're all right?'

'Except for a few letters, I haven't talked to Patsy in ten years. If she wants to know how they are, she can call me.'

'Maybe she's tried, Hoke? It's hard to get you at the hotel.'

'I'll tell you what. Get her phone number from Sue Ellen, and you can call her. Reverse the charges, and if she won't accept the call, the hell with it.'

'Sure you don't want to talk to her?'

'Positive.'

'I'll call her then. If I were their mother, I'd want to know that they got here okay.' Ellita cracked the door to the bedroom, then

329

closed it softly. 'Aileen's sleeping like a baby. That was awfully kind of you, Hoke, taking her braces off.'

'What the hell.' Hoke shrugged. 'She was in pain. I'm her father, for Christ's sake.'

Ellita started to cry. Hoke looked at her for a moment, then picked up his leisure jacket, left the suite, and took the elevator down to the lobby. He didn't know why he felt so lousy, so useless.

He got into his car, switched on the engine, and tried to think of somewhere to go. He didn't have anywhere to go, so he drove to the police station in Miami. He looked for the Mary Rollins file, and read through it. He leafed through two more cases – hopeless, hopeless, both of them – and then locked his office. He went down to the cafeteria for a cup of coffee and sat down alone at a table to drink it.

Lieutenant Fred Slater came in, and Hoke watched him as he got a carton of milk and a glass, and paid the cashier. Slater was grinning. He looked around the room, spotted Hoke, and came over to the table. Slater's thin lips split his pockmarked face into two ugly parts. He opened the milk carton and filled his glass.

'I just heard a good one, Hoke,' he said. 'How do you know when you're sleeping with a fag?' He took a sip of milk and wiped off the milk mustache with a paper napkin. 'How? His dick tastes like shit!' Slater laughed and took another sip of milk.

Hoke didn't laugh. 'Let me tell you something, Slater, and I want you to get it straight. You ever tell my girls a joke like that, and exec officer or no exec officer, I'll kick the living shit out of you.'

'I don't know what you're talking about. It's just a joke, for Christ's sake. All I was …'

But Slater was talking to Hoke's back as he walked out of the cafeteria.

Chapter Sixteen

On Sunday morning Hoke awoke at six, as usual, dressed, and drove to the 7-Eleven. He bought a dozen bagels, a quart of milk, a package of cream cheese, and three large cans of Dinty Moore stew. He also picked out a large Spanish onion, which he planned to dice and add to the canned stew for extra flavor. Back in the suite, he heated water on the hot plate for instant coffee, and when it boiled he woke the girls for breakfast. Then he walked down the hall and knocked on Ellita's door, telling her to join them in his suite for bagels and coffee.

Ellita wasn't wearing pantyhose with her skirt when she joined Hoke a few minutes later, and when she sat down and crossed her legs, he caught a glimpse of the inner side of her thighs. Her soft thighs were as white as ivory, which surprised Hoke so much he stared a little longer than he had intended. Hoke had always assumed that Ellita was the same golden tan all over – like her exposed face, neck, and arms. Hoke knew that most Cubans thought of themselves as white, but he had always considered them as Third Worlders – an island mixture of Spanish, Caribe Indian, and black – and as being brown all over. For that reason, he had never objected to the department Affirmative Action program, which gave preference to minorities, both in hiring practices and on promotion lists. In Miami, however, although the majority of the population was Latin, they were still counted as a minority group. If Ellita was white as well as Cuban, Hoke figured, maybe she hadn't really deserved a promotion to a detective's slot in the Homicide Division. Ellita's white thighs were a revelation to him, opening up a whole line of new thoughts. One of these days, he'd have to talk to Bill Henderson about this as something that should be discussed at the P.B.A. On the other hand, even though Ellita had been given preference, as a Cuban, over several

WASP policemen who also deserved to be detectives, she had paid her dues after working all those years as a police dispatcher. So what difference did it make? None at all. It was just nice to know that Ellita was a white woman, after all – even if she was a Cuban. Henderson liked her, and so did he, and they could hardly blame her for taking advantage of the program to get out of a boring, dead-end job.

The girls were still in the bedroom, and taking turns in the bathroom. Ellita stirred her coffee and sat back a little in the desk chair.

'I called Patsy last night, Hoke,' Ellita said. 'Collect. Sue Ellen also talked to her for a few minutes. She said she'd send a check to the girls to make up the difference between what you gave them as an allowance and what she usually gave them. Sue Ellen told her you were giving them a dollar a week, so she said she'd send them each a check for forty-six dollars every month.'

'What else did she say?'

'She wanted to know who I was, so I told her I was your partner. But then, when Sue Ellen talked to her and told her we were all living here together, she probably got the wrong idea.'

'Does it bother you?'

'What a woman who deserts her children thinks of me is not worth bothering about.' Ellita added more Sweet 'N Low to her coffee.

'She's probably relieved that there's a woman around to look after the girls, but I'm sorry she got the wrong idea about you.'

The girls emerged sleepily from the bedroom and mixed their coffee in the red plastic cups Ellita had brought from her room.

'I don't see why we have to get up so early on a Sunday,' Sue Ellen said.

'There're bagels and cream cheese in the sack,' Hoke explained. 'This evening I'll cook some beef stew, and we'll still have enough bagels to go with it. Do you think, Sue Ellen, that your mother'll send you allowance checks, like she said?'

'I know she will.'

'In that case, I'll lend both of you girls five dollars, and you can pay me back when you get your checks. That way, if you want, you can buy some cigarettes.' Hoke gave them five dollars apiece. Aileen put her money into her pocket, then soaked her bagel in her coffee to soften it.

'How're your teeth this morning?' Hoke asked.

'Fine, Daddy. But I slept awful hard. I don't think I moved all night.'

'Good. But if they start to hurt again, and they might, ask Ellita for another T-3.'

Aileen nodded.

'How about you, Ellita?' Hoke said. 'Did you call your mother too?'

'Three times, but each time my father answered, so I hung up. Then I called my cousin Louisa and asked her to tell my mother I was staying here, and that I'd call her Monday.'

Hoke opened his notebook and tore out a page. 'I went to the office last night and took a look at the Mary Rollins file. Here's the address of that woman up in Boca Raton. Her name is Wanda Fridley, Mrs Fridley. If you don't have anything else planned today, why not take the girls and drive up there and talk to her? Mrs Fridley's the woman who called the department and said she saw Mary Rollins in Delray Beach. Then when MacGellicot drove up and talked to her about it, she changed her story and said she wasn't sure. His notes, that she probably didn't like him because he was a man, may or may not be valid. But maybe she'll talk to you. I was going to send you up there tomorrow, but it might be best to get this interview out of the way today, so we can work on our other cases tomorrow. This way, we can at least tell Brownley we're working on the Rollins case. I'll drive out to the site where they found her shorts and T-shirt and look around the area. I know I won't find anything out there now, but it'll be something else to add to the report. But if you don't want to go today, that's all right, too. You can buy a bathing suit, and you girls can spend the day on the beach.'

'That's no choice at all.' Ellita laughed. 'You couldn't pay me enough money to wear a bathing suit!'

'Why not?'

Ellitta patted the top of her leg. 'Fat thighs. Cellulite. I don't wear a bikini, and I don't go to the beach.'

'I know you can swim. You had to pass the swimming test at the academy.'

'I did. But then I sat on my ass for seven years developing cellulite. I don't mind driving up to Boca. We should be back by noon or a little later, and the girls can still go to the beach. I'll go with them and watch them from a chickee.'

'Okay, that's settled. I'm going to check on that apartment in the Grove for you, and then see if I can run down Jerry Hickey's former landlady. I got the address you left on my desk last night.'

'What can she tell you?'

'I don't know. I just wonder where he got the money and the white lady, that's all. There's something weird about this case, and I'm not ready to close the file on it yet. Don't you think it's a little unusual for a white boy to take a room in a black woman's house in the black Grove?'

Ellita smiled. 'Not for a junkie. Besides, aren't you trying to get me a garage apartment in the black Grove?'

'But you'll be paid for living there. It isn't the same thing.' Hoke recalled his reflections of a moment before, about Ellita's color, but decided to keep his counsel.

'Maybe Jerry was paid to live there, too,' Ellita said.

'That's another question I could ask, I suppose. Well, look, I'll be back this afternoon, and if I'm not back, I'll call the desk and give Eddie a number where you can call me. Then tonight we'll fix the stew and all have dinner, the way we did last night. I enjoyed that.'

Hoke turned to Sue Ellen and Aileen. 'Remember, Ellita's going to be on police business. So you do whatever she tells you, understand?'

Hoke's daughters assured him that they did.

Hoke parked in front of the Coconut Grove Library, the only attractive public building in the Grove. With its fieldstone façade, curving wooden walkway, and the shady branches overhanging the weathered steps, the building looked as though it had grown out of the ground. A police officer was sitting in his squad car reading *Penthouse*. The officer, still in his early twenties, was so absorbed by the magazine he didn't look up until Hoke tapped him on the shoulder.

'Open the back door.' Hoke showed the officer his shield. 'I'm Sergeant Moseley. Homicide.'

The officer clicked up the door lock, and Hoke slid into the back seat. The officer picked his cap up from the seat, slapped it on his head, and shoved his magazine under the front seat.

'What's up, Sarge?'

Hoke looked across the street to Peacock Park. A women's softball game was in progress. The harbor was filled with anchored Hobie Cats and other small sailboats with furled sails. Two bearded, shirtless men holding their shirts in their laps, their faces raised to the sun, sat on the stone wall that bordered the park. Hoke looked back at the officer. 'How long you been assigned to the Grove?'

'About six weeks now. I like it better'n Liberty City. I got hit with a rock during a fracas at Northside Shopping Center.' The patrolman pointed to a jagged red scar on his chin. 'Fourteen stitches. After that, my squad leader thought I might be a little prejudiced, so he had me transferred to the Grove. Best thing that ever happened to me. I been working days, and things've been pretty quiet compared to Liberty City. Some chain and purse snatching, a little loitering, that's about it. On Friday nights there's been a kind of teenage invasion from all over, but I haven't been on nights yet.'

'Did you know a kid named Jerry Hickey?'

'Uh-uh, but my partner might. He's been in the Grove for 'most three years.'

'Where is he?'

'Up at Lum's.' The officer pointed up the sloping street. 'He's getting himself a Lumberjack burger. At first, we used to eat together, but now, when we take a break for a sandwich or coffee, we take turns. That way, Red said, somebody's always with the radio.'

'In other words, you two don't get along.'

'I didn't say that, Sergeant. We get along fine. I've learned a lot from old Red.'

'Okay. You go up to Lum's and get old Red and tell him I want to talk to him. Then you can stay in Lum's and get your own Lumberjack burger.'

'I was plannin' on a tuna fish.'

The officer started up the mild incline, and Hoke wondered how this incredibly stupid young officer had managed to get through the police academy. But perhaps he expected too much; the kid wasn't so much dumb as he was young, that was all.

The police car was nosed into the curb, so Hoke recognized 'old' Red as he limped down the street from Lum's. Red Halstead was thirty-nine, and he had been shot in the foot by a woman he had tried to disarm before she could pump her last bullet into her husband's inert body. As a consequence, Halstead had worked in Property for more than a year. The woman's husband had died, and she had been given ten years' probation by a sympathetic judge. But Halstead, after narrowly missing out on a disability discharge, had endured the necessary therapy and the boring job in the Property office and had finally regained his old job on the street. The widow had married a man a lot wealthier than her dead husband. Now she lived in a condo in Bal Harbour.

Hoke got out of the car and shook hands with Halstead. 'Hoke Moseley, Red. I remember you from Property. How's the foot?'

'Fine, Sergeant, 'cept when it gets cold, but I haven't had to worry much about cold weather lately. It's eighty-eight already, and it's only ten A.M.'

'Sorry to interrupt your break.'

'That's okay. I was finished anyway. Who's dead?'

'A kid named Jerry Hickey. He died from an overdose at home. But he used to hang out around Peacock Park. I thought you might know him, or know someone who did.'

Halstead nodded. 'I knew him. He had an allowance of some kind from his father, the drug lawyer. Some of the kids around here would hit him up for small change once in a while. He also sold weed, but I never caught him with any, and I must've shook him down three or four times. He was also a junkie, and he hung out sometimes with Harry Jordan. Jordan used to be a Hare Krishna, but was kicked out of the cult for skimming off the top, or something like that. But he kept his yellow robes, and now he's in business for himself. Instead of just skimming, he keeps everything he begs now.' Halstead laughed. 'They should've kept him on and just let him take his percentage. But Jordan's straight – I mean he's not into dope. I don't think he even drinks. He's something of a guru around the Grove. He lives on Peralta, over in the black section.'

'1309 Peralta?'

'I don't know if that's the number, but I know where he lives on Peralta. He lives in a garage out back.'

'A garage apartment?'

'No.' Halstead shook his head and grinned. 'A garage. What's going down?'

'Not much of anything. I'm doing a little backtracking, that's all.'

'You just want to talk to somebody who knew Hickey, right?'

'That's it.'

'Well, Harry Jordan knew him as well as anybody. He used to crash at Harry's, but I think he had a room somewhere here in the Grove besides. I could tell you how to get to Harry's, but the easiest way would be to just drive by. You could follow me. When I pass the house I'll flash my turn signal once and keep going. The garage'll be around to the back. I won't stop, because if I did, everyone in the neighborhood would know you were a cop.'

'Okay. And thanks, Red.'

Hoke trailed two hundred yards behind the police car and followed it down Main Highway, parallel with Grand Avenue. Halstead signaled and made a right turn into the black Grove. After two more blocks, Halstead slowed, flashed his signal, and then accelerated. Hoke made a sharp turn into a dirt driveway beside a pink two-bedroom house and parked in the backyard.

A girl, sixteen or seventeen, was sitting in a webbed beach chair, nursing a baby. Her heavy bare breasts seemed disproportionately large for her slender body. Her acorn-brown hair reached almost to her waist, and she wore a soiled eggshell-colored skirt down to her ankles. Her dirty, slender feet were bare. A blue T-shirt was draped over the arm of the chair. As Hoke got out of his car, she looked at him incuriously with sienna eyes and drummed on the baby's bare back with the tips of her fingers. Her left eye was black and swollen, and there were mottled black-and-blue marks on her puffy left cheek.

337

The fenced-in backyard also contained a redwood table and two benches, a drooping clothesline hung with drying diapers, and several rows of vegetables – carrots, green peppers, and plum tomatoes. The garage at the end of the dirt driveway was being used as a residence. The wide garage door was missing, and the unpainted front of the small building, except for a normal door-sized entrance covered by a dusty blue velvet curtain, was composed of plywood and other odd-sized pieces of scrap lumber. The garage had an unpainted corrugated-iron roof that looked new.

A monk came through the blue velvet curtain. He was wearing a clean saffron robe and leather sandals without socks. He was about thirty, and his head, except for a short tuft of blond hair at the crown, was shaved. Despite his shaven head, he was noticeably balding. He looked at Hoke with narrowed blue eyes.

'Get in the house, Moira,' he said.

The girl, carrying her baby and the blue T-shirt, got up from the chair and sidled through the curtain.

'How old's the girl, Harry?'

'Old enough to have a baby.'

'Does her mother know she's here?'

'No. If she did, she'd send someone like you to take her home again. And then it would take Moira another month or so to escape like she had to do the last time. Why don't you people quit hassling us?'

'Moira's mother didn't send me here. It's just that I've got a daughter about that age.' Hoke took out his cigarettes, and then returned them to his pocket. 'What I want is some information about Jerry Hickey. I'm a police officer.'

'I think he left Miami, probably Florida.'

'What makes you think that?'

'A couple of guys came around and searched his old room.' Jordan pointed to the pink house. 'Then they talked to me. He was supposed to deliver a package or something to a Holiday Inn in North Miami, but apparently he never got there. They didn't say what was in the package, but they searched my place, too, which I didn't appreciate.'

'Were they police officers?'

Jordan smiled, and wiped his mouth. 'Hardly. They were both Latins in silk suits. I hadn't seen Jerry for two days, not since – did you get a look at Moira's face?'

'It's quite a shiner —'

'Worse than that. Jerry chipped a piece of bone from her cheek, and she's in a lot of pain. I don't understand it, any of it. I felt sorry for Jerry because I thought he needed a place to be, you know. But when I was out, he tried to jump Moira. When she resisted, he hit her.'

'He tried to rape the girl? That doesn't sound like junkie behavior. Could be, now that Jerry's dead, you're blaming him for something you did yourself.'

'I didn't know Jerry was dead.' Jordan's face became a solemn mask. Jordan held his hands out, palms up, and showed Hoke his forearms. They were covered with tiny red welts. 'Ant bites, Mr Policeman, from my garden. But I won't kill those ants, or any of God's creatures. And I wouldn't hit my wife.'

'You're married, then?'

'In the eyes of God, yes. Moira could also tell you I didn't hit her, but you probably wouldn't believe her either. But I didn't know Jerry was dead. I'll pray for him now, and for you, too, whether you want me to or not. Did those men kill him?'

'No. It was an overdose. Heroin.'

'May God rest his troubled soul.' Incongruously, Jordan crossed himself.

'Can you show me Jerry's room?'

'That's up to Mrs Fallon. I rent the garage from her, and Jerry had a room in her house up till about a month ago. She caught him shooting up, and she kicked him out. Then I took him in.' Jordan shrugged. 'He needed a place to be, and I still think I did the right thing, but I'm finding it hard to forgive him. I'm still working on that, but it'll be easier now, now that I know he's dead, I mean. Mrs Fallon's a member of the Primitive Baptist Church, and they're down on junkies, but she'll probably let you look at his old room. I know she hasn't rented it out again.'

Hoke took out his wallet and gave Jordan a dollar bill. 'Here. Better get some Tylenol for Moira.'

The dollar bill disappeared inside Jordan's robes. 'God bless you, sir.' Jordan bowed from the waist, turned, and went into the garage through the curtain, colliding with Moira, who had been standing right behind it.

Hoke knocked at the back door of the pink house. The door opened immediately because Mrs Fallon, a large black woman in a shapeless gray housecoat, had been watching Hoke through the kitchen window as he talked to Jordan. Hoke had seen her sullen face when she pulled the white curtain to one side. Hoke showed her his shield and ID.

'I'm a police officer, Mrs Fallon, and I'd like to take a look at Jerry's old room.'

'You got a warrant?'

'No. But I have reason to believe that you're holding Mr Hickey's dog a prisoner in your house. And dognapping's a serious crime.'

'I don't know nothin' 'bout no dog. Jerry didn't have no dog, and he's been out of the house 'most a month now, livin' with the reverend.'

'Who'd you sell the dog to? I know there's been a dog here because of that digging around the bush over there – over there' – Hoke pointed – 'by those oleanders.'

'I done that diggin' myself, weedin'.'

'Did you know oleanders were poison? If you burn oleander bushes and breathe in the smoke, you can poison yourself and a dog, too.'

'There's never been no dog here!'

'I'd like to see for myself. I'd also like to see your landlord's license for renting out rooms. You've got one, haven't you?'

'I don't need no license. Jerry was staying here, but I just let him stay as a favor, that's all.'

'Did you charge him rent for the favor?'

'Jerry didn't have no room – not exactly. I just let him sleep in the utility room. I don't run no roomin' house. I told the other two mens that, who pushed their way in here.'

'I'd like to see where he slept.'

'I reckon I can show you where he slept. But you got no right to look in the rest of my house.'

'That's all I want to see. Just where he slept.'

340

Mrs Fallon stepped back, and Hoke came into the kitchen. She opened the door to the utility room, off the kitchen. There was a canvas cot, a three-legged wooden stool, and some nails on the wall where clothes could be hung, but the spotlessly clean room was bare otherwise. There was no window. A single 40-watt bulb dangled on a cord from the ceiling. A long piece of brown twine was attached to the light chain. It would be possible for someone to lie in bed and turn the light on and off without sitting up.

'Did Jerry have kitchen privileges?'

'No, sir. He didn't eat much, but I fed him sometimes. I always got somethin' or other on the stove.'

'You didn't let him keep things in your refrigerator then?'

'No, but he never ast.'

'At least he was a clean housekeeper.'

'I cleaned up after he left. And you can see there ain't no dog in here.'

'The two men who searched his room – what did they look like?'

'They was white mens, but they spoke Spanish to each other. They was driving a green Eldorado with the top down. They didn't stay long. I was gonna call the police after they left, but I didn't want to get involved. I had a little cardboard box packed up with some of Jerry's clothes he left here, but they took that along. It was just some underwear and socks and a blue work shirt. I always did Jerry's laundry with mine, and it was in the wash when he left. He was staying with Reverend Jordan after that, but I wasn't going to carry it down to him. He knew it was here, and he could've come and got it.'

'Did those men take Jerry's dog, too?'

'Jerry didn't have no dog! I done tol' you that ten times!'

'All right. Thank you, Mrs Fallon. But if those two men come back, or if Jerry's dog comes back, call me at this number.' Hoke gave her one of his cards. 'And thank you for your cooperation.'

As Hoke drove out of the yard, Mrs Fallon started to walk toward the garage. She'll pump Harry Jordan, Hoke thought. Jordan will tell her that Jerry's dead, and then she'll pray for Jerry, too. Mrs Fallon's Christian prayers, Hoke decided, would help Jerry just about as much as Harry Jordan's.

Chapter Seventeen

A wire fence separated the Bajan sculptor's garage apartment and yard from the Robert E. Lee housing project. At least thirty black kids were playing some kind of grab-ass on the other side of the fence. They came over to the fence to stare at Hoke while he pulled into the narrow backyard and parked. There was a huge sculpture of a birdlike creature in the yard, blocking the way to the closed door of the garage. The wings were fashioned from automobile fenders, and the body was formed with welded auto parts. The 'bird' had been painted with red rust-proofing primer, and its eyes were red glass taillights. The eyes were unlighted, and Hoke wondered for a moment if the sculptor would wire them for electricity when he was finished with the sculpture. He then realized that he didn't give a shit what the sculptor decided to do, because he would never have to look at it again.

Ellita, if she moved into the small apartment above the garage, would be an object of curiosity, and she would be harassed by the kids in the project. Nor could he take the place himself; there was no way that he could leave his girls alone all day in this neighborhood. Without getting out of his car, he backed out of the yard. Before his back wheels reached Tangerine Lane, a rock hit the windshield on the passenger's side, but it didn't crack the glass. The kids on the other side of the fence, squealing, ran off in a dozen directions.

Hoke turned east to South Dixie Highway and then drove south to North Kendall Drive. He took Kendall west to 136th Avenue, and turned into a Kendall Lakes shopping mall. He parked in the lot, and then paced off the approximate distance to where Mary Rollins's hot pants and T-shirt were discovered. The location was now a chain sandwich shop, featuring roast beef sandwiches. The 'Sunday Special' was a roast beef sandwich with a free Coke for

$2.99. Hoke went inside, ordered the special, and doused his sandwich with the chain's special horseradish sauce. The teenagers behind the counter wore oversized red muslin tams and little red jackets that didn't meet in front. Their white muslin shirts had balloon sleeves. They wore their own blue jeans, however, which diluted by about five hundred years the medieval effect intended by the management. The tables and benches were bolted to the floor, and the benches were set too far back from the table for comfortable seating. Three years ago, this shopping center had been a U-pick pole-bean field. Now it held fifty different shops, anchored by a Publix supermarket and a K-Mart. The mall was filled with Sunday shoppers, most of them wearing Izod alligator shirts and shorts, or running togs. There were a great many small children. Every one of them was eating something or other as the parents walked aimlessly around the mall.

Perhaps, Hoke thought, this cold-case idea of Brownley's was not such a good one after all. West Kendall was the fastest-growing area in the county, and there were hundreds of condos filled already, with more under construction. Not only did Miami have hundreds of new permanent residents moving in every day, there was also a daily tourist influx of at least thirty thousand strangers staying from one day to two months or more on vacations. A colder case than Mary Rollins – missing only, with no body – would be hard to imagine. It was perfectly possible that her body was buried somewhere under the thirty acres of asphalt parking lot.

Of course, Hoke hadn't expected to find anything out here anyway, but it had been more than two years since he had been this far out on Kendall Drive, and he hadn't realized how much the area had boomed. Hoke finished his sandwich and Coke, then showed the kid behind the counter his badge.

The phone was in the small back storeroom, and the kid stood uneasily beside Hoke as he dialed.

'This is police business, sonny. Get out and close the door.' The boy left reluctantly but didn't argue.

Eddie Cohen answered on the twelfth ring.

'This is Sergeant Moseley, Eddie. Did Ms Sanchez phone and leave a number for me to call?'

'Just a second. I got it written down.'

Hoke waited, and then Eddie gave him a number in Delray Beach. 'It's a pay phone, she said, and she'll either wait there, or be there at exactly two o'clock. If you don't call by two, don't call at all, and she'll drive back to the hotel.'

Hoke looked at his Timex. It was 12:30.

'All right, Eddie. If she calls again, tell her I'm on my way to the station, and I'll call her at two from there.'

'I'll tell her. Anything else?'

'Yeah. Don't pull the plug on the air conditioning in my suite or in Ms Sanchez's room.'

'I already did. Mr Bennett told me –'

'I don't care what he said. You plug 'em in again right now, understand?'

'I'll see if I can find Emilio.'

'Never mind Emilio. You do it yourself. Now.'

'If you say so.'

'I say so.' Hoke replaced the receiver.

Before leaving the sandwich shop, Hoke bought an eight-ounce bottle of the special horseradish sauce from the boy behind the counter and thanked him for letting him use the phone.

When Hoke got to his office and turned on the desk light, two detectives on Sunday duty wandered over. They stood in the doorway, not quite coming into the small room, waiting for an invitation they didn't get. They both wore tattered jeans, ragged running shoes, and filthy sport shirts. They both had scruffy beards and long hair. Quevedo was a few years older than Donovan, but they had both been in the Homicide Division for more than three years. They looked like the bums who hung out in Bayfront Park and the Miamarina, because that was where they were working. In the last month, two sleeping bums had been doused with gasoline and set on fire, and they were trying to get a lead on the killer(s).

'I hear,' Donovan said, 'you're on a special assignment.'

'You hear a lot of things around here,' Hoke said.

Quevedo pointed to the stack of files. 'Looks like a lot of cases to have out at the same time.'

'It is indeed,' Hoke said. 'What's new on the torchings?'

'We got some leads.'

'Well, don't let me keep you. I've got some reading to do and some phone calls to make.' Hoke belched, and got a second, searing taste of the horseradish sauce. His stomach burned.

'We're going downstairs for coffee,' Quevedo said. 'Want me to bring you a cup?'

'No thanks.' Hoke took the bottle of horseradish sauce out of his jacket pocket. 'Here, Quevedo. You like hot stuff. This horse-radish sauce is *muy sabroso*.'

'You don't want it?' Quevedo said, taking the bottle.

'I've got another bottle in my car. Keep it. It goes great on hamburgers.'

'Thanks. Thanks a lot.'

The two detectives left. Hoke got up and shut the door. He sat at his desk again, watching the detectives as they crossed to the elevator.

The word was out already, Hoke realized. Quevedo and Donovan already knew about the cold-case assignment and were fishing around for confirmation. That meant his problems would soon multiply. Someone would notify the press, and then when the state attorney arraigned Captain Midnight, there would be reporters coming around to the division looking for details.

And what could he tell them? That the Captain Morrow collar had been merely a lucky break? That they hadn't even read through the old cases yet? It was impossible to keep anything secret in Miami; despite its huge population, Miami was like a small town where everybody knew everyone else's business. And there was too much business in the Homicide Division.

The phone rang. It was Ellita, calling from Delray Beach.

'I called Mr Cohen again, Hoke, and he said you were going to the office. I called early because the girls are getting restless hanging around the mall here. Besides, the news is good for a change. I found Mary Rollins. She's alive and working as a waitress in Delray Beach.'

'Are you sure?'

'Positive. It was fairly simple, although I had to talk to Mrs Fridley for a long time before she would tell me where Rollins worked. It's

345

a long story, but now that I've found Rollins – which we didn't expect – I don't know the next step. Wanda Fridley and Mary Rollins both went to Miami High together. In the same class. Mrs Fridley married a pre-development salesman in Boca, and she's been living in Boca ever since. She just happened to run into Mary by accident at the Delray Beach café where Mary works. Mary told her not to tell anyone she was there. Apparently, Mary staged her own disappearance as a way to escape from her mother. Mary worked at an S and L in Miami, and lived at home. She had to turn over her paycheck each week to her mother, and she was a virtual prisoner. Then she met a guy in the S and L one day, and dated him. He's a married man with three children, and he lives here in Delray Beach. Mary got a raise at the S and L, but didn't tell her mother about it. She started saving her extra raise money, telling her mother the company was paying in cash now each week instead of by check. That way, her mother wouldn't know about the extra money –'

'Can you shorten this a little?'

'Not very well. Then, when Mary had two hundred dollars saved, she planted her bloody shorts and T-shirt in the pole-bean field out in Kendall, and caught a bus to Delray Beach. She thought if her mother figured she was dead, she wouldn't look for her.'

'Where did the blood come from?' Hoke said.

'Most of it came from a bloody nose. When she gets excited, she said, her nose bleeds. The rest was from a cut finger. She already had a suitcase with some other clothes and things in it stashed away at the bus station in a locker. She rented a room here in Delray, got a job as a waitress, and she's been up here ever since. Her affair with the married man is still ongoing, as they say, and she gets to see him once a week – sometimes twice a week. This is the story she told Mrs Fridley, and the same one she told me. Mrs Fridley would've kept the secret, she said, but Mary borrowed fifty dollars from her, promising to pay her back the following week. Then, when she didn't pay it back, Mrs Fridley got mad and called Homicide and said she'd seen Mary Rollins. By the time we finally got around to sending MacGellicot up to Boca, Mary had already seen Mrs Fridley again and paid her ten dollars on account. She was short, and could only pay her back at ten dollars a week. So then, when MacGellicot talked to Mrs Fridley, she'd decided not to turn in her old school friend and she stalled MacGellicot. She was ashamed, she told me, for not trusting Mary to pay her back the fifty bucks. Mary lives in a ratty little room here in Delray, and she only spends an occasional afternoon in a motel with her boyfriend.

'Actually,' Ellita chuckled, 'Mrs Fridley was dying to tell someone the story. Once she got started talking, it all tumbled out.

'Anyway, I drove up to Delray and found Mary. She's working at the Spotlight Café, so I got her address from the manager. I talked to her then, and I believe her. She knew, she said, that her mother was using her for support, and that she'd never have a life of her own unless she ran away. I feel sorry for her, Hoke. She's not too bright, and for a thin girl she's not bad-looking, either. But she doesn't seem to realize that this guy's using her just as much as her mother did. Eventually, she believes, after her boyfriend's children are grown, he'll divorce his wife and marry her, you see.'

'But did you get a positive ID?'

'Of course. Driver's license and birth certificate. She showed me both of them. Do you want me to pick her up and bring her back down with me, or what? I hate to turn this young woman over to her mother again, although –'

Hoke laughed. 'Sure. Bring her in! And then, after we return Mary to her mother, I'll drive you home and return you to *your* mother and father.'

After a five-second silence, Ellita said, 'I guess I wasn't thinking.'

'No, you weren't. Just borrow Rollins's license and birth certificate, and we'll make Xeroxes down here and mail them back to her. Major Brownley can then call Mrs Rollins and tell her that Mary's alive and well. That'll be the end of it. We don't have to tell Mrs Rollins where her daughter lives. Twenty-six years old, she can live anywhere she wants. We don't have to tell her mother shit. But before you come back down here, reassure Mary that we won't give her address to her mother. Otherwise, she might stage another fake disappearance and take off again.'

'She's really afraid of the mother, Hoke. Do you want to talk to her?'

'Hell, no. Just get her address and place of employment so I can write a memo on it to Brownley. We'll attach the Xeroxes to it, and the case is closed.'

'I can give you the address now.'

Hoke wrote the information Ellita gave him on a yellow legal pad.

'You did a good job, Ellita. You know I can't give you any overtime, but if you put in a voucher for mileage up there and back, I'll sign it. Did you have lunch yet?'

'We ate at the Spotlight Café, where Mary works.'

'Okay. Add your lunch receipt to the mileage, and I'll reimburse you for lunch on the voucher, too. See you back at the hotel.'

Hoke chopped up the onion and added it to the three cans of beef stew simmering in the pot on his hot plate. He set the switch to Low-Low and sniffed the aroma. This was one of Hoke's favorite meals. The girls would enjoy it.

Ellita and the girls didn't ask for seconds, however, when they ate dinner. Hoke told them they could reheat the stew for lunch the next day. While they ate, Ellita retold the story about Mary Rollins and showed Hoke the birth certificate and driver's license.

'Has she got a new license under a new name?'

'She doesn't have a car, and she didn't change her last name. She just calls herself Candi now, with an *i* and no *e*. She's got a little nameplate on her uniform. She was pretty happy when I told her – convinced her, rather – that we wouldn't tell her mother where she was living. She showed me a photo of her boyfriend. He's about fifty, and he's got a gut out to here.' Ellita made a circle with her hands to demonstrate and burst into tears.

'What's the matter, Ellita?' Sue Ellen said.

'Nothing.' Ellita wiped her eyes with the back of her hand. 'I've got to wash my hair.' As she got up from the table to go to her room, Hoke's phone rang.

Hoke picked it up and gestured for Sue Ellen and Aileen to stay seated and not follow Ellita to her room.

'Tony Otero's down here, Sergeant Moseley.' It was Eddie Cohen. 'He wants to talk to your daughter Sue Ellen. Shall I send him up, or does she want to come down here?'

'Tell him to wait at the desk. I'll be right down.'

Hoke hung up the phone. He told the girls to clear the card table, fold it up again, and put things away. 'I'll be back in a few minutes, and then we'll have a little talk.'

Tony Otero, wearing a white linen suit, white shoes, and a red silk necktie, smiled at Hoke and shook hands with him when Hoke met him in the lobby. When Tony smiled, Hoke noticed a dark line above Tony's four upper front teeth. He realized that the little boxer was wearing an upper plate. He hadn't noticed it when Bill Henderson had introduced him to the lightweight a few weeks ago.

'Let's sit over here, Tony.' Hoke gripped the boxer's elbow with a thumb and two fingers and led him over to a tattered divan in the lobby, away from the desk. The divan was well separated from the old ladies watching the TV set on the wall.

Tony was looking past Hoke's shoulder, toward the elevators.

'Sue Ellen won't be coming down, Tony. What gave you the idea you could talk to my daughter?'

'I was going to ask her out to dinner. Take her out for a steak maybe.'

Hoke shook his head. 'How old are you, Tony?'

'Twenty-four.'

'D'you know how old Sue Ellen is?'

'Seventeen, she told me.'

'She's *six*teen. Just barely sixteen, hardly going on seventeen.'

'Sixteen? Seventeen?' Tony shrugged. 'What's the difference? I was just going to ask her out to dinner, no shit.'

'Why?'

'She's a pretty girl, and I got nothing else to do tonight. I just thought that – oh, I see! You think I –' Tony laughed. 'No, Sergeant, I'm not wanting to screw the girl, no shit. I'm in training, you know. I won't be able to do nothin' like that till after the fight next month. My manager'd kill me, no shit.'

'But after the fight you'd make your move, right?'

'After the fight, I go back to Cleveland.'

'Do you know what "propinquity" means, Tony?'

'Pro – propinquity? Sure, I'm a pro. I been fightin' five years now, man. I'm number twenty-two in *Ring* magazine, no shit. Number twenty-two.'

'Not pro. Propinquity. It's a word. And what it means is close together. Two people, in propinquity, eventually get married, you see. If there's no propinquity, there's no marriage. So if you only have propinquity with someone you'd be willing to marry, you'll never make a bad marriage.'

'I don't want to get married, man. I *been* married, but I'm not married now, no shit.'

'I know you don't want to get married again, Tony. That's why I can't allow any propinquity between you and Sue Ellen. Sue Ellen's only allowed to go out with a man who'd be a suitable husband for her, and no one else. Because, you see, without propinquity there can be no marriage. So inasmuch as you don't want to marry Sue Ellen, and she doesn't want to marry you, you can't take her out to dinner. Or talk to her down in the lobby here, or ever see her again. Get my meaning?'

'Well, I don't want to get married, no shit. I got a Jaguar out in the lot, man. I can always find a girl to take to dinner, no shit. Just tell her I stopped by to say hello.'

Tony got to his feet, and so did Hoke.

'No, I won't tell her that, either. If I did, she might get the wrong idea, that you were trying to develop some propinquity. The best thing for you to do is to get into your Jaguar, drive away, and forget all about Sue Ellen.'

Tony threw his shoulders back and looked around the shabby lobby. 'This place is a dump, Sergeant Moseley, no shit. I got to get going.'

'Good luck on the fight.'

'I don't need no luck, no shit. I'll put that Filipino away in the third round.'

Hoke held out his hand. Tony Otero ignored it and walked stiff-backed to the double doors without looking back.

Hoke took Sue Ellen and Aileen up to the roof. He took three webbed chairs off the stack and arranged them on the duckboards so that he could face the girls as he talked with them. Hoke had the view across the bay to the city, and the girls, looking past him, saw the steel elevator door. It was hot on the roof, but a damp wind from the Atlantic, gusting occasionally, made it bearable. The girls had changed back into their shorts and T-shirts. They had never been out of Florida, and they paid no attention to the heat, but Hoke was perspiring beneath the arms of his clean sport shirt. His face was oily with sweat, and he cleared the perspiration off his forehead with a sweeping forefinger.

A Chalk's Airline amphibian, coming in for a landing on the water, was almost level with the roof of the hotel. As the three of them turned to watch the plane, it honked its horn three times.

'Did you hear the goose honk?' Hoke said.

The girls nodded. 'I thought I did,' Aileen said.

'The pilot always does that to alert the ground crew on Watson Island that it's coming in for a landing. The last time I came in from Bimini there was a nervous guy aboard. When it honked three times, he said, "Why'd it do that?" I told him that the pilot was honking for the bridge tender to open the bridge, and the guy almost crapped his pants.'

The girls giggled. 'That's for boats,' Sue Ellen said. 'They have to blow a horn three times to get the bridges lifted.'

'I guess he knew that much,' Hoke said. 'That's why he believed the amphibian had to do the same thing.'

'Will you take us over to Bimini sometime?' Aileen said.

'Sure, but there's nothing there. It's only sixty miles and twenty minutes away by Chalk, and it's a nice place to take girls for a weekend. Just don't try to pin me down to any definite time. You know by now we have a cash-flow problem. This is all family talk, understand, just between the three of us. I don't tell my partner everything, and you're not to say anything to Ellita, either.'

'What's the matter with her, Daddy?' Sue Ellen said. 'Why was she crying?'

'She's got a few problems of her own, but I can't discuss Ellita's personal problems with you, either. If she wants to tell you, she will. All I can say is that she's been living at home, and now she's left home and she's going to get a place of her own somewhere. She's never lived alone before, and I guess she misses her mother.' Hoke smiled, and patted Sue Ellen's left knee. 'I suppose you girls miss your mother, too?'

The girls looked at each other.

'Not me,' Sue Ellen said, lighting a cigarette with her disposable lighter.

'Me neither,' Aileen said. 'I thought I would at first, but I haven't so far.'

'Maybe it hasn't caught up with you yet. Besides, Cubans aren't like us. What's that you're smoking, Sue Ellen?'

'It's a generic cigarette. That's the only kind the machine downstairs carries, and they don't taste like much of anything.'

'I should've warned you about that. That's Mr Bennett's personal machine. He stocks his own machine, you see, and at a buck and a half a pack he makes a bigger profit on generics than he would on real cigarettes. From now on, buy your cigarettes at the supermarket, you'll save fifty cents a pack.'

'I've never seen Mr Bennett, or Emilio either,' Aileen said. 'Everybody's always looking for Emilio, but no one ever finds him.'

'Mr Bennett gets the kind of help he pays for. But Emilio's around. You can see the evidence of his work. Didn't you notice how neatly the gravel driveway was raked this morning? That's Emilio. But Mr Bennett only comes around late at night, when he comes around at all. Otherwise he'd be bothered by the residents complaining to him all the time. But it works out. Any time an old lady gripes to me or Mr Cohen, we refer her to Mr Bennett. But that's not what I wanted to talk to you about. Your mother's house in Vero Beach. What's she going to do with it? Will she sell it or rent it out?'

'She'll never sell it,' Sue Ellen said. 'She and Curly'll live in it when the Dodgers come back for spring training next year. She could probably rent it, but I can't see her doing that, not with all her nice things and all.'

'It was just a passing thought,' Hoke said. 'If Patsy would give me the house, I could try for a job on the police force up in Vero, and –'

'No, Daddy.' Sue Ellen shook her curls. 'Momma wouldn't give you anything. You might not believe it, but Momma doesn't like you very much. Isn't that right, Aileen?'

'She hates your guts, Daddy,' Aileen said, nodding in agreement. 'That's a fact.'

'I've often suspected that,' Hoke said, 'especially when her lawyer calls me. But it was just a thought. I'd hate to live in Vero anyway. But we're going to have to be practical. Tomorrow morning, when I go to the station, Sue Ellen, I'll take you with me. Then you can start looking for work at all the places of business closest to the police station. The cafés, shops, drugstores, dry cleaners, whatever. Go to each place in turn, but the closer to the police station you find work, the easier it'll be for both of us. That way, when you get a job, I can drop you off each morning on the way to work, and then bring you back here, or wherever we move to next Friday, when my shift is over.'

'I've never had a job before. What do I say?'

'First, you have to look nice. Wear a dress and pantyhose, and some shoes with heels – not those running shoes. Fix your hair and put on some lipstick. Then, you walk in and say, "I'm looking for a job." The guy or the woman who runs the place will then say, "We don't need anybody." What you do then is point out that they do need someone. Show them how dirty their windows are, and that they need washing. Point out the dust, and other dirty things. Then tell them that you'll clean the place up for three dollars an hour. About every third place, especially the smaller shops, is always crummy. So you'll get some work all right. A cleanup person for only three bucks an hour's a bargain, so they'll hire you instead of doing it themselves. Do you have any problems with that?'

Sue Ellen frowned. 'What about stuff to clean with? Should I buy some –'

'No. At only three bucks an hour, they'll have to furnish the equipment and cleaners and whatnot. All these places have brooms and rags and soap, but they're too lazy to use it. Concentrate on shoe stores. Did you girls ever use a restroom in a shoe store?'

'I asked once,' Aileen said, 'but they said it was for employees only.'

'You know why they said that? It's because the rest rooms in shoe stores are the dirtiest johns in the entire United States. Shoe salesmen, wearing suits and ties, think they're too good to clean up their john, so they let it go to hell. You can get two hours' work, or six bucks, for every shoe-shop john you clean. They're filthy.'

'What about me, Daddy?' Aileen said.

'Until you're sixteen, you can't get a work permit, but you can go into private enterprise. There's a good way to make some money. When I was a kid up in Riviera, I washed dogs one summer, and you can do the same. I used to get two dollars a dog, but times have changed with inflation. You can charge five bucks a dog now, and they'll pay up without a word, because people hate to wash their own dogs. We'll get you a bucket and some laundry soap from the utility room, a dozen towels or so, and you can hit up the dog owners in the apartment houses around here. No dogs are allowed in the hotel, but a lot of these old people in the apartment houses have them. So you can wash their dog, dry it off with towels, and pick up five bucks a dog. If you wash four in the morning, and four more in the afternoon, you'll make forty dollars a day.'

'If it's so easy to make forty dollars a day, why doesn't Emilio do it?' Aileen said. 'You told us he worked in the hotel for nothing except his room and tips. These old people around here aren't going to tip him much – they can't even find him.'

'It's hard to explain, honey' – Hoke took a breath – 'but Emilio's a Cuban refugee who was raised as a Communist in Cuba. The Communists don't understand the American way of life. They don't allow free enterprise in Cuba, and their government finds everybody jobs, jobs they have to take whether they want them or not. When there are no jobs, they give them free food and a place to stay anyway. Besides, Emilio gets a check for eighty-five bucks a month from some Cuban refugee organization here in Miami Beach, just because he's a Marielito. If he started to make any money on his own, they'd stop giving him the check. He wouldn't jeopardize losing that check for anything. He was brought up to think that way in Cuba, you see. If he wanted to work and make a lot of money, he'd leave Miami and make fifteen or twenty bucks an hour in the East Texas oilfields. But you girls are WASPS, and you've got to realize that you've got to make your own way in the world. As girls, you've got two choices. Either you work, or you marry some guy who'll support you.'

'I don't want to get married,' Aileen said. 'Ever!'

'Okay, then. You can wash dogs. Don't be disappointed at first, when you get turned down a lot. You may not get a single dog to wash. But when someone does see you washing a dog out in the yard, they'll bring theirs over to you, too. People are like that. They don't want to be the first one, you see. Later on, when we get settled in Miami, you'll get repeat business, too, a regular route. Then you can go around and wash the same dogs every month or so. But for the rest of the week, you can practice here on South Beach, and get some experience.'

'What about dog bites? A lot of dogs don't like strangers.'

'I used to have a muzzle I put on them first. So just wash small dogs at first. Then, after you get your first five bucks, pick up a muzzle at a pet shop. Don't wash any pit bulls, Dobermans, or Chows. Do you know what these dogs look like?'

Aileen nodded. 'Curly Peterson's got two Dobermans. Twins.'

'That figures. Okay, now, everything's settled. Except now I have to tell you about sex. First, though, what did your mother tell you about sex?'

'She already told us everything, Daddy,' Sue Ellen said, looking at her fingernails. 'You don't have to talk about sex.'

'She tell you about the clap, syphilis, AIDS, herpes, shit chancres?'

'Not about AIDS,' Sue Ellen admitted.

'AIDS you don't have to worry about. That comes from anal sex. If you avoid anal sex, you won't get AIDS, but the point is, I want you girls to avoid sex altogether. There'll be a lot of pressure on you down here. Miami isn't Vero Beach, you know.'

'There was pressure in Vero, too,' Sue Ellen said.

'I know, I know, but the young guys running around down here are different. They'll tell you anything. They'll start by asking you to feel their dong. Then the next thing you know, they'll ask you to jerk it a few times. First thing you know they'll talk you into giving them a blow job. Bang! You've got herpes or gonorrhea of the throat. So, no sex, period. Any guy who gets laid won't ask you to marry him, either. That's something else to remember. But I'm not unreasonable, Sue Ellen. If some guy wants to marry you, bring him around and I'll talk to him. You're sixteen, so you can get married with my consent, but I'll have to check the guy out first.'

'How do you mean, check him out?'

'His father. I can check his father's credit rating in Dun and Bradstreet. I can check the boy's school records and find out what kind of I.Q. he has. You wouldn't want to marry a moron, would you?'

Sue Ellen giggled.

'Then there's his family. I'd have to see his family, find out if there's a dwarf or something in his family. You wouldn't want to have a baby dwarf, would you?'

'No!' Sue Ellen laughed.

'It isn't funny, Sue Ellen. Some of these guys have rap sheets, and I can check that out. Or else the guy might be married already, and be lying to you. That's why you shouldn't have sex until after you're married, you see. Because once he gets it, he won't marry you. Meanwhile, I know you girls are normal, and you'll have normal urges. That's natural. But to relieve your urges, just go into the bathroom, lock the door, and masturbate. But remember this, masturbation is a private matter. Do it alone, and not to each other, and don't ever talk about it.'

'Not even to Ellita?' Sue Ellen asked.

'Especially not to Ellita. Jesus. She's a Cuban and a Catholic. She'd be shocked if you told her about any of this stuff I'm telling you. But VD is the worst. A dose of clap'll make an old man out of you before you're thirty.'

Both girls laughed.

Hoke grinned. 'That's what my old first sergeant used to tell us every payday, when I was in the army. So it won't make an old man out of you girls, but clap's harder on a woman than it is on a man because it can make you sterile. Got any questions?'

The girls looked at each other. Aileen smiled; Sue Ellen studied the tip of her cigarette. 'Can I let the hair grow under my arms? Like Ellita?'

'Not yet. Wait until you're eighteen. Okay? And any questions you have, ask me, and if I don't know the answer, I'll find out for you. If you can't trust your father to give you the straight goods about sex, who else have you got? Okay, run along now. I'm going to stay up here for a while.'

The girls kissed him and took the elevator down. Hoke lit a cigarette and walked to the parapet. The sun was down, but the entire western sky was still a watercolor wash of red, purple, and orange. Low on the horizon, there were darker, slanting shafts of blue-black, indicating the rain that was passing through the Everglades.

All in all, Hoke thought, his little talk had gone fairly well, but he was glad it was over. He had left out a lot, but there were some things the girls weren't ready for, even though they were brighter than he had thought they were. They had made it easy for him, too, by not asking a lot of dumb questions. But he still didn't know what he was going to do about finding a decent place to live.

Chapter Eighteen

Hoke let Sue Ellen off near the county courthouse in downtown Miami and told her to meet him across the street at the Government Center Metrorail station at 5 P.M.

Ellita had left the hotel earlier that morning, and she had dropped a note on Hoke's desk at the station, explaining that she was meeting her mother at her cousin's house. Her mother had two boxes of clothing and some other things for her to pick up. She intended to be back at the station by eight-thirty, if not before. Before leaving the station, Ellita had taken all of the files to the interrogation room and aligned the three piles on the deal table. She had left the Mary Rollins file and the Xerox copies of Rollins's birth certificate and driver's license on Hoke's desk.

Hoke typed a short report about finding Rollins, made a Xerox copy of the report for Lieutenant Slater, and then took the closed file into Major Brownley's office. Brownley looked up and frowned when Hoke entered without knocking.

'The Rollins girl's alive, Willie, and living in Delray Beach. Sanchez found her yesterday. But she also promised Rollins that she wouldn't tell her mother where she was living. So now you can call Mrs Rollins and tell her that her daughter's alive and well.'

'Are you positive?'

'It's all in the report. If you don't want to call Mrs Rollins, I'll do it.'

Brownley was reading the report, and he didn't lift his head. 'No, I'll call her, Hoke. It'll be a pleasure to withhold the girl's address. The mother really bugged me about her daughter.'

Hoke left Brownley's office, put the Xerox copy of the report in Slater's in-box, and went down to join Bill Henderson in the interrogation room. He told Bill about Sanchez's finding Rollins. They both read silently for a half-hour. Then Ellita came in at a

358

quarter to nine, bringing them some coffee and doughnuts she had picked up in the cafeteria.

'Everything go all right?' Hoke said.

'Much better than I expected. My mother's on my side now, and she even agreed with me that it was time I found a place of my own. Meanwhile, my furniture and the rest of my things will just have to stay there till I find an apartment. But I feel a lot better after talking to my mom.'

'If you're looking for a house to rent,' Henderson volunteered, 'I can ask Marie to find you something. She handles a lot of rental properties in Little Havana.'

'Thanks, Sergeant Henderson.' Ellita shook her head. 'That was my original plan, to find a place near my parents, but I think a one-bedroom apartment in a different area would be better. I don't even want to be in the same neighborhood now, and I don't want to live in Little Havana either. Talking to Mary Rollins taught me a lot about my own feelings. I know they didn't do it consciously, but my parents were taking advantage of me.' She smiled at Hoke and sat at her place at the table. 'What did Major Brownley say about Mary Rollins, Hoke?'

'He said he'd call her mother.'

'Is that all?'

'He won't kiss you, Ellita. Willie isn't much for patting people on the head. But he's happy about it. Now that we've arrested Captain Midnight and cleared the Rollins file, he'll probably get together with Slater and give the media the info on our cold-case assignment. I've decided that none of us will talk to reporters. No matter what you tell these people, it's never enough. They'll be after us every day for progress reports. We can't say what we're working on, because it might alert someone we're checking on. So let's just say nothing at all. I'll talk to Brownley about this later and tell him that he'll have to be the spokesman – he or Slater. Slater loves to talk to reporters, as if you didn't know, and I've already told him I'll send him the same progress reports we send the major.'

'So we just say, "No comment," right?' Henderson said.

'No, not "No comment," just refer reporters, either on the phone or in person, to Slater.'

A few minutes later Major Brownley came into the room. He puffed on his pipe, then pulled his jacket down in the back.

'Seeing as to how yesterday was Sunday, Sanchez,' he said, 'I don't mind authorizing four hours of overtime pay.' He placed a hand on Hoke's shoulder. 'Add Sunday's overtime to the voucher, Hoke, when you send it through.' He left the room and closed the door.

Bill Henderson grinned at Ellita. 'That's about as close to ecstasy as Willie ever gets, Ellita. Congratulations.'

'I didn't ask for overtime,' Ellita said.

'Don't reject it,' Henderson said. 'You may never get it again. On this assignment, we aren't even entitled to comp time – are we, Hoke?'

'It's just us three,' Hoke said, 'so we'll adjust our hours to what we have to do, that's all. I've got to take some time off this week for house hunting, and so does Ellita. Any time you need a few hours off, Bill, just tell me.'

Henderson tapped the file he was reading. 'I haven't run into a promising case yet. All this shit is just too old, Hoke. I really should be out there on the street with Teddy Gonzalez, working on the triple murder.'

'We haven't winnowed 'em all out yet, Bill. Out of fifty, we should get four or five –'

'We've solved two already,' Ellita said.

'That doesn't help us,' Henderson said. 'With two out of the way already, Brownley's gonna expect miracles now, and we may not resolve another case in the next two months.'

'In that event' Hoke smiled, 'consider the assignment a vacation. Slater's running Teddy around in circles out there.'

'I know.' Henderson shook his head. 'The poor bastard. But he was happy as hell when I told him about Leroy's crap game.'

At ten-thirty, Hoke went into his office to check the distribution. He skipped through the junk, looking for the lab report on Jerry Hickey. There was no lab report, so he took the elevator to the forensic lab.

Dan Jessup, the chief technician, was lighting a cigar with a Bunsen burner. His long left arm was covered by the sleeve of a dark blue cardigan, but the right arm of the sweater dangled. The rest of the sweater was bunched up and pinned to the back of his shirt. He looked like he was either taking the sweater off or putting it on, but Hoke knew that Jessup always wore it that way because his arthritic left arm was always cold. Jessup was a bald, wiry man in his late thirties. The corners of his short mouth pointed down; it gave him a petulant expression.

'I didn't get the lab report on Hickey, Gerald,' Hoke said.

'No shit.'

'It was promised for today.'

'Today isn't over. You'll get it through normal distribution.'

'It isn't in this morning's distribution.'

'Should be. I remember initialing it.' Jessup went to his desk and searched through three file boxes. One was marked NOW, the second NEVER, and the third SOME DAY. The Hickey report, together with a half-dozen others, was in the NOW box. Jessup put his glasses on and read it.

'That was good shit the kid had, Hoke. About as close to pure heroin as you'll ever see. It was only five percent procaine and thirty percent mannitol. The rest was almost pure H, with a few impurities.'

'Mannitol? That's the baby laxative, isn't it?'

'You might say mannitol's also used as a baby laxative. The dealers probably use more mannitol to cut coke and heroin nowadays than they ever used for babies. Anyway, if Hickey wasn't used to shit this strong, it could've been an accidental OD.'

'Dan. You know an overdose can't be proved either way.'

'I know that. I'm just saying that an accidental OD was possible. I know what you can prove and what you can't. I've spent ten fucking years in this freezing lab. Did Hickey have piles?'

'I don't know. They haven't done the P.M. yet. He could have, but I don't know.'

'Well,' Jessup said, 'if he had 'em, he had 'em bad, because the blue tinfoil wrappers you sent came from Nembutal suppositories. To get Nembutal suppositories, you need a doctor's prescription.'

'Can't you buy them on the street?'

'You can buy anything on the street, Hoke. But I never heard of anyone selling hemorrhoid suppositories on the street. Have

361

you? You can't get high on 'em. They just relieve your pain and put you to sleep, that's all.'

'There are people in Miami who'd pay damned near anything for a good night's sleep.'

Jessup smiled. 'I wish they had 'em for arthritis. I could slip one under my arm at night. That's all I can tell you, Hoke.' Jessup handed Hoke the typed report. 'It don't make no never-mind anyway. If Hickey had piles, they don't bother him now.'

Hoke nodded, folding the typed sheets in half. 'Thanks, Dan.' Hoke hesitated at the door. 'You know, Dan, I can remember when we used to go out to lunch once in a while.'

'Me too, and it's my fault. It's just that I've been so damned busy lately. Why don't you call me some time? I still have to eat, and we can have lunch anywhere you want except the cafeteria.'

'Okay. I'll call you. Not this week, but maybe next week.'

'Good. And another thing, Hoke. A lot of my old records have been sent into storage at the warehouse on Miami Avenue. So if you're going to need any old lab reports from four or five years back, you'd better send me a memo on it soon and give me a little lead time.'

'What do you mean?'

'I mean if you need any old lab reports for those cold cases you're working on.'

'Sure, Dan, I'll let you know. But there's nothing I need right now.'

Hoke left the lab and returned to the interrogation room. If Dan Jessup knows about the cold cases, he thought, everybody in the damned building must know about it by now. How, Hoke wondered, did the word get out so fast! The Morrow case, that was it. The detectives in the division had talked among themselves about that old case and put two and two together.

At eleven-thirty, Bill Henderson was called away from the interrogation room to answer a phone call. Sue Ellen came into the room a few minutes later with her thin lips compressed. She clutched her banana-shaped purse so hard her knuckles whitened.

'What's the matter, honey?' Hoke said, getting up from his chair. Ellita rose, then sat down again.

362

'I couldn't do it, Daddy.' Sue Ellen shook her head. 'I just couldn't do it. It was hard to go into any stores, and when I did they were always speaking Spanish and all, and I couldn't ask for a job. I knew I wouldn't get one anyway, and I was too scared to ask. All I did was fill in an application at the Burger King across from the downtown campus of Miami-Dade, but the manager there said he usually just employed college students part-time. He let me fill in the application, but I know he won't hire me.'

'Did you eat lunch yet?'

'I'm not hungry. Are you mad at me, Daddy?'

'Of course not.' Hoke patted her shoulder. 'Now, didn't you take Spanish in school?'

Sue Ellen shook her head and bit her lower lip. 'You couldn't take a language at my high school unless you passed an aptitude test, and I didn't pass it. Instead of a language, they gave me civics.'

'It doesn't matter. Maybe it'll be better if you just help your sister wash dogs this week. We'll get you a job later, after we move next Friday.'

'I'll drive Sue Ellen back to the hotel, Hoke,' Ellita offered. 'She can help me unload the stuff from my car. Then I'll see that the girls both have lunch before I come back.'

'If you don't mind.'

Bill Henderson came back to the room, and Hoke introduced him to Sue Ellen. Bill bent over and shook hands with the girl. 'You've certainly got your father's eyes, but you're a lot prettier.'

'Thank you,' Sue Ellen said. She looked down at the floor, still on the verge of tears, and edged away.

Ellita got her purse and opened the door.

'When you get back, Ellita,' Hoke said, 'type up the overtime and mileage voucher and leave it on my desk. It'll take five working days to get your money, so we'd better send it in today.'

Sue Ellen kissed Hoke goodbye. Hoke hugged her. 'Cheer up, baby. Don't worry about it.' She and Ellita left together.

'She's not a bad-looking girl, Hoke, but she shouldn't be running around downtown by herself.'

'She's been looking for a job. But she's a little shy.'

363

'School's been out for a while, Hoke. Most of the part-time jobs've been grabbed off already. That's what Marie told me.'

'It won't hurt her to look. I'll find her a job later, after we move back to the city.'

'I just had a call from the Dade County Stockade. Louis Dyer. He's a corrections officer now, but he used to be a Metro policeman when I knew him. Have you run across the Buford homicide in your pile? A black guy, a drifter and can collector, killed under the Overtown bypass.'

Hoke shook his head as he glanced at his list. He looked at Ellita's pad. She had crossed out a Tyrone Buford; the accordion file on Buford was in her reject pile.

'Here it is.' Hoke read the summary sheet on top, frowning. 'I would've rejected this one myself. Buford was a wino, and he was found on a strip of cardboard under the overpass. A dozen or more bums sleep in that area every night, and he could've been killed by anybody. Those guys fight each other every night just to have something to do. I don't see why Brownley picked this one in the first place. It isn't even a possibility.'

'Probably because he was black, Hoke. He couldn't very well pick all white cases.' Bill read the summary sheet, then leafed through the notes in the file. 'I remember this Buford. He was an obnoxious sonofabitch. There were several complaints about him, but no arrests. He collected aluminum cans, and I remember seeing him in the old Jordan Marsh lot, before they built the parking garage at Omni. He usually worked parking lots, and he would stomp on the cans before he put them in his Hefty bag. He would tell people, when they walked through the lot, that stomping the cans gave him a headache. Then he would hit 'em up for three dollars and forty-nine cents to buy a bottle of Excedrin. When he was turned down, he cursed them out. Some people complained, but there was no point picking him up for panhandling, and no one ever swore out a complaint.'

Hoke grinned. 'Brownley probably liked the man's style, asking for three dollars and forty-nine cents. Some people, especially young women, would dig a rap like that and give him a dollar or so. Some of these secretaries downtown'll believe anything.'

'But somebody killed him, Hoke. And Dyer said on the phone he's got a prisoner over in the stockade who wants to see a Homicide detective about Buford.'

'Okay, let's go over and talk to him. We can't solve any cases sitting around here on our ass.'

'I already told Dyer we'd be coming over,' Henderson said, slipping into his seersucker jacket. 'If Dyer didn't think it was an important lead, he wouldn't have called me.'

Henderson drove his car, and they decided to stop for lunch before driving to the stockade. They ate at the Tres Cubanos Café on Seventh Street, both ordering the $3.95 *Especial*, which included *café con leche* and *flan* with the *arroz con pollo* main dish.

At the Dade County Stockade they identified themselves, asked for Louis Dyer, and put their pistols and handcuffs into a metal-bound wooden box. The jailer locked the box with a padlock and took them down the hallway to a small, pastel-green interrogation room with a door of heavy wire mesh. There was a folding table, a pair of straight chairs and a coffee-can lid on the table. The brown linoleum floor was freshly waxed.

Louis Dyer, a stocky, serious man in his late forties, joined them a few minutes later. He shook hands with Henderson, who introduced him to Hoke. Dyer then handed Henderson the stockade file on an inmate named Ray Vince.

'I don't know if there's anything to this or not,' Dyer said. 'The guys in here are always looking for an angle, trying to make some kind of deal. Vince is pulling a single for assault, with six months suspended. But the chances are good now that he won't get the six-months suspension. He broke his wife's jaw, and her parents filed the charges when she was in the hospital. When his wife could talk again, she begged the judge to let him out. She needs the paycheck, you know. But before the judge decided what to do, Vince made another inmate eat a towel, so I don't think the judge'll release him now. He'll probably have to do the full twelve months.'

'How can a man eat a towel?' Hoke said.

'He didn't eat all of it, he only ate part of it. Then when he started to choke to death, another inmate pulled the towel out and tore about half the guy's vocal cords out at the same time. He's still in the locked ward at Jackson Hospital. If he ever talks again, he'll be lucky if he can whisper.'

'What was it?' Henderson asked. 'A face towel or a bath towel?'

'Bath. This guy stole Vince's towel, you see, and when Vince found out who took it, he told the guy if he wanted it so bad, he could eat it. Then he made him eat it.'

'So now Vince wants out,' Hoke said, 'and wants to make a deal?' Hoke opened the stockade file and read the first page.

'It's all in the file,' Dyer said, 'the kinda prick Vince is. If it was me, I wouldn't trust him at all. But then, it ain't up to me, is it? I guess it won't hurt to talk to him, if you're working on old cases, Bill.'

'Who told you we were working on old cases?'

'When I called Homicide and mentioned Buford, the duty officer said you were on the cold cases, and I told him I knew you, that's all. So he called you. Why, is it some kind of a secret?'

'Not anymore,' Henderson said.

'We'll talk to him,' Hoke said. 'This case is four years old, and there're no leads at all.'

Dyer let himself out and returned a few minutes later with Ray Vince. Dyer opened the door and then locked Vince in with the two detectives. Hoke closed Vince's file and handed it to Henderson.

'Just holler when you're through.' Dyer walked away.

Ray Vince was heavy set, with a soft white paunch that drooped in folds over his jail denims. His white T-shirt was immaculate, but it didn't cover his pasty, hairy midriff. His russet hair was long, combed straight back. His nose had been broken at one time and reset poorly. He stared at the detectives with flat blue eyes.

Hoke, who had glanced hurriedly through the file, had learned that Vince was a truck driver who had made two round trips a week to Key West from Miami. He had earned about eight hundred dollars a week. No wonder his wife wanted him back. There was one previous arrest in addition to the current assault charge and conviction, though that case hadn't gone to trial. Vince had broken a hitchhiker's arm with a tire iron, but there were no witnesses, and Vince claimed that the man was trying to break into his truck.

The man who had his arm broken claimed that he had merely asked Vince if he could get a ride back to Miami with him.

Hoke lit a Kool, then offered the pack to Ray Vince.

Vince shook his head. 'I don't smoke.'

'We're from Homicide, Vince,' Henderson said. 'What do you have to tell us?'

'I want outa here. I was supposed to get out next month, and now it looks like I'll have to spend six more in here. I want to make a deal of some kind.'

'You shouldn't've fed the man the towel,' Hoke said.

'What was I supposed to do? He shouldn't've stole it. If the guy had asked to use my towel in a nice way, I might've loaned it to him. But he stole it.'

'I don't think you'd've let him use it, no matter how nicely he asked,' Henderson said.

'Maybe not, but the sonofabitch stole it. Can I sit down? I was playing volleyball, and I'm a little pooped.'

'Grab a chair,' Hoke said. 'What kind of deal do you have in mind?'

'Just tell the judge that I'm cooperative, and to give me a little consideration, that's all. My wife wants me out, and so does my boss. So I shouldn't have to pull another six months in the stockade because some sonofabitch in here's a thief. It ain't fair.'

'We can't promise you anything,' Henderson said. 'You'll just have to tell us what you've got.'

'It may not be anything, and I'll admit that. But I'm trying to be cooperative with the law. I've had some domestic problems, just like any married man, but I'm a good citizen.'

'So talk,' Henderson said.

'Well, the other night some guys were in the latrine drinking bang-bang, and they were all bragging to each other about how tough they were. Usually it don't mean nothing, they're just mouthing off, you know.'

'Were you drinking bang-bang with 'em?' Henderson asked.

'No, I don't drink that stuff. It makes you crazy. I was just in there takin' a shit. Then this one guy, Wetzel's his name, bragged about killing a nigger in Overtown a few years back.'

367

'What was his name, the black man's name he said he killed?'

'Wetzel was slurring his words, being pretty drunk, but it was either Burford or Buford, something like that.'

'Was it the man's first name, or last name?'

'I don't know. He didn't say, but people in here ain't much on first names. They usually call a guy by his last name.'

'Did he say how he killed him?' Hoke said.

'He torched him. That's what he said, but he said he took eighty dollars off him first. He might've been lyin', but Wetzel's an arson suspect, and he's in here now for carryin' a can of kerosene. He's been over in the city jail, but he was transferred over here last week because of the overcrowding order. So I figgered it all adds up. He's a firebug, he had a can of kerosene, so maybe he did torch himself a nigger a few years back.'

'Thanks,' Henderson said. He crossed to the wire-mesh door and called out to Dyer. 'We're ready to go, Mr Dyer.'

'Is that all?' Vince said. 'What about our deal? Will you talk to the judge for me? I cooperated with you guys, didn't I?'

'Sure you did, Vince,' Hoke said. 'Are you sure you'll get your old job back when you get out?'

'I'd better!' Vince thrust out his jaw.

'We can't help you, Vince,' Hoke said. 'But there are two other Homicide detectives who can – Detectives Quevedo and Donovan. They'll be over to talk to you a little later. Just tell them what you told us, and try to remember any details. They'll take care of you. In the meantime, see what else you can find out about Wetzel. Detective Quevedo is very interested in firebugs.'

'Can't you guys say something nice about me, too?'

Bill laughed. 'It's hard to say something nice about a guy like you, Vince, but we'll put a note in your file.'

Dyer unlocked the door. He took Vince down to the end of the corridor and turned him over to another corrections officer, who would escort him back to the yard.

Dyer rejoined Henderson and Hoke, and Hoke returned Vince's stockade file.

'He wasn't much help to us, Louis,' Henderson said. 'But there'll be two more Homicide detectives coming over to see him later. Quevedo and Donovan. Vince told us our man was torched to death, but Buford was killed with an icepick through the ear. The handle was still in his ear when they found him, and he wasn't burnt. But Quevedo and Donovan are looking for a firebug.'

'Quevedo?' Dyer said, frowning. 'I know him. He was the guy who fell in love with a painting, wasn't he?'

'That's the rumor,' Bill said, 'but he got over it. If I was you, I wouldn't mention it to him, though.'

Bill and Hoke retrieved their pistols and handcuffs, and headed back to the station.

When they got back to the interrogation room and the files, Hoke sent Henderson out to the bullpen to fill Quevedo and Donovan in on the information Vince had given them about Wetzel. Hoke then called the morgue from his office and asked the secretary if he could talk to Doc Evans.

'He can't come to the phone now, Sergeant Moseley,' the woman told him. 'He's doing a P.M. and can't be interrupted. But I can give him a message.'

'Do you know if you've done the autopsy on Hickey, Gerald?'

'Let me check ...' Hoke waited for almost two minutes before she came on the line again. 'No, not yet. But they might get to him tonight. Evans is supposed to get a part-time pathologist in tonight to help out with the Descanso Hotel victims. We've been pretty busy around here.'

'Okay, but just ask him to check – when he does the P.M. on Hickey – and see if the man had piles. And if so, what kind of suppositories he was using.'

'You mean like Preparation H?'

'That, or whatever. Whether he had piles or not – I mean hemorrhoids.'

'I've made a note. Where should he call you?'

'I don't know where I'll be yet, but tell Doc I'll call him back about this later on.'

'You spell "Moseley" with an *e*, don't you?'

'That's right. Most people leave out the second *e*. And thanks a lot.'

Hoke looked at his Timex. It was only 3 P.M., but he couldn't face the idea of reading files for another hour and a half. There were times, he knew, when he could no longer look at the outside world from inside the asshole. This was one of those times. He left his office and returned to the interrogation room.

Sanchez looked up from her file and frowned. 'Bill told me you'd been over to the Dade County Stockade. You should've left me a note. I didn't know where you were.'

'You don't need to know everything, and we weren't gone long.'

'I know that. But if someone wanted to know where you were, and I couldn't tell them, it would make you look bad. How could I cover for you?'

'All right. Next time I'll leave you a message. What else?' Jesus, Hoke thought, she's already practicing to be a mother.

'Did you sign my voucher?'

'I didn't see it.'

'I put it in your in-box.'

'I didn't look in my in-box. I'll sign it now, and then I'm going back to the hotel. You can put the files away, and tell Bill to go home, too. He can fill you in on what we found out at the stockade. Okay?'

'It's only a little after three.' Ellita glanced at her gold watch.

'I know what time it is. I've got to go out tonight, and I don't know what to do about the girls.'

'Go ahead. I'll take them out to dinner, and maybe we'll go to a movie.'

'That would be very kind of you.'

'Not really. That hotel depresses me as much as it does the girls. Maybe instead of a movie I should look for an apartment. I've circled some classifieds in the *Miami News*.'

'Hold off on that for a while, Ellita. I've got an idea I want to talk to you about later. All right?'

Ellita shrugged. 'There's no great hurry, I guess.'

'Just put the stuff away and go back to the hotel, Ellita. As far as I'm concerned, it's quitting time.'

Hoke signed Sanchez's voucher, placed it in Lieutenant Slater's in-box, and left the station. Hoke would need Ellita to help him with the girls, but this wasn't the right time to suggest that they share a house together.

Sue Ellen and Aileen were waiting for Hoke in the lobby of the Eldorado. Aileen ran to meet him when he came through the double doors, hugged him, and stood on tiptoe to kiss him on the cheek when he pulled back. She handed him seven one-dollar bills.

'I washed two dogs, Daddy,' she said, looking down at the floor, 'a dachshund and a little toy poodle. The lady who owned the dachshund paid me five dollars, but the man who had the poodle only gave me two. He said the job wasn't worth more than two.'

'Did you tell him in advance that you charged five?'

'Yes, I did. But he only gave me two.'

Hoke returned the seven dollars. 'Here, put it in your purse. You earned it, and it's your money. Do you remember where this guy lives?'

'The Alton Arms.' She nodded and pointed. 'On Third Street.'

'What's his name?'

'Mr Lewis.'

'Okay, we'll go over and talk to him.'

'Can I go too?' Sue Ellen said.

'No. Ellita'll be here in a few minutes, and you can tell her we'll be back soon. Otherwise she'd worry about where you were.'

Hoke and Aileen walked the three blocks to the Alton Arms, a fading pistachio-colored apartment house two stories high with a pink Spanish tile roof. There was a veranda in front, and a half-dozen residents – four old ladies and two old men – were sitting on plastic-webbed chairs and looking across the street. Their view was another two-story apartment house, with four old people sitting on webbed chairs looking back at them.

'Is that Mr Lewis, honey?' Hoke asked. 'The man with the poodle in his lap?'

'That's him. He's holding Thor. That's the dog's name.'

Hoke and Aileen climbed the porch. Hoke took out his badge and ID case and showed it to the old man. Mr Lewis, who had gray hair and a gray face, turned pink, and his arms and legs trembled.

'Police Department, Mr Lewis,' Hoke said. 'I understand that you owe this little girl three dollars.'

Mr Lewis got to his feet and handed the miniature poodle to the old lady in the next chair. The tiny dog snarled at Aileen and began to bark. Mr Lewis took out his wallet, removed three dollars, and held them out to Hoke. His fingers were trembling, and he worked his mouth in and out. Hoke shook his head and inclined it toward Aileen.

'Give it to the girl.'

Mr Lewis gave Aileen the three dollars. 'I was planning to eat on that money this week,' he said. 'I hope you're satisfied.'

'Bullshit,' Hoke said. 'If you can pay a hundred a week to live at the Alton, you can pay for getting your dog washed. You can also apologize to the little girl.'

'I'm sorry,' Mr Lewis said. He put his wallet back into his hip pocket and retrieved Thor from the old lady. The dog stopped yapping immediately. Mr Lewis walked to the doorway that led into the apartment-house foyer. He opened the door and turned. 'I'm *not* sorry! I'm *not* sorry!' he said in a high reedy voice. He then stepped swiftly through the door and into the foyer, pulling the door closed behind him.

On their way back to the Eldorado, Aileen said, 'If Mr Lewis needed that money to eat on, Daddy, I'd rather not take it. But he never told me that this morning.'

'He's a liar, Aileen. Don't feel sorry for him. A miniature poodle like the one he had, if he's got the papers on it, sells for two or three hundred bucks. If he gets hungry enough, he can always sell the goddamned dog. At any rate, you've washed your last dog over here. Some of these people over here on South Beach are crazy as shit-house rats. You and Sue Ellen put on your bathing suits and we'll all go over to the beach for a swim. If we're lucky, maybe we can get an hour or so on the beach before the rain starts.'

Chapter Nineteen

Hoke only had one credit card, a Visa card from an obscure bank in Chicago. He had applied for it in person when he had taken a prisoner to Chicago, and the bank never checked his abysmal credit rating. He called two different seafood restaurants before he made a reservation; he wanted to make certain that his Chicago card would be honored. The card itself was good because Hoke always paid the ten-dollar minimum charge every month. He knew it was the only credit card he was ever likely to have.

La Pescador Habañero's maître d' assured Hoke over the phone that his Visa card was acceptable. Jackets were required at La Pescador, but if Hoke didn't have a jacket, there was a suitable selection in the cloakroom, and he would be furnished with a jacket at no extra charge. Ties, of course, were not required, but if the visitor from Chicago found the evening too humid, he could have a corner table in the courtyard, where the absence of a jacket would not be noticed by the other patrons.

'Never mind,' Hoke said. 'We prefer the dining room, where it's air-conditioned. And I'll be wearing a leisure suit.'

'Excellent!' the maître d' said. 'As I understand it, leisure suits are coming back into style again.'

'And I'll want a bottle of wine. Bordeaux, if you have it –'

'Any particular vintage?'

'I don't care. Just have it uncorked and breathing on the table when we get there.'

That'll cost me, Hoke thought, but what the hell? He hadn't been laid in a long time ...

Hoke had mixed feelings about having dinner with Loretta. He was horny, but he was far from confident that he would end up in Loretta's bed. Was she interested in him as a lover, or did she take him up on his invitation just because she wanted an expensive dinner? In a way, Hoke knew he was indirectly trying to buy a piece of ass, but a man could spend a lot of money on a woman and end up without so much as a goodnight kiss.

This woman was sexy as hell, and physically attractive, but Hoke knew how *he* looked. He had no idea how Loretta felt about him. One thing Hoke knew for sure: Some women liked to fuck cops just because they were cops, and he hoped that Loretta was one of them. This was something he and Henderson had talked about and taken advantage of often enough in their police careers.

Women were attracted to power and money – not just to a man's looks. They were interested in a man's personality, his occupation, especially interesting occupations. How a man *looked* was way down there, about seventh on the list. As Henderson had put it once, 'Every woman wants to fuck her daddy, Hoke. A cop's got a badge and a gun, so he's an authority figure. She can't screw her daddy, so a cop's the next best thing.'

Henderson's opinion was oversimplified perhaps. Still, look at Harold Hickey. He had power and confidence, *plus* good looks, or Loretta wouldn't have married him. Hickey had been on the verge of big fees when she had married him, and she had known he would make it. That's why Hoke hadn't believed Hickey when he said Loretta had been sleeping with Jerry. She was too smart to jeopardize her marriage by sleeping with a skinny, run-down junkie. It didn't make sense – unless there was something going on Hoke didn't know about.

On the other hand, Hickey took himself so seriously that he didn't recognize sarcasm when he heard it. What did the kid say when Hickey had charged the boy with screwing Loretta? 'I didn't think you'd mind, Mr Hickey.' If that wasn't sarcasm, what was it? And if the fat next-door neighbor had really told Hickey about the so-called affair, how had she found out? Did she peep through the windows? She was purportedly a friend of Loretta's, but it didn't seem likely that Loretta would confide that kind of information to anyone. More likely, Ellen Koontz had merely suspected it, then reported her suspicions to Hickey as fact. And he had bought her story.

Loretta was attracted to power all right. Otherwise she wouldn't want to own her own shop – a business she could run her own way – instead of working as a designer for someone else who would have all of the problems. The problem was, Hoke didn't know Loretta well enough to make any educated guesses about her. The best thing to do, Hoke decided, was to get Loretta to talk about herself. Once he got to know her a little better, everything would work out fine.

Before Hoke left the hotel, he shifted his holstered pistol from the small of his back, where he usually carried it, to the front. When they got to the restaurant, he would unbutton his jacket so Loretta could see the butt of his revolver showing above the waistband. As Henderson once said, 'Showing a woman your pistol is just like showing her your cock.' Maybe so, and maybe not, Hoke thought, half-amused at Henderson's ready theories; but with a face like mine, I need every advantage I can get.

The dinner went very well, Hoke thought. The bottle of wine was only twenty-eight dollars and the bouillabaisse for two, as recommended by their waiter, only thirty. A green salad and a rice pudding with raisins were included with the dinner, and they finished their meal with two dollar-fifty espressos.

Loretta Hickey, in a low-cut white chiffon dress, looked lovely to Hoke. She was wearing a lavender orchid (Hoke had ordered it and charged it to the Eldorado's telephone) pinned to her narrow waist. Hoke had told the Vietnamese girl at the Bouquetique to hand the orchid to Mrs Hickey when she left the shop, figuring that if he was going to order a corsage, he might as well give Loretta's shop the business. Loretta was delighted with her orchid.

'You may not believe it, Hoke,' she'd said when he picked her up at her house in Green Lakes, 'but it's been years and years since I've been given any flowers. People think that because I have my own shop, I can get all I want free. That may be true, but I do love flowers, and I certainly didn't expect such a lovely orchid. Even if I did pick it out myself.'

'On the phone I told the girl to pick it, and to hand it to you when you left.'

'Oh, no, Dotty wouldn't dare risk her taste against mine. She's a Vietnamese refugee, you know, and she's practically helpless around the shop. But she's all I can afford at the moment. What I really need is a good designer. Because I'm usually working in the back, I miss a lot of gift sales in front. Dotty Chen couldn't sell a Cuban a cup of coffee.'

Hoke grinned. 'And they drink ten cups a day.'

Three strolling guitar players came to their table in the dining room and played and sang a song. Although Hoke's Spanish was limited, he got the drift that the three singers wanted to die in combat in Cuba with their faces turned up toward the sun. He gave the player nearest him a dollar bill and they strolled off, singing lugubriously, to another table.

'The only thing worse than three Spanish guitars,' Hoke said, 'is one violin.'

'That's right. Three are okay, but one violin sounds screechy.'

'How's business, Loretta?'

'Not all that good, lately. It should be good, but it isn't. There're too many street people on corners selling old cheap flowers, and the prices I have to pay are ridiculous. I have to sell roses for five dollars apiece, and people just won't pay that much for roses. I'll be glad when summer's over and the season starts.'

'I guess you have to borrow money before holidays?'

Loretta nodded. 'At sixteen percent. And it's always a guessing game. For Mother's Day I bought too many carnations. For some reason, no one wanted any this year, so even though I was busy for three days, I had to eat the carnations. I just barely broke even. If I could find a buyer, I sometimes think I'd sell the shop.'

'Then what would you do? It might be hard to work for someone else after you've owned your own business.'

'But I wouldn't have the headaches. A good designer, and I'm a good one, can work anywhere in the country. And people in the business know me, too. I put on design demonstrations at the last two floral conventions in Miami Beach. And I'm not so crazy about Miami that I want to stay here forever. If I wanted to, I could go to Atlanta like that!' Loretta tried to snap her fingers, but they wouldn't.

'Why don't you, then?'

'What?' Loretta laughed. Her face was flushed from the wine and the food. 'And give up my own shop? I'd be crazy to give up my shop in Coral Gables to work in Atlanta. At least we can still walk down the street in the daytime. The last time I was in Atlanta, I was afraid to walk down Peachtree by myself at high noon.'

'Do you want an after-dinner drink, a post-prandial? A short Presidente brandy maybe?'

'We can have a drink back at the house. I've got beer and a bottle of bourbon at home.'

Hoke grinned. 'Sure you don't want to go out to a disco first?'

'Please!'

Although Hoke had to pay another dollar for valet parking, and the attendant had stolen his toll change from the ashtray, he thought he got off lightly for the evening. The wine had been good, but Hoke had poured most of it for Loretta. She was feeling the effects of it, too. On the drive to her house, Loretta gripped his arm with both hands and once in a while rubbed her face against his shoulder.

When they got into the house, Hoke took off his jacket and tossed it on the couch. Loretta went into the kitchen and came back with an unopened bottle of Jack Daniel's. Black label.

'I usually don't buy bourbon,' she said, 'because no one ever drinks it. I've had a few parties here, but most people want Scotch or vodka. Miami's mostly a vodka town, isn't it?'

'Or a pot town, a coke town, and a 'lude town.'

'Do you want some pot? Being you're a policeman and all, I thought –'

'No, no pot. I'll just have a short Jack Daniel's with a little water. If I have too many drinks, I can't perform, and I can feel the wine a little. I'm mostly a beer drinker, but what I want most right now is you.' Hoke pulled Loretta into his arms and kissed her. She tasted like wine, and she forced her hard, hot tongue between his dentures.

Hoke unbuttoned his shirt and tossed it on top of his jacket on the couch. He unbuckled his belt in front and unclipped his holstered pistol.

Loretta looked at the picture window and the opened draperies, and laughed. 'The neighbors across the street can see you. Maybe you'd better undress in the bedroom.'

'I understand.' Hoke grinned. 'You want the neighbors to think you're after me for my money.'

Loretta, carrying the bottle, led the way to the bedroom, and Hoke followed her.

Loretta switched on the bedside lamp. The unmade bed was a mess. While Hoke undressed, she swept the long-legged dolls to the floor, removed the crumpled quilt and top sheet, and pulled the flowered bottom sheet tight. Hoke plumped up the pillows, stretched out on the round bed, and clasped his hands behind his head.

Hoke's erection throbbed with anticipation. Loretta went into the bathroom; Hoke listened to the water run in the sink and thought he could hear his heartbeat above the sound of the running water. He sat on the edge of the bed and picked up the bottle of Jack Daniel's from the bedside table. He unscrewed the cap, took a mouthful of whiskey, and swished it around for a moment before he swallowed it. He took another, shorter drink and recapped the bottle. He felt fine now. Because of his dentures, he always worried a little about his breath. A man never knows for sure whether he will get laid or not, Hoke thought, even if he's married. Especially if he's married. The woman, finally, always selects the man, the time, and even the place.

Once, when Hoke had thought he had a sure thing, he had driven the woman home, locked his car, and walked to the front door, expecting to spend the night. She had unlocked her door, stepped inside, said good night and slammed the door right in his face. He had been astonished. The next time he took her out – and he had called her again – everything had worked out well. He asked her why she had slammed the door on their first date.

'You locked your car,' she said. 'And when you locked your car, so damned confident and macho, I said to myself, the hell with you, boy.'

Women, sometimes, were hard to understand.

Loretta had scrubbed the makeup off her face, removed the barrettes from her hair, and brushed it out. Her thick hair was fluffy around her shining face. Her breasts were fuller than he had thought they would be, with prominent pink nipples. The triangle of pubic hair was darker than her long blonde mane.

'Should I switch off the lamp?'

'No. I like to see what I'm doing. And you've got a damned nice figure.'

'Lay back,' Loretta said, 'the way you were before, with your hands behind your head.'

Hoke stretched out again, clasping his hands behind his head. Loretta, on her knees, crawled between his spread legs and sat back slightly. She reached beneath Hoke's balls, searching for his anus with a greased forefinger. She found it and shoved her finger in.

'Don't!' Hoke said. 'I don't like that.'

'It got you hard, didn't it?'

'Hell, I was already hard. I've been hard all day.'

Hoke reached for Loretta, but she ducked below his hands and buried her face in the hair on his stomach. She bit into it, sucked up some skin, hard, very hard, and made slobbery sounds. This is what she did to Jerry Hickey, Hoke thought. She put those hickeys on his neck the night he died.

Hoke's erection collapsed suddenly and, he thought, irrevocably.

'That'll do,' Hoke said.

'What's the matter?' Loretta laughed. 'Don't you like love bites? You can give me one if you want.'

'Turn over.'

'What?'

'I said, turn over. On your stomach.'

'Why?'

'I want to put it up your ass, that's why.'

'Oh, no you won't! I'll do anything else you want, but not that –'

'Why not? Haven't you ever had an anal orgasm?'

'No, and I don't want one, either. Why don't you just let me suck you off? I'm very good at it, I really am.' She licked her lips and smiled. 'I'll give you an around the world –'

'You can blow me next time, after I've put it up your ass.'

'I can't, Hoke,' she said. 'I've got hemorrhoids; it would hurt too

379

much. Hemorrhoids go with floral designing. I'm on my feet all day, every day, and I've sure got them. If you don't believe me –'

'That's okay. I believe you.'

Hoke got off the bed, put on his shorts, and started toward the bathroom.

'Where're you going?'

'To the bathroom. I'll just be a minute.'

Hoke closed the bathroom door and slid open the mirrored door to the medicine cabinet. There was a bottle of Dexedrine, some Bufferin, a half-dozen bars of bath-size Camay soap, dental floss, four packets of tomato-flavored Kato (potassium chloride for oral solution), a bottle of peroxide, a four-ounce bottle of iodine, seven unused Bic razors, a half-tube of family-sized, mint-flavored Close-up toothpaste, and an empty plastic bottle that had once contained Breck shampoo. On the tank top of the toilet there was an opened tube of K-Y jelly, a box of tampons, and a small leather kit of tools for taking care of finger and toenails.

Hoke rummaged around in the small plastic wastebasket beside the toilet. There were used Kleenex tissues, some honey-colored hairballs, a cardboard tube from a used toilet-paper roll, and at the bottom of the basket, a tiny ball of blue tinfoil.

Hoke was perspiring heavily. The smell of Pine-Sol cleaner was strong in the room. He washed his face and hands, dried them on a dinky, delicately embroidered guest towel and concealed the ball of tinfoil in his hand as he went back into the bedroom.

'What's the matter, Hoke?' Loretta said, sitting up on the edge of the bed. 'Are you sick?'

'No, I'm okay. I'm just a little nervous is all. I'll get my cigarettes from my jacket.'

Hoke went into the hall, then ran to the living room. Loretta's purse was on the round coffee table in front of the couch. Hoke rummaged through the purse and found a narrow cardboard box of suppositories, each of them wrapped in blue tinfoil. There was a typed Ray's Pharmacy label on the cardboard box.

*

282 454 Dr Grossman
One at bedtime. Mrs L. Hickey.
Nembutal 200 mg. Sups/
(Renewable, but dr must be called)

Hoke put the suppositories back in the purse and took out Loretta's checkbook. He glanced at the total in the bank, and then tore a blank deposit slip from the back of the checkbook. He put the deposit slip and the ball of tinfoil into his leisure jacket pocket, then started back down the hall. He ran into Loretta at the bedroom door. She had slipped into a robe. He hoped she hadn't seen him come out of the living room.

'Are you sure you're all right, Hoke?'

'Yeah, but I could use a beer.'

'Lie down. I'll get you one.'

Loretta went into the kitchen, and Hoke went into her bedroom. He lit a cigarette. His hands were shaking. He pulled on his socks and was putting on his pants, when she came back into the bedroom with a red can of Tecate beer. She handed it to him.

'Look, Hoke, it's no big deal. So you lost your hard-on, and now you're embarrassed. You were too anxious, that's all.'

Hoke opened the can and took a sip of beer. 'This has happened to me before, Loretta, but this time I've also got a knot in my stomach. I've ... I've had a hard week and I'm keyed up. I should've taken a nap or something this afternoon.'

'Don't get dressed. Lie down. Take a nap now. In an hour or so, you'll be fine.' Loretta sat on the edge of the bed and let her robe fall open. 'Come on, baby. Lie down, and let me hold you. You'll fall asleep in no time.'

Hoke took another sip of beer, then dropped the butt of his cigarette into the can. 'No, not tonight. I just don't feel right. I'll call you tomorrow.'

Hoke sat on the chaise longue and laced his shoes.

'Don't brood about this, Hoke. These things happen to men once in a while, but it doesn't mean anything. We should've taken our time and necked a little in the living room before rushing into bed. All you've got is an anxiety attack.'

'I know. Next time it'll be different. But the best thing for me to do now is to go home.'

Loretta went with him as he retrieved his pistol in the living room. He knew he had to kiss her good bye at the doorway, and he managed to do it, but it was the hardest thing he had ever done. He wasn't positive – not yet – and he still couldn't prove it, but he knew in his heart that after Loretta Hickey had fucked her stepson, she had killed him herself.

He just didn't know why.

Hoke unlocked the door to his suite at 12:40 A.M. He looked in on his daughters, and they were both asleep. The girls wore short, white cotton nightgowns, and they had kicked off the sheet. Sue Ellen, sleeping with her mouth open, was on her back. Aileen was curled into a knot, hugging an eyeless teddy bear. In their sleep they looked much younger than they did when they were up and running around. With her eyes closed, Aileen didn't look too old to be sleeping with a teddy bear. Hoke covered the girls with the sheet and left the door open to the sitting room so they would get more cool air from the chuffing air conditioner.

Hoke took the elevator down, stopping and locking the elevator at each floor as he sniffed for cooking smells and listened for the sounds of loud talk and laughter. But the hotel after midnight was like a mausoleum.

Eddie Cohen had been asleep on a couch in the lobby when Hoke first arrived, but he was awake now, playing a game of Klondike on a burn-scarred card table. Except for a standing bridge lamp beside the table, and the fluorescent lights above the desk, the lobby was dark.

'What's the matter, Eddie? Can't you sleep?'

'I slept a little. Mrs Feistinger's on my mind.'

Eddie gave up his game and gathered his cards together. He shuffled them three times and offered them to Hoke to cut. Hoke tapped the top of the deck instead of cutting them, and Eddie laid them out for a new game.

'Mrs Feistinger didn't pick up her paper this morning, or yesterday's either,' Eddie said.

'Shit. Have you seen her around?'

Eddie shook his head, looking at his cards.

'Did you check her room?'

'Hell, I've got enough to do around here. But I thought I'd tell you about it when you came in, and now I have.'

'Have we got another one, Eddie?'

'How the hell do I know?'

'What's her room number?'

'Four-oh-four.'

'Want to come up with me?'

'I can't.' Eddie shook his head and put a queen of hearts on a king of spades. 'I gotta stay here and answer the switchboard.'

Hoke walked to the elevators.

Mrs Feistinger was dead, all right, and she had been dead for a day or two, but the room didn't smell so bad because the air conditioning, on high, was going full blast. She was in her eighties, and almost bald. Her blue-tinted wig, complete with ringlets and Mamie Eisenhower bangs, was on a Styrofoam head on the bedside table. She was wearing a blue flannel nightgown and was covered by a sheet and a multicolored afghan. Her pale gray eyes stared sightlessly at the cracked ceiling. Her jaw was rigid; Hoke wouldn't be able to get her false teeth into her mouth without using a lot of force, so he dropped them back into the glass of water. He put the wig on her, though, knowing that she would have wanted it that way, and would have put it on herself if she had known she was going to die in her sleep.

Hoke returned to the lobby and told Eddie to call Kaplan's, the funeral parlor the Eldorado had an arrangement with. It would be a half-hour before Mr Kaplan arrived with his hearse. While he waited for Kaplan, Hoke looked up Mrs Feistinger's guest card and discovered that she had listed a cousin in Denver as her next of kin. He wrote down the Denver address for the funeral director.

Kaplan arrived with his two grown sons and sent them upstairs on the elevator with a folding stretcher. Hoke handed him the slip of paper with the information.

'Mr Bennett'll check out her effects, Mr Kaplan. If she's got an insurance policy, or some money, he'll see that you're paid.'

'I understand that. There's usually something. We always work it out together. Me and Mr Bennett go back a long way.'

'But in case there isn't any insurance, she's wearing a diamond ring. Don't mention it to the cousin, and if she doesn't come up with the funeral expenses, the ring will more than cover it.'

'Don't worry, Mr Moseley. I take care of everything. I notify Social Security, I get the necessary six death certificates – everything. I've had this arrangement with Mr Bennett for several years now.'

After the hearse left, Eddie brought out a bottle of Israeli slivovitz and two glasses. They drank at the desk, then Eddie poured two more shots before locking the bottle in a cabinet behind the counter.

'We saved a full day,' Eddie said, 'and this time no one saw the hearse. Some of them around here get very upset when someone dies. I wish everybody subscribed to the morning paper. It was almost a week that time when Arnie Weisman passed away. Nobody checked his room because somebody said he was visiting his son in Fort Lauderdale. It turned out he didn't have no son in Lauderdale or anywhere else. I still remember how his room smelled. That's why I didn't want to go up there with you tonight, Sergeant Moseley.' Eddie looked down at his shot of slivovitz. 'I wasn't really worried about the switchboard.'

Hoke grinned. 'I thought as much. I also suspect that you knew she was dead because you didn't pull the plug on her air conditioner the last couple of days. But it makes no difference to me, Eddie. Mrs Feistinger had a long life.'

'She was eighty-four, she told me once. But she probably took off a few years. Either that, or she added on a few. Sometimes the old ladies like to add on a few so you'll say they don't look that old.'

'You've seen your share come and go, Eddie.'

'I've seen a few all right. I'll type up a little notice and put it on the bulletin board tomorrow.'

'Cheers, Eddie. For Mrs Feistinger.'

'For Mrs Feistinger.'

Hoke went into the manager's office and typed his report for Mr Bennett, adding that he had told Mr Kaplan to keep the old lady's ring for the funeral expenses. There were two or three deaths a month at the retirement hotel, and Mr Bennett and Kaplan always took care of the paperwork. Deaths weren't Hoke's responsibility, but he kept a carbon of his report to cover himself.

It was after 3 A.M. before Hoke could fall asleep. On the other hand, he had thought, when he first went to bed, that he wouldn't be able to sleep at all.

Chapter Twenty

Hoke awoke groggily at 6 A.M., heated water on the hot plate for instant coffee, put his teeth in, and shaved in the bathroom. He had learned already that if he didn't get to the bathroom first in the morning, the girls spent an unconscionable length of time in there. They also managed, somehow, to use every dry towel, and they consumed an unfathomable amount of toilet paper.

When Hoke was dressed, he filled two cups with strong instant coffee and walked down the corridor to Ellita's room. He banged the door twice with his knee and called out to her. Ellita, wearing her nightgown and a pink quilted robe, opened the door. She had on her large silver circle earrings; she actually does sleep in them, he thought.

'Sorry to wake you so early, but I wanted to talk to you.'

'I was awake, but I didn't want to get out of bed yet.' She lifted the cup in a toast. 'This is exactly what I needed. Come on in.'

Hoke sat in the straight chair, and Ellita sat on the edge of her unmade bed. She had turned off the air conditioner, and the odor of her Shalimar and musk was strong in the small room, but not unpleasantly so; maybe he was getting used to it.

'No use dragging it out,' Hoke said, 'so I'll get right to the point. We've both got a problem, but I think we can work it out together. I've been through some of this before, and you haven't, but in the next few months some strange things will happen to you. You'll start getting sick in the mornings, and later on, when the baby starts growing inside you, it'll take over your entire body. You'll get these periods of extreme lassitude, and your ti – your breasts, I mean, will hurt. You'll still be able to work okay, right up until the eighth month, but there'll be days when you'll have to force yourself to do anything. You'll also have to see a doctor at least twice a month. You'll have to give up spicy foods, and coffee, too.

386

Then, when the baby comes, you'll either have to take an extended leave without pay, or else have someone take care of it when you go back to work.'

'I know all this, Hoke. And I'm sure that my mother will –'

'Your mother'll help some, yes. But with your father's attitude, her help will be limited at best. So let me finish. What I thought was this: When I get a house in Miami, it'll be easier to get a three-bedroom than a two-bedroom, so why don't you move in with me and the girls?'

'I still have to pay the rent for my parents' house, Hoke –'

'I know. You told me that already. But money won't be a problem, or not so big a problem as it is now. I'll have my entire pay, now that I don't have to pay half of it for child support. And what I'm gonna do, I'm going to go to one of these credit places where they consolidate all your debts and then you pay it off at so much a month with just one payment. In a few months, we'll be in good shape financially. Sue Ellen'll be working, and you can just pay a small portion of the expenses if you want – say half the Florida Power bill, or something like that.'

'I've got quite a bit of money saved, Hoke.'

'You won't have to touch your savings. You'll need your money for the baby. We can drive to work together, and if we need another car during the day, we'll get one from the motor pool.'

'It takes an hour to get a pool car, sometimes longer than that.'

'We're partners, and we'll be together anyway. So we'll still be able to use one car most of the time. The point is, I need you as much as you need me. The girls like you, and you can help me out with them. I know you've never lived alone before, and you shouldn't be all alone while you're pregnant. And certainly not after the baby's born. The girls can watch the baby, and it'll be good for them to learn what it's like.'

'It doesn't seem right to move in on you, Hoke. I love the girls, but –'

'They love you, too, Ellita. You're a role model for them. We're scheduled to go to the range next month, and I thought maybe we'd take the girls along and you could teach 'em how to shoot a pistol. I'm too impatient to teach 'em, I know.'

'I don't have to move in on you to teach them how to shoot –'

'Don't say move in *on*, Ellita, say move in *with* us. We'll be like a kind of family. You can have the big bedroom, the master bedroom, all to yourself. We'll get your bedroom furniture, and that way there'll be plenty of room for you and the baby when it comes.'

'When *he* comes.' Ellita smiled.

Hoke grinned. 'He or she, it doesn't make any difference. Girls are all right, too. My girls have been spoiled rotten by their mother, but they'll get straightened around gradually. Right now, they're still confused about things. But once they start working, they'll change their attitudes in a hurry.'

'The girls are fine now, Hoke.' Ellita finished her coffee. 'I'm touched, Hoke, I really am. And I guess you can see how half-hearted my protests are. Last night I was just sitting here in this crummy little room, and it got to me. I kept thinking, this is the way it's gonna be from now on. Alone every night, and on long weekends, too. I'm pretty tough, you know that by now, but I'm not ready to live by myself. Not yet, anyway, even if I had a nice furnished apartment. So I don't have to think about it, Hoke. I'm ready to move when you are.' Ellita got up, and Hoke hugged her awkwardly. He kissed her on the cheek, then took her cup.

'I'm glad, Ellita. We move on Friday. The girls will stay in the hotel today, and I'll give 'em lunch money. After you're dressed, come down for more coffee. There're still a few bagels left, too.'

Hoke opened the door. 'I'll let you tell the girls you're going to live with us. They'll be as pleased as I am.'

Hoke, Bill and Ellita read their files and took notes with very little small talk until nine-thirty. Hoke was called to the phone by the duty officer. There were six cardboard boxes to be picked up at the Greyhound baggage office.

'How late are you open?' Hoke asked the clerk.

'Till six.'

These boxes were the things Patsy had shipped to the girls from Vero Beach. Hoke had forgotten all about them, but he was glad they had arrived at the station. Now he had a legitimate excuse to get out of the office. Of course, he didn't need to have a reason to come and go as he pleased (after all, he was in charge), but

Henderson would rather do almost anything than paperwork and usually wanted to come along.

When Hoke returned to the interrogation room, Armando Quevedo was talking to Henderson and Ellita. Quevedo had shaved off his beard and was in a light gray polyester suit, a white shirt, and a dark blue necktie imprinted with silver pistols. He hadn't cut his long hair, but he had tamed it with some kind of hair oil. He reminded Hoke of an M.C. at a wet T-shirt contest. For a moment, Hoke hardly recognized his fellow detective.

Quevedo flashed his teeth in a smile. 'I gotta go to court today, Hoke. That's why I'm in disguise. I was just telling Sergeant Henderson here that the lead you guys gave us on Wetzel didn't pan out. As it turned out, we couldn't hold him for anything. We had to let the bastard go, and he was the only suspect we had on the torchings and the Descanso Hotel fire. He was picked up downtown by a patrolman right after the hotel fire because he was carrying a can of kerosene. But you can't charge a man with anything just because he's got a can of kerosene. Wetzel stuck to his dumb story, and he wouldn't change it.'

'Did he live at the Descanso?' Hoke asked.

'No. He usually lives under a tree in Bayfront Park. Wetzel claimed he bought the can of kerosene to fill his Zippo lighter. He had a Zippo filled with kerosene, so we were stuck with his story and so was he.'

'But what about Buford? Did Wetzel say anything about that?'

'When Buford was killed three years ago, Wetzel was in jail in Detroit. That checked out, so we released him. But then we drove him up to Fort Lauderdale and dumped him in Broward Country. I think we managed to scare him enough to keep him out of Dade County, anyway. But on the hotel fire and the other torchings, we're back to square one.'

'What did you think of our boy Ray Vince?' Henderson said, broadening his metal-studded smile.

'That sonofabitch is scary, isn't he? He probably heard something, or he wouldn't've come up with Buford's name. But when those guys get high on bang-bang, they're liable to say anything. A lot of squeals come out of the stockade, but this one didn't pan out, that's all.'

'What exactly is bang-bang?' Ellita asked.

'It's a drink the inmates make in the stockade under the barracks. They save potato peelings from the kitchen, the syrup from canned pineapple, raisins from the canteen, and then they get some yeast and brew it up in any kind of container they can get. When it ferments there's a high alcoholic content, but I wouldn't drink it for a million bucks. You can go blind from drinking shit like that. Pardon me, Ellita.'

'*Claro*, Armando! I wouldn't drink shit like that either.' She smiled at Quevedo.

'Maybe you and I can go out for a drink sometime –'

Ellita shook her head. 'I'll take a raincheck, Armando. I've got to lose some weight.'

'I thought you said you had to go to court,' Hoke said.

'You're right.' Quevedo looked at his watch. 'I gotta get to court.'

After Quevedo left, Hoke told them that he had to pick up his daughters' baggage at the bus station and see a real-estate woman about a house.

'You want me to help you with the stuff, Hoke?' Bill said, getting up from his chair.

'No, it's just a few cardboard boxes. You'd better stay here and take a look at the distribution. By tomorrow sometime, I'd like to have a shortlist of cases we can get started on – even if it's only one case we can all agree on.'

'I'm ready to start on Bill's pile now,' Ellita said.

'Okay. Bill can start on yours when he's finished. I'll just have to get back to mine later.'

Hoke put on his jacket and left. He drove to the Fina station a block away from the police department where he always traded and used the phone in the office while the manager filled his tank and checked under the hood. Hoke called the morgue and asked for Doc Evans.

'What made you think the Hickey kid had piles, Hoke?' Doc Evans said when he answered the phone.

'The lab report. There were some tinfoil balls in the ashtray by his bed, and they checked out as Nembutal suppositories. Nembutal can kill a man, can't it?'

390

'If you take enough of it, yes. But Hickey only had one, or maybe two, gobs up his ass. There was enough to put him to sleep, but it didn't kill him. He died from too much heroin, Hoke.'

'Did he have piles?'

'No. He had diverticulitis, but no piles. He was a little young to have diverticulitis already, but it wasn't bad enough to bother him. About forty percent of us over forty have got diverticulitis, but most of us don't even know it. I've got it myself, but it doesn't bother me because I don't eat tomatoes, cucumbers, or anything with little seeds. You avoid little seeds, you won't have a problem.'

'If Hickey didn't have piles, why would he use Nembutal suppositories?'

Doc Evans laughed. 'Maybe he wanted to get high and have a good night's sleep at the same time. Nobody knows how a junkie's mind works, Hoke, but they'll try damned near anything. I can remember, a few years back, when they were all smoking banana skins. They'd bake the skins in the oven, scrape off the inside, and roll cigarettes. There was no dope in the bananas at all, but they got high anyway.'

'I remember that.'

'If you want a nice sleepy high, Hoke, mix paregoric with some pot. Then when it dries, you've got a smoke that'll make you high and sleepy at the same time. It's a lot cheaper than heroin and Nembutal. I don't know what else to tell you, Hoke. Do you need the autopsy report right away?'

'No. Not right away.'

'In that case, you'll have to wait three or four days, before we can get it typed. We're a little swamped over here right now.'

'That's okay. I can wait.'

'Fine. Why don't we have lunch?'

'I can't today, but I'll call you. In the meantime I just have one more question, Doc. My daughter's got a strip of gold glued to her bottom teeth. The orthodonist put it on too tight, and I can't get it off. Is there some kind of solvent I can get to remove it?'

'Jesus Christ, Hoke! A solvent strong enough to dissolve gold would burn holes in her gums. When we have lunch, just bring your daughter by the morgue, and I'll take it off for you. After twenty years in pathology, I could make a fortune by repairing the iatrogenic work done here in Miami.'

'What kind of work?'

'I'm busy, Hoke. Remind me, when we go to lunch, and I'll tell you more than you want to know. It's one of my pet peeves.'

'Thanks, Doc. I'll call you soon.'

'See that you do, or I'll call you.' Doc Evans hung up.

Hoke drove to the Greyhound station, identified himself, and picked up six cardboard boxes that he loaded into the back seat of his car. The boxes were sealed with gray plastic tape and were heavier than he had expected. Possessions. The six boxes containing his daughters' worldly possessions dissolved any lingering doubts, if he had ever had any, that their move was only temporary. There was no disputing it; Sue Ellen would be with him for two more years, and Aileen for four. At least when they were eighteen he could send them out into the world legally and get them off his hands. But in the next two and four years it was still his responsibility to prepare them in some way to earn their livings. He had never really thought about it before, but the responsibilities of fatherhood were mind-boggling or, to use the current term, seismic.

When he got to Coral Gables, Hoke found an unmetered parking space on Murcia and walked to the International Bank of Coral Gables. He showed his shield to the uniformed bank guard, a frail, white-haired man who had a long-barreled .357 magnum in a low-slung leather holster. Hoke told the old man he would like to talk to the bank officer who handled old accounts and made loans.

'That could be either Mr Waterman or Mr Llhosa-Garcia.'

'I think I'd rather talk to Llhosa-Garcia.'

'That's him back there.' The guard pointed.

'Thanks. If you got a lighter gun, old-timer, your kidneys wouldn't hurt you so much at night.'

'I know, I know!' The old man cackled and slapped his holster.

There were several desks behind a mahogany rail in the back of the lofty, cavernous room. There were four desks in a column of twos in front of each officer's larger desk. Four busy young women occupied the desks in front of Mr Llhosa-Garcia's, and the loan officer was talking into a beige telephone, the same color as the blotter in his leather desk pad. The banker had thick, curly gray hair surrounding a mottled bald spot, and a narrow, carefully trimmed black mustache. His round face was sallow, and there were dark half-circles beneath his brown eyes. He was wearing a vest over his shirt and tie, but when he noticed Hoke approaching his desk, he got to his feet, took the suit jacket from the back of his chair, and slipped into it with an easy practiced motion. He indicated the customer's seat with a courteous gesture and sat down again in his well-upholstered leather chair.

'Yes, sir.'

Hoke placed his badge and ID case on the blotter. Llhosa-Garcia read the ID card first and then examined the badge.

'Homicide? I've never seen one of these badges before. Is it solid gold?'

'Gold-plated. Maybe at one time, when gold was thirty-five bucks an ounce, they were solid gold, but if so it was a long time ago. I've never checked into it.'

The banker nodded. 'How may I help you, Sergeant Moseley?' There was no trace of accent in his voice, which surprised Hoke a little. This guy, apparently, had been in the United States a long time.

'I've got an irregular request. I want to get some information on one of your accounts.' Hoke opened his wallet and took out the blank deposit slip he had removed from Loretta Hickey's checkbook. He smoothed it out and passed it across to the banker. Llhosa-Garcia read the name and address printed on the slip, frowned, and then placed the slip on the blotter so Hoke could easily pick it up again.

'I'm afraid I don't understand ...'

'There's not much to understand. Mrs Hickey has an account here. She's a businesswoman in the Gables, and she has been for several years. What I'm interested in are any and all transactions she's made during the past few days – say, the last week.'

Llhosa-Garcia shook his head and smiled. 'We don't give out information like that about our clients.'

'You do if there's a court order. I'm conducting a homicide investigation, and this information may or may not prove to be important. But I need it anyway. Sometimes, to save taxpayers' money, and in the cause of justice, we cut a few corners to expedite matters. For example, you, as a banker, have to report all cash deposits of ten thousand dollars or more to the federal government. Isn't that right?'

Llhosa-Garcia nodded. 'In most cases, yes, although there are certain transfers and revolving accounts that –'

'But you don't have to report any deposits of nine thousand, nine hundred, and ninety-nine. Isn't that also correct?'

Llhosa-Garcia laughed. He sat back and clasped his hands behind his head. 'Who told you that, Sergeant? This is a venerable bank. One of the founders was William Jennings Bryan, and he ran for the presidency three times.'

'And he lost three times. You know, things have changed a good deal since Bryan hyped real estate in Coral Gables. I want – I need – to know what kind of transactions Mrs Hickey made in the last few days. Any information you give me will be confidential, just between the two of us, and I won't contact my friend in the DEA no matter what I discover.'

'What's this homicide investigation of yours got to do with the Drug Enforcement Agency?'

'Absolutely nothing. But there's a DEA agent I know, a guy I used to ride patrol with a few years back, who would also like to know what's in Mrs Hickey's account. That is, he would if he knew what I know about Mrs Hickey. But he doesn't know what I know, and I'm promising you I won't tell him. Any information you give me will be strictly between us, and no matter what comes up later, your name'll never be mentioned.' Hoke pushed the deposit slip back toward the banker.

Llhosa-Garcia got up, went to the desk in front of his, and said something quietly to the young woman sitting there. She nodded and left her desk. Llhosa-Garcia sat at her desk, and Hoke came up behind him to look over his shoulder. The banker rubbed his fingers on the lapels of his suit coat for a moment and then started to key some numbers into the desktop computer terminal. Hoke had his notebook out, but green numbers appeared and disappeared on the screen so quickly there was no time to make any notes. Llhosa-Garcia logged out, the screen went blank, and they returned to the banker's desk.

'I'm not giving you anything in writing. Understand?'

Hoke nodded. 'Of course not. It isn't necessary.'

'She's got four hundred and eighty-two dollars in her checking account.'

'That much I know is true.'

'She owes the bank eighteen thousand dollars, and she hasn't paid the last two installments on her loan. But that doesn't mean anything to us, because she's been late before.' He shrugged. 'That's the flower business, Sergeant. It's feast or famine. But over the years, Mrs Hickey's been a good customer, and her credit's good with us. She also rented a safe-deposit box last Wednesday, a Class C box at thirty dollars a year. There are also a few outstanding checks, but the names don't matter. If you want to look into her safe-deposit box, come back with your court order. We don't know, or care, what people put in their boxes, except in the case of the lady last year who put a bluefish in her box because she didn't like us. We had a hell of a time finding where the smell was coming from.'

'Thank you. I appreciate your cooperation, Mr Llhosa-Garcia,' Hoke said.

'Don't patronize me, you slimy sonofabitch,' the banker said hoarsely, lowering his voice. 'I didn't tell you a fucking thing.'

'Maybe not. But I've got a hunch that Mrs Hickey will pay her overdue installments in a few days. And maybe the entire loan.'

'I don't give a shit whether she pays it off or not. My salary doesn't go up or down on a little business loan like hers.'

'You speak English very well, Mr Llhosa-Garcia.'

'That's because I was born in Evanston, Illinois – not Cuba, where you think. My surname helped me get this job, but it also makes me vulnerable to pricks like you, and you took advantage of me. If you told your DEA friend you suspected a Latin banker of laundering, he'd be down here interrupting our work, even though we have nothing to hide. But if you'd gone to Bruce Waterman with this crap instead of coming to me, he'd've called the Coral Gables chief of police.'

'We've got a Latin quota in the Miami Police Department, too.'

Hoke stood up and extended his hand. Llhosa-Garcia got to his feet to remove his jacket and draped it over the back of his chair.

He ignored Hoke's hand and sat down again, without looking up, to remove some papers from his in-tray. Hoke picked up the deposit slip, put it back in his wallet, and walked out of the bank.

Two doors down from the bank, Hoke went into a shoe store. There was only one customer, a heavyset Latin woman who was trying on a pair of gold-satin pumps. The clerk who was helping her had a dozen shoe boxes scattered around him on the floor. The other clerk was sorting sales slips behind the cash register.

'I'd like to use your phone,' Hoke said, showing the clerk his badge.

'Right there. On the counter.'

Hoke looked up the number in his notebook and then dialed the Bouquetique. Loretta Hickey answered.

'This is Hoke, Loretta. I want to take you to lunch.'

'Oh? Just like that? After the way you acted?'

'Yeah. I had a lot on my mind. The thing is, I want to talk to you, and I can't talk to you privately in your shop, not with customers coming in. Besides, you have to eat lunch anyway, and so do I.'

'I don't know that I want to see you again.'

'Yes, you do. But whether you want to see me again or not is irrelevant. I want to see you. Have you got your car?'

'How do you think I got to work?'

'You have your car, then.'

'Of course.'

'Do you know where Captain Billy's Raw Bar is, in Coconut Grove?'

'Off Bayshore Drive?'

'That's it, about two blocks north of City Hall, on the bay. Meet me there at one o'clock. I'll get there a little earlier and find us a table on the outside patio.'

'What's this all about, Hoke?'

'You, me, Jerry, a cold beer, and lunch.' Hoke hung up the phone.

'Thanks,' Hoke said to the clerk.

The clerk, who had been listening to the call, said, 'That didn't sound like police business to me.'

'No shit. When was the last time you cleaned your rest room? It's filthy in there.'

'What makes you say that? We got a woman comes in every Friday night.'

'In that case, I'll send an inspector over next Thursday to take a look at it.'

Hoke left the shop as the clerk headed for the back of the store.

Chapter Twenty-One

Hoke parked in the Coconut Grove marina lot near the boat launch ramp and walked the block back to Captain Billy's Raw Bar. Captain Billy's had been owned and lost by eight different owners during the last ten years, but the neon sign that flashed CAPTAIN BILLY'S off and on had never been changed. The sign had cost the original proprietor a good deal of money, so the name of the restaurant didn't change when the owners did. The current owner had finally made a success out of the place by enlarging the patio and having Seminole Indians construct palm-thatched chickees over more than half of the outside tables. Some patrons still preferred to sit at tables in the sun instead of beneath the roofed chickees, because they were afraid that a lizard might fall from the fronds into their conch chowder. The patio was popular with a younger crowd in the evenings. There was a small raised stage in the center of the patio, and at night a bluegrass group played until 2 A.M. At lunchtime, however, rock music was played over outside speakers, so Hoke got a table by the edge of the pier, as far away from a speaker as he could get.

Hoke sat with his back to the bay under the shade of a chickee. He was only about ten feet away from the restaurant's tame pelican, which sat on a post at the base of the short wooden pier. This pelican had squatted on this same post for more than three years, and he had lost his ability to fish because restaurant patrons fed him chunks of their leftover fish sandwiches. In the beginning of his residence, the pelican had eaten pieces of fish with the breading still on them, but now he wouldn't accept any fish unless the breading was removed. Every time Hoke came to Captain Billy's, he looked for the pelican. He was always glad to see that the bird was still there.

The short luncheon menu was printed in black ink on a polished empty coconut. Hoke's teenage waiter, wearing a T-shirt that read I EAT IT RAW AT CAPTAIN BILLY'S, sauntered over to Hoke's table.

'For now,' Hoke said, 'just bring me a pitcher of Michelob draft. I'm waiting for a friend, and we'll order later.'

Hoke took out his notebook, glanced through it, and then listed on a blank page the points he wanted to make with Loretta Hickey. The possibility that she might not show up never entered his mind, although he had finished four of the six glasses of beer the pitcher held before she arrived at one-thirty.

Loretta was wearing a lemon-colored silk blouse and a green linen suit skirt. She carried the matching jacket over her left arm. Her dark green lizard purse matched her pumps. The purplish eye shadow she was wearing made her cornflower-blue eyes seem paler, and her bare arms were very white and lightly freckled. Hoke waved to her when she came through the gate, and she crossed the gravel patio slowly, teetering slightly in her high heels.

The wooden benches to the hatch-cover tables were affixed permanently to posts driven into the ground, so Hoke just got to his feet and nodded when she reached the table.

'It's hot out here, isn't it?' she said, as she sat across from Hoke.

'A breeze comes and goes, and a beer helps.'

'I'd rather have a drink, I think.'

'They just serve wine and beer here.'

'A white wine spritzer then.'

Hoke handed her the coconut shell menu and signaled the waiter.

'What're you going to eat, Hoke?'

'The fried clam sandwich is always good, but I'm going to have a dozen oysters on the half-shell.'

'Bring me a cup of the conch chowder,' Loretta told the waiter.

'And bring the lady a white wine spritzer and another pitcher of beer for me.'

The waiter left, and Loretta took a package of Virginia Slims out of her purse. Hoke leaned across the table and lighted her cigarette with a paper match.

'This has been a hectic morning for me,' Loretta said, watching him. 'That's why I'm a little late.'

'That's okay. It's been hectic for me, too. I got a court order this morning and had a temporary seal put on your new lock-box at the Coral Gables International Bank.'

'You what? You had my lock-box opened?'

'No, I didn't say that. I had it sealed so that no one can open it. A temporary seal, that's all. I can get the seal removed at any time, and I won't have to open it first.'

'I don't understand –'

'That's why I invited you to lunch, Loretta, so I could explain some things to you. The box is sealed temporarily, and it won't be opened until after the indictment. If I do ask for an indictment, they drill it open if you won't turn over your key, and then they'll also charge you for the drilling fee.'

'What's this all about, Hoke?'

'Jerry Hickey. I don't know how much money's in your lock-box, but I think it'll either be nine thousand or twenty-four thousand bucks. But you left a thousand of it on Jerry's dresser. Not a large sum for drug dealers either way, but a big score for Jerry Hickey and a woman with a small business going down the tubes. If there was more than twenty-five thousand involved, the guys Jerry ripped off might've looked for him a little harder. And if there had been much more than that, you'd have been afraid to kill Jerry.'

'Kill Jerry? Me?' A hint of dampness appeared above the lipstick on her upper lip. 'Jerry died from an overdose, and you know it!'

'Let me tell you what happened, Loretta.' Hoke held up his hand as the waiter approached the table. The waiter brought the conch chowder and the oysters on a tray. He also gave them silverware, wrapped in paper napkins. He placed Loretta's wine spritzer in front of her. Hoke poured the last of the beer into his glass and topped it off with a head from the fresh pitcher. The waiter put the empty pitcher on his tray.

'Anything else?'

'Bring me some freshly grated horseradish,' Hoke said.

'Yes, sir. I'll be right back.'

Hoke squeezed lemon juice on his oysters and shook a few drops of Tabasco sauce on each oyster. Loretta sat rigidly on her

bench, with her back straight and her hands in her lap. Her cigarette, forgotten in the abalone shell ashtray, sent up a thin column
of smoke. Perspiration was dotting her upper lip.

The waiter returned with a saucer of horseradish and two packets
of oyster crackers in little plastic bags. Hoke put a spoonful of
horseradish on each oyster.

'I'm off on some details, Loretta, but I can give you a broad
outline. The missing details will come out during the investigation.
Jerry was a bag man for some dealers in town. His father probably
got him the job to give him something to do, or perhaps as a favor
for one of his clients. Most of his clients were dealers. Jerry ripped
off the dealers. I don't know what his motivation was. For all I
know, you put him up to it, or suggested it. Jerry probably didn't
know himself, because junkies never make long-range plans.

'Then he came to you and asked you to hide the money for
him, and maybe to hide him as well. You needed this money for
your business. The whole amount, I mean. You were already two
payments behind in your bank loan, and you didn't know what to
do about getting any more. At any rate, when Jerry trusted you
with the money, you rented a lock-box and put it away, except
for a thousand bucks. Then you went home and made love to Jerry
that night. Or at least you tried to. When a junkie's got his fix,
he's not all that interested in sex.'

Hoke forked an oyster into his mouth, chewed for a moment,
and then took a long swig from his glass of beer.

'But you had another little trick to get him aroused, didn't you,
Loretta? Only this time you had a different variation. You slipped
a Nembutal suppository into his ass along with your finger. I think
he had shot up already. Then, when Jerry fell asleep, you gave him
a second shot of heroin in the same punch-mark he'd made before.

'The combination killed him. Good shit, and prescription-quality
Nembutal. More than enough to kill a skinny run-down junkie like
Jerry Hickey.'

Hoke ate another oyster and took another swig of beer.

'That's the most preposterous story I've ever heard,' Loretta said.

'But it's a hell of a story, isn't it? A weird case like this one'll
make the front pages, not just the local section. Harold Hickey's

name'll come into it, too, so when I take it to the state attorney's office, they'll love to pry into your ex-husband's activities. This will give them the excuse they need.'

'Why are you doing this to me, Hoke? What have I ever done to you?'

'I don't have to do anything at all, Loretta. What I'd like to do is something *for* you instead.'

'What do you mean?'

'A proposition. What do you pay on your mortgage at Green Lakes?'

'My house, you mean? The mortgage is one sixty-eight a month, but it goes up every year when the taxes change. What's this got to do with anything? I never did anything to Jerry, and you can't prove I did.'

'I don't have to *prove* anything, Loretta. I'm a detective, an investigator. I turn in my findings, and based on my report the state attorney either makes an indictment herself or turns the information over to the grand jury. The guilt or innocence is determined by a jury of your peers, and half of that jury will be Roman Catholics with very little English. But either way, the trial will get a lot of notoriety. No matter what the jury decides, by the time the trial's over, you'll be lucky if you can get a job hawking flowers at a stoplight. No matter what happens, your career as a Coral Gables businesswoman is finished.'

'I'm innocent, Hoke. I've got some money in my lock-box, I'll admit that. But this was money a man in Atlanta owed me for a long time, and –'

'What's his name and address?' Hoke said, taking out his notebook. 'I'd like to talk with him.'

'I can't tell you that.' Loretta shook her head. 'He wouldn't want his name brought into this. He's a married man … His wife doesn't know he paid me the money back.'

'Sure.' Hoke put his notebook away and ate another oyster.

'You're not going through with this, are you?'

'I don't have to, no. I've got a little plan where you and Jerry can redeem yourselves. Jerry never did anything for anyone while he was alive, and you're as selfish as he was. But I've got a proposition for you. Move to Atlanta, and take that designer's job you've been offered up there. Sell your shop in the Gables for whatever you can get for it, and clear out. Stay in Atlanta for four years. During those four years I'll live in your house in Green Lakes and pay the mortgage payments of one sixty-eight a month. At the end of this exile you can have your house back, and if you save your money in Atlanta, maybe you can open a new business down here again. I don't give a shit what you do. All I want is the use of your house for four years, and I'll maintain the place.'

Loretta stubbed out the butt of her smouldering cigarette. For a long moment she stared at the brown pelican on the post. 'None of this makes any sense,' she said at last. 'Why do you want my house? If you think I've got money hidden in the walls, or anything like that, you're crazy.'

'I need a house to live in for four years. It's that simple. There's nothing crazy about it.'

'You have no evidence against me. Zero. If you went to the state attorney with a wild story like that, she'd laugh at you.'

'I wouldn't go today. I have a few more loose ends to tie up first. That's why I only put a temporary seal on your lock-box. But when I file my report, all the gaps will be filled. Meanwhile, it'll just say in the newspapers tomorrow that you are being investigated in the alleged homicide of your stepson, Jerry Hickey. Sex, drugs ... your Gables customers will like that, won't they? And so will the bank, when you ask for another loan.'

'What about my furniture?'

'Take it, leave it, or put it in storage. Just be out of the house by noon Friday, and I'll drop everything. I'll come by your shop tomorrow for a few minutes and bring a written agreement for a four-year lease. Then I'll take the seal off your lock-box, you can get your money, and you're off to Atlanta. Or wherever you want to go.'

'It isn't that easy to sell a business, not that quick. Not a flower shop.'

'Move into a hotel. Get an agent to handle it. But I want that house by Friday noon. That's the deadline.'

'You're a rotten sonofabitch!'

'If you don't want your conch chowder, try one of my oysters.' Hoke refilled his beer glass.

Loretta lit another cigarette, using her own lighter. 'You're getting into something a lot deeper than you realize, Hoke. Can you wait here for a while? I want to make a phone call.'

'If you're going to call a lawyer, you'd better call your ex-husband. You might ask him how he found out you were fucking Jerry.'

'Jerry told him, and it was a lie.'

'Uh-uh. Your fat friendly neighbor, Mrs Koontz, told him. Jerry just confirmed it, that's all.'

'Ellen? I don't believe it.'

'Ask your husband when you call him.'

'I'm not calling Harold. I want you to talk to a couple of friends of mine. Will you wait?'

'Sure.'

Loretta picked up her purse and crossed the patio to the bar. She passed something to the bartender, and he put a phone on the bar. As she talked into the phone, she gestured with her left hand, making circles in the air. Hoke had a good idea about who these two men would be, but he wasn't certain. Maybe, despite what she'd said, she was just talking to Harold Hickey. Or maybe to her own lawyer. Hoke took out his pistol, set it on his lap, and covered it with a paper napkin. Loretta came back to the table and sat down.

'I don't want to move to Atlanta, Hoke. My business is going to get a lot better now, and if I had to stay away for four years before coming back, it would mean starting all over again.'

'Look at it this way. If the case goes to trial, a good attorney could probably get the charge reduced to manslaughter. At most you'd get three years, and you'd be out in one. But with a dope lawyer like Harold Hickey on the stand as your chief character witness, probation would be out of the question with the tough judges we've got down here. Believe me, Loretta, four years of living well in Atlanta will be a lot better than a year in the women's prison working in the laundry.'

'None of this makes any sense, Hoke. It was only a matter of time before Jerry died of an overdose or got killed by the people he was working with —'

'Just shut up about it before I change my mind.'

'My friends'll be here in a minute. I want you to talk with them first. Then, if we can't work something out, you can have my house – if that's all you want.'

'That's all I want.'

'I'll wait – over by the gate.' Loretta got up and left the table. Hoke watched her teetering walk as she crossed the gravel to the gate in the wooden fence. He drank another glass of beer. Five minutes later, two young men came into the patio. Loretta talked to them for a moment before the three of them came over and joined Hoke at the chickee. Loretta sat down, but the two men on either side of her stayed standing. Both were in their late twenties, and they both wore linen jackets, open-collared sports shirts, and lightweight slacks. The taller of the two had a St Christopher medal the size of a silver dollar on a gold chain around his neck, and there was a bulge under the left armpit of his white linen jacket. They were sleek and well fed, with the expensive sculptured haircuts of TV anchormen, but Hoke wasn't deceived by their appearance. He had seen too many like them in the courtrooms, accompanied by attorneys in three-piece suits.

'Loretta here,' the taller man said, 'told us that you've got something that belongs to us.'

'What's that?'

'Twenty-four thousand dollars.'

'Why not say twenty-five, and round it off?'

'Because she returned a thousand already.' He turned sideways and pointed to the top of a brown envelope in his jacket pocket.

'Doesn't the envelope say one thousand and seventy?'

'It says that, but there's only a thousand in it. She told us you've got the other twenty-four.'

Hoke looked at Loretta. She stared back at him with a determined expression, but there was a tic in her left eyelid.

'When you lose something, and somebody finds it, the finder gets to keep it,' Hoke said. 'If you "found" Loretta's thousand, that's her tough luck. But you'll never find my twenty-four. I've got it, and you've lost it.' Hoke put his pistol out on the table, turned on its side. Holding onto the grip, he used his free hand to cover the weapon with a paper napkin. 'Your trouble is, there's no way you can ever prove I've got it.'

'We've got the serial numbers written down —'

'Did you tell Jerry Hickey you had the serial numbers written down, too?'

The man said nothing, meaning he had.

'He took it anyway, didn't he?' Hoke said. 'If you were dumb enough to use a junkie like Jerry as a courier, you deserve to lose the money. Write it off to experience, and forget about it. But I'm not going to forget what you two bastards look like. From now on, any time I see you – either one of you – you're going to jail.'

'On what charge?' the smaller man said, lifting his chin. 'You don't even know our names.'

'I could bust you right now for making a disturbance in a public place, resisting arrest without violence, and for carrying a concealed weapon. Now both of you get the hell out of here! You stay, Loretta.'

The two men looked at each other for a moment. Then they backed away. They walked to the gate, stopped, and looked over at the table.

'You should've warned me, Loretta,' Hoke said, forcing a grin. 'I'm not as convincing a liar as you are. They'll talk to you some more, your friends over there, but if you can really convince them that I've got the money, it'll be all yours, safe in your lock-box. I don't want it. Like I said, all I want is the house.'

'I'm afraid of them, Hoke.'

'I'm not. But you should be. When they tell their bosses what happened, they might try for some kind of retaliation against me, but I think they'll write it off instead, or cover it out of their own pocket if they have to. To you and me, it's a lot of dough, but it isn't that much to them. So do we have a deal on the house?'

Loretta stared at him, then at the two men in the distance. 'I don't have any choice. That's what you're saying.'

'That's right. And if you decide to leave in the morning, leave the key in your fake rock, but put it in the backyard, near the back door so I can find it. Put all the mortgage papers and stuff on the dining-room table, and when you send me your new address in Atlanta, I'll see that you get a legal lease on the house.'

Loretta shook her head and stood up. 'I can't figure you out, Hoke.'

'It's simple, really. I need the house. And I'll take good care of it for the next four years till you come back – if you decide to come back to Miami.'

'I don't know what I'm going to do. Nothing worked out the way I planned.'

'Nothing ever does. You'd better go. Your friends are getting impatient. Just stick to your story, whatever it is you told them, and they'll let you go. At least I hope so, for my sake. I need the house.'

Loretta started to say something else, changed her mind, and turned abruptly away. She joined the two young men at the gate and they left together, one on either side of her as they headed for the parking lot.

Hoke returned his pistol to its holster. He forked another oyster, and then put it down again. His appetite was gone. His stomach burned and his throat was constricted. He was letting the woman get away with murder – and with the money she had killed for as well. But the fact was that his case against her was weak on a number of counts and probably wouldn't make it past a grand jury, despite everything he'd just made her believe. She'd be back out in no time, and laughing at him. The two slimeballs were still in town, but they would learn the true meaning of police harassment, and he knew every trick in or out of the book. Within six weeks, or two months at the most, they would leave Miami, move to Yuba City, California, and consider their new home a paradise.

Hoke didn't like himself very much. He never had, now that he thought about it. Still, a man had to take care of his family.

At least he had the house in Green Lakes.

Ellita and the girls would love living in Green Lakes, especially after staying at the Eldorado for a few days. Later on, after they got settled, he could go down to the Humane Society and pick up a puppy for the two girls. He would make them take care of the dog, too, teach them something about responsibility.

On Thursday he would send Ellita down to the water department and Florida Power to put down their deposits and to get the name changed on the service. The phone could wait; a cop always had a little priority when it came to getting a new phone. Yes, Thursday would be plenty of time for the deposits. By that time they'd be finished reading all the cases and they could start working on a few of them that were getting colder every day.

Hoke took one of his oysters, still in the shell, over to the pelican and offered it to him. The pelican turned its bill and head away, refusing the oyster. Either he doesn't like the horseradish, Hoke thought, or he doesn't like me.

Hoke paid his tab. Then he borrowed the phone at the bar, called his lawyer, and told him he was coming over to get a lease made up for his new house.

Chapter Twenty-Two

When Hoke got to the station on the following Monday morning, he paused to read the bulletin board before going to his office. A new promotion list was posted. Slater had been promoted to captain; Bill Henderson had made commander; and Armando Quevedo had been promoted to Sergeant, now that Henderson's sergeancy was open.

The new rank of commander was a compromise, after the city manager vetoed the colonelcies the new chief had wanted. The rank of commander was to be higher than a sergeant but lower than a lieutenant, something like a warrant officer in the army. Each division in the department had been allotted one of them. A commander would be entitled to a salute and a 'Sir' from the lower ranks, but wouldn't be in command of any men or task force. His major function would be paperwork, plus taking the responsibility for property and keeping track of it, thereby relieving captains and lieutenants of these irksome chores. This would give the latter more time for supervisory duties, and allow them to get away from their desks more often.

Major Brownley would never get that eagle for his uniform now, Hoke thought, but he was happy about Henderson's promotion.

Henderson was in the little office, glowering into a Styrofoam cup of coffee.

'Good morning, sir, Commander Henderson, sir,' Hoke said, throwing Henderson a salute.

'Fuck you,' Henderson said. 'I don't know why they picked me. You and two other guys outrank me by date-of-rank, and I didn't take any exam or ask for this promotion.'

'We'll find out when we talk to Willie Brownley at ten, I suppose. But congratulations, Bill. If anyone around here deserves a promotion, you do.'

'But I'm not so sure I want it. The rank doesn't make sense. Why call a man a commander if he doesn't command anybody or anything except a desk?'

'They had to call it something, I suppose. And they couldn't use warrant officer because everybody's already an officer, including the lowliest rookie on the street.'

'I don't like the insignia, either. It's a silver lozenge. When I think of a lozenge, I think of a piece of candy.'

'Don't look at it that way, Bill.' Hoke grinned. 'Just think of the extra fifty bucks a month you'll get.'

'Big deal. I could make that much in one night, wearing my uniform and watching the polka dancers at the Polish-American Club.'

'You still can –'

'No I can't either. A commander has too much rank for that. But I'm going to take it because of Marie and the kids. I just talked to Marie on the phone, and she's happy as shit.'

'I'm happy for you, too, Bill, all shitting aside.'

'Thanks, Hoke. But you should've got it instead of me.'

'I think Brownley wants to keep me on the cold cases. But I don't know what you'll be doing. You won't stay with me and Ellita, not as a commander.'

'I know that. Where's Ellita, anyway? Didn't she come in with you?'

Hoke shook his head. 'She's got a doctor's appointment at ten, so she won't be here for the meeting either.'

'Are you settled in yet, in the new house, I mean?'

'We're getting there. We haven't picked up Ellita's bedroom suite, but we'll get it sometime this week. But Saturday, Sue Ellen got a job at the Green Lakes Car Wash. She started this morning.'

'Doing what?'

'They trade off. Part of the time she'll be vacuuming the cars before they go through the wash, then they trade places and she dries the cars with towels after they've been through it. Vacuuming is best, she said, because if she can talk the customer into a pine spray or a new-car spray, she gets a fifty-cent commission. Also, all the people pool tips, and they're divided equally at the end of the day. But otherwise, she gets minimum wage.'

'That's a good job for a kid. What about the little girl?'

'I don't know. I'm going to see if I can get her an afternoon paper route in the neighborhood, delivering the *Miami News*. But I want to keep her close by, in the neighborhood. Sooner or later a route'll open up. Otherwise, everything's working out fine so far.'

'What do you want me to do this morning?'

'I don't know. You might just summarize all of the cases you've read so far, what your thoughts are on them. We've picked the first five, but you won't be working on them now, so I don't know what else to tell you.'

'I've done that already, but it isn't typed.'

'You don't have to type it. I'm closing out the Gerald·Hickey case as a probable accidental OD this morning, and we won't start on the Dr Raybold case until I've talked to Ellita about it. Raybold's the first one on our list.'

'It's got good potential, Hoke, and I'd like to work with you on it.'

'Why not? You're staying in the division, no matter what else they give you to do, and you'll still be able to help with some of these cold cases.'

Teddy Gonzalez knocked on the door, which was open, and then came into the office. Gonzalez was in his early twenties, with an A.B. in History from Florida International University. He had wanted to teach history, but joined the police force instead when he couldn't find a teaching job. He wore a suit and tie, and his shoes were shined, but he had a nervous habit of biting the cuticles on his fingers.

'Congratulations, Commander Henderson,' Gonzalez said, smiling.

'Thanks, Teddy,' Henderson said. 'What's on your mind?'

'Not much of anything, right now. I just wanted to congratulate you, that's all. I followed up on that tip you gave me about Leroy's floating crap game, and it's still in operation. Leroy Mercer, who ran it all these years, has been dead for about eight months. His son Earl runs it now, but they still call it Leroy's game. I checked around at Northside, and found out that the game was held up about a month ago by three men. And those three guys who were killed could've been the holdup men. If so, they could've been found and killed for holding up the game. That sounds reasonable, although it doesn't seem likely that they'd be killed for the small amount of money they took from the game.'

'How much was in the game?'

'I don't know. But according to the snitch I talked to, there was never more than five or six thousand bucks in any of those games.'

'In Liberty City,' Hoke said, 'five thousand bucks is a hell of a lot of money. Did you talk to Earl Mercer? Question him, find out who was playing when the game was held up. Then run down each guy, and see where he was on the night of the murders.'

'Earl isn't in town, and the game isn't playing right now. My snitch said he went back to Tifton, Georgia, to stay with his mother for a vacation.'

'Who's your snitch?'

'The old black man who takes tickets at the Royale Theater. All they play at the Royale is kung-fu movies, and Shaft reruns. They got a double-feature Shaft movie on now, and old Bert says he hasn't been able to get around much lately because they've been so busy. Anyway, that's where the case stands. I really don't know what to do next. You got any more suggestions, Sergeant – I mean, Commander?'

'I don't know, Teddy. It seems to me you've got reasonable cause to get the chief up in Tifton to pick up Earl Mercer. At least for questioning. Then you can go up there and talk to him. What do you think, Hoke?'

'I think that Slater should turn the case over to a black detective. Nobody in Liberty City's going to tell Teddy much of anything. And hearsay isn't enough to pick up Mercer either. What did Slater tell you, Gonzalez?'

'I haven't talked to him about the crap game yet. He won't be in today, anyway. He's lecturing at the police academy.'

'We've got an appointment at ten with Major Brownley,' Henderson said. 'I'll suggest to him that the case go to a black detective.'

'I'm not trying to get out of anything,' Teddy said. He put a finger in his mouth and began to chew it.

'We know that, Teddy. But you've taken it about as far as you can. Haven't you got anything else to work on?'

'A DOA on Fifth Street, but it looks like a suicide. I won't know for sure till I see the P.M.'

'Work on that, then,' Henderson said, 'and I'll talk to either Slater or Brownley about taking you off the triple murder. If we were still working together, Teddy, if it makes you feel any better, I'd ask to get off the case myself. If Lieutenant Slater won't take you off, he ought to at least get a black detective to work with you on it.'

'*Captain* Slater,' Hoke said, grinning.

'That's right.' Henderson smiled. 'He was insufferable before. I wonder what he'll be like now with two bars.'

'The same,' Hoke said. 'Actually, now that he finally made captain, he might mellow out a little.'

'Thanks a lot,' Teddy said. 'And congratulations again, Sergeant Henderson. Commander.' Teddy left the office, and they watched him through the glass as he crossed the squad room toward his desk.

'What do you think of Gonzalez, Bill?'

'I don't know yet. But he's got a lot of guts. It takes nerve for a white man to go down to the Royale Theater and hang around in the men's room there for a chance to talk to an old ticket-taker. I know he's armed, and all that, but I wouldn't want to hang around in there alone for very long. Jesus, look at Armando!'

Armando Quevedo was coming toward the office from the men's room. He had a short haircut, with white sidewalls, and he was wearing a brown silk suit with an opened collar shirt, and a wide grin.

Quevedo stood in the doorway and spread his arms. 'Congratulations, Bill,' he said. 'Thanks to your promotion, I finally got my three stripes.'

'And a haircut,' Hoke said.

'You would've got your three stripes no matter who got the commander rank,' Henderson said. 'So you don't have to thank me. Besides, your score was the highest on the division list.'

'I know, but thanks just the same.'

'If you guys haven't got anything else to do,' Hoke said, 'why don't you do it somewhere else. I've got work to do, and people will be coming around all morning to congratulate you.'

'Come on, Bill,' Quevedo said. 'I'll take you down to the cafeteria and buy you a second breakfast.'

'Why not?' Henderson got up from the desk. 'Can I bring you anything, Hoke? Coffee?'

'No, I don't think so. Ellita fixed a pot of Cuban coffee at home this morning.'

After the two detectives left, Hoke closed the Gerald Hickey case, wrote a summary memo in longhand, and then placed the file next to the typewriter on Ellita's side of the desk. 'Accidental OD.' The folder, thickened now with additional papers, would go into the closed files. He wouldn't have to think about it again, Hoke thought, for at least four more years. And in four more years, he'd only have another four to go until retirement. And maybe, just maybe, Loretta Hickey wouldn't come back. After a few months, or a year, when he had saved some money, he might even be able to write to her and offer to buy the damned house in Green Lakes.

At 10 A.M., Hoke and Henderson knocked on Major Brownley's door. He beckoned them in, got to his feet, and came around the desk to shake hands with Henderson.

'Congratulations, Bill.'

'Thank you, sir,' Henderson said, towering over the major.

'Sit down, sit down,' Brownley said. He went behind his desk and picked up his burning cigar from the piston ashtray. 'Where's Officer Sanchez?'

'She's got a doctor's appointment,' Hoke said as he sat down.

'Couldn't she make it for another time?'

'Female trouble. She had to see her gynecologist.'

'Oh, that's different. Well, we don't need her anyway. You can fill her in, Hoke. You probably think I'm disappointed about the colonelcies being shot down, and I am – a little. But I knew the money wasn't in the budget in the first place. Of course, the money wasn't in the budget for the commanders either, but the city manager just didn't want that much brass in the department. When he gets fired – and no manager lasts more than two or three years in Miami – the chief may get through to the next one. Anyway, even though I left the choice of the commander promotion up to

Captain Slater, I approved of it because the final decision was mine. You outrank Henderson, Hoke, and I want to clear up any resentment you might have.'

'I don't have any.' Hoke sat back in his chair. 'I'm happy doing what I'm doing, and I don't think you could find a better candidate in the division than Bill. After all, we worked together for more than three years.'

'Okay, Hoke. Henderson will be Captain Slater's assistant, and Slater felt that he could work better with Bill than he could with you. It's that simple. And I agreed with him, because I think Bill can work with almost anybody.'

'Slater isn't all that easy to get along with,' Henderson said. 'What's my job description?'

'I'm getting to that. You'll take Slater's desk out in the bullpen, and he'll take back his old office. That means that you'll have to furnish an office in Room 3 for Hoke and Sanchez. I'm leaving them on the cold cases, as a permanent assignment. So get them some filing cabinets, a typewriter, and a typing table. You can take the big double desk in there for yourself and replace it with Slater's smaller desk. You'll need the double desk because you're getting a secretary. You'll need one, because all of the paperwork in the division will go through you before you take it to Slater.'

'Will I still report directly to you, or do I report to Captain Slater?' Hoke said.

'To me. But send copies of your weekly reports to Bill here. He'll have to know what's going on. Still, I want to give you as much leeway as possible. Another thing, Bill. When you get your secretary, make an inventory of everything in the division, supplies and all, because you'll have to sign for all the division property.'

'Jesus Christ,' Henderson said. He took out a handkerchief and wiped his face.

'What's the matter?' Brownley said.

'That's a lot of paperwork.'

'I know. That's what the rank calls for. You'll also be responsible for shift assignments, overtime, things like that. But Captain Slater'll fill you in on the specifics. It's a desk job, Bill, and you won't have to go out into the hot sun any longer. It might sound

415

a little tough now, but you'll work into it all right. Besides, you'll have a secretary. What would you rather have, a male or a female?'

'Female. I don't want any gay secretary.'

'A male secretary isn't necessarily gay, Bill. The way unemployment is in Miami right now, I could get you a male secretary with a degree in economics. The line-item pays ten thousand a year, with COLA increments every six months.'

'I'd rather have a woman.'

'Okay. But when you advertise the position, remember that you can't specify that you would rather have a woman. You and Slater can work out the ad. Now we haven't got a written job description for you yet, but there's no hurry. None of the divisions know exactly what to do with this new rank. But I'll work on it with Captain Slater, and you can put any suggestions you have in writing and send them to me. Okay? I guess you'd better get going. You've got a lot to do.'

'Yes, sir.' Henderson got up, gave the major a half-hearted salute, and left the office. Hoke stood up, too.

'Just a minute, Hoke, I want to talk to you.'

Hoke sat down again, and took out his cigarettes. He lit a Kool and put the match into the major's ashtray.

'I understand,' the major said, 'that Officer Sanchez is living with you now.'

'She's renting a room from me in my new house in Green Lakes. But that doesn't mean she's *living* with me, if that's what you're implying. I've got my two daughters with me now, and she's been a big help to me with them.'

'I didn't mean to imply anything.'

'Yes you did, Major, but that's your hang-up, not mine. I know you're a deacon in your church and all, but there's no rule against us living together, even if we were. We're partners, and without any regular hours, so our arrangement will work out fine.'

'Maybe I'm old-fashioned, but I don't want any criticism. People like to talk, you know.'

'Not as much as you think. At any rate, you'll have to talk to Ellita about this, not me. She told me already that she wanted to talk to you.'

'All right. My door is always open. Tell her to come and see me. But meanwhile, I'm leaving you two on the cold cases for an indefinite period, not just the two months I originally planned. A time limit of any kind is too restricting, and sort of defeats the idea. What are you working on now?'

'The Dr Raybold homicide. It's four years old, but it's our best bet. He was shot in his driveway at six-fifteen in the morning. We know the approximate time because the man on the paper route discovered the body when he threw the paper on the lawn, and the body was still warm. But nobody saw the shooting. Mrs Raybold was still asleep, and didn't hear the shots. There were two of them, one in the head, and one through the heart. There were no clues at all, but six months later Mrs Raybold married Dr Sorenson, who was Raybold's partner in the clinic. This was a professional hit, and whoever did it probably knew that Raybold had an operation scheduled at St Mary's Hospital at 7 A.M. He wasn't robbed, for example –'

'So you think Dr Sorenson and Mrs Raybold wrote the prescription?'

'Yeah, but there's more to it than that. If you want, I'll get the file and we'll go over it, but right now all I can say is that it's promising. There's nothing definite yet.'

'Never mind. You know what you're doing. Just keep me up to date in the weekly reports. I'm not looking for any miracles. You've done a hell of a job so far, and the best thing I can do for you is stay out of your hair.'

'Yes, sir.' Hoke stood up. 'Is there anything else, Major?'

'No – yes. You know Henderson better than I do. He didn't seem very enthusiastic about his promotion.'

'He's happy enough, Willie. It's just a lot to absorb all at once, that's all. But no one would be thrilled, knowing he had to work with Captain Slater every day.'

'Maybe that's it.' Brownley stood up. 'Thanks for coming in, Hoke.'

'Yes, sir.' Hoke went back out to his office and opened the drawers to his desk. Now that he had to move, he decided to clean out all the accumulated junk first and throw it away before toting the rest of his things down to the interrogation room. Henderson, with all of the work he had to do, would be needing the big desk right away ...

The phone rang a few minutes after eleven. Ellita Sanchez was on the phone. 'I called earlier, Hoke, but I guess you were still in with Major Brownley. I just left the doctor's office. I got there at nine forty-five, but I didn't get in to see the doctor till ten-thirty. But the nurse took my urine specimen at ten, so I didn't have to hold the jar in my lap.'

'What did the doctor say?'

'I'm fine. No problems. I don't have to see him again for six weeks.'

'Good. You can come in then, and help on the move. We're moving permanently into Room 3. Tonight we'll take the girls out to dinner and celebrate.'

'Celebrate what? Moving out of the office?'

'No. Bill Henderson got promoted. He made commander, the new rank the paper mentioned yesterday. Remember?'

'Bill made it? How come he got it instead of you?'

'Dumb luck. That's why we're celebrating. It could have been me.'

BOOK 3

Sideswipe

Life is an effort that deserves a better cause.
KARL KRAUS

There's a lot of bastards out there!
WILLIAM CARLOS WILLIAMS

To Betsy and the boys

STOREOWNERS GUNNED DOWN IN DARING DAYTIME HOLDUP

Los Angeles (U.P.I.) – In a daring daylight holdup, Samuel Stuka, 53, and his wife, Myra, 47, owners of Golden Liquors, 4126 South Figueroa Street, were shotgunned and wounded fatally by a tall man wearing a gray cowboy hat at ten this morning, according to Detective Hans Waggoner, University Station, investigator of the case.

'There was an eyewitness,' Waggoner told reporters, 'and we are tracking some leads now. The man was alone and drove away in a red vehicle that was either a Camaro or a Nissan two-door with a horizontal fin across the trunk.'

The eyewitness, who was not named, heard the two shots, the detective said, and dived behind a hedge next to the store. He looked up when the killer got into the vehicle and drove away, but did not get the license number.

'The M.O. is familiar,' Waggoner said, 'and we have some good leads.' He did not elaborate, because the investigation was continuing.

Mrs Robert L. Prentiss, the couple's daughter, who resides in Covina with her husband and two children, Bobby, 4, and Jocelyn, 2, said that her father had bought the store three months ago, after moving to Los Angeles from Glen Ellyn, Ill., to be closer to his grandchildren.

'He was semi-retired, but needed a place to go every day,' she said, 'and that's why he bought the store. My mother was only helping him out temporarily –' Mrs Prentiss broke down then, and could not continue.

The robbery of Golden Liquors was the third liquor store robbery this week in southwest L.A., but the Stukas were the only proprietors killed, Waggoner said. A shotgun was employed in the other two holdups as well.

'Mr Stuka probably put up some kind of resistance,' Detective Waggoner said, 'which is a mistake if the robber has a sawed-off.'

Chapter One

Detective-Sergeant Hoke Moseley, Miami Police Department, opened the front door of his house in Green Lakes, looked to the left and to the right. Then, barechested and barefooted, and wearing droopy white boxer shorts, he dashed out to pick up the *Miami Herald* from the front lawn. At six A.M. there was little need for this modesty. His neighbors were not up, and the eastern sky was barely turning a nacreous gray.

The paper was usually delivered by five-thirty each morning by an angry Puerto Rican in a white Toyota, whose erratic throw from his speeding car never found the same spot on the lawn. The driver was still angry, Hoke thought on those mornings when he stood behind the screen door waiting for the paper, because Hoke had returned the delivery man's stamped, self-addressed Christmas card without including a check or a five-dollar bill as a tip.

In the kitchen, Hoke pulled the slippery transparent cover from the paper, wadded it into a ball, and tossed it into the overflowing grocery bag that served as a garbage receptacle. He read the first paragraph in all of the frontpage stories. Another American hostage had been killed by a Shiite skyjacker in Lebanon. The new fare for Metrorail would (perhaps) be a quarter, a half-dollar, or a dollar, but the newest fare system would probably depend on which station the rider used to board the train. An eighteen-year-old Haitian, a recent graduate of Miami-Norland High School, had miraculously managed to obtain an appointment to the U.S. Air Force Academy, and the congressman who had appointed him had just discovered that the boy was an illegal alien and was awaiting deportation at the Krome Detention Center. This item reminded Hoke of the tasteless joke Commander Bill Henderson had told him yesterday in the department's cafeteria.

'How can you tell when a Haitian's been in your backyard?'

'How?'

'Your mango tree's been stripped and your dog's got AIDS.'

Hoke hadn't laughed. 'That won't work, Bill.'

'Why not? I think it's funny.'

'No, it doesn't work, because everyone doesn't have a mango tree in his backyard, and not every Haitian has AIDS.'

'Most of them have.'

'No. I don't have a mango tree and neither do you.'

'I mean AIDS. Most Haitians have AIDS.'

'Not so. I think the figure's less than one-half of one percent.'

'Go fuck yourself, Hoke.' Henderson got up from the table and left the cafeteria without finishing his coffee.

Hoke's reaction to Henderson's crummy humor had been another sign, but Hoke hadn't spotted it and neither had Bill Henderson. Ordinarily, when Bill told one of his jokes, Hoke at least grinned and said, 'That's a good one,' even when it was an out-of-context gag Bill had written down from the Johnny Carson monologue.

But Hoke hadn't smiled for more than a week, and he hadn't laughed at anything for almost a month.

Hoke sprinkled a liberal helping of Grape-Nuts into a plastic sieve and ran hot water from the tap over the cereal to make it soft enough that he could eat it without putting in his false teeth. When the cereal had softened sufficiently, he dumped it into a bowl and covered it with Half-and-Half. He then sliced a banana into the cereal, upended a pink packet of Sweet 'N Low over the mixture, and took the bowl and the newspaper out into the Florida room.

The sun porch had open, jalousied windows on three sides, and a hot, damp breeze blew through them from the lake. The Florida room faced a square lake of green milk that had once been a gravel quarry. The backs of all of the houses were toward the lake in this Miami subdivision called Green Lakes. Not all of the homeowners, or renters, had glassed-in porches like Hoke. Some of them had redwood decks in back; others had settled for do-it-yourself concrete patios and barbecue pits; yet all of the houses in Green

427

Lakes had been constructed originally from the same set of blue-prints. Except for the different colors they had been painted, and repainted, and the addition of a few carports, there was little discernible difference among them.

Hoke sat at a glass-topped wrought-iron table in a webbed patio chair and then realized that he didn't have a spoon. He returned to the kitchen, got a spoon, sat at the table again, and slowly gummed his Grape-Nuts and chopped bananas as he read the sports section. Ron Fraser, the Miami Hurricanes' baseball coach, who had coached the team to its second win in the college World Series in Omaha, said he might retire in three, maybe four more years, or he might even renegotiate a new contract. It must be hard, Hoke thought, for a sports writer to turn in something every day when there was nothing worthwhile to report.

Hoke then turned to Doonesbury, which was poking fun at Palm Beach for requiring mandatory ID cards for non-resident blue-collar workers on the island. Hoke was overwhelmed instantly with a formless feeling of nostalgia. Palm Beach was right across the inlet from Singer Island, and Singer Island, at the moment, was where Hoke wanted to be. Not in his father's huge four-bedroom house up there, on the Lake Worth intracoastal waterway, but in a hotel or motel room facing the sea where no one could find him and force him to read the fifteen new Incident Reports, with their fifteen attached Supplementary Reports, or 'supps' as they were called in the department.

Hoke shook his head to clear it, glanced at the box scores, and noticed that the Cubs had dropped another game to the Mets – three so far in a three-game series. He threw the paper down in disgust. The Cubs, he thought, should be able to beat the Mets every game. What in hell was the matter with them? Every season it happened this way. The Cubs would be three or four games ahead of everybody, and then drop into a mid-season slump, and then down and down they would plummet into the supps, the supps, the supps ...

The drapes were pulled back suddenly inside the master bedroom by Ellita Sanchez. Hoke turned slightly and waved languidly with his right hand. Ellita, still in her pink shorty nightgown and wearing a purple satin peignoir, smiled broadly and waved back. Then she waddled away from the sliding glass doors toward the bathroom, the one she shared with Hoke's daughters, Sue Ellen and Aileen – and with Hoke when he could find it unoccupied.

The morning had begun, another broiling, typically humid June day in Miami. It was Thursday, but it could just as easily have been a Tuesday or a Friday. The summer days were all alike, hot and blazing, with late-afternoon thundershowers that did nothing to relieve the heat and only added to the humidity. Ellita Sanchez, eight months pregnant and now on indefinite maternity leave from the department, would make a pot of Cuban coffee and bring it out in a Thermos to Hoke. She would have one quick cup with Hoke before returning to the kitchen to fry two eggs, sunny side up, and to toast four slices of Cuban bread that she would slather with margarine. Ellita's doctor had told her not to drink any more coffee until after the baby was born, but she drank the thick black Cuban brew anyway, at least one cup, and more often two.

'My baby,' she explained to Hoke, 'will be half Cuban, so I don't see how one or two little one-ounce cups of coffee can hurt him before he's born.'

Ellita didn't know the father's last name. His first name was Bruce; she had picked him up for a one-night stand (her first, she had told Hoke) and gotten pregnant as a result. Bruce, whoever he was, did not know that he was going to be a father, and he had probably never thought of Ellita again after the two hours he spent with her in his Coral Gables apartment. A blond, blue-eyed insurance salesman, twenty-five years old – that was almost all Ellita knew about Bruce. That much, and that he had two black tufted moles one inch below his left nipple. Ellita was thirty-two years old, and she was not only reconciled to having the unplanned baby, she was looking forward to it. If it was a boy, she was going to name him Pepé, after her uncle who had died in one of Castro's prisons; and if it was a girl, she was going to name her Merita, after her aunt, Pepé's wife, who still lived in Cuba. Ellita didn't care whether it was a boy or a girl, just as long as she had a healthy baby. She had prayed that her child would not have any tufted moles beneath its left nipple – in either case – but she was prepared to accept them if that was the will of God.

When her eggs and toast were ready, Ellita would bring her plate out to the glass table and rejoin Hoke. With her knife and fork she would fastidiously cut away the white part surrounding the barely cooked yellow yolks and eat the white part first. Then she would eat the yolks, scooping them up one at a time and shoveling them into her mouth without breaking them. This was the part Hoke could barely stand to watch, the runny yellow yolk oozing through Ellita's strong white teeth. But he couldn't say anything to Ellita about this practice, this disgusting habit, because she paid half the rent and half the utilities on the Green Lakes house. Ellita was Hoke's partner in the Homicide Division, and she would be his active partner again when her maternity leave was over and she came back to work, so Hoke could only give her criticism or suggestions as a police officer. His supervisory status did not extend to the home, to her eating habits, to her sleeping with earrings on, or to her wearing a layer of sprayed musk on top of her overdose of Shalimar perfume.

Hoke did not sleep with Ellita; he never had, and he never would. She was an investigator assigned to him as a junior partner in the Homicide Division, and that was that. But Hoke needed her in the house, and not just because he wouldn't have been able to swing all of the expenses by himself. Ellita had also helped him considerably with his two teenage daughters.

The girls had been living with Hoke for six months now, after being sent back to Hoke by their mother, who had moved from Vero Beach, Florida, to Glendale, California, to marry Curly Peterson, a black pinch hitter for the Dodgers. Sue Ellen, sixteen, had a job at the Green Lakes Car Wash and planned to drop out of school permanently when high school started again in September, so she could keep making monthly payments on her new Puch moped. Aileen, fourteen, had been helping around the house and had found a few baby-sitting jobs in the neighborhood, but she would be required by law to go back to school in the fall. Aileen wanted to quit school, too. Both girls adored Ellita Sanchez, and they ate their fried eggs each morning in imitation of Ellita. Hoke

430

could not prevent the girls from continuing this disgusting habit; anything he said to them would be construed by Ellita as an indirect critique of *her*.

Hoke had discussed this dilemma with Bill Henderson, his previous partner, and Bill had told him that the only thing he could do was to eat his breakfast alone, preferably before Ellita and the girls got up in the morning. If he didn't watch them eating their eggs, and if he tried to put it out of his mind, perhaps, in time, he wouldn't think about it. And as a rule, this was what Hoke did. He would eat his Grape-Nuts out on the porch, and then when Ellita joined him with her plate, he would pour his coffee and take it into the living room, there to sit in his La-Z-Boy recliner in front of the television while he watched the morning news.

Hoke preferred to get up before the females anyway, so he could take his shot at the bathroom for his shower and shave. Once the rest of them were up, the wait for the bathroom could be interminable. One bathroom was not enough for four people, but that was the way the contractor had saved money when he built the Green Lakes subdivision in the mid-fifties, and there were several families much larger than Hoke's in the subdivision making do.

Ellita brought out the Thermos of coffee, an empty regular-sized cup, and a demitasse cup. She poured the coffee – four ounces for Hoke, one ounce for herself – and asked what was new in the paper.

'I'm finished with it.' Hoke shrugged. He took his filled cup into the living room and sat in his La-Z-Boy, but he didn't switch on the television.

When Ellita had started her maternity leave, two weeks before, Major Brownley, the Homicide Division chief, had told Hoke he wouldn't be able to replace her. Hoke had Ellita and a young investigator named Teodoro Gonzalez (immediately nicknamed 'Speedy' by the other detectives in the division) working for him on the 'cold case' files. In the beginning this was supposed to have been a temporary assignment, but the three of them had so handily solved a half-dozen old murder cases that the major had made it a permanent assignment, with Hoke in charge. Without Ellita, and without any replacement for her, Hoke would have to depend solely on Gonzalez – a bright young investigator, but a man without a sense of direction – for most of the legwork. Gonzalez had a B.A. degree in economics from Florida International University in Miami, and had served only one year as a patrolman in Liberty City before being promoted to plainclothes investigator in the Homicide Division. He hadn't actually earned this promotion, but had been elevated because he was a Latin with a bachelor's degree. His black patrol sergeant in Liberty City had recommended Gonzalez for the promotion, but that was because the sergeant had wanted to get the man the hell out of his section. Despite the map in his patrol car, and the simple system of streets and avenues in Miami (avenues run north and south; streets run east and west), Gonzalez had spent half of his patrol hours lost, unable to locate the addresses he was dispatched to find. Gonzalez was willing and affable, and Hoke liked the kid, but Hoke knew that when he sent him out to do some legwork, an important function on cold cases, Gonzalez would spend most of his time lost somewhere in the city. Once Gonzalez had been unable to get to the Orange Bowl, even though he could see it from the expressway, because he couldn't find an exit that would get him there.

Gonzalez had, however, prepared Hoke's income tax return, and Hoke had received a $380 refund. Gonzalez had also prepared Ellita's Form 1040, and she had received a refund of $180 when she had expected to pay an additional $320, so they thenceforth both admired Gonzalez's ability with figures. Hoke had given Gonzalez responsibility for the time sheets and mileage reports, and they had had no trouble in getting reimbursed. Beyond this, however, Hoke didn't know quite what to do with Gonzalez and the fifteen new supps that had been deposited in his in-box the day before.

These supps all represented new cold cases which, in Hoke's opinion, were still too warm to be considered inactive. What these cases really were were difficult cases that other detectives in the division considered hopeless. But they were also much too recent to be hopeless, as Hoke had discovered by glancing through them yesterday afternoon. Hoke was getting them via interoffice mail because Major Brownley had put a notice on the bulletin board directing detectives in the division to turn over all of the cold cases they were currently working on to Sergeant Moseley. These new cases, added to the ten Hoke had selected already from the back files to work on, because they had possibilities, were not, in Hoke's opinion, beyond hope. Even his cursory reading of the new supps had indicated that the detectives could have done a lot more work on them before putting them on his back burner. What it amounted to, Hoke concluded, was a way for these lazy bastards to clear their desks of tough investigations and shift them over to him and Gonzalez. All fifteen supps had yellow tags affixed to the folders, meaning that there was no statute of limitations on these crimes because they were homicides, rapes, or missing-person cases. Hoke realized that his desk would be the new dumping ground for more and more cases from detectives who had run out of routine leads and gotten down to the gritty part of thinking about fresh angles that were *not* routine. The chances were, he thought gloomily as he finished his coffee and put the cup on the magazine table next to the La-Z-Boy, that there would be a few more of them in his in-box when he got down to his cubbyhole office on the third floor of the Miami Police Station.

Hoke stopped thinking about this new idea. Then he stopped thinking altogether, closed his eyes, and sat back in the chair.

The girls got up. (They shared a bedroom, Ellita had the master bedroom, and Hoke had the tiny eight-by-six-foot bedroom that was originally supposed to be either a den or a sewing room at the back of the house next to the Florida room.) They used the bathroom, took their showers, and fixed their breakfasts. They jabbered with Ellita out in the Florida room but didn't disturb Hoke when they saw him with his eyes closed, sitting in his chair. At seven-forty-five, Sue Ellen kissed Hoke on the forehead (he apparently didn't feel it) before getting on her moped and riding off to work at the Green Lakes Car Wash. Ellita and Aileen washed and dried the dishes in the kitchen, and then, at eight o'clock, Ellita touched Hoke's bare shoulder gingerly, told him the time, and said that the bathroom, if he wanted it, was clear again. But Hoke did not reply.

At eight-thirty Ellita said to Aileen:

'I think your father's gone back to sleep in his chair. Why don't you wake him and tell him it's eight-thirty? I know he has to work because he told me last night he had fifteen new supps to read through today.'

'It's eight-thirty, Daddy,' Aileen said, her right hand ruffling the stiff black hairs on Hoke's back and shoulders. Aileen, every time she got an opportunity, liked to feel the hair on Hoke's back and shoulders with the tips of her fingers.

Hoke didn't reply, and she kissed him wetly on the cheek. 'Are you awake, Daddy? Hey! *You* in there, old sleepyhead, it's after eight-thirty!'

Hoke didn't open his eyes, but she could tell from the way he was breathing that he wasn't asleep. Aileen shrugged her skinny shoulders and told Ellita, who was sorting laundry from the hamper into three piles, that she had given up on waking her father. 'But he's really awake,' she said. 'I can tell. He's just pretending to be asleep.'

Aileen was wearing a white T-shirt with a 'Mr Appetizer' hot dog on the front; some of the egg yolk from her breakfast had spilled onto the brown frankfurter. Ellita pointed to it, and Aileen stripped off the T-shirt and handed it to her. Aileen did not wear a brassiere, nor did she need one. She was a tall skinny girl, with adolescent chest bumps, and her curly sandy hair was cut short, the way boys used to have theirs trimmed back in the 1950s. From the back, she could have been mistaken for a boy, even though she wore dangling silver earrings, because so many boys her age in Green Lakes wore earrings, too.

Aileen returned to her bedroom to get a clean T-shirt, and Ellita went into the living room. 'Hoke,' she said, 'if you aren't going downtown, d'you want me to call in sick for you?'

Hoke didn't stir in his chair. Ellita shrugged and put the first load of laundry into the washer in the utility room off the kitchen. She then made the bed in her bedroom (the girls were supposed to make their own), hung up a few things in her walk-in closet, and gave Aileen $1.50 for lunch money. Aileen, together with her girlfriend Candi Allen, who lived on the next block, were going to be driven to the Venetian Pool in Coral Gables by the girl's mother. They would be there until three P.M., and then Mrs Allen would pick them up and bring them back to Green Lakes. Aileen left the house, carrying her bathing suit in a plastic Burdine's shopping bag, after kissing her father again and running the tips of her fingers through the hair on his back and shoulders.

By eleven A.M., when Hoke had not stirred from his chair – he had urinated in his shorts, and there was a large damp spot on the brown corduroy cushion – Ellita was concerned enough to telephone Commander Bill Henderson at the Homicide Division. Bill Henderson, who had been promoted to commander a few months back, was now the Administrative Executive Officer for the division, and all of the paperwork in the division – going and coming – crossed his desk before he did something about it or routed it to someone else. Bill did not enjoy this newly created position, nor did he like the responsibility that went with it, but he liked the idea of being a commander, and the extra money.

Ellita told Bill that Hoke had been sitting in the chair since breakfast, that he had pissed his underpants, and that although he was awake, she could not get him to acknowledge her presence.

'Put him on the phone,' Bill said. 'Let me talk to him.'

'You don't understand, Bill. He's just sitting there. His eyes are open now, and he's staring at the wall, but he isn't really looking at the wall.'

'What's the matter with him?'

'I don't know, Bill. That's why I called you. I know he's supposed to go to work today, because he got fifteen new supps yesterday and he has to read through them this morning.'

'Tell him,' Bill said, 'that I just gave him five supps on top of that. I handed them to Speedy Gonzalez about fifteen minutes ago.'

'I don't think that will make an impression.'

'Tell him anyway.'

Ellita went into the living room and told Hoke that Bill Henderson just told her to tell him that he now had five more supps to look at, in addition to the fifteen Bill had sent him yesterday.

Hoke did not respond.

435

Ellita returned to the phone in the kitchen. 'He didn't react, Bill. I think you'd better tell Major Brownley that something's wrong. I think I should call a doctor, but I didn't want to do that without talking to you or Major Brownley first.'

'Don't call a doctor, Ellita. I'll drive out and talk to Hoke myself. If there's nothing radically wrong with him, and I don't think there is, I can cover for him and Major Brownley'll never know anything about it.'

'Have you had lunch yet, Bill?'

'No, not yet.'

'Then don't stop for anything on your way over, and I'll fix you something here. Please. Come right away.'

Ellita went back into the living room to tell Hoke that Bill was coming to the house, but Hoke was no longer sitting in his chair. He wasn't in the bathroom, either. She opened the door to his bedroom and found him supine on his narrow army cot. He had pulled the sheet over his head.

'I told Bill you weren't feeling well, Hoke, and he's coming right over. If you go back to sleep with the sheet over your face, you won't get enough air and you'll wake up with a headache.'

The room air conditioner was running, but Ellita turned it to High-Cool before closing the door. Low-Cool was comfortable enough for nighttime, but with the sun on this side of the house, it would be too warm in the afternoon.

Bill arrived, and after pulling the sheet away from Hoke's face, talked to him for about ten minutes. Hoke stared at the ceiling and didn't respond to any of Bill's questions. Bill was a large man with big feet and a huge paunch, and he had a brutal, metal-studded smile. When he came out of Hoke's room, he carried his brown and white seersucker jacket over his left arm, and he had taken off his necktie.

Ellita had fixed two tuna salad sandwiches and heated a can of Campbell's tomato soup. When Bill came into the kitchen, she put his lunch on a tray and asked him if he wanted to eat in the dining room or out in the Florida room.

'In here.' Bill pulled out an Eames chair at the white pedestal dining table and sat down. 'It's too hot out there without any air conditioning. The announcer on the radio coming over said it would be ninety-two today, but it seems hotter than that already.'

Bill bit into a tuna salad sandwich, sweet with chopped Vidalia onions, and Ellita put two heaping tablespoons of Le Creme into his steaming tomato soup.

'What's that?' Bill said, frowning.

'Le Creme. It turns ordinary tomato soup into a gourmet treat. I read about it in *Vanidades*.'

'When you called me, Ellita, I thought maybe Hoke was just kidding around, and I was half ready to kick him in the ass for scaring you. But there is something definitely wrong with him.'

'That's what I was trying to tell you.'

'I know. But I still don't think we should tell Major Brownley. Was Hoke sick to his stomach, or anything like that?'

'No. He was all right when I fixed his coffee this morning, and he'd already read the paper.'

Bill stirred the soup in his bowl; the creamy globs of Le Creme dissolved in a pinkish marble pattern. 'I don't want to scare you any more than you are already, Ellita – but – how's the baby coming, by the way? All right?'

'I'm fine, Bill, don't worry about me. I've put on ten pounds more than the doctor wanted me to, but he doesn't know everything. He told me I'd have morning sickness, too, but I haven't been sick once. What about Hoke?'

'What it looks like to me, and I've seen it more than once in Vietnam, is "combat fatigue." That's what we used to call it. A man's mind gets overwhelmed with everything in combat, you see, and then his mind blanks it all out. But it isn't serious. They used to send these guys back to the hospital, wrap them in a wet sheet for three days, put 'em to sleep, and they'd wake up okay again. Then they'd be back on the line as if nothing had happened.'

'It's all psychological, you mean?'

'Something like that – and temporary. That wasn't a big problem in the Army. In the department, though, it could be. If Major Brownley calls in the department shrink to look at Hoke, I'm pretty sure that's what he'd call this. I mean, not "combat fatigue," but "burnout" or "mid-life crisis," and then it would go on Hoke's record. That's not the kind of thing a cop needs on his permanent medical record.'

'Hoke's only forty-three, Bill. That isn't middle-aged.'

'It can happen at thirty-three, Ellita. You don't have to be middle-aged to go through a mid-life crisis. Instead of telling Brownley, it might be best if we keep this to ourselves. I'll fill in the papers, and we can put Hoke on a thirty-day leave without pay. I can forge his name easily enough. I did it plenty of times when we were partners. Then I'll call his father up in Riviera Beach and get him to take Hoke in for a few weeks. If Hoke's up there on Singer Island, instead of here with you, Brownley won't be able to come and check on him.'

'I don't think Mr Moseley'll like that, Bill. And I know his wife won't. I met her once, when the two of them were going on a cruise, and she's one of those society types. The sundress she had on when she came to the ship must've cost at least four hundred dollars.'

'There's not even any back to a sundress.'

'Make it three-fifty then. But she looked down her nose at me. She doesn't approve of lady cops, I think.'

'Hoke's old man's got all of the money in the world. I'll talk to Mr Moseley, and he can get his own doctor to look at Hoke. A visit to the department shrink is supposed to be confidential, but it always gets out sooner or later. This thing with Hoke'll blow over soon, I know it will, and if we can get him out of town for a few days no one'll ever know the fucking difference.'

'What'll I tell the girls?'

'Tell them Hoke's gone on a vacation. I'll call Mr Moseley on your phone after I finish eating – the soup's good with this stuff, by the way – and you can drive Hoke up there this afternoon. You can still drive, can't you?'

'Sure. I go to the store every day.'

'Okay, then. Take Hoke's Pontiac. Your car's too small for him, and you can drive him up there right after I call and explain everything to Mr Moseley. You'll still be back in plenty of time to fix dinner for the girls. If not, you can always send out for a pizza.'

Ellita nibbled her lower lip. 'You really think Hoke'll be all right?'

'He'll be fine.' Bill looked at his wristwatch. 'It's one-fifteen. If anyone ever asks you, Hoke's been on an official thirty-day leave of absence since eight A.M. this morning.'

Hoke hadn't planned it that way, but that's how he got back to Singer Island.

Chapter Two

Stanley and Maya Sinkiewicz lived in Riviera Beach, Florida, in a subdivision called Ocean Pines Terraces. The subdivision was six miles west of the Atlantic Ocean and the Lake Worth waterway. There were no pines; they had all been bulldozed away during construction. There were no terraces, either. Not only was the land flat, it was barely three feet above sea level, and flood insurance was mandatory on every mortgaged home. Sometimes, during the rainy season, the canals overflowed and the area was inundated for days at a time.

Stanley was seventy-one years old but looked older. Maya was sixty-six, and she looked even older than Stanley. He had retired from the Ford Motor Company six years earlier, after working most of his life as a striper on the assembly line. During his last three years before retiring, he had worked in the paint supply room. Because of his specialized work on the line for so many years, Stanley's right shoulder was three inches lower than his left (he was right-handed), and when he walked, his right step was about three inches longer than his left, which gave his walk a gliding effect. As a striper, Stanley had painted the single line, with a drooping striping brush, around the automobiles moving through the plant as they got to him. These encircling lines were painted by hand instead of by mechanical means because a ruled line is a 'dead' line, and a perfect, ruled line lacked the insouciant raciness a hand-drawn line gives to a finished automobile. Stanley's freehand lines were so straight they looked to the unpracticed eye as if they had been drawn with the help of a straightedge, but the difference was there. During Henry Ford's lifetime, of course, there were no stripes on the black finished Fords. No one remembered when the practice began, but Stanley got his job as a striper on his first day of work and had kept it until his final three years.

He had been transferred to the paint shop when it was decided by someone that a tape could be put around the cars; then, when the tape was ripped off, there was the stripe, like magic. Of course, it was now a dead stripe, but it saved a few seconds on the line.

Stanley and Maya had lived in Hamtramck, and they had paid off their mortgage on a small two-bedroom house in this largely Polish community. On a Florida vacation once they had spent two weeks in a motel in Singer Island. During this time they had enjoyed the sun so much they had decided to retire to Riviera Beach when the time came. The Ocean Pines Terraces development had been in the planning stages, and because pre-phase construction prices were so low, Stanley had made a down payment on a two-bedroom house and hadn't had to close on it for almost two more years. After Stanley retired, he and Maya trucked their old furniture from Hamtramck down to the new house and moved in. The house Stanley had closed on for fifty thousand dollars, six years earlier, was now worth eighty-three thousand. With his U.A.W pension and Social Security, Stanley had an income of more than twelve thousand a year, plus three ten-thousand-dollar certificates of deposit in savings. Their son, Stanley Jr., now lived with his wife and two teenage children in the old house in Hamtramck, and Junior paid his father two hundred a month in rent. Maya, who had worked part-time, off and on, at a dry-cleaning shop a block away from their house in Hamtramck, also drew Social Security each month, and both of them were on Medicare.

Despite their attainment of the American Dream, Maya was not happy in Florida. She missed her son, her grandchildren, and her neighbors back in Michigan. She even missed the cold and snow of the slushy Detroit winters. Maya didn't like having Stanley at home all of the time, either, and they had finally reached a compromise. He had to leave the house each morning by eight A.M., and he wasn't allowed to return home until at least noon. His absence gave Maya time to clean the house in the morning, do the laundry, watch TV by herself, or do whatever else she wanted to, while Stanley had the morning use of their Ford Escort.

After eating lunch at home, which Maya made for him, Stanley usually took a nap. Maya then drove the Escort to the International

Shopping Mall on U.S. 1, or to the supermarket, or both, and didn't return home until after three. Sometimes, when there was a Disney film or a G-rated film at one of the six multitheaters in the International Mall, she took in the Early Bird matinee for a dollar-fifty and didn't come home until five P.M.

When they first moved to Florida, Maya had telephoned Junior two or three times a week, collect, to see how he and his wife and the grandchildren were getting along, but after a few weeks, when no one ever answered the phone, she had called only once a week, direct dial, on Sunday nights. She then discovered that Junior would be there to talk – for three minutes, or sometimes for five. Her daughter-in-law was never at home on Sunday nights, but sometimes Maya would be able to talk to her grandchildren, Geoffrey and Terri, a sixteen-year-old boy and a fourteen-year-old girl.

Stanley was a clean old man, and very neat in his appearance. He usually wore gray or khaki poplin trousers, gray suede Hush Puppies with white socks, and a white short-sleeved shirt with a black leather pre-tied necktie that had a white plastic hook to hold it in place behind the buttoned collar. The necktie, worn with the white shirt, made Stanley look like a retired foreman (not a striper) from the Ford Motor Company, and he always said that he *was* a retired foreman if someone asked him his occupation. He hadn't been able to make any new friends in Florida, although, at first, he had tried. For a few weeks, Stanley had been friendly with Mr Agnew, his next-door neighbor, a butcher who worked for Publix, but when Mr Agnew bought a Datsun, after Stanley had told him that the Escort was a much better car, and an American car to boot, he no longer spoke to Mr Agnew, even if Maya was still friendly with Agnew's wife.

When Stanley left the house in the mornings, he wore a long-billed khaki fishing cap with a green visor. He always carried a cane, even though he didn't need one. He wore the cap because he was bald and didn't want to get the top of his head sunburned, but he carried the cane to fend off dogs. The gnarled wooden cane had a rubber tip and a brass dog's-head handle. The handle could be unscrewed, and Stanley had a dozen cyanide tablets concealed in a glass tube inside the hollowed-out shaft of the wooden cane.

Stanley had appropriated these cyanide tablets from the paint shop at Ford because he found them useful for poisoning vicious dogs in Hamtramck, and later in Florida. Stanley was afraid of dogs. As a boy, he had been badly mauled by a red Chow Chow in Detroit, and he didn't intend to be bitten again. During the last three years, he had used three pills to poison neighborhood dogs in Ocean Pines Terraces, and he was ready to poison another one when the opportunity arrived. Stanley had a foolproof method. He would make a hamburger ball approximately an inch and a half in diameter, with the cyanide pill in the center. Then he rolled the ball in salt and put the ball in a Baggie. When he took a walk and passed the house where the targeted dog lived, he would toss the ball underhand onto the lawn, or drop it beside a hedge or a tree as he continued down the sidewalk. When the dog was let loose in its yard, it would invariably find the hamburger by smell, lick the salt once or twice, and then gulp down the fatal meatball. Thanks to Stanley's skill, the neighborhood was shy one boxer, one Doberman, and one Pekingese.

Stanley's cane had also helped to make him a fringe member of the 'Wise Old Men,' a small group of retirees that congregated each weekday morning in Julia Tuttle Park. This small two-acre park had been constructed by the developer as a part of his deal to get the zoning variance that he needed for Ocean Pines Terraces. There was a thatched shed in the park, where a half-dozen retirees played pinochle in the mornings, and there was a group of rusting metal chairs under a shady strangler-fig tree, where another, smaller group of elderly men sat and talked. The group that met under the tree was called the 'Wise Old Men' by the pinochle players, but they meant this sarcastically. The two groups didn't mingle, and if a man went to the park every day he would eventually have to decide which one to join. Stanley didn't play pinochle, and he didn't talk much either, having little to say and a limited education, but for the first few weeks, after silently watching the boring pinochle games, he had joined the group under the tree, to listen to the philosophers. The dean of this group was a retired judge, who always wore a starched seersucker suit with a bow tie. The other Wise Old Men wore wash pants and sport shirts, or sometimes T-shirts, and comfortable running shoes. Except for the judge, Stanley was the only one who wore a necktie. The group had changed personnel a few times since Stanley's retirement – some of the older men had died – but the judge was still there, looking about the same as he had in the beginning. Stanley, when he looked in the mirror to shave each morning, didn't think that he had changed much either. He realized deep down that he must have aged somewhat, because the others had, but he felt better in Florida than he had ever felt back in Michigan when he had had to go to work every day.

One morning the topic under discussion was the 'dirtiest thing in the world.' Theories and suggestions had been tendered, but they had all been shot down by the judge. Finally, toward noon, Stanley had looked at his cane, cleared his throat, and said: 'The tip of a cane is the dirtiest thing in the world.'

'That's it,' the judge said, nodding sagely. 'There's nothing dirtier than the tip of a cane. It taps the ground indiscriminately, touching spittle, dog droppings, any and everything in its blind groping. By the end of a short walk, the septic tip of a cane probably collects enough germs to destroy a small city. I believe you've hit upon it, Mr Sinkiewicz, and we can safely say that this is now a closed topic.'

The others nodded, and they all looked at Stanley's cane, marveling at the filthy things the rubber tip had touched as Stanley had carried it through the years. After that triumph, Stanley had contributed nothing more to the morning discussions, but he was definitely considered a fringe member and was greeted by name when he sat down to listen.

But Stanley didn't go to Julia Tuttle Park every single day like the others. He was too restless. He sometimes drove to Palm Beach instead, parked, and walked along Worth Avenue, window shopping, marveling at the high prices of things. Like Maya, he visited the International Mall on U.S. 1, or parked in the visitors' lot of the West Palm Beach Public Library. He would browse through the obituaries in the Detroit *Free Press*, looking for the names of old acquaintances. The fact was, Stanley didn't quite know what to do with his long free mornings, yet although he was frequently bored, searching for something to do to pass the morning hours, he was unaware of his boredom. He was retired, and he knew that a man who was retired didn't have to do anything. So this was what he did: nothing much, except for wandering around.

Once a week he cut the lawn, whether it needed it or not. In the rainy season, lawns had to have a weekly cutting; in the winter, when the weather was dry, the lawn could have gone for three weeks or more. But by mowing one day every seven, on Tuesday afternoons, he broke up the week. Maya did all the shopping and paid all the monthly bills from their joint checking account. Stanley cashed a check for thirty-five dollars every Monday at the Riviera Beach bank, allowing himself five dollars a day for spending money, but almost always had something left over at the end of the week.

In the evenings, Stanley and Maya watched television. They were hooked up to the cable, with Showtime and thirty-five other channels, but they rarely changed the channel once they were sitting down. Sometimes they watched the same movie on Showtime four or five times in a single month. Maya went to bed at ten, but Stanley always stayed up and watched the eleven o'clock news. Because of his afternoon nap, he could rarely fall asleep before midnight. He rose at six A.M., though, got the *Post-Times* from the lawn, drank some coffee, and read the paper until Maya got up to fix his breakfast.

On a Wednesday afternoon in June, Stanley was asleep on the screened porch behind the house at three-thirty when Pammi Sneider, the nine-year-old daughter of a retired U.S. Army master sergeant who leased a Union gas station out on Military Trail, came through the unlocked screen door. Pammi was a frequent visitor when Maya was home, because Maya would give the girl cookies and a glass of red Kool-Aid, or sometimes, when she had been baking, a slice of pie or cake. The Sneiders lived four doors down from the Sinkiewiczes, and once Mrs Sneider had told Maya that if Pammi ever pestered her to just send her home. Maya had said she liked to have the little girl drop by, and that Pammi reminded her of her granddaughter back in Michigan, whose name was Terri, a name ending with an *i*, just like Pammi's. Despite that conversation, the two women were not friends. There was too much difference in their ages, and in just about everything else. Mrs Sneider was only thirty-six, and she belonged to Greenpeace, the La Leche League, Mothers Against Drunk Drivers, and the West Palm Beach chapter of N.O.W. Mrs Sneider was away from home a good deal, but this was a safe neighborhood, and Pammi was allowed to play with other children and was also authorized to go to Julia Tuttle Park in the afternoons, by herself. In the afternoons, very few of the older men went to the park. It was too hot to sit there, for one thing, and when school was out, the older men did not like to hear the small children squealing on the playground equipment and chasing each other around. There were almost always a few mothers there with smaller children, so the park was considered a safe place to send children to get them out of the house.

Pammi was barefooted, and she wore a blue and white striped T-shirt and a pair of red cotton shorts with an elastic waistband. She carried a leather sack in her left hand, a sack that had once contained marbles. She tiptoed over to the webbed lounger, where Stanley was sleeping on his back, and gave him a French kiss.

Stanley spluttered and sat up suddenly. Pammi giggled and held out her grubby right hand.

'Now,' she said, giggling again, 'you gotta give me a penny.'

Stanley wiped his mouth, blinking slightly. 'What did you do?'

'I gave you a kiss. Now you gotta give me a penny.'

'My wife's at the store,' Stanley said. 'But she should be back soon. I don't know if she's got any cookies for you or not, Pammi. I haven't been in the kitchen —'

'I don't want a cookie. I want a penny for my collection.' The girl held up her leather bag and shook it. The coins inside rattled.

'I didn't ask you for a kiss, and you shouldn't kiss a man like that anyway. Not at your age. Who taught you to stick out your tongue when you kissed?'

Pammi shrugged. 'I don't know his name. But he comes to the park every day when it begins to get dark, and he gives me a penny for a wet kiss, and five pennies for a look. You owe me a penny now, and if you want a look you'll have to give me five more.' Pammi put her sack on the terrazzo floor and stripped off her red shorts. Stanley looked, and shook his head. Pammi's hairless

446

pudenda, which resembled a slightly dented balloon, did nothing to excite the old man.

'Put your shorts back on. What's the matter with you, anyway?'

As Stanley got off the lounger, Pammi laughed and danced away. He picked up her shorts from the floor and stalked the little girl, trying to drive her into a corner so he could put her shorts on again. Maya drove into the carport in the black Escort and parked, then came into the kitchen with a bag of groceries and looked through the sliding glass doors to the porch. By this time, Stanley had Pammi by one leg and was trying to insert it into the shorts, while Pammi giggled and tried to get away from him.

'You owe me six cents first!' Pammi said. 'You looked, you looked!' Then, when Pammi saw Maya's face through the glass doors, she stopped giggling and began to cry. Maya hurried through the living room and went out the front door, slamming it behind her. When Pammi began to cry and ceased struggling, and the front door slammed, Stanley let go of the little girl's leg. He was still holding her shorts in his right hand when Pammi ran out the back screen door and into the yard. She cut through the unfenced backyards and, bare-butted, raced home, four doors away.

Still holding Pammi's shorts, Stanley went into the kitchen. He looked into the bag of groceries on the sideboard by the sink. There was a quart of milk and a dozen eggs in the bag, as well as some canned things. He put the eggs and the milk into the refrigerator. He wondered where Maya had gone; she had, apparently, taken her handbag when she'd gone back out the front door. Maya's car keys were still on the counter beside the bag of groceries.

It did not occur to Stanley that he was in an awkward position. Instead, he was irritated because Maya had left the house without telling him where she was going. He was also a little concerned about Pammi. A girl that young shouldn't be French-kissing a man old enough to be her grandfather – or great-grandfather, for that matter – and showing off her dimpled private parts for pennies. He wondered who had taught her those games, but he couldn't think of any of the old men in the park who would do any such thing. Later on that evening, he decided, he would go down to Mr Sneider's house and talk to him about it.

Stanley picked up the leather bag of coins and looked inside. He dumped the pennies on the kitchen table and counted them. There were ninety-four. He guessed that Pammi had needed six more pennies to make a hundred, so that was why she had kissed him and showed him her private parts. If she had a hundred pennies, she could change them for a dollar bill.

Stanley put the rest of the groceries away and sat in the living room waiting for Maya to come back. Twenty minutes later, Maya came briskly up the walk, accompanied by Mr Sneider. Stanley, still holding Pammi's red shorts in his lap, got out of his chair as Maya unlatched the front door. When it swung open and he saw the expression on Mr Sneider's face, Stanley started to run out toward the back porch. Sneider, rushing past Maya, moved uncommonly fast for a man his size and he hit Stanley in the mouth before Stanley could say anything to either of them.

An hour later, Stanley was in the Palm Beach County Jail.

Chapter Three

Hoke Moseley spent the next three days in the back guest bedroom in his father's house. Hoke's father, Frank Moseley, had been upset when Ellita Sanchez arrived at his Singer Island home with his son, even though Bill Henderson had telephoned and explained things before Ellita drove the seventy miles up from Miami. Frank, a spry seventy-five-year-old, had rarely been sick in his life and had never missed a day of work in his hardware store and chandlery in Riviera Beach. He had been a widower for many years after Hoke's mother had died of cancer, and had then married a wealthy widow in her early forties named Helen Canlas.

Frank had called his doctor, as Bill Henderson had suggested, a physician he had known for thirty some odd years in West Palm Beach, and Dr Ray Fairbairn, who had a dwindling practice, had driven over immediately. Dr Fairbairn, whose breath always smelled like oil of cloves, examined Hoke privately in the guest bedroom. He then told Frank and Ellita that Hoke was all right but needed rest. Lots of rest.

'I've given him a tranquilizer, and I've written out a prescription for Equavil,' Dr Fairbairn said, handing the slip of paper to Frank. 'I think he'll be okay in a few days.'

'What did he say?' Frank asked.

'He didn't say anything.' Dr Fairbairn shrugged. 'He's in good shape physically, but the fact that he won't talk to me indicates that he's probably decided to avoid everyday life for a while.'

'I don't understand,' Frank said, running his fingers through his thick white hair. 'How in the hell can a man avoid everyday life? Hoke's a homicide detective in Miami, and every time I've talked to him on the phone – about once a month – he tells me how busy he is.'

Ellita, who had been listening, cleared her throat. 'Hoke's on a thirty-day leave without pay, Dr Fairbairn. Will that be enough time for him to rest? I mean, if he needs additional time, Commander Henderson can probably get his leave extended.'

'I haven't kept up too well with all of these new psychological theories, madame,' Dr Fairbairn said, addressing Ellita thusly because he had already forgotten her name and could see that she was pregnant. 'But Hoke has what they now call "burnout." I've known Hoke since he was a little boy. He's always been an over-achiever, in my opinion, and these types frequently have attitude problems when they mature. Hoke's heart is fine, however, and he's as strong as a mule. So when someone like Hoke turns away from everyday life, as he's apparently decided to do, it's nature's way of telling him to slow down before something physically debilitating does happen to him. And the buzzword, according to pop psychology, is "burnout." I read an interesting article about it last year in *Psychology Today*.'

'Then this could be partly my fault,' Ellita said. 'I'm his partner, and I started my maternity leave two weeks ago, so I'm not around to help him on the job anymore.'

'You're a police officer?' Dr Fairbairn raised gray eyebrows. 'You don't look like a police officer.'

'That's because I'm eight months pregnant. A pregnant woman, even in uniform, doesn't look like a police officer.'

'Are you going to stay here with him?'

'No, I've got to get back to Miami. I share a house with Hoke and his two daughters, and I have to look after them. But I won't drive back right away if I'm needed here and can help Hoke in any way.'

'Will my son need a nurse?' Frank asked. 'Of should I send him to the hospital?'

'No hospital, Mr Moseley,' Ellita said, shaking her head. 'If this is just a temporary condition, like Dr Fairbairn says, it wouldn't look good on Hoke's record to have a hospital stay. Rather than do that, I'll take Hoke back to Miami with me and look after him myself.'

'He doesn't need a nurse,' Dr Fairbairn said, 'or hospitalization either. Just let him rest tonight, Frank, and I'll come by tomorrow and take another look at him.' The doctor consulted his watch. 'It's too late to go back to my office now, so I could do with a drink.'

'What'll you have?' Frank asked. 'Bourbon? Gin?'

'I could use a martini, but no vermouth, please. And before I leave, Frank, I'd better give you a prostate massage. You haven't been into the office for more than two months.'

Frank flushed slightly and glanced sideways at Ellita. 'Helen gives them to me now, Roy. That's why I haven't been in.'

'In that case, I'll just settle for the martini.'

'Would you like something, Miss Sanchez?'

Ellita shook her head. 'Not till after the baby. I'll just go in for a second and say good-bye to Hoke. Then I'd better head back to Miami.'

'Why not stay for dinner first? Helen'll be back from her Book Review Club soon, and Inocencia's cooking a roast.'

'Thanks, but I'll have to fix something for the girls. And they'll want to know that their father's all right. What book are they reviewing?'

'I don't know the title, but it's something by Jackie Collins. She's Joan's sister, you know. Jackie's the writer, and Joan's the actress. We saw Joan in *The Stud* on cable the other night, and Helen said their new book reviewer is so good at explaining the good parts she no longer has to read the books.'

'I'll just look in on Hoke.'

Hoke was lying on his back on the king-sized bed, still wearing his stained boxer shorts, but he wasn't under the covers. The room was cool, and there was a whispering hiss from the central air-conditioning duct above the door. The sliding glass doors to the backyard were closed, but the draperies were pulled back partially, giving Hoke a view, if he wanted to raise his head and look at it, of the swimming pool, the gently sloping back lawn, a short concrete dock, and Frank's Boston Whaler tied to the pilings. Across the narrow blue-green waterway there were mangroves, and high above the mangroves black thunderclouds were billowing toward the island from the Everglades.

Ellita tapped Hoke on the arm. He flinched slightly, but didn't look at her. 'The doctor said you were going to be all right, Hoke.

You're going to stay here with your father for a while. I'm going back to Miami, and I'll look after the girls. If you want your car, call me, and I'll have someone drive it up. Don't worry about me or the girls. We'll be all right. Okay?'

Hoke turned on his side and looked out the window.

'Your robe's over on the chair. I put your toilet articles in the bathroom. Your teeth are in a glass in the bathroom, and there's plenty of Polident. There are slacks, sport shirts, underwear, and socks in the suitcase, I forgot to pack your shoes, but your gun and buzzer are in the bag with your wallet. Tell your father to get you some sneakers or something from his store, and I'll send up your shoes when you want your car. I guess that's it, then. I'll be in touch with your dad if you need anything.' No response. 'Well, good-bye, then.'

Ellita closed the door behind her, said good-bye to Frank Moseley and Dr Fairbairn and drove back to Miami.

Later that evening, when Inocencia, the Moseleys' Cuban cook, brought Hoke's dinner in to him on a tray, Hoke was sitting in a chair by the sliding glass doors. He had taken a shower and was wearing his white terrycloth shaving robe. Inocencia put the tray on the table beside the chair and left the bedroom without trying to talk with him.

The rain was coming down hard on the patio tiles outside the sliding doors, and it was difficult to make out the mangroves across the waterway in the driving rain. Hoke put in his teeth in the bathroom, then made a roast beef sandwich with one of the rolls Inocencia had brought. He didn't touch the Waldorf salad, the broccoli, the baked potato, or the wedge of blueberry cobbler. He drank a glass of iced tea, took another Equavil, and went to sleep on top of the covers.

Later that evening, when Frank and Helen looked in to see him, Hoke was asleep on his back, breathing through his mouth and snoring.

Frank and Helen had a long talk about what to do with Hoke when they went into their bedroom that night after watching TV. Helen didn't want Hoke to stay with them, even though they had a large house with two spare bedrooms. Frank told her that Hoke would stay as long as it was necessary. Helen patted off her makeup with cold cream, stared at her handsome face in the mirror for a moment, and then hunched her plump shoulders combatively.

'I want to know that he'll be leaving,' she said.

'We can't decide anything now, Helen. We'll see what the doctor says tomorrow or the next day, and if it turns out that the police department's too much for Hoke to handle any longer, I can always let him clerk in the store. He worked in the store summers and Saturdays when he was in high school, and he was one of the best clerks I ever had.'

'He's forty-three years old now, Frank, and he's been a cop for fourteen years. He can't go back to being a clerk in the store.'

'Why not? Mrs Grimes has been in the store for thirty-two years, and she's sixty years old. I still go to the store every day, and I'm seventy-five. What makes you think forty-three's too old to be a hardware clerk?'

'That isn't what I meant.'

'What did you mean?'

'I just meant that he's too old to be coming back home to live. Especially after being a police detective. It wouldn't work out for Hoke, and it wouldn't work out for us.'

'We'll talk about that tomorrow. By the way, Dr Fairbairn said I was overdue for my prostate massage.'

Helen sighed, and then she smiled. 'I'll get the Crisco.' She got up from her vanity table and padded lightly down the hall toward the kitchen.

Later on, when Hoke recalled this dormant three-day period, he remembered every detail of this long first day: Ellita's frequent reminders of the time, his daughter's kisses, the drive up the Sunshine Parkway from Miami, and Steely Dan playing 'Rikki Don't Lose That Number' on the car radio. Hoke had huddled on the back seat of the old Le Mans with his terrycloth robe pulled over him. He had tried, for a while, to count the kingfishers poised above the hyacinth-choked canal, clinging to telephone wires. The kingfishers, loners to a bird, had been spaced out along the wire about five miles apart, with their heads pulled in as if they had no necks. But he soon lost count, and wondered if it could be the same kingfisher he was counting each time, the same old bird flying ahead endlessly to fool him.

He didn't know why he couldn't bring himself to answer Ellita, his daughters, Bill Henderson, or old Doc Fairbairn, who had set Hoke's broken arm when he was eleven, but he had known somehow, cunningly, that if he didn't say anything to anyone, eventually they would all let him alone and he would never have to go down to the Homicide Division and work on those cold fucking cases again.

It was funny-peculiar too, in a way, because he had been thinking about Singer Island while he was reading the newspaper, wishing he were back on the island, and now, without any conscious effort, here he was, all alone in his father's house, lying on a firm but comfortable mattress in a cool and darkened room. And no one was bothering him, or trying to force him to read all of those new Incident Reports and supps that were piled up on his desk.

Hoke did not, after his first night's troubled sleep, take any more of the tiny black Equavils. They hadn't made him feel funny while he was awake (although they must have been responsible for his weird and frightening dreams), but while he *was* awake, they had robbed him of any feelings, and his mind became numb. If he took four of them a day, as the doctor ordered, he would soon become a zombie. Besides, Hoke didn't need any chemicals to maintain the wonderful peace of mind he now enjoyed. The bedroom was cool, and although he wasn't hungry, the little he did eat when Inocencia brought in his trays was delicious. He told himself that he would never have to go back to the police department. All he had to do was lie quietly on the bed, or sit by the glass doors and look out at the blue-green pool or at the occasional boats that passed on the inland waterway ignoring the NO WAKE signs, and everything would be all right. There was no need to think about anything, to worry about anything, because, as long as he kept his mouth closed and refused to react to anybody, he would be let alone. When a man didn't talk back or answer questions, people couldn't stand it for very long.

When Hoke looked back later, those three days had been the happiest he had ever known, and he often wondered if he would

454

ever have such peace again. But he had also known, or suspected – even at the time – that it was too wonderful to last.

On the fourth morning, Hoke awoke at six, his regular time, opened the sliding doors, and dived bare-assed into the swimming pool. He swam ten slow laps in the tepid water, showered, dressed, put in his teeth, shaved, and then, because he had no shoes, walked barefooted into the kitchen and made a pot of coffee. When Inocencia arrived at seven, driving her whale-colored VW Beetle, Hoke asked her to make him a big breakfast.

'You want to eat now, Mr Hoke, or wait and eat with Mr Frank?'

'I'll wait for Mr Frank.'

Hoke took his coffee into the living room to get out of Inocencia's way, and sat on one of the tapestried chairs that were spaced evenly around the polished black mahogany table. There were twelve of them, and room at the table for two more. These other two chairs flanked the arched entrance that led down a step to the sunken living room. Inocencia, when she had let herself into the house with her key that morning, had brought the newspaper in from the lawn and dropped it on the table. Hoke didn't open it. He just waited for his father, sipped his coffee, stared at the bowl of daisies in the centerpiece, and wondered what he should say to the old man.

Anyone who saw the two together would notice a family likeness. It would be difficult to explain where it was, however, because the two Moseley men, except for their chocolate eyes, did not resemble one another. They were both a quarter-inch over five-ten, but Frank's shoulders slumped and he was stooped slightly, making him look much shorter than his son. He was also thin and wiry, and not more than 150 pounds, whereas Hoke weighed 190. When he had lived alone, Hoke had maintained an off-and-on diet and had once got down to 180 pounds, but after his ex-wife returned his daughters to him and Ellita had moved into the house in Green Lakes, Ellita had done all of the cooking. The starchy foods she liked – rice and black beans, fried plantains, baked yucca, chicken and yellow rice, pork roasts and pork chunks – had soon restored his lost poundage, and then some.

Frank Moseley had a full head of white hair. When a few people had told him that he resembled the ex-auto maker John DeLorean, the old man had let his hair grow and had fluffed it out on the sides, which made his resemblance to the automobile designer almost uncanny. But Frank, oddly enough, looked much younger than DeLorean. Perhaps it was because he had led such an untroubled life.

Hoke's face was as long as his father's, but it looked longer because he was balding in front, and his high brown dome and sunken, striated cheeks made his face seem a good deal narrower as well. Hoke had sandy hair, with no gray in it as yet, but he wore it roached back and without a part. His barber had suggested once that he comb it straight forward and let it grow a bit, which would give him a fringe effect. That style would minimize his baldness, he said. But Hoke thought that men who wore bangs looked like fruits, and he rejected the suggestion. A suspect would not, in Hoke's opinion, take a cop seriously if he looked the least bit gay.

Hoke's face was almost as dark as iodine from his lifetime exposure to the Florida sun, and his hairy forearms were deep mahogany because he always wore short-sleeved shirts. When he took off his shirt, his upper arms were ivory-colored; the rat's nest of black chest hair, and the long black hairs on his shoulders and back, looked like tangled nylon thread against the whiteness of his skin. As a teenager, when Hoke had worked on a live-bait ballyhoo boat out of Riviera Beach during the summers, he had been tan from the waist up as well, but he no longer went out in the sun without a shirt, and, like most Miamians, he rarely went to the beach. Because of his cheap blue-gray dentures, Hoke looked older than forty-three; but then, when one looked into his eyes, he seemed younger than that. Hoke's eyes, so dark it was difficult to see where the iris left off and the pupil began, were beautiful. Here, then, in the eyes, was where the family resemblance had concentrated itself. To see one man with eyes like that was remarkable; to see two men with eyes like theirs together was astonishing.

'Morning, son,' Frank said, picking up the paper and turning to the business section. 'How d'you feel?'

'Okay.'

The old man put on his glasses and checked the stock market reports with a forefinger. He grunted, shook his head, and removed the glasses. 'You going back to Miami, or what? You've been mighty quiet the last few days.'

'I've been thinking, Frank. I've decided to resign from the department, and I'm never leaving the island again.'

'You mean you're moving back here to Riviera Beach?'

'No, not exactly. I'm not going to leave the island, or cross the bridge to the mainland. I'm going to get a room here on the island, and find a job as a fry cook, maybe, or something like that.'

'You can come back to work at the store.'

Hoke shook his head. 'Then I'd have to drive across the Blue Heron bridge to Riviera every day. I don't want to leave the island. I intend to simplify my life.'

'That ain't the way to do it, Hoke. You've got the two girls to look after –'

'They can go back to Patsy. That ballplayer she married makes three hundred and twenty-five thousand bucks a year. He can take care of them, or put them in a boarding school. I'm concerned with my survival.'

'If it was just me, Hoke, you could stay here, I think you know that. But Helen wouldn't want you to live with us on a permanent basis. Now, I've got a little place near the Ocean Mall you can have. I own the apartment house – eight units in all, all efficiencies – and you can have one of 'em. You can live in the apartment rent-free, and I'll give you a hundred dollars a week to manage them for me. They rent for a thousand a month during the season, and six hundred a month the rest of the year. There's a two-week minimum on rentals, and it's three-fifty for just two weeks. Paulson Realtors has been managing the place, but he hasn't been doing what I'd call a bang-up job. I had me some trouble over there last month. A single man rented an apartment for two weeks, and then moved in six of his buddies from Venezuela. It was an entire professional soccer team, and they almost ruined the apartment before Paulson even found out about them. I need someone on the premises, you see, not sitting in an office in Riviera Beach. If you're there all the time, you can rent out the units, take care of problems like that, and sort things out for me.'

'Are you talking about the El Pelicano Hotel?'

'It was a hotel, but I had it converted a couple of years back to efficiency apartments. I thought maybe at first I'd make it a time-shared condo, but it works out better as rentals. Those time-share apartments are more trouble than they're worth. Three of the units are rented out already on annual leases to people working here on the island, and they get a special rate. I'll drive you over there right after breakfast, and you can move right in.'

'I need to stop at Island Sundries first and buy some sneakers.'

Frank nodded. 'This'll be a better deal for you than working as a fry cook.'

Hoke shrugged. 'I really don't care what I do, Frank. I'm not leaving the island again. I'll be glad to run the hotel for you.'

'It's not a hotel now, Hoke. I had the sign changed and call it the El Pelicano Arms. I had the boy paint a brown pelican on the sign, too. It looks nice.'

Hoke had a substantial breakfast of fried eggs, bacon, grits, and biscuits, but the old man ate a single piece of dry toast and a small dish of stewed prunes. In January, the single cool month of the year, Frank sometimes had oatmeal as well; otherwise this was his standard breakfast throughout the year. This was a frugal meal, but Hoke knew that the old man would leave his office in the hardware store at ten-thirty and go next door to Matilda's Café, eat two jelly doughnuts, and drink a cup of chocolate. Frank did this every working day, and he went to the hardware store six days a week.

On the drive to the El Pelicano Arms, Frank stopped at Island Sundries, and Hoke bought a pair of sneakers, paying for them with his Visa card. Frank drove a new Chrysler New Yorker, and told Hoke it handled a little on the stiff side. For a few months he had driven a Bentley, just because Helen had wanted one, but business had dropped off at the store because the towns-people had thought he was doing too well. So he had sold the Bentley and bought the New Yorker, and business was back up to normal again.

The sign was new, but long strips of ochre paint hung from the rest of the building like the shredding skin of a snake. There was an empty apartment on the second floor facing the ocean. Hoke put his suitcase on one of the Bahama beds, opened the window, and took a long look at the sea, two hundred yards away across the wide public beach. A one-legged man in a skimpy bikini was hopping across the sand toward the water. Three teenage girls in bikinis played a listless game of volleyball, two of them on one side, one on the other of a sagging net. By noon the beach would be crowded with bathers, and all of the parking spaces on Ocean Drive would be full.

'This is perfect, Frank. It's only a block away from the Giant Supermarket, and I won't even need my car.'

'You might feel different in a few days, Hoke. But I'll get a "Manager" sign from the store and bring it back tonight. You can tack it to your door. There's a bulletin board downstairs with the rates posted and all, and you can put up a note saying the manager's living in 201.'

'Anything you say, Frank.'

'Here's your first hundred in advance.' Frank handed Hoke five twenties. 'If you need more now, just holler, and I'll give you a second advance.'

'No, that's plenty. Thanks.'

'I've got to get over to the store. But I'll call Paulson and have him come over here with the books and explain things to you.'

'I could walk to his office –'

'You'd better rest easy for a while. I'll send him over. There's a black-and-white TV over there, but no phone. I better order a phone for –'

'I don't want a phone, Frank.'

'You'll need one in case you want to call someone, or if someone wants to call about a rental.'

'I don't want a phone. I want to simplify my life, like I told you. If someone wants to rent a unit, and one's available, they can come over here and look at it. I'll be here.'

'You might like to call the girls, or Ellita.'

'I don't think so, but if I do, there's a pay phone over at the mall. If Ellita calls you, tell her to send someone back up with my car.

She can get one of the kids in the neighborhood to drive it up. I'll give him twenty bucks and he can take the bus back to Miami.'

'I'll call her. Anything else?'

'I guess not. Mr Paulson'll fill me in on what I need to know. And thanks, Frank. I think everything's going to be all right. I don't want you and Helen to worry about me.'

'I'm sure it will, son.'

The old man left, and Hoke closed the door.

Frank Moseley wasn't so sure that everything was going to be all right. Hoke had seemed to be his old self again, but he was still a little preoccupied. Perhaps the pills Dr Fairbairn had ordered made him like that. At any rate, Frank had gotten his son out of the house, and Helen would be pleased about that. This afternoon she had her bridge group coming to the house, and she had been worried last night that Hoke might lurch out into the living room in his urine-stained boxer shorts.

Chapter Four

Instead of throwing Stanley into the twenty-man tank with the assorted drunks and coke-heads, the jailer put him in a two-man cell with an alleged holdup man named Robert Smith. One of the tank drunks looked hostile, and the jailer thought he might pick on the old man if he found out that he was accused of a short-eyes offense. Stanley had had to take off his belt and remove his shoelaces. He held his pants up with both hands, and he scuffled, dragging his feet as he came down the corridor, to keep from stepping out of his shoes.

Robert Smith, *né* Troy Louden, was lying on his back in the lower bunk with his hands clasped behind his head. Troy was wearing scuffed cowboy boots, a blue-denim cowboy shirt with pearl snap buttons, and a pair of gray moleskin ranch trousers with empty belt loops. His tooled leather belt and silver buckle were with his other effects in the property room. Troy's blond hair was cropped short, but he had retained thick sideburns, and they were down to the level of his earlobes. His deep blue eyes were slightly hooded. Sometimes a woman would tell him, 'Your eyes are the same blue as Paul Newman's.' When a woman said this, Troy would always smile and say, 'Yeah, but he puts drops in his.' In other respects he bore no resemblance to Paul Newman. Troy was tall and rangy, an inch or two over six feet, with long ropy arms and bulging biceps. His nose had been broken and poorly reset, and the lines that ran from the wings of his nose to the corners of his slightly crooked mouth looked as though they had been filled with coal dust. His wide lips were about the thickness of two dimes. When he grimaced occasionally – he had a slight tic – he reminded Stanley of a lizard. Stanley didn't mention this, and neither did anyone else, but Stanley was not the first man to notice the reptilian look that appeared on Troy's face whenever he pulled his lips back hard for a split second, then relaxed them.

The cell was four feet by eight, with a two-tiered bunk bed, and there was a stainless-steel toilet without a seat at the back of the cell. There was a steel sink in the back corner, but it only had one tap, and that drizzled cold water. There were no towels or soap. The bars were painted white and were flaked away here and there, indicating that they had been repainted many times. There was no window, and a single forty-watt bulb in the ceiling, covered with heavy wire, lighted the cell dimly. With Troy stretched out on the bottom bunk, there was no place for Stanley to sit, unless he climbed into the upper bunk or sat on the rim of the toilet.

'I've got to use the toilet,' Stanley said, after clearing his throat.

'Go ahead. It's right in front of you.'

'I can't go with you looking at me.'

Troy closed his eyes; then he put his fingers into his ears. 'Okay. I won't look and I won't listen.'

Stanley urinated, and then washed his hands and face at the sink. There was a deep cut on his upper lip, and he wished that there were a mirror so he could see how badly it was split. There was a lot of blood on the front of his shirt, but his lip had stopped bleeding.

'Let me take a look at that lip.' Troy didn't sit up, so Stanley had to bend over the bunk for Troy to examine it.

'If it was me,' Troy said, 'I'd have a couple of stitches put in. Otherwise, you're gonna have a nice little scar. Seems to me you're too old to be brawling, anyway. A man your age'll lose more fights than he'll win, Pop.'

'I wasn't fighting. My neighbor hit me, and he didn't have no call to do it. I was going to explain, but he hit me and then twisted my arm up behind my back while my wife called the police.'

'Did you hit your wife?'

Stanley shook his head. 'I been married forty-one years, and I never hit her a single time. Not once.' He said it as though he'd had ample reason to.

'Then why'd your neighbor bust you in the mouth?'

'My wife told him I molested his little girl, and I didn't do a darned thing to her, nothing at all, but he wouldn't listen to me.'

'How old was the girl you showed your weenie to?'

'I didn't show her nothing. She showed *me*, and she's nine, going on ten.'

'You're lucky there, old man. If she was eight or under you'd be looking at twenty-five years. But once they hit nine they're old enough to take instructions in the Catholic church. So eight's the magic number in most states. But when they hit nine or ten, sometimes you can make a deal with the state attorney. Unless you hurt her. Did you hurt her?'

'I didn't touch the girl. I was taking a nap out on my back porch, and she came in the screen door and woke me up by putting her tongue in my mouth.'

Troy nodded and made the lightning grimace. 'You must've seemed irresistible to her, laying there with your mouth open. I had a girlfriend once in San Berdoo who used to wake me up by sticking her tongue up my asshole. But she was thirty-five and didn't have very much else going for her. What did she do then, Pop, pull your pants down?'

'No, she took off *her* pants, her shorts, red shorts. I was still half asleep, or half awake, and didn't quite catch on to what she was doing at first. She had a bag of pennies, you see, and she wanted one penny for the soul kiss, and then asked for another five pennies after she took off her shorts.'

'That's cheap enough, God knows.'

'She said some old man in the park – Julia Tuttle Park – was giving her pennies for doing this, and I guess she thought that because I was old I'd do the same thing.'

'But you didn't start anything?'

'No, I was asleep, I told you. Then Maya, that's my wife, came into the house while I was trying to catch Pammi and put her shorts back on. She ran down the block and told Mrs Sneider. She called her husband at the gas station, and he came over and hit me in the mouth. Nobody would listen to me. I don't know what Pammi told her mother.'

'Pammi? Short for Pamela?

'No, just Pammi, with an *i* at the end and no *e*.'

'Did you make your phone call? You're entitled to a phone call, you know.'

'The deputy said I could make a call, but the only one I could think of to call was Maya, and my wife knows I'm in here already.' Stanley began to cry.

Troy got to his feet and told Stanley to sit down on the bunk. He pulled Stanley's shirttail out of his pants and wiped the old man's face. 'Crying ain't gonna help you none, old-timer. What you need's a good jailhouse lawyer. You listen to me, and I'll help you. Then you can do something for me. Okay?'

'It's all a big mistake,' Stanley said. 'I'd never do nothing to that little girl in a million years. I ain't even had a hard-on for more'n three years now. I'm seventy-one years old and retired.'

'I believe you, Pop. Just listen a minute. Here's what'll happen to you. This father, Mr Sneider –'

'He's a retired Army master sergeant, but he leases a Union station now.'

'Okay, Sergeant Sneider. What he'll do is file a complaint, and then they'll send you out of here for a psychiatric evaluation. That'll mean three or four days in a locked ward at the hospital. The doctor'll listen to your story, just like I did. Psychiatrists don't say much, they mostly listen, and I have a hunch he'll tell the state attorney to let you go. Meanwhile, this sergeant'll be thinking things over, and he'll realize if this case goes to trial his little girl will have to take the stand. After he and his wife talk about it, they'll decide they don't want to put the kid through the trauma of a courtroom appearance. So whether you're guilty or not, this case won't go to trial. But how you handle yourself when you talk to the psychiatrist is very important. He'll ask some very personal questions. How often do you masturbate?'

Stanley shook his head. 'I don't do nothing like that.'

'That's the wrong answer, Pop. Tell him once or twice a week. If you tell him you don't do it at all, he'll put it down on his report that you're evasive. And in shrink jargon, "evasive" means lying. How often do you have relations with your wife?'

'None at all. Not since we came down to Florida, and that's been six years now. I still wanted to at first, but Maya said she wanted to retire, too, just like me, so we just quit doing it. I wasn't all that keen myself, to tell you the truth.'

'For Christ's sake, Pop, don't tell the analyst that. Tell him once a week, at least. Otherwise, he'll think you're abnormal and you need little girls for an outlet.'

'I don't need any little girls! I never touched Pammi. I told you that already.'

'I *know* that, but you've got to tell a shrink what they want to hear. You'll have to persuade him that you have a normal, regular sex life.'

'Maya'll tell him different.'

'He won't talk to her. She's not accused of anything; you are. Apparently she believes what she thought she saw, so she'll be on Sneider's side. You understand what I'm talking about?'

'I think so. But it seems to me that Pammi, if she tells the truth, could clear all this up in a minute.'

'Of course she could. But she'll want to cover her own little ass. Little girls lie, big girls lie, and old women like your wife lie, too. Come to think of it, all women lie, even when the truth would do 'em more good. But you've got an honest face, old man, and the psychiatrist'll believe you when you lie.'

'My name is Stanley. Stanley Sinkiewicz. I don't mind being called Pop, because that's what they used to call me on the line at Ford, but I don't much like "old man."'

'Okay, Pop, fair enough. My real name's Troy Louden, but I'm signed up in here as Robert Smith. Let me finish telling you what to do, and you'll be out of here in no time. Stick to the same story you told me, but keep it simple. Maybe, when one of the detectives questions Pammi, she'll break down and tell the truth. But whether she does or not, it's still your word against hers. I realize your wife says she saw something, but all she saw was you trying to put the girl's shorts back on. Right? Admit this much, and that'll probably be the end of it. But I can guarantee you that you won't do any time if this is your first offense. This *is* your first offense, isn't it? You didn't get caught with any little girls before?'

'I never did nothing with a little girl, except when I was a little boy, and I never got caught then. I worked on the line at Ford all my life, and most of the time I was sick at night from smelling paint and turpentine all day.'

'You haven't got a record, then?'

'None. I never been in jail before.'

'Then you're in the clear, Pop. Feel better?'

'I think so.' Stanley nodded. 'My lip still hurts though.'

'I can't do anything about that. But when you get out, you should get a doctor to take a couple of stitches in it. Or, if they send you to the psychiatric ward in the morning, ask the nurse to get it sewed up for you. If I had a needle and thread I'd do it for you myself.'

'You know how to do things like that?'

'Sure. I'm used to taking care of myself when I get hurt. I'm a professional criminal, a career criminal, and when I get hurt on the job, or someone with me does, we can't go to a doctor – not a regular one, anyway. I've set bones, and I even took a bullet out of a man's back once. If I hadn't, he'd of been paralyzed.'

'How come you're in jail, Troy?'

'Call me Robert, Pop, while we're in here. Robert. After we get out, then you can call me Troy. Remember I told you I'm signed in here as Robert Smith.'

'Sure, Robert. I'm sorry. I'm still upset, I guess.'

'No need to be. You'll get out of this okay, Pop. But to answer your question, I'm a professional criminal, what the shrinks call a criminal psychopath. What it means is, I know the difference between right and wrong and all that, but I don't give a shit. That's the official version. Most men in prison are psychopaths, like me, and there are times – when we don't give a shit – when we act impulsively. Ordinarily though, I'm not impulsive, because I always think a job out very carefully before I get around to doing it. But I misjudged this truck driver this morning. I thought he was a little simple-minded, in fact, just because of the way he talked. But he turned out to be devious. He didn't have much education, but apparently he had more native American intelligence than I gave him credit for – Somebody's coming.'

Troy crossed to the bars and watched the black trusty coming down the corridor with an enameled metal plate and a cup of coffee.

'Who was it missed supper?' the trusty asked as he reached the cell.

466

'Just pass it through. I'll give it to the old man.'

'I'm not hungry,' Stanley said.

'Never mind,' Troy said. 'Somebody'll eat it.'

The trusty passed the plate and the cup through the slot in the cell door, and Troy sat beside Stanley on the bottom bunk. The plate contained beef stew, mustard greens, lime Jell-O, and a square of corn bread. There was a tablespoon in the cup of black coffee, which had been heavily sugared.

'Sure you don't want some of this, Pop? It'll be a long time till breakfast. Here, eat the corn bread, anyway.'

Stanley ate the corn bread, and Troy ate the stew and the lime Jell-O, but not the mustard greens. He sipped the coffee and grimaced. 'I don't mind food mixed up on the plate, because it all goes to one place anyway, but I can't eat greens without vinegar. Can you?'

'I'm not hungry. But this is good corn bread.'

'I'm not hungry either, but I never pass up a chance to eat when I'm in jail. Ever been in jail in Mexico, Pop?'

'I never been in jail before. I already told you that. I never been in Mexico, either.'

'I was in jail in Juarez once, right across the border from El Paso. They only feed twice a day there, at ten and four, and the guys who're doing the most time take half your beans. All you get is tortillas and beans twice a day, and the guys who've been there longest need the extra calories. They presume that a man who just got in's been eating good already, and they need to keep up their strength. There's more of them than there are of you, so you have to give up half your beans.'

'What did you do to get thrown in a Mexican jail?'

'That's another story, Pop. Let me finish telling you what went down this morning, 'cause you're gonna help me with my situation. I'm on my way to Miami, and I got stuck just outside of Daytona, hitchhiking. Hitchhiking ain't what it used to be, unless you're a soldier or a sailor in uniform, because there are a lot of criminals on the roads these days, and people aren't picking up strangers the way they used to. I waited on U.S. One for almost three hours before I got a ride. Finally, a guy named Henry Collins gave me a lift. D'you know him, by any chance?'

'No, I don't. But I don't know many people.'

'He lives right here in West Palm Beach.'

'I don't live in West Palm. I live in Ocean Pines Terraces, over in Riviera Beach, the retirement settlement the other side of the canal.'

'Well, Collins lives here, and he told me West Palm was as far as he was going when I first got into his car. He drives a 1984 Prelude.'

'That's a Japanese car. You know, it's un-American to drive one of them. The foot pedals in a Honda are too small, and there's more leg room in a Ford. A Ford'll do anything a Honda'll do, too.'

'I'm not complaining about the car, Pop. After three hours standing in the sun, I was willing to ride in the back of a pickup with a load of sheep. Anyway, Collins is a truck driver, and works out of Jacksonville. But he had two full days off, and he was coming home to spend it with his wife. I got to thinking about standing on the highway for another three hours or so, and the more I thought about it, the more I hated the idea. So I decided to take Collins's car and drive to Miami myself.'

Stanley widened his eyes. 'You mean you stole the man's car, after he was good enough to give you a free ride?'

'No, it didn't work out that way. I took my pistol out from under my belt and shoved it into his side, but before I could explain that I was only going to borrow his car, and that I wasn't going to hurt him, Collins jerks the wheel and we pile into a concrete bridge rail. About a mile north of downtown Riviera Beach. I'd already seen the sign marking the city limits. The damned fool could've killed us both.'

'That's right. 'Specially in a tinny Japanese car.'

Troy laughed. 'He was frightened, I suppose. He banged his head against the windshield, and he was stunned for a minute, but I was braced and wearing my seatbelt. I always wear a seatbelt. Seatbelts save lives.'

'I don't wear mine. I figure if I'm hanging on to the wheel I'm braced enough.'

'It didn't work out that way for Henry Collins, Pop. The swamp was right there, with water going under the bridge, and it looked pretty deep there, so I tossed my gun as far as I could into the

468

water. Collins was only out cold for a few seconds, but then he came to and glared at me.'

'You should've run,' Stanley said. 'If I'da been you I'd've started running.'

'I never run, Pop. What could Collins prove? It was only his word against mine. We didn't wait long anyway, because people stopped right away to see if we were hurt. Within three minutes there was a state trooper there to investigate the accident. It was just inside the city limits, so he called for a Riviera cop. Meanwhile, Collins was filling the trooper in about me pulling a pistol on him.'

'What did you say?'

'I told the trooper and the cop both that Collins was either drunk or crazy. They made him walk a straight line and then take a breath test. And he wasn't drunk. They didn't think he was crazy either, so after he said he'd prefer charges, they locked me up. Hell, he's a homeowner here, and I don't have any fixed address. Not at the moment anyway, except for this cell.'

'Did they ever find your gun?'

'Not yet, and they won't try very hard, not in all that stinking muck out there. But even if they find a gun they can't prove it's mine. There must be hundreds of guns thrown off bridges here in Florida.'

Frowning, Stanley took the plate and cup from Troy and put them down by the door. 'You're in a lot of trouble, son. That's an awful thing to do, pulling a gun on a man that way. Whatever made you do it?'

'I explained that to you. I'm a criminal psychopath, so I'm not responsible for the things I do.'

'Does that mean you're crazy? You don't look crazy, Troy – I mean John.'

'Robert.'

'Robert. Of course, pulling that pistol on that man –'

'Let me finish, Pop. I don't have time to go into all of the ramifications of my personality, it's too complex. I've been tested again and again, and it always comes out the same. Psychopath. And because I'm a criminal, I'm also a criminal psychopath. You follow me?'

'Yeah, I think so. But if you aren't crazy, what are you?'

'It's what I told you already. I know the difference between good and bad, but it makes no difference to me. If I see the right thing to do and want to do it, I do it, and if I see the wrong thing and want to do it, I do that, too.'

'You mean you can't help yourself then?'

'Certainly I can. I'll put it another way. I can help myself, but I don't give a damn.'

'And because you don't give a damn, you're a criminal psychopath, is that it?'

'You've got it.'

'But why' – Stanley made a sweeping movement with his arm – 'don't you give a damn?'

'Because I'm a criminal psychopath. Maybe, when they give you some tests, you might be one, too.'

'No, I'm a responsible person, Robert. I worked hard all my life, took good care of my wife and son, and even put my boy through junior college. I own a home up in Detroit, and I own my own home here in Florida. I never done nothing wrong in my life, except for – well, I won't go into some little things, maybe.'

'Even after they test you, Pop, you still won't know how they came out. They never tell you. I had to give a man at Folsom two cartons of Chesterfields to get a Xerox of my medical records. That's how I know. Otherwise I wouldn't know that I was a criminal psychopath, and I would think I was doing strange things instead of acting naturally. I read a lot, you see, even when I'm not in jail.'

Stanley pointed to the dish and cup on the floor. 'Do I have to wash this plate and cup?'

'Hell, no, just leave it for the trusty. Until a man's been adjudicated and found guilty, he don't have to do anything in jail. They'll try to get you to do things, but you can tell them to go fuck themselves because you're innocent until you're proven guilty. You and me are both innocent, so we don't have to do a damned thing. Sit down over there, Pop, I want to talk to you.'

'I don't want to hear no more about those tests.'

Stanley sat beside Troy, and Troy put an arm around the old man's shoulders. 'Never mind the tests. I want you to do me a

470

little favor, Pop. If you don't want to help me, say so, and I won't ask.'

'Sure, I don't mind helping you, Robert, I guess. But in here, I don't know –'

'You won't be in here much longer. If you call a lawyer he can get you out right away on your own recognizance.'

'My what?'

'Rec – The fact that you know who you are and that you're a property owner. Just listen to me a minute. I'm not wanted anywhere at present, but the first thing the sheriff'll do is send my fingerprints up to Charleston, South Carolina, to see if there's any criminal record on me, or if I'm wanted by some southern state. Florida's still the South, you know, despite all the snowbirds who moved down here from the North. And in the South, they always send the prints to Charleston first, because it's the southern version of the FBI records center. They won't get a make on my prints in Charleston, because I did all my time in California.'

'They didn't take my prints yet. Will they send mine to Charleston, too?'

'I don't think so. As I said, you probably won't even be booked. Let me finish, then I'll answer your questions.'

'Sorry, Robert. It's just that this is so darned interesting. How come they don't just send your fingerprints to the FBI in Washington?'

'They will. But later. They're interested first in whether a southern state wants a man or not. In the South, they really don't give a shit about the rest of the United States. If there isn't any make on the prints in Charleston, *then* they send them to Washington. And that's what I'm worried about, you see. It'll take about three days to get a negative report from Charleston, and then they'll forward my prints to Washington, which'll give me another three days. So I only have about six days altogether before they find out who I am. Washington's got a list on me about this long' – Troy spread his arms – 'beginning with my yellow discharge from the Army and everything else. Right now, I'm okay. With just the two of us involved, me and Henry Collins, the state attorney, when he looks at the case, wouldn't be too eager to prosecute.

But when he sees my record I'll be arraigned, and the judge'll be all set to convict me even though I'm innocent, just because of my record.'

'But you aren't innocent, Robert. You already said –'

'I'm innocent until they prove otherwise. They can't prove anything, but my record'll make me look bad. That'll put me in a tight spot.'

'I'm not seeing how I can help you.'

Troy crossed to the bars, looked down the corridor, then sat down again. He pulled off his left boot, extracted a nail from the heel, and slid the lowest layer of the heel to one side. From a hollowed-out recess in the heel he removed three tightly folded newspaper clippings. Troy unfolded the clippings, thumbed through them, and handed one of them to Stanley. He replaced the other two clippings in the heel, twisted it back, and reinserted the nail.

'Go ahead and read it, Pop.'

The clipping contained three short paragraphs. Stanley didn't have his reading glasses, so he had to hold it at arm's length to read it. Stanley read it three times before returning it to Troy. 'I don't understand, Robert –'

Troy smiled and patted the old man on the knee. 'What did you get out of it, Pop? Tell me.'

'Maybe I missed something, I don't know. All I got out of it was that a man held up a liquor store in Biloxi, Mississippi, and then beat the owner unconscious because there wasn't enough money in the cash register to suit him.'

'What's the dateline? Up at the top?'

'Biloxi, Mississippi.'

'Right. That shows that the item was printed somewhere else. If something happens here in West Palm Beach, they don't put the name of the city down, but if something happens up in Jacksonville, and they run an item here, they put Jacksonville in the dateline, you see. Anyway, all you're supposed to get out of it is the story.'

'This wasn't you, was it, son?'

'Of course not.'

'Then why ... I mean, what –?'

'You don't have to keep asking me questions, Pop. I'll tell you what I want you to do for me. First, put the clipping away – in your shirt pocket.'

Stanley refolded the clipping and put it away. Troy rubbed his nose for a moment, then looked intently at the old man. 'It's really simple, Pop. When they turn you loose, later tonight or tomorrow morning, look in the phone book and find out where Henry Collins lives. As a truck driver, he's bound to have a phone, but if he doesn't, check the city register for his address.'

Stanley nodded. 'I can do that easy enough.'

'Fine. Then go to his house and see him for me. Hand him that clipping, and tell him to read it.'

'Is that all?'

'Not quite. After he's read the clipping, tell him to drop the charges against me or I'll kill him. But tell him I won't kill him until after I've killed his wife and child first.'

'I can't do that!'

'Of course you can, Pop. I wouldn't hurt a fly, any more than you would. But Collins doesn't know that. Just tell him what I said. Then he can tell the desk sergeant he was dazed by the accident and only thought I had a pistol, and now that his memory's come back he wants to rectify his mistake and withdraw the charges.'

'But you really did have a pistol –'

'That's right, a thirty-eight Smith and Wesson.'

'And Mr Collins knows you had the pistol.'

'That's right.'

'I don't think he'd do it.'

'I do.'

'Well ...' Stanley thought for a minute. 'I don't think I could do nothing like that. You've been mighty nice to me and all, telling me about things and cheering me up, but that's a lot to ask – even if I do get out.'

'You'll get out, don't worry.'

'You really think so?'

'I know so. And what I asked you to do, a small favor for me, won't take much of your time. You're retired, so what else have you got to do with your time?'

'It ain't the time, son. I'm afraid. If I went to Mr Collins with a message like that one, he might think I'm in on it and call the police. Then I'd be back in here with you.'

'I see what you mean. There's a way around that. Write out the message. Print it on a plain piece of paper, and keep it short. Then put the message and the clipping in an envelope, and print Mr Collins's address on the outside.'

'I don't know his address.'

'You can look it up, like I already told you, in the phone book. Then you can take it to Collins, and tell him you found the letter on the street, and it didn't have any stamp on it, so you thought you'd bring it to his house because it might be important. In fact, you might even ask him for a reward, or a tip. That might be even better. And if he or his wife aren't home, just drop it in his mailbox.'

'I could put a stamp on it and mail it instead.'

'No, that would take too long, and mailing it could get you into trouble with the Post Office – if they found out about it. I haven't got that kind of time.'

'I guess I could do that much all right.'

'Sure you could. And this way, you'll just be a good Samaritan delivering a letter you found on the street, the way any good citizen returns a lost wallet to someone who's lost it.'

'All right. If I get out, I'll do it.'

'Thanks, Pop. I really appreciate it. Now you better let me tell you some more questions the shrink'll ask you, in case you get a psychological examination. Suppose you're playing baseball, and you knock your ball into a circular field surrounded by a ten-foot wall. How do you find the ball?'

An hour later, Stanley was out on the street again. They had given him back his wallet, his belt and shoelaces, an unused Kleenex tissue, and eighty-four cents in change. John Sneider, Pammi's father, was waiting outside the jail in his tow truck to drive Stanley back to his empty house in Ocean Pines Terraces.

Chapter Five

The El Pelicano Arms apartment house was a hundred yards north of the public tennis courts, about sixty yards south of the Ocean Mall, and on the Atlantic side of Ocean Road. There was direct access to the public beach through a wooden gate to the left of the lobby entrance. There were reserved parking spaces for each apartment, and a special parking place for the manager – a marked slot next to the lobby entrance. There were no visitor spaces, but visitors could usually, except on weekends, find parking in the Ocean Mall lot.

The Singer Island beach, an important asset of the Riviera Beach municipality, was one of the widest beaches in Florida. In most respects, it was the best public beach in the state. The Gulf Stream was closer to shore here than anywhere else, making the water warm enough to swim all year round. During January, the cool month, the ocean was always warmer than the air, which made the water easier to get into than it was to get out. Now, toward the end of June, the water temperature was eighty-five degrees, the same as the humid air.

Across from the El Pelicano, in the older business section of Singer Island, there was a row of one- and two-story office buildings and shops, and a three-story hotel. Several shops sold T-shirts and other resort clothing, and there was a discount drugstore. Back in the 1970s, one of these stores had been the office of *Alfred Hitchcock's Mystery Magazine*, but the magazine had moved to New York, and now there was a realtor occupying the spot. Most of the space between these older buildings and the new Ocean Mall was taken up with a macadam parking lot that had no meters.

The mall had three restaurants, a dozen or more stores, a game room, and several small offices above the stores at the northern end of the mall. The Ocean Mall was 'new,' as far as Hoke was concerned, because the mall hadn't been there during the 1960s, when he grew up on Singer Island. There had only been one building then beside the municipal beach, a drive-in hamburger restaurant with girls on roller skates who waited on the parked cars that encircled the building. It had been a favorite place for the younger people in Palm Beach County to hang out, day and night. Sometimes the cars had been parked three deep, which meant that there was a constant movement, backing and filling, as people sought to get out or get in, and there was considerable visiting between cars.

The new mall was still a favorite place for young people. In bikinis and trunks they slouched and ran up and down the sidewalks on both sides of the mall, or cut through passageways and through the stores. There were also a great many tourists, and hundreds of middle-aged and elderly condominium residents stumbled and tottered about the mall.

There were a dozen motels and more than thirty high-rise condominiums along the single island highway, with more condos under construction. There was a narrow bridge exit at the northern end of the island, which led into North Palm Beach, as well as the Blue Heron bridge at the southern end, which took people into downtown Riviera Beach. The traffic on Blue Heron Road was always heavy.

In recent years, especially during the summer, Miami's Latins had discovered Singer Island, thanks to the Sunday *Miami Herald* travel section, where motel ads announced cheap weekend rates. It was possible for a couple (with children under twelve free) to get a motel room on the ocean, a free piña colada, two free breakfasts, and a three-day, two-night stay for as low as fifty-eight dollars a room (tax not included). A few motels, anxious for summer business, offered even lower rates if the room was rented during the week and if the couple vacated it before the weekend. Miami's Cubans, who had a long-standing tradition of going to Veradera Beach in Cuba for holidays, now flocked to Singer Island on weekends, bringing their parents, their aunts, and from three to five children per family. There were plenty of trash barrels on the beach, but the weekenders usually disdained them.

When Hoke picked his way among the sunbathers to take his first morning swim, he stepped on a discarded sanitary napkin with his bare left foot. Backing away from that and saying 'Shit,' he stepped into a pile of the very thing with his bare right foot. No dogs were allowed on the beach (a rule that was strictly enforced), so Hoke was worried that he had stepped in human shit. He scraped it off with an empty beer can and decided, then and there, that he would not rent out any of his El Pelicano apartments to Latins.

Hoke swam beyond the surf for almost an hour, then walked up the beach, staying close to the hard-packed sand of the littoral. By the time he reached the third condo, the beach was almost deserted. The condos, especially the older ones, were sold out completely, but only about thirty percent of the owners lived in their apartments full-time. The majority came down at Christmas and at Easter, or spent three or four winter months there; most of the year their apartments were unoccupied. At least, Hoke thought, they aren't all year-round residents, like the condo owners in Miami and Miami Beach. If all of the apartments and motel rooms on Singer Island were occupied at the same time, there probably wouldn't be enough room on the island to hold all of their cars. The island population would triple overnight. He wondered if the people buying into those condos under construction were aware of the population glut that was coming if they kept putting up these twenty- and thirty-story buildings. The condos all had heated pools on the ocean side of their buildings, explaining why very few condo residents took advantage of the warm Atlantic. Hoke decided that from now on he would walk down here and swim in front of one of these condos instead of swimming at the public beach.

As Hoke started back toward the public beach, he noticed a man seated in a webbed chair beneath a striped beach umbrella behind the Supermare, a twenty-story condo with a penthouse on top. The man had a blanket, an open briefcase, and was talking on a white portable telephone. As Hoke stopped to look at him, the man put the phone on the blanket and made a notation with a gold pen on a yellow legal pad.

Hoke crossed over to the blanket and looked down at the man. He was balding in front, but he wore a thick gray mustache, and there was a thick cluster of curly silver hair at the back of his head. He wore a rose-colored *cabaña* set with maroon piping on the shirt and on the hems of the swimming shorts.

'Good morning,' he said, not unpleasantly, taking off his sunglasses.

'Morning. D'you mind if I use your phone?'

'Local or long distance?'

'Long distance. Miami. But I'll call collect.'

'No need to do that.' The older man shrugged as he handed Hoke the phone. 'I've got a WATS line. Don't worry about it.'

Hoke dialed Ellita Sanchez in Green Lakes, and she picked up the phone on the third ring.

'Ellita? Hoke.'

'How are you, Hoke? I've called your father a couple of times, and –'

'I'm fine. You won't have to call him again. I'm living in a new place. You got a pencil?'

'Right here.'

'It's the El Pelicano Arms. Apartment number 201, upstairs, here on Singer Island.'

'What's the phone number?'

'No phone. The address is 506 Mall Road, Singer Island, Riviera Beach. I'm going to need a few things. My checkbook, bankbook, and probably my car. I bought some surfer trunks yesterday, but the legs are too long, so pack my swimming trunks when you send someone up with the car.'

'What other clothes will you need?'

'None. I've got a new plan. I've still got my gun, badge, and cuffs, and I won't need them either. Maybe you can turn them in at the department for me?'

'*Espera*, Hoke! Let's wait awhile on that. You've got thirty days of leave, and Bill Henderson's covering for you just fine. Don't rush into any rash decisions. Your dad told me you were going to stay for a while, but you might change your – What's that roaring sound?'

'Roaring sound? Oh. I guess that must be the surf you hear coming in. I've borrowed a portable phone from a guy on the beach.'

The owner of the phone laughed. Hoke moved twenty feet away from the blanket to keep him from listening in on their conversation. 'I guess that's about it, Ellita.'

'There must be a few other things you need.'

'I don't want to tie up this man's phone, Ellita. He's working.'

'On the beach?'

'Yeah. We're on the beach side of the Supermare condo – or in the back. I thought Frank already told you, I'm going to manage the El Pelicano for him, so I won't be coming back to Miami.'

'What? What about the girls – and the house?'

'You can have the house. I'll send you my half of the rent from my savings until you can get someone else to share it with you. The girls will have to go out to California and live with their mother.'

'Suppose Patsy won't take them back?'

'I don't want to think about that. I've still got some other things to sort out, but that's my immediate plan.'

'Don't you want to talk to Aileen? She's home, but Sue Ellen's out.'

'I do, yes, but I don't want to tie up this man's phone. There's no hurry about the car. But I'll need my bankbook and checkbook so I can buy a few things and send you the rent money.'

'You didn't ask, but the baby's fine. I'll see that you get your car –'

'Thanks, Ellita.' Hoke cut her off. 'It was nice talking to you.' Hoke walked back to the blanket and handed the man the telephone. 'I don't mind paying for the call. You can check the amount, and I'll bring you the money later. It should be about a dollar eighty-five, but I don't have any money with me.'

'That's okay. It won't matter to my WATS line.' The older man balanced the phone on his bare knee. 'I didn't mean to eavesdrop on your call, but I had to laugh. She asked about the roaring sound, didn't she?'

Hoke nodded.

'That's one of the reasons I come down to the beach to make my morning calls. I've got the penthouse up there, but they always ask me about the sound. Then I tell them I'm on the beach under my umbrella, and that's the surf they're hearing twenty feet away. It puts me one up, you know, because then they know I'm wearing swimming trunks and sitting on the beach here in Florida, while they're in an office wearing a three-piece suit in New York.' He chuckled. 'Or else they're sweating down there in an office in Miami, on Brickell Avenue.'

'It's been a long time since I wanted to be one up on anyone –'

'Everybody needs an edge, my friend. You've got an edge with your badge and gun. What are you, a detective?'

'How'd you know?'

'Just a guess. I heard you mention your gun and badge. If you'd just said gun, I might've figured you for a holdup man.'

'I'm a detective-sergeant, but I'm retiring from the Miami Police Department.'

'To manage the El Pelicano Arms?'

'Yeah. For now, anyway.'

'Have you heard about the burglaries here on the island? Pretty soon the island'll be as bad as Miami.'

'What burglaries?'

'In the condos. We've had three right here in the Supermare. And whoever it is, he's only taking valuable items. The cops in Riviera Beach aren't doing a damned thing about it, either.' He smiled smugly.

'You don't know that. They must be working on it. They don't always tell you everything they're doing.'

'I don't know about that, Sergeant. But stuff is disappearing. People are gone for a few weeks, or months, and when they come back paintings and other valuables are missing. We've got a security man on the gate twenty-four hours a day, so who's taking the stuff?'

'There's no guard back here,' Hoke pointed out, 'on the beach side. I could climb those steps to the pool, walk into the lobby, and take an elevator right up to your apartment. This is a public Florida beach. Anyone can walk or jog all of the way up to

Niggerhead Rock and back. In fact, when I get settled, that's what I plan to do every day.' Hoke edged away.

'I'd like to talk to you again about these burglaries sometime.'

'I'm not a detective any longer. I was in Homicide, not Robbery. Was. Now I'm an apartment manager.'

'Take my card anyway. Some evening, if you've got nothing better to do, stop up for a drink. If you're not interested in the burglaries, we can talk about something else. I have two martinis every day at five o'clock.'

Hoke read the card he was handed. E. M. SKINNER. CONSULTANT. 'What's the E. M. stand for?'

'Emmett Michael, but most people call me E. M. My wife used to call me Emmett, but she's been dead for three years now.'

'Hoke Moseley.' The two men shook hands.

'Any relation to Frank Moseley?'

'My father. You know him?'

'I know his wife. I only met him once, but Helen has an apartment here in the Supermare. I knew Helen before they got married. She still owns her apartment here.'

'I didn't know that. With the big house they have, why would Helen still keep an apartment here?'

'As an investment, a tax write-off, probably. Some owners live here for six months and one day to establish a Florida residency, just because we don't have any inheritance or state income tax. They might make their money in New York or Philly, but legally they're Floridians.'

'That's not my family, Mr Skinner. We go back a long way in Florida. The original Moseleys lived here before the Revolutionary War and then went to the Bahamas during the war because they were Loyalists. Then, after the war was over, they came back to Riviera Beach.'

'Not many families in Florida go that far back.'

'I know. There are still a few here in Riviera Beach, and even more down in the Keys. That's why we're called "Conchs," you know. Originally, we were conch fishermen, both here and in the northern Bahamas. The term's been corrupted now, because they call any asshole born in Key West nowadays a Conch. But the Moseleys are truly Conchs in the original sense.'

'What's the difference between a Conch and a Cracker?'

'Crackers are people who moved to Florida from Georgia, from Bacon County, Georgia, mostly. Farmers and stock people. So they're called Florida Crackers instead of Georgia Crackers. I don't know how the word "Cracker" got started. All I know is there's a helluva difference between a Conch and a Cracker.'

The phone rang, and Skinner picked it up. Hoke moved away down the beach, and Skinner waved. Hoke nodded back and headed for his apartment. The guy loved attention, Hoke concluded, and would have talked all morning.

Hoke was mildly curious about E. M. Skinner. The old man had everything, including a penthouse overlooking the Atlantic, but he was obviously lonesome as hell, looking for adventure or something. All the guy needed was a phone and a pencil, apparently, and he could sit under a beach umbrella and make money. Lots of money. Old Frank Moseley was like that, too, but his father's knack for making money hadn't been passed along to Hoke. Frank had once owned the land now occupied by the Supermare condo, and he probably still had a few points in the building as well, though Hoke didn't understand exactly how points worked. Hoke knew the difference between being alone and being lonely, however, and he knew he would never be lonely as long as he stayed on Singer Island.

Hoke showered, slipped into slacks and a sport shirt, and walked to the Tropic Shop in the Ocean Mall to see if his jumpsuits were ready yet. He had ordered two yellow poplin jumpsuits when he bought his surfer trunks, but had asked the shop owner to have the sleeves cut off and hemmed above the elbow. This was Hoke's first positive step toward simplifying his life. He would wear one of the jumpsuits one day, wash it at night, and then wear the other one the next day. That way he wouldn't need any underwear, and he could wear his sneakers without socks. He had selected the jumpsuits because they had several pockets, including zippered pockets in the back. He had wanted the long legs, however, instead of cutoffs, because they could be Velcroed at the ankles. Insects were not a big daytime problem on the island, because of the prevailing breeze from the ocean, but when the direction changed and the winds came from the 'Glades, it usually brought in swarms of tiny black mosquitoes at night.

The woman at the Tropic Shop told Hoke that she hadn't got the jumpsuits back from the tailor yet, but would send them over to the El Pelicano when her daughter came back from the mainland.

'She doesn't have to do that. I don't know where I'll be, so I'll check back later this afternoon or tomorrow morning.'

'I could call you when they come back.'

'I don't have a phone.'

Hoke left the shop and crossed Blue Heron Road to the Giant Supermarket. He picked out potatoes, onions, celery, carrots, summer squash, and two pounds of chuck steak. He bought a dozen eggs and three loaves of white sandwich bread. He added a bottle of Tabasco sauce, and a jar of peppercorns for seasoning, and carried the two bags of groceries back to his apartment. His new plan was to eat two meals a day. He wanted to lose at least ten pounds, so he would eat two boiled eggs and a piece of toast for breakfast each morning, and skip lunch. At night he would eat one bowl of stew, and he had enough ingredients to make a stew that would last for five days. Then, the following week, he planned to make enough chili and beans to last for five evening meals. This would solve his cooking problems, and he could eat two slices of bread with each bowl of stew or chili. On the other two days, when the beef stew or the chili ran out, he would just eat eggs and bread for breakfast, and perhaps go out at night for either a hamburger or a fried fish sandwich. With a plan like this one, he wouldn't get bored with his meals, because when the stew started to bore him, it would be time for two days without stew, and then the following week he could look forward to chili and beans.

Hoke was taken with the simplicity of his plan. He chopped the vegetables for the stew while he browned the cut-up chunks of meat in the cast-iron Dutch oven. Then he dumped in the vegetables, added water, and turned the electric burner to its lowest setting. He threw in a handful of peppercorns, then sat at his dining table to examine the account books Al Paulson had brought him last night.

Three units were rented on one-year leases: to a schoolteacher, to a salad man at the Sheraton Hotel, and to a biology professor from the University of Florida who was on a one-year sabbatical. Hoke, of course, had 201, so there were only four other apartments. Two were already rented to two elderly couples from Birmingham, Alabama, who were vacationing for two months on the island. So two units were still unrented. The sign on the bulletin board in the lobby said that there was a two-week minimum, but the sign hadn't deterred a few people from coming up to Hoke's apartment and asking about weekend rentals. All he could do then was to repeat what the sign said, but that hadn't kept one asshole from Fort Lauderdale from arguing with him about it. There would be more assholes like that, Hoke suspected, from his experience in living at the Eldorado Hotel in Miami Beach for two years. The Eldorado had also been a hotel for permanent or semi-permanent guests, and it didn't take overnighters or week-enders either. Poor old Eddie Cohen, the day and night manager of the Eldorado, must have had a hundred arguments with tran-sients who just wanted an overnight stay. The best thing to do, Hoke decided, was to try and get all permanent residents for one-year leases, if he possibly could. If he could manage that, he could just collect the rent from everyone once a month and hang out a NO VACANCY sign. Perhaps the best way to start was to change the policy from a minimum rental of two weeks to a two-month minimum. Hoke went downstairs, crossed out 'weeks' and wrote in 'months' above it. His father might not like the new policy, but then he wouldn't have to tell him about it – not until he had the empty units rented, anyway.

Paulson had also given him a list of people to call when things went wrong – a plumber, an electrician, a handyman, and a phone number for Mrs Delaney, a widow who lived in a private home two blocks away. She cleaned apartments when they were vacated, and was paid a flat rate of thirty-five dollars, no matter how dirty or clean the apartment was when the tenants left. Hoke recalled her name vaguely from when he was a boy, but couldn't remember what she looked like. Perhaps, when the time came to clean the next vacated apartment, he could do it himself and pocket the thirty-five bucks. He could see already, from the cost of the groceries at the Giant Market, that a hundred bucks a week wasn't going to go very far.

When he resigned, he could either take his retirement-fund money in a lump sum, or leave it and wait until he was fifty-seven, and then draw a small monthly retirement check. He didn't know which one was the best course to follow. He didn't like the idea of living on one hundred dollars a week for the next fourteen years. But he didn't want to think about money right now. He didn't want to think about Ellita and her baby, Sue Ellen, or Aileen. He didn't want to think about anything at all.

Hoke stripped down to his shorts and went to sleep on the Bahama bed, with a warm, damp wind blowing over his body from the window facing the sea.

Chapter Six

When Stanley saw Mr Sneider standing beside his tow truck waiting for him, he involuntarily put the fingers of his right hand to his cut lip and considered darting back inside the jail.

'Everything's all right, Mr Sinkiewicz,' Sneider said, holding up a hand. 'I'm here to drive you home.'

Sneider opened the door to the cab, and Stanley climbed into the passenger seat. After Sneider got into the cab, he sat for a long moment with both hands on the wheel, staring through the windshield. Sneider was a hairy, ursine man, who had grown a bushy black beard after retiring from the service. His fingernails were black with embedded grease, and Stanley could smell beer on Sneider's breath.

'This whole thing's been a damned farce, Mr Sinkiewicz, and I want to apologize. I had no reason to hit you, even though I thought you were going to run. I just wasn't thinking clearly, that's all, after talking to my wife and Mrs Sinkiewicz. Besides, I had a bad day. A bastard in a blue Electra stiffed me for twenty bucks' worth of gas. He filled up at self-service and tore out of there at sixty miles an hour. But that's beside the point. I'm still sorry, but that's what happens when you listen to two hysterical women talking at the same time.'

'I – I didn't do nothing bad to Pammi.'

'I know that now, but I didn't know it at the time, you see. After I got back home from here I had a long talk with Pammi in her bedroom and managed to get the truth out of her. I know now you didn't instigate anything, because Pammi has been carrying on with a couple of old geezers in the park in the evening. We've been letting her go out after dinner, because she was supposed to play with her friend Ileana down the street. Instead, she's been meeting one old fart or another in the pinochle shed in the park. Apparently this has been going on for weeks. She's still a virgin, however. I checked that out myself, and her hymen's still in one piece. But she's been doing some other dirty things with these old men that I'd rather not go into just now. I think you know what I mean.'

'I was asleep, and she stuck her tongue in my mouth and asked for a penny.'

Sneider sighed. 'I know. She told me. You're off the hook, Mr Sinkiewicz, and I'm sorry if I caused you any trouble. But that fucker in the blue Electra had me going to begin with – well, what difference does it make? Did you get any dinner? If not, I'll spring for a Big Mac and a shake before I take you home.' Sneider started the engine and put the stick into first gear.

'I'm not hungry. I had a piece of corn bread, and my lip's too sore to eat anyway.'

'You could probably use a stitch or two, but if you've got some adhesive tape at home, I can put a butterfly stitch on it for you, and it'll be good as new in a day or so.'

'There's some tape in the medicine cabinet. It's old, though.'

'That don't make no difference. Adhesive tape, unless it gets wet or dried out in the sun or something, is good for years.'

On the drive to Ocean Pines Terraces, Sneider told Stanley about a kid he caught breaking into his Coke machine a couple of weeks back. 'He didn't get anything, but when I took the kid home to his father, I told his old man that the kid had stolen about ten dollars' worth of Cokes from me during the last month or so, and the guy came up with ten bucks.' Sneider laughed, relishing the story.

When Sneider pulled into Stanley's driveway, Stanley noticed that his Escort wasn't in the carport. 'Is Maya still with your wife, Sergeant Sneider?'

'No. My wife went off to one of her meetings, and I made her take Pammi along. I don't know where your wife is. Let's go inside, and I'll fix up your lip.'

Stanley found the roll of tape and got a pair of scissors from Maya's sewing basket, and Sneider put a neat butterfly bandage on Stanley's lip. 'Just leave it there for two or three days. Shave around it, and the old lip'll be as good as new.'

487

The two men shook hands at the door, and Sneider apologized again before driving off down the street in his tow truck. Stanley looked around the house for a note, but didn't find one. Then he stopped looking, realizing that if Maya knew that he was in jail, she wouldn't leave a note for him because she wouldn't expect him to be coming home to read it. Stanley went next door to the Agnews' and rapped on the front door. The jalousies on the door opened slightly, but not the door.

'Go away!' Mrs Agnew said.

'Is my wife in there with you, Mrs Agnew?'

'No, she isn't, and if you don't go away, you pervert, I'll call the police!'

'Do you know where she went?'

The jalousies were cranked closed. Stanley could hear Mrs Agnew's tapping footsteps as she walked across her terrazzo floor toward the kitchen. Stanley returned to his house and sat in his recliner. He knew he was too restless to watch television. After a few moments, he went into the bedroom and took off his bloodied shirt. As he threw the dirty shirt into the hamper beside the open closet door, he noticed that the Samsonite two-suiter wasn't on the closet shelf. He looked through the clothes in the closet. There seemed to be a few things missing, but he wasn't sure. He looked for Maya's photo album, where she kept the family snapshots, including the ones of the grandchildren Junior sent down from time to time. When he couldn't find the album, he knew that Maya was gone. Her checkbook was missing from the little corner desk in the living room where she worked on the household accounts, and so was her little recipe file box.

She was gone. No question about it.

Stanley looked up the number and direct-dialed his son in Hamtramck. Junior's voice was a little garbled at first because his mouth was full of food.

'It's me,' Stanley said, 'and I'm calling long distance from Florida. Have you heard from your mother?'

'Just a sec, Dad.' Junior finished chewing. 'Are you calling from the jail?'

'No, I'm home. I'm calling from home.'

'Mom said you were in jail when she called me. How'd you get out? She said you were arrested for molesting some little kid.'

'It was all a mistake, son. Maya didn't see what she thought she saw, and that's all been cleared up now.'

'Is Mom still there, Dad? I'd like to talk to her.'

'No, she isn't here. I just wondered if she called you. I don't know where she is.'

'In that case, she's already left, Dad. She said she was coming back here to Detroit, that's what she called to tell me, and that was that. Now, I realize you own the house up here and all that, but I told her we didn't have any room for her. Christ, Dad, we've only got two bedrooms and one bath, so where'll we put Mom?'

'She's driving up, then? I don't think she can find her way to Detroit, and the Escort's due for an oil change, too.'

'If she's already left, there's nothing we can do about it, I guess. But when she gets up here, I'll send her back after a couple of days. We really can't put her up for more than one or two days. Maybe I can make reservations for her at the Howard Johnson's, or some motel near the house. Too bad you didn't get out of jail soon enough to stop her from leaving. A woman Mom's age shouldn't be driving all the way across the country by herself.'

'She'll get lost. There's no doubt about that.'

'No, I don't think she'll get lost, Dad. She can always ask the way to Michigan at a gas station. D'you want to talk to the kids while you're on the phone?'

'No. Did you call the jail, Junior, and try to get me out?'

'I didn't call anybody. I was trying to talk Mom out of coming up here, and then she hung up on me. I'm trying to eat dinner now. I've really had a bitch of a day. Mom was in a hurry and told me she'd give me the details when she got here. What happened, anyway?'

'Nothing happened. When your mother gets there, she can give you her version of the details. And you can also tell her for me that I won't take her back. Tell her to keep the damned Escort and look for a job. You can also tell her not to cash any checks with the checkbook she took with her either, because the account is now closed!'

Stanley hung up the phone. His face was flushed and his fingers trembled. He went into the kitchen and heated water to make a cup of instant coffee. Before the water boiled, the phone rang. At first he wasn't going to answer it, figuring it was Stanley Junior calling him back, but when it kept ringing he finally picked it up on the eighth ring.

'Listen, Dad,' Junior said, 'and please don't hang up. If the trouble's all cleared up, and if Momma calls me again from wherever she is on the road, I'll just tell her to go back home. Okay? Of course, she knows what she saw, and all that, but I think I can talk her into going back, especially now that you're out of jail. I'd like to see her, of course, and so would the kids, and all, but we really don't have any room here for her – and that's a fact.'

'I won't take her back, Junior. Mom's your problem now, not mine. If that's the way Maya thinks about me after all these years, I don't want the woman around. She never liked it down here in Florida anyway. So from now on, she's your –'

'Let's talk a minute, Dad.'

'There's nothing else to talk about. She made up her mind, and I've made up mine. Just make sure you keep sending me the rent money every month, and don't give it to Maya. I still have to pay the mortgage down here. Understand?'

'Okay, Dad, but I think we'd better discuss this later, after you and Momma have a chance to cool off some. We'll work some –'

'It's already worked out, Junior. Just give my love to the kids. You called *me* this time, and you're on long distance, you know.'

'Right, Dad. Do you need any help from me? Can I get you a lawyer? If you need a lawyer, I can check around here, and see if –'

'I don't need no lawyer, because I'm not in any trouble. Your mother's in trouble, not me. Get a lawyer for Maya. Good night, son.' Stanley hung up the phone.

Stanley tried to calm down. He drank his coffee at the kitchen table. His heart was beating rapidly, and he could almost feel it inside his chest. He was disappointed in his son, as well as in Maya. If the situation had been reversed, and he had learned that Junior was in jail for molesting a child, he would have been on the phone, or gone to the jail with a lawyer immediately. And no matter what they said, he wouldn't have believed Junior guilty of doing something like that. But Junior hadn't even called the jail to find out what they were doing with his father.

With Maya gone, his life would be a little harder now. He would have to cook his own meals, clean the house, and do his own laundry, but he would rather do that than take her back. That's what their marriage had come down to anyway, a division of labor, just two people sharing the same house. For months Maya had tried to talk to him about moving back to Hamtramck, and every time she brought it up he had refused to discuss it.

'We made our decision when we came down here,' he told her, 'and we're settled in now. If you want to go up there on a visit, you can go by yourself. I don't ever want to see ice and snow again. Just call Junior and tell him you're coming back to visit for a couple of weeks or a month – and see what he says!'

Maya hinted to Junior on the phone a few times that she would like to visit, but she didn't get an invitation, and she didn't come right out and ask for one because she knew she wouldn't get one, and Stanley knew she wouldn't ever get one. So this 'incident' with Pammi was the first real excuse she had to leave, her first opportunity, and she had taken it because Junior couldn't turn her away if Stanley was in jail. Well, as far as Stanley was concerned, she could stay there, too. He had his pride, and he wouldn't take her back. He might if she begged him, but he didn't think she would do that. In her own way, she was as stubborn as he was; she didn't like Florida, and she didn't need Stanley any more than he needed her.

Well, he could take care of himself. It was all over, and he was too exhausted to think about it any longer. Without finishing his coffee, Stanley went into the bedroom to lie down for a moment, to quiet the rapid beating of his heart.

A minute later, Stanley was asleep, and he didn't awaken until morning.

It was still dark when Stanley got up at five A.M. and shaved. He scrambled two eggs in butter and toasted himself two slices of bread. He made instant coffee instead of using the Mr Coffee machine, because he didn't know how to work it and he couldn't

491

find the directions in the kitchen drawer where Maya kept all of the warranties for their appliances.

Stanley was disappointed in his son, but no longer angry with him. The boy (Junior was almost forty years old) hadn't turned out as well as he should have, even though Stanley had paid for Junior's two years of community college. Junior had been fired from both Ford and Chrysler because he had been unable to adjust to working on the line. After a series of low-paying jobs, he had finally found a job selling new cars for Joe 'Madman' Stuart Chrysler in Detroit. The last time Stanley had talked to his son on the phone, the boy had been on the verge of tears. Junior worked for an unrealistic and demanding sales manager who'd had an old-fashioned cardboard outhouse built, complete with a cutout quarter moon on the door. The salesman with the lowest sales each week had to stay seated in the 'shithouse' during the weekly sales meetings and pep talks. Any salesman who ended up in the shithouse for three weeks in a row was fired automatically. Junior spent one or two meetings a month in this mock-up and had barely escaped the terminal third week on two different occasions. For some time, it had been in the back of Stanley's mind to suggest to Junior that he move down to Florida when he got fired, as he was bound to be sooner or later, so he could get a fresh start in life. But that was out now. And if Junior fell behind in the rent payments, Stanley would have him evicted. It was just a token rent he paid anyway; the Hamtramck house should be renting for $325, or even $350 a month.

After breakfast, Stanley got a notebook from the desk and made a list of things he had to do. He used to make a similar list first thing every morning when he had worked in the Ford paint shop, and the methodical planning of his days there had worked well for him since.

First, he would close his bank account, move to another bank, and put the account in his name only. He would also cash in his three ten-thousand-dollar CDs and pay the early-withdrawal penalty. He could then take out three new CDs under his own name. He hated to lose money to the penalty, but if Maya cashed any of them he would lose every cent.

Should he buy a new car? No, he could wait on that for a while. The municipal bus ran into downtown Riviera Beach every hour, and he could ride it into town. He had never been without a car, as far back as he could remember, but he could watch the list of repossessed cars that the banks posted every week until a good deal came along. It didn't pay to rush into buying a car, whether it was new or used. And maybe a used car would be the best buy after all. It was the same when Saul, Maya's old Airedale, died. She had wanted to buy a new puppy to replace the old dog, but he had reminded her that at their age any dog they bought now would probably outlive them and that there would be no one left to take care of it when they were gone. Stanley had hated the flatulent Saul and didn't want another stinking dog hanging around the house and begging at the table. At his age, he wouldn't outlast a new car, either, so why not buy a cheaper, secondhand one?

On the way back from the bank he would stop at the supermarket and buy a dozen or so TV dinners. They were simple to fix. All he had to do was put them into the toaster oven for twenty-five minutes at 425° and his dinner would be ready. He had often asked Maya why she didn't fix TV dinners instead of preparing time-consuming meals from scratch every day, but she wouldn't hear of it. Probably because she didn't know what else to do with her time, he supposed.

Before going into town he would do his laundry, and when he came back he could put it into the dryer. There was nothing to that. He knew how to use the washer and the dryer. Then, while the laundry was drying, he could go down to the park and tell the Wise Old Men that he was a bachelor now.

Stanley's mind froze.

They would know that already. They would also know by now that he had been arrested as a child molester. He was innocent, of course, but Sergeant Sneider had told him that there were two other old geezers involved with Pammi, and it was quite possible that one, or both, of them were Wise Old Men. Whoever it was would lay low now, but any man once accused – as he was, even though he was innocent – would always be suspect. He didn't think any of the Wise Old Men would actually say anything to him about it, but they would think about it – and figure it was him – and he didn't want to sit there while they looked at him sideways and speculated about his guilt. No, it would be a long time before he could go to the park again – if ever. On the other hand, the longer he stayed away from the park, the more they would consider him guilty.

He couldn't win either way.

Stanley separated his clothes from Maya's and put her dirty clothing into a brown-paper grocery bag. He sure as hell wasn't going to wash *her* things. When she got around to sending for her clothes, he would pack them up and send them to her dirty. He looked through the pockets of his bloodied shirt and came across the news clipping Troy Louden had handed him. He hadn't forgotten about it; he had merely put it out of his mind, which wasn't the same thing. This errand had priority over everything else he had to do, but he was reluctant to deliver a message like that. It wouldn't do the young man any good. But he had said that he would do it, so he might as well. There was a Big 5 writing tablet on Maya's desk. Stanley printed out the message in block letters:

IF YOU DON'T DROP THE CHARGES, I'LL KILL YOUR BABY AND YOUR WIFE AND THEN YOU.

The printed message looked sinister all right, but it also looked unreal. Stanley then printed ROBERT SMITH under the message and sealed it in one of Maya's pastel-pink envelopes, along with the clipping. Then he printed Collins's address on the envelope. There was only one Henry Collins listed in the West Palm Beach section of the phone book.

Even if the message didn't help Troy, it couldn't hurt him any. If Mr Collins brought it in to the police station, Troy could deny that he sent it. How could he? He was in jail. Stanley put the sealed envelope into his hip pocket, collected his checkbook, certificates of deposit, and passbook, but he paused at the door. It was eight A.M., and the sun was blazing. He put on his billed cap and his sunglasses, and got his walking stick from the umbrella stand beside the door, but still he hesitated. Mrs Agnew was out in her yard, watering the oleanders that grew close to her house. She would turn her back on him the moment he stepped outside. He could count on that. But all the other neighbors on the two-block walk to the bus stop would peer through their windows and point him out as the dirty old man who had molested little Pammi Sneider. Except by sight, Stanley didn't know his neighbors very well. But Maya knew them all because they often met at each other's houses in the morning when the bakery truck stopped on their street. The housewives would come out in their wrappers and buy sweet rolls and doughnuts and take turns meeting in each other's houses for coffee. Maya had picked up gossip this way about the various neighbors, and had often tried to tell him about how Mrs Meeghan's dyslexic son was failing in school, or about Mr Featherstone's alcoholism (he was a house painter), but Stanley had always cut her off. He didn't care anything about these people, didn't know them, didn't want to know them, and didn't want to know anything about them. If they had been men he worked with, or something like that, he might have been interested in their private doings, but he wasn't interested in these housewives or their husbands or their noisy children.

But he realized now that these women would be gossiping about him and about Maya's leaving him, because that's what they did best – pry into other people's lives. Stanley steeled himself and walked to the bus stop, without looking either to the right or the left.

Stanley got off at the Sunshine Plaza Shopping Center when the bus stopped in front of the Publix. The bank wasn't open yet, so he drank a cup of coffee in Hardee's and slipped a dozen packets of Sweet 'N Low into his pants pocket. When the bank opened (it was really a Savings & Loan Association, but it also operated as a bank), Stanley had no trouble cashing in his CDs and collected a cashier's check for the money in his savings and checking accounts. He had expected an argument. But why would they argue? They made a handsome profit off him when he cashed in his three one-year CDs early. As he left the bank officer's desk, Mr Wheeler said:

'We're sorry to lose you as a client, Mr Sinkiewicz, but I suppose you need your money for bail –'

'Bail? What're you talking about?'

'It was on the radio this morning – your, ah, trouble, and all, you know. So I assumed you required funds for a lawyer, and to post bond.'

'No.' Stanley shook his head. 'That matter was all a mistake. It's all cleared up now.'

'I'm glad to hear it, Mr Sinkiewicz,' Mr Wheeler said, smiling. 'It was a pleasure to serve you.'

Stanley walked over to U.S. 1 and waited for the bus to West Palm Beach. He realized now that all the time he had been talking to Mr Wheeler, the banker had been staring at the bandage on his lip. He had probably wanted to ask about it, but didn't have the nerve. And all the time, Wheeler figured he was dealing with a child molester out of jail temporarily, on bail. If there had been something about his arrest on the radio, maybe there had been something on the local TV newscast, too. Stanley felt his heart pound again, and he slumped on the bus-stop bench.

The bus came at last, and he rode into West Palm Beach, getting off at the downtown Clematis Street stop. He deposited his cashier's check of $38,314.14 in a money-market checking account and withdrew fifty dollars with his new temporary checkbook before leaving the new S & L. Interest rates on CDs had dropped, and he could earn almost as much interest in the new money-market account as he could from buying new CDs. Besides, he wanted to have his money readily available in case he wanted to buy a car. He also filled out forms to have his U.A.W. pension and Social Security checks transferred to his new account.

Before leaving the S & L, he asked the young woman who had opened his new account how to get to Spring Street, in West Palm Beach. She gave him complicated directions that would entail two bus transfers, and he couldn't understand what she was talking about. Being without a car gave a man an entire new way of looking at the world. He thought he knew West Palm fairly well, just from driving around and going to the library, but he didn't know it at all when it came to public transportation. He walked to the Greyhound bus station and got a Veteran's cab. The driver, a black man wearing a woman's nylon stocking cap with a little topknot in it, didn't know where Spring Street was, either. He had to call the dispatcher on his radio for directions. It was a three-fifty ride to Mr Collins's house, where Stanley got out and told the driver to wait for him.

Collins's house was a two-bedroom, lemon-colored concrete-block-and-stucco building on a short dead-end street with eleven other houses constructed from the same plans. A pudgy young woman was listlessly spreading sand on a dying front lawn. There was a baby, eighteen months or perhaps two years old, in a plain pine playpen on the front porch. The barefooted woman wore faded blue shorts and a lime-colored elastic tube top. The pile of yellow sand was about six feet high, and she was taking a small shovelful at a time from the pile and sprinkling it awkwardly on the lawn. She was perspiring freely. Stanley checked the house number against the address on the envelope.

'Excuse me. You Mrs Collins?'

She nodded, a little out of breath, and looked incuriously from Stanley to the cab, then back at Stanley. The driver had his door open and was reading a comic book that had Bugs Bunny on the cover.

'Is Mr Collins home?'

She shook her head. 'No, he ain't. He's out gettin' estimates on the car. He had a accident yesterday, and he has to get three estimates before he can go to the insurance company for the money. At least that's what they told him on the phone. Tomorrow he has to go back up to Jax, so he has to get the car fixed today. I don't know when he'll get home.'

Stanley felt a great sense of relief. It was much easier this way, dealing with a young woman instead of a truck driver. 'I don't have to see your husband, Mrs Collins. I found this envelope downtown on Clematis Street. I figured it might be important, and since there wasn't any stamp on it, I got a cab and brought it on out.' He tried to hand the woman the envelope, but she wouldn't take it.

'I'm pretty busy right now, and I can't spend no time listening to you tryin' to sell me something. I'm tryin' to spread some of this sand around this mornin' before it gets too hot, and it's almost too hot to be out here now.'

497

'You better take it. I don't want nothing for my trouble, but as you can see, the meter's ticking on my cab, so I can't stay and talk with you.'

She dropped the shovel on the ground, wiped the palms of her hands on her shorts, and took the envelope. As Stanley started to back away, she tore it open and frowned as she read the short message. She looked up, puzzled, and started to unfold the news clipping.

'I don't understand this at all. Who are you?'

'I'm a retired foreman,' Stanley said, pausing beside the taxi, 'and I was shopping downtown when I found that envelope, that's all. All I am, I guess, is a good Samaritan. But I'll tell you something else I've learned living down here in Florida. If it was chinch bugs and army worms that killed your lawn, sand won't get rid of them. You'll have to get an exterminator out here to spray your lawn, and it'll run you about thirty-five dollars.'

Stanley tapped the driver's comic book with the end of his stick, got into the back seat of the cab, and closed the door. Mrs Collins rushed over. 'Just a minute! What's all this mean? I don't understand what this is all about!'

'I don't know either,' Stanley said, pushing down the door lock. 'It's addressed to your husband, so maybe he knows. Let's go, driver.'

The driver closed his door, put down his comic book, and made a U-turn back toward Pierce Avenue. The woman stayed at the curb, staring at the retreating cab for a moment, and then unfolded the clipping again.

Stanley caught the bus back to Riviera Beach and got off at the International Shopping Mall. He watched a demonstration class of middle-aged aerobic dancers perform in the plaza section for about a half-hour, then had a slice of pizza and a Diet Coke at Cozzoli's while he waited for the movies to open at one o'clock. He got an Early Bird ticket and sat through two showings of *The Terminator* before coming out into the mall again. Because of daylight-saving time, it still wasn't dark enough to go home, so he wandered around the mall until the nine P.M. bus left for Ocean Pines Terraces.

It had been awful to walk those two blocks that morning, with all the neighbors looking at him, so he wanted to make certain it was dark before he went home. He was exhausted from the long day, and he had missed his afternoon nap. There was so much shooting going on in the movie, he hadn't been able to sleep in the theater, either. Stanley went to bed and fell asleep immediately. He forgot to put the damp wash in the dryer, and the next morning the laundry was covered with mildew and he had to wash it all over again.

Chapter Seven

That afternoon, after taking his nap, Hoke knocked on the door of each occupied apartment and introduced himself as the new manager. The schoolteacher, a Ms Dussault, had already left the island to spend a month of her summer vacation with her parents in Seffner, Florida. One of the Alabama couples claimed that their toilet kept running after it was flushed. Hoke showed them – both of them – how to jiggle the handle to make it stop.

'And if that doesn't stop it,' Hoke said, 'take off the lid, reach down in there, and make sure that the rubber stopper's covering the drain.'

'That's inconvenient,' the woman said. Her tiny lips were pursed, and her abundance of hair had recently been blued.

'That may be,' Hoke said, 'but if I called a plumber out here for thirty-seven dollars and fifty cents an hour, he'd tell you the same thing.'

'At the rentals you all charge, we shouldn't have to spend five minutes or so jiggling the handle every time we use the bathroom.'

'I can move you to another apartment if you like. But you've been living here for two weeks already, and if I move you, you'll have to pay a thirty-five-dollar cleaning charge for moving before your two months' rent are up.'

'That's all right, Mr Moseley,' the woman's husband said quickly. 'I don't mind jiggling the handle.'

Hoke used his passkey to check Ms Dussault's apartment, and turned off her water heater. He made a note in his policeman's notebook to turn it on again a day before she would return. The salad man wasn't home, but the college professor was in. He wanted to talk, and Hoke had a difficult time getting away from him. He was a tall, rather stooped Ohioan in his middle thirties, with long chestnut hair in a ponytail down his back, secured by some rubber bands. He wore a 'Go 'Gators' T-shirt, blue-denim cutoffs, and Nike running shoes without socks. He said his name was Ralph Hurt, but everyone at the University of Florida called him Itai, because *itai* meant 'hurt' in Japanese. He had once spent an entire year in a Zen monastery in Kyoto, and had talked so much about his experiences in Japan that his colleagues in his department had come up with the nickname. Itai had a year's sabbatical leave at three-quarters pay, to write a novel.

'You teach English, then? My dad told me you were a biology teacher.'

'I am. But I couldn't get a grant to do the research in my field, so I told the board I'd write a novel instead. Sabbaticals are given out on a seniority basis anyway, so the board didn't give a rat's ass what I did so long's I put something down on paper as a project. So I said I'd write a novel, and now I'll have to write one to have something to show my department chairman when I get back. It doesn't have to be a publishable novel, although that would be nice, but I'm going to have to come up with two or three hundred pages of fiction.'

'What is your field?'

'Ethiopian horseflies. I'm probably the only American authority on Ethiopian horseflies. Most of the original work on Ethiopian Tabanidae was done by Bequaret and Austen, back in the late twenties, but these early studies were incomplete. Other hotshots in the field are Bigot, Gerstaeker, and, of course, Enderlein, but there's still a lot to be done. And there hasn't been much recently. The problem, you see, is that these flies can be as troublesome after they die as they are in life. The fact that the fly is only caught in the act of aggression seems to lead to a lamentable display of force by collectors.'

'You mean it's slapped down on when it bites?'

'Exactly. As a consequence, it's almost impossible to get an Ethiopian *Haematopta* intact, you see. What I really wanted to do was to go to northern Ethiopia and do my own collecting. There's only so much a man can learn from plates, and I only have a half-dozen preserved specimens up at Gainesville to study. A man could

501

write a long and very important book on wing variations alone, if he had the specimens. But I've only got one wing specimen that's halfway intact. I didn't know you were so interested in horseflies, Mr Moseley.'

'I'm not. But I guess it must be an important field of study.'

'It is, definitely. There's no such thing as a group of immaculately preserved specimens, and until there is, all we have is a somewhat spurious appearance of accuracy in the studies published so far. At any rate, in lieu of going to Africa, I have to write a fucking novel to get my year off. Please excuse me. Sometimes I don't watch my language, although I'm careful around students.'

'I don't always watch mine either,' Hoke admitted.

'The novel's coming along, though. I'm writing about a college professor at Gainesville, a history professor, who's having an affair with one of his students – an orthodontist's daughter from Fort Lauderdale. She works part-time in a wicker-furniture factory, and they meet there at night to make love.'

'Does she have bad teeth?'

'Yes. How'd you know that?'

'I don't know, but it seems to me I've already read a novel like that in a paperback – or maybe it was a movie?'

'You must be mistaken, Mr Moseley. This is a true story, based on my own experiences. But I've disguised it by making the hero a history professor instead of an entomologist. The girl actually worked in a seat-cover shop – for cars – and her father was a peridontist, not an orthodontist.'

'That's a fairly thin disguise.'

'You're probably right, but entomologists aren't expected to be particularly inventive. The manuscript won't be publishable anyway, and the department chairman won't even read it, so it doesn't matter. He'll just count the pages, and if there're more than two hundred he'll be satisfied. Writing it, though, is a kind of therapy for me. I'm lonely down here, and I'd much rather be in Ethiopia, collecting. Maybe you can come down some evening and have a drink? I can tell you a lot more about horseflies, or we can talk a little about Zen –'

'I don't think so. My father owns the El Pelicano, and he told me he'd rather not have me socializing too much with the tenants.'

'That's absurd. Well, take these along anyway.' The professor got a three-volume set of H. Oldroyd's *The Horse Flies (Diptera: Tabanidae) of the Ethiopian Region* from the pile of books beside his desk and handed them to Hoke. The three books were heavy; altogether, Hoke figured, they weighed ten or twelve pounds.

'I'll get these back to you as soon as I can, Dr Hurt.'

'Itai. Just call me Itai, and there's no hurry. If you have any questions, I'm home most of the time, at least when I'm not on the beach.'

Hoke returned to his apartment and put the three volumes on his dining table, a small, round affair with a green Formica surface and aluminum legs. There were four straight chairs with foam rubber seats, covered with plastic sheeting, and they too had aluminum legs. The floor was covered with brown linoleum with a square tile design, with narrow beige lines that were supposed to look like grout. There were no rugs in any of the apartments, because sand would get into the carpeting as the tenants came in from the beach, and there was no daily maid service to vacuum up. There was a narrow galley (it wasn't big enough to be called a kitchen), with a Formica counter between it and the living-bedroom. Two sturdy oak stools stood at the counter. The bathroom had a shower but no tub, and this room was so narrow that when Hoke sat on the toilet his knees touched the wall. The two single Bahama beds were in one corner of the living room, with the top third of one bed pushed beneath a square coffee table that held a clear glass lamp, two feet high, filled with seashells. When the El Pelicano was a hotel, only one door was required, but now Florida law required two doors for apartments. When Frank converted the rooms into efficiency apartments, he had added the extra door right next to each entrance door, but this useless exit was blocked inside each apartment by the dining table. The two doors, the galley, and the windows took up most of the wall space on three sides. There was room enough on the remaining wall, however, for a picture. The framed print, a cheap reproduction of Winslow Homer's *The Gulf Stream*, was the same in all eight apartments, and was bolted to the wall to prevent its theft. Also bolted to the wall and chained in the galley were a toaster oven and an electric can-opener. Like the picture, these were highly pilferable items. A window air conditioner occupied the bottom half of one window, but the view of the ocean from the other window by the Bahama bed was excellent. Hoke usually sat at the table instead of the counter, because when he looked up he liked to see the semi-naked black man lying in the damaged boat floating in the current. The black man seemed indifferent to his fate, whatever it was going to be, and appeared to be contented with his hopeless condition, drifting along with the Gulf Stream.

The stew in the big iron pot, simmering on the small stove, smelled wonderful to Hoke, but although he was hungry he planned to put off eating for as long as possible. If he ate too early, it would be a long time until breakfast, and he was limiting himself to only one bowlful.

Hoke opened Volume I of *Horse Flies of the Ethiopian Region* and read the introduction. He didn't understand most of the technical terms, but the plates in the book were beautifully delineated, with an attention to detail that seemed painstakingly precise. By studying the plates closely, Hoke could see what Dr Hurt – Itai – meant by damaged specimens. Some of the segments on the antennae were missing, and so were parts of the legs. The delineator had not guessed, or filled in the missing parts, but that, Hoke supposed, was what real science was all about.

In science, if it wasn't there, you couldn't just guess at something and fill it in, whereas detective work was just the opposite. You took what you had, the facts you could find, and then tried your best to fill in those missing parts until you came up with a complete picture. Well, he wouldn't have to worry about detection any longer. No more guesswork. These books, which he had been so reluctant to accept, were just the right sort of reading. He could read them when he didn't feel like working out a chess problem (after he got settled in, he planned to buy a board and chessmen and a book of problems), and he wouldn't get emotionally involved with the horseflies. He might have to buy a biology dictionary, however, to learn the definitions of some of the special words entomologists used. Maybe Itai had one; if so, he could borrow the professor's, a little later on –

There was a knock on the door, a rat-tat-tat of one knuckle.

Hoke opened the door, and there was his daughter Aileen. She exposed her crooked, overlapping white teeth in a wide grin. She was wearing jeans, a pink T-shirt, and tennis shoes. As she encircled Hoke's naked waist to hug him, and stood on tiptoe to kiss him, Hoke pulled back and looked over her shoulder.

'Did Ellita drive you up, or what?'

'I drove up myself. I didn't have any trouble at all.'

'But you don't have a license!'

'Sure I do!' Aileen giggled and put her leather drawstring purse on the table. She opened the drawstring, found her wallet, took out a Florida driver's license, and handed it to her father.

'This is Sue Ellen's license,' Hoke said. 'If a trooper'd stopped you, you couldn't have passed as your sister. You girls don't look anything alike.'

'But I wasn't stopped, Daddy. Now that I've proved I can drive, you ought to help me get a learner's permit so I can at least drive around in the daytime.'

'I don't want you driving yet, honey, you aren't aggressive enough to drive in Florida. Where'd you park my car?'

'Over there – in the mall lot.'

'Give me the keys. I'll move it to the manager's slot next to the entrance.'

After they got the car, and Hoke reparked it by the entrance, he asked her what were in all of the cardboard boxes in the back seat.

'I brought my things, too, Daddy, along with stuff for you. I'm going to stay with you for the rest of your leave.'

'Who told you that?'

'We had a family conference, me, Ellita, and Sue Ellen. Sue Ellen's got her job at the car wash, and Ellita'll be having her baby soon, so I had to be the one – and I *wanted* to be the one – to come up and look after you. Besides, Ellita's mother's going to move in before the baby comes.'

'I can take care of myself. You girls are going out to California to live with your mother.'

'No.' Aileen shook her head. 'We voted against that. Sue Ellen decided she isn't going back to school in September. She's sixteen and she's got a good job, so she can drop out legally. We don't want to live with Mom and Curly Peterson. And you know that Curly doesn't want us around.'

'Just take what you need upstairs, and we'll leave the rest of the stuff in the car for now.'

'Won't someone break in and steal them?'

'This is Singer Island, not Miami. Besides, there's no room for all of that stuff upstairs. When your grandfather converted the hotel to apartments, he had to use the closets for kitchens. So except for a few hooks by the galley doorway, and that little alcove in the bathroom, there isn't much room to store anything.'

Aileen paused in the small lobby, holding her train case in her right hand. 'What about the room behind the counter, Daddy?'

'That was the old office, when this place was a hotel. It's full of odds and ends now, a couple of rollaway beds and some other crap.'

'If I cleaned it out I could make it into a bedroom, or we could store some of our stuff there.'

'Never mind the "we." You can stay tonight, but I'm sending you back on the bus tomorrow.'

'I'm not going back. You need someone to look after you; we decided.' She walked into the apartment ahead of him. 'I know you aren't sick, or anything like that, but you're still acting funny, and Ellita doesn't want you living all by yourself.'

'What I do is none of Ellita's business.'

'She's your partner, Daddy, and she's concerned about you.'

'I'm quitting the department. I already told her that. I just haven't put my papers in yet because I've had a lot of other things to do. So Ellita won't be my partner much longer.'

Aileen began to leaf through the books on the table. 'These books are all about Ethiopian horseflies.'

'I know. I've been studying them.'

'Horseflies? I don't know, Daddy. You say you're all right and all that, and I believe you because you look fine – rested and all. But if I called Ellita and told her you were studying a three-volume set of books on Ethiopian horseflies, I think she'd be up here like a shot –'

'Don't get smart. There's a college professor who lives here, and he lent them to me for a few days. He's writing a novel.'

'Really? What about?'

'It's about – I haven't read any of it. But don't bother him about it, either. A man writing a novel doesn't want to be bothered by some nosy kid asking a lot of dumb questions.'

'Okay, Daddy, I won't say anything to him. That stew smells awful good.'

'I guess you want some stew, too.' Hoke said it in a way that would let her think he didn't care whether she ate any of it or not – but he did care. Aileen never seemed to gain any weight, but she was a voracious eater, so he knew she would want at least two helpings of stew. There went his plan. The stew wouldn't last two people for any five meals, and Aileen always ate a substantial lunch, too. And she liked to eat sweet things between meals. He didn't know what to do with the girl. He hated the idea of calling his ex-wife and asking her to take Aileen back – especially if Sue Ellen refused to go, too. Sue Ellen was bullheaded, and if he insisted that she return to her mother, Sue Ellen might just move out of the house and find a room somewhere in Miami. She was already making more than $150 a week at the Green Lakes Car Wash, and if she started to work overtime on Saturdays she would be more than able to support herself. But at sixteen, Sue Ellen shouldn't be living all by herself in Miami. Christ, how in the hell could a man simplify his life?

Aileen came up behind him, put her long arms around his waist, and rubbed her cheek on his hairy back. 'I missed you, Daddy. I – we were all so worried about you. But you're going to be fine. I'll take good care of you, you'll see.'

'I'm fine now. Just look in the cupboard above the sink, and set the table. You'll find plastic plates, two plastic bowls, and some wooden-handled silverware in the drawer beside the sink. So set the table, and I'll dish up the stew.'

After they finished eating, Aileen excused herself and left the apartment, saying that there was something she needed in the car. She was gone for more than fifteen minutes. While she was gone, Hoke put the leftover stew in the refrigerator and washed the dishes and silverware. When she came back empty-handed, Hoke asked what it was she had forgotten in the car.

'Chewing gum.' She opened her mouth to show him the gum. 'But while I was downstairs I took the old broom that was behind the counter and swept the lobby. It really needed it, and so do the hallways, upstairs and down.'

'Jesus.' Hoke shook his head. He remembered then that on top of acting as a rental agent, he was also responsible for keeping the apartment house clean; for keeping the small lawn mowed; and for checking that all of the garbage was put into the dumpster outside, if and when the tenants left stuff lying around. Maybe it might not be a bad idea to keep Aileen around for two or three days until he could get things policed up, and *then* he could send her back to Miami.

Aileen took her Monopoly game out of one of the cardboard boxes she had brought upstairs earlier and began to set it up on the dining table. 'Let's play some Monopoly, Daddy. What do you want to play? The slow game or the fast game?'

'The slow, regular game, I guess. What's the hurry?'

Chapter Eight

After Stanley rewashed the laundry and put it into the dryer, he sat in his recliner and wondered what to do with himself. He had forgotten to stop at the supermarket to buy the TV dinners, but there were all kinds of canned goods in the storage cabinet. There were also eggs, milk, hamburger, and a few tomatoes in the refrigerator, so he could get by without going to the market for a few days.

He didn't want to leave the house and have people stare at him and whisper. Perhaps one of the Wise Old Men would come by and offer him some moral support? He dismissed this thought at once. He had never invited any of the old men to his house, and none of them had invited him to visit them either. Most of these retirees were a lot like him, he supposed. Their wives ran them out so they could clean up, and the park had just been a place to go – either there, or one of the malls. Stanley didn't have a close relationship with any one of them.

As he had gotten older, Stanley recalled, especially after he had been assigned full-time to the paint shop, he had lost most of the friends he once had on the line. He had lost interest in drinking beer in a noisy tavern. It was more comfortable to sit at home in his underwear, and a lot cheaper to drink a six-pack at home after work. The number of men he had known well dwindled as many of them were replaced by robots; and the new employees were all so much younger than Stanley that he hadn't had anything in common with them. The new men had called him Pop, or sometimes Grandpop, but they hadn't asked him to go bowling with them after work. At one time, Stanley had been keen on bowling, but he hadn't bowled a line now in – hell, it must be fifteen years, at least. In fact, he had given his bowling ball to Junior when he left Hamtramck for Florida.

In other ways, it was kind of pleasant to have the house to himself in the morning. He certainly didn't miss Maya. He didn't have to leave the house and wander around for hours. He could watch *Donahue* himself if he wanted to, instead of getting Maya's secondhand opinion about what the people had said that morning about sexual deviance. He had never been satisfied with her summaries; she always seemed to leave out something important or get it wrong somehow.

He decided he would do all his shopping at night. The market was open until eleven, and the bus ran until ten. In the late evening, he would be much less likely to run into any of his neighbors at the supermarket.

Stanley got his deck of Jumbo index playing cards and laid them out for a game of Klondike on the kitchen table. With the big numbers, he didn't need to wear his reading glasses. He played for almost an hour before he tired of the game, but he didn't beat the cards a single time. There were ways to cheat and win, but Stanley never cheated because he would only be cheating himself.

At ten-thirty the mail came. Stanley waited until the postman got to the next house before opening the door. There was another offer for supplementary insurance for people on Medicare (he got one or two of these solicitations a week) and a circular from Sneider's Union Station offering a free car wash with an $11.95 oil-and-lube job. If he still had the Escort, he would have taken Sneider up on that one, but Maya had the car. No catalogs today. Sometimes Maya received a short letter from one of the grandchildren, usually asking for something or other, which she immediately bought and mailed to them. But Stanley never got any personal mail. He no longer read the children's begging letters either, because they made him so angry. Louise, Junior's wife, encouraged her kids to write Maya and ask for things, Stanley suspected, because brand names were never misspelled, unlike the longer, and even shorter, words in their letters.

Stanley tossed the mail in the trash can. He folded the dry laundry and put it away. The blood on his shirt hadn't washed out altogether, so he put it back into the hamper. He would rewash it a third time the next time he did the laundry, and if it didn't come out then he'd just throw it away. He had plenty of shirts.

Finally it was noon, so he could fix lunch. He heated a bowl of tomato soup, but he wasn't hungry. When Maya fixed it, she put whipped cream in it, but there wasn't any Cool Whip in the refrigerator. He didn't finish the soup. By the time he washed the saucepan and his bowl and spoon, it was only twelve-thirty. Stanley changed the sheets on his twin bed and put the dirty sheets into the hamper. He took a long shower, put on clean underwear, and stretched out on his sweet-smelling bed for a nap. With the venetian blinds closed and the window air conditioner turned to High-Cool, he fell asleep almost immediately.

He was awakened at five by the telephone. When he heard the phone he didn't know how long it had been ringing. It was on the kitchen wall, and Stanley, who was wearing his socks but not his shoes, slipped on the terrazzo floor and almost fell when he rushed to answer it. He picked up the receiver.

'Hello.'

There was no answer.

'Hello. Who is this?'

The person at the other end hung up. Stanley hung up, too. He hated it when people did that. If they had a wrong number he expected them to say so, not just hang up without a word. But what if it was intentional? Someone trying to harass him. He could expect that – if someone thought he was a child molester. Well, he wouldn't let that bother him ... but it *did* bother him. He poured a six-ounce can of prune juice into a glass, added ice cubes, turned on the television, and watched a rerun of *Kojak*. He had missed the first few minutes, and it was one he hadn't seen before.

A little after six, just after the news came on, a taxi pulled up outside and stopped at the curb. Stanley went to the window, then hurried to open the front door as Troy Louden came up the walk.

'Evening, Pop. Let me have a five, will you? I've got to pay the cabbie.'

Stanley took out his wallet and gave Troy a five-dollar bill.

'Better give me one more, Pop – for a tip.'

Troy paid the driver and then came back to the house.

'Sit down, sit down, Troy,' Stanley said, indicating the recliner and switching off the TV. 'It's good to see you, son! I delivered your message, the way you said, even though I didn't want to. Mr Collins wasn't at home though, so I gave it to his wife.'

'I know, Pop, that's why I'm here. To thank you. The message was just an empty threat, but it worked out just like I told you it would. Collins came down to the lock-up and told them that he'd been mistaken. The knock on his head had confused him, and being dazed that way, he only *thought* I had a gun. The sergeant wasn't too happy about it, but Collins had this bandage on his head so he couldn't say that Collins had intentionally filed a false arrest charge, either. When they let me out, I told the sergeant I wanted to see Collins and tell him there was no hard feelings, but he'd already left. Did you tell Mrs Collins your name? When you talked to her, I mean?'

'No, I just told her I was a messenger.'

'Did you get my clipping back?'

'She kept it. I guess she showed it to Mr Collins when he got home. He was out getting insurance estimates for his car.'

'That's okay, Pop. It was a nice little story, but I've still got a few more clippings.'

'Would you like some coffee, Troy? I don't have any beer, but –'

'Coffee'll be fine, but let me fix it. You had dinner yet?'

'I was going to wait till after the news.'

'Watch the news, then. I'll fix dinner for both of us, and you stay out here while I work in the kitchen. Hell, that's the least I can do for you.'

Instead of watching the news on television, Stanley sat at the pass-through counter while Troy prepared dinner. He delivered a bitter diatribe against his wife for leaving him, against his son, and Sergeant Sneider, and his neighbors, and Mr Wheeler at the bank. Troy didn't interrupt him until Stanley told him about the mysterious phone call.

'That must've been me, Pop. I borrowed a phone at the station and called to see if you were here. I didn't have any money for a cab or a bus, but I knew if you were home you'd take care of it. I didn't say anything else because I didn't want the sergeant listening in, you know? Ordinarily, I wouldn't've come directly to your house in a cab, but would've taken the bus, got off a couple of stops away from your house. Cab drivers keep a log, so I can be traced to your address. But inasmuch as I'm leaving for Miami, it won't matter. I didn't want to leave for Miami without thanking you –'

'I'm glad it was you, Troy. I don't like the idea of getting scary calls like that.'

'You still might get a few crank calls, Pop. But don't worry if you do. People who phone instead of facing you in person aren't the ones you have to worry about. You might get some eggs or rocks thrown at your house at night, too. But that'll be teenagers. They'll hear their folks talking, you see, and they'll consider you fair game. But after the word on your innocence gets around, it'll all blow over. That is, if word does get around. It doesn't seem likely that this Sneider guy and his wife will go around the neighborhood telling everyone that their daughter's a prepuberty hooker.'

'I wish you hadn't told me that.'

When dinner was ready, Stanley set the dining-room table. Troy had cooked individual meat loaves, parsley potatoes, and beets *à l'orange*, using a covered bowl of leftover beets he had discovered in the refrigerator. There was no lettuce, but Troy had arranged a decorative pinwheel of alternating tomato and cucumber slices, garnishing the platter with stuffed deviled egg halves. He made eight cups of coffee in the Mr Coffee machine and showed Stanley how to work it in the future.

'Seems to me, Troy,' Stanley said, with his mouth full, 'you can do most anything. I never had to learn how to cook, so I never got around to it.'

'What you need,' Troy advised, 'is a housekeeper. A half-day would be plenty. She could clean your house, fix your breakfast and lunch, and then leave your dinner in the fridge to warm up at night.'

'I couldn't afford that. I'm on a fixed income.'

'Wouldn't cost you much. If you got an illegal Haitian woman, you could pay her a buck an hour and change your luck on the side.'

Stanley put his fork down on his empty plate. He had eaten the beets, a vegetable he detested. 'Know what I been thinking, Troy? I was kinda hoping you'd stay here with me for a while. I've never lived alone before, and I'm just rattling around this house. It's only two bedrooms, and the porch, but it seems like a big place for a man all alone. There's a single bed in the guest room, and you can have that all to yourself. And if you want to find a job of some kind in town, you can live here free. Won't cost you a cent.'

Troy grimaced. 'I don't like the confinement of a steady job, Pop. I thought I explained that to you. I've got a little deal working in Miami, however, which'll bring me in some quick cash – quite a lot of it, if it all works out. But I won't be sure till I get down there and check it out. I'll need to borrow a few dollars from you to get to Miami, for the bus fare, because the desk sergeant advised me to leave town. In fact, he was pretty emphatic about it.'

'I can let you have thirty dollars. That's about all I've got on me now, but if you want to wait till tomorrow I'll cash a check and give you some more. But I sure wish you'd stay with me for a few days. Hard work never hurt nobody, and a smart young fella like you could get a job easy in Riviera Beach –'

'That's enough!' Troy said. The white scar on his forehead had turned pink. 'Who in the fuck are you to tell me how to live? You don't know a damned thing about living. You don't understand your wife, your son, or even how your mind works, and that's because you've never had to use it. I've learned more about living in thirty years than you have in twice that long.' Troy got up from the table, took his coffee into the living room, and sat in the recliner.

The old man followed him and put his hand gingerly on Troy's shoulder. 'I'm sorry, son. I didn't mean to rile you none. You don't have to get a job to stay here. I didn't mean that. I never got along good with my son, but I've been able to talk to you, and I've got enough money coming in each month that the two of us can live here pretty good. I'm worried about you, that's all. Going down to Miami, broke as you are, you might get into some trouble.'

'I might at that.' Troy grinned. 'But I don't think so. If everything works out, I won't need any money for a year or so, maybe longer. But I appreciate the offer. Maybe I'll come back from Miami and spend a few days with you – in a couple of weeks or so. How does that sound?'

'It sounds fine. I'll write my phone number down for you, and you can call me when you're coming and I'll get some steaks and stuff.'

'Good. How about some kind of dessert?' Troy put his cup on the cobbler's bench that served as a coffee table. 'Anything you like. I'll fix it.'

'No thanks, Troy, I'm not much on sweets.'

'Suit yourself.' Troy tapped the cobbler's bench with a forefinger. 'I worked in a shoe repair shop once, a program for young offenders in L.A. I really hated the smell of cobbler's glue.'

'Now that's a good trade –' Stanley started to say something else, but changed his mind.

Troy cleared the table and washed the dishes, pots, and pans. If Troy had asked him to help, Stanley would have been glad to, but the thought of volunteering never occurred to him. Finished, Troy re-entered the living room, drying his hands on a dish towel.

'It's a peculiar thing, old-timer, but a man your age can learn something from me, although it should be the other way 'round. First I'll tell you something about me, and then I'll tell you about you.'

'A man can always learn something new.' Stanley filled his pipe. 'There's an extra pipe if you want to smoke. I don't have no cigarettes.'

'I don't smoke.'

'Smoking is a comfort to a man sometimes. I like to smoke a pipe sometimes after dinner, but I don't smoke during the day –'

'Smoking comforts ordinary men, but I'm not an ordinary man. There aren't many like me left.' Troy drew his lips back, exposing small even teeth. 'And it's a good thing for the world that there isn't. There'll always be a few of us in America, in every generation, because only a great country like America can produce men like me. I'm not a thinker, I'm a doer. I'm considered inarticulate, so I talk a lot to cover it up.

'When you look back a few years, America's produced a fair number of us at that. Sam Houston, Jack London, Stanley Ketchel, Charlie Manson – I met him in Bakersfield once – Jack Black. Did you ever read *You Can't Win*, Jack Black's autobiography?'

'I been a working man most of my life, Troy. I never had much time for reading books.'

'You mean you never *took* the time. I've just named a few men of style, my style, although they'd all find the comparison odious. Know why? They were all individualists, that's why. They all made their own rules, the way I do. But most of us won't rate a one-line obit in a weekly newspaper. Sometimes that rankles.' Troy paused, and his brow wrinkled. 'There was a writer one time … funny, I can't think of his name.' Troy laughed, and shook his head. 'It'll come to me after a while. What I'll do is pretend I don't want to remember it, then it'll come to me. Anyway, this famous writer said that men living in cities were like a bunch of rocks in a leather bag. They're all rubbed up against each other till they're round and smooth as marbles. If they stay in the bag long enough, there'll be no rough edges left, is the idea. But I've managed to keep my rough edges, every sharpened corner.

'But you, old-timer, you're as round and polished as an agate. You've been living in that bag for seventy-one years, man. They could put you on TV as the perfect specimen of American male. You're the son of a Polish immigrant, and you've worked all your life for an indifferent capitalistic corporation. Your son's a half-assed salesman, and you've had the typical, unhappy sexless marriage. And now, glorious retirement in sunny Florida. The only thing missing is a shiny new car in the driveway for you to wash and polish on Sundays.'

'I've got a car, Troy! A new Escort, but Maya took it when she left.'

'I'm not running you down, Pop. I like you. But life has tricked you. You fell into the trap and didn't know you were caught. But I'm a basic instinctive man, and that's the difference between us. Instinct, Pop.' Troy lowered his voice to a whisper. 'Instinct. You've survived, but mere existence isn't enough. To live, you have to be aware, and then follow your inclinations wherever they lead. Don't care what others think about you. Your own life is the only important thing, and nothing else matters. Want some more coffee?'

'I better not. I got me a little bladder problem. If I drink more than one cup it gets me up at night.'

Troy got another cup of coffee. He returned to the living room and grinned at the puzzled expression on the old man's face.

'If I were in your shoes, Pop, I'd enjoy the situation. Quit feeling sorry for yourself. All of a sudden you've departed from the norm, and now people are noticing you. Yet you're upset because your neighbors are disturbed. Why should you worry about what they say or think about you? You survivors think you're living out here in Ocean Pines Terraces. What you're doing, you're dying out here.'

'I worked hard all my life, and I was a fine craftsman. I took pride in my work –'

'Did you? You hated it, Pop. You told me you got sick every day from the smell of paint and turpentine, but what about the bathroom back there? Did you get sick when you painted the bathroom?'

'No, but that ain't the same as working on the line.'

'Sure it is. The paint's the same and the smell's the same. But you didn't get sick because you were working for yourself, and you painted it the color you wanted. I don't want to hurt your feelings, but maybe you should take off the blinders. Where's the phone book? I want to find out when the bus leaves for Miami.'

'Right there.' Stanley pointed. 'Under that pile of *Good Housekeeping* magazines, on the counter.'

While Troy looked up the number and called, Stanley's mind raced, trying to think of something to say in his defense. He wanted Troy to have a good opinion of him.

'Two-thirty, Pop. If you'll let me have the thirty bucks now, I'll be on my way.'

'You don't have to leave just yet.' Stanley put his pipe down, looked into his wallet, and handed Troy thirty dollars. 'Sit down awhile, Troy. There's plenty of time. I can always call you another cab when the city buses stop running. I don't want you to think you've hurt my feelings, either. A man don't mind hearing what others think about him, even if they've got it all wrong.'

'I don't, Pop, and I don't care what people think of me.'

'Well, I like to listen to you, anyway. I liked that part about the rocks in a leather bag. That makes a lot of sense. But a man's born where he's born. And if he's raised in a city, he can't help being a city man.'

'I was raised in a city, too. Los Angeles. But if you follow what I'm saying, it's all a matter of awareness and instinct. Today the times are so damned good it's hard to be an individualist. What you should've done, the first time you came home and puked up your guts, was quit striping cars.'

'I couldn't quit, Troy. It was the best job I ever had. I was newly married, too. I guess I can't really explain it, but most people in Detroit'll work for an auto company if they can. The union did a lot for us, too, you know.'

'Have you got an alarm clock? Maybe I'll take a little nap before the bus leaves.'

'Sure, you can sleep in my wife's bed, Troy.' Stanley led the way into the bedroom and switched on the bedside lamp. 'I'll just sit up, and wake you in plenty of time for the bus.'

Troy put his arm around Stanley's shoulders, then dropped it. He pinched the old man's skinny buttocks, and Stanley flinched.

'Ever fool around, Pop? Want to go to bed with me? I wouldn't mind a little round-eye. It'll make me sleep better.'

'No, no.' Stanley shook his head and looked at the floor. 'I never done anything like that.'

Troy shrugged, sat on the side of the bed, and pulled off his boots. 'I won't press you. But I advise you to keep away from little girls. Next time you're liable to land up in Lake Butler. And some of those cons up there would rather have a clean old man than a young boy.' Troy unsnapped the buttons on his shirt. 'If you've got an alarm clock, go to bed. You look like you need some sleep yourself. I won't bother you.'

'I don't need any sleep. I had me a long nap this afternoon. I'll wake you in plenty of time.'

Stanley closed the bedroom door. He poured a cup of coffee and pulled the plug on the machine. If he was going to stay up anyway, the coffee couldn't bother him too much.

What made Stanley uneasy was the way Troy had hit the nail on the head about his alleged allergy to the smell of paint. When Maya had wanted the all-pink bathroom, he had wondered about it at the time. He had enjoyed painting the bathroom, taking his own sweet time, and he had done a beautiful job in there. But the bathroom was small, and he had often worked with the door closed. And he hadn't been sick or nauseated during the three days it took him to complete the job.

But he didn't recall actually hating his job at the plant, either. He'd been too happy to have a good job, especially when a lot of men in his neighborhood had been laid off. There had been days when he had been sore about something or other, but that was only natural with any kind of work. Besides, Troy had never had a regular job, he said. What could he know about the comfort and security it gave a man to know that he had a paycheck coming in every week? With a paycheck, a man could plan things, build up some savings, even buy on credit if he wanted something bad enough. He knew exactly how far the money would go every month. Except for strikes. The budget went to hell then. But after the strike, he would be better off than before, with a higher paycheck and other fringe benefits. Reuther had been a genius; that's probably why they had killed him. There were a lot of things he would like to talk about with Troy if he would only stay a few days ...

At one-thirty, Stanley made a fresh pot of coffee in the Mr Coffee machine. It wasn't so hard. At two he awakened Troy.

'I made some fresh coffee, and I already called for the cab.'

Troy, fully dressed, joined him in the kitchen and poured a cup of coffee.

'What's your all-fired rush to get to Miami, Troy? Staying here a couple of days won't hurt you. If the police don't know you're here, they won't be out here checking on you.'

'I'm not worried about the cops, I'm looking for a fresh stake. I wouldn't mind staying here a couple of days, but I want to visit the West Indies. Sit down a minute, Pop. There's this guy down in Miami I met in New Orleans. He's a Bajan nonobjective painter, and he told me about a job in Miami that could make us both a bundle.'

'What kind of a painter?'

'A Bajan. Barbadian, from the island of Barbados. They call themselves Bajans.'

'I mean the other. Nonobjective, you said.'

'Right. It's different from abstract. In abstract art, part of something is recognizable, but in nonobjective art nothing is.'

'I don't understand –'

'Hell, you told me you were a painter, a striper.'

'I am. But I never heard of nonobjective art. It don't make any sense.'

'Now you've got it. It isn't supposed to make any sense, Pop. But James, that's his name, can't draw worth shit, so he became a nonobjective painter. He's a remittance man, in reverse. His father's a black man, and his mother's white, an Englishwoman. His father owns some kind of catchall store in Bridgetown. Dry goods, English china, peanut butter, and he also has the island concession on two different European cars, James told me. That's the way they work down there. His old man has the peanut butter concession, so anybody wants peanut butter he has to get it from James's father. James is the only legitimate son, although he has a few illegitimate brothers and sisters. When his father made enough money, he went to England and got himself an English wife before he came back.

'James's father wants him to go into business with him, but James talked his family into letting him study painting in the United States. His old man sends him an allowance of two hundred bucks a month, and he keeps this allowance low so that James'll give up painting and come back to Barbados. Evidently, legitimate sons are a premium in Barbados, and having light skin is good for business, too.

'If he wanted to paint on the side, James told me, his old man wouldn't care, but full-time nonobjective painting is too much for his father to tolerate. His aunt sent him some extra dough on his twenty-sixth birthday, and he used it for a sketching trip to New Orleans. I met him on the levee one day. He had a sketchbook, and he was trying to draw the *Dixie Queen*. It was like some little kid drawing. We got to talking, and we became friends. He mentioned this setup in Miami when he learned that I was experienced in that line. He's desperate, you see, to study art in New York at the Art Students League, on Fifty-seventh Street. He thinks if he could get a one-man show in New York, he'd get some recognition, and then he'd never have to go back to Barbados.

'To cut this short, I dropped James a card that I was on my way to Miami, and I'm a few days late already – because of what happened in Jacksonville.'

'What happened in Jacksonville, Troy? You never told me nothing about that.'

'I don't think you want to know about it, Pop. It was just a misunderstanding I had with some guy I met in a bar.'

The cab pulled up at the curb, and the driver honked his horn. Troy opened the front door and waved to the cabbie to let him know he had heard.

'Thanks for everything, Pop. I'll send your money back to you in a few days.'

'Never mind the money, Troy. I – I suppose it's too late for me to go with you, ain't it?' The old man's lower lip quivered.

Troy rubbed the flat place on the bridge of his nose. 'It's never too late to do anything, Pop. I can't promise you anything, but if you want to come to Miami with me, the cab's waiting.'

The cabbie sounded a long blast on his horn. Troy opened the door again. 'Don't blow that horn again.' His voice carried in the night air, and the driver jerked his hands away from the wheel as if it were red-hot.

'I can't go right this minute, Troy. But I can come in a day or so.'

'Get a pencil and paper. I'll give you James's address.'

Stanley got a ballpoint and a piece of paper from Maya's desk. Troy scribbled the address. 'That's James Frietas-Smith, with a hyphen between the names. I've never been there, but the house is in the neighborhood they call Bayside – not far from downtown. There's no phone, so come right out to the house. There's a big house in front, belongs to the Shapiros, and James has the garage apartment in back.'

'I can find it. I can't come today, but Thursday or Friday for sure. At least I'm pretty sure.'

Troy winked and kissed Stanley lightly on the lips. He opened the door, stepped outside, and snapped his fingers. 'Pop! The writer's name. The guy who made the statement about the rocks in the bag. Somerset Maugham, the Englishman. And he lived to be a helluva lot older than you.'

Troy got into the cab, and Stanley turned off his porch light. He wondered if any of his neighbors had seen Troy kiss him, but he didn't much care if they had. It had been a sweet kiss, the way his son had kissed him when he was seven or eight years old and left for school in the mornings. Then one morning Junior had stopped kissing him, and even pulled away when Stanley had tried to hug him. Boys were like that. Junior would still let Maya hug him in the house, but if she tried to kiss or hug him in public, the boy had a fit, and pulled away from her, too. But Troy had liked him well enough to kiss him good-bye, and the old man was touched by it. Well, maybe he would go to Miami, and maybe he wouldn't. Despite what Troy said, a man couldn't do anything he felt like doing without thinking it over first.

Chapter Nine

On Sunday, Hoke and Aileen went to his father's house for dinner. Sunday dinner was always served at three P.M., because the Moseleys usually had a late breakfast and skipped lunch. It was an early dinner for Inocencia, too, so she could finish up and go home to her own family in time to attend evening church services. There was a standing rib roast for dinner, and if anyone got hungry later, they could make sandwiches. Frank had always followed this practice on Sundays, even after he became a widower, and he hadn't changed the tradition when Helen came into his life.

Hoke and Aileen got to the house at one, so Aileen could swim in the pool before dinner. Aileen didn't like to swim in the ocean. She was afraid of jellyfish, and had once been bitten on the toe by a bluefish in Vero Beach. The El Pelicano didn't have a pool, so her grandfather had given her his permission to use his pool any time she wanted to walk the mile and a half to his house on Ocean Road. Frank and Helen rarely swam in their pool, but they had white cast-iron chairs and an umbrella table beside the pool, and they often sat out there in the early evenings to have a drink and watch the traffic on the intracoastal waterway. There was an old back-scarred manatee that often came to the dock in the evenings. When it did, Helen fed it a few heads of iceberg lettuce. Because iceberg lettuce was eighty-nine cents a head, Helen had tried to feed the manatee Romaine, which was much cheaper, but the manatee didn't care much for it, so she had gone back to giving it iceberg. While Aileen splashed in the pool, Hoke looked for the manatee, but it never showed up.

Hoke was wearing a new yellow poplin jumpsuit, tennis shoes, and a pair of Ray-Ban aviator-style sunglasses he had owned for ten years or more. He occasionally missed the tug of his gun at the back of his belt, where he usually wore it, but he no longer carried it, or his badge, or his handcuffs. On the right leg of his jumpsuit there was a square cargo pocket that closed with a zipper, but the outline of the gun was clearly visible when he put it into this pocket, so he had decided to quit carrying his weapon. Inasmuch as he was on leave, and not in Miami, he wasn't required to have his gun on his person at all times. Still, he felt a little funny without it.

Frank was in his den, watching a lacrosse game on cable, and Helen was in the living room. She sat at her fruitwood desk, addressing envelopes and enclosing mimeographed letters requesting donations for the Palm Beach Center for Abused Children. She was on the last few envelopes when Hoke joined her in the living room. He poured three ounces of Chivas Regal at the bar, added two ice cubes, and gave himself a splash of soda. Helen looked over her shoulder and smiled. 'I'm about finished, Hoke. Could you fix me a pink gin, please?'

'Tanqueray or Beefeater?'

'It doesn't make any difference when you add bitters, so I'd just as soon have Gordon's.'

Because it did make a difference, Hoke poured three ounces of Tanqueray into a crystal glass, added ice cubes, and put in a liberal sprinkling of Angostura bitters. He took a cocktail napkin from the stack and put the napkin and drink on the edge of the desk where Helen could reach it.

'Thank you.' Helen sipped her drink. 'This is Tanqueray.'

'There is a difference, then.'

'I know that, but what I meant was that it didn't make any difference to me. There, that's the last of the list. I wanted to have these letters printed, but I was argued out of it. The committee thought if we had them mimeographed instead, the letter would be more convincing as a dire need for funds. In my opinion, mimeographed letters look tacky. I'm not sure anyone'll read them.'

'Copiers are best. A Xeroxed letter looks like the typed original nowadays.'

'I may suggest that to the committee next time, although there's no urgent need for funds. We only have one abused child in the program so far, and we're sending him up to the Sheriff's Boy's

Ranch in Kissimmee for the rest of the summer while his mother dries out in Arizona. She's paying the tab for both ranches, the one in Kissimmee and the one in Tucson.'

'When did you get interested in abused children, Helen?'

'I'm not, really. But I thought I should serve on some kind of committee, and this is less onerous than some of the others. What I really want to get on is the Heart Fund Ball Committee, but there's a waiting list a mile long for that one.'

'I met a man on the beach the other morning, Helen, who told me you still have an apartment at the Supermare. A guy named E. M. Skinner. D'you know him?'

Helen laughed, shook her head, and dampened the flap of an envelope with a sponge. 'I know him all right. He has the pent-house, and he was president of our condo association for almost a year before we got rid of him. When the condo first opened, he was the only owner who wanted to be president, so we all voted for him. But he was a busybody and started making all kinds of foolish rules, so the other members of the board, especially Mr Olsen and Mary Higdon, got him voted out. Mr Olsen's our new president now, and Mr Skinner's no longer even on the board. One of the rules he wanted, for example, was a wristband with your apartment number on it. You were supposed to wear it at the pool at all times. This band, he claimed, would keep tourists and strangers from using our pool without permission. The manager, Mr Carstairs, knows everyone in the building and doesn't need to check a wristband to see if you're a resident or not.' She put her envelopes down. 'But I'm a little annoyed that Mr Skinner told you about me. Why would he tell a stranger he met on the beach that I still have my apartment there?'

'I told him I was Frank's son, that's why. But I was surprised that you still had an apartment there.'

Helen looked toward the hallway, and then lowered her voice. 'I'll tell you a little secret, Hoke, but don't mention it to Frank. Okay?'

'How secret is it?' Hoke sipped his drink. 'Frank and I are a little closer now than we've been in some years, and I don't want to jeopardize our relationship. After all, he's made it possible for me to stay here on the island –'

'I'll tell you, and if you want to tell him you know, it won't hurt him any. It might embarrass him a little, but that's all. When we went to Nassau on our honeymoon we were supposed to get married there, but we didn't. We both needed our death certificates from our former spouses in order to get a license. We didn't bring them along, so we couldn't get a license without them. We'd already sent out announcements that we were married, so we had our honeymoon anyway. Then, while we were there – a week in Nassau's like a month anywhere else, you know – and we got to talking, we decided not to go through with a wedding. After all, what difference would it make? Except for making our lives more complicated legally? In the long run, marriage would cost us both money, you see. Of course, everyone thinks we're married because it was in the newspapers, but by remaining single I still get my homestead exemption on my condo at the Supermare, and he gets an exemption on this house. That saves us twenty-five thousand a year apiece. We also save on our income taxes. They're punitive for married people, as you know. Anyway, that's the secret, or our little secret, and if you want to tell Frank you know, go ahead. But please don't tell anyone else.'

Hoke grinned, leaned over, and kissed Helen on the cheek. 'I'll carry your secret to the grave, Helen. I, too, have lived in sin, and it's better than being married.'

'Sin has nothing to do with it. It's just common sense and economics. I have plenty of money, and I don't need Frank's. We've both made out separate wills, and that'll take care of everything if one of us dies.'

'Inasmuch as Frank is thirty years older than you, it shouldn't make much difference.'

'Frank's in pretty good shape, Hoke.'

'Thanks to you. I was glad when you two got married, Helen. Although I knew about the girlfriend he had in Lantana. He used to see her two or three times a month, even when my mother was still alive.'

'Well, he doesn't have a girlfriend in Lantana any longer. And that's no secret. I put an end to that by threatening to tell her husband.'

Hoke finished his drink and shook his head. 'Don't tell me anything else, Helen. I'm trying to simplify my life, and everything I'm learning today makes it more complicated.'

Helen laughed. 'Let me show you one more secret. Come on. Follow me.'

'Do I need another drink first?'

'No.' She laughed. 'Come here.'

Hoke followed Helen to the kitchen, and then through the kitchen exit to the two-car garage. Helen pointed to a girl's Schwinn ten-speed bicycle that was leaning against the garage wall. The bike was painted Latin red, and there was a brass nameplate on the slanting bar of the frame. THIS BICYCLE WAS MADE ESPECIALLY FOR AILEEN MOSELY was engraved on the brass plate.

'Frank bought it for Aileen so she can ride up here any time she wants and use the pool. Do you think she'll like it?'

'Of course she will. But it'll make it that much harder for me to get rid of her. Oh, I don't mean that the way it sounds. I love Aileen, but I think she should be living with her mother. Now that she has a bike, it'll be that much harder for me to persuade her to go out to California.'

'There's no hurry about that, Hoke. We both think Aileen should stay with you for a while. You've had a difficult time for a few days, and you need her – or someone – with you for a few months. When school starts, she can catch the bus into junior high in Riviera Beach.'

'I don't think Patsy'll take her back anyway. There isn't a helluva lot of room in our efficiency, but she seems happy enough.'

'Why shouldn't she be? I'd've given anything to live alone with my father when I was her age. And in a way, I'm doing that now, living with Frank.' Helen blushed and turned away. 'I hardly ever saw my father when I was a girl. I was away at school most of the time, and he was too busy making money to have any time for me.'

'Well, at least I'm not making any money.' Hoke grinned. 'Apparently the less money you have, the more likely you are to have your children living with you. That ballplayer my ex-wife married makes three hundred and twenty-five thousand dollars a year with the Dodgers.'

They returned to the living room, and Hoke poured a shorter drink. He added ice cubes but skipped the splash of soda. Hoke and Helen were almost the same age, and he had always been comfortable around her, although he had rarely talked to her alone. She was blonde and plump, but not heavy, and she had been a positive influence in his father's life. The old man was thinner and much happier since he married – began living with – Helen. She dressed him better, too. Frank wore slacks and colorful sport shirts now, instead of the wrinkled seersucker suits he had favored, and she had thrown away the black leather bow ties he had worn every day to the store.

'Would you like another pink gin, Helen?'

'I don't think so. We're going to have wine with dinner, so one'll be plenty.'

'When was the last time you visited your condo at the Supermare?'

'About a month ago. Why?'

'Was anything missing? Skinner told me that you had some burglaries there recently. The thief's been hitting the empty apartments.'

'That's the first I've heard about it, but I haven't been going to any of the monthly meetings.'

'Do you have a bolt lock on your door?'

Helen nodded. 'A regular through-the-doorknob lock, and a bolt lock too.'

'If you want me to, I'll check it out for you.'

'I don't keep any jewelry there. Just furniture and furnishings, and a few clothes. Frank and I change clothes there once in a while when we go to the beach. And I have to live there, or be physically present, on January first, to get my homestead exemption.'

'When's the last time you went to the beach?'

Helen laughed. 'About four months ago. During the season. It's too hot for me in the summer.'

'We'd better drop by and check it out.'

'I've got some extra keys. I'll give them to you, and you can drop by some morning when you go swimming. In fact, you can use the apartment any time you like, or swim in the pool. I'll call and tell Mr Carstairs that you're my guest. But Aileen can't use the pool, or even hang around the building. No children are allowed.'

'Don't people there have grandchildren?'

'Sure they do, but they're not allowed to visit. The no-children rule was one of the major selling points for an apartment at the Supermare. A lot of people don't want to have grandchildren around, Hoke, or even their own adult children. Not everyone's like Frank and me.' Helen got the extra keys from the center drawer of her desk and put them into an envelope. She handed the envelope to Hoke, and he dropped it into his front pocket. 'You'd better get Frank now, Hoke. Take him a drink, and by the time he's finished, dinner should be ready.'

'What does he like? He used to drink bourbon on the rocks, or with a little Coke –'

'Give him a Beefeater on the rocks, but put an olive in it. He thinks vermouth ruins a martini.'

'He's right.'

Helen went into the kitchen, and Hoke fixed his father a stiff gin on the rocks. It occurred to him for the first time in his life, as he headed toward the den, that one of these days, if he was lucky, Frank might leave him the El Pelicano Arms in his will. And if he did, he would be able to stay on the island until he died without any more worries. Even if Frank didn't leave him the apartment house, and left everything to Helen, he was sure that Helen would let him stay on as manager.

But he had better prove that he was worthy of the job by renting out those two empty apartments as soon as possible …

Aileen was shown the new bicycle before dinner, and she kissed Frank, Helen, and Hoke. Hoke had told her that she would not be allowed to drive his car again; now she could go almost anywhere she wanted to go on the island with her bicycle.

'I'll get you a basket for the handlebars,' Hoke said, 'and you can do our shopping at the supermarket.'

'I don't need a basket. I can carry groceries under one arm, and steer with one hand.'

529

'Just don't ride through the mall parking lot,' Hoke said. 'A lot of sick Yankees back out without looking, and they might run over you.'

Aileen ate swiftly so she could ride her new bike, but still she put away two helpings of rare roast beef, with mashed potatoes and gravy, before she excused herself from the table.

After dinner, Frank and Hoke went into the den with their coffee. Frank turned on the cable to a women's mud-wrestling match in Buffalo, New York. Frank, who'd only had the cable channels for a few months, had never known about lacrosse, mud wrestling, four-wall volleyball, and knife-, star-, and hatchet-throwing contests until he signed up for cable, so he was still interested in these new – to him – sports. He was also fond of Dr Ruth's sex show in the evenings, and rarely missed her program.

At a quarter to five, Hoke got to his feet. 'I've got to go, Dad. I left a note on my door saying I'd be back at five. Someone might be there looking for an apartment.'

'Stick around, son. There's a man coming over after a while I want you to meet. Let Aileen ride back on her bike; she can tell anyone there to wait for you.'

Hoke found Aileen outside and told her to take herself and her wet bathing suit back to the apartment house.

'If someone's there, you can show them an empty apartment, but tell them to stick around till I get back.'

'I know how to show the apartments, Daddy.'

'I know you do, honey, but I want to screen people. I don't want any Latins to get in there for two months or more. Or some drunk. Okay?'

'What's the matter with Latins? Ellita's a Latin.'

'Nothing's the matter with them, but our efficiencies are for one or two people, not for families of six or more. There're only two single beds, you know.'

Aileen let this pass. 'I put a sack of mangoes in the front seat of the car, Daddy. Helen said we could have all we wanted from the tree in the backyard.'

'Fine. How're the brakes on the bike?'

'I *know* how to ride it, Daddy – and I won't ride through the parking lot.'

Hoke fixed another Scotch and soda in the living room, but he didn't return to the den. He went into the kitchen. Inocencia had cleaned up in there and had gone home. Before leaving she had made four roast beef sandwiches and put them into a sack for Hoke to take home. Hoke took the bag of sandwiches out to his car and put them on the seat next to the mangoes. As he closed the car door, a black Buick Riviera pulled up behind Hoke's Le Mans in the driveway.

'I'm leaving in a few minutes,' Hoke called over to the man who got out of the car. 'So you'd better let me back out first, then you can pull in ahead of me.'

'I'm only going to be here a few minutes myself. You're Sergeant Moseley, aren't you?'

'That's right, but I don't live here. I'm just visiting my dad.'

'You're the man I've come to talk with.' He introduced himself as Mike Sheldon, chief of police for Riviera Beach. 'Your father called me yesterday and said you'd resigned from the Miami Police Department.'

'Well, I haven't resigned yet, Chief, I'm still thinking about it. My problem right now is what's best for me, Chief. You know how it goes. I can either take my pension money out in a lump sum, or I leave it in till I'm fifty-seven and then start drawing it monthly. I haven't got around to sitting down with a pencil and paper and figuring out what's the best thing to do.'

'If you take it out in a lump sum, you'll have to pay income taxes on it as earned salary this year.'

'I know that, but my income for the next six months with be negligible, so I still have to go over the figures.'

'I was in the same position.' Chief Sheldon rubbed a deep white scar on his chin. He was a heavyset man in his late forties, and his face was severely sunburned. His nose was peeling, and when he took off his dark sunglasses, as he did now, the freckled skin below his blue eyes was paper-white. 'I've only had this job for six months. The old chief was indicted, you know, and I had to make up my mind in a hurry when the city commission offered it to me. I was a homicide lieutenant up in Trenton – that's in New Jersey – and I'd put in for chief at three or four small towns, answering ads in the journal. Riviera Beach made me the best offer. So I had to make the same kind of decision you're up against. I left my money in the pension fund. I'm making less money as chief here than I did as a lieutenant in Trenton, but life's a lot easier here on the Gold Coast. Money isn't the most important thing in a man's life.'

'Not unless you don't have any.'

'Your father said you'd had it with Miami, but you might be open to an offer here in Riviera Beach.'

'That's impossible.' Hoke shook his head. 'The police station's on the mainland. I've decided never to leave the island again.'

'Never's a pretty long spell. Just hear me out. I looked over your record from when you were still a patrolman here on the Riviera force, before you went down to Miami. You were a good officer here. No reprimands, and five commendations, which isn't bad for three years. Then I called your Homicide Chief, Major Brownley, in Miami, and he said you were one of his best detectives –'

Hoke laughed. 'You called Major Brownley? He doesn't know I'm quitting! As far as he knows I'm on a thirty-day leave without pay. I told you I hadn't put any papers in yet. He must've shit his pants when you called him.'

'He was a little disturbed at first, yes. But I was discreet. I just told him I wanted to offer you a lieutenancy as my Homicide Chief here, but when I mentioned the salary he just laughed. All I can offer you, except for the lieutenant's bars, is fifteen thousand a year.'

'I make thirty-four as a sergeant in Miami.'

'That's what he told me. But then, if you're fed up with Miami – and I can't blame you for that – the higher rank and the job itself might be more to your liking. We don't have many homicides, although we do have a lot more abuse cases and missing persons every year, and they come under Homicide, too. A lot of things have changed in Riviera since you left here. Ten years ago, most of the residents were WASPs; now we've got sixty percent blacks.'

'You must be kidding. I don't think there're more than one or two black families living on the island.'

'That's here on Singer. They can't afford to live over here. But there's been a big influx in town. For a couple of years we had a drop in population, but now it's on the upswing with more blacks moving in. The WASPs have moved out to North Palm Beach, or to those new suburbs in West Palm. That's one of the reasons I was hired. I had to deal with a lot of black crime in Trenton.'

'Major Brownley's a black officer.'

'I figured that when I talked to him on the phone. But he told me you'd worked in Liberty City and Overtown, so you've dealt with black crime.'

'What you need is a black lieutenant, Chief. You don't need me. I've never taken the lieutenant's exam in Miami, and I'm not sure I could pass it if I did.'

'That's no problem. If you were a sergeant already on my force, you'd have to pass the exam before you could get a promotion. But if you come on the force from outside, I can appoint you as a lieutenant immediately, based on your experience and my personal evaluation. The city commission gave me the job, and so far they've been letting me run it my way. Why don't you sleep on the idea tonight, and then come by the station in the morning? I'll show you what the job entails. You'll have a free car, you know, and that's worth at least four thousand bucks a year. And you'll only have two detectives to supervise – a black and a Puerto Rican.'

'I already told you, Chief, I can't come over because I've made up my mind not to leave the island.'

'You aren't making a helluva lot of sense, Sergeant Moseley.'

'Maybe not. But I'm living in a six-hundred-dollar-a-month apartment, rent-free, and I'm making another four hundred in salary, so I can survive without ever going into town. Everything I need's right here on the island – laundromat, supermarket, restaurants, and the best beach in Florida. Complete with no hassles. The worst that can happen to me is to step on a tin can on the beach and cut myself.'

'No job's any safer than Homicide, Moseley. When you report to the scene, the victim's already dead, and the killer's long gone. Or he's still there, crying and saying he didn't mean to do it.'

'But then there's all the paperwork and the headaches. It was time for a change. But I want to tell you I appreciate the offer, Chief Sheldon.'

'It wasn't exactly unsolicited.' Sheldon shrugged. 'After all, your father has a lot of clout in this town. He used to be on the city commission, and he owns half of Singer Island. I'm not saying you aren't highly qualified –'

'I think some of that's exaggerated. Dad used to own a lot of the island, but all he has left now are a few beachfront lots –'

'Which appreciate about a thousand bucks per beach foot every year.'

'I suppose. What about those burglaries in the condos? Who's handling them?'

'At the Supermare? Right now, Jaime Figueras. He's a homicide detective, the Puerto Rican I told you about, but I gave them to him. He hasn't found out much of anything. Who told you about them?'

'Things get around. If you live on the island, you find out about everything sooner or later. I might be able to help him. Why not ask Figueras to drop around and see me at the El Pelicano? Tell him to bring an inventory of the missing stuff. That is, if you don't mind a little civilian help.'

'If you haven't resigned yet, you're still a police officer, and I need all the help I can get. I'll send him around tomorrow.'

'We'd better go inside and see the old man.'

'I don't need to see Mr Moseley. He asked me to talk to you, and I have. I'll just back out and go.'

'Better see him for a minute. If you leave without talking to him, it'll hurt his feelings. Have a drink, at least, and then tell him you've got some pressing business. But he's funny about things like that.'

'A man can always use a drink.'

They went inside, and the chief had two drinks and made some small talk with Frank before leaving. He didn't mention his offer to Hoke, and Frank didn't ask him about it.

But after the chief was gone, Frank said, 'Did you take Sheldon up on his offer, Hoke?'

534

'No. I couldn't take it because I'd have to leave the island and work in the Riviera Beach station. And please, Dad, don't do any more favors for me. I'm happy at the El Pelicano. But I sure didn't know that the black population was up to sixty percent in Riviera.'

'Seems like more than that. But it's been good for the hardware store. They have to fix up those old fifties houses they move into, and my business has increased almost twelve percent in the last year.'

'Why don't you sell the store, Frank? You and Helen could take life easy and do some traveling or something. You don't need the money.'

Frank grinned. 'Going to the store gives me a chance to leave the island every day, that's why. I'm just as stubborn as you are. And I already saw the world on that trip Helen and me took on the Q. E. II last year. It wore me out, and I don't want to see it a second time.'

'I'm sorry, Dad. I shouldn't've mentioned it.'

'I'm the one who should apologize. I shouldn't've called Chief Sheldon, not without checking with you first.'

'Don't worry about me, Frank. I'm fine now, and I appreciate you getting Aileen the bicycle. I'll just say good-bye to Helen, and then I'd better get back and see about renting those empty apartments.'

As Hoke drove back to the El Pelicano Arms, he turned over in his mind the information he had picked up. He had discovered that Frank wasn't married to Helen, which was something he wouldn't have thought possible a few years back; and he had been offered a job that he would have leaped at if it had been offered to him six months ago. But he couldn't take it now. If he did, he could still reside on the island, but he would be spending most of his time investigating knifings and shootings in Riviera Beach – that is, when he wasn't waiting around in the Palm Beach County courthouse to appear as a witness. He had liked Chief Sheldon; they had similar backgrounds in police work, and Hoke knew exactly how Sheldon's mind worked. But Hoke had almost insuperable problems just trying to manage a place like the El Pelicano Arms.

The rents were too high, for one thing. And he needed a coin-operated washer and dryer for the residents to use, because it was a two-block walk to the laundromat. Both of the Alabama couples had complained about that. The ice machine in the lobby was broken, and he couldn't get a man to come out until next Tuesday, if then. He would have to find a new service, one that would come out on weekends. But worst of all, he was under the old man's thumb again.

When he'd been married to Patsy, and still on the Riviera Police Department, he and Pasty used to have dinner with the old man every damned Sunday, and now he would be expected to spend every Sunday afternoon with Frank again. There was no way out of it. Frank would expect it, and no excuse would be acceptable.

There was a blue Camaro with Dade County plates parked in Hoke's manager's slot at the El Pelicano Arms. Hoke pulled in behind the car and blocked it so it could not back out. Then he walked over to the mall and used the pay telephone to call the towing service. After the tow truck had showed up and towed the Camaro away – it would cost the Camaro owner sixty dollars to redeem his car – Hoke felt good for the first time that day.

Chapter Ten

Unlike Troy Louden, Stanley Sinkiewicz was a homeowner with responsibilities. He couldn't just pick up and leave in the middle of the night, and he would never have gone down to Miami by himself to spend money on an expensive hotel room. But Troy had invited him to stay with him, and he wouldn't be all alone down there in the city. He wanted to get away from the Terraces for a while, even if it was only for a week or so, to let 'the incident,' as he now thought of it, blow over. He wouldn't get in Troy's way, and he wouldn't wear out his welcome down there. From all accounts, Miami was a dangerous place, but nothing would happen to him if he was down there with Troy and that Bajan fella.

But the first thing he would have to do was to buy a car. A man without a car would be helpless down there, and he didn't know anything about the bus routes, or how to use the new Metrorail, either. In a city that widely spread out, a car was an absolute necessity.

He rode the bus into West Palm Beach and made arrangements at his new bank to buy a brown Honda Civic, a repossessed 1981 model with 42,000 miles on the odometer and a new roof rack. He felt guilty about buying Japanese, but being six years old the Civic was only $1,800, not counting taxes.

He paid with a check and filled in the insurance transfer from his Escort at the bank, applying its coverage to the Honda. This transfer meant that Maya no longer had any insurance on their Escort, but that was her problem now, not Stanley's. He also got another five hundred dollars in traveler's checks and another forty in cash at the bank before driving home in his new – practically new – car.

He found the mortgage book in his wife's desk and wrote out two monthly mortgage checks in advance. He didn't know how long he would stay in Miami, but at least he had this worry off his mind. He called the telephone company and, after being transferred three times to people who didn't seem to understand what he wanted, managed to get his telephone placed on a hold, or standby, basis. This way, if someone called, the caller could hear it ring, but the phone would not actually ring at his home, nor would he be able to make any calls from his home until it was taken off standby. The fee for this was nine dollars a month. Stanley argued with the supervisor he had finally been transferred to, telling her that it was outrageous to charge him this much money for an inoperable phone, but the company wouldn't budge. Stanley then sent a check for the current phone charges – and for ten dollars more – to the address the woman gave him, which was different from his regular billing address.

The business with the phone company was such an ordeal, Stanley decided to do nothing about paying any of his other utility bills in advance. If they cut off his water and electricity while he was gone, he would pay up and get them reconnected when he returned.

He then drove into Riviera Beach, mailed the mortgage payments, and signed a 'hold mail' card at the post office for an indefinite period, writing on the card, 'Will pick up at PO when I return from vacation.'

If Maya had still been with him – instead of running away – these were all little chores that he could have delegated to her. And he knew his life would be complicated in a lot of other respects by her desertion. But it was worth it. He wouldn't have been able to take Maya to Miami with him anyway, even if she had been willing to go. Being without a wife gave a man a whole different way of looking at the world, and it looked even better now that he had a car to drive again. If it came to a tossup, a car or a wife, most men, or at least the ones Stanley had known in Detroit, would certainly give up their wives.

After packing some white shirts and some wash pants in a cardboard box, and putting on a new blue and white seersucker suit he had bought when he first came to Florida, but had never worn, Stanley wondered what to do about the storm shutters. If he closed them, and turned off the electricity, everything would be mildewed when he returned. He decided not to pull them down, but to crack all of the windows a little for circulation after he turned off the air conditioning. He drove over to Sneider's station to have the tank filled and asked Mr Sneider to pull down the storm shutters from the outside if there happened to be a hurricane while he was gone.

'If you'll do that for me, Mr Sneider, I'll give you a dollar for your trouble when I get back.'

'No problem, Mr Sinkiewicz. It's the least I can do for a neighbor. You takin' I-95 into Miami?'

'I thought I would.'

'They've been having some highway robberies down there, you know. They throw a mattress or a set of box springs on the off-ramps, and then when you stop another guy throws a concrete block through your window and robs you. It's been in the papers. So what you should do is carry a tire iron on the other bucket seat in front, so you can chop off the man's fingers when he reaches in for your wallet and wristwatch.'

Stanley checked the trunk, but there was no tire iron. Sneider got one from the shop and handed it to him. 'I'll lend you this one, Dad. You can return it when you get back. But if I were you, I'd stay in the center lane on I-95 and keep your doors locked. When I drive down to Miami in my tow truck for parts sometimes, I carry a shotgun loaded with birdshot. I don't want to kill nobody, but a load of birdshot in the face will discourage most of these robbers.'

'I could stop at Moseley's Hardware and buy a shotgun –'

'The tire iron'll be enough. I use my shotgun for dove hunting, too, but for you, I wouldn't go to that extra expense just for a trip down I-95.'

'How's little Pammi, Mr Sneider?'

'I sent her up to Camp Sparta for the rest of the summer. She called last night to tell us she won fourth place in the archery contest. They know how to straighten little girls out in Camp Sparta. You get a little girl, or a little boy, interested in sports, it gets their mind off their private parts.'

'I never had the advantage of going to a summer camp when I was a kid.'

539

'Me neither. But there was a time there in the service, for about five years, when I didn't own a damned thing that couldn't be left out in the rain. Kids have it good nowadays, but they're too dumb to know it.'

Hoping he hadn't neglected anything important, Stanley drove to I-95 and headed south for Miami, seventy miles away, and without a single stoplight on the interstate.

The painting on the upright easel in the garage had a meaning so private that the artist himself, James Frietas-Smith, didn't know what it was.

James always worked slowly, on one large canvas at a time, and without a preconceived notion of what the final product would look like. He piled on paint and then more paint until every inch of the canvas was covered with multiblobs of color three-quarters of an inch thick.

James stepped back about ten feet and studied the painting for a few minutes. The composition definitely held the eye within the rectangle, and the magenta blobs on the right balanced the three wide smears of lamp-black on the left. But the overall picture needed a touch of luminosity. James squeezed a large tube of zinc white. The thick paint oozed out like diluted toothpaste onto his palette knife. Moving in close to the canvas and spreading his short, slightly bowed legs, James applied the globule of white to the center of the canvas. He brought his pursed lips close to the blob and blew steadily, flattening it into the shape of an amoeba with the jet of air he forced through his lips.

That was all it needed, he thought, as he stepped back and looked at the picture again. Finished. A wave of depression engulfed him as he wiped his fingers on a turpentine-soaked rag. It was always this way when he completed a picture. Always. Painting them was a joyful suspension of life, but it was a downer to finish them. Who would buy a picture like this one, anyway? The canvas was sixty inches wide and forty inches high, and a frame would make it larger still. James always made his own stretchers, tacking down the canvas and sizing the surface with white lead himself. The money he invested, including the tubes of paint, was a large sum for a man in his financial position. And if he were to consider the time consumed in actually painting and finishing a work (the cost of framing was out of the question), he would have to charge a great deal of money for each finished picture. But so far, he couldn't sell any of them; he couldn't even give them away.

The primary colors he was fond of would overpower most living rooms, and the hotels he had tried were not interested. A few weeks ago, before his trip to New Orleans, James had stacked four of his paintings on top of his little Morris Minor, tied them down with rope, and driven to a half-dozen small hotels in Miami Beach. The two managers who consented to look merely shook their heads; the rest of them wouldn't even come out to the parking lot. He didn't intend to let them humiliate him again. He would just have to wait until he was somehow discovered, and his work recognized by someone.

The picture was finished now, but what could he do with it? Maybe the best thing to do would be to scrape off the paint and begin another. But he didn't feel like starting another painting. Not now. Not when he was frightened half to death – and part of his fear, he noticed, had somehow managed to work its way into the new painting. He didn't recall using so much magenta in anything else he had done.

The temperature in the four-car garage was in the high eighties, but James's hands were cold and clammy. He wiped his palms on his blue-denim cutoffs and sighed. If this thing with Troy Louden didn't work out, he would be in the hands of the Allambys for certain. James shivered and left the garage studio for the bright sunlight of the jungly backyard. James didn't know the precise origin of the expression 'in the hands of the Allambys,' although he presumed it had been a slave-owning family of unusual cruelty during the early years of Barbados. But Bajans, when they still used the archaic expression, knew for certain that when a person was 'in the hands of the Allambys,' hope was gone, the worst that could happen to a man had already happened, and from that day forward the man was lost ... doomed.

Like many Barbadians whose families had been on the island for a dozen generations or more, James wasn't completely

Caucasian, even though in Barbados he was considered a white man. His hair was reddish brown and curly. His eyes were blue. His nose, although high at the bridge, was wide at the base, and his large round nostrils flared slightly when he got excited. His even teeth were white and strong, and his lips were pronounced and thick. His jutting hips and the carelessly swinging arms that gave an island rhythm to his loosely disjointed walk also hinted at his ancestry and upbringing. But only once since he'd come to the United States – in New Orleans – had James been recognized as a man who was half black.

Every time James recalled the incident in New Orleans, a wave of shame, fear, and revulsion hit him, like a man with a case of the dog bitters. He had gone into one of those intimate, candle-lit, side-street, open-air restaurants to sample some of the city's famous French-Creole cooking. The patio setting was attractive, with flowers growing in ceramic pots along the intricate wrought-iron fence. There were colored lights trained on the fountain in the center of the courtyard. The waiter had seated James at a glass-topped wrought-iron table, with a pink plastic table setting and pink linen napkin. He handed James a menu printed in French and left him alone for five minutes.

When James had looked up again from the menu, he was confronted by two white-jacketed men who were studying his face by the flickering light of the double-candled hurricane lamp on his table. The headwaiter nodded briefly to his table waiter and then said softly and firmly, 'We'll serve you this time, sir, but don't come back again. Many of our patrons prefer not to dine with black men.'

No one overheard the headwaiter, but for a moment James had been petrified with fear. Without protesting, without even ordering, he had slunk out of the restaurant. He hadn't eaten anything that evening. He had walked for hours, thinking about the things he should have said to the waiters. He could have shown them his Barbados passport; he could have forced a showdown of some kind – but he hadn't. Two days later James had left New Orleans on the Greyhound bus and come back to Miami, even though his vacation money would have stretched for another week.

He had a good setup here in Miami, and he was sorry now that he had gone to New Orleans in the first place. If he had only stayed put, when his aunt had sent him the birthday check, he wouldn't be involved now with Troy Louden and that horribly mutilated woman! James could hardly look at her face without feeling sick to his stomach, and he couldn't meet her eyes at all. Her face was so badly disfigured, he knew that the horror he felt in his heart would show in his eyes.

And now another man was coming in on the deal – Pop Sinkiewicz, Troy Louden's old cellmate. Another professional criminal and ex-con. Troy had told James that Sinkiewicz had done a little time with him for trying to crack a small safe, and that James should be nice to the old man because he would be financing their operation. How many more would be in on it before Troy was through? He had never dreamed that Troy would come to Miami in the first place. James had been rather vague about the job at the time he had suggested it to Troy in New Orleans, but he hadn't been able to concentrate fully on his painting since he received the postcard from Troy saying he was on his way to Miami.

The postcard alone had been an omen. A symbol, and an ugly one, too. As a nonobjective painter, James thought often about symbols, even though he avoided them in his work, and just the sight of that four-color postcard had shaken him before he read it. Naturally, James hadn't told Troy about the incident in the courtyard cafe; he would never tell anyone about that, ever. Yet the card from Troy had featured a typical New Orleans wrought-iron gate, and filling the background behind the gate (not in front, which would have made a big difference, symbolically, but *behind*) there was a bed of roses – yellow, pink, and dark red. What had made Troy take that particular card at random out of a drugstore rack? There were literally thousands of postcards he could have chosen. Did the gate represent prison bars? Or did it mean the color bar? The symbols meant something awful; he knew that much.

Suppose, just suppose, everything went wrong? The robbery would fail – or *could* fail – despite Troy's assurances to the contrary. Then where would he be? In prison, that's where, and if he went to prison, would the authorities list him as a black man or a white man? But that wasn't as important as *going* to prison ...

Oh, man, he wouldn't be able to stand being in prison either way.

On the other hand, Troy knew what he was doing. This sort of thing was old stuff to Troy, and if everything worked out smoothly, as Troy claimed it would, James would be off to New York with four or five thousand dollars – maybe more – in his pocket. And if there was a place that deserved to be robbed in Florida, it was the Green Lakes Supermarket.

On the tenth of every month James received a check for $200 from his father, mailed from Bridgetown, but it wasn't enough, not nearly enough to live on and buy expensive art supplies, too. When the Green Lakes Supermarket had announced its grand opening in the newspaper, James had driven out there and applied for a part-time job as a bag boy. He had worked on Fridays until eleven, and all day Saturdays. The minimum wage, plus his tips, had added almost forty dollars a week to his income. But this extra money wasn't enough either, not when he had to buy art supplies and pay for the upkeep on his Morris Minor. To supplement his supermarket pittance, James had done a little pilfering every Saturday he worked at the market. He hadn't taken much, only little items he could stuff into his pockets – a can of sardines, a can of tuna, some candy bars, apples, toothpaste, and once a pound of hamburger, which had turned bad before he got home that night. Then on his way back inside the store after delivering a load of groceries to a customer's car in the parking lot, James would drop off his pilfered items behind the front seat of his Morris, which he always parked close to the store's entrance.

At four P.M. on the last Saturday he worked at the market, the day manager crooked a finger at him as he came back in from the lot, pushing a half-dozen carts he had collected. The day manager was in his early forties and wore a Fu Manchu mustache, a red tie, and a pink button-down shirt.

'You're fired, James.'

'Why?'

'For stealing, that's why! Now get the fuck out of here, you goddamned thief, and don't stop at the cage for your check on the way out!'

Two of the girls on the checkout line heard every word.

'Yes, sir,' James said, and hurried out of the store as the two checkout girls giggled.

That was a week before his twenty-sixth birthday, and before he received the sizable and welcome check from his Aunt Rosalie. Now he had no money, and a lot on his mind.

The Green Lakes Supermarket had suited Troy perfectly when James had driven him out there yesterday to show it to him. After spending fifteen minutes in the store, with James outside in the car, Troy had rejoined him with two apples he had bought. He handed one of the apples to James and bit into the other.

'Lush,' Troy had said. Then, gesturing toward the entrance, 'It's just like you said, James.'

From a professional's point of view, the layout of the store and the location of the market were ideal. Eventually there would be an entire Class B shopping center in the Green Lakes subdivision of Miami, with thirty different stores, but at present only the supermarket had opened, and the rest of the buildings were still under construction. The supermarket would anchor one end, and there would be a Kmart at the other. The twenty-five-acre parking lot had been completed, but had not yet been striped for parking spaces. The new supermarket was about 250 yards away from State Highway 836, which led to the Miami International Airport cut-off. Troy couldn't have selected a better location, or a better time, for a successful robbery if he had been allowed to design one himself. The employees were new, and security was lax, and as James had said, the safe was supposed to be locked but in practice never was until the store was closed for the night.

When they got back to James's garage apartment, after the quick surveillance of the supermarket, Troy had borrowed the Bajan's last five dollars, taken the Morris Minor, and driven away. James hadn't seen him again until he returned later that night with the woman –

'Pardon me, son.'

James leaped two feet off the garage floor and whirled in midair before he landed again. 'Man!' he said to Stanley Sinkiewicz, 'you shouldn't sneak up on a man like that, man!'

'I didn't mean to scare you none, son. I knocked at the door of the big house in front, but when no one answered I just came around here to the back.'

'That's all right, sir.' James had recovered his breath. 'I live back here over the garage. The Shapiros own the big house, and they let me live here free for taking care of the place while they're up in New England for the summer.'

'You're James Frietas-Smith, with a hyphen?'

'Yes, sir.'

'You're the fella I'm looking for, then.' Stanley stared curiously at James. Stanley had never seen a Bajan before, but the young man, except for the size of his splayed bare feet, looked about the same as any other well-tanned Floridian wearing cutoff shorts and a paint-stained T-shirt. 'My name's Stanley Sinkiewicz. Senior,' he added. 'I'm a friend of Troy Louden's.'

'Yes, sir. We been expecting you, Mr Sinkiewicz. Troy and Miss Forrest have gone over to her motel to get her suitcase. She's moving in with us, too.' James forced a smile. 'They should be back just now.'

'Miss Forrest? I haven't met her –'

'I only met her last night myself, Mr Sinkiewicz. She's Troy's friend, not mine. If you're parked out front, you better pull into the yard back here and park over there.' James pointed to the utility shed.

Stanley nodded. 'The grass out front needs cutting. It didn't look like nobody lived here, and I was afraid for a minute there I had the wrong house.'

'I'm supposed to cut the grass every two weeks, but I was away on a trip and missed a few weeks.'

Stanley got his car and parked it by the shed. He brought his box of clean clothes and toilet articles into the spacious four-car garage, and James tried to take the box away from him.

'I'll take that upstairs for you, Mr Sinkiewicz.'

'I'm not in any all-fired hurry, son.' Stanley surrendered the box and looked at the huge paintings stacked against and hanging from the garage walls. 'Troy told me you were an artist. I'd like to look at your work, if you don't mind?'

'I don't mind at all.' James put the box on the steps that led upstairs to the apartment, and crossed to the easel. 'I finished this one just now, but I haven't got a title yet. Sometimes when I can't think of a title I give it a number. But I haven't thought of a number, either.'

Stanley studied the painting, frowning with concentration. He put on his reading glasses and moved in a little closer. 'I wouldn't know, myself – although it looks a little scary.'

'It's a nonobjective painting,' James explained, 'and some kind of emotion is all you're expected to get out of it. Two years ago there was a German painter staying over on the Saint James coast – that's in Barbados – and I showed him some of my work. He told me I was probably the only primitive nonobjective painter working today. He's the same man who advised me to go to New York and study at the Art Students League. And when we finish our job, that's where I'm going.'

Stanley nodded. 'You could use a little more study, I guess. I used to do some painting myself. One thing you need's a steady hand.' Stanley pointed to a canvas on the wall, a crosspatch of thin vertical red lines and thinner horizontal black lines on a lemon background. 'Now that picture over there. You put all them lines on with a straightedge, didn't you?'

'Yes, sir. That was just an experiment, Mr Sinkiewicz. But even Mondrian used a ruler to get certain effects.'

Stanley shook his head. 'If you've got a steady hand, you don't need no straightedge. You got any clean canvases and a striping brush? I'll learn you how to do it.'

'Yes, sir.' James didn't want to have the old con spoil one of his unused canvases, but he didn't want to offend him either.

James removed the newly finished painting from the easel and replaced it with a recently sized blank canvas. 'There's a can of brushes on the workbench, Mr Sinkiewicz. Take any one you like.'

Stanley moved to the cluttered workbench. He opened a can of turpentine and held the spout to his nose. He sniffed experimentally, inhaled deeply, and screwed the lid back.

'Do you like the smell of turpentine, son?'

'I don't mind it. But I don't particularly like it.'

'One good thing about turpentine. It always smells the same.'

'Yes, sir,' James said uneasily. 'It always smells the same.'

Stanley rummaged around in a coffee can full of brushes and selected a short-handled camel's-hair brush about a half-inch in width. 'This ain't no regular striping brush, but it'll do. A real striping brush is wider, and slants back aways, and the bristles are longer on one side than on the other. I'll just stir up some of this cadmium orange and turpentine, and then I'll show you how to make a straight line without looking at the canvas.'

As Stanley mixed the new tube of cadmium orange with turpentine, James scowled and bit his lower lip. The paint had cost him $4.95 in U.S. dollars, and the old man had squeezed out half the tube.

'All right, young fella,' Stanley said, his cheeks flushing, 'just watch me now.'

Stanley held the paint-loaded brush at his side, resting his forearm on his hip, and stared up at the cobwebby ceiling. He took two swift steps in front of the canvas, turned, and winked at James. James's jaw dropped. The bright orange line on the canvas was exactly one-eighth of an inch wide, and straight as a die. The line was as vibrant as a tightly stretched guitar string. It looked to James as if it would hum to the touch, and the old man had drawn this perfect rule in less than a second!

'That's what I mean by a steady hand,' Stanley said, with a short laugh.

James clucked and shook his head. 'I don't know how you did that, Mr Sinkiewicz. I couldn't draw a line that straight, even with a yardstick.'

'There's a knack to it, son. Here. Take the brush and I'll show you how to hold it. You've got to put the right amount of paint on the brush, too. With a little practice, you can learn how to do it.'

For the next forty-five minutes James and Stanley were engaged in painting straight lines. The once-white canvas was an almost solidly colored orange rectangle when Troy Louden pulled into the driveway outside the garage and honked the horn of the Morris Minor. They both went outside to meet him. Troy embraced the old man, hugging him to his chest, and kissed him wetly on the cheek.

'By God, I'm glad to see you, Pop! To tell you the truth, I wasn't sure you were going to pry yourself loose from up there. If you hadn't come today, I was going to call you tonight. You've met James, I see.'

'He sure has, Troy,' James said. 'Mr Sinkiewicz has been teaching me how to paint a straight line.'

'That's nice of you, Pop.' Troy frowned at James. 'I hope you thanked him.'

'Yes, I did.'

'It'll take him a while to get the hang of it,' Stanley said. 'A man can't learn nothing overnight.'

Troy punched the old man lightly on the arm, and then snapped his fingers. 'Jesus. I was so glad to see you I forgot to introduce you to Dale Forrest. Hop out of the car, honey, and meet Mr Sinkiewicz.'

Stanley had seen the woman in the car the moment he had stepped out of the shady garage, but he had hurriedly looked away again. As Dale Forrest advanced toward him timidly, holding out her limp right hand, Stanley forced himself to look at her face again. The young woman had a voluptuous figure, with long straight legs. She wore green-denim clamdiggers and a short-sleeved white silk blouse with the top three buttons undone to reveal her cleavage. Her heavy breasts, without a brassiere, strained against the thin silk. Her skin was a golden bronze, and her hair was almost the same shade, although bright highlights shimmered at the crown. Her long thick hair softly framed her face, and there Dale's beauty stopped.

There were four knobby irregular bumps on her forehead, as if someone had been beating on her with a hammer. Instead of eyebrows, Dale had two hairless dents above her eyes, both of them crisscrossed with red scars where stitches had recently been removed. She had filled in these crescent-shaped depressions with black makeup, which made them more obvious. Her nose was crushed almost flat, and the left nostril was partly missing, as if cut away with a razor blade. Both of her sunken cheeks contained rough and jagged scars, and some of these holes looked large enough to contain marbles. Her jaw had been broken, and reset off-center, and her tiny recessed chin jutted to the right at a puzzling angle. Although Dale still had her lower front teeth, her six upper front teeth were missing, and her gummy smile was like a grimace of intense pain. Stanley recognized that the grimace was a smile, but when he looked at it he felt like crying. Her scarred and puffy lips reminded him of the sewn end of a sack of potatoes.

'I'm happy to make your acquaintance, Mr Sinkiewicz,' Dale said. She shook Stanley's hand, then dropped behind Troy as if she were trying to hide.

'Likewise,' Stanley said, clearing his throat.

'James, boy!' Troy said. 'Where'd you put Stanley?'

'We haven't been upstairs yet, Troy. But I thought I'd give him the bed out on the porch, if that's all right with you?'

'That'll be fine. Get Dale's bag out of the car.'

The six-bedroom, two-story house faced Biscayne Bay, and the Shapiros, the elderly couple who owned it, spent three winter months there every year. They had, at one time, kept the garage apartment as servants' quarters, but they no longer employed live-in servants, even when they were in residence, so the garage apartment hadn't been redecorated for more than ten years. Even so, the garage, like the bayside house, was constructed of the coquina stone that was once quarried in the Keys, and its exterior showed almost no deterioration. All of these residences along the bay, put up in the late 1920s, when there had been a good view of Miami Beach, were built to last, and they had. In return for staying on the premises, and for looking after the grounds, James Frietas-Smith had the rent-free use of the apartment and garage, with his utilities paid for by the Shapiros.

The empty garage below the apartment was huge, and with all four doors swung up against the ceiling there was ample light for his painting. The apartment above, however, was shabby, filled with discarded furniture and other items from the large house in front. In addition to the screened porch on the east side, furnished with a sagging three-quarter-sized bed and several odd pieces of antique furniture, there was a living room, a bedroom, a bathroom with a tub but no shower, and a kitchen large enough to include an old-fashioned breakfast nook, as they were called in the 1950s.

The view from the porch and from the breakfast nook provided a good prospect of the bay. All of the rooms were large, with high, paneled ceilings. The pink wallpaper, with tiny rosebuds of darker pink in the design, had pulled away in various places and hung down in scattered tatters. A musty, nose-tingling odor of dust, mildew, and stale bacon grease pervaded the rooms, and there was no air conditioning. There was a large overhead ceiling fan in the living room, but it didn't work any longer.

'You can have the bedroom, Pop,' Troy said, 'if you don't want the porch, but Dale and I don't mind it in there, and you'll have a better breeze on the porch at night.'

'Whatever you think, Troy.'

'Good. The bathroom's at the end of the hall next to the kitchen, and I'll have James put some clean towels in there for you. You don't mind sleeping here in the living room, do you, James? You can sleep on the Empress couch.'

James shrugged. 'I don't care where I sleep.' He took Dale's overnighter into the bedroom, and she followed him in. When James came out again, she closed the door and stayed in the bedroom.

'Take your jacket off, Pop,' Troy said. 'We've got some errands to run this afternoon, so you might as well be comfortable.'

Stanley had put on his suit jacket after getting out of his car, but he shucked out of it now and removed his tie. Troy took them and handed everything to James.

'Hang these up for Pop, James. Okay, old-timer, let's get going.'

'Where to?'

'James.' Troy snapped his fingers. 'Have you got any more money?'

'The five I gave you was my last cent.'

'Well, it doesn't make any difference, I guess, now that Pop's here.' He put a hand on the old man's thin shoulder. 'Pop, you'd better give James twenty bucks or so, to go to the store. Talk to Dale, James, before you go, and find out what she needs. She can cook dinner for us. We should be back around six or six-thirty.'

'I don't know where you're going, Troy, but I'd like to go along,' James said as he accepted two ten-dollar bills from Stanley.

'And I'd like to take you, too, James, but Pop and me've got some business to discuss. Ask Dale if she knows how to cook pork chops.'

Troy crossed the bedroom door and rapped on it. 'Dale, honey.' The door opened, and Troy planted a long kiss on the woman's ruined mouth. 'Pop and me are going out for a while. James'll get you what you need, and you can fix dinner for us. All right, sweetheart?'

'Yes, sir, Mr Louden.'

'There's a good girl.' He patted her exquisite buttocks.

Stanley followed Troy down the stairs. Troy wanted to drive, so Stanley handed over the keys to his Honda.

Chapter Eleven

At seven-thirty that Sunday evening, Hoke and Aileen ate one roast beef sandwich apiece and decided to save the other two for Monday's lunch. Hoke wasn't hungry, and neither was Aileen, but they chewed methodically through the sandwiches, washing them down with tall glasses of iced tea. Aileen wanted something sweet afterward, and Hoke told her to eat one of the mangoes, suggesting that she either eat it over the kitchen sink or take it into the shower – preferably the latter – because it was so ripe.

Aileen took the mango into the bathroom, closed the door, and moments later the shower was running full force. Hoke cleared the table, rinsed the plates and glasses, and put them on the sideboard. Because the water was running at the sink and in the bathroom, he didn't hear the first knock, but when he turned off the faucet, he heard a very loud pounding at the front door. Hoke opened the door, trying to hold back his rage. There was no need for anyone to bang so hard. Louis Farnsworth, the salad man at the Sheraton Hotel, was at the door. Hoke would have said something sharp to him, but there was a woman standing there too.

Farnsworth was a thin man with a pot belly. He wore his white pants above the pot, and it looked as if he had a bowling ball below his belt. His hair was gray and thinning, and he had a sour expression on his lined face. The young woman behind Farnsworth was shorter than he was, but she outweighed him by sixty or seventy pounds. Her face was round, and her cheeks were so fleshy they sagged almost to her lips. Her puckered mouth was a small round O, and she stood there blinking pale blue eyes. She – or someone – had plucked away most of her eyebrows. She had given herself – or someone had – a home permanent that didn't take, and her brownish hair had frizzed up all over her head. A port-wine-colored birthmark covered most of the left side of her face, including the left eyelid. Her heavy breasts inside her white T-shirt sagged nearly to her waist, and she wore a waitress's brown mini-skirt with a skimpy red apron.

'You didn't have to break the door down,' Hoke said.

'I'm sorry,' Farnsworth said. 'I guess you didn't hear me knock the first time. I knew you was in there because I could hear the water running.'

'Okay – what can I do for you, Mr Farnsworth?'

'I need me another key. This here's Dolly Turner. She's just come down from Yeehaw Junction, and she's got herself a dishwashing job at the hotel. Until she gets a couple of paychecks and can rent her own place, she's gonna bunk in with me. So I need us another key.'

'Why can't you both use the same key?'

'We're on different shifts, that's why. What's the big problem about a second key?'

'No problem.' Hoke went into the kitchen and opened the drawer where he kept his books and the extra keys. 'You're 204, right?'

When Farnsworth didn't reply, Hoke brought him the extra key with the apartment number written on an attached cardboard tag. 'That'll be a buck-fifty deposit,' Hoke said. 'When you return the key, you get the buck-fifty back.'

'I didn't pay no deposit on my key,' Farnsworth protested.

'That's because you paid a one-month security deposit rent, along with your first month's rent. If you lose your key, I can take it out of that. But each extra key's a buck-fifty deposit.'

Dolly Turner looked sideways at Farnsworth. He took out a blue-green package of Bugler and some white papers, and rolled an economical cigarette. Dolly had a black wool Peruvian handbag with a white embroidered llama on one side. She rummaged in the interior, which was filled with odds and ends, including a flannel nightgown, and managed to find $1.38 in change.

'That's twelve cents short,' Hoke said, after counting the pennies.

She glanced over at Farnsworth again, who took a long drag on his thin cigarette, and then watched black ashes flutter to the floor.

'That's all I got on me,' Dolly said, in a tiny voice, 'but I'm supposed to get paid next Saturday, if I work out all right.'

'Okay. I'll trust you for the rest. But we don't make any profit on lost keys. It costs a buck-fifty to have one made.'

Aileen, wrapped in a bath towel, came out of the bathroom, noticed the couple in the doorway, and quickly dodged back inside. Farnsworth and Dolly Turner left, and a few minutes later, Aileen, in jeans and a T-shirt, came out of the bathroom.

'Who was that with Mr Farnsworth, Daddy?'

'Dolly Turner. She's going to be living with him until she's saved up enough money to rent her own place. She just got a job at the Sheraton, and he was good enough to take her in.'

'But they aren't married. Isn't it against the law to rent to an unmarried couple?'

'They aren't exactly a couple. He's renting the place, not her, so she's merely his guest.'

'But isn't it against the law for two people to sleep together if they aren't married?'

'No. They can sleep together. There's no law against that. But fornication between them is against the law. In fact, the missionary position is the only position allowed by law in Florida, and even then you have to be married. But it's a law that's rarely enforced.'

'What's the missionary position?'

'That's when the woman lies on her back, and the man gets on top.'

Aileen giggled. 'That ain't the only way they do it up in Vero Beach.'

'*Isn't*, you mean, or anywhere else. But that's the Florida law. It just isn't enforced, that's all.'

'If they did, it would sure spoil things in the parking lot at Beach High.' Aileen laced up her running shoes and went to the door. 'I'm gonna go out for a while and walk off that sandwich and mango.'

'Aren't you going to ride your bike?' Aileen's new bicycle was wedged between her Bahama bed and the wall.

'I'm just gonna walk around the mall. But tomorrow I'm gonna clean out that old office downstairs and keep it down there. The apartment's too crowded, and if I leave it outside somebody'll steal it, chain and all.'

'That's a good project for you. The dumpster people come on Tuesday, so I'll help you tomorrow. Most of the stuff in there is junk, anyway. If we clean it up, maybe we can use it as an office again.'

After Aileen left, Hoke was restless. He slapped his chest with both hands, and then he slapped his front pockets. He shook his head when he realized that he was feeling for his cigarettes, although he had no real desire to smoke one. He hadn't had a cigarette since the first day of his mid-life crisis, and he didn't really want one now, except that was what he had always done when he was bored or restless – smoke a cigarette. To give his hands something to do he went into the kitchen and cleaned the burners with a wet Brillo pad. As the foam formed between his fingers he recalled a description of eating pussy he had read in a novel last year. The description had been exaggerated, but the fact that he was thinking about pussy again was a good sign. He would have to do something about that, as soon as he got things organized around the El Pelicano. The best place for pickups used to be the Sand-Shell Villas, in its small dark bar in Singer Island Shores. A lot of New York secretaries, usually in pairs, took a villa on the beach during the off-season at the attractive package rates, which included round-trip fare from Kennedy. They were easier to pick up with two guys, but now that he had his own apartment, he could probably break up a pair and bring one home for the night – except for Aileen. He would have to do something about Aileen soon. If she absolutely refused to go out to her mother in L.A., he would have to persuade her to go back to Green Lakes. After all, Ellita could use Aileen's help as well as her mother's when the baby came. But that was still a few weeks away. He wanted Aileen out of his apartment sooner than that –

There was a light tapping on the door. Hoke washed his hands at the sink and dried them on a dish towel as he crossed to the door to open it. Dolly Turner, clutching her wool handbag, blinked vacantly at him a few times, then took two hesitant steps inside as Hoke backed away from the door. She reached into her bag and handed him the extra key to 204.

'I want my deposit back.'

'Leaving already? I thought you two were an ideal couple.'

Dolly worked her tiny mouth in and out and shook her frizzed head. 'He wanted me to do something.'

'What did you expect? When Mr Farnsworth didn't come up with the twelve cents, I figured he wasn't into altruism.'

'What?'

'Kindness to strangers, with no strings attached.'

'I don't mind the regular way, I expected that. But I'm not gonna do nothing that ain't natural.'

'How're you going to get back to Yeehaw Junction?'

'I'm not going back. He didn't get me my job, and I'll just sleep on the beach till I get paid. It won't cost me nothing to eat in the hotel kitchen.'

'You won't be able to sleep on the beach, Miss Turner. The public beach closes at ten, and the beach is patrolled at night. You'd get picked up for sure. Why don't you keep your key and go over to the mall till about ten or ten-thirty, and then come back. Tell Mr Farnsworth you're afraid of catching AIDS –'

'What's AIDS?'

'Mr Farnsworth knows. By ten-thirty, he'll probably be ready to settle for something rather than nothing. If not, knock on my door again. I'll be up till at least eleven, and I'll give you your deposit back and let you sleep in my car. But just for one night. Tomorrow you'll have to find someone else or make other sleeping arrangements.'

'I wouldn't mind sleeping in your car right now.'

'Do it my way. You should've thought of these things before you left Yeehaw Junction, but you can think about them now, sitting on the bench over at the mall.'

'I had to leave. When my daddy died, I didn't have no place to stay.' She began to cry.

'It's a hard world, Miss Turner, but it's not as bad as you think. You've got a job. You can eat, and you've got two places to sleep – either with Mr Farnsworth or in the back seat of my car. And even if you do something unnatural with Mr Farnsworth, you still won't actually have to *sleep* with him afterwards. He's got two Bahama beds in his apartment, just like I have, so you'll have a comfortable bed all to yourself.'

'You've given me something to think about.' She wiped her face with the back of her hand.

Hoke opened the door a little wider. 'Good. As I said, I'll be up till at least eleven, so go over to the mall and think about your options.'

'I think maybe I'd better go back down the hall and talk to Mr Farnsworth again.'

'Whatever.'

Hoke closed the door behind her, wondering if he had handled the situation diplomatically. The girl was only twenty-one or -two, and he was no expert on giving advice to the lovelorn. Perhaps he should have returned her deposit, and let it go at that. But if he had, she would have ended up in the Palm Beach County Women's Detention Center without her new dishwashing job, and with the beginning of a rap sheet. He wondered what he would do if he were in Dolly's position – there was a double rap on the door – but he was a man, and would never be in Dolly's position. Hoke shook his head and picked up his car keys from the dining table. That was quick, he thought. I'll tell Dolly to keep her head down in the back of the car, even though the night patrol cars hardly ever check the apartment-house parking lot. He would wake her at six, take her a cup of coffee, and she would be fine.

Dr Ralph 'Itai' Hurt was at the door. He wore a light blue muscle shirt exposing stringy arms, swimming trunks, and canvas skivvy slippers.

'Good evening, Professor.'

'Itai. Just call me Itai,' he said with a half-smile. 'You aren't eating dinner now, are you?'

'No, we finished a while ago.'

Itai nodded. 'That's what I figured. I'm a little embarrassed about this, Mr Moseley, but I've got a strong sense of *locus parentis*, held over from when kids were still "kids" at college until they were twenty-one. I still volunteer advice sometimes to eighteen-year-olds, and they're pretty quick to tell me it's none of my business. Now that kids are considered adults at eighteen –'

'I know. It's easier to put them in jail. I suppose you want your books back. They're over here on the table –'

'No, no, that isn't what I've come to see you about. I want to talk to you about your daughter for a moment. I've been thinking about it, and I know how young she is, so perhaps you won't think I'm out of line if I – what's the word – "rat" on her.'

'We don't call them rats anymore. The new term is "confidential informant." What's your beef with Aileen, Professor?'

'None at all. There are, as you know, some hibiscus bushes right outside my window where I work –'

'How's the novel coming along?'

'Not bad. I got a page and a half today. Actually it's a page and a quarter, but that's because I stopped halfway through the last sentence. When I finish the sentence tomorrow it will be about a page and a half. Hemingway said that was the way to do it.'

'It works that way on Incident Reports, too. Look, what's on your mind, Itai?'

'Incident Reports? Right. Well, your daughter's been vomiting behind the hibiscus bush. That's what I wanted to tell you.'

'When?'

'The last time? Just a while ago. But she's also been down there throwing up after breakfast in the mornings. Is she sick? Has she said anything to you about being sick to her stomach?'

'No. She eats a lot for being so skinny. More than I do, in fact. But she seems healthy enough.'

'She isn't healthy, Mr Moseley. I suspect she's got bulimia – a form of *anorexia nervosa*. Remember that singer a few years back, Karen Carpenter? That's what she died from. She kept vomiting, sticking her finger down her throat until she lost so much weight she finally starved to death. It's fairly common at the university. Even Jane Fonda had bulimia as a girl, she said, although she managed to kick it later on.'

'I don't see how Aileen could catch anything like that. She hasn't been around anyone with a disease like bulimia, or I'd've known about it. She's never complained about being too full, either. If anything, she seems hungry most of the time, like any other normal teenager.'

'If you threw up everything you ate, you'd be hungry, too, Mr Moseley. It's called an eating binge. Then they get rid of it, and they still stay thin, or get thinner. How old is Aileen now, exactly?'

'Fourteen. Almost fifteen.'

'Does she menstruate?'

'I think so. I haven't noticed any of the pads and what-not around here yet, but down in Miami, living with three females, I'd sometimes see the Carefree boxes they came in – you know, in the garbage. But I don't know for certain about Aileen.'

'At fourteen, she should be. But once you develop bulimia, and stick with it, even if you've started menstruating, you'll stop again. Just like female runners stop when they get up to six miles a day. And that's what they like, you see. When they stop menstruating they consider it a good sign. Their diet's working and they're getting thinner.'

'Christ, how thin does she want to get?'

'This is a psychological disease, Mr Moseley. If they've got bulimia, they'll never believe that they're thin enough. So if that's what this is with Aileen, she needs treatment right away. I don't want to alarm you, but I thought I'd tell you what I thought. Because if I'm right, your daughter needs to see a shrink.'

'Jesus Christ.'

'I'll talk to her if you want me to, because I could be wrong, you know.'

Hoke shook his head. 'I think you may be right, Itai. I should've noticed the signs myself. She always disappears after every meal, saying she's got an errand, or she's going out for a walk – even down in Green Lakes.'

'I've got some Early Times downstairs. Come down and I'll buy you a drink.'

'I'd better wait for Aileen to come back.'

'I know where she is. I can point her out to you from my window downstairs. After she throws up, she lies down on the bench by the parking lot. It makes you weak, you know, throwing up that way, so she always stretches out there to rest afterwards. Come on.'

They went downstairs to Itai's apartment and the professor pointed through his window to Aileen. She was lying on her back on the concrete bench, with both hands clasped behind her head.

560

'You want to look at the vomit?' Itai suggested. 'We can go outside, and I can show it to you behind the bush.'

'Fuck no, I don't want to see the vomit! Where's the Early Times?'

Itai brought out the bottle and glasses, and they had two shots apiece, without water or ice.

'I feel like a bastard, Mr Moseley. But this is pretty serious business, and if the girl doesn't get psychiatric treatment she could actually die.'

'Whatever happened to the brother?'

'What brother?'

'Karen Carpenter's brother.'

'I don't know. But he wasn't a bad musician. I imagine he found a job playing in a cocktail lounge somewhere. But they made so much money as a couple, he might've retired. Their records still sell pretty well. You hear them on the goldie-oldie stations sometimes.'

'Bulimia must be a female disease. I never heard of a man getting it, did you?'

'No way! Most men'll diet for a few days at a time, but men don't have the intestinal fortitude to starve themselves to death the way women do.'

'Thanks for the drinks, Itai. I appreciate you coming to me with this – and I owe you one.'

'I feel like a prick, being the informant, and I may be wrong. But it won't hurt anything to look into it.'

Hoke went back to his apartment, wishing he had hit up Itai for a third drink. He made a pot of coffee instead and waited for Aileen. She returned about fifteen minutes later. He told her to pour herself a cup of coffee and to join him at the table.

'You want to play some more Monopoly, Daddy? We can play the fast game –'

'No, I want to talk to you.'

'I don't want any coffee.'

'Sit down, anyway. When's the last time you had your period?'

'Oh, Daddy ...' Aileen blushed and looked away.

'When?'

'I haven't started yet.'

'That isn't true. Ellita told me once that both of you girls were menstruating. I'd been complaining to her about all the paper products that were coming into the house. She told me then, and I remember.'

'I did a few times, but then it stopped. I talked to Ellita about it, and she told me not to worry about it. Every woman's not the same, she said. Some are regular and some aren't, at least at first. Let's play Monopoly, Daddy. It's embarrassing to talk about this grungy stuff.'

'I want you to change into a dress and your good shoes.'

'What for?'

'Because I said so. And do it now!'

Aileen took a backless sundress into the bathroom to change, and Hoke put her canvas carryall on her bed. She wouldn't need much, but he packed the bag with underclothing, jeans, and T-shirts, taking them out of the cardboard box at the foot of the bed. He then put Aileen's sweater into the bag; she would need the sweater in L.A.

Hoke's jumpsuit was too tight under the arms for his shoulder holster, so he strapped on his stiff ankle holster instead. At least he could get his pants leg over it. He put his .38 Chief's Special in the holster, his shield and ID case in his right front pocket, and dropped his handcuffs into his rear pocket.

'Let's go,' Hoke said, when Aileen, dressed now and wearing a new pair of Mushrooms with her sundress, came out of the bathroom. He picked up her bag.

'What did you put in my bag?'

'Everything you'll need.'

They went downstairs. As Hoke unlocked his Le Mans, Dolly Turner emerged from the shadows of the building and clawed at his arm.

'You said I could sleep in your car, Mr Moseley, and now you're driving away.'

The car door was open, and Hoke could see by the dome light that Dolly Turner's left eye was black and blue. It was swollen, and the discoloring did not blend in well with her birthmark.

'We're using the car right now, Dolly. You can sleep in it when I get back.'

'There's 'skeeters out here,' Dolly whined.

'Okay. Hold onto this bag, and hop into the back seat.'

Hoke put Aileen into the passenger's seat in front, got in himself, and locked the doors. There was no release on Aileen's door; Hoke had had it removed to keep suspects from jumping out at red lights when he transported them in his car. Dolly sat in the middle of the narrow back seat, cradling Aileen's canvas bag in her ample lap.

Aileen sulked during the ride to the West Palm Beach International Airport, but after Hoke parked in the visitors' lot, and she realized she was actually being sent back to her mother, she said, 'I don't want to go back to Momma, or to Miami either. Grandpa said I should stay with you!'

'I'm your father, not your grandpa. Fathers don't always know best, but they do the best they can. Let's go. You too, Dolly.'

When they got inside the airport, Hoke told them both to sit down. He handcuffed Aileen's right wrist to Dolly's left wrist. 'Now you girls sit here while I get the tickets, and I'll be right back.'

Hoke went to the Eastern window and used his Visa card to buy two one-way tickets on the red-eye flight to Los Angeles. There was a half-hour stopover in Houston, the clerk said, and the flight left West Palm at two A.M.

'Don't you have a flight that goes straight through?'

'Sure, but not till ten A.M. tomorrow morning. I wouldn't wait for it if I were you. The stop in Houston isn't very long, and if you're asleep you probably won't even be aware of it.'

'I have a little problem. The "D. Turner" isn't me. It's the nurse over there on the bench. She's accompanying a mental patient to L.A., and I don't want her to try and get off the plane in Houston.'

The ticket seller, a long-armed young man with a fuzzy brown mustache, looked to where Hoke was pointing. He frowned when he noticed the handcuffs. 'Which one's the mental patient?'

'Don't be funny. The young girl's the patient.'

'I wasn't trying to be funny, it's just that I've never seen a nurse in a brown mini-skirt with a red apron. I just wanted to be sure which one so I could get word to the captain, that's all. She won't cause any trouble on the plane, will she?'

563

'Of course not.' Hoke showed the clerk his badge and ID case. 'This is a family thing, and we want to keep it quiet. The young girl's Curly Peterson's adopted daughter, and he'll meet the plane at LAX.'

'The pinch hitter for the Dodgers Curly Peterson?'

'That's the one.'

'I didn't know he had a daughter. Somehow, you don't think of a rich ballplayer, with all that dough they make, being dumb enough to get married. But a lot of 'em are married, I guess.'

'And they have daughters. Sometimes sons.'

'Right. You don't have to worry, Sergeant. I'll see to it that the captain's informed when the plane comes in. It'll be past my shift, but I'll stick around anyway to tell him. You couldn't pick a better airline than Eastern. We really do earn our wings every day.'

'I appreciate it.'

Hoke returned to the bench, removed Dolly's handcuff, and then locked Aileen's wrist to the bench rail. 'Come with me, Dolly. I want to talk to you for a minute.'

Hoke led Dolly over to the coin lockers, out of Aileen's earshot. Dolly's black eye looked worse under the bright lights than it had in the car, and there was a smear of blood on her T-shirt he hadn't noticed before. The white of her half-closed eye looked like a piece of red celluloid, and her fat cheek was puffy.

'Mr Farnsworth really hit you, didn't he?'

She nodded. 'But I got him back in a good place.'

'Okay. Here's what I want you to do, Dolly. You fly out to L.A. with my daughter, and when you get there her mother'll meet you and keep you on for a few days as a trained nurse –'

'I ain't never had no nurse's training, 'cept for the things I did for my daddy and all.'

'My ex-wife doesn't know that. Just tell her you're a trained nurse, and she'll want to pay you off – probably within a day or two – and then you ask her for fifty dollars a day.'

'That much?'

'That's right, including today. You've already earned fifty bucks, and you aren't even in L.A. yet. Then, after she pays you off, go to the Welfare Department in downtown L.A. and apply for emergency relief. You can't get on regular welfare till you've lived there a year, but in California all new arrivals qualify for emergency relief. They'll fix you up with a room, food stamps, or a meal ticket, and then you can look for a job out there. It's easy to get a job in a kitchen in California, and you'll have a better future there than in Riviera Beach.'

'Don't I need permission or something to leave the state?'

'No. Who told you that?'

'I don't know. I was born here, up in Yeehaw Junction, and I thought I had to get permission.'

'Hell, no, Dolly. You can go anywhere you like. This is practically a free country. And if you don't like California, you can always ask them at the welfare office to send you back. But I know you'll like it out there. The important thing is to not let the girl get off the plane when it stops in Houston. My ex-wife, Mrs Peterson, will be waiting for you at the L.A. airport. Okay?'

'Do they feed us on the plane?'

'Sure, you get two breakfasts on the red-eye. One between here and Houston, and another breakfast somewhere around the Grand Canyon. Meanwhile, I'll get you something out of the machine. Here's the key to the cuffs. Go back and cuff yourself to Aileen again.'

'And a diet Orange Crush, if they have it.'

'There's an orange juice machine, I'm sure.'

'If they don't have an Orange Crush, I'd rather have a Classic Coke.'

Hoke got some change from the change machine and bought two ham-and-cheese sandwiches, two bags of Doritos, and two half-pints of orange juice from the machines. He brought them back to the bench. He handed one sandwich to Aileen, and gave the rest to Dolly.

'If it was Sue Ellen instead of me,' Aileen said, 'you wouldn't send *her* out to Los Angeles. You've always loved Sue Ellen better than me. But someday you're going to be sorry you did this, just wait and see! I won't forget it, neither, handcuffing me like a criminal!'

'Eat your sandwich.'

565

'I'm not hungry.'

'You should be, after throwing up your dinner.'

'Who told you that?'

'Never mind. I love both you girls the same, and if Sue Ellen had the same problem you have I'd send her to L.A. too.'

'You always wanted a boy instead of me!'

'Is that what you think?'

'I heard you tell Ellita once you wished you had a son.'

'That was in addition to you two girls, not instead of, for Christ's sake. Is that why you're trying to stay thin? Are you trying to look like a boy instead of a girl?'

'You don't know or care anything about me!' Aileen's brown eyes filled with tears, and she shook her head to clear them away. 'Nothing!'

'Don't cry, honey,' Dolly said, offering the opened bag. 'Have some Doritos.'

Hoke went to the bank of pay telephones and used his Sprint card to call Patsy in Glendale. The phone rang ten times before Patsy picked it up. Hoke sighed when she answered.

'Patsy, this is me, Hoke.'

'You caught me as I was going out the door, so make it short. I've got to pick up Curly at the studio. He's doing a commercial for the new California Chili-Size people. You know how much he gets for a thirty-second spot?'

'No, and I don't give a shit. This is an emergency, Patsy, or I wouldn't've called. Aileen came down with bulimia, and I'm sending her out to you with a trained nurse on the Eastern red-eye, Flight 3. I want you to meet the plane with a doctor and get her into a hospital right away.'

'What's she got?'

'Bulimia. It's a wasting-away disease, and if she isn't treated by an expert she can die from it.'

'Can't she be treated there in Florida?'

'No, it's a California-type disease. They know more about it there than they do here. Jane Fonda had it, and Karen Carpenter died from it. Aileen needs a specialist. Your doctor'll know who to call in for a consultation. So you'd better bring him along when you meet the plane. I don't know if you'll need an ambulance or not. Probably not, but you'd better ask him about that too.'

'How long's she had it?'

'I don't know. I just found out today myself. But she's a very sick girl. She only weighs about eighty pounds.'

'She weighed ninety-five six months ago!'

'See what I mean? You got a pencil and paper?'

'Just a sec –'

Hoke repeated the flight number and gave her the time of arrival at LAX. 'Please call me at Dad's house when she gets there, and let me know what the doctor says.'

'Are you up at Grandpa's?'

'I'll wait for your call at his house. I'm staying at the El Pelicano, here on Singer Island, and I haven't got a phone.'

'What are you doing up there?'

'I quit the force, and I'm managing the El Pelicano for Frank.'

'What about my alimony? You owe me three checks already.'

'Jesus Christ, Patsy, your husband makes three hundred and twenty-five thousand bucks a year!'

'More than that, counting commercials, but what's that got to do with our final agreement?'

'Let's talk about money later, okay? Right now you've got to get a hold of a doctor, so he can have Aileen admitted to a hospital when she gets there.'

'When the girls lived with me, they were never sick for a single day.'

Remembering the pediatrician's bills Patsy had sent him in the ten years the girls had lived with her, Hoke almost said something about it, but he restrained himself.

'In that case,' he said, 'you shouldn't have sent 'em back to me.' He racked the phone before she could reply. Perhaps he had overstated Aileen's illness, but with Patsy he always had to exaggerate to get her attention. He only hoped now that he had elaborated Aileen's condition sufficiently so that Patsy would get the girl some help.

The wait for the two A.M. departure seemed interminable. Aileen stared at Hoke with loathing and tightened lips, but gradually her mood changed for the better. Hoke got the key from Dolly Turner and took off the handcuffs when Dolly said they had to go to the bathroom.

'Okay, Dolly, but don't let her throw up in there.'

When they returned, Hoke didn't cuff them again. He returned the handcuffs to his hip pocket. When the flight was called, Hoke walked them to the gate. Aileen seemed resigned to the trip to L.A. She gave him a weak smile and took his hand.

'I love you, Daddy.'

'I love you, too, honey. And just as soon as you're well again, I want you back. I hope you know that.'

Aileen nodded. 'I'll be back soon, Daddy.' He hugged her, and kissed her on the cheek.

'If you happen to see Mr Farnsworth tomorrow,' Dolly said, 'ask him to tell 'em over at the hotel that I've done quit and went out to Hollywood.'

'I'll tell him.'

Hoke drove back to the island, feeling embarrassed and guilty at the same time. It was embarrassing to have a stranger – a tenant – tell you that your daughter had a psychological disease like bulimia, and he felt guilty for not picking up on the signs himself. He had been so wrapped up in his own concerns, he had neglected both of the girls; and for that matter, he had been pretty abrupt with Ellita when he had talked to her on the phone.

Hoke parked in his slot at the El Pelicano and checked his mailbox in the lobby, the first time he had looked into it since Thursday. There was an advertising flyer from Es-Steem-Cleaners, offering a $21-per-room rug shampoo, and there was a Mailgram from Ellita in the box.

On Mailgrams, Hoke knew, they telephoned the message and sent the letter the next day. But he didn't have a phone, so the Mailgram could have been in his box since Friday or Saturday morning. The message was short: HOKE, CALL ME AT YOUR EARLIEST CONVENIENCE. ELLITA.

Hoke left the lobby and crossed the lot to the pay phone beside the brightly lighted 7-Eleven store. The Singer Island store was open twenty-four hours a day now, which made the 7-Eleven sign meaningless. It took Hoke three tries on the pay phone to get Ellita. To use his Sprint card he had to dial thirty-six numbers altogether: the 1-800, the 305 area code, and his Green Lakes number. Then he had to dial his Green Lakes number again, and finish with his authorization code number. Even when he took his time dialing, it was hard to keep all of the numbers straight in his head in the dim light of the booth.

Ellita answered on the fifth ring. 'Allo?'

'It's me, Ellita. I know it's late, or early, but I just picked up your Mailgram.'

'What time is it? I was asleep.'

'A little after three.'

'And they just delivered the Mailgram? I called it in Friday.'

'It's my fault, Ellita. I just now got around to checking my mailbox. You could've called me at Frank's house. We spent almost all afternoon over there.'

'I didn't want to bother him. When I called before to ask after you, he was a little cross, I thought. But a problem's come up, Hoke, and I wanted to talk to you about it. You remember when Dr Gomez told me I should have the amniocentesis, and you told me not to do it?'

'You're damn right I did. You don't need a needle stuck into your belly, and he's only trying to gouge you for more money.'

'Insurance pays eighty percent, Hoke –'

'I know, but the other twenty percent comes out of your pocketbook. Besides, it's the principle of the thing. We discussed this –'

'But here's the problem, Hoke. He wants me to sign a paper absolving him of responsibility for any birth defects in the baby – just because I turned down the amniocentesis. My mother says I should have it, and not sign the paper.'

'Look, Ellita, it's the same as I told you the first time. You're a healthy woman, and you don't need to know whether you're going to have a boy or a girl –'

'It's a boy, Hoke. He kicks like a boy.'

'All right, then. And if they discovered any birth defects, you'd have him anyway, wouldn't you?'

'Of course. He's my baby. I know I'm going to love him no matter what.'

'Then sign Gomez's paper and let him off the hook. Your mother's old-fashioned and still thinks that doctors know everything. She's into authority figures, that's all. But don't let me influence you either way, Ellita. If you want to do it, go ahead. I'm just telling you what I think.'

'I don't think I need it, either, Hoke, but I wanted to talk to someone about it first. I'll just go ahead and sign his paper.'

'I'm sorry I didn't phone you earlier, but like I said, I just now got your Mailgram.'

Hoke was going to tell her about Aileen's affliction, and sudden flight to California, but he decided that this was not the best time. It would be better to wait on that, until after he had heard from Patsy.

'I'm a little curious, Hoke. How come you checked your mailbox at three in the morning?'

'Oh? I thought I heard a disturbance downstairs, so I checked it out. But it was just a couple of cats fighting. While I was downstairs, I checked the box, that's all. How's Sue Ellen?'

Ellita laughed, but quickly suppressed it. 'Sue Ellen? I don't know about Sue Ellen, whether she's all right or not.'

'What do you mean? She isn't sick, is she?'

'No, she's fine, but she did something awful to her hair. She had it cut short on the sides, and then had it dyed green – right down the middle.'

'That doesn't sound like something she'd do willingly. Do you suppose that –?'

'She dyed it for the concert, she said. The whole gang at the car wash is going to the Dead Kennedys concert at the Hollywood Sportatorium. And Sue Ellen wanted the new punk look, she said.'

'That's okay, then.' Hoke sighed with relief. 'I thought she might be sick or something. I see a lot of young girls with dyed hair here on the beach.'

'Green?'

'Sure. Green, blue, different colors. It's just a fad; next month, or next year, they'll dream up something else.'

'You don't mind, then?'

'No, why should I mind? After all, Sue Ellen's the only girl working with those blacks and Cubans at the car wash, so she's got to prove she's just as tough as they are. So give her my love, and tell her to have a good time at the concert.'

'I will. She was a little worried about what you'd think. She also paid thirty-five dollars for her ticket.'

'That much? Well, why not? As the song says, she works hard for her money. Tell her to take a Saturday off sometime and come up here for the weekend. If she takes the bus, I can drive over and pick her up at the Riviera Beach station.'

'Not this weekend. She's going to the concert.'

'I know, but maybe next weekend. And tell her that Grandpa sends his love, too. Are you okay now, Ellita?'

'Sure, I'm okay. I'm feeling pretty good. I just wasn't going to sign Dr Gomez's chit without talking it over with you first.'

'Good. Go back to sleep, and I'll call you in a couple of days.'

Hoke bought a four-pack of wine coolers in the 7-Eleven and drank all four bottles before he fell into a fitful sleep. His alarm woke him at six-thirty. He showered and shaved, put on a clean jumpsuit, and drove to his father's house to wait for a call from Patsy. He missed Aileen already, and he was glad that he had told the girl he wanted her to come back. Maybe Sue Ellen actually would come up for a weekend. Frank, he knew, would like to see her, green hair and all, and while she was here she could ride Aileen's bike.

Chapter Twelve

After Stanley and Troy left the house, Troy drove in silence until he was stopped by a red light. He turned and winked at the old man. 'I think it's hot enough for a beer.'

'I can always stand a beer. Sometimes two,' Stanley agreed.

'I've been thinking about this little car of yours, Pop. We'll need a much bigger car for the rest of us. Besides, the clutch slips on James's little Morris.'

Troy parked in front of a beer-and-wine bar on Second Avenue, and they went inside. Except for a middle-aged bartender and a few buzzing insects beating against the red neon Budweiser sign in the window, the dark bar was deserted. There were three booths and a half-dozen stools – most of the seats crisscrossed with gray duct tape – at the aluminum-topped bar. Troy ordered two long-necked bottles of Bud and told the bartender to bring them over to the booth with cold steins. Pop paid, and Troy filled the frosted mugs.

'Beer from a long-necked bottle tastes better than it does from a short-necked bottle,' Troy said. 'But I suppose you know that?'

Stanley nodded. Troy took a swallow, and so did Stanley.

'This is just right,' Troy said. 'Tell me something, Pop, what do you think of Dale Forrest?'

'I just met her, Troy, so I haven't thought much of anything about her. She seems like a nice enough girl, but what happened to her face? Was she in an automobile accident?'

Troy laughed. 'No, not in an "automobile accident." It's a funny thing, but people call cars "cars" until they refer to accidents, and then all of a sudden it becomes an *automobile* accident. Let me tell you something, Pop' – Troy snapped his fingers – 'I'm going to help that girl. And if you feel any compassion at all for Dale, I want you to help me help her.'

'Sure, Troy. I'll do what I can, but I don't –'

'You can do a lot, Pop, a helluva lot. Just to look at her now, you'd never guess that she was once Miss Bottlecapping Industry of Daytona Beach, would you?'

'She's got a nice shape.' Stanley wet his thumb. 'I can say that much.'

'You noticed that, did you?' Troy grinned.

'I ain't making fun, son. It's just that it's easier to look at her figure than her face. That's all I meant.'

'Maybe, Pop, I see something in Dale you don't see. I see the shining inner beauty of the woman. To me, what's inside is much more beautiful than a battered exterior. Do you know what I'm talking about?'

Stanley nodded. 'Sure. Beauty's only skin deep. I won't argue none about that.'

'Yes' – Troy nodded and took another sip of beer – 'but it's much more than that, Pop, in a spiritual sense. I'm gonna fill you in some on Dale's background, and then you can appreciate what a beautiful woman she really is – not only in her body but in her soul. A man must help himself in this world, but sometimes he needs a bit of understanding from other people. I think Dale's taken a step forward into a better and richer life by listening to me, but now that this responsibility has been thrust upon me, I feel it right here, deep inside.' Troy tapped his chest, took another sip of beer, and sighed. 'Not only am I responsible for Dale Forrest, but I've got a duty to James Frietas-Smith, and an even greater debt to you.'

'You don't have to worry none about me, son. I been looking after myself for a good many years now, and I can keep on for a few more.'

'Exactly!' Troy thumped the table with his fist. 'That's what I mean! Why should you? Why should any man your age have to look after himself? Because nobody loves you, that's why. Well, all that's changed now, Pop. You aren't alone in the world any longer. One man, at least, cares what happens to you, and that man is me! Why, you've got more get-up-and-go than any of these Miami yuppies. And certainly more than those slugs up in Ocean Pines Terraces. How many up there – think for a minute – would pack up and come down here to Miami to help me out the way you did? Just to help a friend in need?'

'Not many, I guess,' Stanley said uneasily. 'But I –'

'No excuses, Pop, please. I needed you and you came. It's that simple. Let's forget about it, and I won't embarrass you by trying to thank you. Instead' – Troy reached across the table and took Stanley's right hand in both of his – 'I'll try to be the son you always wanted to have but never had ...'

Stanley's eyes blurred a little. To cover his emotion, he drank the rest of his beer. He opened his mouth to say something, but Troy shook his head.

'Let me tell you about Dale Forrest, Pop. Right now, that girl and that young Bajan painter need our help, and we've got to do something to help them. Tell me the truth, Pop, what do you think of James's painting?'

'Well, I ain't any art expert, Troy, but I'd say that the boy needs some lessons from an art teacher of some kind. He seems willing enough to learn, all right. I was showing him how to stripe, and he was catching on a little bit when you drove up with Miss Forrest.'

'I've really got to hand it to you, Pop. You grasped James's problem immediately, and you stuck the needle into the nerve. James needs art instruction desperately, even though he's bulging with native Bajan talent. You and I can see to it that he gets to the Art Students League up in New York. And then, someday, we'll be sitting back, after James becomes a famous painter, and we can say, "We helped that boy when he needed it most, and we're proud we did!" Isn't that right?'

'Just a minute, Troy.' Stanley leaned forward and frowned. 'I'd like to help that Bajan just as much as you, but I'm on a fixed income –'

'Christ, you didn't think I wanted money, did you? I'm the one who's putting out the money for James's studies in New York. It'll all come from my end. What I want from you is a steadying influence. I want you to give James and Dale the benefit of your wisdom and experience, that's all. You must've misunderstood me. I don't imagine you brought more than a few hundred dollars down here with you anyway. Right?'

'Well, I didn't know exactly how long I'd be staying. I brought along five hundred in traveler's checks. Of course, I've got my checkbook with me, and Visa card.'

'That'll be enough. Your needs are simple, and while you're staying with me you're my guest, of course. The last thing I want you to worry about is money. But you have to let me tell you about Dale.

'A few months ago, believe it or not, she was on her way to stardom on the Gold Coast here. She was already the featured stripper at the Kitty Kat Theater, and she sang a solo, "Deep Purple," before her act. They have these live acts between showings of Triple-X movies at the Kitty Kat, see? Eight girls altogether, and Dale was one of the featured stars, with a life-sized cutout on a poster board in the lobby. She already had a slogan her manager wrote for her, "You can't see Dale Forrest for the trees!"' Troy shook his head. 'She was on her way up, no question about it.

'Her manager had a new gig lined up for her in East Saint Louis. The next step would've been burlesque on State Street, in Chicago. Then, inevitably, New York, and into television. Eventually, and I'm sure of it, she could have been one of those pretty girls on daytime TV, on one of the talk shows, leading guests on and off the stage. And then, blooie!' Troy slapped the table so hard the bartender jumped.

'Yes, sir!' the bartender said. 'Two long-necked Buds, coming up!'

'What happened?' Stanley picked at the scab on his upper lip.

Troy sat back and lowered his voice. 'She fell in love.'

The bartender took some money from the pile of bills and change in front of Stanley. 'Take a dollar for yourself,' Troy told him.

'Thank you, sir.'

'Now there's nothing unusual about falling in love,' Troy was saying. 'Dale's young. She won't be twenty-one for another five months, even though she looks older. And the guy she fell in love with was a handsome young cab driver. He was also a part-time student at the community college, taking a course in real estate. He was an athlete, too, Dale told me, playing slow-pitch softball every Sunday at Tropical Park. They were star-crossed lovers, Pop. Dale was already a flickering star, with only one way to go – straight

575

to the top. But here was a guy who only wanted a real-estate license so he could sit around in empty houses on Sundays instead of playing softball. Compared to Dale, the boy had no future at all. See what I mean?'

'I think so. She was riding in his cab and they had a car wreck.'

'No, that isn't what happened. I'm just filling you in on the background so you'll see that marriage was out of the question. Here was a handsome man, but he had no real purpose in life. Dale was heading for stardom, but if she'd married him, she would've had to give up her dream. That's the American way, Pop. If a man can't support his wife, he's got no business getting married.'

'That's right. But it's okay if his wife works part-time.'

'I didn't mean part-time. It's nice for a woman to get out of the house for a few hours every day, but Dale would've had to give up show business.'

'What happened?' Stanley refilled his glass.

'None of us are saints, Pop. All of us are human, so Dale started fucking the cab driver. If that was all there was to it, there wouldn't've been no problem. Once something like that starts, they get tired of each other after a while, and it would have ended. She would've gone on to stardom, and he, in all probability, would've finished his real-estate course. But it also happened that Dale was fucking her manager. After all, he had discovered her, picking her out of a group of girls in a wet T-shirt contest up in Daytona Beach. He gave Dale her first break, and he was pushing her toward the top. He was entitled to screw her for his trouble, and she wasn't making any big money yet. In show business, that's the way things are done. You've probably seen the same thing in movies.'

Stanley nodded. 'On TV, too.'

'But this is a real-life story. Dale isn't too smart; her manager wasn't too shrewd either. But he found out about the cab driver, and that's what happened to Dale's face. Her manager busted in on her in the middle of the night and beat the hell out of her, and that was the end of her stage career. No matter how beautiful her body still is, her face would frighten the customers.'

'That man should be put in jail for ruining her face that way.'

'Not so fast, Pop. You aren't looking at this objectively. Things are more complicated than that. It could be argued, for example, that Dale deserved to be worked over a little. After all, her manager was putting in a lot of time and effort in furthering her career. She had no business risking it with a cab driver. And the fact is, her manager didn't intend to mark her up that way, either. She was his bread and butter. But unfortunately, he was drunk at the time, and he forgot to take off his rings. He had a great big signet and a pinky, and that's what cut up her face so bad. And, being drunk, he kept on hitting her for a long time after he should've quit. You've got to admit she had a whipping coming.'

'No, sir.' Stanley shook his head. 'A man should never hit a woman with his fists.'

'What would you have done, if you were her manager?'

'I don't know, Troy. It takes a lot to make me mad, but I wouldn't've hit her, drunk or sober.'

'Exactly. You'd have punished her, and so would I, but we've both got enough sense not to hit a woman where it'll mark up her face. Now that Dale's put herself under my protection, I can't look at her situation objectively. It's up to me to get her fixed up again, so she can go on with her career. I just don't believe that a beautiful girl like Dale should suffer for one mistake, do you?'

'Of course not. But what –?'

'Here's the answer, Pop, right here.' Troy unsnapped the top buttons of his shirt and withdrew a brown envelope. He opened it and handed Stanley a color brochure of Haiti, with a photograph of the Gran Hotel Olofsson on the cover. 'Haiti. That's the answer, Pop. When I met James in New Orleans, he told me a lot about the West Indies, and he sold me on the idea of living in the islands. I went to a travel agent here and looked at folders on all the different islands, and Haiti looks best of all. Except for visiting border towns in Mexico, Tijuana and Juarez, I haven't been out of the United States.'

'Me neither, except for Canada. I been in Canada lots of times, but not Mexico. Where is this Haiti?'

'The other side of Cuba. My original idea was to just go island-hopping, taking a plane from one island to another till I found one I really liked. But Dale has changed my plans. There's a plastic surgeon over in Haiti, a German doctor who lost his license in the States, but he can still practice in Haiti. A con I knew in Soledad told me about him – you know, in case you ever wanted to change how you look? He's supposed to be a top man. Well, I'm going to Haiti, Pop, and I'm going to find that surgeon for Dale.'

Stanley tapped the folder. 'That'll take a lot of money, won't it?'

'Don't you think Dale's worth it? And doesn't James deserve a chance to study art in New York?'

'Sure.' Stanley nodded.

'And what about you, Pop? Wouldn't you like to see Haiti?'

'I don't rightly know. I'm not sure where it is, even.'

'It's only two hours away from Miami, Pop, on Air France. And that's where you, me, and Dale are going next Sunday morning.'

'I don't know about that. That's pretty short notice. Don't you need a passport and some shots and things like that?'

'Not to go to Haiti you don't. I already checked it out with the travel agent. You can stay sixty days without a passport or visa, and as long as you've got money and a return ticket they'll keep extending your stay. Indefinitely. You don't need any shots, either. Round trips for the three of us, not counting taxes, will cost six hundred and sixty-nine dollars. Two-twenty-three apiece.'

Stanley whistled softly. 'That's a lot of money.'

'Not for me it isn't. By Saturday night I'll have twenty-five, maybe thirty thousand dollars. Four thousand'll go to James, for New York, and then, after I pay you back two thousand, plus the vig, that'll still leave plenty for the three of us to go to Haiti, live in a nice hotel, and pay for Dale's operation. And while we're there, everything's on me, Pop. Transportation, hotel, drinks, anything you want, and for as long as you want to stay.'

'What's this about paying me back two thousand?' Stanley straightened in the booth.

'I figure it's no more than right, Pop. I know it's only a short-term loan, but you're entitled to interest all the same. I'll need two thousand from you now, and on Saturday night I pay you back twenty-five hundred. I think that's fair, don't you?'

'Where're you gonna get all this money? The twenty-five or thirty thousand, I mean, to pay me back?'

'I'm holding up the new Green Lakes Supermarket, here in Miami. I thought I already told you. And I'm letting James and Dale help me.'

'No, you never told me nothing like that. I can't loan you no money to commit a robbery! One of the main reasons I came down here was to keep you out of trouble. And why do you need two thousand anyway?'

'To pay for our airplane tickets, for one thing. There's a flight leaving Miami at twelve-forty Sunday, and we'll be on it, me, you, and Dale. I also need some cash to buy some things for the job. These are all ordinary business expenses. You know as well as I do, it takes a little money to make a lot of money.'

'But if you get caught, you'll go to jail, Troy. And then where'll you be?'

'This job is foolproof, Pop. I've never seen a better setup than this one. Christ, this is what I do for a living. Hey – you're not prejudiced, are you, just because James is a black man?'

'Black? James? You said he was a Bajan. He don't look black to me.'

'Well, he is black, as well as being a Bajan. He's at least a fourth black, maybe more, so that makes him a black according to southern laws. But that's just another reason he needs my professional help. If he tried to do this job on his own, as he intended to at first, he'd get caught. You ever hear of Affirmative Action, Pop?'

'Of course. We had it at Ford. Ford's an equal opportunity employer.'

'All right, then. Chew this over for a few minutes. Blacks in this country are only about ten percent, or perhaps a little more. But in prisons, about *forty* percent of the prisoners are black. In city jails, the percentage is even higher. Why do you think this happens, Pop? So many black men in jail?'

'I don't know. I never thought much about it.'

'Well, I have. It's because there's no Affirmative Action plan for black ex-criminals, that's why. Without proper guidance and training, they almost always get caught and end up in prison. But

I believe in Affirmative Action, and that's another reason why I want to help James. This particular job was originally his idea, but I planned it, and I'll see that it's carried out properly. James is a pretty desperate nonobjective painter, and he needs my help almost as much as Dale does. But I never thought you were prejudiced –'

'I'm not prejudiced, Troy. I'll admit that with Affirmative Action, you sometimes got a pretty dumb black foreman on the line. But some of the white foremen were just as dumb, I always thought. When you consider the aggravation and responsibility that goes with being a foreman, the extra money isn't worth it.'

'That's true, Pop. I could never understand why the so-called correction officers worked for such low pay, either, but there's always someone dumb enough to take a guard's job. But you won't find many professional white criminals like me who'll train a black man under Affirmative Action. And this'll be my last professional robbery. When we go to Haiti, and after the surgeon starts work on Dale, which'll take several months, I'm going to start a business over there, one way or another. The Haitians make and wear these voodoo masks, you see. I figure Dale, with her figure and strip act, and wearing a voodoo mask, can get work at one of the tourist nightclubs. That way, she'll keep up with her dancing while her face is healing, and be ready to take up her career back here when it's all over. We can rent us a beach house and eat fresh lobster for lunch every day. How does that sound?'

'It sounds fine, Troy, but two thousand dollars –'

'Two thousand loaned for twenty-five hundred back is a profit-able deal, Pop. Besides, I don't even need cash. I'll just borrow your Visa card, and by the time your bill comes in a month from now, you'll have already been paid back your twenty-five hundred in cash. Of course, if that isn't enough interest for you, tell me what you want.'

'It ain't the interest, Troy. I want to help you, but –'

'And James and Dale?'

'Them, too. But I don't want you to go to jail.'

'You're worried about the loss to the supermarket? Is that it? Well, don't worry about that. They have insurance, so they won't lose a dime. In fact, they'll probably pad their loss, saying it was more than it was. In an operation like this one, nobody loses and everybody gains.'

'Tell me a little more about the job.'

'I'd rather not, Pop. The less you know, the better off you'll be. After this is all over, and you come back from Haiti, some cop might ask you about it. And if you don't know anything, you won't be able to tell him anything. I want to keep you out of this thing altogether, Pop. See what I mean? I want to protect you just like I'm protecting James and Dale.'

'Let me think a minute, Troy. It's a lot to take in all at once, if you know what I mean ...'

'Of course. Take all the time you want. There's no big rush about this. We've got till Saturday night. Want some pretzels?'

'A little too salty.' Stanley shook his head. 'But I'd like one of those small packs of barbecue chips.'

Troy picked a dollar up from a small stack of bills and went over to the bar to look through the snack rack. Stanley took a sip of beer.

What would happen, he thought, if he turned Troy down? Everything between them would change, and quickly. If he still stayed on for a few days, the relationship between them would be strained, and he had truly been enjoying himself. It was all so interesting and exciting, being in the city with Troy, with James. Even Dale, now that he knew about her show-business background, was a more exciting woman. On the other hand, if he lent Troy the money – which wouldn't hurt him too much, since it was out of savings, even if it wasn't paid back for a while – and Troy carried out this big robbery, Troy might end up in prison again. And he didn't want to be responsible for that, even indirectly ...

Troy was back at the booth, handing Stanley a bag of Wise barbecue potato chips. 'These are just as salty as pretzels, aren't they?'

'Maybe so, but the barbecue flavor gives 'em a better taste. They go good with beer.' Stanley opened the bag, poured a handful of chips into his left hand, and offered some to Troy. Troy shook his head and made his lightning grimace.

'What happens, Troy, if I don't loan you the money?'

Troy shrugged, grimacing again, pulling his thin lips tightly over his small teeth. 'James and me'll have to cowboy it, that's all. We'll have to drive around at night and hold up some liquor stores and gas stations. Two thousand isn't much. In two or three nights we'll have the stake. That's what I usually do when I need some quick cash. But James is inexperienced, and a little on the nervous side. That's why I asked you instead.'

'In other words, you're gonna go through with this big robbery you planned, whether I help you or not?'

'You know I am, Pop. I already told you before, this is what I do. But I won't press you. If you don't think you're getting a good return on your investment, forget I asked you. And if you don't trust me –'

'I trust you, Troy.' Stanley licked his fingers. 'Hell, if I can't trust you, who can I trust? Besides, as they say, one hand washes the other.'

'Now you're talking. Just let me borrow your Visa card, your union card, and voter's registration for ID. You can then drive back to the house, and I'll get a cab to take care of business.'

'I don't have no voter's registration card. Down here in Florida, if you register to vote they make you serve jury duty.'

'Your Social Security card'll do just as well.'

'That ain't supposed to be used for identification. It says so right on the card.'

'The man I'm dealing with will accept it, Pop. Trust me.'

Stanley took out his wallet, found the cards, and handed them over to Troy. Troy slipped them into his shirt pocket. He snapped the flap shut. 'I'll take the rest of the change here on the table for cab fare. You keep the travel folder and show it to Dale when you get back to the apartment. She hasn't seen it yet. You better cash one or two traveler's checks, too. But keep a record of every cent you give Dale for groceries. We can add that in on top of your twenty-five hundred next Saturday.'

Troy dropped the Honda keys on the table and slid out of the booth. 'Finish the rest of my beer, Pop –'

'Just a minute, Troy. Whatever happened to the cab driver?'

'What cab driver?'

'You know, the one who was carrying on with Dale.'

'Oh, him? He visited Dale in the hospital, took one good look at her, and she's never seen him again. Some men are like that.'

'That poor girl.' Stanley shook his head and poured the rest of Troy's beer into his stein. 'She's lucky she found you.'

'I think she knows it, Pop.' Troy kissed the old man on the cheek and left the bar.

Stanley trusted Troy about the money. After all, he thought, everything so far had happened the way Troy said it would, so Stanley had no reason not to trust him, and he could tell that Troy genuinely liked him. Stanley had worked with other men all of his life, and he could tell whether someone was sincere or not, and Troy was the only person who had paid any attention to him since he had moved to Florida. On the other hand, the credit limit on Stanley's Visa card was all the way up to $2,200. Without even asking him, the bank had automatically raised the limit by two hundred dollars when he had renewed the card two months ago. Any way he looked at the matter, he couldn't afford to outright lose two thousand dollars, even though, as Troy said, his intention was to pay back five hundred in interest just for using the money till Saturday. Stanley picked up his beer and his cane and crossed to the bar.

'Can I use your phone?'

'There's a pay phone in the hall, back there by the john. You need any change? It takes quarters.'

'No. I've got change. But I can't read phone numbers too good, even with my reading glasses. Would you look up the eight-hundred number of Visa for me? And write it down?' Stanley put a dollar bill on the bar and pushed it toward the bartender. The bartender put the bill into a glass beneath the bar, then got the battered L–Z telephone book from the shelf to look up the number.

Stanley called the Visa number the bartender gave him and told the woman who answered that he had lost his Visa card.

'Do you have the number?'

'No, but I can give you my Social Security number and address.'

'Let me have your name first.'

Stanley gave her his name, Ocean Pines Terraces address, and Social Security number.

'When did you lose your card?'

'Yesterday, I think. But I didn't miss it till just now.'

'All right. You'll get a replacement card in a week or so, but it'll have a new number. Not exactly a new number, but four additional zeros will be added in the middle. And this time please write it down and keep it in a safe place, in case you lose it again.'

'If someone finds and uses my card I won't be charged more'n fifty dollars, will I?'

'That's correct. But you should be very careful with your Visa card. It's not the same as money, it's better than money.'

'Yes, ma'am. I might've just misplaced it, but far's I know now, it's lost.'

'Yes, sir. Now if you do find it, don't use it. Just cut it in half and mail it in to us. Wait until you get your replacement card before you charge anything again.'

'Yes, ma'am. I'm sorry I lost my card.'

'We're sorry, too. But thanks for reporting the loss promptly, and have a rainbow day.'

'Yes, ma'am.'

Stanley folded the slip of paper with the Visa phone number on it and put it into his wallet. It would take the Visa people a day or two, perhaps more, to get the missing number on their lists, and by that time, Troy would have an ample opportunity to charge whatever he wanted. He felt a little guilty about reporting his card as lost, but if everything worked out all right, he could call Visa again and tell them he had found it after all. A fifty-dollar loss wouldn't hurt him too much, but a two-thousand-dollar loss, when a man was on a fixed income, was simply too much. What he would do, Stanley decided, was to just ask Troy for two hundred dollars in interest, instead of five hundred, when he got his money back. After all, the money Troy was going to make was primarily for Dale's and James's benefit, and Stanley felt sorry for both of them.

Stanley filled his car with gas and cashed a fifty-dollar traveler's check before driving back to James's garage apartment.

Chapter Thirteen

Patsy didn't call Hoke at Frank Moseley's house until almost noon. On the advice of Curly Peterson's doctor, Patsy said, Aileen had been placed in a clinic at a Catholic convent in the Verdugo Woodlands section of Glendale. There she would be watched around the clock by the live-in sisters who ran the school.

'It's much better than a regular hospital, Hoke,' Patsy said, 'because as far as anybody knows, she'll be just another student there. Curly worries about his image, and it wouldn't look good for him if it got into the papers that his stepdaughter was starving to death. Not with his income.'

'She isn't Curly Peterson's daughter. She's *our* daughter.'

'Well, it wouldn't look good for you or me either, would it, if Aileen starved to death? Besides, Dr Jordan'll look in on her every day. Curly said Dr Jordan practically wrote the book on sports medicine, and he has a lot of confidence in him.'

'She needs psychiatric help, not sports medicine. All those guys know how to do is shoot people in the knee with painkillers.'

'That's easy for you to say. If you saw the bone spurs on Curly's feet, you'd want shots, too. But the Mother Superior will talk to Aileen every day, and she told me she's had a lot of experience with anorexics. Apparently some of the nuns have had it, and some of the convent girls come down with it on Novenas, she said.'

'What are Novenas? One thing I know for sure, Aileen doesn't take any drugs –'

'I don't know what they are, and I didn't ask. I'm just telling you what the Mother Superior told me, that's all. The important thing is she knows all about anorexics, and she'll watch Aileen like a hawk and supervise her diet. She's got little black eyes like shiny caraway seeds.'

'How serious is Aileen's case? And when'll she be cured?'

'It just takes time and patience, Dr Jordan said. But first she's got to gain some weight and accept the idea that she's not too fat. I already promised her that when she gets up to one hundred pounds I'd take her home. So we'll just have to wait and see, that's all. She ate breakfast before the doctor gave her a shot, and that's a good sign. I already fired that weird nurse you sent out with Aileen, by the way. Where'd you find her, anyway?'

'On short notice, it was hard to get a nurse willing to fly out to L.A. I hope you paid her –'

'I did, and you owe me another hundred dollars.'

'You'll get it, Patsy, just as soon as my pension money comes in. After my retirement papers go through, I'll take all my money out of the pension fund in a lump sum. And as soon as Aileen's well again, I want her back. But right now, money's tight.'

'You *have* to take her back, Hoke. I go on all the road games with Curly, and we can't take her with us. If Curly told me once he told me a dozen times, he married *me* – not my daughters. Sometimes, when he's at bat, the camera points at me, and they tell the TV audience I'm his wife, and he likes that.'

'I can understand all that. But if you handle the clinic and doctor bills, I'll take Aileen back, and gradually pay you back. Sue Ellen's got a good job in Miami, so I don't have to worry about her' – Hoke didn't mention the green Mohawk haircut – 'but Aileen'll have to go back to school in September.'

'Sue Ellen's got a job? That's hard to believe. I couldn't even get her to pick her clothes up off the floor in Vero Beach.'

'What can I tell you, Patsy? She's getting minimum wage, plus tips, at the Green Lakes Car Wash.'

'She has to go back to school, too, doesn't she?'

'No, she's dropping out. They like her at the car wash, and the manager gave her a permanent job.'

'What kind of career is that for a girl? Only wetbacks work in car washes here in California.'

'It's mostly Haitians down here. Sue Ellen's the only white girl there. But that gives her an advantage, she says. It won't hurt her to work for two or three years. Then, if she wants to go to college, she can take the G.E.D. test and go to Miami-Dade Community

College. Don't worry about Sue Ellen. You've got enough to think about with Aileen. And please tell her to call Grandpa's house collect any time she wants, and I'll get back to her when they let me talk to her. Okay?'

After Patsy inquired after the health of Frank and Helen, and asked Hoke to give them her love, she rang off.

Hoke was vaguely dissatisfied and resentful after the conversation. Somehow, either on the phone or in person, Patsy had always managed to put him on the defensive. Hoke and Patsy were not Catholics, and he knew very little about the religion except that nuns were supposed to be tough disciplinarians. But maybe that was what Aileen needed. In religious matters, Hoke and Patsy were both nonbelievers, and they had never sent the girls to Sunday school, figuring that they could make up their own minds about that when they were old enough to think such things out for themselves. The nuns would undoubtedly go to work on Aileen, but Hoke had already warned the girls about religious cults and their brainwashing techniques, and he was sure Aileen could handle whatever propaganda the nuns tried to give her. Curly Peterson, the ballplayer Patsy had married, was probably a Southern Baptist, if he was anything, so it was probably the sports doctor – with his somewhat biblical name – who had insisted on the Catholic clinic.

Hoke had eaten breakfast with his father, but Frank had been unperturbed by the news of Aileen's affliction. 'When a girl's sick,' he said, 'she should be with her mother, and you did the right thing. When we find out exactly where she is, I'll wire her some flowers.'

'Under the circumstances, it might be better to send her a basket of fruit.'

'What? Oh, sure, I see what you mean. I've got to get down to the store.'

Helen usually slept until noon, so Hoke managed to get out of the house before she called Inocencia for her breakfast tray.

Hoke became very busy at the El Pelicano. Before he could shave, Mr Winters, a man in a khaki safari suit, had showed up wanting to rent an apartment for two months, and perhaps through October as well. He had a cashier's check for twelve thousand dollars, but no cash and no bank account. To obtain the first and last month's rent in advance, Hoke had to break his rule again and drive Mr Winters to the bank in Riviera Beach so that he could cash the check and open an account. The drive to the bank was what Hoke would have called once a 'two-cigarette' drive, one on the way over and another coming back, but he no longer smoked. Mr Winters, or 'Beefy' Winters, as the new tenant called himself, was an elephant trainer. He had been fired from the Ringling Brothers Circus in Kansas City. He tried to explain why, as they drove over the bridge into the city, but Hoke couldn't follow the complicated politics of the dismissal. Winters had also left his wife, who still worked for the circus 'in Costumes.' After returning to Sarasota, their winter home, Beefy Winters had cashed in their savings, and then had driven over to Singer Island to hide out from his wife until the season ended. He had a permanent winter job every year in Sarasota as a pharmacist, so he had decided to sit out the rest of the circus season in Singer Island and let his wife worry about where he and the money had gone. He was pretty sure that by the end of September she would take him back. He already missed the three elephants he trained, but not his wife – at least, not at the moment. But he would be glad enough to see her when the circus returned to its winter quarters in Sarasota.

Back at the El Pelicano, as Hoke gave him his key and a receipt, Beefy said that as a pharmacist he could make thirty thousand a year if he worked at a drugstore all year round, but circus life got into a man's blood.

'You have something in common,' Hoke told him, 'with Professor Hurt on the first floor. He's a horsefly man, and would probably enjoy talking to you about elephants and Africa ...'

Hoke shaved, showered, and washed his dirty jumpsuit while he showered. He put the damp suit on a hanger and hung it over the showerhead to dry. The poplin material would be bone dry in about three hours. So far, the jumpsuits were the only items that had simplified his life. Everything else seemed to be as complicated as ever, and he still hadn't managed to slow his life down to the leisurely pace he had envisioned when he had accepted the management of the El Pelicano.

There were several cardboard boxes of Aileen's things in the apartment, and the small room was much too crowded. He decided to clean out the old office downstairs and store her bicycle and boxes there. The boxes had been opened, and he noticed the yellow and black Cliff Notes for *Catcher in the Rye*. He remembered reading the novel, and a simpler story would be difficult to find. Why would Aileen need the help of Cliff Notes to understand a boy like Holden Caulfield? He riffled through the pages of the Notes. Holden Caulfield was sixteen, but that was back in 1951, when the book was first published, so Holden was fifty-two years old now. Hoke took two boxes downstairs, one under each arm, thinking that Caulfield was probably either a balding broker on the stock exchange or one or those gray-faced corporation lawyers who had never been inside a courtroom. Either way, the thought was depressing.

Hoke unlocked the office door behind the short Formica counter. He put his cardboard boxes on the counter and looked inside the office. The room was about six by eight feet with an enclosed half-bath – a toilet and a washbasin, but no shower. If he cleaned it up and redecorated, and if he could somehow squeeze in a shower stall, he could probably rent this little room out as a one-person efficiency. Either that, or use it as an overflow bedroom for some family with an adult son or daughter. If he added a hot plate, he might be able to rent it to some permanent worker on the island – say, a dishwasher like Dolly Turner – for one hundred fifty or two hundred dollars a month. Then, if he didn't tell his father about it, he could pocket the money and Frank wouldn't know the difference. Fat chance. Frank would know about it within an hour; there were no secrets on the island.

The room was a mess now. A dusty metal desk took up most of the space, and there were two rusty rollaway beds on top of it. Boxes of discarded sheets and battered cooking utensils were stacked haphazardly against the walls. Hoke tried the toilet, but it didn't flush. The water didn't run from the washbowl taps, either.

'Maybe the water's turned off, Sergeant Moseley?'

Hoke looked over his shoulder. A thin, dark man in his early twenties with a fluffy bandito mustache stood in the doorway. He had dark blue eyes, but Hoke recognized a Latin when he saw one. He wore a light tan summer suit with a yellow shirt and an infantry-blue tie. He held a large brown envelope with the tips of his fingers.

'I'm Jaime Figueras,' he said, shaking Hoke's hand. 'You're a hard man to find, Sergeant Moseley. I came over about ten, hung around awhile, and then had a couple of beers at The Greenery. I decided to try again, and then if you weren't here I was going back to the station. How come you don't have a phone?'

'There's a pay phone fifty yards away in the mall.'

'I didn't know that number. Besides, when you call a pay phone, nobody answers. And if someone does, he always tells you it's a pay phone and hangs up.'

'I'm trying to simplify my life a little, that's all. If I had the only phone in the building, I'd be the message center for all my tenants. They'd also be knocking on my door at midnight wanting to use it. Anyway, what can I do for you, Figueras?'

'I haven't got a clue. Chief Sheldon said you might be able to help me out with these burglaries.' He tapped the envelope against the Formica counter. 'That's about it. He said you were a famous homicide detective from Miami, and that I could probably learn something from you.'

'Famous? What else did he say about me?'

'That's about it. Except that you were Frank Moseley's son, and that you used to be on the Riviera force before you went down to Miami.'

'You're pretty young to be in plainclothes already.'

'I'm twenty-four, and I've been a cop for more than three years now. I joined when I graduated from Palm Beach Junior College. I was going to transfer up to Gainesville, but I decided that two more years of education at the U.F. wasn't worth borrowing twenty thousand bucks, plus the interest. Besides, I was offered a job here, so I took it.'

'As a cop, you'd make more money in Miami.'

'I know. I went down there and talked to some of the Latin contingent on the P.B.A. But they discouraged me when they found out I was a *Mondalero*.'

Hoke laughed. 'What did you expect? Cuban cops think that anyone who didn't vote for Reagan is a Communist sympathizer. If you voted for Mondale, you should've kept that information to yourself.'

'I meant to, but I'm a Puerto Rican, not a Cuban. The trouble with Cuban-Americans, even when they're born here, is that they think of themselves as Cubans first, and *then* Americans. We love our island as much as they say they love theirs, but we know that without some kind of welfare, an island with a growing population can't support itself. All these Reagan cuts are killing us down there, man.'

'You're probably right.' Hoke shrugged. 'You must've made the right choice, staying here in Riviera, or you wouldn't be a detective already. Want some coffee?'

'No, but I'd like to use your john. Like I said, I had a couple of beers in The Greenery.'

Hoke put the two boxes inside, re-locked the office door, and led the way upstairs. Hoke pointed to the bathroom door and took the envelope from Figueras. It contained two Xeroxed rosters listing the names of the residents with stolen items at the Supermare. The items each resident was missing were typed beneath the names. Many of the items were small objects, but there were also three paintings and a Giacometti sculpture on the list. The dimensions of the Giacometti weren't noted, but the paintings included a Corot, a Klezmer, and a Renaissance cartoon, artist unknown. The artists' names, except for the Klezmer, were vaguely familiar to Hoke.

'What've you done so far?' Hoke asked, as Figueras, zipping his fly, came back into the living room.

'I've talked to these people, and to the manager, Mr Carstairs. These residents come and go, you know. Mr Olsen – he's the president of the Supermare board of directors – he and his wife went on a two-week trip to the Galapagos a couple of months back, but they didn't miss their stuff right away. The cartoon was in the hallway, he said, and he never liked it much anyway. But it was plenty valuable. He didn't know whether it was missing before they left or not. His wife lost a diamond ring and a half-dozen elephant-hair bracelets. She had another diamond pin in her jewelry box, but that wasn't taken.'

'What was the cartoon about?'

Figueras grinned. 'I asked her the same question. It isn't a comic cartoon. It's a preliminary drawing of a Madonna and child, and it's supposedly after Raphael, Mrs Olsen said. In other words, it's a brown-tone drawing, the kind the artist makes before he does the painting, and it's called a cartoon. "After Raphael" means that it might've been drawn by Raphael but probably wasn't. It could've been done by one of Raphael's apprentices.'

'It couldn't be worth much.'

'I don't know. Mr Olsen said it's worth quite a bit. Just as it is, without authentication, it's valued at twenty grand. And if it's ever authenticated, the value would triple. Mrs Olsen isn't so worried about the diamond ring, but she wants the elephant-hair bracelets back because her granddaughter gave them to her last Christmas.'

'Who gave you this list?'

'The manager. Carstairs. Then I talked to the tenants.'

'Let's take another trip down there, Figueras. My father's wife's got an apartment there, and I promised her I'd check it out. She hasn't been in it for several months, so she might have something missing, too.'

'Your stepmother has an apartment there?'

'Stepmother – come on. We're about the same age; she's just my father's second wife.'

'Sorry.'

'No cause to be. Technically, I guess she is my stepmother, but I've never thought of her that way. My kids call her Helen, not Grandma.'

'Want to take my car?'

'No, you go ahead. I'll ride my daughter's bike down and take my trunks. After we check things out, I'll swim in the pool. I'd invite you, too, but a guest can't invite another guest.'

'I got plenty to do back at the station. I really should come over here to the beach more often, but somehow, when I get through work and go home, I just don't think about it.'

'You married?'

'No, but I got a live-in. Girl works at the International Mall. Suave Shoes. Nothing serious. She just wanted to get away from her parents and couldn't afford a place of her own.'

'Lot of girls like that nowadays, it seems.'

Figueras shrugged. 'One, anyway.'

Mr Carstairs, a tanned, middle-aged man wearing khaki cargo shorts, a short-sleeved blue workshirt, and a pair of blue felt house slippers, was outside by the Supermare swimming pool. With a twelve-foot skimmer he was scooping dead dragonflies and bits of dried grass from the surface of the pool. When Hoke introduced himself, Carstairs put the skimmer down, nodded at Figueras, and lighted a menthol True.

'Your stepmother already called me about you, Mr Moseley. The pool's open from nine to nine, but there's no lifeguard so you swim at your own risk. And no children are allowed.'

'That's what Mrs Moseley told me. Suppose I want to swim earlier, say, six or six-thirty in the morning?'

'I don't enforce the rules. I live over in Riviera, so I don't get here till around eight. But Mrs Andrews, who lives right over there in 101-A, has threatened to shoot anyone who goes in before nine A.M. with her BB gun.' Carstairs laughed harshly, and it brought on a paroxysm of coughing. His body doubled over and his face turned bright red. He clutched the back of an aluminum beach chair for support, coughed some more, and finally managed to take another short drag on his cigarette. That seemed to work; he stopped coughing.

'You okay?' Hoke asked.

Carstairs nodded, catching his breath. 'It's the damned menthol. I might as well have stuck with the Camels. 'Course, I don't think she'd really do it, Mrs Andrews, with the gun. But she said she would, and ever since she made her threat at the monthly meeting, nobody's taken a chance. She brought her Red Ryder BB rifle to the meeting to show she had one.'

'In that case,' Hoke said, 'I'll abide by the rules.' He took one of the folded lists out of his pocket and handed it to Carstairs. 'You got any more additions to your list? Any more reported thefts?'

Carstairs ran a finger down the list and shook his head. 'No, this is complete. But a lot of people are still away for the summer. When people get back, there may be more. I haven't inventoried any of the unoccupied apartments because I don't know what's supposed to be there in the first place. And even if the apartments are messed up, the owners could've left them that way when they went north.'

'I understand.'

'As a matter of routine,' Figueras said, 'I checked both pawnshops in town, but nothing showed up. These aren't the kind of things people would pawn anyway. A Corot, for example, worth maybe a hundred thousand bucks, wouldn't be fenced, either. A painting that valuable's usually held for ransom from the insurance company.'

'I don't know what else to tell you, Mr Moseley,' Carstairs said. 'We've got a twenty-four-hour guard on the gate, but the owners voted down a TV surveillance system. Most of the people living here are old enough to go to bed early. After ten at night, the gate guard checks the lobby and the pool area every hour or so.'

'Have you got the keys to all of the apartments?' Hoke asked.

'Sure. It's the law. I've got a master through-the-door-knob key, and those who've added bolt locks are required to give me the extra key. I keep 'em on a board in my office.'

'What about the exterminator?'

'He's on a monthly schedule. I send out a mimeographed notice for the day and hours he's here, and they're supposed to let him in to spray. When he finishes all of the occupied apartments he comes back to me, and then I go with him while he works through the unoccupied units. If people are here, and don't let him in, they don't get sprayed, that's all. Our contract's with Cliffdweller's Exterminators, and they're bonded. They do most of the condos on the island.'

'What about U.P.S., and other deliveries?'

'The gate guard signs, and then takes the packages up himself. And that includes pizza deliveries. That way' – Carstairs laughed – 'the guard gets the tip the delivery man should get. Why not? We only pay the guards four bucks an hour.'

'When he's on an upper floor making a delivery, the gate isn't covered.'

'That's true. But it's locked. Nobody has to wait very long, and all the owners can open the gate with their plastic cards. There haven't been any complaints – except from pizza delivery men.' Carstairs laughed harshly and fell into another spate of coughing. He sat heavily on a webbed beach chair, gasping for almost a minute before he recovered his breath. 'Not everybody living here knows about these burglaries, but when the place begins to fill up again in November, and it turns out that some more absentee owners have been ripped off, there'll be hell to pay, and I'll be blamed. I like this job. I managed a condo in North Miami Beach for three years before coming up here, and they all complained down there because they thought I was overpaid. Twenty-two thousand a year, and they thought I was overpaid. Here, everybody thinks I'm *under* paid, and I get plenty of tips and sympathy.'

'How much do you get here?'

'The same twenty-two a year. It's the going scale for a condo this size, but these wealthy people, who think I'm scraping along, don't ask me to do much of anything. Down in N.M.B., some of those old ladies even expected me to drive 'em to the fucking grocery store. I do real well here at Christmas, too. Absentee owners send me fruit from that place in Oregon. Last year I got four lugs of Comice pears.'

'Next time you have a meeting,' Hoke suggested, 'why not have Detective Figueras give the owners a little pep talk on security. Anybody who's away for six months or more and leaves jewelry in his apartment is also leaving a cold trail if it's stolen.'

'Would you do that, Officer Figueras?' Carstairs asked.

'Sure. It might take the pressure off both of us. Just call me at the station a day or two before you have a meeting.'

'Thanks, Mr Carstairs,' Hoke said. 'We're going to look around a little.'

The manager nodded and lighted another cigarette with his Zippo. Hoke and Figueras got into the elevator, and Hoke punched the PH button.

'Thanks for the volunteer lecture,' Figueras said. 'But it's a little late now, isn't it, for a talk on security?'

'If they aren't doing the things you tell 'em, it might get Carstairs off the hook. He seems like a decent guy.'

'Yeah, he does. But he ought to switch back to Camels soon. Those menthol cigarettes are killing him.'

The elevator stopped at the roof exit, and the door opened automatically. They stepped onto a railed redwood deck that covered a fifty-foot square of the flat roof. Part of the deck had aluminum roofing, in blue and white panels. There was a metal blue and white patio set of table and four chairs beneath the roof section. The table and all four chairs were bolted to the deck to prevent strong winds from blowing them away. One twin-glass floor-to-ceiling window faced the deck, but the red vertical Levolors were closed. Hoke pressed the white button beside the double-door entrance to the penthouse. Figueras took out a crumpled package of Lucky Strikes and a book of matches from his jacket pocket, looked at them for a moment, and put them back. While they waited, Hoke looked out over the ocean. From this height it resembled an ironed sheet of Mylar. Out in the Gulf Stream, four or five miles away, three tankers steamed south. Thanks to them, Hoke reflected, the soles and toes of hundreds of feet would collect little pieces of tar when they walked on the beach. All of the motels and apartment houses kept metal containers of benzine and paper towels by the outside showers so that bathers could clean it off their feet. The tar was worse this year than Hoke could ever remember it.

Mr E. M. Skinner, wearing royal-blue slippers and a yellow silk happi coat over his purple silk pajamas, opened the door. He blinked in the strong sunlight.

'I was taking a nap,' Skinner said. 'I thought I heard the bell, but I wasn't sure. Today's Hirohito's day off.'

'Hirohito?' Hoke took off his sunglasses.

Skinner smiled. 'My Japanese houseboy. Actually, he's a Nisei, and his real name's Paul Glenwood. I sometimes call him Hirohito just to kid around. Come in, gentlemen.'

'This is Detective Figueras,' Hoke said. 'He's the Riviera officer investigating the burglaries you were telling me about down on the beach.'

Skinner nodded and shook hands with Figueras. 'I think Carstairs mentioned your name to me.' Hoke walked inside before Skinner could shake his hand and looked around the living room.

The room was large but seemed bigger because it was so sparsely furnished. There was a polished parquet floor, with no rugs to hide it. At the northern end of the room there was a grouping of leather overstuffed chairs and small black lacquered tables. A bar, covered in black leather and with two red-cushioned rattan stools, was directly behind the grouping. The other end of the room, apparently a dining area, was furnished with a glass-topped mahogany table and eight cushioned, wrought-iron chairs. A Nautilus machine, with four brown leather roller pads, incongruously occupied the space between the conversation area and the dining setup. There was a long passway counter into the kitchen, but the counter had a pull-down door, and it was closed. Hoke could see only part of the kitchen through the opened doorway. There were a half-dozen closed doors along the hallway, so Hoke concluded that Skinner had separate rooms for work and for play, and at least three bedrooms.

'I was telling Sergeant Moseley, Mr Figueras,' Skinner said with a thin smile, 'I don't have my daily martinis until five, but that restriction doesn't hold for you. What will you gentlemen have?'

'I guess I could stand a beer,' Figueras said.

'Nothing for me, thanks,' Hoke said.

Skinner went behind the bar and rubbed his hands together. 'Michelob okay?'

'Anything that's cold,' Figueras said.

Skinner opened the bottle and poured part of it into a glass, then set the glass and bottle on the bar. Figueras had his Luckies and matches out. He looked at the bar, and at the tables, but there were no ashtrays. For the second time, Figueras put his cigarettes away. One of the small lacquered tables held two elaborately carved wooden fishes. There were floor-to-ceiling windows on three of the walls, but the closed vertical Levolors darkened the room. The track lighting above the bar was on dimly. There was a chandelier above the dining table, but it wasn't lighted.

'When you first heard about the burglaries, Mr Skinner,' Hoke asked, 'did you check your own apartment for missing items?'

'I didn't have to check. I'm here all year round. And when I'm not here, Hirohito's here.'

'You two are never out at the same time?'

'I didn't mean that. I mean, Paul lives in. He has his own bedroom. Sometimes when I go out at night he drives me. When I go to a party in Palm Beach I like to have two or three drinks, and I won't risk a D.U.I. Two double martinis, even watered down with ice, will register a big point one-four on the breathalyzer, I've heard.'

'It depends on the size of the person,' Figueras said, taking a sip from his glass. 'But they've been cracking down on drunk drivers. People who used to get a warning are now either doing a little jail time or community service.'

'What kind of community service would I do,' Skinner said, smiling, 'if I happened to get caught? Not that I ever will, of course.'

'It's up to the judge. But a Palm Beach corporation lawyer, two weeks ago, was assigned to work for sixty days putting on a new tar-and-pebble roof on school buildings in the county. Working with boiling tar, out in the sun all day, is pretty rough community service for a lawyer. But a barmaid I know got off easy. She licked stamps in the judge's office when he ran for re-election. They haven't established any firm guidelines yet, so it's still up to the whim of the judge.'

Hoke cleared his throat. 'So you haven't missed anything?'

'Not a thing. And if something was missing, Paul would tell me.'

'I notice you don't have any paintings.'

'I have paintings. A man has to have some collectables for diversification. But I keep my paintings in my strong room, together with my certificates and krugerrands and so on. No one goes in there but me. Not even my houseboy has the combination. I had the strong room put in while the Supermare was still under construction.'

'What kind of paintings?'

'Well, I've got five Picassos – drawings, not paintings – and two Milton Averys.'

'Could we take a look at them?'

'They're investments, not for showing. I'd be glad to show them to you, but they're wrapped up in brown paper and sealed. When

Milton Avery died, my Averys almost doubled in value, but I don't like either one of them. Collectables are just a hedge against inflation, as we say.'

'Figueras,' Hoke said, 'would you mind going outside on the deck to finish your beer and smoke a cigarette for a few minutes?'

'Why?'

'Because I asked you in a nice way, and I know you want a smoke.' Hoke put his sunglasses on the bar.

Figueras gave Hoke a look and poured the rest of the beer into his glass. Then he lighted a Lucky, took the glass of beer with him, and went out through the front door. As the door clicked behind Figueras, Hoke took a step forward and hit Skinner in the stomach with his right fist. The blow was hard and unexpected, and air whooshed from Skinner's lips in a strangled scream of fear, pain, and surprise. He clutched his stomach with both hands as he dropped to the floor, and kept making little *ah, ah, ah* sounds as he struggled for breath. This man, Hoke thought, has never been hurt before. Except for a toothache, maybe, he has never known any real pain. Certainly Skinner was handling his pain in a craven way. He drummed on the floor with his heels until his slippers fell off. When he regained his breath he began to cry, and he crawled backward away from Hoke. His fingers, scrabbling behind him, could get very little purchase on the polished floor. It took almost half a minute before his back hit the black leather chair behind him. His eyes popped wildly as he stared up at Hoke, and tears ran down his cheeks. He pressed his fingers into his stomach gently. 'You – you broke something inside ...'

Hoke nodded. 'Lots of little things. Capillaries, for the most part, and some muscle shredding, but I was an inch or so below the solar plexus. Haven't you ever been hit in the belly before?'

Skinner shook his head. 'Jesus Christ that hurt! It still hurts!'

Hoke took Skinner's right hand and pulled him to his feet. He twisted the unresisting arm behind Skinner's back, and then put some upward pressure on it.

Skinner squealed. 'Jesus Christ, man!'

'Let's go take a look in your strong room, Skinner. I want to check your collectables against my property list.'

'It's all there, Sergeant, every bit of it! You're breaking my goddamned arm!'

It was all there: the brown-tone cartoon; the tiny Corot, only twelve by fourteen inches, but with a gilded frame; and the Giacometti sculpture, an anorectic figure a foot high, mounted on a thick ebony base. The Klezmer turned out to be a painting of a tiny piece of yarn, about one inch in length, but the picture was in a two-by-two-foot black frame. A small magnifying glass was attached to the frame by a chain so a viewer could see all of the yarn's delicately painted hairs. The jewelry, and there was a good deal of it, including the elephant-hair bracelets, was all wrapped neatly in white tissue paper and packed in a cardboard box.

Skinner now sat in a leather chair. His face was a mixture of pink and gray. He was calmer now, but he covered his face with his hands. After Hoke checked off all the items on his list, he patted Skinner on the shoulder.

'Don't worry,' he said, 'you aren't going to jail. I wouldn't want something like this to get into the papers. It would be bad for the island and bad for the Supermare. My father's wife still has an apartment here, and it might make the value go down.'

'I wasn't going to keep any of these things,' Skinner said, looking up and wiping fresh tears from his eyes. 'I'm not a thief – I don't even know how you knew I –'

'I didn't know. But I suspected you. I've got a good memory for details sometimes, Skinner. When Helen told me that Mr Olsen and Mrs Higdon were instrumental in getting you out of office, and then their names popped up on the list, I figured it had to be you. As the ex-president of the board, you still had a key to the office, so you probably found a way to get into any apartment you wanted to. Isn't that right?'

'I gave my master key back to Carstairs, but I had a duplicate made first in your father's hardware store. I thought that was how you found out.'

'I never considered that. I suppose he still has a sales slip on file. But I just figured you went into the office at night, took the extra bolt-lock keys, and then swiped the stuff at your leisure. If I wasn't on the verge of quitting the police force, I wouldn't have hit you. I've been a cop for more than fourteen years, and you're the first suspect I've ever hit. I'd better get Figueras.' Hoke put on his dark glasses and adjusted them.

'What'll he do? I mean –'

'By now, he'll need another beer. Put your slippers back on and open him another cold one.'

Hoke went to the front door, opened it, and beckoned to Figueras. When Figueras came in, Skinner was behind the bar, opening a bottle of Michelob. 'Would you like another beer, Officer Figueras?'

Figueras looked at the paintings and the cardboard box beside the leather chair. He looked sharply at Hoke. 'What the fuck's going on?'

'Last night Mr Skinner found all this stuff on the fire stairs. He didn't turn it over to the manager immediately, because he thought they might think he took it. That's why he wanted to talk to me alone. He was about to phone the police, in fact, when you and I showed up. So what we'll do, Figueras, we'll just say we found it on the stairs ourselves. Okay? Then we can turn it all over to Carstairs, and no one'll ever know the difference. Mr Skinner's a rich man, with his own strong room full of collectables. He doesn't need stuff like this. But he's got a few enemies in the building, he says, and this way it won't even make the newspapers.'

'If that's the way you want to handle it,' Figueras said.

Skinner came gingerly from behind the bar and handed the open bottle of beer to Figueras. Figueras took it and poured the beer over the two carved wooden fish on the lacquered table. He tossed the empty bottle behind the bar and listened appraisingly as it crashed. Then he picked up the cardboard box containing the jewelry. 'I'll ring for the elevator, Sergeant. Want to give me a hand?'

'Sure,' Hoke said. 'But I get off at the twelfth floor. You can take everything down to Carstairs, and he can return the stuff to the owners. I'm going to take that swim in the pool.'

Figueras went out the door with the cardboard box.

'What about me?' Skinner said, in a hoarse whisper. 'What's going to happen to me?'

601

Hoke hit Skinner again with a hard right fist, and Skinner, clutching his stomach, fell to the floor. Hoke picked up the skinny sculpture and opened the door. Figueras came back in for the paintings, then rejoined Hoke at the elevator. If he was curious about Skinner, writhing and groaning on the parquet, he didn't say anything.

Hoke pulled out the red knob to release the elevator; then he pushed the button for twelve.

'One of these days,' Figueras said, when Hoke got off the elevator at the twelfth floor, 'I'd like to drop by and talk to you some about homicide work.'

'Sure. I'm home every night. You ever play Monopoly?'

'Not since I was a kid.'

'The short game is still fun. But if you come by, you'll have to bring your own six-pack. I'm trying to lose some more weight, so I don't keep any beer in the fridge to tempt me.' Hoke patted his stomach and walked down the hallway to 12-C.

Chapter Fourteen

Dale already had most of the dinner on the table by the time Troy Louden returned to the garage apartment. Stanley watched everyone's comings and goings from his chair beside the window. Troy came in carrying a large Naugahyde suitcase in his left hand and his cowboy boots in his right. He paused for a moment and, with his eyes closed, sniffed the aroma of the steaming food. Then he disappeared into the bedroom. He was wearing a dark gray *guayabera*, pleated khaki trousers, and a new pair of gray leather running shoes with slanted purple stripes on them.

A moment later, Troy reappeared in the bedroom doorway and crooked a finger at James. As James crossed the room, Dale whispered to him, 'Tell him dinner's ready any old time.'

James nodded, followed Troy into the bedroom, and closed the door.

Stanley got up from his chair and surveyed the table. 'Everything sure does smell good.'

'That's the pork chops,' Dale said. Her face was flushed, and the hair at her temples was damp. 'What I do, I pepper 'em real good and dip 'em in a simple egg-and-flour batter. Then I fry 'em in bacon grease. There's candied sweet potatoes, with little marshmallows on top, turnip greens in wine vinegar, spicy applesauce, and buttermilk biscuits. I'll finish up the milk gravy now, and that'll be dinner. I've got a Mrs Smith's apple pie warming in the oven, and that'll be dessert. Mr Louden does so much for all the rest of us, I want him to have a decent dinner.'

The table was set for four, although there were not enough matching plates, cups, and saucers. There were only three silverware forks; Dale had put a plastic one at her setting, Stanley noted. A few minutes later, Troy and James came back from the bedroom, and they sat down to eat.

James was visibly nervous during dinner. He plucked at his ears, his lips, and his eyebrows, and he only ate one pork chop. Troy praised the meal, and Dale's puffy lips twisted into a grimace of pleasure.

'I had two brothers and two little sisters,' Dale said, 'and Momma taught all of us how to cook. She said us girls needed to know how to catch a husband, and the boys needed to know how so they could teach their wives when they got married.'

'Let's not get into your family,' Troy said. 'We've got our own little family, right here. We're all starting out new, and the past is past. Why, James, are you picking your nose at the table?'

'I'm just nervous ... it's ... it's these greens, Troy,' James said. 'I don't like vinegar on my greens.'

'Whether you like them or not you have to eat them. Otherwise you'll hurt Dale's feelings. And in America, you don't pick your nose at the table. Everyone, from time to time, has to pick his nose. That's a given, but it's a private thing, James, and should be done where people don't have to watch you. I remember once when I was in Whittier – that's the reform school in Orange County, California – a boy was picking his nose at the table and the guy sitting beside him jammed the boy's finger right into his nostril all the way up to the last knuckle. The kid's nose got all swollen, so fast that he couldn't pull his finger out. Finally, the matron led him out of the dining hall and took him to the clinic. It was funny to see, and we all laughed, of course, but it was a lesson in manners for us boys, too. No one after that ever picked his nose in the dining hall. Not only is it impolite, it's un-American. I realize that as a foreigner and as a black man, you'll find some of our customs strange, James, but you'll just have to abide by them.'

'I'm sorry,' James said. 'I won't do it again.'

'When you get up to New York, James,' Troy continued, 'you should rent a room with an American family instead of moving in with the other Bajans up there. Then you can learn our ways. Otherwise, when you have your first one-man show, and you're standing around in the gallery with two fingers up your nose, no one'll buy your paintings.'

'I won't *do* it again, Troy.'

'Good. Now eat your greens. At Whittier, if we didn't clean our plates, we didn't get any dessert. You could eat all you wanted, but once you put it on your plate you had to eat it.'

'I didn't put the greens on my plate,' James said. 'Dale did.'

'I'll eat your greens, James,' Stanley offered. 'I like the greens.'

'If you want more greens, Pop,' Troy said, 'Dale will get them for you. James will have to eat his own greens.'

James wrinkled his nose and ate.

'I'll get the pie,' Dale said, rising from her chair.

'Put a scoop of ice cream on mine,' Troy said.

'I don't have any ice cream,' Dale said, hesitating in the doorway.

'Then cut a wedge of cheddar to go with it. I like cheese just as well.'

'There isn't any cheese either.' Dale put a hand over her mouth.

'In that case, skip me on the pie, and just bring me some coffee.'

Dale cleared the table and served slices of pie to Stanley and James. She poured coffee for the three of them and retreated to the kitchen. James put three spoonfuls of sugar into his coffee and stirred it noisily. The spoon slipped from his fingers and fell to the floor.

'Maybe you shouldn't drink any coffee,' Troy said, 'if it makes you so nervous.'

James glanced at Stanley, licked his lips, and looked back at Troy 'It ain't the coffee making me nervous. I'm afraid of what you want me to do.'

'Do you want me to send Mr Sinkiewicz instead? Send an old man to do a boy's job?' Troy shook his head and pulled back his lips in a lightning smile.

'I didn't say that, Troy. I *want* to do it. It's just that I've never done nothing like that before.'

'What is it, James?' Stanley asked. 'Maybe I can help you?'

'Please stay out of this, Pop.' Troy held up a warning hand. 'You've done enough already. I don't want you to be connected with this operation in any way. I told you that already. Dale, James, and I are the three who will benefit most, so we have to do the dirty work. And we each have to pull our own weight.

605

As the head of the family and director of the operation, I've got to make the decisions on what each person has to do. You, of course, are retired, and although you are an important part of our little family – I hope you know that – you're also our honored guest. Here, before I forget, let me give back your cards.' Troy took Stanley's Visa card, Social Security card, and a folded yellow receipt out of his wallet and pushed them across the table.

Stanley put the two cards away and examined the receipt. There was a letterhead that read: Overseas Supply Company, Inc. The address was a Miami post office box. At the bottom of the yellow sheet, in italics, *Se habla Español* was printed. The bill, for 'used hunting supplies,' was $1,565, but the supplies were not itemized. Stanley's Visa receipt was stapled to the bill.

'Where is this place?' Stanley asked. 'The Overseas Supply Company?'

Troy laughed. 'It isn't a place, Pop, it's an idea. Today it's a room in the Descanso Hotel. Tomorrow it's a house in San Juan, Puerto Rico. Everybody, nowadays, needs hunting supplies.'

Stanley was unable to follow this line of thinking. He looked down, folded the bill and receipt, and tucked them into his wallet.

'But as you can see, Pop, I didn't need the full two thousand. And I still got everything I needed, including these new pants, goatskin gloves, the shirt, and the running shoes. Boots look good on a man, but for running, when you have to run, they aren't worth a damn.'

Stanley cleared his throat. 'I been thinking, Troy. And I think five hundred's too much to give me in interest. Now that you've only used fifteen hundred, let's cut it down to maybe a hundred and fifty.'

Troy shook his head and smiled at James. 'Look at this guy, James. Without Pop's help, we'd be sitting here without any tools, and we'd either have to borrow money on the street at leg-breaking vig, or hold up a half-dozen liquor stores. Nothing doing, Pop. You still get your five hundred, and you get it Saturday night. But James here, who stands to benefit more than you do, is getting cold feet on a little project I gave him.'

'I'll *do* it, Troy,' James said quickly. 'I never said I wouldn't do it. I just said I was afraid to do it because I've never done nothing like that before.'

'I know you'll do it,' Troy said, nodding, 'because you have to. But I don't want you to be nervous. If you want me to, I'll go over everything with you again.'

'Suppose I can't find one? What'll I do then?'

'All right, I will go over it again. First, I'll drive you to the Brickell Metrorail station. You ride it down to Dadeland North station, and then walk over to the Dadeland parking lot. This time of night, there'll be at least a thousand parked cars, probably a lot more. At least one in a hundred drivers leave their keys in the car, right in the ignition. It's one of those statistical truisms, I read about it in the paper. There was this Boy Scout troop that wanted to do a good deed on a Saturday morning, so they had little cards printed up, saying, "Don't leave your keys in your car. It invites theft." They found that almost a fifth of the cars they looked at in the Westchester Shopping Center had keys in the ignition. They then left the little card under the windshields, you see, so the owners would find them when they came back. So when you say you don't think you'll find at least *one* car out of a *thousand* with the keys in it at Dadeland, you're simply full of shit.

'I could do it myself, and I'd be back here within an hour with a nice big car for us to use, but I want you to do it as part of your on-the-job training. I've got other things to do. Dale can't go because her face is too conspicuous, even though she'll drive the car later on. Also, because of Dale, you have to get a car with an automatic transmission. She can't drive a stick shift. What else did I tell you?'

'You said dark blue or black.'

'Right. But any dark color'll do. Just don't come back with some bright yellow or red car, or I'll send you right back. I don't want any Blazer, either, all shiny with chrome and those tires with big white raised letters. Understand?'

'I'm ready,' James said, getting up from the table.

'What are you doing, Troy?' Stanley asked. 'Are you sending James out to steal a car?'

'I'm trying to keep you out of this, Pop. You really should save your questions till it's all over. But the answer is no, James is not going to steal a car. He's going to *obtain* a car for our use in the operation, which we'll drive to the airport later, on Sunday morning. The owner will be notified by postcard where we parked his car at the airport, and I'll leave a generous rental fee for the use of his vehicle in the glove compartment. I guarantee that the person whose car we use'll benefit. Are you with me? You can see I'm explaining to you as we go along on a need-to-know basis.'

Stanley nodded. 'Sure, Troy. I just thought, from the way you were talking, that James was going to steal a car, that's all.'

'Renting is a long way from stealing, Pop. While I run James over to the Brickell station, see if you can find some hacksaw blades down there in the garage. There's a vise on the workbench where James keeps his paints, and I remember seeing a box of tools under the bench. Then, when I come back, you can help me out.'

Troy and James left in the Morris, and Stanley went into the kitchen. 'That was a nice dinner, Dale, and I really enjoyed it. Want me to carry that bag of garbage down to the yard?'

'No, I'd better do it myself.' Tears trickled down her cheeks. 'You've got to look for the hacksaw blades like Troy said. When he tells you to do something, he means it. How was I to know he wanted ice cream on his pie? If he'd said, then I could've gotten ice cream and cheese, too. If you only knew how many rejections I've had in my life, Mr Sinkiewicz, you'd feel sorry for me.'

'I feel sorry for you already, Dale. That's why I loaned Troy the money he needed.'

'Did I ever tell you about the lawyer I lived with once in Coconut Grove?' Dale wiped her eyes with her wet hands and then had to use the dry edge of a dish towel to get the soap out of her eyes. 'I'd been living with him for two months in his apartment, you know, and I thought he really liked me. Jesus, I used to go down on him every morning before he went to the office, and I never had any complaints. Then one night, it was after midnight, he said, "Get your coat." I was wearing a nightgown, so I started to get dressed. Then he said, "No, just your coat." I had this fur coat he'd given me, but I'd never worn it. It was a good fur – dyed rabbit – but you never need a fur coat down here. Anyway, I put it on over my nightgown, and slipped on some sandals. I didn't have on panties or pantyhose or nothing else. Just the nightgown and the fur coat. We got into his Mercedes, and he drove to Biscayne Boulevard, downtown, and then he stopped the car and told me to get out. Nothing else. Not a word of appreciation or thanks or nothing. And after two months. I didn't have my purse, my clothes, my money, anything. Lucky for me, just after he drove away, another car picked me up – an insurance man from Hialeah. We went to a motel on Seventy-ninth Street, and I was back in business again. But my life's been one rejection after another like that, and sometimes I just don't think I can stand any more of it.'

'You're lucky you have Troy now.' Stanley patted her on the shoulder. 'I'm sure he didn't mean to hurt your feelings about the ice cream. You saw the way he made James eat his greens. That shows how sensitive he is to your feelings. Next time, you'll know to get ice cream when you fix apple pie.'

'I guess I should look on the bright side, huh?' Dale's twisted, toothless smile made Stanley turn his head away. 'I like you a lot, Mr Sinkiewicz, and if you ever want a little action and Troy ain't around, you just let me know. Hear?' She reached amiably for Stanley's crotch, but he backed away before she could touch him.

'I'd better go down to the garage and look for those blades.'

Stanley found a metal toolbox beneath the bench, but the box had been left open and the unused tools were rusty from long exposure to the humidity. There were a half-dozen hacksaw blades wrapped in waxed paper, and the rusty saw was usable. The garage was well lighted with several overhead 150-watt bulbs. One of the shadeless bulbs was directly above James's easel so he could paint at night. Stanley looked at James's paintings until Troy returned, thinking that James was lucky that he didn't need subject matter to paint. The Bajan could paint day or night, or anytime he felt like it, and it wouldn't make any difference. He wondered if they would make James paint objects of some kind when he enrolled in the Art Students League up in New York. If they did, James was going to be in trouble ...

Troy returned in the Morris and parked it beside Stanley's Honda. Stanley showed him the blades, and Troy went upstairs to get what he called his 'new, but used' shotgun from his suitcase. He came down to the garage again, locked the shotgun in the vise, and sawed off the barrels as close as he could to the forestock. Then he turned the gun around in the vise and sawed off the rear stock. It took him a great deal longer to get through the wood than it had to shorten the metal barrels. When Troy finished it was an odd-looking weapon. He would have to hold it like a pistol to fire it. It looked unwieldy to Stanley.

'Won't that thing kick out of your hand when you shoot it?' Stanley asked. 'It won't be accurate, neither, if you go dove hunting.'

'I'm not going to *fire* it, Pop. Jesus, there'll be double-aught shells in it. If I shot it, especially at close range, it would blow great big holes in a man's body. I just sawed off the barrels so it wouldn't look like some kind of sporting gun you see in the Sears catalog, but would look like a sawed-off shotgun, which it is now. It's a psychological ploy, Pop. A person associates long barrels with bird-shooting. But he associates a sawed-off shotgun with gangster movies, and he's afraid of it. This way, you don't have to shoot anyone, all you have to do is show the thing. If I do shoot it, I'll just shoot it up at the ceiling or something, and carry a few extra shells in my jacket pocket.'

'It looks wicked that way, and you've sure ruint it for shooting birds.'

'It was more accurate, or wicked as you say, with long barrels, Pop, and you just proved my point. But I'd never shoot birds with a shotgun. I think hunting for game of any kind stinks, and I'm against it. The only way to justify hunting is if you're lost in the woods or something, and you have to kill a bird or a rabbit to survive. Otherwise, hunting for sport is cruel. It ought to be outlawed. You don't think so?'

'I like quail, and there was a neighbor of mine up in Hamtramck who –'

'I don't want to hear about it, Pop. If you want to eat quail, Dale can get you some at the supermarket. All you want. They raise 'em for that purpose, and you can buy 'em fresh frozen. You don't hunt, do you?'

'No, not me, but I had this neighbor, and he used to –'

'I said I don't want to hear about it. Where's Dale?'

'After she finished the dishes I think she took a shower. I heard it running a while ago.'

'What do you think of Dale, Pop, now that you've met her and had a chance to talk with her?'

'She seems like a nice enough girl. A little forward, maybe.'

'She come on to you while I was gone?'

'Oh, I don't know. A little bit, maybe. She felt bad about you not eating the apple pie.'

'That's my fault, not Dale's. I'll have to make a list of the things I like and don't like, so she won't make mistakes like that again. I can't blame Dale for my own oversights. But she'll learn soon enough what I like and don't like. It's her face that makes her so sensitive, Pop. Dale's life's been one rejection after another, so if she offers you head, you'd better accommodate her. Otherwise, she'll think you don't like her.'

'I like her fine, Troy, but I haven't done nothing like that in three or four years now, and I guess I don't have the desire anymore. But if there's any leftover pork chops, I wouldn't mind a cold pork chop sandwich before I go to bed.'

'Good. I'll tell Dale how you feel, and I know she'll be happy to fix you a sandwich later on. Or, if you want, you can have my piece of apple pie and a glass of warm milk.'

'I'd rather have the pork chop sandwich.'

The doctored weapon was still in the vise. Troy used a file to smooth the ends of the jaggedly cut barrels, which were not cut off evenly, and then he filed off the splinters from the stock.

James drove a navy-blue Chrysler New Yorker into the yard and parked beside the Honda and the Morris Minor. The big Chrysler dwarfed the two foreign cars. James honked the horn once and then jumped out of the vehicle as if it had been set on fire. He walked toward them, wringing his hands.

'Oh, a terrible thing happened, Troy! And I didn't know what to do! I was chased, and if I hadn't cut off a pickup at the Miller exit they'd of caught me for sure!'

'You didn't lead anybody back here, did you?'

611

'No, I made sure of that. But I didn't mean to take the baby! I didn't see it back there when I got the car. There was this old lady with packages at the curb in Dadeland, and a younger woman was driving –' He was trying to catch his breath. 'Then, when the woman got out to help the old lady with the packages, I jumped in and drove off. The keys were in the car and the motor was running. Both those ladies came running after me, and then a taxi chased me down Kendall Drive. I went through the red light and so did he, right on my back, all the way down the Palmetto to Miller –'

'What baby?' Troy said, going over to the New Yorker and opening the back door. 'Oh, shit,' he said as he looked at the baby strapped in its car seat in the back.

'I never looked in the back, Troy. There wasn't time. I just took the car 'cause I only had a second or so to get into it and go. He didn't even start crying till I got onto Kendall Drive.'

'This is a nice car, James, exactly what I wanted, but it's useless to us now. Everybody in town'll be on the lookout for this vehicle. I try to think of everything, but I didn't tell you not to steal a car with a baby in it. I thought you'd have more sense than that.'

'I didn't *see* him,' James said. 'Then, when the cab started chasing me, I couldn't stop and get out. I had to lose him first.'

'What is it,' Stanley asked, 'a boy or a girl? The way it's bundled up and all ...'

'Boy or girl doesn't make a helluva lot of difference, Pop,' Troy said. 'Whatever it is, they'll want it back, and the cops'll be looking for this New Yorker all over the damned county. Are the keys still in the car, James?'

'Yes, sir.'

'I told you before not to say that anymore, James. We're all equals here, so I don't want to hear any more of that no, sir, yes, sir crap. I just asked if the keys were in the car.'

James nodded and gulped. The night was hot and humid, and James's shirt was soaked. Water ran down his flushed face as if he had just been doused with a hose.

'All right,' Troy said. 'I'll get rid of this car and come back with another. You two go on upstairs, but don't tell Dale about the baby. Women get upset over misunderstandings like that. I don't know when I'll be back, but when I do get back, James, I hope you realize that I'll have to punish you for this mistake.'

James nodded and wiped his face with his fingers. 'It ain't altogether my fault, Troy. These things happen.'

'I understand. And I'll take under consideration that you're a foreigner here on a student visa. But if I don't punish you in some way, you might make more mistakes that are even more serious. So go on upstairs now, both of you. And ask Dale to fix your pork chop sandwich, Pop.'

'I don't want it right now.'

'When you do.'

Troy took his shotgun out of the vise, loaded it, and put some extra shells into his *guayabera* pocket. He then got into the Chrysler New Yorker, backed and filled, and drove out of the yard.

James took a shower and put on a clean pair of jeans. His old jeans, which he had worn to Dadeland, were stained from when he had wet his pants during the chase by the taxicab. James rolled the soiled jeans into a ball and took them, together with the garbage bags, down to the trash can in the yard.

Stanley stripped to his underwear and went to bed on the porch. It was too warm to cover himself with a sheet, although a breeze from the bay made the porch a little cooler than the living room. The moon was up, and he could see everything in the yard from his window. The enormous two-story house was an ominous dark mass beyond the circle of light flooding from the bulbs inside the garage. James, apparently exhausted, slept on the couch in the living room, naked except for his jeans. Stanley couldn't sleep. He was worried about Troy driving around in the city with the baby in the back of the car. If they caught him in the car, he would be charged with kidnapping, as well as car theft. Troy should have made James take the car back to Dadeland. But that wasn't Troy's way; he was too responsible for that, despite all his other faults.

Dale, wearing her nightgown, came out to the porch and sat on the edge of the bed. 'Do you mind if I lay down here with you, Mr Sinkiewicz? Just till Troy gets back. I can't sleep all alone. It's scary in the big bedroom all by myself.'

'I don't mind. But don't roll up against me. It's too hot for anything like that.'

Dale curled into a ball, sighed once, and fell asleep. A moment later, she was snoring through her damaged septum.

It was well after two A.M. before Troy drove into the yard and parked a dark blue Lincoln town car beside the back porch of the two-story house. Stanley woke Dale up and told her to go back to the bedroom. Troy came upstairs, woke James, and whispered something to him that Stanley couldn't hear. The two of them went downstairs again. The garage lights were switched off. Without the lights, Stanley could barely see them in the yard as they walked to the Lincoln. He heard the trunk of the car being raised, and then heard it slam down again. For a few minutes, the lights in the big house were on, and then they were switched off again. It was about ten minutes or so before the two men came up the stairs quietly. Stanley pretended to be asleep. James went back to sleep on the couch, and Troy went into the bedroom and closed the door.

Now that Troy was back safely, Stanley got so sleepy he could barely keep his eyes open. But then, why should he keep them open? He wondered, for a moment, what Troy and James had been doing in the big house, but he supposed that Troy had been bawling James out for taking the car with the baby in it. It didn't matter. As Troy said, if he needed to know, he would be told. After all, he was a guest here, and not part of the operation.

Chapter Fifteen

Hoke was wearing his swimming trunks under his jumpsuit, but after he let himself into Helen's apartment, he decided that he didn't want to swim in the pool. His right shoulder throbbed, and he rubbed it briskly. Massaging didn't help it any. He had a touch of bursitis, which came and went periodically and was back now because he had put too much shoulder into popping Skinner in the belly. Hoke had enjoyed hitting Skinner – both times – and he wouldn't mind going back up to the penthouse right now and hitting him again. But he would never hit the millionaire again, and he probably shouldn't have hit him the first time. Skinner was undoubtedly on the phone with his lawyer right now, getting some twenty-five-dollar-a-minute advice.

And what would his lawyer tell him? If Skinner had a good counselor, and there was no doubt that he did, he would be told to count his blessings. That would be the end of it. Hoke wasn't angry, although Skinner had apparently taken him for a fool. Otherwise, he wouldn't have asked Hoke so disingenuously if he had known about the so-called burglaries when he first met him on the beach.

Hoke looked incuriously around Helen's two-hundred-thousand-dollar apartment, taking in the beige leather furniture and the Dufy-blue carpet that picked up the tints in the Hockney painting of a swimming pool above the five-cushioned couch. He decided that Skinner was as bored with his life at the Supermare as Helen had been. Like John Maynard Keynes, who had purportedly picked up the phone every morning and made two or three hundred pounds before getting out of bed, Skinner led a dull existence. After checking the market each morning, and then selling and buying stocks, Skinner didn't know what else to do with his spare time. Helen hadn't known what to do with her time either, living in this designer-decorated apartment, so she had moved in with Frank. Helen still slept until noon, but at least now she had started to engage herself in a few social activities, and she and Frank could always discuss which channel to watch at night. The fact that they had never actually gotten around to getting married didn't really matter.

The spacious apartment had two bedrooms, two baths, and an enormous walk-in dressing room. Very few of Helen's clothes were in the closet. There was a layer of dust over everything, and an anthurium, leaning at a desperate forty-five-degree angle toward the window, had drooped and died from lack of sun and water.

Hoke poured himself two ounces of Booth's gin from an opened bottle at the bar beside the television-hi-fi console. The refrigerator door was propped open with a yellow kitchen stool, and the plug had been pulled from the wall, so he drank his gin without ice. Except for Helen's ocean view, and it was an excellent one, especially from her bedroom floor-to-ceiling windows, Hoke decided that her apartment wasn't worth two hundred thousand – in fact, *no* apartment was. After the residents of the Supermare looked at their view in the morning, what did they do with the rest of their day?

Frank was wise to go to the hardware store every day, Hoke concluded as he unlocked the chain from Aileen's bicycle down in the lobby. Of course, Frank had little or nothing to do with running the store any longer. Mrs Renshaw now ran every aspect of the business. But Frank had his private office in the back, and he was on the telephone a great deal. There was big responsibility in handling a fortune. Occasionally, when Frank left his office, to go to the bank or to see his lawyer, he would wait on a customer – just to keep his hand in. But at least he had a place to go in the mornings.

What did he, Hoke, have now, now that he had decided to leave the police department? In Miami, except for his job and his two daughters, his life had turned to shit – a big *nada*. But when they began to overload him and crap on him in the department, too, his unconscious mind must have rebelled against the work as well. Now his two daughters were almost gone, too, or soon would be.

Hoke was feeling so sorry for himself that he was almost

splattered across the pavement by a white Mercury convertible as he allowed his bike to wobble into the middle of the lane on Ocean Boulevard. Before reaching the mall parking lot, Hoke dismounted and pushed his bike for the rest of the way to the El Pelicano. He locked the bicycle in the small downstairs office, deciding to clean out the cluttered room some other time.

The door to Hoke's apartment was ajar. He knew that he had locked it when he left, so he stood to one side of the door and kicked it open with his foot. Major Willie Brownley, the M.P.D. Homicide Chief, Hoke's boss, was sitting at the dining table playing Klondike with Hoke's deck of cards. There was a steaming cup of coffee in front of him on the table, and he was smoking a cigar. He looked up at Hoke and tapped some ashes into the saucer that held the cup.

'I understand you're managing this apartment house now,' Brownley said as he counted off three cards and looked at a three of hearts. The chief was wearing a Miami Dolphins No. 12 T-shirt, with 'Free Mercury Morris' in white cutout letters across the chest. Hoke had rarely seen the major out of uniform, and it looked strange to see this relaxed black man sitting at his dining table.

'I – I'm trying to, Willie,' Hoke said, at last. 'How'd you get in here?'

'With my passkey. I hung around downstairs for a while, waiting for you, but people kept looking at me funny, as if they'd never seen a black man before. So I decided to wait up here in your apartment. If I were you, Hoke, I'd put a bolt lock on the door – especially if you're going to be fucking off somewhere instead of staying here to rent out your apartments.'

'I had some other business to attend to.'

'You know, the ten of diamonds and the four of clubs are missing from this deck, and I don't think you're playing with a full deck either. I lost two games before I found out.' The major gathered the cards together and shuffled them. Willie Brownley's face was the color of an eggplant, and the corners of his mouth dropped sharply. His gray kinky hair was clipped short, with a razor-blade part on the left side. The yellowish whites of his eyes made him look jaundiced.

'Sit down,' Brownley said, putting the cards down and indicating a chair with his left hand. 'Don't make me look up at you, you sneaky bastard.'

'Who's sneaky?' Hoke sat across from the chief. 'You broke into my apartment.'

'You and Bill Henderson aren't half as smart as you think you are, Hoke. I signed your emergency leave without pay because I believed him when he told me your father was dying. But just because I believed him at the time didn't mean that I wouldn't check it out later. And I did. Your daddy told me on the phone that he was fine, that you seemed to be your old self again, and that it was nice to have you home.

'Then I asked my secretary to call Ellita. Ellita, of course, gave Rosalie a full report and told her that you were under a doctor's care up here in Singer Island. Then I braced Bill Henderson, and he told me what really happened. As a reward for Bill's disloyalty I gave him all of your unprocessed homicide cases to work on – in addition to his other duties, of course. That should keep him so busy for a while that he won't be able to cover up anything else on me for a few weeks. While I pondered various disciplinary measures, if any, I wondered why you hadn't come to me with your problems, even if they were imaginary problems. Surely, by now, I thought, Hoke trusts me to do the right thing. Hoke' – Brownley shook his head and tapped his chest with his right palm – 'it hurts me right here to have my trust in you violated.'

Hoke cleared his throat. 'I can't explain myself, Willie. But I wasn't trying to bypass you, or anything like that. I was suddenly overwhelmed, that's all, and sort of blacked out. What I needed, I guess, was a rest. I'd been pushing hard, and I –'

'Spare me the bullshit, Hoke. I had a call from Mike Sheldon.'

'Who?'

'Mike Sheldon. The Riviera Beach police chief. Are you going to pretend you haven't talked with him?'

'Oh, sure, Chief Sheldon. I met him at my father's house. He seems like a nice guy. Used to be a homicide detective up in New Jersey. What's wrong with that?'

'He called me and asked for a written recommendation, that's what. It appears that you applied for a lieutenancy in his department, and he wanted a letter so he could start on the paperwork.'

'He made a tentative offer, but I turned him down, Willie. I didn't *ask* him for –'

'Bullshit! What hurts me, Hoke, you went behind my back. Why didn't you tell me you wanted to be a lieutenant? How many times, in the last three years, have I suggested that you take the exam?'

'Several. But I told you I don't want to be a lieutenant.'

'What you mean is you don't want to be a lieutenant in Miami, working for me, but you'd like to be a lieutenant up here at half the salary you already make as a sergeant. That doesn't make any sense.'

'No, I don't want to be a lieutenant here, either. I do plan on taking an early retirement, but I'm not joining the Riviera force, Willie. The job's too much for me – at least I think it is. I don't really know any longer.'

'If you wanted an easier job, why didn't you come in and see me? My door's open at all times.'

'I *have* seen you! I've bitched about my overload plenty of times, for Christ's sake.'

'Everybody has a lot to do, Hoke. Didn't I give you Speedy Gonzalez as an assistant?'

'He spends half his time in gas stations, asking for directions –'

'He's getting to know the city, Hoke, and you just proved my point. It takes a long time to train a man for homicide work, and that's why I can't afford to lose you to some jerkwater little town like Riviera Beach. Hell, you'd die of boredom here. And you've already proven you can't run this little apartment house.'

'How's that?'

'There was no note on your door saying when you'd be back. And some old redneck from Alabama, who thought I was the janitor, asked me to fix his toilet for him. He said no matter how much he jiggles the handle, the toilet still keeps running. You'd better do something about things like that.'

'Fuck him.'

'See what I mean? Here, I've got something for you.' Brownley opened his briefcase, which was on an adjacent chair, and took out a large brown envelope. He put it on the table. 'You don't have to open this now, Hoke, but when you come to your senses again, it'll come in handy. I put your name down for the lieutenant's exam next month. You'll have to write your own essays, on Part Two of the exam, but here are all one hundred and fifty answers to the multiple-choice questions in Part One. With these answers memorized, you should be at the top of the list when the results are posted. Only minority applicants will have any priority on you on the next vacancy. That's because of Affirmative Action, and there's nothing I can do about that. But otherwise you should head the list.'

Using his thumbnail, Hoke opened the envelope and took out the Xeroxed answer sheets.

'I said you didn't have to open it now,' Brownley said. 'Memorizing all of those answer sheets'll take several hours of uninterrupted study.'

Hoke laughed. 'Hell, these aren't the answers, Willie, they're just letters. Without the questions that go with 'em, they don't make any sense.'

'They don't have to make sense, and you don't need to know the questions. Besides, I couldn't get a copy of the questionnaire. The right answers have all been blacked in, so all you have to do is memorize them in order. See? Number one is C. Number two is A. Number three is C again. You go over them again and again until you've got 'em in your head, like reading them off a blackboard. Hell, you've got a month. I give you a beer, and now you want an egg in it, for Christ's sake.'

Hoke returned the sheets to the envelope. 'Why are you doing this, Willie?'

'I want to keep you in the division, and I like you, Hoke. It also occurred to me that I might've been working you too hard. But that's the way it always is, Hoke. People who can do more than other people always get more to do. I'll tell you right now, though – when your leave is over, I'll see that you get a lighter load.'

'I don't want the answer sheets, Willie. When I decide to go for a promotion, which I doubt, I'll study for it just like everyone else. Besides, I haven't made any decisions. Let me finish my leave, and I promise I won't make up my mind till I've talked to you first.'

'Fair enough. But keep the answer sheets anyway, in case you have a change of heart.'

'No.' Hoke shook his head. He put the envelope back into the major's open briefcase and shut the lid. 'I wouldn't feel right about it. Besides, I have a hunch I'd be pretty high on the list even if I didn't study for the exam. You may not remember, but I was first in my class at the FBI course.'

'I remember. How many years have you got left to go? Exactly?'

'For regular retirement? About seven and a half years.'

'That isn't too long, Hoke. And if you weren't a cop in Miami, you'd still have to be a cop somewhere. You don't know how to do anything else.'

'You might be right. But I can learn.'

'I know I'm right.'

There was a knock on the door. Hoke got up from the table. It was Professor Hurt, and Hoke introduced him to Major Brownley.

'I came up to invite you to dinner, Mr Moseley, but there's plenty, so you're included in the invitation, Major Brownley.' Hurt shook hands with Brownley.

'I've got to drive back to Miami.'

'No use going back on an empty stomach. Besides, I've got four liters of Riunite on ice.'

'I guess I could have a glass or two with you, but I really have to get back to Miami.'

'Let the traffic thin out a little, Willie,' Hoke suggested. 'Eat dinner with us.'

'Beefy Winters is coming, too,' the professor said. 'He's an elephant trainer with Ringling Brothers, Major.'

'He was,' Hoke amended. 'But that'll make four of us, and then maybe we can play some Monopoly?'

'I should go back –' Brownley said. 'But I guess I can stay for one game. If we play the short game. The regular game takes way too long.'

'I like the short game myself,' Hoke said.

'Okay,' Hurt said, rubbing his hands together. 'I've got a dozen Swanson Hungry Man dinners. What'll you have? There's fried chicken, macaroni and cheese, spaghetti and meatballs, you name it. What I've found out with Swanson's is that one isn't quite enough, but two of them are too much. So what I usually end up doing is heating up two different kinds, and I eat what I want from both of them at the same time. I suggest that you do the same. I'll pop 'em in the oven, and they'll all be ready in a half-hour or so. Meanwhile, we can start on the Riunite and the game.'

'You two go ahead,' Hoke said. 'I'll dig out the Monopoly set.'

Major Brownley picked up his briefcase and went with the professor, telling him he liked the kind of dinner with the little square of apple pie better than he did the kind with the little square piece of cake. Otherwise, he said, he didn't much care whether he ate macaroni and cheese or the ham with the sweet potatoes.

Before joining them downstairs, Hoke took the Monopoly game out of the cardboard box and arranged the property cards so that when he dealt them around for the short game he would end up with Boardwalk and Park Place. Hoke knew that if he played Monopoly against Major Brownley, he would need an edge.

Chapter Sixteen

It was 10:29 exactly when Stanley Sinkiewicz parked his Honda in the asphalt lot outside the supermarket in the Green Lakes Shopping Center. There were seven cars in the lot, not counting his own – more than he had expected – but some of them, he concluded, belonged to store employees. The uneven façade of unfinished buildings, dark and unoccupied, stretched for almost three hundred yards down the lot before the two-story windowless department store blocked and anchored the northern end. Only the supermarket was lighted. There were dozens of tall street lamps scattered at intervals throughout the lot, but none of the sodium-vapor light clusters was turned on. A few four- and five-foot palm trees, propped up by two-by-fours, had been planted recently in some of the concrete islands in the lot.

Stanley locked his car, and then remembered his cane. Troy had told him to take it with him. The cane gave him a distinguished look, he said – meaning, Stanley supposed, that he'd look like a harmless retiree whom nobody would notice. Stanley unlocked his car, retrieved his cane, buttoned his suit jacket, and walked purposefully toward the glass doors of the supermarket, reviewing Troy's instructions. Once more he marveled at how Troy had managed to make him a part of the operation, yet had allowed him to remain aloof from anything untoward and not become a part of the robbery itself. The store closed at eleven, but as a general rule one of the bag boys, or the assistant manager, would then stand by the doors to let late shoppers out, but he wouldn't admit anyone. Stanley's assignment was to walk into the store at ten-thirty and to shop for small items. He was to keep shopping until ten-fifty, or a little later than that, before getting into the line at the checkout counter.

'If possible,' Troy had told him, 'and it is possible, you should be the last shopper in the line. See that you are before you get

623

into the line. By ten-thirty they'll be down to only one lane anyway. The other checkers will turn in their trays and leave by ten-fifteen, James says. So all you have to do, Pop, is dawdle. If you overlooked someone, and they get behind you, let them go ahead of you in the line and say you forgot something.'

'Like what?'

'It doesn't matter. Bread, toilet paper, anything. You leave your cart in place, and you don't come back until you're positive you're the only one left. With only small items to check off, and your cart loaded, it'll take the checker a long time to ring up all your stuff. When you're the last customer in the store, I'll bang on the door. The boy won't let me in, of course, and that's when you say to the checker, "That's my son. I forgot my wallet at home, and he's brought it." I'll wave the wallet at the boy. They'll see the mountain of groceries in your cart, with some of 'em rung up already, and the boy'll let me in.'

'What do I do then?'

'When I tell 'em it's a stickup, you just hold up your arms like any other smart customer, and you're in the clear.'

'Suppose they ask me later why I said you were my son?'

'You don't have to worry about that. But if they do, just say you're old, which is obvious, and that you were confused for a moment when you couldn't find your wallet. So you *thought* I was your son. The point is, Pop, I don't want you involved in this in any way. That's why I've come up with this foolproof method of letting you help us, but one that'll keep you out of it at the same time. But if you think it's too much for you to handle, let me know now, and I'll work out another way of doing it.'

'No, no, Troy, I'm sure that I can handle it. It's just that … well, after the robbery, what?'

'You can't leave with us, naturally. So you just stay there, and when the police come you act a little dazed and scared. If you can avoid it, don't say anything at all. Just pretend that you were overwhelmed by the whole thing, and you don't remember what any of us looked like. Finally, after they've let you rest for a while, tell the cops we were wearing masks and plastic gloves, but you think we were black men from the way we talked. They'll jump on that idea. Just don't change your story. Then they'll let you go.'

'Suppose, just suppose, they ask me why I've driven all the way down to the Green Lakes mall in Miami to buy groceries, when I live seventy miles away in Riviera Beach?'

'That's easy. They won't ask you that, but if they do, tell 'em you were down here in Miami to see the sights, and you stocked up at this new Green Lakes market because the prices were cheaper down here.'

'They aren't, Troy. Things are a lot cheaper up in Riviera than they are down here.'

'Christ, Pop, the cops don't know that! They aren't going to give you any third degree. You're wearing a suit and tie, you're a property owner, and you own your own car. You're above suspicion. Can't you see how this all works?'

'I guess so, Troy. But these questions just come to me, and I want to do everything right, that's all.'

'You'll do fine. Take off your shoes now, and let James give 'em a good shine. Also, clean out your pockets and give everything to me. I already collected James's stuff, so he can't be identified. If you don't have your wallet on you, your story'll hold up. Put your traveler's checks in Dale's purse, over there on the table. She'll keep things safe for you, just in case.'

'In case of what?'

'Unforeseen eventualities. Sometimes there are unforeseen eventualities that no one can predict. At any rate, when they let you go – which won't take long – drive back here to the house. Then we'll get ready to leave in the morning for Haiti.'

'Maybe it would be best, Troy, if I didn't go with you. To Haiti. Right away, I mean.'

'Hell, I've already got your ticket.'

'You can turn it back in when you leave. I can buy another one later. I'd better go back up to Ocean Pines Terraces first, then I can join you later on. Maya might have some second thoughts, and if I'm missing and she calls the police, they might be out looking for me and then they'll find you and Dale. But I can go back home for a few days, call my son, and then a few days later I can call him again and tell him I'm going to the islands on a vacation. You know, I can sort of set things up. If I leave my car in the carport, and tell my neighbors I'm going on a vacation, too, nobody'll look for me.'

'Okay, Pop, if that's the way you want to do it. Dale and I will be in Haiti waiting for you. By the time you get there, I'll have a house rented and a room for you. When you get to Port-au-Prince, go to the American embassy; I'll leave the address there for you. Either that, or I can call you from Port-au-Prince and tell you where we are.'

'Can you phone from there?'

'Sure.'

'I've already had my phone disconnected. Maybe you'd better just leave the address at the embassy. How do I find it?'

'Take a cab from the airport to the embassy. Then you hang on to the cab, get our address, and join us. If we don't have a house yet, we'll be at the Gran Hotel Olofsson. The hotel doesn't take reservations, but all of the hotels have empty rooms down there because of the troubles they've had. So we'll be easy enough to find. People have a tendency to remember Dale's face. You'll find us all right.'

They had left it at that.

During the last few days, there had been a great deal of tension in the apartment. James was so apprehensive, he jumped at the slightest sound, and Troy had given him money to buy rum at the liquor store. James picked at his food, and instead of sleeping at night he sat on the lumpy couch smoking one cigarette after another. He drank Mount Gay rum from the bottle, without even a water chaser. He would finally fall asleep well after midnight. Once James fell asleep with a cigarette still burning between his fingers, and Stanley had seen it just in time. As a consequence, Stanley was afraid to go to sleep until after James had passed out on the couch.

During the daytime, James, because of his trembling fingers, was unable to paint. He spent the day looking at his pictures, wondering what to do with them. After James received his share of the money, five thousand dollars, he figured on driving directly to New York, but there was no room in his little Morris Minor for all of his paintings. He had already packed his paints and clothing in the car, and his plan was to keep driving until he got to Valdosta, Georgia, before stopping at a motel. Finally he asked Stanley for advice.

'What I'd do, James, I'd just leave the old paintings here and forget about them. Let the Shapiros have them. You owe them something for not taking care of the grass and the yard. You'll be going to school, and starting over again anyway. After you've had some instruction, you won't want to be reminded of your old work. That's what I think.'

'They're a part of me,' James said. 'I hate to just leave them.'

'I know how you feel. I used to feel the same way after I striped a new car. It was a part of me, I guess you could say, and now it was leaving the line for the whole world to see. But you'll be painting new pictures in New York, and these old paintings'll just clutter up your new studio.'

'I won't have a studio. I'll just rent a little room somewhere. I'll have to use the studio at the school to paint.'

'So leave the pictures and forget 'em.'

James nodded grimly and stacked all of his paintings in a corner of the garage. Even so, he would return to the pile from time to time, examining the compositions as if he were trying to memorize them.

Dale kept busy. She washed and scrubbed and cooked plain but ample meals, as well as baking cakes and pies. For breakfast she served them not only fried eggs, but bacon, sausages, and pancakes. She scrubbed and waxed the hardwood floors of the apartment, then washed all of the windows. She polished the furniture, using Lemon Pledge, and the apartment smelled like a lime grove. She used Bon-Ami and elbow grease and managed to get almost all of the mildew off the tiles in the bathroom.

Troy taught James and Dale how to hold and aim their pistols. There was a .38 Smith and Wesson for James, and a small .25-caliber pearl-handled semi-automatic pistol for Dale. James refused to load his pistol. He remained firm that he would just take an empty pistol to hold during the robbery, but Troy still made him aim and practice dry-firing at a target he drew on the garage door.

'Even if you don't intend to shoot it,' Troy said, 'you have to look like you know what you're doing. It's like with the shotgun. People have to think that you'll shoot. Now Dale, on the other hand, has to keep her pistol loaded because she might have to fire it from the car to warn us when I come out of the market. That way, if someone tries to follow me out, her firing into the air will make 'em stay inside.'

Troy oiled and loaded his shotgun. He bought a khaki windbreaker at Sears, one like James had, and crammed double-aught shells into the pockets.

Sometimes Troy was silent for hours at a time. He would sit in the backyard with his shirt off, brooding, not moving, soaking up the sun.

In the evenings, after dinner, and after Dale had finished cleaning up the kitchen, Troy made her dance for them. She needed to keep in practice, he said, to be ready for her nightclub debut in Haiti.

Dale was not, in Stanley's estimation, a very good dancer, but he kept his opinion to himself. Troy tuned to a rock station on the radio, and Dale would gyrate in her G-string, and her bare breasts would bounce up and down; but she was awkward; she stumbled frequently; and she seemed to be out of synchronization with the music, Stanley thought. But Stanley figured that nightclub patrons in Haiti wouldn't be so critical. After all, Dale had a spectacular figure, and as Troy said, she would be wearing a voodoo mask to hide her face.

James, drinking his rum neat, watched Dale gloomily and without comment. One evening, joyous on rum, he showed them all how to limbo. With Stanley and Dale holding a broom, and with salsa blaring on the radio, James kept saying, 'Lower, lower, limbo like me!' Finally, he writhed under the broom without touching it while it was held less than a foot above the floor. Troy and Stanley both tried it, but they couldn't get below three feet. Dale, bottom-heavy, couldn't limbo as low as Stanley and Troy. Stanley had enjoyed watching James limbo, but he hurt his stiff back after his third try and had to lie down.

After the heavy meals and the dancing, everybody except James went to bed early. Stanley missed his color TV set. He still took afternoon naps, and he couldn't go to sleep so early. He would lie there on his bed on the porch, listening to Troy and Dale make love in the bedroom. Afterwards, Troy always sent Dale out to sleep with Stanley, because Troy didn't rest well if there was another person in the bed with him. Dale, exhausted from her long day of housework, dancing, and love-making, and wearing her shorty nightgown, would fall asleep immediately. Sometimes, in her sleep, she would snuggle up against Stanley, and her body was so hot she reminded him of an overloaded heating pad. By this time, James would be quite drunk, muttering to himself and dropping ashes on Dale's clean floor. It would be better, Stanley thought, when the job was all over and James was up in New York, and they were down in Haiti. He was looking forward to the trip. After Dale got her operation, and was recuperating, he and Troy could bum around town together, just the two of them, taking in the sights, and they could eat some of that Creole food Troy had talked about. But he really couldn't go with them right after the job, not with all of his responsibilities. In Detroit, if a man left his car at the airport for a week or so, when he came back the car – or at least the battery – would be missing. It was undoubtedly the same way at the Miami airport. Besides, he did have the house to worry about; he would have to arrange with the bank to have his mortgage payments made while he was away. And there was Stanley Junior. If Junior couldn't get ahold of him, he would report him missing to the police. The best thing to do was to go home first, call Junior, and tell him and the neighbors that he would be away on a vacation. That way, he could leave his car in his own carport, take the bus to the West Palm Beach airport, fly to Haiti from there, and save ten dollars a day in airport parking fees. He could get a plane to Haiti just as easily from West Palm as he could from Miami. Besides, he didn't know how long he would be away. This way, if he didn't like it down there, he could use his return ticket to fly back to West Palm whenever he felt like it.

Troy hadn't liked it much when he told him he would join them later in Haiti. He could tell, by the way Troy squinted his eyes. He should have worked it around so that Troy could have been the one to make that suggestion, the way Maya had got around him when she wanted to do something. But Troy would get over being mad about it, once he had joined them down there ...

Stanley pushed his cart to the back of the store, passing a pimpled teenage employee who was mopping the floor with a wet mop and whistling tunelessly. The boy wore a black bow tie, a white short-sleeved shirt, and blue jeans. A red plastic tag, with white letters spelling RANDY, was pinned to the pocket of his shirt. Stanley stopped at the meat counters, but the meat had all been collected and put away for the night. The refrigerated bins were bare, and the butchers had left. He went to the gourmet section and began to drop small items into his cart, taking them at random from the shelves – a can of anchovies, a bottle of capers, a flat can of smoked oysters, a jar of cocktail onions, an oval tin of pâté. He felt in his pocket for his car keys; for a panicky moment he thought he had left them in the Honda. But the keys were there ...

Stanley looked at his watch. Ten-fifty-five. His cart was filled to the brim; it was so full of canned goods it was hard to push. On the shelf below the basket, he had placed an orange, an apple, a sweet potato, one tomato, one head of cabbage, and a six-pack of Stroh's light beer. Stanley headed for the front of the store. Randy, the boy who had been mopping the floor, now stood beside the locked front doors. The key was in the lock. The night manager, a middle-aged man with a long-sleeved white shirt and a loosened maroon wool tie, was in the open-topped cage behind the service counter with a gray-haired woman employee in a blue and white uniform. There was a woman checker at the second checkout counter, and she was ringing up sales for a plump, very pregnant Latin woman who had driven three blocks from home to buy a loaf of Cuban bread, a dozen eggs, a quart of skim milk, and a box of Fruitful Bran. The checker, a young woman with tight yellow curls, purple lipstick and eyeliner, and with too much blusher on her cheeks, was asking the pregnant woman how much longer she had to go when Stanley stopped behind the woman's cart. The checker glanced over at Stanley's overloaded basket and groaned good-naturedly at the sight of all his groceries.

'At least another week, maybe ten days,' the Cuban woman said, with a little laugh, 'but it might be sooner' – she picked up her bag of groceries – 'if he feels like it.'

Stanley took his cane out of his cart and tucked it under his left armpit. With his right hand he began to take out the items, one at a time, and place them on the counter.

"Evening, sir,' the girl said cheerfully. 'Looks to me like you're starting your own store.'

'Just stocking up a little,' Stanley said, not looking up from the cart.

At the door, Randy tried to take the pregnant woman's bag of groceries from her, but she smiled and shook her head. 'I can manage it all right – Randy,' she said, glancing at his name plate. 'Are you?'

'Am I what, ma'am?'

'Randy?'

'Yes, ma'am,' he said, letting her out of the store. He relocked the door.

'Maybe,' Stanley said, 'I'd better get this stuff off the bottom first.' He bent over and got the six-pack. As he straightened up, he saw Troy at the door. Troy waved the wallet in his hand and grinned wolfishly at Randy through the glass.

As he had been instructed to do, Stanley patted his empty pockets. His heart was fibrillating slightly, and he found it difficult to breathe. He clutched the handle of the cart for support, and his cane clattered to the floor.

'That's my son at the door,' Stanley said to the checker. 'I forgot my wallet at home, and it's got all my money in it.'

The checker, by this time, had run up $28 worth of groceries, and the cart was still two-thirds loaded.

'For God's sake, Randy,' she called to the bag boy, 'let him in.'

Randy unlocked the door and let Troy in. Before he could relock the door, Troy kneed the boy in the crotch.

Randy dropped to the floor, keening and clutching his genitals with both hands. James slipped through the unlocked door, carrying a black, doubled-up Hefty garbage bag in his left hand and his .38 pistol in his right. James had pulled one leg of a pair of Dale's pantyhose over his head and face, and both legs trailed down his back in foxtails. The pistol danced in his gloved hand, and it looked, for a moment, as if he was going to drop it.

'This is a holdup!' Troy announced, taking the sawed-off shotgun from beneath his jacket. He lifted the hinged top at the service counter to enter the cage.

James stood midway between Randy, who was still on the floor, and the second checkout counter. First, he would point the pistol at the checker, then he would wheel and point it at Randy. In his fear and excitement James kept pulling the trigger, and the empty pistol clicked away like a cheap alarm clock.

The safe was open, as James had said it would be. The night manager and his assistant had their arms high above their heads as Troy entered the crowded cage. The manager kicked back with his left foot and hit a buzzer on the wall. Bells clanged all over the store, and a red light began to flash outside, above the entrance door.

Troy shot the manager in the stomach, and a dark red splotch the size of a grapefruit appeared instantly on his white shirt. The dark blood was a much deeper shade than his maroon tie. As the heavy pellets came out of his back and the blood splattered the woman beside him, the pattern got larger. The gray-haired woman yelped once as the shotgun fired, and her slightly popped eyes rolled back in her head. Her legs gave way, and she fell over sideways in a faint on the manager's dead body. Troy stuck the short barrel against the back of her neck and fired the second round, half severing her head from her body.

Troy reloaded his shotgun and left the cage, pocketing the used shells. James managed to slip his pistol into his own pocket and came through the opened counter into the cage. He knelt by the two bodies, shuddered, and began to transfer the money from the safe into his Hefty bag.

At the sound of the first shotgun blast, Stanley had dropped to the floor and crawled over to the next checkout counter. He stretched out on the floor and covered his head with both hands. Something, he thought, has gone wrong. Troy had told them there would be no shooting at all. The manager must have tried to pull a pistol on Troy.

The checker, except for quivering, hadn't moved from the moment Troy announced the holdup. Her face had a greenish pallor beneath her heavy makeup, and there was a thin ring of white encircling her purple lips. She began to urinate, couldn't stop, and a large puddle formed around her feet. Her lips quivered, but she couldn't make any sound come out of her dry throat as Troy walked toward her with the shotgun extended in his right hand. When he was about two feet away, Troy shot her in the face, and blood and brains erupted from her blond head. She fell backward and slid to the floor. With his left hand, Troy scooped the bills from her register and jammed them into the pocket of his windbreaker. As he turned back toward the cage, Randy, crouched low, was on his feet again, hobbling as fast as he could toward the dairy section at the back of the store.

Running lightly in his Nikes, Troy overtook the boy and shot him in the back of the head. The boy's body fell forward and slid across the clean floor into a six-foot pyramid of canned peaches. The stack toppled, and the heavy cans bounced and gurgled on the brown linoleum.

Stanley lifted his head above the counter, high enough to see Troy shoot Randy. As the pyramid collapsed, Stanley dropped to his hands and knees and crept as rapidly as he could to the square U that made up the produce section. There was no place to hide, but he wedged his body as close as he could against a large bin of White Rose potatoes.

'Be sure you get the change, too, James!' Troy called out above the clanging bells as he reloaded his shotgun.

'I got it! I got it *all*, man!' James shouted. He came out of the cage and slipped sideways through the passway at the service counter. There were stacks of banded bills in the bag, but the rolls of halves, quarters, dimes, and nickels made the bag heavier than he had expected it to be. Troy raised the shotgun, put the muzzle against James's chest, and fired. Troy picked up the bag and jumped up on the nearest counter, surveying the store.

'A change in plans, Pop!' he shouted. 'Instead of staying here, you'd better come with me now. I mean it, Pop! Those bells are ringing in the police station, too, and I can't hang around here while you make up your mind!'

There was no movement anywhere.

'Pop, let's shake it. Come *on!*' Troy jumped down and took a step toward the closest aisle, cereals, but then he stopped. There were altogether at least a dozen aisles in the store. In the back, there were two open service doors leading to the stockrooms. 'Shit,' he said under his breath.

Troy turned around and walked to the door, carrying the bag slung over his left shoulder.

'Okay, Pop, see you in Haiti, and thanks for the help!'

Awkwardly, with his shotgun hand, Troy unlocked the door. He pushed it open and stepped into the humid night.

Ellita Sanchez had reached her car and unlocked the door when the first shotgun round was fired. She dumped her groceries behind the seat as the second round was fired, and took her .38 Chief's Special out of her purse. She did it all automatically, without thinking about it, but now, with her pistol in her hand, she hesitated and stared at the brightly lighted supermarket and the flashing red light. She was on a maternity leave, so technically she was not even an off-duty cop. She had no radio. Perhaps she should drive away, find a pay phone, and call 911? No one could blame her for that. On the other hand, if someone was shooting a shotgun inside the store – and the sound was unmistakably that of a shotgun – there was no way after nine years on the force that she could just jump in her car and drive away without investigating what was going on. The clanging bells were insistent. She could at least try to get a look inside.

Ellita took her badge out of her purse. She held the badge in her left hand and the pistol in her right as she lumbered heavily toward the lighted glass doors of the store. As two more shotgun rounds were fired, she gripped her pistol tighter. She hesitated, looking around for suitable cover as the shotgun went off for the fifth time. She knelt behind a newly planted palm tree, a few yards away from a brown Honda with a roof rack on it, where she could watch the door. A tallish man, carrying a Hefty bag and a sawed-off shotgun, came bursting out of the store. He was silhouetted against the lights inside, his features in such dark shadow that Ellita couldn't see what he looked like. The flashing red light made his movements seem jerky.

'Freeze! Police!' Ellita yelled, trying to keep her large body behind the tree. She fired a warning shot into the sign above the doors.

The robber fired once in her general direction and dropped into a crouching position. Then he fired again. The double-aught pellets scattered all over the lot at this distance, but one of them hit Ellita in the face, and another tore into her right shoulder. She could hear some of the buckshot hitting and ricocheting off the Honda. Ellita dropped to the asphalt and tried to wedge her pregnant body under the Honda, without success. Her face and shoulder seemed to be on fire. Her right arm was numb, so she fired the rest of her rounds blindly toward the store, trying to steady the pistol with her left hand.

Dale Forrest, who had been parked around the corner of the building with the engine running, pulled up in front of the double doorway and stopped while Ellita was still firing. One of Ellita's bullets hit the right front fender of the Lincoln town car. Troy threw the Hefty into the back seat through the open window and told Dale to move over so he could get in and drive. Dale shot him in the face with her .25, and Troy fell sideways onto the pavement, dropping his shotgun and clutching his face with both hands. Dale drove away, flooring the gas pedal so hard she almost killed the engine. She made a wide circle in the parking lot and exited onto State Road 836, heading west.

Ellita felt the first strong contraction of what she feared was early labor. She rolled over on her back and bit her lower lip as two matching pains gripped her unexpectedly, beginning at the small of her back, encircling her waist, and then meeting in front to interlock. The pain didn't last long, and when it subsided she got onto her knees. She watched an old man come out of the store, leaning heavily on his cane. She crawled backward into the darkness as she realized that the old man was coming toward the brown Honda, but she kept behind his car and he didn't see her. She ducked her head. Her pistol was empty, useless. Where the hell was her purse?

The old man got into his car without seeing Ellita. He drove up beside the wounded man who was still holding his face and kneeling on the sidewalk. The old guy got out, helped the groaning man get into the car, and then drove away. When he reached the State Road 836 exit, he turned east and disappeared into the traffic.

Ellita walked unsteadily into the store, surveyed the dead bodies, and leaned against a pay phone while she called Commander Bill Henderson at home. As she explained what happened, another contraction gripped her hard, and her water broke with a rush of fluid down her legs.

'Everyone's dead, Bill. Everyone. But you'd better have an ambulance sent anyway. I'm slightly wounded, but the pains are getting closer together, and oh Jesus I'm going to have this baby any minute!'

But Ellita's baby, a nine-and-a-half-pound boy, wasn't born until ten the next morning at Jackson Memorial Hospital. A nerve in Ellita's right shoulder was half-severed, and there was an ugly hole in her face. Her right cheekbone was chipped off cleanly, right below the eye, and there was a jagged two-inch tear in her right cheek.

The pantyhose robber with the empty gun had died instantly. His partner with the sawed-off shotgun had wounded Ellita Sanchez and murdered four store employees for what was estimated to be less than twenty thousand dollars.

Chapter Seventeen

The supermarket robbery-massacre got considerable play in the Miami press and on the radio and television stations. Very little information was released to the media by the Homicide Division, but pictures were printed in the papers, and the headline, SUPER-MASSACRE AT SUPERMARKET, frightened everyone who read it, especially old-line Miamians. The story revealed that all the victims were white, Protestants, and native-born Americans. There had been mini-massacres in Miami before, with four or five men and their women and children killed all at once, but those victims had been Colombians, or other Latins, or blacks; and usually they had been connected in some way with the drug industry or with organized crime. These innocent victims, on the other hand, were not only white, they were respectable middle-class people, and all of them were residents of the predominantly native-born Green Lakes subdivision.

The night manager, Victor Persons, forty-five, was married, the father of three children, and a paid soloist on Sunday evenings at the Green Lakes Methodist Church.

His assistant, Ms Julia Riordan, fifty-eight, was a former school-teacher who had taught fourth grade in Dade County, at various schools, for twenty-two years. According to one of her Green Lakes neighbors, she had retired under the old Florida Retirement System, before Social Security had been withheld from teachers' pay, and she had taken the night-shift job at the supermarket so she could build up enough credits to obtain a second retirement from the Social Security system when she reached sixty-two. The gruesome photographs of Mr Persons and Ms Riordan beside the open safe, which appeared in both Miami papers, though not on television, brought dozens of angry letters to the editors of both papers, protesting their publication.

Sally Metcalf, twenty-three, the blond checker, or 'scanner-assistant,' as her position was called by the supermarket chain (her job, apparently, was to assist the electronic scanner in its task), had been a member of the Miami-Dade Community College's South Campus volleyball team before she graduated, and she was engaged to be married to her high-school sweetheart as soon as he finished his first hitch at Fort Benning, Georgia.

Randolph Perkins, seventeen, the bag boy, a high-school student at Miami-Norland, was remembered by his fellow students as 'a real good guy who was always ready with a joke, and liked to kid around a lot (sic).' His principal also told the same reporter that Randy had already passed Florida's 11th Grade Achievement Test, and that he had a 'very high C average' in all of his classes. There was a black and white photograph of four of Randy's buddies and two crying girls in the paper, all of them wearing black ribbons pinned to their T-shirts, in mourning for their classmate.

Fred Pickering, twenty-eight, the produce manager, who had rushed through his closing work at the store so he could leave early to watch a tape of *Ghostbusters* his wife had rented that afternoon, credited his Sony VCR with saving his life. 'God,' he told the TV reporter, 'evidently has other plans for me!' He broke down, then, on camera, and cried. 'Here I was,' he sobbed, 'laughing my head off at home at *Ghostbusters*, while Ms Riordan was getting her head blown off down at the store! It could've been me. It could've been me!'

Letters were written to the Cuban-born mayor and to the multi-ethnic members of the city commission. The tone of the letters varied, but the essential message was the same, reminding the commissioners that when they ran for their six-thousand-dollar-a-year seats that they had all claimed that they would serve *all* of the people in Miami if elected, not just their ethnic groups. They were also reminded that WASPs, although they only numbered approximately eight percent of Miami's population, still had a lot of money to spend in future elections.

The mayor and the other members of the commission put considerable pressure on the city manager. The city manager, who had the authority to hire and fire police chiefs, applied even more pressure on the chief of police to find the killers. He, in turn, appointed a Special Task Force to solve this crime, to be headed by Major Willie Brownley. Major Brownley, in turn, made Commander Bill Henderson his operations officer, to coordinate activities, and Bill Henderson, in turn, canceled Hoke Moseley's leave without pay and called him back to do the actual work on the investigation with the help of Detective Speedy Gonzalez.

Hoke and Gonzalez had lots of help from within the division and the department. Ellita, not only because she was a wounded cop, but because of her cheerful disposition and willingness to lend small sums of money, was popular with all of the detectives in the Homicide Division. They volunteered their off-duty time to Hoke the moment their shifts ended. Hoke gave them things to do, like the routine roundup of tall, black holdup men with previous convictions, who were then interrogated about their whereabouts at the time of the robbery-massacre. These interrogations didn't get any concrete results, but were considered necessary to eliminate possible suspects and on the off-chance that some information would turn up.

Gonzalez and Sergeant Armando Quevedo interviewed the day-shift employees at the supermarket, and the day manager quickly identified the dead mulatto's photograph as that of a bag boy he had fired for stealing a couple of months back. The man's name, according to the three-by-five employment card, was John Smith, but the rooming-house address on the card did not exist, and the Social Security number on the card belonged to a forty-seven-year-old John Smith in Portland, Oregon.

'We don't run background checks on bag boys,' the manager said. 'They don't handle money, and they come and go too fast. Smith had a Caribbean accent, so maybe he gave us a phony name and Social Security number because he was here in Florida illegally. That sometimes happens with foreigners on student visas, who ain't supposed to work either. All I know about Smith is, he was a thief, and as soon's I spotted him stealing I canned him.'

Quevedo then checked the dead man's clothes in the lab with the head technician. Here their luck changed, and they got a valid lead.

Hoke, of course, had to read and cross-check every supplementary report with the others, and the pile of paper mounted hourly on his desk. Hoke's phones, as well as Bill Henderson's, were busy night and day, after the numbers were listed in the newspapers. But Hoke welcomed the activity, knowing, from experience, that it was the kind of things they were doing now that eventually provided a breakthrough in any investigation.

Hoke would have returned to Miami anyway, whether his leave had been canceled or not. He considered himself partly responsible for his partner's injuries. If he had been home instead of trying to 'find himself again' up in Singer Island, he would have been the one to go to the store instead of Ellita, and she wouldn't have been wounded. Her face, the surgeon told him, when Hoke talked to him at some length in the hospital, would be okay when the surgery healed. The hole could be filled in with a piece of plastic, and the skin would stretch over it. Except for a small dent, and a fine line across her cheek, which could be camouflaged easily with pancake makeup, no one, unless he looked very closely indeed, would notice the repair work. The arm, unhappily, was a more serious injury, because of the nerve damage. In time, Ellita would regain partial use of her arm, eighty to eighty-five percent perhaps, with a lot of therapy, but the disability meant the end of her career insofar as full-time police work was concerned.

The surgeon would recommend a thirty-percent disability pension for Ellita Sanchez, and because disability pensions paid a higher sum than regular police pensions, Ellita would make almost as much money as she would have made if she had stayed on the force for twenty years. In fact, in the long run, she would make a little more, because she still had eleven years to go for normal retirement, and she would be drawing the disability pension for those eleven years without working. Moreover, the disability payments would continue for the rest of her life, with a three percent COLA every year. She also received a Heroism medal from the Chief of Police, and considerable space in the newspapers.

On the even brighter side, she would be able to stay home and raise her son, and the boy, Pepé Roberto St Xavier Armando Goya y Goya Sanchez, was a healthy, beautiful blue-eyed baby. And, the surgeon added, he wished that Hoke, if he had any influence with Ellita at all, would ask her to reconsider and let him circumcise the boy before she took him home from the hospital.

Hoke told him that he would think about it, although he didn't intend to say anything about it.

Mr and Mrs Sanchez, Ellita's parents, were in Ellita's hospital room when Hoke and Sue Ellen visited her. One or the other had been there every minute since the time she had been brought back to a private room from Recovery. They sat quietly on metal folding chairs beside the bed. Mr Sanchez, who had disowned his daughter when he had discovered that she was pregnant, still didn't speak to her, but the fact that he was there, and smiled in spite of himself when the baby was brought in for nursing, was a sign that there might be, eventually, some kind of a reconciliation. Hoke shook hands with the tight-lipped Mr Sanchez, and smiled at Mrs Sanchez, who merely pursed her lips and shook her head. Hoke kissed Ellita lightly on the forehead.

'Have you seen the baby?' Ellita asked, smiling.

'I sure did. He's a monster with black hair and blue eyes.'

'Didn't I tell you he would be a boy?'

'I never doubted it. They wouldn't let Sue Ellen go up there, though, and she's dying to see him.'

'She can see him in here, when they bring him back to nurse. But you'll have to leave then.'

'I've quit my job, Ellita,' Sue Ellen said. 'So I'll be there to help you with the baby when you come home.'

'You didn't have to do that –'

'It was my idea,' Hoke said. 'Aileen's coming back from L.A. next Saturday, and she's going to spend the rest of the summer with my dad in Singer Island. Those sisters at the convent straightened her out in a hurry. But she'll be back home when school starts, and the manager at the car wash said Sue Ellen could have her job back any time she wanted it.'

'How's the investigation going?'

Hoke turned to Sue Ellen. 'Wait in the waiting room, honey. You can come back when they bring in the baby. Could you ask your parents to leave while we discuss this, Ellita?'

Ellita said something to her parents in Spanish. They didn't reply, but they didn't move, either.

'They won't leave, Hoke.' Ellita shrugged. 'But they won't repeat anything you say, don't worry.'

Sue Ellen went out, closing the door softly behind her.

'The dead guy with the stocking cap was identified,' Hoke said. 'There was a numbered yellow cleaning tag stapled on his jacket, and I gave it to Sergeant Quevedo to track down. He was on the phone for four hours, tracing it to Bayside Cleaners. He went down there, but they didn't have any slip for the cleaning on file. The woman in the shop, though, a woman from Eleuthera, recognized his picture, because of his little car. He had an old Morris Minor, and when he came in she told him she hadn't seen a car like that since she left Nassau fifteen years ago. They had talked some about the islands, and she remembered that he told her he brought the car from Barbados with him. So Quevedo did some legwork in Bayside, found the mail carrier on the route, and the mailman knew him because he delivered his mail from Barbados. He was living in a garage apartment that belonged to Sidney Shapiro, watching their house while they were up in Maine. His name was James Frietas-Smith, and the little Morris was parked in the yard, all packed up with his stuff, and there were some weird paintings stacked up in the garage. Quevedo called Smith's father in Barbados, and he's going to make some kind of arrangements with a shipping firm to take the body back to the island.'

'That was good police work on Quevedo's part.'

Hoke grinned. 'That's why Quevedo's a sergeant, and also why I'm thinking about sending Gonzalez back to duty in Liberty City. Gonzalez ain't gonna make it as a detective, and he should be back in uniform.'

'Give him time, Hoke.'

Hoke shrugged. 'Anyway, that garage apartment was incredibly clean. The furniture was polished, and you wouldn't believe how neat it was. Not a dirty dish. But there was no evidence of anyone else living there. But that wasn't the main discovery. Quevedo asked Shapiro to come down to see if anything valuable was missing from the big house in front of the garage. Shapiro flew down, and when he and Quevedo went through the house, they found a dead guy and a dead baby rolled up in a carpet in one of the guest bedrooms on the second floor.'

'A dead baby? I don't under –'

'The baby, about eighteen months old, had been strangled, but the dead man, a guy named James C. Davis, had been shotgunned. The baby had been kidnapped at Dadeland, and we got an ID from the mother already. They took the car and the baby, and then dumped the car and kept the baby to kill it. Davis was a detail man –'

'A detail man?'

'From a pharmaceutical firm. Lee-Fromach Pharmaceuticals, in New Jersey. A detail man is a guy who goes around and talks to doctors about his products. These guys work alone, you see, and Dade County was Davis's territory. That's why no one reported him missing. He was a bachelor with a pad in the Grove. We found his car, a blue Lincoln town car, parked at a Denny's on Biscayne Boulevard.'

'I still don't understand why they would kill a baby, Hoke.' She brushed her eyes with the back of her hand. 'An eighteen-month-old baby couldn't identify anybody. He'd hardly know his mother!'

'It was a little girl. I know, it was totally senseless. But what we're dealing with, Ellita, is a crazy double-donged sonofabitch. The same guy who shot you probably killed the baby, and they must've shot Davis when they took his car for the robbery. This killer's a scary guy.'

'What about prints on the car?'

'Nothing, except for smudges and Davis's prints. You said the person driving could've been either a man or a woman, probably a woman because there was the scarf over her head, but we can't verify that. You can't describe the guy with the shotgun because he was in silhouette, so we don't know if he was black or white.'

'That red light, flashing off and on, was like a strobe, Hoke. I couldn't tell anything for sure.'

'Well, we know the Bajan was a high yellow, so we've been figuring the guy with the shotgun's probably black, too. But that still doesn't explain the old white man. You say he was a shopper in the store, but he must be a member of the gang if he left with the one who was shot. The collection of groceries in his cart was such a weird mixture, he was obviously killing time in there for some reason or another.

'Anyway, we circulated the Identikit picture of the old man you described, and now I've asked the TV stations to run it in the *Crime Stoppers* series. At first, we thought the way you did, that the old man was a customer, just somebody doing a good-Samaritan act and driving the wounded man to the hospital. But none of the hospitals have reported any gunshot men who haven't been accounted for in some other way. If the gunshot killer was hurt as badly as you say, he needed medical attention. We've been checking clinics and hospitals by phone from Key West to West Palm Beach, but so far, nothing. There were no prints on the two weapons found either, so the guy must've been wearing gloves.'

'How much did they get in the robbery?'

'About eighteen thousand. There should've been more, but because of those armored-car robberies last month, Wells-Fargo's been varying their pickup schedules. They picked up at noon on Saturday instead of waiting for Monday. The chain had insurance for the money, but they may have to close the supermarket. People are scared shitless. It's not open at night anymore now, and a few of the businesses that had signed leases to move into the new mall have just canceled them. Willie Brownley asked the chain to increase the reward from ten to twenty-five thousand, and they probably will. If we don't catch the killer, nobody'll visit that mall when it finally opens – not at night, anyway.'

'I should've been more alert, Hoke. I was crouched right behind the Honda and I didn't get the license number. It didn't even occur to me. I noticed the roof rack, however, and those aren't standard.'

Hoke patted her arm. 'If I'd been shot in the face and was going into labor, I wouldn't have thought of the license either. The Identikit drawing's a good one, you say, but do you realize how many old men there are who've retired to Florida and look like that? Every pensioner in Dade County owns at least one wash-and-wear seersucker suit.'

'What about the cane, Hoke? There was a brass dog's head on the cane, I think. Not every old man carries a cane. So why not run a picture of that along with the Identikit photo?'

'What kind of dog was it?'

'I don't know. But it was a shiny brass dog's head, not a duck or a snake, I'm almost positive.'

'Were the ears up or down?'

'Down, like flaps, and the nose was a little pointed, I think, but it wasn't any special breed. I didn't pay that much attention, but I did notice the cane when he put it under his arm at the checkout counter.'

'Okay. We'll get 'em to run a picture of the cane, too. A cocker spaniel, maybe.'

'I wish there was something else, Hoke.' Tears formed in Ellita's eyes again. 'When I think about that dead baby ...'

'Don't think about it. I'll leave Sue Ellen here so she can see your baby, and I'll pick her up tonight on my way home. Do you need anything?'

'Well, if you can, smuggle me in a can of Stroh's.' Ellita wiped her eyes with the corner of the sheet. 'My mother says that an occasional beer makes your milk richer. Because of the hops, and all. And the doctor said I couldn't have any.'

'Sure, I'll sneak you in a couple of beers, kid. Do you need anything for pain? I can bring you some codeine tablets if you want some.'

'No, I'm okay there. It's a steady kind of pain, in my shoulder, and it shoots down my arm once in a while, but I can stand it. They've been giving me Darvon every four hours, and that helps.'

'I know how these bastards are, Ellita. Doctors call pain "discomfort," and they don't give a shit whether you're suffering or not. If it gets too bad, you tell me, and I'll get you some codeine.'

Hoke patted Ellita on her good shoulder, nodded good-bye to the Sanchezes, and left to drive back to the police station. The Sanchezes, to Hoke's amusement, suspected that he was the father of Ellita's baby, and hated him for not acknowledging it, and for not marrying their daughter after getting her pregnant. Ellita had told them that Hoke wasn't the father, but they had never believed her. Hoke, of

645

course, didn't care what the Sanchezes thought about him, or what they had thought his reasons were for telling them, in his halting Spanish while Ellita was in surgery, that he'd find the son of a whore who shot at her and her baby if it took him twenty-five hours a day.

The next break in the case came when a black man giving his name only as Marvin telephoned Commander Bill Henderson and said he had some information on the robbery. But he wanted to make a deal, he said, before he would pass it on. Marvin also said he wanted the reward money, and a statement, in writing, that he was entitled to it, before he gave Henderson any information.

'We get a lot of strange calls, Marvin,' Henderson told him. 'What've you got?'

'Do I get my deal first?'

'That depends on your information, and the deal you want.'

'I'm out on bond,' Marvin said, 'for soliciting a minor for prostitution, and I want the charges dropped.'

'That's a serious charge. How old was the girl?'

'It wasn't no girl, it was a boy. He's fourteen, but he was already hustling when I recruit him. It's a bum rap, but they don't like me over here on the Beach and they set me up.'

'You realize that Miami and Miami Beach are two different jurisdictions?'

'I knows that, but I also knows that deals can be made, 'specially on something like this massacre.'

'I'll see what I can do, Marvin. But you'll have to come to the station to talk to me.'

'I can't do that. I done been told by a Miami vice cop never to come over to Miami again, or he'd shoot me on sight.'

'Who told you that? What's his name?'

'A Miami vice cop. I don't know his name, but he knows mine and he knows me. I'll meet you this afternoon at four-thirty at Watson Island. In the Japanese garden, at the gate. I'll show you some proofs of what I'm saying, and then we can dicker.'

'Okay, Marvin. See you at four-thirty.'

Bill Henderson passed this intelligence on to Hoke, and then returned to making up duty schedules for the following week. He also had a supplementary payroll for the division to get out.

That afternoon, Hoke and Gonzalez drove to Watson Island, only an eight-minute drive from the police station, and parked in the lot outside the Japanese garden. The garden, donated to Miami by a Tokyo millionaire in 1961, hadn't been maintained, but it was still open to the public every day until five.

There was no one at the gate. Gonzalez looked at the jungly growth in the garden and shook his head. 'This place was really something a few years ago, Sergeant. I remember bringing my girlfriend over here on Sundays, just to walk around and look. There used to be a beautiful stone lantern over there, right by the bridge.'

'Somebody probably stole it. The city can't afford to have twenty-four-hour security on a place like this.'

'Maybe not, but it's a shame to let it run down this way. You think this Marvin guy'll show up?'

'You never can tell, Gonzalez. Usually, anonymous callers don't show the first time, but if they really have something, they'll call again. That's the usual pattern. If this guy's got anything at all, he'll meet us eventually. Reward money brings them out, and it was in the paper this morning, about the reward being increased to twenty-five thousand.'

At four-thirty, Marvin Grizzard left his hiding place behind the Japanese teahouse with the sagging roof, ambled over the arching bridge, and introduced himself. He was a tall black man, wearing pleated gray gabardine slacks, a long-sleeved flowered sport shirt, and shiny white Gucci shoes. The left sleeve had been rolled back one turn to show a gold Rolex watch on his wrist. He handed Hoke a square piece of black plastic, approximately six by six inches.

'Here's part of it,' Marvin said.

'Part of what?' Hoke said.

'Evidence, man. I cut that out of the Hefty bag.'

'What Hefty bag?'

'The bag that held the money taken in the robbery.'

'Shit,' Gonzalez said. 'A piece of plastic cut out of a Hefty don't mean anything.'

'It does,' Marvin said, raising his chin, 'when you got the rest of the Hefty, which is complete 'cept for this piece I cut out. In

647

fact, it's two Hefty bags, one inside the other. And I've got all the money, too.'

Marvin unbuttoned his shirt and took out a stack of banded twenty-dollar bills. The paper band was green, and the initials 'V. P.' in black ink were scrawled on the band. Hoke riffled the bills and studied the initials for a moment.

"Cuff him,' Hoke said to Gonzalez. Hoke then moved to a stone bench, sat down, and carefully counted the money. It was a thousand dollars even. It was almost too much to hope for, but the initials should be those of Victor Persons, the murdered night manager of the Green Lakes Supermarket.

Chapter Eighteen

Marvin protested about being handcuffed, but to no avail. Hoke told him to sit on the bench and explain how he obtained the banded one thousand dollars.

'What about my deal and the reward?'

'Don't worry about the reward. That money's paid only if an arrest leads to a conviction. But if you're a perp in this case, you can't collect it.'

'I'm not! I didn't have nothin' to do with it, and I got an alibi for the robbery. I was at the Dania fronton till it closed, and I got friends who was with me.'

'You aren't charged with anything yet,' Gonzalez reminded him. 'And you don't have to tell us anything. We can take you in on what we have, and anything you say can be held against you.'

'You can have a lawyer present, too, if you want one,' Hoke added. 'And if you can't afford one, we'll get one for you. D'you understand that?'

'I don't need no lawyer. I ain't even no 'cessory after the fact. I'm a good citizen doing his public duty for the reward money, and a registered voter.'

'You're a convicted felon,' Gonzalez said. 'How can you be a registered voter?'

'Who told you 'bout that? Besides, I registered once, and I thought it was still good. My card's right there in my wallet.'

'Just tell us where the money came from, Marvin,' Hoke said. 'We'll check out everything you tell us, and if you're in the clear, getting the reward money won't be a problem.'

'What about the soliciting charges?'

'That'll be up to the state attorney. But she's a reasonable woman, and if you help us, I'm sure she'll do something for you. We can't speak for the state attorney, but we can make a

649

recommendation. And that's it. We won't promise you doodly squat.'

A middle-aged Latin man drove up to the gate, got out of his car, closed the gate, unlocked the padlock on the dangling chain, and then re-locked the padlock on the chain.

'Hey!' Hoke called out. 'Don't lock the fucking gate! Can't you see us over here?'

'¡Cerrado!' The man tapped his wristwatch, got back into his Escort, backed up, and drove down the gravel road to the causeway.

'Jesus,' Hoke said, 'the assholes we've got working for this city –'

'That includes us, Sergeant,' Gonzalez said, 'for arguing overtime with this funky bastard. I've got some legirons in the trunk. Why don't we put 'em on Marvin here, and put him under the bridge overnight and come back tomorrow morning some time. If it's five o'clock, it's our quitting time, too, and I could stand a beer.'

'We don't have to do that,' Hoke said. 'Marvin wants to tell us all about it. Don't you, Marvin?'

Marvin did, and he did.

His story took them back to the night of the robbery. Dale Forrest, who had parked around the corner of the supermarket, with the nose of the Lincoln extended out far enough so she could watch the glass doors, had been instructed to wait for three minutes before driving up to the doors to pick up Troy and James. Troy had estimated that the job would only take three minutes, four at the most. When Dale heard the first two shots and the clanging bells, however, she had panicked and almost driven away without them. It was an instinctual feeling, but she didn't leave because she knew, an instant later, that if she did drive away Troy would find her, no matter where she went, and kill her. Besides, Dale had never acted that independently. A man had always told her what to do, for as long as she could remember, beginning with her father, and her Uncle Bob, who had lived with the family and seduced her when she was eleven, and all of her brothers, and the men she had lived with, off and on, since she had left home. So she had gripped the wheel hard with both hands and kept her eyes on the luminous dashboard clock. She twitched and bit her lip when the shotgun fired again, but she waited till the three minutes were up before she left the concealed parking spot. She looked through the window just in time to see Troy deliberately kill James. She knew then that Troy was probably going to kill her as well, that Troy did not intend to take her with him to Haiti, and that there wasn't any plastic surgeon in Haiti to fix her face, either. The pearl-handled .25 semi-automatic pistol was in her lap. When Troy threw the Hefty bag into the back seat and told her to move over so he could drive (that wasn't the original plan; *she* was supposed to drive), she knew damned well that he would kill her, and she panicked, and with a swift motion she picked up the little weapon, fired, took her foot off the brake, and pushed the gas pedal to the floor. The heavy car, already in drive, sprang forward with the tires squealing as Troy dropped to the sidewalk. Dale heard him scream, so she knew as she turned onto State Road 836 that he wasn't dead. She hadn't seen Mr Sinkiewicz either, so she suspected that Troy had killed him, too.

At first, Dale was going to follow the original plan and drive back to the garage apartment, but she quickly changed her mind. Her packed suitcase was already in the back of the Lincoln, and so were Troy's things. And with Mr Sinkiewicz's Honda still in the parking lot, Troy would undoubtedly follow her back to the apartment in the old man's car. At the next exit, Dale got off the overpass and drove through unfamiliar neighborhoods until she reached Biscayne Boulevard. She stopped at a Denny's, parked and locked the car in the back lot, and went inside, taking a booth in the corner. She ordered a ham sandwich she didn't want, to go with the coffee she did, and tried to figure out what to do next. She couldn't think very well at all, and she had to hold the cup of coffee, which was only lukewarm, with both hands to drink it. Dale was truly afraid for her life. Everything Troy had told her about going to Haiti and getting plastic surgery for her face and buying a nice home on the island where she could lie on the beach and recuperate, everything, including her dancing career, had been destroyed when she shot him in the face. Now that she had a little time to think it over, she decided that maybe he wouldn't have hurt her. In all probability he had just killed James and

Mr Sinkiewicz so he wouldn't have to share the money with them. After all, Troy had loved her, and told her so, lots of times, especially when they were doing it in bed. For the first time in her life she had met a man who loved her, who appreciated her for herself instead of just for her body, and she had spoiled it all by panicking and shooting him. But if Troy found her now, he would *surely* kill her, and she could hardly blame him. Troy would believe – and how else could he think? – that she had intended all along to shoot him and keep the money for herself. She didn't know what to do, she didn't know where to go, and she couldn't think of anywhere to hide where Troy couldn't find her. With her face, her badly disfigured face, she could be tracked down no matter where she went.

Not only that, but the car she was driving was stolen. Troy and James had hidden the owner's body in the big Shapiro house. Mr Sinkiewicz hadn't been told about that because, as Troy had said, it might upset the old man, but the man and his car had been missing for three days now, and the chances were that the police were looking for the car. And if they found her driving it, and then found the owner's body, she would be blamed for his murder and then it would all come out about the supermarket robbery plus the death of James and Mr Sinkiewicz and she would be charged with those murders, too. Troy, of course, was way too smart to be discovered or caught, so she would be blamed for everything! And that could mean the electric chair.

She ordered another cup of coffee.

'Anything wrong with the sandwich?' the waitress asked as she refilled Dale's cup.

'It's fine. But I think I'll take it home and eat it. Have you got a doggie bag?'

'No problem.' The waitress left with the sandwich.

Doggie bag, Dale thought. She had all the money in that sack in the back seat of the Lincoln. She needed some advice and a place to hide and she needed it right away. That's when Dale remembered Marvin Grizzard, the pimp she had hustled for when she had first moved down to Miami Beach from Daytona. Because of the way she looked she had been lucky to get as much as ten dollars a trick hustling Mariel Cuban refugees on the Beach. She hadn't brought in enough income for Marvin, so after two weeks he had driven her across the causeway, dropped her off on Biscayne Boulevard, and told her she was on her own. He had been nice enough to give her a twenty-dollar bill, so she could rent a motel room, but he said that with her face she simply didn't bring in enough money for him to take care of her. What little she did bring in each night wasn't enough to pay the lawyer he had on retainer to get his girls out of jail when they were picked up by the vice cops. Dale hadn't blamed Marvin. In his own way, Marvin had been decent to her, but business was business to Marvin, and he had a lot of expenses.

But now she had a lot of money in the car.

If she gave the money to Marvin, he would help her get out of town, or he'd come up with some way to hide her from Troy. She was sure she had never told Troy anything about Marvin. In fact, she had almost forgotten about Marvin until now. He was the only man she could think of who would know what to do.

Dale paid for her sandwich and coffee at the cashier's, then threw the foil-wrapped sandwich and Mr Sinkiewicz's signed traveler's checks into the Dumpster on her way to the car. She retrieved her suitcase and the Hefty bag from the car, wiped the steering wheel and door handle with a paper napkin from the restaurant, walked to the taxi stand at the Omni Hotel, and took a cab to Miami Beach. She checked into Murgatroyd Manor, a pink-and-green art deco hotel on Ocean Boulevard, paid a week's rent in advance, and got a room overlooking the sea. She looked up Marvin's telephone number, called his apartment, and spoke into his answering machine after the little ding.

'Marvin, this is Dale Forrest. I've got the money I owe you. Five thousand dollars. If you're interested, I'm in room 314, at the Murgatroyd Manor.' She hung up the phone, waited for a minute, and then called the desk and asked the clerk to send up a bottle of Early Times and a bowl of ice.

An hour later, after she had had three drinks and had calmed down some, and decided not to drink any more, there was a knock on the door.

Marvin, worried about some kind of a trick, but keenly interested in the sum of five thousand dollars, although Dale Forrest didn't owe him any money – no one ever owed Marvin any money for very long – had sent Hortensia, one of his girls, to check on the situation while he waited in his Cadillac a block away. Dale handed Hortensia two hundred dollars in twenty-dollar bills.

'Tell Marvin this is a sample, but tell him I want to talk to him in person.'

Hortensia walked back to the car, gave Marvin the money, and told him that Dale was alone in her hotel room. She hadn't seen anyone else lurking around, either. There was no one in the lobby, and the desk clerk was half-asleep behind the desk.

Marvin went down the alley, climbed the fire escape to the third floor, walked down the corridor, and knocked on Dale's door.

The money, almost nineteen thousand dollars, had been counted and stacked on the double bed. The rolls of coins were beside the rows of stacked bills, and the Hefty bags, folded neatly into squares, were side by side on top of the pillows.

Dale poured Marvin a drink over ice cubes in a plastic glass and told him about the robbery. She also told him that she had shot Troy, but that Troy, though he was wounded, was undoubtedly looking for her and the money, and that he was, in all probability, driving a brown Honda Civic. Marvin had nodded, asking a few questions but looking at the money instead of Dale. When she finished talking, he took another drink from her bottle of Early Times, this time drinking from the bottle instead of pouring a shot into his glass.

All of this had taken considerable time. Dawn arrived before they finished discussing the situation. What he would do, Marvin told Dale, he would get her out of the country. He would get her a ticket to Puerto Rico, and a passport so she could enter that country, but he would drive up to West Palm Beach and buy a ticket to the island from the Palm Beach airport, instead of Miami's, because it would be unlikely that Troy Louden would think she would leave from Palm Beach. Troy might have the Miami airport covered, but he wouldn't cover the Palm Beach airport.

It would cost, Marvin told her, three thousand dollars to get her a false passport. The remainder of the money, except for a thousand dollars, which she would need to get started on in San Juan, would be his fee for these services. It might take a couple of days to get the passport, but she would be safe here in the hotel if she didn't leave the room; meanwhile, he would drive up to West Palm and buy the ticket. He realized that his fee was high, but this Troy she told him about was a dangerous bastard, and he, Marvin, was putting his ass on the line –

At this point, Gonzalez broke in: 'You asshole. You don't need a passport to go to Puerto Rico. It's part of the United States!'

'Since when? I thought it was like El Salvador –'

'Never mind,' Hoke said. 'Tell us the rest of it, Marvin.'

'I reckon Dale don't know that about Puerto Rico, either,' Marvin said, shrugging. 'Anyway, that's the plan I came up with. I took three thousand for the passport, and two hundred more to get the ticket, but I left the rest of the money in the room – to show my good faith and all. Then I left. I ate breakfast back in my apartment and watched TV. There was something about the robbery and massacre, but not too much details. I went down for the *Miami Herald*, you know, but there was nothing in the paper about it. The story had happened too late at night to get in. But at ten, when the *Miami News* came out, the first street edition, with the pictures and all, I realized that this situation was too heavy for me. I was gonna help Dale get away. I was gonna have a fake passport made up, and drive her up to Palm Beach myself, just like I said. But this was a big Murder One thing, so I put off doing anything, you see, trying to figure out what was best for me. If there's one thing I don't need, it's a 'cessory rap to a Murder One rap, and on top of that, whenever I thought about this Troy dude my balls turned to ice cubes.

'I went back to Dale's room late that afternoon and told her it would take more time than I thought to get the passport. I also took a Polaroid snapshot of her, which I said the passport man needed. I been stalling for three days now.'

'What's the passport man's name?' Gonzalez asked.

'There ain't no passport man. I was just gonna paste Dale's picture on Hortensia's passport. Hortensia's here on a student visa from the Dominican Republic. But the more I thought about it, the more worried I got. Then when they come out in the papers this morning with the new reward, which is more than the nineteen thousand, I got this new idea – to turn Dale in.'

'Where's Dale now?' Hoke asked.

'Like I said, 314, Murgatroyd Manor.'

'Okay, Gonzalez,' Hoke said, 'let's go over to the Beach and get her.'

'Shouldn't we notify the Beach cops we're picking her up?'

'We should, but we won't. This is an emergency, and the massacre was in Miami, not in Miami Beach. In the state she's in, she's liable to take off any second. Would you trust an asshole like Marvin?'

'Not for a minute,' Gonzalez said.

'I resent that,' Marvin said. 'I done told you everything, like a good citizen. Besides, she's quiet because I been giving her Percodans. Hortensia's outside watching the building, and if Dale leaves she'll follow her.'

They left the handcuffs on Marvin and boosted him over the gate before climbing over it themselves. Marvin, because his wrists were handcuffed behind his back, fell on his face, and some flinty pieces of gravel got embedded in his right cheek. They put Marvin in the back seat of their unmarked Fairlane and took the MacArthur Causeway to Miami Beach.

When Hoke rapped on Dale's door at the hotel, there was no answer. The television was on in the room, however, so Gonzalez went downstairs and got the extra key to the room from the desk clerk. When he came back, Hoke unlocked the door and pushed Marvin in ahead of him, in case Dale decided to take a shot at them. Gonzalez covered Hoke and Marvin with his pistol.

Dale was on her back, snoring, and a half-eaten Domino's pizza was on the bed beside her with the stacks of bills and rolls of coins. She had finished the first bottle of Early Times, and she had made sizable inroads into a second bottle. Two grinning Channel Ten newscasters were making kidding remarks to the weatherman on the TV set. Gonzalez turned off the television and picked up Dale's purse from the bedside table. The little .25 pistol was inside. Gonzalez re-clasped the purse without touching the weapon and tucked the leather purse under his arm. Hoke was unable to rouse Dale from her drug-and-alcohol slumbers. Hoke unfolded the Hefty bags and put the money inside without counting it.

'Where's the place on the Hefty where you cut out that little square?' he asked Marvin.

'I didn't cut it outa that bag 'cause I couldn't give Dale no reason for doing it. I cut it out of another Hefty I had in my apartment.'

'Jesus Christ, Maria,' Gonzalez said, shaking his head.

Before they left, Hoke and Gonzalez shook down the room, found nothing of interest in Dale's suitcase, and then drove back to Miami to book Marvin and Dale. Hoke had carried Dale downstairs over his shoulder, and Gonzalez had brought the bag of money, Dale's suitcase and purse, and a small sack of toilet articles that belonged to Troy Louden.

Marvin was isolated in Interrogation Room Two. The story he told and retold several times to Major Brownley and Bill Henderson was substantially the same as the one he had told Hoke and Gonzalez.

By the time Dale sobered up enough in the female annex of the city jail to realize that she was going to be charged with murder and robbery, she had decided not to say anything else to anyone. In jail, she knew she would be fairly safe from Troy Louden, and the prospect of spending a few years on Death Row, or with good luck, twenty-five years in prison, seemed for the moment like a reasonable exchange for her life.

Dale regretted telling everything to Marvin, but they couldn't use most of what she had told him against her in court. And she certainly wasn't going to tell the police anything she knew about Mr Sinkiewicz and Troy. Troy was mad enough at her already, and even the women's prison wouldn't be safe enough distance from him if he knew she blew the whistle on him to the cops.

For the next two days, Hoke and Gonzalez spent hours at their desks writing up their reports and supps, supps, supps.

Chapter Nineteen

On Saturday morning, Hoke picked up Aileen at the Miami International Airport and drove her up to Singer Island. Aileen – if there had been anything seriously wrong in the first place – seemed to have made a prompt recovery. She had gained eleven pounds, and she wore a pair of black velvet toreador pants and a matching bolero jacket her mother had bought her for the trip. Curly Peterson, elated to see her departing his home and life, had put two crisp fifty-dollar bills into her purse as a going-away present. Aileen was happy to be back, although the trip and all of the excitement had been an adventure to remember and she had met this boy who lived three doors down from her mother's house in Glendale. His name was Alfie, and his father was a composer who scored music for movies. She had a snapshot of Alfie, which she had shown Hoke, and she told her father that she and Alfie were going to be pen pals.

Hoke looked at the photo – a grinning teenage boy with unkempt hair and a cotton string for a backbone – and told her that he was a handsome boy indeed. The boy, in Hoke's private opinion, looked like a congenital idiot, but he took it as a favorable sign that Aileen was taking an interest in boys. After all, Aileen was his daughter, so she was certainly smart enough to know by now that boys were not interested in skinny, bony girls who looked more like boys than they did girls.

Still, Hoke would be watching her and Sue Ellen both a lot more carefully now. And maybe that wasn't so bad, either.

After they got on the Sunshine Parkway, Hoke told her in more detail than he had on the phone about the supermarket murder-robbery, and the progress they had made on the case, so far. Aileen, however, was more concerned about Ellita than she was about the manhunt. She was also disappointed that she hadn't had a chance to see Ellita and the new baby.

'Instead of staying with Granddad, wouldn't it be better for me to stay home? I can help Sue Ellen with the housework and the baby while Ellita's going through her therapy.'

'I thought about that, honey. But Mrs Sanchez's going to live with us for a month or so when Ellita comes home, and the house would be too damned crowded. Besides, I want you fattened up a little, and Inocencia's going to keep you on a separate diet the doctor gave us. I've been worried more about you than Ellita. I should've paid more attention to you instead of being so damned wrapped up in my own problems. I probably shouldn't've sent you out to L.A. in the first place.'

'No.' Aileen shook her curls and laid a hand on Hoke's arm. 'It was my fault, Daddy. I know now I was only trying to get more attention from you than I deserved, and it worked too well. That's why I always vomited by the professor's window. I guess I knew he'd tell you about it sooner or later.'

'From now on, baby, no matter what's bothering you, come to me and we'll talk about it, okay? Lately I've been busier than a cat covering shit on a marble floor, and sometimes I might forget to be a father.'

Aileen started to cry, but stopped just as abruptly. She wiped her cheeks with the back of her hand, leaned over, and kissed Hoke's right hand, which was holding the steering wheel.

'What's that thing on the chain around your neck?'

'It's a Saint Joseph's medal,' Aileen said, holding it up for him to see. 'Mother Superior gave it to me. She said I was a pretty girl, and when I gained more weight, boys would want to kiss me. Instead of letting them kiss me, she said I should tell them to kiss the Saint Joseph's medal.'

'That's good advice if you ever date Cuban boys in Miami, but it won't work with WASP boys. By this time next year you'll be beating off boys with a stick.'

'Maybe next summer Alfie can come and visit us from California? He's never been to Florida, but his father's got lots of money.'

'Why not? But a year's a long time. Ask me again next summer, and if you still want him to visit, then I'll write and ask his father – or phone him.'

'Would you?' Aileen sat back and looked at Hoke with new regard. 'Sure. Why not?'

Hoke stopped at the El Pelicano to collect his belongings, Aileen's boxes, and her bicycle, before driving to Frank's house. Once the car was packed, he told Aileen to ride her bike to the house while he took a last look around the apartment and said good-bye to Professor Hurt.

Hoke's small apartment needed cleaning, but it still looked good to him, and he knew that he would miss living in it. He hadn't forgotten anything. For a long moment, he looked out the window, across the crowded beach to the water. As an experiment, it hadn't worked out, but it had still been worthwhile, despite the negative results. Scientists always considered negatives as positives because they didn't have to try the failed experiment again. They could go on to something else. Hoke had learned that there was no way a man could simplify his life. In managing the apartment house, as simple as that had seemed to be, he would have had just as many problems as he had as a detective-sergeant. They would all be petty problems, however; little annoying things that would have to be done, but would occupy his time without producing any sense of satisfaction or accomplishment. Right now, he was stymied in his manhunt for the killer, but he knew in his heart that he would find him eventually.

He didn't like the idea of the grim-faced Mrs Sanchez moving in with them, but at least Mr Sanchez wasn't coming with her. That meant the move would be temporary. Without his wife to look after him, old man Sanchez would be almost helpless, so she wouldn't stay any longer than necessary. By the time school started again, everything would be back to normal, except that he would never have Ellita back again as his partner at work. The girls would have to take more responsibility for their lives, but they were maturing fast, and Sue Ellen, in spite of her green hair, was as stable as a stone house. Hoke shrugged, picked up the three volumes on horseflies, and went downstairs to Dr Hurt's apartment to return the books.

Itai was glad to see him.

'How about some wine?' Itai said, grinning. 'I got a case of last year's Beaujolais Nouveau at Crown on a special sale.'

'I haven't got the time, Itai. I'm going to have lunch with my father, and then I've got to get back to Miami.'

'We're going to miss you around here, Hoke, but I've decided to go back up to Gainesville in September myself. In the last two days I've only written eighteen words. So I've decided to abandon my novel for a while – the way Valéry said you should abandon a poem. I miss teaching and my lab, and I'm vacationed out.'

'What'll your chairman say, if you don't come up with a complete manuscript?'

'He'll be glad to have me back, and I've already written to tell him I'm cutting my leave short. Now he won't have to hire a substitute. Besides, I may finish the book back at school. I've got enough down on paper to still plug away at it. But there're too many novels already, and not nearly enough books on horseflies. I'm going to save my dough and take a leave without pay in another year or so and go to Ethiopia. The flies will still be there, waiting for me.'

Hoke gave him his card. 'Keep my card, Itai, and drop me a line. Or if you ever come down to Miami, call me and we'll have a few beers. I really enjoyed our little dinner party.'

'I did, too, even though Major Brownley won every damned game. A game with dice should be a game of chance, but his luck was uncanny, I thought. He never landed on anyone else's property but his own.'

'He plays Monopoly with his kids all the time, that's why he's so good. But at least I didn't let him talk you into playing for real money.'

'Sure you won't have a glass of wine?'

'No, I've got to go.'

'I'll walk you to your car. By the way, Hoke, that Riviera Beach detective was here this morning looking for you.'

'Detective Figueras?'

'Yeah, that's his name.'

'Did he say what he wanted?'

'No, just that you should get in touch with him. I guess he heard you were leaving, and wanted to say good-bye. Everybody on the island's following this case, you know. Your name's been in all the papers, although most of the people around the mall call you "the man in the yellow jumpsuit."'

Hoke laughed. 'I still wear 'em around the house.' They shook hands. 'Anyway, if Figueras comes around again, tell him I'll call him.'

Aileen was given the large guest bedroom at the back of the house, the same room where Hoke had spent three happy days in quiet contemplation. With this room she could open the sliding doors to the patio and swim in the pool anytime she wanted. Hoke and Frank carried her boxes into the bedroom, and Helen stayed with her to help put her things away. Frank and Hoke had a glass of iced gin apiece while they waited for lunch.

'I'm not very hungry, Frank,' Hoke said. 'And I really ought to get back to Miami. You should see my goddamned desk. It's piled up to here with autopsy reports, folders, and paper. You wouldn't believe how much paper a case like this generates. Everything has to be written down, checked, rewritten, distributed –'

'It'll all wait another hour or so, son. Detective Figueras called me earlier, and I told him you'd be here for lunch. He said he'd come by at noon.'

Hoke looked at his Timex. 'It's eleven-thirty now. I'll call him at the station and save him the trip.'

Hoke used the phone in the kitchen to call the Riviera Beach police station. 'What's up, Jaime?' he said, when he got Figueras on the line. 'This is Hoke Moseley.'

'I think I've got a tentative lead on your supermarket massacre, Hoke. It may turn out to be nothing, but it looks pretty good, and I was going out this afternoon to check it out. But when your father told me you were going to be here today, I thought maybe you'd like to go with me. Like I say, it may be nothing, but I got what looks like a positive ID on the old man's picture. It's not him so much as it is the cane. The woman says that the old man was carrying a cane like that – the one with the dog's-head handle.'

'What woman?'

'Mrs Henry Collins. Her story was weird enough to have some truth to it, so I checked it out. What happened, she said, was that this old man told her to tell her husband to drop charges against a guy named Robert Smith, or her husband would be killed. This guy was a hitchhiker Collins had picked up, who then pulled a gun on him. Collins wrecked his car at a bridge outside Riviera, and then the hitchhiker was booked in the Palm Beach County Jail. At any rate, Collins believed this threat and dropped the charges. No weapon was found in the case, so Smith was released. I took a gander at the jail records, and this old man, Stanley Sinkiewicz, Senior, was Smith's cellmate for a few hours. He was arrested for molesting a child, but wasn't booked because the father of the little girl said it had all been a mistake. Interesting parallel, you know? Charges dropped by the complainant in both cases. The old man was released, and the father of the girl, a guy named Sneider, drove him home.'

'And Mrs Collins gave you a positive ID from the picture in the paper?'

'That's right. Her husband was up in Jacksonville when she called me, and I went out to talk to him yesterday when he came home. He's a truck driver, and he didn't get back home till yesterday. He was really pissed off at his wife for calling me and didn't want to get involved. Being away from home three, some-times four days a week, he was afraid that this Smith guy would do something to his wife and kid while he was on the road. Anyway, I checked back, and the fingerprint report, when it finally came in from the FBI, was just filed away because Smith had already walked, and nobody did anything about it. But this Smith is a career criminal named Troy Louden. He's wanted in L.A. for killing a liquor-store owner and his wife in a robbery. When I got the printout of his rap sheet, it was two fucking feet long. He's a dangerous sonofabitch, and Collins was smart to drop the charges.'

'D'you have the old man's address?'

'Sure. You want to go with me and see if he's home? I doubt if he'll be there, but maybe we can find something there that'll lead to something else.'

'Where should I meet you?'

'I'll meet you in the parking lot behind the Double X Theater at Dixie and Blue Heron Road.'

Hoke hung up and told his father that he couldn't stay for lunch. He might be back a little later to say good-bye, but right now he had to go check on something with Jaime Figueras.

'I understand,' Frank said. 'But I'll have Inocencia fix you some sandwiches before you drive back to Miami.'

'That'll be fine.'

Figueras drove, and it took only a few minutes to drive out to Ocean Pines Terraces.

'When I left Riviera,' Hoke told him, 'this was all dairy farm land.'

Figueras cruised slowly down the curving streets, taking the speed bumps at an angle and looking for Sinkiewicz's house.

'It's a mixed subdivision now, Hoke. About half retired people, and half working people with kids. I don't think Riviera'll get any more subdivisions like this one. Most white people are building north of North Palm Beach now. In another ten years, this'll probably be an all-black subdivision if the interest rates come down a few points.'

There was a brown Honda parked in Stanley Sinkiewicz's carport. Figueras pulled in and stopped at the curb, two houses down. 'There's a car. Somebody home, after all.'

'And the Honda's got a roof rack. You go to the front door, Jaime, and I'll slip on around to the back. Nobody locks Florida rooms, and I'll come in the back way.'

'Don't you think we should get some backup first?'

'If no one's there, we won't need any backup. And if someone's home and resists, I want to take a shot at the bastard. What do you want to do?'

'I'm with you, Sergeant. Why don't we see what happens?'

Hoke took out his pistol. He circled behind the house to cut through the two backyards. Figueras waited, to give Hoke enough time to reach Stanley's yard, then walked up the concrete path to the door. He rapped on it with the barrel of his pistol.

Stanley Sinkiewicz opened the door, left it open, and walked back to his dining-room table. Stanley didn't say a word, but sat at the table and began to spoon tomato soup into his mouth. Figueras followed him inside and closed the door with his foot, covering the old man with his weapon. Hoke entered the dining room from the screened porch, also holding his pistol on Stanley. He looked at the old man's lined, pigeon-gray face, and shook his head. Hoke knew an old lag when he saw one, and he could tell, just by looking at this old con, that the man had spent most of his life in prison. When they finally got his record, it would probably be three feet long.

'Sinkiewicz?' Hoke asked. 'We're both police officers.'

'I been waiting.' Stanley nodded. 'But I ain't ate nothing for two days now. I just fixed this soup, not really wanting it, but knew I had to eat something pretty soon. Maya – that's my wife – when she fixed it for me, used to put a little whipped cream in it. The milk in the icebox went sour on me, and I had to fix it with water instead of milk. But it still tastes pretty good, once I got started on it.'

'Are you alone, Sinkiewicz?' Figueras asked.

Stanley nodded and crumbled two soda crackers into his soup.

'Do you know Troy Louden?' Hoke said.

Stanley nodded.

'D'you know where he is?'

Stanley pointed down the hall with his spoon. 'In the bedroom.'

'I thought you said you were alone.' Hoke had reholstered his pistol, but he quickly withdrew it again. ''Cuff him, Jaime.'

Hoke started down the hall. Figueras handcuffed Stanley's wrists behind his back. Hoke hesitated outside the closed bedroom door, waiting for Figueras to cover him. Figueras, holding his pistol with both hands, stayed ten feet behind Hoke. Hoke twisted the knob, threw open the door, and jumped inside with his gun in front of him.

There was no one else in the room. Figueras joined him. The bed was piled high with a half-dozen sheets, a comforter, a bedspread, and was topped by a woman's red plastic raincoat. There was a discernible mound beneath all of these coverings. Hoke peeled them back from the head of the bed, one at a time, and uncovered Troy Louden as far as his waist. The corpse was ripe, and the washcloth over Troy's face had dried. Hoke picked it gingerly away and thought he could detect the odor of burning almonds, but later he was never sure whether he had or not. Dale Forrest's little .25-caliber slug, a crisscrossed lead dumdum, had hit Troy's left cheek, penetrating the bone, and then fragments had been deflected upward, exploding the left eye and skating through the eye socket. Troy had suffered a good deal of pain before he died. Hoke covered the dead man's face back up with the dry washcloth, then drew the bottom sheet over the upper body and head. He and Figueras went back into the dining room.

Stanley, with his thin arms handcuffed behind his back, was staring at his cooling soup, but he had apparently lost interest in it.

'How long's he been dead?' Figueras asked the old man.

'Three days. I didn't know what else to do. He was suffering, but he wouldn't let me call no doctor or let me take him to the hospital. I brought him home, and when I thought he couldn't stand it no more I gave him two cyanide pills. I didn't know what else to do for him.'

'Cyanide?' Hoke said. 'Where in hell did you get cyanide?'

'Inside my cane. Sometimes people keep vicious dogs that bite strangers and little kids. They won't bite their owners because they feed them, you know, but you can walk down any sidewalk and they'll come right at you before you know it. So I always kept some pills to poison a bad dog once in a while, when I got the chance. Troy was a good boy, good to me, anyway, maybe because I fed him, too, I guess. But he was a lot like a bad dog. I didn't want to do it, but I didn't know what else to do. I even thought about taking some pills myself. But then I thought, Why should I? I ain't done nothing wrong. Troy managed to keep me out of everything so I wouldn't get involved, so all I'm responsible for is putting to sleep the only person who ever really loved me. Anyone who ever heard Troy cry and carry on that way would've done the same. You just can't imagine.'

'Why did he kill all those people?' Hoke said. 'Did he say?'

Stanley shook his head. 'He never said, but I think I know why. It was the responsibility. Me and Dale and James. We was all too much for him, and he couldn't stand the responsibility. That's what it was ...'

Stanley began to cry then, and Hoke didn't try to stop him. He realized that the old man had been holding it in for a long time, and that it would be best to let him get it all out. There would be time for more questions later.

'I'll Mirandize him, Jaime, while you call Chief Sheldon. This is going to be a jurisdictional ordeal, but no matter what you people up here in Palm Beach County think you want to do, I'm taking this old fart back to Miami with me to be tried first for the supermarket murders.'

'What difference does it make, Hoke,' Jaime said, 'whether he's tried down there first, or for the guy?' Figueras pointed down the hall.

'There're lots of reasons, but I'll give you one you can understand. Before the old man and the whore are tried to fry in Raiford, I'm going to make lieutenant out of this case. When the next promotion list is posted, I'm going to be at the head of it.'

Hoke was so pleased with the way it sounded that he left off the part about the answer sheets Major Willie Brownley still had in his briefcase.

It was well after nine P.M. that night before Hoke got onto the Sunshine Parkway and headed south for Miami. Stanley, handcuffed to the D-ring Hoke had welded onto the passenger door, sat quietly beside him in the dark. Stanley had promised not to try and run, so Hoke hadn't put legirons on him. Ordinarily, the drive to Miami would have been a six- or maybe a seven-cigarette ride, and for the first time, Hoke truly missed his Kools. But he was over the habit, and he wouldn't smoke again. Not smoking, and counting the weight he had lost, his blood pressure was almost normal again for a man his age.

To get around the heavy, crazy traffic at the Golden Glades exchange, which every wise Floridian avoided, if possible, Hoke left the Sunshine Parkway at the Hollywood exit and picked up I-95 for the rest of the way into the city. As the thousands of lighted windows in the tall Miami buildings came into view, Stanley spoke for the first time on the trip.

'What's going to happen to me, Sergeant?'

'Hell, Pop,' Hoke said, not unkindly, 'except for the paperwork, it already has.'

BOOK 4

The Way We Die Now

No one owns life.
But anyone with a frying pan owns death.

WILLIAM S. BURROUGHS

For Lou, Betsy, Tom and Cheryl

Chapter One

Tiny Bock heaved his bulk from the sand chair.

He stood silently in the clearing for a moment listening, but all he could hear was the whirr of insects and the scuttling of a few foraging wood rats. He folded the red-and-green webbed chair, took it to the black pickup truck and threw it into the back. He opened the cab door on the passenger's side and reached for the paper sack on the seat. There were two bologna sandwiches wrapped in oil paper and two hard-boiled eggs in the sack. He unwrapped one of the sandwiches, noticed that the lunch meat had turned green on the outer edge. He rewrapped the sandwich, put it back in the sack, took one of the hard-boiled eggs. He cracked open the egg and peeled it, but when he split the egg in two he realized that the yolk had turned purple and there was a strong smell of sulphur.

Twenty feet away a raccoon, also smelling the egg and the sulphur, rose on its hind legs and waved its forefeet, sniffing the air.

Tiny Bock noticed the raccoon and placed the two halves of the egg on a tuft of grass. As Tiny moved to the cab of the truck the raccoon, a female, scurried forward and scooped up the two egg halves. The coon took the two halves to a muddy pool of water and rolled the egg in the water to wash it preparatory to eating. Tiny Bock, who had taken his shotgun from the cab of the truck, fired once. Eight of the twelve slugs hit the raccoon, reducing it to an unrecognizable spot of fur and blood. Bock reloaded the shotgun before replacing it on the gun rack above the seat.

Listening again, Bock could hear the airplane sound of the airboat long before he saw it. Then he spotted the boat; it was returning to the hammock from a different direction than he had expected, but Chico de las Mas was heading unerringly toward Bock and the parked truck. Skimming across the wet sawgrass of the Everglades, it resembled a giant but harmless insect.

Skidding the aluminum boat sideways, Chico stopped short of the dry brushy hammock. After Chico turned the engine off, and the whirling propeller had run down, Bock said, 'What took you so long?'

'Had a hard time finding a deep enough sinkhole. But it won't matter. When the rains come this whole area'll be under a foot of water. You won't be able to drive out to the hammock here for another six months. I thought I heard a shotgun, but I wasn't sure.'

Bock grinned and pointed to what was left of the raccoon. 'I shot a coon.'

The two men pushed the airboat into the clearing and well into the brush on the other side. Chico chained the prow of the boat to a cypress tree, and then padlocked the chain. They climbed into the cab of the truck. Chico took the wheel and drove across the dry sands, avoiding occasional puddles, toward the dirt and oolite access road, some ten minutes away. The access road had been built illegally by a group of Naples hunters almost five years ago in the Big Cypress. They had also planned to build a weekend lodge, but their plans had fallen through, so now the road, a foot above the water level, was a road to nowhere.

'There's blood on the front of your shirt,' Bock said.

'I know.' Chico took a bloody Baggie out of his shirt pocket and handed it to Bock.

'What's this?'

Chico laughed. 'A bonus. Remember the tall one, the one they called C'est Dieu? I cut that out of his asshole.'

Bock removed the soggy wad of money from the Baggie, tossed the Baggie out the window. He unfolded and counted the money. 'One ten, and thirty ones. Forty bucks. Did you cut the others?'

'Didn't have to. I've been watching them close, and no one ever let old C'est Dieu out his sight. Always one or two with him. So I knew he was holding it for all of 'em.'

Bock folded the bills and put them into his back pocket. 'There's a couple of bologna sandwiches left in the sack if you want 'em.'

'Sinking Haitians in a swamp is hard work, Mr Bock. I thought we'd drive into Immokalee and get a decent meal at the cafeteria.' Chico slowed down, ripped off his shirt and tossed it out the window.

'Why not? But you won't be able to eat in the cafeteria without a shirt.'

'I'll buy a T-shirt at the sundry store. It's no big deal.'

When he reached the access road, Chico got onto the raised road without any trouble using first gear. The road ran west for two miles before it met the state highway. Chico turned north and headed for Immokalee.

Chapter Two

Commander Bill Henderson, homicide division executive officer, Miami Police Department, entered Sergeant Hoke Moseley's cubicle, removed the *Miami Herald* from the chair beside the desk, tossed it toward the overflowing wastepaper basket, and sat down heavily. He looked at the sheet of paper on his clipboard and sighed.

'I'm running a little informal survey, Hoke.'

'I'm busy right now, Bill. I think I've finally got a worthwhile lead on the Dr Paul Russell killing.'

Hoke's messy desk was littered with a half-dozen sheets of bond typewriter paper, supplementary reports, and a red accordion file. He had been drawing diagrams on the bond paper with a ruler and a ballpoint.

'This is an important survey.'

'More important than solving a cold-case homicide?'

Bill pulled his lips back, exposing large gold-capped teeth that were entwined with silver wire. 'Depends on whether you smoke or not. Have you quit yet?'

'Not exactly, but I'm down to about ten a day. I've tried to quit cold turkey, but the longest I've managed to go was about six hours. Now I time it and smoke a Kool every four hours, with maybe few extra at night when I watch the tube. If I can hold it down to only ten a day, it's almost like not smoking at all.'

Bill shook his head. 'I switched over to cigars, but I still inhale, so I'll probably have to go back to cigarettes. After five cigars my throat's raw as a bastard, and I've been coughing up all kinds of shit in the morning.'

'Is that the end of the survey?' Hoke picked up a Telectron garage-opener device, the size of a king-size pack of cigarettes, and showed it to Bill Henderson. 'Know what this is?'

'No, I don't, and no, I'm not finished. This really is important. I attended the new chief's weekly briefing this morning, and he's come up with a terrible plan. He wants to stop all smoking inside the police station. His idea's to set up a smoking area in the parking lot, and anytime you want to smoke you have to sign out for personal time and go out to the lot. Then, when you finish your smoke, you sign back in again and return to your desk or whatever. A lot of guys have already quit smoking, you see, and they've complained to the new chief that smoke from heavy smokers is invading their space.'

'What about the men's room?'

'No smoking inside the building, period. That includes interrogation rooms, suspect lockup, everywhere except the outside parking lot.'

'It won't work, Bill. Lieutenant Ramirez, in Robbery, smokes at least three packs a day. He might as well move his fucking desk out to the parking lot.'

'That's what we tried to tell the new chief. But he figures if he makes it hard on smokers, they'll either cut down radically or quit.'

'Does the new chief smoke? I never noticed.'

'Snoose. He dips Copenhagen. He usually has a lipful of snuff, but he doesn't spit. He swallows the spit instead.'

'That figures. The rule won't bother him any, so the bastard doesn't give a shit about the rest of us. But I don't think a rule that dumb can be enforced. Guys'll sneak 'em in the john or even at their desks.'

'Not if they get an automatic twenty-five-dollar fine they won't.'

'Jesus.' Hoke took a Kool out of his pack and lighted it with his throwaway lighter. He took one drag and then butted it in his ashtray. 'I lit that without thinking, and I've still got an hour to go.' He returned the butt to his pack.

'That's why I'm running this survey, Hoke. If a big majority complains, he probably won't put in the rule. So I'll put you down as opposing the new rule, right?'

'Right. Now let me tell you about this little gadget –'

'Some other time. I've got to see some other guys before they go off shift.' Henderson got to his feet. 'One other thing – I almost forgot to tell you.' Henderson snapped his fingers and turned in the doorway. At six-four and 250 pounds, his body almost filled the doorframe. 'Major Brownley said to tell you to let your beard grow, and he'd call you Sunday night at home and let you know about the meeting –'

'This is only Thursday, and I work tomorrow. Does he mean that I let my beard grow out now, or do I shave tomorrow?'

'All he said was what I told you. So I suppose he means to let it grow from now till he tells you to shave.'

'Did he say why? Perhaps I should talk to him about this first.'

'You can't. He went down to the Keys and won't be back till Sunday night. He'll call you at home then and explain it to you, and also about the meeting.'

'What meeting?'

'He didn't say. He's got a visitor, an old fraternity buddy he went to A and M with in Tallahassee, and they went fishing down in the Keys. Off Big Pine, I think.'

'I've never grown a beard, Bill. Even if I go a day or two without shaving, it makes my neck itch. Did he give you any hint –'

'I'm only the executive officer. Major Brownley's the division chief, and he doesn't take me into his confidence on every little thing. I'm just passing along the message he gave me over the phone. He didn't come in today, and that's why I went to the new chief's meeting instead of him. If it was important for me to know, he would have told me the reason. Don't worry about it.'

'Why shouldn't I worry? Wouldn't you be concerned if Willie ordered you to grow a beard?'

'I'd like to stay and talk about this with you, although it's a fruitless discussion. I say fruitless because anything we say would only be idle conjecture, based on inadequate information. But I suspect sometimes that Willie Brownley pulls shit like this once in a while just to keep us off-balance. My son Jimmy's like that. Only yesterday Jimmy asked me if he could grow a mustache.'

'Jimmy's only twelve years old.'

'Eleven. But I gave him permission anyway. I figure it'll take another six years before it grows out long enough to be noticed. But he was happy as hell when I told him to go ahead.'

'At least Jimmy asked for permission. Sue Ellen had her hair all kinked up and then dyed it electric blue right down the middle. She didn't say anything. She just did it.'

'But she's seventeen. If Jimmy was seventeen, he'd grow his mustache without asking me for permission.'

'She looks terrible. She looks like the kind of girl who goes with boys who've dropped out of school.'

'If she's still working at the car wash, that's the only kind of boy she's likely to meet. I'm not criticizing – at least she's got a job. But she's probably the only white girl in Miami working full-time at a car wash.'

'I know. She's even picked up some black dialect. But I've discouraged her from using it around the house.'

Henderson disappeared from the doorway. Hoke gathered his work sheets together and put them into the red-flagged Dr Russell file. He locked the file, together with the supplementary reports, in his two-drawer file cabinet. He slipped into his blue poplin leisure jacket and dropped the garage door opener into the left leather-lined outside pocket before leaving his cubicle on the fourth floor of the Miami police station. Hoke always carried several loose .38-caliber tracers in the outside pocket of his jacket, and he'd had it lined with glove leather for this purpose.

Hoke rode the elevator down to the garage and climbed the ramp to the outside parking lot. He paused at the exit, inhaling the hot, humid air, and wondered where the new chief would put the smoking area in the lot. The fenced-in area would be crowded as hell if three hundred cops on each shift made trips back and forth to smoke. Not all of them smoked, however. But even one hundred and fifty cops going and coming from the building would crowd the elevator and stairways. It would take approximately twenty minutes for each cop who smoked to make his round trip and smoke a cigarette, and if each cigarette was charged to personal time, without pay, six smokes a day could mean a loss of two hours' pay for each smoker. That meant that many would be sneaking cigarettes and then get a twenty-five-dollar fine when they were caught. All this extra money coming into the department would mean that the new chief would probably meet his annual budget for the first time in the city's history.

Hoke climbed into his battered 1973 Pontiac Le Mans and lighted a cigarette for the drive home to Green Lakes. If the rule went in, despite the advice not to do it, the odds were good that it would be rescinded within three days. Tomorrow he would get together with Bill Henderson, and they could make up an office pool on how long the rule would last. After they made up the card, Hoke decided he would take number three before they sold the other slots around the office. This would be like found money. A rule that stupid couldn't possibly last for more than three days ...

The Green Lakes subdivision, where Hoke lived in northwest Miami, bordered Hialeah, Dade County's second-largest city, but it was still primarily an enclave for WASPs, rednecks, and well-paid blue-collar workers who were employed, for the most part, at the Miami International Airport. There were a few Cuban families in the subdivision, but not very many, and one entire block had filled up with immigrant Pakistanis. The houses were all concrete block and stucco, three-bedroom, one-bathroom buildings, constructed during the mid-fifties. The homeowners' association had managed to stop more Pakistanis from buying houses by passing a new rule that limited the occupancy of each house to only six residents – unless a second bathroom was added to the building. The sewer system, also installed during the mid-fifties, was considered inadequate for any more added bathrooms, so no new permits for additional bathrooms were granted. This rule effectively kept out any additional Pakistanis, with their families of twelve or more – and often up to twenty-five – and it excluded large, extended Latin families as well. There was a grandfather clause, of course, so original WASP homeowners, with several children apiece, were not affected by the new ruling.

Most of the houses, but not all, backed up to a series of small square lakes – formerly rock and gravel quarries – that looked as though they were filled with green milk. The houses all were built from the same set of blueprints, but many owners, over the years, had added garages, carports, Florida rooms, and short docks for small boats. There were a few swimming pools, but not very many, and even a few gazebos. Because of drowning accidents, swimming was prohibited in the lakes. This rule wasn't enforced, and sometimes, late at night, a few bold people did some skinny-dipping. The lakes were bordered by tall Dade County pines, and the residents had planted their yards with orange, grapefruit, and mango trees, hedges of Barbados cherry and screw-leaf crotons, and several varieties of palms, including a few stately Royals. At one time coconut palms, planted by the original construction company, had lined the vertiginous streets, but when lethal yellow attacked the trees in the late seventies, they all had been removed by the Metro government. Nevertheless, the subdivision was a green oasis in the middle of a highly urbanized city, and Green Lakes, with its own Class B shopping center and mall, was considered a desirable location for white Americans to live. There was a zealous Crime Watch program, and the curving streets had large speed bumps spaced out every fifty yards and a fifteen-mile-per-hour speed limit. Drivers who ignored the limit and the high, rounded speed bumps soon needed new shocks for their vehicles.

Hoke, with the windows of his car rolled down (although he had air conditioning), observed the speed limit, easing his car over the bumps at an angle, and tried to open garage doors with the door opener whenever he passed a garage with a closed door. Not every garage had an electric door opener; but many of them did, he knew, and he was trying to see if the late Dr Russell's door opener would work on any of them. He tried it on at least a dozen garages before he pulled into his own driveway, but it didn't open any of them. Apparently each garage door opener had its own frequency.

Hoke's house had an open-sided carport but no garage. Ellita's Honda Civic was in the carport, and Sue Ellen's Yamaha motorcycle was chained and padlocked to the left steel roof support. Hoke parked behind the Civic and entered the house.

Pepe, Ellita's one-year-old, was crying and shrieking as Hoke came through the front door, and Hoke's two daughters, Sue Ellen, seventeen, and Aileen, fifteen, were setting the table in the dining room.

'What's the matter with Pepe?'

'He needs changing,' Aileen said.

'Why don't you change him then?'

'We're setting the table now, and Ellita's in the kitchen.'

Hoke lifted Pepe out of his crib in the living room and carried the screaming, writhing body into the bathroom. He removed the soiled Pamper and tossed it into the black plastic Hefty bag that was kept in the bathroom for this purpose. The bag was half-filled with dirtied Pampers, and the fetid odor permeated the small bathroom. Hoke turned on the water in the shower, adjusted the taps one-handed until it was warm, and then, holding the boy by his wrists, hosed him down with the hand-held shower head. He dried Pepe with Ellita's face towel, sprinkled the boy's bottom with Johnson's baby powder, and put on a clean Pamper.

Pepe had stopped crying now, and Hoke returned him to his crib in the living room.

Hoke went down the hall to his own small bedroom at the far end of the house and changed from his leisure suit into a pair of khaki shorts and an old gray gym T-shirt that had the arms cut off at the shoulders. He lay on his cot and looked at the cracked ceiling, holding the garage door opener in his right hand. The device was simple enough. It worked on radio waves, or something, and each garage mechanism was set a little differently. You pressed the button, aiming at the radio box in the garage ceiling through the closed door, and the door opened. If you pressed the button again, still aiming, although you didn't even have to get close to the box in the garage ceiling, the door closed. There was also a button inside the garage, usually by the door to the kitchen. If you pressed that, it also opened the door. When the door was closed, no one could open it manually from the outside, although it could be raised manually from inside the garage. An opener like this was not supposed to assist in a murder – and yet it had. Of that much, he was positive.

But he wasn't certain; he merely had an intuition, and that meant that he was getting anxious again, pressing too hard. When he was first assigned to the cold cases, together with Bill Henderson and Ellita Sánchez, they had been lucky, solving three three-year-old cases during the first ten days. Then Henderson had been promoted to commander, and Hoke and Ellita had worked alone.

He had pushed, trying too hard and putting in too many hours, and had come very close to suffering a breakdown. A month's leave without pay had given him enough distance to realize that this was just a job, not a mission. After Ellita had been shot and retired on disability, he had worked alone until they gave him González, a young investigator too inexperienced to provide much help. Hoke hadn't come close to solving a cold case since he had returned from his month's leave, and now, what with the shortage of detectives in the Homicide Division, this was an assignment Major Brownley couldn't keep him on much longer. He was needed for regular duty, and so was González; but it would be rewarding to solve at least one more case before he returned to straight duty.

Hoke shook his head. It didn't pay to become obsessed with anything, especially a case as gelid as the Russell murder. If he solved it, fine; if he didn't, what difference would it make a hundred years from now? Hoke clicked the door opener several times, aiming at nothing. Then Ellita called to him that dinner was ready. He tossed the opener onto the dresser and, barefoot, padded down the hall to the dining room.

Chapter Three

Hoke shared a leased house with Ellita Sánchez; her baby son, Pepe; and Hoke's two teenaged daughters from his broken marriage.

Patsy, Hoke's ex-wife, had kept the two girls, following their divorce, for ten years. She had then married a pinch hitter for the Dodgers, a black ballplayer named Curly Peterson, and moved to Los Angeles. Before she left Vero Beach, Florida (she had met Curly Peterson there during spring training), she had shipped the two girls down to Miami and Hoke on a Greyhound bus. Hoke had not seen or heard from the girls in ten years, when they had been six and four years old. Because there was no way he could think of to get out of the responsibility for them, he had, of course, taken them in. Ellita had moved in with him to share the expenses when her father had thrown her out of his house when she became pregnant. Hoke was not the father of Pepe Sánchez; that honor belonged to a one-night stand Ellita had picked up in Coconut Grove, but Ellita's parents suspected strongly that Hoke was the father because Ellita had moved into the house with Hoke and his two daughters.

Then, one night, Ellita had been shot in the shoulder by an escaped holdup man. As a result of the wound, she had lost approximately twenty percent usage of her right arm, and now she stayed home full-time with Pepe. Because of the rehabilitation exercises she had had to perform to get her arm and body back into shape, she looked better now than she had before she had been wounded. She had trimmed down to 120 pounds, her pretty face was thinner, and although she was thirty-three, she could pass easily for twenty-nine.

Sue Ellen and Aileen helped Ellita with her baby, so she had ample time to shop every day and have a 'standing' every Thursday at the beauty parlor. By living with Hoke and his daughters, instead of living under her father's tyrannical thumb, she had unlimited freedom and no longer had to hand over half her salary to her father. Her disability pension was more than adequate to pay her share of the expenses, and she intended to stay home with Pepe and keep house until he was old enough to go to school before she looked for a part-time job.

The girls adored the baby and were always willing to baby-sit if Ellita wanted to go out with one of her old girlfriends to lunch or dinner, or to attend mass at St Catherine's in Hialeah. After the baby was born, Ellita's father had forgiven her and asked her to move home again, but she had refused. At thirty-three Ellita had no intention of giving up her freedom again. Ellita's mother, who sold Avon products in Little Havana, visited the house frequently, and Ellita took Pepe home occasionally (Señor Sánchez, a security guard, would not set foot in Hoke's house) to see his grandfather.

Hoke did not even pretend to be the titular head of this household. He accepted his responsibility for the girls as their father, and he would feed and clothe them and give them a home until they reached maturity (or got married); but they were allowed to do pretty much as they pleased so long as no one else in the house was inconvenienced. Sue Ellen had dropped out of school to take a full-time job in the Green Lakes Car Wash and was allowed to keep all of her weekly paycheck and tips. She was also encouraged to buy her own clothes, now that she had a steady income, and so long as she was paying for them, Hoke didn't feel that he could tell her what to wear. She had bought a motorcycle, on time payments, without his permission, and he wasn't happy about that; but he taught her how to ride it and insisted that she wear a helmet, leather pants, and jacket every time she mounted the vehicle. If she skidded across the asphalt, he explained, in an accident (and the chances were sixty-forty that she *would* have an accident), the leather clothes would prevent the pavement from scraping her skin and flesh right down to the bone.

Sue Ellen and Aileen both were sensible girls, so even when the heat and humidity reached the nineties in Miami, Sue Ellen wore her helmet and leathers when she rode her Yamaha. Hoke had ridden a motorcycle when he had been assigned to Traffic, and he knew how dangerous it could be. He had explained the dangers, but that was as far as he went with it. He had had some narrow escapes as a motorcycle cop, and the fact that he would not ride Sue Ellen's bike, under any circumstances, had helped make her take his warnings seriously, but not enough to give up the motorcycle. The bike, she insisted, gave her a certain status at the car wash, and she needed an edge to put her on equal terms with the male black and Cuban teenagers she worked with every day.

Aileen was filling out nicely after recovery from bulimic anorexia, but at fourteen she had been so thin Ellita had nicknamed her *La Flaca* ('The Skinny One'). She now ate everything within reach at the table and snacked between meals as well. She was reconciled to being a female now, and her curly chestnut hair fell down to her shoulders in soft waves. Her pointed breasts had swelled, and because she didn't wear a brassiere, they bobbed under her T-shirt as she helped set the table. Aileen's teeth were slightly crooked, and she had a noticeable overbite; but her generous mouth provided her with a big white smile.

Sue Ellen, who toweled down wet cars under a blazing sun every day, was sunburned a deep golden brown and was almost as dark as Ellita. Her short, curly hair, clipped an inch from her skull and dyed electric blue down the middle, gave her the punk look she coveted, but she was attractive in spite of herself. She wore two pairs of plastic earrings and was considering the idea of having third holes punched into her earlobes for another pair. Both girls, when they were home, wore shorts and T-shirts and usually went barefoot around the house as well. Ellita, unless she was going out, almost always wore jeans, sensible heels, and a long-sleeved blouse. She thought her thighs were too fat to wear shorts, but the Miami heat didn't affect Ellita as much as it did Hoke and his daughters.

It was habit – not a rule – but everyone did his or her best to eat dinner at home every night, and it was the only time of the day they all were together as a family. Hoke, of course, as a homicide detective with odd hours at times, couldn't always make it home in time for dinner. But when he couldn't, he phoned, and Ellita always saw to it that he had a hot meal when he did come home. The rest of the time each family member went his or her own way, getting up at a different time and preparing personal meals other than dinner.

Hoke took care of the finances, the rent and the utilities, and Ellita purchased everything else that was needed for the house, including food, cleaning materials, or the odd plumbing job that called for a professional. At the end of each month Hoke and Ellita sat down and figured out how much each owed, and then they paid the bills.

Hoke ate and slept much better than he had when he was single and unencumbered, and he also spent more time watching television than he had when he had lived in a hotel room as a single man. Even with Pepe to care for, Ellita still managed to keep the house neat and clean, and she prepared enormous meals at night.

The major drawback to living as a family man (when the girls' stereo made too much noise, Hoke could always retreat to his small bedroom and close the door) was that Hoke couldn't very well bring a woman home with him to spend the night. He knew that Ellita wouldn't mind, but he had to set an example for his daughters. He was afraid that if he brought a woman home, they might decide to bring boys home to their room overnight. As a consequence, when Hoke managed a rare conquest, which now happened at longer intervals, he had to take the woman to a hotel or motel. Miami hotel rates are expensive, even during the off-season, and there had been times that he had dropped a promising pursuit when he knew he would have to pay at least seventy-seven dollars, plus tax, for a hotel room. Hoke was forty-three and looked every single day of it. The women he attracted, divorcées and widows he met in bars, were not, in most instances, worth that much money to him. Unhappily the divorcées and widows who were interested in sleeping with Hoke were usually in their late thirties, or older, and more often than not had teenaged children of their own; that also denied them the use of their own houses and apartments. It had been more than four years since Hoke had slept with a woman who didn't have stretch marks. But he didn't mind the stretch marks so long as she didn't complain about his middle-aged paunch.

For several months Hoke had carried on a long-distance affair with a married woman from Ocala, who would fly down to Miami once a month for a shopping trip. They would check into the Miami Airport Hotel, which had reasonable day rates, and spend the afternoon. Then she would fly back to Ocala. A few days before she flew down, she would telephone Hoke and tell him what she was shopping for, and he would buy the items and have them ready in the hotel room when she checked in. She would reimburse him for the packages, of course, and they would spend the afternoon in bed. Hoke paid for the room. Once a month was better than nothing, but Hoke didn't like to do the shopping for the woman (which cut into his off-duty hours), and after their fourth monthly liaison they had more or less run out of things to talk about. She hadn't called Hoke for several weeks, and Hoke had a hunch she had found someone else to do her Miami shopping. When he thought about it, as he did when he got horny, he discovered that he was just as happy that she hadn't called, and he wouldn't really mind if he never heard from her again.

Now that Hoke had a family again, he had all the advantages of a family man (except for a regular sex life), and few, if any, disadvantages. Ellita respected him, and he got on well with his daughters. His clothes were always clean; Ellita did his laundry and put it away for him, and on Saturday mornings Aileen shined his policeman's black, high-topped double-soled shoes. He was one of the dozen men in Miami who still wore shoes with laces. He didn't like low-cut, slip-on shoes. Ellita was a wonderful cook, and in the past year Hoke had regained the twenty pounds he had dieted away and was back to his prediet weight of 210. This was at least twenty-five pounds too much for a man of five-ten. Hoke's waist had swelled from thirty-eight to forty-two, and he had been forced to buy two new poplin leisure suits in the cut-rate Miami fashion district because his old pants couldn't be let out any farther. Every day he promised to cut down on his eating but could seldom manage to do so. He also found it difficult to hold himself down to only two cans of Old Style a night when the refrigerator was always stocked with at least a dozen cans of his favorite beer.

Hoke was also doing well professionally. He had a permanent assignment as sergeant in charge of the cold-case files, which gave him almost unlimited time to work on the old and all but hopeless unsolved homicides. He had passed the examination for lieutenant and was at the head of the WASP list. Being at the top of the WASP promotion list meant that he had passed the exam with a higher score than any other candidate in the department, but it did not mean that he would be the next sergeant promoted to lieutenant. Because of Affirmative Action, there were three Latins and two blacks ahead of him for promotion (all with much lower scores than Hoke's), but if the department ever *did* get around to promoting a white American to lieutenant again, Hoke would get the promotion. He had a little more than five years to go for retirement, and he was positive – or almost positive – that he would be promoted before he retired. And if not, whoever said that life was fair?

When Ellita called him to dinner, Hoke broke his rule and decided to have a beer with his meal instead of waiting an hour after eating. To justify it, he decided he would drink only one more that evening and would hold off until 10:00 P.M., when the rerun of *Hill Street Blues* came on the tube.

Dinner was roast pork loin, accompanied by boiled yucca, fried candied plantains, black beans, boiled pearl rice, hard Cuban rolls, and a salad of sliced tomatoes, avocados, and iceberg lettuce, with Ellita's homemade Thousand Island dressing. There was a bottle of garlicky *criollo* sauce for the pork, a bowl of mixed green and black olives, and butter and guava jelly for the rolls. Hoke was served a baked potato instead of yucca (he didn't like yucca). After he had split and mashed the potato, he spooned black beans over it and added a jigger of sweet sherry to the mixture. Ellita and the girls took ample portions as well, but unlike Hoke, they wouldn't eat seconds. Ellita, who starved herself during the day, always felt entitled to at least one decent meal at dinnertime, so she still managed to keep her weight on a fairly even basis. Hoke took second helpings but ate only one baked potato.

After everyone was served and eating, Hoke told them about the new chief's planned no-smoking-in-the-station rules.

'Henderson was taking a survey in the division, and it could be a narrow margin. A lot of guys have quit already, and it may be a majority for the new chief. If so, I'll have to go outside every time I want a smoke.'

'You've been trying to quit,' Ellita said, 'and if he makes the rule, it'll be that much easier for you to stop.'

'That isn't the point, Ellita. Smoking's still a legal activity in this country, and cigarettes are still sold in the stores. If it's legal to buy 'em, it should be legal to smoke 'em. It's a hard habit to break, and I don't think the new chief can enforce a rule like that for very long without a rebellion from the PBA. So tomorrow I'm going to get together with Bill and start a little office pool. I think, if the rule goes in, it'll last for only three days.'

'I'd say five,' Ellita said. 'Put me down for number five in the pool. How much for each ticket?'

'I hadn't thought about it. Five dollars, do you think?'

'That's too much. Make it two dollars a ticket. I'll give you the money after dinner. Save me number five.'

'I still say three.'

'According to the *Miami News*,' Sue Ellen said, 'the army's already stopped soldiers from smoking in their vehicles and inside all government buildings.'

'Where'd you see that?'

'In the paper. A few weeks ago.'

'How come I didn't see it?'

'I don't know, but it was in there.'

'The army won't be able to enforce that rule either. At least they wouldn't've been able to when I was in the service, and I was an MP.'

'When you were in the army,' Aileen said, 'they didn't know that cigarettes caused cancer. Not back in the world war.'

'I wasn't in the world war. I was in the Vietnam War.'

'They still didn't know, not way back then.'

'They don't know now either,' Hoke said. 'They only suspect cigarettes cause cancer. There's no real proof.'

'The surgeon general says they do,' Sue Ellen said.

'Who're you going to believe?' Hoke asked. 'The Tobacco Institute or the surgeon general?'

'The surgeon general,' both girls said in unison; then they giggled.

Hoke grinned. 'Me, too.'

Hoke put two slices of white pork on his plate, cut off the fatty edges, and frowned as he looked around the table.

'Aileen,' Ellita said, 'please get the Tabasco sauce for your father. You didn't bring it in when you set the table.'

Aileen went into the kitchen for the Tabasco. Ellita put her utensils down and looked sideways at Sue Ellen. 'As a favor to me, Sue Ellen, I'd like to ask you one more time. Please dye your hair back to its natural color for Sunday, and I'll help you dye it blue again on Monday. Mama wants Sunday to be a very special party for Uncle Arnoldo, and she says it would upset him to see blue hair on a woman. Tío Arnoldo's a very conservative man, and he wouldn't understand.'

Sue Ellen shook her head. 'No, Ellita. If he's going to live here, he'll have to accept America as it is, and it might do him good to see blue hair. Miami isn't Cuba. We can do what we please here.'

'He understands that, but he's been waiting in Costa Rica for four years for his visa, and every relative we have will be at the party Sunday. He's my father's older brother and very dignified.'

'I'm conservative, too,' Sue Ellen said. 'But if you think the color of my hair'll bother your uncle, I'll just go to work instead. I can get more overtime in the car wash. In fact, I can work every Sunday if I want.'

'I think you'll enjoy the party, and I want you to come. It's just that Mama wants everything to be nice for him. He was in prison for twenty-two years before he got to Costa Rica.'

'I don't speak Spanish anyway.' Sue Ellen shrugged. 'I'd just as soon go to work.'

'If you don't come now, Sue Ellen, Mama'll think it's her fault, and you know she loves you.'

'I like your mom okay, too, but I won't dye my hair back just to go to a dumb party.'

Hoke cleared his throat. 'I don't think I'll be able to make it either, Ellita. I meant to tell you earlier, but it slipped my mind.'

'You have to come, Hoke,' Ellita said. 'Tío Arnoldo doesn't know any Americans, and Mama's already told him that I live here with you. If you don't come, he'll think you don't approve of him.'

Aileen returned from the kitchen and handed Hoke the Tabasco sauce. He unscrewed the top and sprinkled his pork liberally. 'That doesn't make any sense,' Hoke said. 'Whether Sue Ellen or I come or not – or Aileen – makes no difference. We're not related to your uncle. He wasn't a political prisoner anyway. You told me he was sent to prison for killing a man, a man who was sleeping with his wife. He served his time and then got a visa to Costa Rica, so he's paid his debt to Cuban society. I don't hold anything against him. Now that he's here in Miami, he's just another lucky Cuban far's I'm concerned. I can't see why your family's trying to make a big hero out of him. If he was a Marielito, with his prison background, he'd probably be locked up in Atlanta, waiting for shipment back to Cuba with the rest of the criminals.'

'Tío Arnoldo's not a criminal!' Ellita said. 'He's a man of honor, and he's family! If you were getting out of prison and then exile after twenty-six years, we'd give a party for you, too. When you were married to Patsy, if you'd caught her sleeping with another man, wouldn't you have shot the *cabrón?*'

'Hell, no! You don't shoot a man just because he falls in love with your wife. What you do, you get a legal divorce.'

'You don't understand Cuban honor.'

'The Cuban judge didn't either. He sentenced your uncle to life, didn't he? Even though he got out in twenty-two years. But I don't hold it against him. I intended to go to the party, but I have to stay home and wait for a call from Major Brownley. This afternoon, just before I left, Bill Henderson told me to let my beard grow and that Brownley was going to call me at home Sunday.'

'What kind of message is that?' Ellita raised her eyebrows.

'It's the message Bill gave me. It's probably some special assignment. We're shorthanded in the division, and Brownley decided to give it to me. What with the suspensions and resignations, I don't think I'll be on cold cases much longer.'

'What time will he call you on Sunday?'

'Bill didn't say.'

'Can Major Brownley do that, Daddy?' Aileen asked.

'Do what?'

'Make you grow a beard?'

'I don't know. One thing I do know – the department can make you shave *off* a beard, and a mustache, too, if they want. That was a concession we had to make with the new PBA contract. But I don't know if they can make a man grow a beard or not. At any rate I won't shave till I talk to him. Willie Brownley's weird sometimes, but he's not frivolous.'

'Why didn't he tell you himself, instead of Bill?' Ellita said.

'He's fishing down in the Keys with one of his old college buddies and won't be back till Sunday.'

'He can call you at my father's house just as easily as he can here. I'll phone Mrs Brownley, give her the number, and he can call you there. You aren't getting out of this party, and neither's Sue Ellen.'

'Okay.' Hoke shrugged. 'Call her then. You heard that, Sue Ellen. We're all going to the party.'

'In that case,' Sue Ellen said, sighing, 'I'll dye my hair brown again – if you'll help me, Ellita.'

'I said I would, and I'll help you dye it back again next Monday night.'

'You don't have to do that, Sue Ellen,' Hoke said, 'if you don't want to – I hope you know that.'

'I know, but it'll make it easier for Ellita. Besides, all afternoon those old Cubans will be whispering about the *chica* with the *pelo azul*, and I'm liable to say something nasty.'

Hoke grinned. 'You've picked up a few Spanish words, haven't you?'

'I hear the Cuban dudes talking behind my back at the car wash. They make jokes about my blue pubic hair, too – but not to my face. They know what kind of temper I've got.'

'If you want my opinion –' Aileen said.

'I don't.'

– I think it looks gnarly. Blue hair, I mean.'

'That's enough about hair at the dinner table,' Hoke said. 'Let's talk about something else.'

Sue Ellen glared at her sister for a moment and then doused her pork with *criollo* sauce without speaking. Pepe awoke and started to cry. Ellita got the baby from the crib, sat in her chair again, rolled up her blouse, and the baby began to suckle the left nipple.

'Which breast does Pepe like best, Ellita?' Hoke asked. 'The left or the right?'

'What kind of question is that? He usually takes the left first, but that's because I hold him that way. He doesn't have any preference.'

'Not according to Melanie Klein,' Hoke said. 'When you took your psych course at Miami-Dade, did they ever discuss Dr Klein's theories about babies?'

'I don't think so. Melanie Klein?'

'Dr Klein. She was a child psychologist, like Anna Freud, one of the first to analyze children. She claimed that babies developed a love-hate relationship with breasts. Breasts are good, both of them, at first. Then, when the babies are weaned, sometime during the first two years, let's say, and the breasts are denied to them, they become bad because they're a source of frustration. Being denied means they're bad objects instead of good objects, and they look at breasts as separate from their mothers. What mothers have to do then is to get them to see the mother as a whole person and not just as a woman who's got two objects hanging off her to be loved or hated.'

'What about the good breast and the bad breast?'

Hoke thought for a moment but couldn't remember. His complete knowledge of Dr Melanie Klein was limited to a book review he had read of her biography in the *New York Times Book Review*. He had picked it up in the men's room on the fourth floor of the police station. He had read the review while he was in the can, sitting on the commode, and he remembered thinking at the time that the theories of Dr Klein were ludicrous.

'It's very complicated, Ellita. It has something to do with transference, but I haven't read any Klein for several years, and I'm not sure exactly how it works. I do remember that Karen Horney supported Klein's theories.'

"We read Karen Horney at Miami-Dade. There was a chapter from Horney's book *Self-Analysis* in our textbook. But I don't remember any mention of Melanie Klein.'

'It's just a theory, I guess, like everything else in psychology. But if Pepe begins to favor one breast over the other, maybe you'd better look into it.'

'I think Dr Klein is full of shit,' Ellita said.

Pepe dug his fat knuckles into Ellita's left breast, trying to increase the flow. Ellita, eating awkwardly with her right hand, dropped a forkful of lettuce saturated with Thousand Island on Pepe's head. She put down her fork and wiped the baby's head with a paper napkin. She smiled.

'Are you making all this up, Hoke?'

'As I go through life' – Hoke shook his head – 'I find that when I tell people something they don't already know, they almost always think it's a lie. Dr Klein was a famous pioneer in child psychology. Just because you never heard of her doesn't make her a nonexistent person.'

'Daddy wouldn't make up a story like that,' Aileen said. 'He doesn't have that much imagination.'

Ellita and Sue Ellen laughed.

'Thank you, sweetheart,' Hoke said, 'for defending your old man.'

Pepe squirmed, and Ellita shifted him over to the right nipple. He suckled and gurgled. The four of them smiled at the red-faced baby's greediness.

'So much for Melanie Klein,' Hoke said.

After dinner Sue Ellen and Ellita cleared the table and retreated to the kitchen to wash the dishes. Aileen, who usually helped, had a baby-sitting job down the street, and she left the house wearing the earphones to her Sony Walkman, listening to her new Jimmy Buffett tape.

Hoke went into the bathroom, scrubbed his false teeth, and then put them into a plastic glass with water and Polident to soak overnight. He sat in his La-Z-Boy recliner, after turning on the set, and tried to change channels with the Telectron garage opener. It didn't work on the TV either, so he turned off the set. He went over his theory in his mind.

697

Three days before his death Dr Paul Russell had parked in his marked space at his clinic – the clinic he owned in partnership with Dr Leo Schwartz and Dr Max Farris. Sometime during the day his garage door opener had been stolen from his white Mercedes. Nothing else had been taken. He missed the garage door opener when he got home because it wasn't in the glove compartment where he always kept it. He parked in the driveway and entered his house through the front door. His second garage door opener – the one Hoke held in his hand – was kept as a spare, according to his wife, Louise, on a small side table in the foyer.

For the next two days Dr Russell had intended to get another opener but hadn't got around to it. He was a busy doctor, and he still had the second opener. However, instead of taking the spare opener with him in his car, where it might be stolen again, he opened the garage from inside, backed his car out to the driveway, got out of his car, closed the door with his opener, and then went into the house through the front door. He put the opener on the little table in the foyer again. The procedure was annoying but not onerous, and he didn't want to have the opener stolen again – not until he obtained another spare.

On the third morning, after he had backed onto his driveway and closed the door, as he crossed the lawn to the front door of his house, someone stepped out from behind an Australian pine on Dr Russell's front lawn and shot him between the eyes with a .38-caliber revolver.

Dr Russell had had a gall-bladder operation scheduled at 7:00 A.M. at the Good Samaritan Hospital and had backed out of the garage at approximately 6:15. His dead body, still warm, had been discovered at 6:30 by the *Miami Herald* deliveryman when he threw a paper onto the lawn. He had then knocked on the front door to call the police. Mrs Louise Russell wasn't home. She had gone to Orlando the day before to visit her younger sister, who taught the second grade. The deliveryman had then gone next door and called the police. He waited until the police came, standing beside the body, and said he didn't touch anything. Dr Russell had been killed instantly, and the garage door opener had fallen from his hand. His expensive gold Rolex wristwatch continued to keep accurate time on his wrist. The Russells' Mexican maid didn't get to the house until 7:30, and when she did arrive and saw the homicide team and the dead body, she became hysterical. It took Sergeant Armando Quevedo, the detective in charge of the case, several minutes to calm her down before she could tell them that Mrs Russell was in Orlando. Sergeant Quevedo had called the clinic to inform the nurse about the murder. Dr Farris had gone to the hospital to take out the gall-bladder Dr Russell had been scheduled to remove.

All this had happened three years before – three years and three months ago – and now the case was very cold indeed. Some of Quevedo's notes were in Spanish, but they were reminders to himself. The supplementary report was written in Quevedo's clear, easy-to-follow English. There were no leads whatsoever, except that the killing had all the earmarks of a professional hit.

Quevedo could discover no motive. Dr Russell had no known enemies. He had been a hard-working professional, and he had put in long days. He earned more than $150,000 a year, and he also owned an eight-unit apartment house in Liberty City. The apartment house was managed for him by a company that specialized in renting properties to blacks, and the company kept fifteen percent of the rents it collected. And it always collected, or the residents were evicted immediately. Although the black people who rented the substandard apartments might have resented Dr Russell if they had known that he was their slumlord, they were unaware of his ownership.

Dr Russell owned the two-story house in Belle Meade, where he lived with his wife, Louise (they had no children), and she had said that they had a limited social life because of his busy schedule. He wasn't robbed. In addition to the expensive gold Rolex, there was a gold ring set with an onyx and a diamond on his ring finger. His wallet contained eighty-seven dollars and a half-dozen credit cards. It was possible, Quevedo suggested in his supplementary report, that the hit man, whoever it was, had hit the wrong man.

Hoke didn't accept that. The stolen garage door opener interested Hoke. Whoever had stolen the opener from Dr Russell's Mercedes had had to be familiar with his habits. The man – or woman – who shot the physician must have known that he would cross the lawn at that point to get back to the front door and put the opener away before returning to his car.

Who had profited from Dr Russell's death? Dr Schwartz and Dr Farris hadn't brought in a new doctor to replace Dr Russell in their clinic. After his death they had split Dr Russell's practice between them. They both had profited because of their partnership insurance. Also, and this is what piqued Hoke's curiosity, four months ago Dr Leo Schwartz had married the widow, Louise Russell. He now lived with her in the Belle Meade house, a house Dr Russell's mortgage insurance had paid off in full at his death. Dr Schwartz now drove the white Mercedes, and Hoke wondered if Dr Schwartz was wearing Dr Russell's Rolex and ring as well. And why, Hoke wondered, had Louise Russell decided to visit her sister in Orlando at that particular time? The sisters were not close; the Orlando sister had never visited the Russells in Miami. All this, of course, was not known by Sergeant Quevedo.

Whoever had stolen the garage door opener from Dr Russell's locked car at the clinic, and then relocked the car door afterward, was probably the murderer or the person who had hired the killer. Hoke suspected that that person was Dr Leo Schwartz, or perhaps it was Dr Schwartz *and* Dr Max Farris – with an assist, perhaps, from Louise Russell Schwartz? All he had to do was find some proof.

The garage door opener, the spare, had been locked away as evidence, and Hoke had checked it out of the property room (it took Baldy Allen, the property man, more than two hours to find it, three years and three months being a long time for evidence to be stored away), but Hoke was convinced that the opener was the key, somehow, to the case.

Perhaps Dr Schwartz had taken the original door opener, and if so, instead of throwing it away, he still had it? If so, and if he had also planned three years ago to marry Louise, and if they had been having an affair at that time, he was currently using the original door opener to get into the garage now that he was married to Louise and living in her house – and driving the white Mercedes. Everything seemed logical; the killer could very well be Dr

Schwartz. Tomorrow, when he got to the office, he would see where Leo Schwartz had been when the murder was committed. There was nothing much in the report about Schwartz, except that he and his partner, Max Farris, both had attended the funeral. Sergeant Quevedo had attended Dr Russell's funeral and had copied down the list of everyone who had signed the register. But Quevedo hadn't checked on any of these people to see where they had been during the murder. It might be a good idea to check the Belle Meade house, too. He would see if this spare opener still opened the garage. If it did, it might mean that Dr Schwartz did indeed have the original opener – the one stolen from the Mercedes. If the spare didn't open the garage, it could mean that a new radio signal and new openers had been ordered and that he was on the wrong track ...

Hoke fell asleep in the recliner. Ellita brought him a cold beer at ten o'clock and woke him in time to watch the rerun of *Hill Street Blues*.

Chapter Four

The next morning, when Detective Teodoro González came into the office, Hoke handed him the garage door opener and told him to go to the late Dr Russell's house and see if it would open the garage door. Hoke didn't tell González why. All he had was a theory, even if the opener did open the garage. If it worked, however, his suspicion would be stronger, and it would confirm that he was at least on to something.

'After I open the garage,' González asked, 'should I go inside, or will I need a warrant?'

'All I want you to do,' Hoke said slowly, 'and I want you to do it as inconspicuously as possible, is open the door – *if* it opens. Then, if it opens, push the button and close the door again. If anybody's around, don't do it. Drive past the house. Keep circling the block, and don't let anyone see you open and close the door. If you think Mrs Schwartz is at home or see her out in the yard, just drive away. Go back later when she isn't home.'

González slipped the opener into his outside jacket pocket. He was wearing an iridescent lime-green linen sports jacket, a black silk T-shirt, with pleated lemon-colored gabardine slacks, and tasseled white Gucci slip-ons.

'And take off that jacket. Your T-shirt's okay, but that jacket isn't inconspicuous, and neither are your slacks. So don't get out of your car either.'

González nodded. He removed his jacket and draped it, silk lining side out, over his arm. 'Don't I check and see what's in the garage after I open it? I mean, take a quick little survey, something like that? What exactly am I looking for?'

'Nothing. Just see if that gadget opens the door. Then come back and tell me. Do you know where the Belle Meade neighborhood is? How to find the address on Poinciana?'

'I know about where it is. There's a Publix market at the corner of Poinciana and Dixie, so all I have to do is turn there and follow Poinciana till I get to the address.'

'Okay, then, move out. And come straight back here when you finish trying the opener.'

González hadn't been promoted to detective-investigator because he had earned it. He had been promoted after only one year of patrol duty in Liberty City because he had a degree in economics from Florida International University. González had a poor sense of direction and often got lost in Miami, even though he had lived in the city for the last ten of his twenty-five years. Hoke almost always found it necessary to brief him about directions before he sent him out of the office to do legwork. On the other hand, González was excellent with figures and had saved both Ellita and Hoke money when he had prepared their income tax returns for them.

Hoke hadn't realized how much he had depended upon Ellita for detail work until she was no longer his partner. González was barely adequate at best, if he was told exactly what to do. He had no initiative, and Hoke had already asked Brownley for a replacement for González at the earliest opportunity. But the Homicide Division was shorthanded, after three recent suspensions and several resignations, and it was unlikely that González would be replaced.

After González left, Hoke took a clean yellow file folder out of the cabinet. He began to grid it with a black felt-tipped pen and a ruler to make up a pool card. There would be forty squares. At two bucks a square, if he sold them all, the winner of the revocation of the no-smoking pool would win seventy-eight dollars. After he finished the card, Hoke wrote his name in number three, and Ellita's in number five and left his cubicle to look for Commander Bill Henderson.

Henderson emerged from the elevator, carrying a Styrofoam cup of coffee in his left hand and his clipboard in his right. He grinned broadly as Hoke approached him, holding up the pool card.

Henderson shook his head. 'Forget it, Hoke. There's been a compromise. There'll be no smoking in vehicles, but it'll still be okay inside the building. Not out here in the bullpen, but in offices like yours it'll be okay. Men can smoke in the john, too. We finally persuaded the new chief that it would be impractical to have men going to and coming from the lot all day and all night.'

'Shit. It took me twenty minutes to make up a pool card.'

'Hang on to it. The new chief's really gung-ho about this no-smoking business and may change his mind back again.'

'I don't see anything wrong about smoking in a patrol car, unless a man's partner objects.'

'I don't either. But that was the compromise. Besides, it doesn't apply to you because you drive your own car. But it will apply to unmarked cars from the motor pool.'

'Unmarked cars, too? That doesn't make sense.'

'That's the rule. I'm going to type up the notice and post it on the bulletin board now – after I finish my coffee.'

'Any other truly important news at the meeting?'

'Yeah, there is. Every division's got to appoint a crack committee. They want us to come up with something or other to help the new Crack-Cocaine Task Force. According to new statistics, Miami's got more crack houses than New York had speakeasies during Prohibition. So something drastic has to be done. You didn't shave this morning, Hoke, so you're the new chairman of our Homicide Crack Committee.'

'You told me yesterday *not* to shave, you bastard!'

'I know I did. But I don't have anyone else available just now. You can pick out two more detectives for your committee, and start thinking of ways to crack down on crack abusers and crack houses.'

Hoke ripped up the pool card, tossed it into a wastebasket, and went down to the basement cafeteria. He got a *café con leche*, dark on coffee, and sat at an empty table. He was due in court at ten-thirty, making an appearance as the investigating officer in an old case that had already been continued several times. It would, in all probability, be continued again because the defendant, who had killed his wife with an aluminum baseball bat, had fired his court-appointed lawyer and the court would have to appoint a new one.

Hoke finished his coffee and lighted a Kool, wondering what, if anything, he could come up with (as a homicide detective) to combat the use of crack in Miami. He couldn't think of anything, except to charge crack sellers with second-degree murder. Crack abusers died off eventually, if they didn't break the habit. But legislation like that was unlikely. He would select Sergeant Armando Quevedo and Detective Bob Levine for his committee. The three of them could go out for a few beers at Larry's Hideaway, kick the idea around, and then come up with a meaningless report of some kind. Hoke hadn't been out drinking with Quevedo and Levine for some months now, and this was a reasonable excuse to have a few beers and shoot the breeze with his old buddies. He was getting too housebound for his own good.

It was unfair of Bill Henderson to make him the chairman, but Hoke didn't resent the appointment. He knew that if he had been in Henderson's position, he would have appointed the first man he happened to see, too. The idea was stupid in the first place. A committee like this one was just busywork, another public relations ploy the new chief could hand out to the media to make it look as if something were being done about drug abuse. Education didn't work, Hoke thought as he stubbed out his butt in the ashtray. He knew he shouldn't smoke, and he knew he shouldn't drink, but that hadn't stopped him from smoking and drinking. So far this year thirty-six Miamians had died from smoking crack, but crack use increased daily.

Hoke returned to his office and slipped into his leisure suit jacket. He decided to drive over to the Metro Justice Building a little early because it was difficult to find a parking space over there. The phone rang.

'Hoke,' Ellita said, when he picked up the phone, 'you know the house across the street, the run-down place that's been for sale for the last year?'

'What about it?'

'A man moved in this morning. They unloaded a van of furniture earlier, and the guy who moved in has a little Henry J. It looks like a brand-new car.'

'You must be mistaken, Ellita. They haven't made any Henry Js since the fifties.'

'It's a Henry J, Hoke, and it looks like a new one. After the van left, the man brought a dining-room chair out to the lawn, and he's been sitting and staring over at our house for the last hour. The grass over there's a foot high, and he looks funny, just sitting there in a chair and staring at our house.'

'What about it? If he bought the house and moved in, he's entitled to sit on a chair on his front lawn, whether he mows it or not. I'm glad the house finally sold. Now someone'll have to take care of the yard.'

'I don't like it, Hoke. I know he can't see me, or anything like that, because I'm here inside. But every time I go to the front window and look over at him through the curtains, he's staring directly at our house. He's wearing a dark blue suit, and it must be ninety out there in the sun. It bothers me.'

'What do you expect me to do about it, Ellita? I've got to go to court this morning.'

'I thought maybe you could find out who he is.'

'Hell, you can do that yourself. Call the realtor and ask him. The sign out there was Paulson Realtor, wasn't it?'

'I already called the realtor, and they let me talk to a Mrs Anderson. She's the woman who handled the sale, but she wouldn't tell me anything. She said if I was interested, the neighborly thing to do would be to go over and introduce myself. Then if he wanted to talk about himself and why he bought the house, it would be up to him.'

'That seems reasonable, Ellita. Why don't you do that?'

'I don't know. It's just that he looks so weird over there. Like a sitting statue or something. Wearing a blue suit.'

'Look, I've got to go to court. If you're afraid of him, take your pistol along –'

'I'm not afraid of him. It's just that it looks – Never mind. If your case is continued again, will you come home for lunch?'

'I don't know. I'll try to call you from the courthouse.'

As Hoke suspected it would be, the case was continued, although the angry judge said it would be the last time. The new lawyer, a young woman from the public defender's office, requested a thirty-day delay so she could prepare a defense. Hoke almost felt sorry for her. This was her first homicide case, and she would certainly lose it. The defendant, an insurance salesman and Little League baseball coach, had killed his wife with a bat because she had berated him for not letting their son pitch. His son could neither pitch nor hit, he told the desk sergeant when he turned himself in and handed the bloody bat over and confessed at the station. Hoke had prepared the supplementary reports on the simple case. If the man's signed confession was allowed as evidence, the guy would go to prison, no matter what kind of defense the attorney attempted.

Hoke called Ellita from the courthouse.

'I've been waiting for your call, Hoke –'

'Go ahead and have lunch without me. I've got too many things to do today to come home for lunch.'

'I found out who that man is, Hoke. And I don't think it's a coincidence. It's Donald Hutton!'

Hoke laughed. 'Hutton's a common name, Ellita. My Donald Hutton's still doing twenty-five years in Raiford. A mandatory twenty-five before he's eligible for parole.'

'You're wrong, Hoke. This is *your* Donald Hutton. I went over and introduced myself. He told me he was waiting outside for the water man and the FPL to turn on his utilities. He said he just moved down here from Starke, that's where Raiford Prison is, and he's had his furniture and little Henry J in storage for the last ten years. Then he told me his name was Donald Hutton. I didn't tell him you lived in the house with me, but I've got a hunch he already knows that. That's why he bought the house –'

'Did you ask him if he was in prison?'

'That isn't something you ask a person you're meeting for the first time, Hoke. I couldn't very well say, "Did you just get out of prison?" could I?'

'I guess not. I'll check it out while I'm here at the courthouse.'

'Call me back. I'm not going out.'

'I'll call you.'

Hoke recalled the Donald Hutton murder case well. This had been Hoke's second homicide investigation, and he had worked hard on it, trying to prove himself as a new detective.

Donald Hutton and his older brother, Virgil (Virgil was five years older than Donald), had moved to Miami from Valdosta,

Georgia, in the sixties. They had started a knotty pine paneling business. They already owned hundreds of acres of pinelands in Georgia, and they specialized in paneling offices and dens in new homes. During the building boom of the early seventies they had prospered in Miami. Eventually they had twenty-two employees. They lived together in an old mansion in the Bayside section of Miami, overlooking Biscayne Bay.

Virgil had married a modestly successful interior designer, a young woman named Marie Weller. She had kept her maiden name when they married, because of her established business. Her new clients were often advised to panel one or two rooms in knotty pine (she could get them a substantial discount). Then Virgil Hutton disappeared.

Donald Hutton had made a nuisance of himself at the police station, demanding that they find his big brother. Virgil had no known enemies, and according to everything Hoke could find out, he had been a 'good old boy.' Virgil did the selling for the two-man firm. Donald took care of the paperwork and also supervised the actual paneling that was put in by their hired craftsmen.

Donald also complained to the media, claiming that the police were not looking hard enough for his brother. How could a two-hundred-and-forty-pound man, six feet tall, disappear into the hot, moist air of Miami?

Marie Weller couldn't understand it either. She and Virgil had been married only for a year and were happy together, she claimed. In fact, they had even talked to the attorney, Randy Mendoza, about the possibility of adopting a child. At thirty-two Marie Weller was capable of bearing a child, but Virgil, forty-three and fifty pounds overweight, had a low sperm count. Virgil had disappeared without a trace. No money had been taken from his bank account, and his Cadillac was still in the three-car garage. His extensive tailored wardrobe was still intact.

One Saturday morning a photograph of Donald Hutton and Marie Weller appeared in both newspapers. Considering the possibility that Virgil might be suffering from amnesia, Marie and Donald had gone downtown and checked the skid-row breadline at Camillus House, believing that Virgil, if he were having an amnesia attack, might be sleeping under an overpass at night and getting mission handouts. They had notified the newspapers of their impending trip downtown, and photographers and reporters had been there to check the breadline with them. Virgil had not been among the homeless men, of course, but some excellent human-interest photos of other bums in the line were published in both papers.

Negative PR like this put additional pressure on Hoke Moseley and the Homicide Division.

Because of their partnership agreement, Donald Hutton, in essence, now owned one hundred percent of the business. Marie Weller, naturally, continued to live with her brother-in-law in the big Bayside mansion. Donald Hutton – although he didn't have to – paid Marie Weller a fair share of the profits from the business, but until Virgil was declared officially dead – not just missing – the business was all his, not Marie Weller's. If the body was found, Marie Weller would inherit her husband's half of the firm.

Hoke discovered the body.

Before he found the corpse, Hoke had learned, during routine checks of Donald's movements in the weeks preceding Virgil's disappearance, that Donald had purchased three pounds of strychnine at the Falco-Benson Pharmaceutical Company, in Hialeah, ostensibly to get rid of rats at his house. Inasmuch as the Huttons had a live-in cook, a daytime maid, and a gardener who spent two days a week taking care of their yard, why would a busy executive like Donald Hutton decide to kill the rats himself? Wouldn't he hire an exterminator, or else tell the regular exterminator who visited the house every month to take care of the rats? It wasn't much to go on, but the third judge Hoke talked to signed a second search warrant. Hoke discovered the body buried under the garage floor beneath Virgil's parked 1974 El Dorado. The house had been searched briefly earlier, when a two-man detective team looked about for evidence in the disappearance, but they hadn't moved the Cadillac during this first, and rather perfunctory, search. Donald Hutton was arrested when the autopsy revealed traces of strychnine in Virgil's body. Marie Weller had been in North Carolina attending a furniture convention when Virgil disappeared, so she was not a suspect.

The evidence was largely circumstantial, and perhaps a good criminal lawyer could have obtained a not-guilty verdict for Donald Hutton, but Donald had retained Randy Mendoza, and Mendoza, a corporation lawyer without criminal law experience, made the mistake of putting his client on the stand. The prosecutor had managed to make Hutton lie, after accusing him of sleeping with Marie Weller, his brother's wife, during a long weekend in Key West. After Hutton had denied the allegation, the prosecutor produced a photocopy of the hotel registration card (obtained by Hoke during his investigation). He also put another witness on the stand, a hotel maid, who claimed that the two of them were in bed together on the morning she entered their room (at their request) to clear away their breakfast dishes. Marie Weller was then put on the stand. She admitted sharing the bed in Key West with her brother-in-law but said that she did so only because all the other rooms were booked up. They had slept together, she said, but they 'hadn't done anything.'

The jury found Donald Hutton guilty of first-degree murder but recommended life imprisonment. The magistrate accepted the jury's recommendation. Life, on a murder-one conviction, meant twenty-five mandatory years in prison before Hutton would be eligible for a parole. Technically Donald Hutton should still have fifteen years to serve ...

Judge Hathorne was not in his chambers, but his law clerk informed Hoke that Hutton's case, on a third appeal, had been granted a new trial by the state supreme court. Hutton's attorney, they concluded, had prepared an inadequate, incompetent defense. Mendoza should not have put Hutton on the stand, and he should have accepted a plea bargain of guilty for the reduction of the charge to second-degree murder. If Hutton had pleaded guilty to second-degree murder, he would have been eligible for parole in only eight years. Rather than retry the case (now that Hutton had served ten years), the state attorney had gone along with the recommendation to release Hutton for 'time served.' And so Hoke learned that Ellita was right. *His* Donald Hutton, a man who had promised to 'get him' someday, a threat Hoke had considered empty at the time, was back on the street, or, more specifically, living in a house directly across the street from Hoke's house.

Hutton had money, lots of money, and if he had let it grow at ten percent interest or more in the bank, while he was serving ten years, he was a lot richer now than when he had been sentenced. Of course, the appeals had cost him considerable sums, but Marie Weller had paid him a good price for his half of the paneling business.

As Hoke drove back to the police station, he concluded – as Ellita had – that Donald Hutton's purchase of the house across the street was not a random coincidence. Perhaps Hutton's threat to 'get him' someday was no longer empty. Hoke was not fearful of Hutton, but the circumstances made him a little uneasy.

When he got back to his cubicle, Hoke called Blackie Wheeler, Hutton's parole officer and a man he had known for several years, and asked Wheeler about Donald Hutton's parole status.

'I've talked to him only once, Hoke,' Blackie said on the phone. 'He has to report to me once a month. He'll have to come in person for the first two or three months, but after that I'll probably just let him call in by phone. He's not exactly a criminal, or wasn't when he went up to Raiford, and he shouldn't give me any problems. In fact, I wish I had a few more like him in my load. He has independent means, so I don't have to see that he has a job and check with his employer, and he has no ex-criminal buddies to associate with. He told me that he intended to start a small business of some kind, once he got settled, just to have something to do.'

'I can tell you where he lives right now,' Hoke said. 'He lives across the street from me in Green Lakes.'

'I've got his address –'

'When he was found guilty, Blackie, he threatened to kill me someday, after he got out of prison. So I don't think it's any coincidence that he moved into that house.'

'He isn't a professional criminal, Hoke. And he's entitled to live anywhere in the city he wants. Of course, if you're afraid of him, we might be able to get a restraining order to keep him off your property. But I'm not so sure a judge'll even do that much. After all, the threat was made ten years ago, and the guy was understandably sore at the time. But I don't think Hutton would relish doing any more time. Even with all his dough, it was still rough on him in prison. Keep in touch, though, and if he does anything funny, let me know. Meanwhile, if you want me to ask him why he bought in Green Lakes, I will. It might be that it's just a nice neighborhood. He's already forbidden to contact Ms Weller. She doesn't want anything to do with him, naturally. I've talked with her on the phone, and she's planning to get married again – to the guy who owns the Cathay Towers over in Miami Beach. I've got his name written down here somewhere –'

'That's okay, Blackie,' Hoke broke in. 'I'm not worried about Weller or Hutton, I just wanted to check with you, is all. She's not dumb enough to take up with him again. It would be bad for her business. But I still don't think it's just a coincidence that he moved in across from me.'

'It could be.'

'Not if you saw the house. The previous owner let it go to hell, and it's been vacant for more than a year. He's gonna have to spend a lot of dough just to get it back into livable shape.'

'He's *got* a lot of dough, Hoke. Look, I've got two guys waiting here to see me ...'

'Thanks, Blackie. I'll keep in touch.'

A few minutes later González came into the office. He handed the garage opener to Hoke.

'It opened the door okay,' he said. 'But when I pressed it again, and I was parked right there in front of the driveway, it wouldn't close again.'

'If it opened the door, it should've closed it.'

'What can I tell you?' González shrugged.

'Did anybody see you?'

'Nobody was around. It's a quiet neighborhood. But I felt bad driving off leaving the door open. Somebody could come along and steal the riding mower that's parked inside the garage.'

'That's Robbery's problem, not ours. Take the opener back down to Property, and turn it in. Bring back the receipt, and I'll put it in the file.'

Hoke hid his disappointment from González. At least he had been half right.

712

Until Ellita had phoned him, Hoke had forgotten all about the Donald Hutton case, but there were some interesting parallels between the Hutton case and the Dr Russell case. When he had more time, maybe he would dig out the old Hutton file and compare the two to see if he could discover anything else that was similar. He needed a fresh idea. But that was the trouble with cold cases. They were cold because everything, or practically everything, had been checked out already before they were abandoned and filed away in pending. That's why they were called cold cases.

Hoke decided to go out and eat lunch before González came back from Property. He had to work with González, but if he timed it right, he didn't have to eat with him.

Chapter Five

After lunch Hoke typed his notes about the opener, his speculations, and put them into the Russell file, together with the receipt González brought back from Property. He slid the accordion file back into his pending drawer. He would let his subconscious mind work on the case for a couple of days before he took the file out and looked at it again.

Hoke and González sat across from each other at a glass-covered double desk in their small two-man cubicle. They shared a phone and a typewriter. A two-drawer file cabinet with a combination lock held the cases they were currently investigating. The other cold case they had been studying for the past week was equally baffling. Instead of two accidental deaths, or suicides, it had turned out to be two homicides, and there were no discernible leads.

Miami has termites, just like every other city, but they breed quickly and eat a lot of wood in the subtropical climate. Once they are discovered in a house, a 'tent job' is the only way to get rid of them. It isn't unusual for a homeowner, once termites have been discovered, to have a new tent job every two or three years. Termite swarms have an uncanny knack for finding their way back to an edible house, and exterminators in South Florida thrive on repeat business. The house is put under canvas, and the tenants must stay away for from thirty-six to seventy-two hours while the Vikane gas kills the termites and other insects inside the house. Food and other perishables are placed in plastic bags during the tenting, and homeowners either stay with friends or put up in a motel until it's safe to return home. Burglaries of tented houses occur frequently, and three or four times a year, and sometimes more often than that, dead burglars, overcome by the Vikane gas, are discovered together with the dead insects when the owners return home. Vikane is a powerful poison, and it kills people as easily as it does termites. Burglars who specialize in tent-job invasions wear gas masks and get in and out quickly with their loot. But amateurs who hold dampened handkerchiefs over their mouths and stay too long looking for valuables can be overcome by the fumes and drop dead to the floor like the roaches and termites. Usually, dead burglars are teenagers, high-school dropouts with low IQs, but occasionally they are mature men who should know better. Warning signs are posted on all four sides of the tented house, in English and Spanish, but more than thirty percent of the Miami burglars are illiterate in both languages and cannot read signs. At one time the exterminator used to post a guard in front of the house. But the insurance rates went up considerably. The insurance companies told the exterminators that the fact that they did have guards meant that they could be sued by a dead burglar's family for failing to keep the man out. While a guard was sitting in his car out front, smoking and listening to a rock station on his radio, a house prowler could sneak under the tent through a back entrance. After this decision exterminators no longer posted guards and merely put up warning signs. Exterminators were not responsible for illiterate burglars because high school principals were not responsible for graduating illiterate students.

No female burglar, teenage girl or mature woman, has ever been found dead from Vikane gas in a tented house. Females, Hoke reflected, taught by their moms about the danger of household cleaners, wouldn't be caught dead going into a tented house.

Two dead black men, well bloated by the heat, were discovered by Mr and Mrs James Magers in the foyer of their home, after a tent job. The Magerses, during the tenting, had made a holiday out of it and had taken the Friday-evening-to-Monday-morning cruise to Nassau on the *Emerald Seas*. When they cleared customs and drove home, it was almost 11:00 A.M., and the canvas had already been removed by the exterminating company. The windows had been opened, and the Vikane gas had blown away. The exterminator was still there, however, and so were two uniformed policemen, who had been called by the exterminator when he reopened the house. The Magerses couldn't identify the two dead men, and they had been removed to the morgue. Except for crude

715

tattoos on the backs of their hands – stars, circles, and two inverted V's – there was no other identification on the two men. It was apparent that nothing in the house had been taken. There were no valuables in their pockets, and the house hadn't been ransacked. After checking, the Magerses said nothing was missing. Mr Magers had left his World War II Memorial .45-caliber semi-automatic pistol (a highly pilferable item) in the house, and it was still safe in its glass display case. Mrs Magers had prudently taken her jewelry with her on the cruise, and the purser had kept it locked in his safe when she went ashore in Nassau.

The two men, or someone, had jimmied the front door open, after slipping under the canvas, and dropped dead in the foyer. Death was caused by the Vikane gas. The medical examiner then discovered bruises on the backs of both skulls, indicating that the men had been sapped and then tossed, still alive but unconscious, into the foyer. Also, the killer(s) knew that the bodies would be safely hidden inside the house for at least seventy-two hours, allowing ample time for a getaway. Hoke's problem, and González's, was to discover the identity of the two men. The case was now two years old, and Hoke had no leads. The original investigator, a detective who was no longer on the force, had given up on the case after three fruitless months of checking. The homemade tattoos on the backs of their wrists indicated that they had once been in a Cuban prison or perhaps in some other Latin American prison, and that was all Hoke had to go on. Latin prisoners, in many cases, tattooed the backs of their hands with their crime specialty – burglar, arsonist, holdup man, and so on. But the stars, circles, and V's were not listed on the tattoo ID sheets Hoke had requested from Atlanta, where a thousand Mariel prisoners awaited shipment back to Cuba someday – if Dr Castro ever decided to take them back.

If the two men had arrived during the 1980 Mariel boatlift, they would have been fingerprinted. But there was no record of their fingerprints in Atlanta or in the FBI files in Washington. There were several Mariel prisoners at the Krome Detention Center in Miami. These men had served their sentences for crimes committed in America and were waiting deportation to Cuba, although they would probably remain incarcerated in Krome until Dr Castro died before they could be returned.

'I'll tell you what, Teddy,' Hoke said. 'Take these Polaroid mug shots and the tattoo photos out to Krome, and talk to some of the Cuban detainees. Even if we can't get an ID, they might know what the tattoos represent. We haven't got anything else. They're black men, but most of the Marielitos were black Cubans.'

'Will they cooperate with me at Krome?' González asked. 'The INS, I mean.'

'The INS, yes. But the Cubans may not. They're bitter, you know. They've served their sentences in Atlanta and want to be released to their families here. But you speak Spanish, and you can talk to them. After all, these poor bastards are in limbo here, with nothing else to do. They might cooperate, just to be doing something, or else think that if they help you, you might help them later by putting a good word in their files.'

'Is it okay to promise them that? That I'll write a favorable report for their files if they help me?'

'Why not? A promise means nothing. They aren't going back to Cuba till Castro says they can, no matter what you tell them. See what you can find out about the tattoos.'

'How do I get out to Krome? I've never been out there.'

'First, drive west on Calle Ocho until you reach Krome Avenue. Turn left, or south, and look for the sign. Then talk your way in, and see if they'll let you interrogate some of the black Marielitos. Be sure to wear your jacket. It'll impress the Marielitos with its sincerity.'

'What's wrong with this jacket? This is a Perry Ellis jacket.'

'Nothing. It's perfect for this job, kid. If I had one like it, I'd wear it out to Krome myself. Take your own car, instead of one from the pool, and go on home when you're finished. I'll see you Monday morning.'

After González left, Hoke wrote redline memos to Quevedo and Levine, appointing them to his crack committee. He placed the memos in their mailboxes. They both were on the night shift, and he would be gone before they read the memos and cursed him for giving them this opportunity to serve their division and community.

When Hoke pulled into his driveway and parked behind Ellita's car, Donald Hutton, wearing a dark blue suit, was still sitting in a dining-room chair on his front lawn. Hoke got out of his car without rolling up the windows first, slammed the car door, and crossed the street. He stopped on the sidewalk, not wanting to trespass on the man's property.

'Why are you sitting there, staring at my house?'

Hutton, who had been a tall, spare man to begin with, unlike his dead brother, Virgil, had lost more weight in prison. He unfolded his long arms, which had been crossed over his chest, and placed his spatulate fingers on his bony knees. Unlike Hoke, he had retained all his hair, and it had been teased into ringlets. A fringe of black curls obscured the hairline on his high forehead. His long nose hooked slightly to the left. His deep-set dark eyes were more violet than blue, and he had long black eyelashes. As he widened his eyes, Hoke could see the outline of the full optic circle. A half-smile made Hutton's full lips curl on the right side only, and there was a tiny square of dentist's gold on his right front tooth. He had been a handsome man at the trial, ten years ago, and he had worn a different suit and tie every day. Now that he had a few craggy lines around his eyes and at the corners of his mouth, he was even more handsome. Or craggy. Yes, that's the word for him, Hoke thought: *craggy*.

Hutton pointed a forefinger at Hoke. 'I think I know you, sir. Aren't you Detective Moseley?'

'Sergeant Moseley.'

Hutton nodded. 'I thought you looked familiar, but you've lost a little hair. And you live over there?' Hutton moved his finger slightly to the right, so it was no longer pointing directly at Hoke. 'Then we must be neighbors. What do you do, Sergeant – congratulations on your promotion, by the way – rent a room from Mrs Sánchez?'

'That's Ms Sánchez, and she lives in my house.'

'You aren't married then? That isn't your baby?'

'No, that's Ms Sánchez's son. My two daughters also live with me.'

'I saw them earlier. Nice-looking girls. How old are they?'

'What are you doing out here, staring at my house?'

'There's not much else to look at. But sitting out in the sun has been a rare privilege for me in recent years. I occasionally look down the street because I'm watching for the FPL man to turn on my electricity. The water man came already; but the FPL promised faithfully to send out a man today, and I don't want to miss him.'

'How come you bought this house? This particular house, right across from mine?'

'Oh, I didn't buy it, Sergeant. I leased it for a year at a very attractive rate, with an option to buy at the end of the year. But I don't think that's any of your business. How much did you pay for your house?'

'I'm leasing it.'

'At least your house is on the lake, and mine isn't. D'you ever swim in the lake?'

'Swimming's forbidden. It was a pretty deep quarry, and some kids drowned.'

'A nice breeze comes off the water, though, doesn't it?'

'A hot breeze. But you haven't answered my question.'

'I thought I did. I got an attractive deal, and I've always thought that Green Lakes was a quiet part of Miami to live. It's not quite as nice as I remember it, but it's convenient for shopping. The new shopping center's only five blocks away.'

'You threatened my life, Hutton. D'you remember that, too?'

'Yes, I did, didn't I?' Hutton smiled crookedly. 'But I was upset at the time. After all, I was an innocent man and was sentenced for a crime I didn't commit.'

'You killed your brother, all right. That was proven to the satis-faction of the jury.'

'A new trial would bring a different verdict. But I was denied a new trial. I took the deal, anyway, to get out of prison. But I still didn't kill my brother. Did you ever ask yourself how I, a man fifty pounds lighter than my brother, managed to get him to eat two spoonfuls of rat poison?'

'Many times. How did you persuade him? There were traces even in the roots of his hair, so he took it over a long period of time.'

'I didn't put it in his shampoo either, Sergeant. I loved my brother and wished him no harm. I only hope that someday you people will catch the real killer. But it's written off now, isn't it? I don't hold a grudge against you or the system. I think now you were only doing your job, as they say, so I don't hold a grudge against you. You may disregard my old threat, Sergeant, if you haven't already. I hope we can be good neighbors.'

'We'll never be good neighbors, Hutton.'

Hoke was perspiring freely. It was only 6:00 P.M., and with DST there would be another two and a half hours of sunlight. Hoke took off his jacket. The heat had no apparent effect on Hutton, despite his heavy blue serge suit.

'The only way we'll ever be good neighbors, Hutton, is if you stay on your side of the street and I stay on mine. And keep away from my family.' Hoke turned on his heel and crossed the street. He imagined that he could feel Hutton's violet eyes boring into his back. He rolled up the windows in his car and went into the house without looking over at Hutton. Hoke realized he had come out badly in the little confrontation. He should have ignored the man altogether, but it was too late now.

Hoke showered and wished that he could shave. The dark gray stubble on his chin and cheeks, and the thick mixture of black and red hairs on his upper lip, made him feel seedy and unclean, even after his shower. He put on a pair of khaki shorts and a clean white T-shirt and sat on the edge of his army cot in his small bedroom.

He was angry about Hutton, but there didn't seem to be anything he could do about it. Ten years was a long time for a man to hold a grudge. Either a man would forget about it altogether, or he would nurse it, hugging it to his chest, and let it become an integral part of his being. Donald Hutton was an educated man, with a degree in agriculture from Valdosta State College. He still had a trace of Georgia accent in his voice, but not very much. Voices flattened out, and accents – except for Latins – eventually disappeared after a man had lived in Miami for a few years. Even Hoke called the city 'Miami' now instead of 'Mi-am-ah,' as he had when he first moved down here from Riviera Beach, Florida.

How *did* Donald persuade his brother to take strychnine? This was a point that Hoke had never been able to clear up, although it hadn't mattered too much at the time. Hoke's part in the process was to find enough evidence to go to trial, and he had. What the state's attorney and the jury and the judge did with the evidence was not important to Hoke. Cases where the evidence had been very strong indeed had been lost by the state; other cases, with little or weak evidence, had obtained convictions. But if Hoke worried about lenient judges and juries letting people off, he would be (as some of his fellow detectives were) in a constant state of rage. In Hutton's case the man was surely guilty. Hoke was certain of that, although it hadn't mattered to him whether or not Hutton was convicted and put away. That part of the process was not his job, and Hoke was objective about the outcome of most murder trials, including the ones he had worked on. Hutton, of course, hadn't shared his objectivity. Perhaps now, with the knowledge he had gained at Raiford, Hutton had mellowed out. What did he say? 'You were just doing your job.' Right. By the time Aileen came back to his room to call him to dinner, Hoke had decided that Hutton was not an immediate threat to him or his family. The girls didn't know anything about the Hutton case, but he would remind Ellita to keep the threat a secret from the girls. There was no need to alarm the girls unless there was a need to alert them.

Hoke went into the kitchen and told Ellita to say nothing about Hutton's ten-year-old threat.

'You don't have to tell me that,' she said. 'I'd never tell them anything without talking it over with you first.'

'I realize that. But I don't want anything to slip out. We don't want the neighbors to find out who he is either. Otherwise, they'll be taking walks every night to take a gander at him out of morbid curiosity.'

Hoke took the platter holding the turkey breast out to the table and began to carve it into even quarter-inch-thick slices. There was Stove Top corn bread dressing, mashed potatoes and gravy, and boiled rutabagas. There were avocado halves filled with shrimp salad as appetizers. Ellita had always laughed at the TV commercials of the housewife tests for Stove Top dressing. 'Did the husbands prefer Stove Top dressing to mashed potatoes?' The husbands invariably wanted the Stove Top dressing, instead of the mashed potatoes, but Ellita knew that most men would want both – not one or the other.

There was a dish of jalapeños for Hoke, black and green olives, and a bowl of jellied cranberry sauce. Hoke distributed slices of turkey and then sat in his chair as Ellita passed around the other plates of food.

There was a knock on the front door. Ellita got up. 'I'll get it.'

'If it's anyone for the girls,' Hoke said as he chopped a jalapeño over his turkey slices, 'tell them we're eating now and to come back in an hour.'

'Ellita,' Sue Ellen said, 'says that little car across the street's a Henry J. How much would a little car like that be worth today, Daddy? I've never even seen one before, and we get just about everything through the car wash.'

'I don't know, sweetie. Back in the fifties you could pick up a second-hand Henry J for about a hundred bucks. A used one, I mean. But after twenty years a car in Florida becomes a classic, so it would all depend on how much a collector would be willing to pay for it.'

'D'you think I could talk the owner into a Simoniz job? I could do it Sunday and give him a better price than he could get down at the car wash.'

'We're going to the Sánchezes' Sunday afternoon. Remember?'

'If I can make thirty-eight bucks on a wax job, I'll skip the party. I'm not all that thrilled about –'

Ellita entered the dining room with Donald Hutton. He was carrying a small aluminum coffeepot in his right hand.

'This is our neighbor from across the street,' Ellita said, 'Mr Hutton. You already know Sergeant Moseley, but these are his daughters, Sue Ellen and Aileen.'

The girls nodded and smiled. Hutton shifted the coffeepot to his left hand and shook hands awkwardly with the two seated girls. He cleared his throat and lifted one corner of his mouth in a lopsided smile. 'I, ah, was only asking Ms Sánchez here for a pot of hot water, thinking I'd brew up some instant coffee. My electricity hasn't been turned on yet, and I don't want to go out for anything because the man could show up at any time. I certainly didn't invite myself to dinner.' He looked at Hoke, who said nothing in return.

'I invited you,' Ellita said, gesturing to Aileen. Aileen got up and brought a chair in from the kitchen and placed it next to her seat. Sue Ellen went into the kitchen for silverware and another plate. Ellita took the plate from Sue Ellen and filled it. Hutton sat in the chair Aileen brought to the table, shifting the empty pot from one hand to the other; then he placed it on the floor between his feet.

'Dig in, Mr Hutton,' Hoke said. 'None of us cares for dark meat, so Ellita usually cooks a turkey breast instead of the whole bird, except when she fixes *mole* sauce.'

Hoke passed Hutton the dressing and the gravy boat. His fingers trembled slightly from rage, although his voice hadn't betrayed him. What he wanted to do was kick Ellita squarely in her big fat ass! What in the hell was the matter with her, inviting this bastard to the table?

'This really looks good,' Hutton said. 'It's been a long time since I've had a home-cooked meal.'

'Did your wife die, Mr Hutton?' Sue Ellen said.

'That's a personal question, Sue Ellen,' Hoke said.

'Oh, that's quite all right,' Hutton said, smiling as he spread a heaping tablespoonful of cranberry sauce on his turkey. 'I've never been married. I came close a couple of times, but somehow I just never got around to it. I'm forty-five now, and it's a little too late to start a family, I guess.'

'We were talking earlier about your Henry J,' Sue Ellen said. 'How much is it worth, a little antique car like that?'

'It isn't for sale. It's the only car I've got left. At one time I collected classic cars, but I kept the little Henry J. It's only got twenty-seven thousand miles on it, and I'll just use it for transportation.'

'Would you like a beer, Mr Hutton?' Ellita asked.

'I'm not allowed to drink.' Hutton shot a quick glance at Hoke. 'Doctor's orders,' he added.

What a bastard, Hoke thought; did Hutton think he would turn him in to his parole officer for drinking a lousy beer?

'I wouldn't mind some coffee, though,' Hutton said, smiling at Ellita.

'We usually have coffee later, with dessert. Cuban coffee. And we're having *Tres Leches* for dessert.'

'Three milks?'

'It's a homemade custard. I haven't started the coffee yet, but –' Ellita started to get up.

'Sit down, please. I'm in no hurry for coffee.'

Ellita sat down, and Aileen jumped up. 'Let me make it, Ellita. I know he wants his coffee now, or he wouldn't've brought his pot over.'

'Please –' Hutton held up his right hand.

Aileen went into the kitchen.

'I work at the Green Lakes Car Wash,' Sue Ellen said. 'But I can do wax jobs for people on my own time. I could do a nice Simoniz job on that Henry J for you at a bargain price. Thirty-eight dollars. It'll cost you fifty at the car wash. I can't do it this Sunday because we're going to a party. But I can do it next Sunday.'

'That sounds fair to me.' Hutton nodded. 'I don't have a garage or a carport, so it might be a good idea. If it's going to sit out in the sun all day, that might be the thing to do.'

'Sunday week, then, Mr Hutton. I'll also bring along a can of new car spray, and you can keep it in your car. It'll look like a new car when I finish, so you'll want it to smell like one, too.'

'Sure. Why not? This turkey's wonderful, Ms Sánchez.'

Aileen came back from the kitchen. 'There's a van over in front of your house, Mr Hutton.'

'That's probably the FPL man.' He started to get up.

'I'll go,' Hoke said. He got up and placed a hand on Hutton's shoulder. 'I know where your meter is. Finish your dinner.' Hoke left the house and went across the street. He hadn't been able to take another bite after Hutton had sat at the table.

After the Florida Power electrician had turned on the electricity, Hoke signed 'D. Hutton' and the time on the man's clipboard. He finished his cigarette before he went back to his house. He had calmed down by this time and was half amused by his former anger. He decided to say nothing to Ellita. It was as much her house as it was his, and if she wanted to invite the killer to dinner, she was entitled to feed him.

When Hoke took his place at the head of the table again, Ellita was nursing Pepe. She had folded her T-shirt back, exposing her large alabaster breasts, with faint tiny blue veins. Hutton, a little bug-eyed, was trying to keep his violet eyes off them but couldn't quite manage it. He stared at his plate, and then cut his eyes over, and then shifted back to his plate again, obviously discomfited.

Hoke was able to eat now. He finished quickly so the others could get to their desserts and coffee. Hoke enjoyed Hutton's uneasiness. Hoke hadn't paid that much attention to Ellita's breasts before, but he saw them with new eyes, thanks to Hutton. Ellita was a D cup before she began nursing, but her breasts were much larger now. Pepe, red-faced, nursed audibly.

Hutton refused a second cup of coffee, finished his custard, thanked Ellita again, and left the house. Aileen walked him to the front door and then came back, hesitating in the archway between the living and dining room. Aileen looked at her sister and giggled.

'Did you notice his eyelashes?'

'Did I?' Sue Ellen rolled her brown eyes. 'I'd give my left ovary for eyelashes like that.'

'His eyes are violet, not blue,' Ellita said. 'Just like Elizabeth Taylor's.'

'Jesus Christ,' Hoke said, and he threw his napkin down on the table. He left the table and went into the living room to catch the last half of the *Kojak* rerun on Channel 33. The women cleared the table, and he could still hear them talking and laughing in the kitchen over the cacophony of the New York traffic coming from the television set.

Chapter Six

Saturday morning after breakfast Hoke mowed the lawn. The lawn mower was old, and the blades needed sharpening; but Hoke enjoyed the exercise. The activity, he felt, was good for him, but he wanted to finish before the sun got too hot. It had been eighty degrees at six-thirty, with humidity to match, when he went out to get the newspaper. The paper stated that the highs would probably be in the low nineties. The Henry J was gone, so Hutton, thankfully, was off somewhere. Hoke was pleased about that. He hadn't relished the thought that Hutton might sit out in his front yard and watch him work for two hours.

At ten-thirty, when Hoke had finished the front lawn and was sweeping grass cuttings off the sidewalk, Ellita called him in to answer the telephone. It was Teodoro González.

'Hello, Teddy,' Hoke said into the phone. 'How'd you make out?'

'They let me talk to four Cuban guys wearing orange jumpsuits out in the yard. What they told me doesn't mean much, but they got my Omega.'

'Your wristwatch?'

'Yeah. One of the bastards took it, but when we shook 'em down later, nobody had it on him. I didn't miss it, you see, until I was leaving and picking up my pistol and cuffs at the main gate. We went right back, but by then whoever took the watch had a chance to ditch it. Security said they'd shake down the barracks this morning and let me know if it shows up. But I'll never see it again, and I paid a hundred and eighty-five bucks for that watch.'

'You should've checked it with your pistol at the gate.'

'Tell me about it.'

'What about the tattoos?'

'They said they weren't prisoner tattoos. Those stars and circles were new to them, and they thought the little V's might be initials.

The dead men could be cane cutters, they said, Jamaicans or Haitians, but whatever they are, they aren't Cubans.'

'What made them so certain?'

'Because the tattoos don't mean anything. And only cane cutters would be dumb enough to make meaningless tattoos. I don't see how any of this'll help. There's no cane in Miami to cut, so when I told 'em how the men were killed, they said they were probably *droguistas*.'

'It's more than we had before.'

'I had my watch before, too.'

'You don't need a watch. You notice I don't wear one. If you need to know the time, there's always some asshole around to tell you.'

'Well, don't ask this asshole again because I no longer have a watch.'

'Maybe it'll turn up in the shakedown, Teddy.'

'I don't think so.'

'I don't either. Buy yourself a nineteen-dollar Timex.'

'I'll do that, Hoke.' González laughed. 'Soon's I make my last two payments on my Omega. They all shook hands with me when I left, so one of those slick bastards must've slipped it off then. Far's I'm concerned, those Marielitos can rot out there in Krome.'

'Write up your notes, and put 'em in the file. We might as well bury it in old cases now and give up on it. If they're alien Haitians or Jamaicans, we'll never find out who they were. Unless we get some new leads, it can't be solved till we get some positive ID. But you did well, Teddy. See you Monday morning.'

Hoke showered and then took Ellita grocery shopping at the Green Lakes Supermarket. Aileen stayed home to give Pepe a sunbath and then a sponge bath. Sue Ellen had gone to work at the car wash. Saturday was the busiest day of her six-day week.

While Ellita fixed Hoke a turkey sandwich for lunch, Hoke tried to phone Quevedo and Levine to arrange a committee meeting. Mrs Quevedo said she didn't know where her son was or when he would be back. Myra Levine said her husband had gone to the races at Calder, and she had no idea when she could expect him home. Hoke thought both women were lying, but he couldn't do anything about it if they were. He'd have to set up a meeting later on next week, when he could corner the two elusive detectives at the station.

Feeling restless, Hoke drove Aileen to the Cutler Ridge Mall, bought her a pair of Wrangler's jeans, and then they went to the early-bird movie at Multitheater No. 5 and watched *Friday the 13th: Jason Returns*. Aileen spent most of the movie with her face buried in Hoke's right armpit. Afterward she told him that this was the best version of the Jason story she had seen so far.

'That's because Jason killed mostly cops this time, as well as yuppies,' Hoke explained. 'People hate cops and yuppies, and old Jason keeps up with the trends in each new movie.'

'You always told us that policemen are our friends.'

'We are, and most people know that, sweetheart. But everybody feels guilty about something or other, and cops in uniform remind them of their guilt.'

'Why do people hate yuppies? I don't hate yuppies.'

'Americans hate anyone who's more successful than they are.'

'I don't know a yuppie from anyone else. How can you tell one? I dress well, but I'm not a yuppie.'

'Ask who they voted for. If they like Ronnie and Nancy Reagan, they're yuppies. It's a simple but effective test.'

'But you voted for Reagan.'

'My vote doesn't count. I didn't vote for Reagan, I voted against Carter. Carter let all those Marielitos in and ruined Miami as a decent place to live. You were still living up in Vero Beach with your mom then, so you don't remember what a pleasant place Miami used to be before they let in all that scum.'

'Maria, my friend at school, is a Marielito, and she isn't scum. She's very nice –'

'I'm not an absolutist, baby. Some of them are all right, I suppose. But crime's gone up twenty-five percent because of the Marielitos since they got here. I was talking to my partner, Teddy González, this morning. I sent him out to Krome yesterday to talk to some Marielitos, and while he was talking to them, one of them stole his wristwatch.'

'Right off his wrist?'

'Right off his wrist, and he never noticed it.'

'But he already knew that the Cubans at Krome were criminals. He should've checked his valuables at the gate before he talked to them.'

'That's right. When you grow up, I'd like to have you as my partner.'

'When I grow up, I'm gonna marry a rich yuppie, buy a penthouse condo on Grove Isle, and tool around town in a red Ferrari.'

Hoke sighed. 'My daughter's a yuppie. Where did I go wrong?'

Aileen giggled and took his arm. They went out to find his Pontiac in the parking lot.

Hoke pulled into his driveway at five-thirty. Two Latin gardeners were finishing their work on Hutton's yard across the street. They had cut the grass, trimmed the Barbados cherry hedges, and lopped off some of the lower limbs of the smelly melaleuca tree in the front yard. A formidable pile of cuttings was stacked on the grass verge at the curb. The yard looks nice, Hoke thought. If he gives the house a new paint job, at least it will improve the appearance of the neighborhood. But he wasn't going to suggest the idea; the less he had to do with Donald Hutton, the better.

Ellita met them in the dining room. She had rolled up her long black hair in empty Minute Maid orange juice cans. Ellita had an abundance of hair, and she had used eight cans. Her face was flushed, and her nails, freshly varnished, were the color of arterial blood. Her fingers were spread wide, to allow her nails to dry.

'Can you baby-sit tonight, Aileen?' Ellita held up her hands, palms outward, fingers spread.

'I'm supposed to sit for the DeMarcoses tonight.'

'Can't you take Pepe along with you? I've already fed and changed him and prepared a bottle of water and another of orange juice. If he wakes later, you can give him one or the other or both.'

'You and Rosalinda going out?' Hoke asked.

'Rosalinda got engaged a month ago, Hoke. I told you all about that.' Ellita blushed and turned her head away. 'I've got a date.'

'You've got a date?' Hoke asked.

'I'll take care of Pepe,' Aileen said. 'But I'd better call Mrs DeMarcos and ask her if it's all right to bring him.'

'I already called her. She doesn't mind. And Sue Ellen will be home later, if you run into any problems.'

'You've got a date?' Hoke asked again.

'For dinner and a movie. But we're going to the movie first and then out to dinner. *Los Olvidados*, at the Trail. It's an old Buñuel movie he made in Mexico about slum children. And I've never seen it.'

'*Los Olvidados?*'

'"The Lost Ones." It's supposed to have a lot of surrealistic symbolism, but I've never seen it.'

'Who're you going with, if not Rosalinda?'

'I have a date. What do you care?'

'I don't care. I think it's nice. It's just that you haven't had a date, since, hell, I don't know –'

'In almost two years. And I don't want you to get all upset about it.'

'I'm not upset. I'm pleased. Why should I get upset?'

'Good. You'll have to get your own dinner. But there's turkey in the fridge, and you can make sandwiches. There's still enough *Tres Leches* for dessert, and there's ice cream, too. Heath Bar Crunch, the kind you like. Can you help me, Aileen?'

'Sure.'

They left for Ellita's bedroom (Ellita and Pepe shared the master bedroom), and Hoke got a can of Old Style out of the refrigerator. He didn't recall being told about Rosalinda, Ellita's best friend, getting engaged. If she had told him, he would have remembered. She hadn't told him; she only thought she had told him.

Sue Ellen roared into the yard on her motorcycle. She stripped off her leathers in the living room. She wore denim cutoffs and a Green Lakes Car Wash T-shirt under her leathers. She tossed the garments and her helmet on the couch and sat on the bean bag next to Hoke's La-Z-Boy recliner. Sue Ellen's nose, prominent to begin with, looked larger because it was plastered with white Noskote.

'I'm really tired, Daddy. Can I have a sip of your beer?'

Hoke handed her the can. She took a sip and returned it. 'It's good and cold, but I still don't like the taste of beer.'

'Sit there. I'll get you a Diet Coke.'

Hoke brought her a Diet Coke and sat in his La-Z-Boy again. 'I think six days a week is too much for you, Sue Ellen, especially out in the sun all day. Why don't you work five days and rest on weekends?'

'On Saturday I get double time. And I usually don't mind because we trade off jobs. But today I was drying all day and never got a job in the shade. Drying's easier than vacuuming, but when you vacuum, you can sometimes talk the driver into a pine spray, and you get ten percent off the spray job. But Arturo hogged the vacuum all day and wouldn't trade off with anyone.'

'Why not take Sunday and Monday off then?'

'Because if you don't work five days, the sixth day isn't a double-time day. You know that. But I'm so tired I'm going to take a shower and go to bed right after dinner.'

'I'm making sandwiches tonight. Ellita, apparently, is going out.'

'Ellita's going out?'

'That's what I said. She's got a date.'

'Where is she now?'

'In her bedroom. Aileen's helping her dress, I guess.'

'Why didn't you tell me before?'

Sue Ellen struggled out of the bean bag and ran down the hall toward Ellita's bedroom. Hoke went into the kitchen and began to fix a platter of turkey sandwiches. There was pork, so he made some pork sandwiches, too. He used mustard on the pork sandwiches and mayonnaise on the turkey sandwiches. He put out another plate of sliced tomatoes, in case someone wanted to add them to a sandwich. He set the table and put the platter of sandwiches in the center. The table looked bare, so he opened a jar of pickles and a jar of olives, put some into bowls, and added the bowls to the table. He put glasses at the girls' plates. There was a quart jar of iced tea in the refrigerator, Diet Cokes, and milk. Hoke was hungry, but he waited to eat with the girls. He sat in his La-Z-Boy and lighted a Kool.

Ellita, when she appeared in the living room, flanked by the two grinning teenagers, was transformed. A vision, Hoke thought. She wore a white organdy dress with a full circle skirt, and it fell just below her knees. She wore a pair of five-inch spike-heeled silver slippers, and a thin silver chain belt engirdled her narrow waist. Some cleavage showed in the V-necked dress, but not too much, and her golden skin seemed to glow. She had combed out her hair, and it hung in black curls to her bare brown shoulders. She wore coral lipstick and had touched her high cheekbones with traces of coral blusher as well. She had also used too much Shalimar perfume and had then added musk to that. Shalimar and musk filled the entire living room.

'Wow,' Hoke said, grinning. 'You really look nice, Ellita.'

'Not nice, Daddy,' Aileen said, 'beautiful.'

'What time is it? Is it six-thirty yet?' Ellita said.

'Six thirty-five,' Sue Ellen said. 'Let him wait another five minutes. He'll wait.'

'Where's my purse? The movie starts at seven.'

'I'll get it,' Aileen said. 'It's in the dining room.' Aileen brought the purse, a large patent leather bag. The shoulder strap had been broken and had been tied instead of mended.

'Your old bag spoils the effect,' Aileen said. 'What you need is a little silver evening bag to go with that dress.'

Ellita shrugged. 'No, I need my big bag. I'm just happy I could get into this dress again. Well, I guess I'd better go.'

'Isn't he coming to pick you up?' Hoke asked.

'No.' Ellita lifted her chin. 'He lives right across the street.'

Aileen and Sue Ellen giggled. Ellita looked at Hoke and smiled, but she blushed.

'You don't mean you're going out with Hutton?'

Ellita shrugged. 'Donald came over this afternoon and asked me, so why not? He told me about the Buñuel movie, I haven't seen it, so I said I'd go.'

'Have you got your pistol?'

'In my bag.' Ellita patted her purse.

'Good luck then,' Hoke said, 'and have a good time.'

'I intend to.' Ellita left, and the girls, watching through the screen door, looked at her as she crossed the street.

'The table's set,' Hoke said. 'And I fixed sandwiches.'

They moved into the dining room and sat down.

'Isn't Mr Hutton a little old for Ellita, Daddy?' Sue Ellen asked.

'He's only forty-five, and she's thirty-three. Men like to go out with younger women, as a rule.'

'That doesn't mean you have to go out with them.' Sue Ellen frowned. 'I was propositioned last week by an old man – he must've been sixty-five – driving a Datsun. I told him to grow up!'

'I'd better take a look at Pepe for a sec,' Aileen said, getting up from the table.

'Don't worry about Pepe,' Hoke said. 'Let him sleep. He knows how to yell when he wants something. Get something to drink from the kitchen. I didn't pour you anything because I didn't know what you wanted.'

'Don't get anything for me, Sis,' Sue Ellen said. 'Did Ellita tell you where they were going for dinner, Daddy?'

'No, she didn't.'

'The Biltmore, in Coral Gables. He made a reservation and everything, for ten o'clock.'

'When I came to Miami, the Biltmore was a VA hospital –'

'Ellita said he told the man on the phone to have the wine opened and burping on the table when they got there. Isn't that funny?'

'Yeah,' Hoke said, biting viciously into a pork sandwich. 'That's funnier than a son of a bitch. I only wish I'd been here to hear him say it.'

Chapter Seven

They took both cars to the party for Tío Arnoldo Sánchez. All of his Miami relatives were there. Except for Ellita's parents, Hoke didn't know any of them. There were cousins and cousins-in-law by marriage and a few old men who had known Arnoldo back in Havana thirty years earlier.

Señor Sánchez (Ellita's father) ignored Hoke, as was his wont, and because everyone at the party was speaking Spanish, Hoke didn't try to mingle – nor did he want to mingle. The girls, both a little shy in this Latin gathering, stayed close to Ellita, taking turns holding Pepe so Ellita could talk unencumbered to her friends and relatives. Pepe began to cry, and Señora Sánchez, Ellita's mother, filled his bottle with two ounces of *jus* from the roast beef platter. He enjoyed this greasy treat and stopped crying immediately. Hoke, with a plateful of pig's feet and a long-necked bottle of Bud, shared a yellow velvet couch with two middle-aged, obese Cuban women who had no English whatsoever.

Hoke wanted desperately for Major Brownley to call him soon. No matter what Brownley told him on the phone, it would give him a chance to bug out early. This is why he had insisted on taking both cars, even though his Pontiac had ample room for the five of them, including Pepe's paraphernalia.

Hoke, when they first arrived, had shaken hands with Tío Arnoldo and welcomed him to America. The old Cuban – who wasn't really all that old in years but had been broken in prison and looked as ancient as God – had wept. He looked a little dazed and confused as well. He cried and smiled at the same time, exposing some snaggled teeth in his purple gums, and said something to Hoke in Spanish in a gargling voice.

This was a very emotional family, Hoke concluded – all of them. They laughed and cried at the same time as they talked rapidly and stuffed enormous quantities of food into their mouths.

Tío Arnoldo, Ellita informed Hoke, was the last one left in her father's family, and now there were no more relatives to get out of Cuba. It had cost her father more than thirty thousand dollars to buy Tío Arnoldo a visa in Cuba and to support the old man in Costa Rica until his entry visa to the United States came through. But everyone in the family had chipped in something or other, even if it was only a food package mailed to the old man during his four-year wait in Costa Rica.

Hoke admired the Sánchez family's loyalty but didn't think that the old man would contribute much, if anything, to America. Mr Sánchez would support him, but within a few days Tío Arnoldo would be signed up for SSI and Medicaid and would be hospitalized eventually, free, of course, because he didn't have a dime and was obviously going to die within a few months – certainly within the year. He was brown skin and frail bones, and the last job he had held – twenty-six years ago in Cuba – was that of a file clerk in an Havana bank. As a matter of 'honor,' Ellita had said, Tío Arnoldo had refused to do any work in Castro's prisons, and the wardens had been hard on him.

On the table the pig's feet had looked appetizing, but now that Hoke had them on his plate he couldn't eat them. They weren't prepared the way he was used to eating pig's feet (pickled, and from a jar), but had been fried in bacon grease saturated with garlic. He couldn't cut the thick skin with the white plastic fork he had taken from the table, and the feet were so slippery with hot grease he couldn't pick them up with his fingers either. Hoke returned the uneaten plate of pig's feet to the table casually and went out on the porch to smoke a cigarette.

He finished his beer and put the empty bottle on the porch rail. There was a shrine to Santa Barbara in the front yard. It was surrounded by a well-tended bed of geraniums, and someone had placed a bouquet of roses in front of the three-quarter-size saint inside the concrete brick and stucco shrine. Hoke wondered if Señor Sánchez practiced *Santería* and if he had sacrificed a goat or a chicken in honor of Tío Arnoldo's arrival. He wouldn't put it past him, but he hoped that Ellita was too civilized for such practices. He didn't know for sure. He had thought he knew her very well, after working with her in the division and living with her for more than a year, but apparently he didn't know her as well as he had thought. He still couldn't get over the astonishment that she would actually go out on a date with Donald Hutton, a man who had murdered his own brother.

Hoke had fixed his own breakfast that morning and had heard Ellita and the girls talking in Ellita's bedroom while he ate his Grape-Nuts and toast in the dining room. When Ellita came out to fix her own breakfast, she hadn't said a word about her date. It was none of his business, and he hadn't asked. But his curiosity was high. If she didn't volunteer any information, there was nothing he could do to find out. He could always ask Aileen, who would tell him anything he wanted to know, but he wouldn't take advantage of his daughter's desire to please him.

Hoke flipped his cigarette butt into the shrine and wondered if he had been at the party long enough to leave without hurting the Sánchezes' feelings. He could drive Ellita's Honda home and leave the keys to the Pontiac so she could bring the girls and Pepe home later. Then Ellita appeared on the porch, holding a bowl of mixed rice and beans (*morosy cristianos*) and a plastic spoon.

'I saw you sneak those pig's feet back on the table,' she said, smiling, 'so I brought you something you could eat.'

'You didn't have to do that.' Hoke took the bowl and spoon. 'There're plenty of things on the table I could eat. But those pig's feet are gross.'

'Major Brownley hasn't called yet, Hoke. But I told my mom I'm expecting him to call, and she's been listening for the phone.'

'There've been about a dozen calls already.'

'It's always that way. At a party like this it rings off the hook. People who can't come want to talk to Tío Arnoldo anyway, and people who're coming later want to know what to bring, or they say they'll be late – you know – Cuban time.'

Hoke nodded. 'I didn't hear you come in last night. I watched the news but didn't stay up for *Saturday Night Live* because I was too sleepy.'

This wasn't the whole truth. Hoke had gone to bed earlier than he had wanted to because he didn't want Ellita to think that he was waiting up for her to come home. There was nothing physical between Hoke and Ellita – no sexual sparks – and he had always considered her asexual. But as he had watched the eleven o'clock news, he had considered the possibility that Donald Hutton, after ten years in prison, had looked at Ellita as a desirable sex object and was probably trying to get his hand up under her dress as he sat beside her in the Trail Theater watching the old Buñuel film. And Ellita, being a mature woman, might very well open her legs and encourage such explorations. Why not? She was entitled, and it was none of his business what she did.

'*Los Olvidados* was a good movie, Hoke. It was in Spanish, with English subtitles, but whoever wrote the titles really didn't understand the street idioms. So I had to explain a lot of them to Donnie during dinner.'

'Donnie?'

Ellita nodded. 'He likes to be called Donnie instead of Don or Donald. His mother always called him that, he said.'

'Jesus Christ, the man's forty-five years old! Isn't that a little old for the diminutive?'

'What about Ronnie Reagan? He's thirty years older than Donnie.'

'But Reagan's primarily an actor, like Swoosie Kurtz.'

'Donnie did some acting in prison, he said. They had a little theater group there for a while.'

'I'll bet he did. He did plenty of acting at the trial, too, but it didn't help him any.'

'He told me he was innocent, Hoke.'

'You don't believe him, do you? Monday, if you like, I'll dig out the old files and bring them home so you can take a look at the evidence.'

'I'm not a fool, Hoke,' Ellita said with a little laugh. 'I was a cop for nine years, remember? They *all* say they're innocent. I told Donnie he should try to put it out of his mind. Innocent or guilty, it didn't make any difference to me. He was free now, I told him, and he could start a new life. All of that was behind him.'

'What did he say to that?'

'That he was trying. But inasmuch as he hasn't been given a new trial, and he accepted the parole, his name will never be cleared now. So when he thinks about it, it still galls him.'

'We proved conclusively that he was fucking his brother's wife.' Hoke put the untouched bowl of rice and beans on the porch rail next to the empty beer bottle.

Ellita nodded and smiled. 'He explained all that to me at dinner. His brother wasn't altogether infertile, he just had a low sperm count, that's all. Marie Weller and Virgil had a regular sex life, but she was impossible for him to impregnate. So Donnie was doing his brother a favor, he said, because Virgil wanted a son. She really wanted a baby, too, and was planning to adopt one. So Donnie said he would impregnate her instead, and Virgil would then think it was his, you see. Being they were brothers, the baby would even look something like Virgil and Donnie, and Virgil would think it was his. Virgil and Donnie even had the same blood type – AB. But Donnie said he couldn't get her pregnant either, and he really tried.'

'What a crock of shit! Jesus Christ, Ellita –'

'Isn't it?' Ellita threw her head back and laughed. 'But he was wonderful, Hoke. He told me all this shit with such a solemn face and was so earnest about it. I could just picture him working on Marie Weller with this proposition. She did go to bed with him, you know. Not only in Key West that weekend, as they proved at the trial, thanks to you, but he met her several times at the Airport Hotel. They have reasonable day rates at the Airport Hotel, he said.'

Hoke cleared his throat. 'That's what I heard, too. Look, Ellita, give me your Honda keys, and you drive my Pontiac home.' He handed her his car keys, which were attached to his old army dogtags with a small chain. 'I'd better go home and wait for Brownley's call there. I've met your uncle and put in my appearance, so your folks'll understand if I have to leave for police work.'

'There's going to be a cake later and –'

'Fuck the cake.'

'I'll bring you a piece when I come home.'

Ellita took Hoke's car keys and left to look for her purse and the Honda keys.

Major Willie Brownley called Hoke at seven-thirty. By then Hoke had finished three beers, and he suppressed a belch when he picked up the phone.

'Good!' Brownley said when Hoke answered. 'I'm glad I tried your house first before I called the Sánchezes. It's always hard to get through to a Latin house. When they hear you speaking English, they think it's the wrong number and hang up on you.'

'We do the same, Willie. When I get an answer in Spanish, I hang up, too.'

'I never thought about that, but I do, too, now that you mention it.'

'I went to the party, Willie, but bugged out as soon as I could. It's a madhouse over there. And just as I was leaving, a neighborhood group of kids was setting up to play salsa. The phone was tied up most of the time anyway. Besides, I was getting eager to hear from you so I can shave off this damned stubble.'

'You haven't shaved, have you?'

'Not yet. I've let my beard grow since Thursday, such as it is, and my neck itches. If this is some kind of joke on your part, Willie –'

'It's not a joke. Here's what I want you to do. Wear some old clothes tomorrow.'

'All my clothes are old.'

'I mean some old jeans, maybe a blue work shirt, if you've got one. An old pair of shoes. And meet me at seven-thirty at Monroe Station.'

'Out on the Tamiami Trail?'

'That's right. It's about forty miles out, maybe a few miles more, on the other side of the Miccosukee Trading Post.'

'What's this all about, Willie? Are we going hunting?'

'Something like that. Have you got a hat, a straw hat?'

'I haven't got any hats. You've never seen me wear a hat.'

'Okay, I'll bring you one. What's your hat size?'

'In the army I wore a seven and an eighth.'

'With a straw, I guess it doesn't make that much difference. I'll see what I can find.'

'What's this meeting all about?'

'I don't want to talk about it on the phone, Hoke. And don't tell Ellita about it either. I'll explain everything tomorrow morning.

Now when you get out to Monroe Station, don't go inside. You can park out front where the trucks and dune buggies are, but then you take a little dirt trail on the right of the restaurant, the other side of the gas pumps. That's west of the building. There's a small clearing in the scrub palmettos and pines there called the wedding grotto. The restaurant owner's a notary public, and sometimes he marries people in the little grotto. You'll see the sign. I'll meet you there, in the grotto. The owner uses that clearing as a marriage chapel.'

'Should I bring a present?'

'A present? What do you mean?'

'If I'm going to a wedding, I thought maybe I should bring a wedding present.'

'Don't try to be funny, Hoke. I'm not up to it. I got badly sunburned down in the Keys. And when a black man gets burnt, it's a lot worse than when a white man does. My neck and shoulders are on fire. It seemed cool out on the water, and I took my shirt off. Anyway, that's it. Seven-thirty A.M. In the wedding grotto at Monroe Station. Got it?'

'I've got it. Did you catch anything?'

'We were fishing for permit, so even when you catch one, you still haven't got anything, if you know what I mean. In the morning then.'

Without a good-bye Brownley hung up the phone. Hoke listened to the dial tone for a moment and then racked the phone himself. Willie Brownley was not a secretive man, and this mysterious business was out of character for him. Well, he would just have to wait and see.

Without the girls around, it was lonely in the house. Hoke went out to the White Shark on Flagler Street. He played bottle pool with a detective he knew from Robbery until ten-thirty, drank four more beers during their games, and then went home.

Chapter Eight

Hoke left the house early, stopped for breakfast at a truck stop at Krome and the Trail, and then drove cautiously down the two-lane Everglades highway toward Monroe Station. The Tamiami Trail was an extension of Eighth Street, renamed *Calle Ocho* by the Cubans, but was still referred to by the old-time Miamians as the 'Trail.' When the two-lane highway had been built from Naples to Miami, road crews had worked toward each other from both sides of the state. Monroe Station had been a supply camp then for workers and had found its way onto the state map.

As ordered, Hoke wore an old pair of blue jeans and a plaid, almost threadbare, long-sleeved sport shirt. Remembering the fierce mosquitoes, he wanted sleeves that rolled down to the wrists. He wore his regulation, high-topped policemen's shoes, figuring they were old enough. Although the temperature was in the eighties, he drove with the car windows rolled down, and it was cool enough with the wind coming through. Except for a few trucks, the traffic was relatively light this early in the morning. On weekends, with cars bunched up in clusters, all waiting for an opportunity to leapfrog along the ninety-six-mile stretch to Naples, the Tamiami Trail was a dangerous highway. Head-on crashes were not infrequent. The Miccosukees and the Seminoles who lived in reservation villages at intervals along the Trail had special licenses and rarely drove more than fifteen miles an hour. The Indians were never in a hurry, and sometimes there would be a string of twenty or thirty cars behind an Indian, all waiting for a chance to pass him.

Although Monroe Station is still on the state map, there are just a two-story building and a few sheds on the property. Behind the restaurant, on the ground floor of the wooden building, two hundred yards south on the old loop road, there's an abandoned forest ranger station and a shaky, unoccupied lookout tower. Now that the Big Cypress National Preserve is all government property, the restaurant is merely 'grandfathered' in. When the current owners die, it will be razed, and only the sign on the Tamiami Trail, MONROE STATION, will be left. At one time a good many people lived on the loop road that wends through the Everglades, and Al Capone once owned a hunting lodge in the area. But that's gone, and most of the shacks and trailers that loners and pensioners lived in out on the loop road have been destroyed, too.

Hoke had been out to the Big Cypress Preserve a couple of times on wild pig and wild turkey hunts, but that had been four or five years ago. It had been fun for the first hour or so to ride in a dune buggy; but the hordes of lancing mosquitoes had always spoiled the day for him, and he had never managed to shoot either a turkey or a wild pig. Now, except for the Indians and a few men with special permission, dune buggies and airboats have been outlawed in the preserve.

Hoke parked beside a rusty Toyota pickup in front of the Monroe Station restaurant and glanced at the homemade signs plastered onto the building as he got out of his car.

STOP AND EAT HERE BEFORE WE BOTH STARVE
COUNTRY HAM BREAKFAST WITH GRITS RED EYE
GRAVY AND HOT BISCUITS

NOTARY PUBLIC – MARRIAGES, BUT NO DIVORCES ...

Near the gas pump, on the side of a whitewashed generator shed, a fading blue-and-white poster proclaimed THIS IS WALLACE COUNTRY. George Wallace, when he ran for president, had racked up a sizable vote in rural Florida, and Hoke had all but forgotten the Wallace frenzy. Hoke found the narrow path to the grotto and brushed away some dew-laden cobwebs before he reached the small clearing in the hammock of pines and scrub palmettos. He sat on a wooden bench, lit a cigarette, and slapped some of the gnats away from his eyes.

At seven thirty-five Major Brownley and another black man joined Hoke in the clearing. The major, a squat man in his early fifties, with skin the color of a ripe eggplant, was wearing a pink T-shirt, with 'Pig Bowl' printed on it in cherry-red letters. He wore faded jeans and unlaced Reebok running shoes. The other black man, who was about the same age, was at least a foot taller than Brownley. He wore khaki trousers and a shirt with the creases sewn in, and he had pulled a snap-brim fedora well down on his forehead. His skin was the color of a dirty basketball, and mirrored sunglasses hid his eyes. His wellington boots, rough side out, had seen hard wear. Brownley was carrying two unopened cans of beer and a new straw hat. He handed the hat and one of the beers to Hoke.

'Try this for size.'

Hoke put on the hat and pulled down the brim. 'It fits okay.' He popped the top of his beer and took a long pull.

'This is Mel Peoples, Hoke. Mel, Sergeant Hoke Moseley.' Hoke shook the tall man's hand. Instead of a beer, Peoples was drinking a Diet Pepsi, and his spidery fingers were damp and cold.

'Let's sit down,' Brownley said. Peoples and Hoke sat on the bench, but Brownley remained standing. His short, kinky hair, with shiny black sidewalls, resembled bleached steel wool, and he scratched his scalp with his right forefinger. There was a razor-blade part on the right side of his head. 'I guess you're wondering what this is all about.'

'Not at all,' Hoke said. He put his beer on the bench and lighted a Kool. 'It's pleasant to meet in the 'Glades like this instead of in your air-conditioned office, although I imagine it'll be pretty hot out here along about noon.'

'It won't take that long. Mel and me go back a long way, Hoke. We were roommates at A and M for two years, and we majored in business administration. We were even in business together for a while, scalping tickets to the FSU games.'

Mel chuckled. 'But it didn't last the full season.'

'You got caught?' Hoke said.

'No.' Mel shook his head. 'Our source at FSU was expelled. He never got caught for the football tickets, but he stole the final exams from the social science department.'

'I thought it was the history department –'

'This is interesting,' Hoke said impatiently. 'Should I tell you now about my year at Palm Beach Junior College?'

'Sorry, Hoke,' Brownley said. 'Mel's a field agent for the State Agricultural Commission. A kind of troubleshooter. Isn't that right, Mel?'

'Something like that, and a little more. For six years I was investigating complaints statewide, concentrating on migrant workers. But for the last two years I've been in Collier County on a permanent basis. In the last few years lots of things have changed. What with unemployment insurance, food stamps, and welfare, a lot of former migrants have quit migratin'. After the harvest season, instead of moving on the way they used to, they stay put and pick up unemployment or go on welfare. Then, too, we've got us a large illegal Haitian population, and they ain't movin' either. They've got a language problem, and they wouldn't have no one to talk to if they moved on up to Georgia, say –'

Hoke nodded. 'So now you stay in Collier County because you've got enough migrant problems without moving around the state?'

'That's the size of it. I check growers' complaints as well as migrants'. Haitians are good people, but they're used to tiny one-man farms back in Haiti, so they can't understand teamwork. This makes for discipline problems, and we've tried to get some training programs started. But that takes money, and the legislature ain't going to give us money for people who've entered the country illegally. Technically they ain't even here. But they *are* here.'

'Discipline? You're punishing Haitians because they don't understand teamwork?'

'No, not at all. Say you've got ten Haitians, and you assign each one to a row of tomatoes. They all start out okay, and then one guy gets a little ahead and sees a nice tomato in the next row. He goes over and picks it. Then he spots another, three rows over, even bigger, so he gets that one, too. The other Haitians do the same, and the first fucking thing you know Haitians are scattered all over the field. And half their assigned rows are unpicked.'

Hoke laughed. 'The bigger the tomatoes, the sooner a man gets a full basket, right?'

'Right. But the growers have to use 'em 'cause, like I said, the old-time fruit tramps have quit pickin' and migratin'. They either sit tight on welfare or find other jobs. Then they put their kids in school and register to vote. We've still got a trickle of illegal Mexicans and lots of Haitians, but our old reliable source has dried up. To get harvests in on time, the big growers've been hiring tougher crew bosses.'

'I still don't see where this is leading,' Hoke said, looking pointedly at Brownley. 'I'm working on the old Russell case right now, and I've got a fairly good lead –'

'Finish your beer, Hoke. Let Mel tell you the rest of it.'

'The thing is, Sergeant,' Mel continued, 'you could put Delaware in Collier County and never notice it was there, and I'm only one man. I had me a clerk, but she quit last month because she can make more money puttin' pickle slices on burgers at McDonald's.' Mel crushed his Pepsi can and placed it on the bench.

'I still don't know what you expect me to do about that.'

'You speak any Creole, Hoke?' Brownley said, taking a sip of his beer.

Hoke grinned. 'I just know their worst swearword. *Guette mama!* I was called it once in Little Haiti, so I checked it out.'

'*Guette mama?*'

'Yeah. That's Creole for *linguette mama*, or "your mama's little tongue." At one time, in Africa and Haiti, they used to cut off a woman's clitoris when she got married. It was called the little tongue, a useless thing to be thrown away.'

'My wife wouldn't agree on that,' Brownley said. 'Why would they cut off a woman's clit?'

'Without a clit, a man's wife's less likely to fool around, Willie. They don't do it in Haiti any longer. But it has a nice sound to it as a swearword, doesn't it?' Hoke lowered his voice and growled: '*Guette mama!*'

Brownley frowned at Mel. 'Tell him, Mel.'

Peoples nodded, and sucked his teeth. 'Haitian farm workers've been disappearing, Sergeant Moseley. We didn't notice it for some time because they stay to themselves. Because of the AIDS scare, American black men don't even go after their women, you see. And Haitians don't complain about things 'cause they're afraid of being sent back to Haiti. But word gradually gets around. A family man'll disappear, and his woman'll ask if anyone's seen him. Then someone'll say, "I think he went over to Belle Glade to work." But a Haitian won't leave his wife without sending her money. And they all send money back to Haiti. They're Catholics and family-oriented. But once one of these Haitians disappears that's the end of him. He ain't in Belle Glade or anywhere else. And we don't know how many are missing altogether.'

'When you say "we,"' Hoke said, 'are you talking about you and Willie here, or you and the clerk who went to work for McDonald's?'

Mel shook his head. 'Me and Sheriff Boggis, in Collier County. I also had a dialogue with a deputy over in Lee County, but he said he wished they all were missing, so I didn't talk with him again. But what happened, we finally found a body.'

'You and Sheriff Boggis?'

'No, a truck driver from Miles's Produce, over in Tice. He picked up a load of melons in Immokalee and then stopped on the highway, a couple of miles past the Corkscrew Sanctuary cutoff, to take himself a leak. He went behind the billboard there, the one that advertises the Bonita Springs dog track, and found some toes stickin' up. It had been raining, the ground was marshy, and the foot had worked its way up. He dug around a little with a stick, enough to see it was a foot, and then phoned Sheriff Boggis when he got to Bonita Springs. Boggis took a look, and then he called me out there to see if it was a missin' Haitian. And it was.'

'How'd you know? Not just because he was black.'

'He had a tattoo on the back of his left hand. *Le Chat*, with a couple of pointed ears below the words. The tattoo had been carved in, probably with a razor blade. Haitians, as you probably know, eat cats.'

'No, I didn't know. These so-called ears, could they be little V's?'

'I guess you could say that. Why?'

'Nothing. I was thinking about another case. Go ahead.'

'They eat cats because they think it'll make 'em invisible. It's a folk myth, because no one's ever become invisible by eatin' a cat. But they hear about it, believe it, and then get a cat and try it, you see. If you go to Port-au-Prince, you won't see any cats at all. Dogs, yes, but no cats. Man owns himself a cat he locks it up inside his house, or someone'll grab it and eat it. This Haitian cat eater had this tattoo on his arm to prove it. The little ears were put there to show that the rest of the cat was invisible and inside the man.

'So he was a Haitian, Sergeant. Afro-Americans don't tattoo French words on their hands. Besides, his feet and hands were calloused, and he'd been a field worker all his life.'

'How was he killed?'

'The ME wasn't positive. He'd been badly beaten around his head, and the ME didn't know whether he was dead or just unconscious when he was buried, so he marked it down as "Death by Misadventure."'

'That's pretty damned vague, especially if the man was buried alive.'

'The ME couldn't say for sure. He'd been in the ground too long.'

Hoke nodded. 'So all you have to do now is find the man – or woman – who buried him and see if he's buried a few more somewhere.'

'Yeah,' Brownley said. 'That's what we want you to do.'

'Me?' Hoke shook his head. 'Collier County's a little far out of our jurisdiction, isn't it, Willie? We can't –'

'I know, but this is a special case, Hoke. I told Mel I'd help him out. And we've got something to go on. It's something you could check out in a couple of days. The ME dug some dirt out from under the corpse's fingernails and toenails, and it didn't match the loam where he was buried. It matched the dirt in a grower's farmyard this side of Immokalee. A man named Harold Bock, nicknamed Tiny Bock. That name ring a bell? Tiny Bock?'

Hoke shook his head. 'I don't know the name.'

'There was a feature article on him a few years back in the *Miami News*. He was an old-time alligator poacher, born in Chokoloskee. Then, when the state cracked down on poachers, and they couldn't sell the skins up North any longer, he bought up farmland in Lee and Collier counties and became a grower. His property's scattered, but he's got about two thousand acres, all in two- and three-hundred-acre parcels. He usually runs three or four gangs of workers, and he grows all kinds of shit. But the farmhouse he lives in is on the Immokalee road between Carnestown and Immokalee. Mel got this sample of soil from his farmyard, and it matched the dirt under the dead man's nails. I had it checked out at the University of Miami by Dr Fred Cussler, the forensic geologist.'

'I met Dr Cussler once,' Hoke said. 'White-haired guy, supposedly the world's authority on oolite. But most of the soil in South Florida's about the same, isn't it?'

'In a way – coquina stone, shale, gravel, sand, oolite. But you give Cussler a sample, and he'll tell you where it came from in Dade County. Besides, this Tiny Bock beat a slavery rap three years ago, you see. He had a bunch of winos living in a trailer and was charging 'em more for their food and rent than he was paying 'em. He wouldn't let anyone leave until they paid what they owed, and they couldn't get even. He also gave 'em free wine.'

'So how'd he beat the rap?'

'One of the winos escaped and told the sheriff about the other men out there. Sheriff Boggis went out there and turned 'em loose, but there was no case. Bock had books proving that all these winos owed him money. He was charging three bucks for a plate of beans and a chunk of corn bread and ten bucks a night for a straw mat in the trailer. So there was no case.'

'They do this in Dade County, too, Willie,' Hoke said.

'But this is different. Because of this incident with Bock, a workers' co-op got started in Immokalee, and the growers blame Bock. Half the migrants' wages must be paid to the co-op each week, and then the co-op gives that money, less expenses, to the workers when they finish the job.'

'What you're telling me is that Bock is disliked by the other growers –' Hoke started to say.

'Hated is more like it,' Mel broke in. 'Because of Bock they all have a lot of paperwork to do now, and they can't hide any income from the IRS. Not very well they can't.'

'So anything that happens, the other growers'll all say it's probably Tiny Bock?'

'That's true,' Mel agreed. 'But Bock's the only suspect we have, and the dirt did match at his farmhouse yard. Him and his foreman live alone, 'cept for a couple of pit bulls he keeps in the yard. I was a little nervous the night I went down there to get the soil samples.'

748

'I still don't see what you expect me to do about it,' Hoke said. 'I don't know shit about farming. I wouldn't even know how to begin to investigate something like this. What did Sheriff Boggis say when you told him you were bringing me in, Willie?'

'Mel and I didn't tell Boggis anything about you, Hoke. Mel tried to get Boggis to assign a deputy in plain clothes, but Boggis said his deputies are too well known in the county to do any undercover work. Any deputy wearing civvies nosing around would be recognized in no time. But Mel and me talked this over, and naturally I thought about you –'

'I'm not right for this,' Hoke protested. 'You need a Department of Law Enforcement man, some stranger from Tallahassee. I don't have any jurisdiction in Collier County. If the sheriff found me nosing around, my ass would be buttermilk, for Christ's sake.'

'That's the whole idea,' Brownley said. 'You won't be official. You'll just be a private citizen. If you find out anything, just get word to Mel here. He'll get in touch with Boggis if there's something concrete to go on. I'm asking you to do this as a favor to me because I owe a big favor to Mel.'

'Okay, let me get this straight, Willie. You want me to visit Tiny Bock's farm, sneak past a couple of vicious dogs, and then dig around the farm to see if I can find a few more dead bodies. That it?'

'Not exactly, Hoke,' Brownley said. 'Bock's advertised for crew chiefs in the *Immokalee Ledger*, but no one wants to work for him. Only someone desperate for money'll work for the son of a bitch. Lately Bock and his foreman, a Mexican named Cicatriz, have had to drive over to Miami to find Haitian laborers. They soon quit and drift back to Miami.

'So when you go out to the farm and ask for a crew chief's job, he'll hire you. Once you're living there, you'll be able to check around with no sweat.'

'It won't work, Willie.' Hoke shook his head. 'He'll ask me some questions about farming, and he'll know immediately that I don't know the difference between my dick and a cucumber.'

'You won't be picking cucumbers or nothing yourself. If he hires you, you'll be supervising pickers, and they know what to do. You should be able to supervise a gang of Mexicans, Haitians, and winos –'

'What about my cases in Miami?'

'González can handle things till you get back. After all, they're all cold cases anyway. A couple of days won't matter. I'll have him report daily to Bill Henderson.'

'What I was going to have González do today was to check to see if Dr Schwartz is wearing the late Dr Russell's Rolex and diamond ring. But González isn't subtle, and I have to tell him how to go about it.'

'I'll explain it to him. Is this important?'

'Might be. Schwartz married Russell's widow and drives his Mercedes, so it might be worthwhile to know whether he's wearing his watch and ring as well.'

'Don't worry. I'll tell Gonzáles how to go about it.'

'How?'

'I'll just have him make an appointment. Then, when he goes in, he can take a look when Schwartz examines him.'

'Examines him for what? What's supposed to be wrong with González?'

'What kind of doctor is Schwartz?'

'Internal medicine.'

'Okay, I'll tell González to say he's got a bellyache.'

'No.' Hoke shook his head. 'Ulcer. Two hours before his appointment, make a peanut butter ball, the size of a marble. Let it dry a little, and then have González swallow it without chewing it. In two hours it'll spread out a little in his stomach and look like an ulcer on an X-ray.'

'You sure?'

'A lot of guys beat the draft that way during Vietnam. And it'll work on Dr Schwartz. I don't want him to suspect anything, so Teddy'll have to get his story straight.'

'I understand that. Anything else?'

'Several things. What're you going to tell Ellita and my daughters? I can't just disappear for a few days without a word –'

'I'll tell Ellita you're on a special assignment when I drive your car back. As an ex-cop she'll understand that.'

'You're taking my car, too?'

'You won't need it. And don't write or call Ellita either.'

'There's one other thing, Willie. It might be important, and it might not. But Donald Hutton got paroled –'

'The man who poisoned his brother? You must be wrong. He got a mandatory twenty-five.'

'I know. But he was awarded a new trial on his last appeal. The state attorney didn't want to retry the case, so he's out on a time-served. It isn't all that unusual.'

'You don't think he's still out to get you, do you? After all, it's been ten years.'

'I don't think so, no. But he bought the house right across from me in Green Lakes. If I'm out of town, he might try to get back at me through one of my daughters or even Ellita. I'm not really worried about it, but this is a bad time for me to be away for a few days.'

Melvin Peoples got up, and shoved his hands into his pockets. 'I don't know what this is all about, Willie, but if Sergeant Moseley's family's in any danger, we'd better forget about this idea or postpone it. This investigation could take three or four days or more –'

'Take it easy, Mel,' Brownley said. 'I can handle this. I've got to drive Hoke's car back anyway, so I'll stop by and talk to Hutton myself. The threat he made ten years ago doesn't mean much. But I'll talk to him, and if I don't like what he says, I'll make him move.'

'I already checked with his parole officer, Willie,' Hoke said. 'He told me Hutton can live anywhere he wants, and there's nothing we can do.'

'He can't do anything, but I can.'

'It's not that important, Willie, but I thought you ought to know about it.'

'I'll check him out. Now empty your pockets and put everything on the bench here.'

'What for?'

'I've got a new ID for you. If Bock finds your gun and badge on you, he won't believe you're a crew chief so down on your luck you're asking him for work. Gun first.'

Hoke took his gun and holster from his belt in back and placed it on the bench.

'Cuffs, too.'

'They're in the car – glove compartment – together with my sap.' Hoke put his badge and ID case on the bench. He removed his money from his wallet – eight dollars – and put the wallet beside his ID case.

'What else you got in your pockets?'

'Cigarettes, about a half-pack. This Bic lighter, some Kleenex, some change. Car keys and fingernail clipper. That's it.'

'Okay. Keep the lighter and cigarettes, and put your money in this wallet. It's your new ID.' Brownley handed Hoke a well-worn cowhide wallet that was torn on one side. There was a yellow business card, advertising Goulds' Packers, Goulds, Florida, with an address and telephone number. There was a letter on lined stationery that had been folded and refolded. Hoke took the letter out of the envelope, addressed to Adam Jinks, General Delivery, Florida City, FL, and read it:

Dear Adam,
I got your money order for ten dollars the one from Farm
Stores, but how long do you think ten dollars will last not
long when I still have rent to pay and Lissies been sick with
the croop and needs to see a doctor. I can't find no work here
in hake City where I can take Lissie with me and I been sick
myself. So if you can send another MO soon I won't bother
you soon again.
All my love EVIE.

'I guess,' Hoke said, 'when I get paid I'd better send my "wife" some more money up in Lake City.'

'If you do, it'll be a shock to Evie. Adam Jinks was killed in a knife fight in Florida City last Friday night. By now she knows it, but no one else down here does. I kept his wallet. They brought Jinks up to Jackson, and he died there. I got his effects, such as they are. And because it happened down in the Redland, it didn't make the Miami papers.'

Hoke nodded and looked at the rest of the wallet's contents. There was an unused condom wrapped in a piece of tinfoil, a photo of a freckled young woman with a little girl on her lap, a fourteen-cent stamp with Sinclair Lewis's face on it, and a coupon torn from a newspaper that would entitle the owner to a free Coke at Arby's if he also bought a roast beef sandwich.

'Is this all?' Hoke asked. 'There's no money.'

'Jinks was fired from the Goulds packinghouse, and he was broke. He got knifed trying to steal a man's change off the bar in Florida City. Put your own money in the wallet, and there's your ID. Adam Jinks is an easy name to remember.'

'There should be a Social Security card.'

'He probably knew his number and lost the card. Hell, I lost my card ten years ago and never asked for another. I know my number.'

'All right,' Hoke said. 'If I'm asked, I'll use mine.'

'Give me your teeth, too, Hoke.' Brownley held out his hand. 'Jinks didn't have any teeth, so you can't either.'

'He had false teeth, didn't he?'

'Not when he was knifed, he didn't. He probably pawned 'em, but there wasn't any pawn ticket with his effects. Hand 'em over.'

Hoke removed his upper and lower dentures, wrapped them in a tissue, and placed them in Brownley's hand. Brownley dropped the teeth into his right front pocket. 'I'll take good care of these, Hoke. Soon's I get home I'll put 'em in water with some Polident.'

'How'm I supposed to eat? Without my fucking teeth?'

'Stick to soft stuff for a while, but your gums ought to be pretty tough by now.'

'Without my teeth I look a hundred years old, 'specially with this gray beard, for Christ's sake!'

'You just look down and out, Hoke, and that's the look you'll need to get a crew chief's job with Mr Bock.'

'On the road to Immokalee,' Mel Peoples said, 'you'll pass by Tiny Bock's farmhouse. It's on the east side of the road. Don't stop. Go on into Immokalee and talk to some of the migrants in town before you do anything else. It's unlikely that Jinks would know anything about Bock's hiring problem down in Goulds or

Florida City, so you'll have to pick up that information in town before going out to his farm.'

'I understand that,' Hoke said, nodding.

'Tom Noseworthy's the man to contact in Immokalee if you find out anything. Contact him, and he'll call me, and then you can go back to Miami. When you get to Immokalee, go down the main drag. Go straight instead of taking the dogleg to Bonita Springs, and continue down the street for two more blocks. You'll pass a drugstore and a Sixty-six station, and then you'll see the sign for Noseworthy's Guesthouse. It's a two-story building with gingerbread trim, a bed and breakfast place. Noseworthy's a Bahamian from Abaco. He isn't doing too well with this bed and breakfast place because not many tourists spend any time in Immokalee. But it's a nice place if you can afford it. Sixty bucks a day, with a free breakfast. It's too steep for hot-bed traffic, so at least he gets legitimate guests. Anyway, Tom knows how to get ahold of me, but don't go near him till you're ready to leave.'

'I'll need some money to eat on,' Hoke said. 'Eight bucks and change won't go far.'

'That's plenty,' Brownley said. 'In fact, it's almost too much. You've got to play the part of Adam Jinks, and he's got to be broke enough to actually hit Tiny Bock up for a job.'

'All right, Willie, I'll play it your way this time. But after this you're going to owe me a big one.'

Mel shook hands with Hoke. 'Good luck, Sergeant. I've got to get moving. I'm due back in Naples before noon.' Mel turned and started up the path.

'Just stay here for about twenty minutes,' Brownley said, 'and then go out and hitch a ride on the Trail.' He turned to leave.

'Just a second, Willie. Is this some kind of test or what?'

'In a way maybe, but don't worry about it. Just look at this as another routine investigation.' Brownley trotted up the path to catch up with Peoples.

Hoke sat on the bench and lighted another cigarette. With cigarettes selling for a buck and a half a pack, he would have to go easy on them for a while – at least until he got some more money. Why didn't he tell Brownley to go fuck himself? The story about the dirt at Bock's farm matching the dead Haitian's toenails and fingernails was thinner than his hair, for Christ's sake. There must be dozens of farms in the Immokalee area with the same kind of dirt. For some reason they wanted to get something on Tiny Bock. He didn't have to take this weird assignment. He was on his own now – without a badge, gun, or authority – and he didn't know exactly what he was supposed to be looking for – except those little V's nagged at him a bit – and neither did Peoples and Brownley. Well, he would find out soon enough. Some branches broke up the path, and Hoke got to his feet.

Brownley came back into the clearing. He wiped his sweaty forehead with the back of his hand. 'Those dogs, Hoke, the pit bulls. D'you know what to do if one of 'em attacks you?'

'Sure. I run like a striped-ass ape.'

'No, that isn't the way. He'll catch you. When one of 'em jumps for your throat, he tucks his front legs up a little, like this, see?' Brownley held up his wrists in front of his chest and let his hands dangle. 'What you do then, you grab these forelegs, drop onto your back, and flip the dog over at the same time. Hang on to his legs. This'll break both of his front legs, you see, and then he can't chase after you again. That's all you have to do.'

'No shit? That's all I have to do, huh? Just hang on to his legs. Suppose both dogs jump for my throat at the same time?'

'You'll have to dodge one when you get the other one. But I wanted to be sure you knew what to do in case you got attacked, that's all.'

'You ever do this, Willie?'

'Not with a real dog, no. But when I was at Fort Gordon, Georgia, during the Korean War, we practiced how to do this with a sack of sand. The sergeant would throw the sack at us, and it had two little legs dangling off it. We practiced grabbing 'em, and it wasn't too hard once you got the hang of it.'

'A sand dog and a pit dog aren't the same, Willie.'

'Sure they are. The principle's the same. You'll catch on in time. I just wanted to make sure you knew how to do it, that's all. Good luck, Hoke.'

Brownley waved and disappeared up the path.

Chapter Nine

When Hoke emerged from the shady grotto to stand on the north side of the trail, his Pontiac was gone. Perhaps he should have argued with Brownley to keep the car, but it wouldn't have done any good. A toothless migrant like Adam Jinks could hardly explain how he came to own a 1973 Pontiac with a new engine and a police radio. The rusty Toyota was still there. A tourist family had parked beside the pickup and was disembarking for breakfast (a middle-aged man in green canvas shorts, two teenage children, and an obese woman – the wife, no doubt, carrying a sleepy two-year-old on her hip). Hoke wanted to follow them into the restaurant and drink another beer, but Brownley had told him not to go inside. Besides, he had to guard his eight bucks and change until, somehow, he managed to obtain some more money.

It was another twenty miles to the hamlet of Ochopee, and then seven or eight more to Carnestown, the crossroads where he would have to take the state road north to Immokalee. The Tamiami Trail continued southwest into Naples at Carnestown, and south of Carnestown, two or three miles, was Everglades City, the major port for marijuana coming into South Florida.

The traffic was thinly spaced, and no cars slowed to his raised thumb. Why would they? Without his teeth, and with the stubble of gray beard on his long face, he looked like a wilderness wino. The sun toasted his back through his threadbare shirt, and he was grateful now for the new straw farmer's hat with its green plastic brim. It protected his balding dome from the direct rays. Sweat dribbled down his sides, and his shirt was wet. His balls were damp in his Jockey shorts. There were fewer mosquitoes out on the highway than there had been in the dusty clearing, but there were still clouds of gnats nibbling at the moisture about his eyes and lips. Two hundred yards up the road, across from Monroe

Station, was a small Seminole village. There were a half-dozen chickees behind the peeled pole palisade, and he could see the tops of the thatched roofs of the chickees. At the gate, on the other side of the canal, across the small bridge, there was a small clapboard store selling Indian artifacts. A pipe rack outside the store displayed multicolored Seminole jackets and aprons.

Hoke walked down to the village parking lot and stood under the shade of an Australian pine. There were no tourists as yet, parked in the gravel lot, but he would wait for one and then ask the driver for a ride as far as Carnestown. It would be much more difficult for a man to refuse his direct request than it would be to ignore his thumb from passing cars.

There were buses on the Tamiami Trail, Trailways and Greyhound, but they went straight through to Naples and didn't stop for passengers on the Trail. If a man lived out here in the 'Glades, he either owned his own vehicle or had to cadge a ride with a friend. The migrant camps had buses and trucks, and if one came by, Hoke might be able to get a ride in one or the other; but his best bet, he thought, was a sympathetic tourist.

Monday morning was not, apparently, a good day for tourists of any kind. An Indian kid, black as tar and with a heavy black braid down his back, came out of the village and crossed the road. Hoke watched the boy go into the Monroe Station restaurant and then come out a couple of minutes later eating a Mounds bar. He nibbled the bar as he walked back and then tossed the candy wrapper into the canal before crossing the little bridge into the village again. Ah, Hoke thought, Indian culture at first hand. The Seminoles and Miccosukees both, in Hoke's opinion, were a surly lot. If you bought gas at their Shark Valley reservation station, near their restaurant, the attendant would merely look at you without expression until you told him what you wanted. After he had filled your car, he would take your credit card without saying anything and walk away. You got no thanks or any other acknowledgment from the pump jockey when he returned with your card or change. It was as if the Indian were doing you a big favor by selling you gas, gas that was ten or fifteen cents more per gallon than you could buy it for in Miami. If you asked the jockey to check under your hood, he didn't hear you. He went back inside his office and waited until you drove away, frustrated and angered by his attitude.

The Indian kid with the Mounds bar had not looked at Hoke either going to or coming from the Monroe Station restaurant when he crossed the highway. It was nice to know that officially the United States and the Seminole Indian nation had not, as yet, signed a peace treaty and that the two nations were still at war. This was a mere technicality to the United States, but perhaps the Indians took it more seriously and therefore refused to fraternize with the enemy – except to take American money.

An hour later the sun was hotter yet, but Hoke discovered that if he walked back and forth on the lot instead of standing still, he could discourage some of the lazier gnats. Smoking also helped keep them away, but he was now down to only six cigarettes in his crumpled pack. No more cigarettes, he promised himself, until he got a ride.

The stillness in the Everglades was appalling. There were six chickees inside the compound, but no noise or talking came from inside. The woman inside the open door to the little shop didn't come out to take a look at him. Indians never offered any help or suggestions and merely grunted the price of something if you asked. There was no dickering either. Except for the striped, multicolored Seminole jackets fluttering on the pipe rack, all the other Indian artifacts they sold were made by other Indian tribes – not by the untalented Seminoles or Miccosukees. The turquoise jewelry came from New Mexico, and the rubber tomahawks were imported from Taiwan. But the Seminoles were getting rich anyway. They sold taxless cigarettes and ran bingo games on their reservation in Broward County, and the federal government couldn't do anything about it – so long as they stayed on their reservation. But Hoke wouldn't live out here in the 'Glades if he made two hundred thousand dollars a year. Hell, it would take more than three hours to get a Domino pizza delivered from West Miami!

What *was* he doing out here anyway? No driver's license, no weapon, no teeth, and no ID except for a handwritten identification card in his beat-up wallet – the kind that comes with a cheap wallet when you buy it. Not even a Social Security card for the unmourned Adam Jinks, stretched out now on a gurney in the Miami morgue with the top of his skull sawed off. He shouldn't have let Brownley take his teeth. Even if Adam Jinks was also toothless, he must have had a set of choppers stashed somewhere. The more Hoke thought about it, the more absurd the mission seemed to be. What was he supposed to do? Exactly. Get hired somehow by Tiny Bock or perhaps by his honcho, Cicatriz, and then poke around on the farm to see if he could discover a few more buried Haitians? Cicatriz ... Cicatriz? The name sounded familiar. Of course. *Cicatriz* in Spanish, means 'scar,' so that couldn't be the Mexican foreman's real name. He would have a scar, and it would be a lulu of a scar if he used it as his moniker. Jesus, what was he getting into, and why should he do it?

Hoke lighted another cigarette and decided to return to Miami. He could cross the road to Monroe Station, buy a fresh pack of Kools, and then pay someone – sooner or later – five bucks to give him a ride back to Miami. This was not a legitimate assignment for a Miami homicide detective, and there wasn't a damned thing Brownley could do about it.

A huge Mack sixteen-wheeler slowed slightly as Hoke held out his thumb and pulled to a wavering stop some two hundred yards past the Indian Village. Hoke ran toward the truck but slowed after the first hundred yards, panting for breath. He was almost out of wind by the time he reached the cab. He climbed the three steep steps, opened the door, and collapsed on the sheepskin seat in the air-conditioned comfort of the monstrous cab.

'Sorry,' the young driver said, grinning, 'I didn't stop a little sooner, but I was afraid she'd jackknife on me.'

Hoke nodded, gasping. 'That's okay.'

'I don't know how to back her very good neither. To go one way, you see, you gotta turn the wheel the other way, and even then it don't always back straight. I'm still learnin' how to drive her. You may not believe it, but this baby's got seven shifts forward and three shifts in reverse.'

'Sure, I believe it. But you'd better move it on out 'cause you're still on the road, and someone might ram into you.'

'Right. I'll just take a quick look at this little diagram on the dashboard here. It's got all the shifts on it and stuff. I don't know what all this shit means yet on the dash. What's the tack-o-meter for? When I get her rolling past fifty, that needle spins around like crazy. So I slow her back down to forty-five.'

'It just measures the engine's revolutions per minute, that's all. Ignore it. But forty-five's a nice speed for a rig this size. What're you hauling, fish?'

'Smells like it, don't it? But I don't think it's fish. The back's all sealed up, but the guy on the loading dock had him a couple of cartons marked "lobster tails," so I think that's what I'm carryin'.'

'Didn't he tell you?'

'No, but it don't matter none to me. For two hundred bucks I'd haul a load of dead babies, wouldn't you?'

The driver, with a long chestnut mane, a silver stud in his right earlobe, and smudgy traces of sparse brown hairs on his upper lip, was about nineteen, Hoke thought. He wore tight, faded jeans, running shoes with red racing stripes, and a rose-colored T-shirt with a white sailboat printed on it. A CAT gimme cap rested lightly on the back of his head. He bit his lower lip with concentration as he studied the gear diagram bolted to the dash and then took the lever noisily through five gears as he accelerated. He didn't double-shift, and the truck jerked at each progression.

'I usually skip four and five,' he said, sitting back, 'and it don't seem to make no difference.'

'It probably won't hurt anything on a flat road like the Trail. There's only a one-foot drop in elevation between Miami and Naples.'

'That's where I'm goin'. Naples. You got a driver's license?'

'Yeah, but not on me. I left it back in Miami.'

'Me neither. That's too bad, pops. The main reason I picked you up was because I thought you might have a license. I don't mean I'd let you drive or nothin', but I wanted to tell a trooper, in case he stopped me, that you were the driver and you was givin' me lessons drivin' across the Trail. See what I mean?'

'Not exactly. Who're you driving for? What company?'

'He didn't say. I was drinkin' a Miami Nice Slurpee and readin' *Auto Trader* outside the Seven-Eleven on Bird Road when these two guys drove up in a brown Volvo. Black guys. I guess I must've looked at 'em a little funny, you know. I never seen a black man drive a Volvo before, have you?'

'Never.'

'Anyway, the driver got out and asked me if I knew how to drive a truck. I told him I sometimes drove my dad's pickup, and then he asked me if I wanted to make two hundred big ones. "Sure," I said, and got into their Volvo. We went to this warehouse over in Hialeah, and this here's the truck they give me to drive. He paid me a hundred in advance, and when I get to Naples, to the warehouse there, I get the second hundred.'

'In that case,' Hoke looked out the window, and peered at the rearview mirror on his side, 'we should have a brown Volvo riding shotgun right behind us.'

'I did, for a while. But they had them a flat tire back at Frog City. I suppose they'll catch up, though, 'cause I've been holdin' her down to forty-five.'

'What you've got here, son, is a load of hijacked lobster tails.'

'I think so, too. But I didn't steal 'em. I'm just a driver, and I was paid to drive a truck to a Naples warehouse for two hundred bucks. So even if I'm stopped, the worst they can do to me is get me for not havin' no license.'

'They're robbing you.'

'What do you mean?'

'This load's worth at least two hundred thousand bucks, maybe more, and you're only getting two hundred dollars. If I were you, I'd ditch this truck somewhere in Naples and then call the bastards and ask for more money before delivering the load.'

'Do you think I should?'

'I would. You can do as you please. But now that nobody's trailing you, you could take the cutoff into Everglades City when we hit Carnestown, hide out overnight, and then make your call tomorrow. By then they'll be ready to dicker. Either that, or they'll find and kill you.'

'I think I'll just take her on in to Naples.'

'Suit yourself. But you can get another thousand, easy.'

'Or a bullet.'

'Or even a burst of bullets. Two hundred grand is a lot of bread.'

'It don't take all that long to fix a flat. They might be right behind me already, just hangin' back a little.'

'They might.'

'But it's sure temptin', what you said.'

'What else you do, son, besides hang around the Seven-Eleven?'

'Well, I worked at Burger King for a while. But I don't really see myself as a fast-food man, not on a regular basis. I been thinkin' about joinin' the army.'

'When?'

'When my two hundred bucks runs out!' The kid laughed. 'I ain't in no all-fired hurry to join no army.'

They passed through Ochopee – a gas station, the world's smallest post office, a grocery store, an abandoned motel, and a restaurant that also offered dune buggy and airboat rides to tourists – and then continued on to Carnestown without talking. Hoke got out of the truck, and thanked the driver for the ride, wished him good luck in the army – that made the kid laugh – and walked across the highway to the ranger station, thinking that he could have made a nice arrest of a hijacked truck. But he was confused by mixed feelings. It still wasn't too late. An anonymous telephone call to Sheriff Boggis in Naples would take care of it. On the other hand, the kid had been good enough to give him a ride, and he had liked the boy. Besides, at the moment, he wasn't Sergeant Moseley. He was Adam Jinks, itinerant fruit tramp. Fuck Brownley, and fuck the law; he didn't even have his badge or weapon.

The gray-haired lady behind the counter handed Hoke a partially filled four-ounce cup of grapefruit juice. Hoke tossed it down and asked for another.

She set her lips in a prim line and shook her head. 'Sorry, only one cup to a visitor.'

'Two ounces isn't much grapefruit juice.'

'T'aint s'posed to be. It's just a sample, that's all. We get tourists in here who'd drink it all day, just 'cause it's free.'

Hoke left the counter and studied the large relief map of Florida on the wall. Carnestown was just a crossroads, and no one lived here. Most travelers would stay on the Tamiami Trail into Naples, but sometimes tourists, to avoid traffic in downtown Naples, took the state road north to Immokalee. From Immokalee, they could take the dogleg road west again to Bonita Springs and then get on the Tamiami Trail again north of Naples and miss all the stoplights downtown. Hoke hoped that some of them would take the longer road into Immokalee today. Hoke walked back to the crossroads and waited in the sun for a ride to Immokalee. An hour later an old black man driving a half-ton Ford truck loaded with watermelons stopped. Hoke opened the door, and the black man shook his head. He pulled his lips back and squinted his eyes. 'In the back! If this was your truck, would you let me ride up front?'

'Sure. Why not?'

'You want a ride, you get in back!' He jerked his thumb.

Hoke slammed the door, climbed into the back, and found a narrow space for his feet on the truck bed. He didn't sit on the melons. He bent forward awkwardly to hold on to the front part of the bed, and the truck lurched away. The load was too heavy for the pickup, and the driver never got above forty all the way into Immokalee. When the old man backed into a loading platform of a packinghouse off the main road, Hoke climbed down stiffly. Both his feet had gone to sleep, and he pounded them awake, stamping on the asphalt lot. His back was sore from holding the scrunched-over position, and he hadn't seen any mailbox with a 'Bock' on it when he had passed the widely spaced farms. As Hoke straightened, his back made little cricking noises. The black driver disappeared inside the warehouse before Hoke had a chance to thank him for the ride.

It had been at least eight years since Hoke had been in Immokalee, driving through without stopping on a trip to Fort Myers, but he didn't think the little town had changed much. There was a fresh coat of oil on the main drag, and he didn't remember the stoplight's being there at the dogleg into Bonita Springs. But the buildings were just as ancient, and there was a fine layer of dust over everything. Hoke walked to the nearest gas station and asked the attendant, a teenager wearing a white 'Mr Goodwrench' shirt, for the key to the men's room.

'Hell, you know better'n that,' the kid said. 'You're s'posed to use the place down by the pepper tree. Get outa here! My john's for customers.'

The rejection astonished Hoke at first, and for a moment he considered taking the key off the doorjamb, where it was hanging, wired to a railroad spike, and using the toilet anyway. But the moment passed. His cover was working; he looked like a tramp, and he was being treated like one.

Hoke looked down the highway and spotted the tall, dusty pepper tree. It was on the edge of a hard-dirt parking lot next to a building painted a dull lamp-black. CHEAP CHEAP GROCERIES had been painted in white letters above the door of the black building. There were seven or eight Mexicans near or under the spreading branches of the pepper tree. One sat in a rubber tire that had been attached to a limb by a rope; three men sat together on a discarded, cushionless davenport; and the others merely stood there, talking and smoking. This was obviously a work pickup spot, but they were all Mexicans here. If someone needed a man for an hour or an all-day job of some kind, he drove to the pepper tree and picked up a worker. Pay for the job would be negotiated, and off the man, or two or three men, would go. There were several of these unofficial pickup stations in Miami, in Coral Gables, Liberty City, Coconut Grove, South Miami, but those were reserved for unemployed blacks. There were no black men here under this tree. Hoke walked across the lot and looked beyond the tree. Behind the tree was a row of dusty waist-high bushes, and behind them a wooden rail was balanced across a sluggish irrigation ditch. This was the open-air john, and the bushes screened it from the road. Clumps of wadded newspaper littered the ground. Hoke took a leak, returned to the shade of the tree. Across the street was a long row of one-room concrete blockhouses. Each house had been painted either pink or pastel green, but most of them were pink. There were several blacks in each house, and he could see them inside through the shadeless windows. A good many children played in the dusty yards. Three skinny black kids were kicking a sock-ball with their feet, passing it to one another without letting it touch the ground. There was no laughter. Not letting the sock-ball touch the ground was a serious matter to these Haitian boys.

Two Mexicans looked at Hoke incuriously when he joined them under the tree. One was tall; the other was much shorter and had a gold tooth. Hoke offered them cigarettes, but they were already smoking, so they shook their heads.

'How's the job situation?' Hoke asked.

'Picky spanee?' the tallest Mexican said.

'A *poco.*'

'*Malo.*' The tall man field-stripped his cigarette and began to roll another with Bull Durhan and wheat-straw paper. Hoke offered his pack again, but the man ignored it.

'You ever hear of Tiny Bock?' Hoke asked.

The shorter Mexican smiled, flashing his gold tooth. '*El Despótico!*'

The taller Mexican lighted his fresh cigarette with a kitchen match and shook his head. '*El Fálico! Buena suerte.*'

The two men moved away from Hoke as he lit his Kool.

Hoke went into the Cheap Cheap Grocery Store. It was more than just a grocery, although there were plenty of canned goods and a small produce section. There were also farm implements, rope and hoses, and bins of hardware items. Tables were piled high with blue jeans, bib overalls, khaki and denim work shirts, and rolls of colored cloth. There was a strong smell of vinegar, coffee, tobacco, and disinfectant. A pasty-faced white man stood behind a narrow counter next to a chrome cash register. There was a heavy mesh screen in front of the counter, with a pass-through window blocked by a piece of polished cedar.

'Let me have a pack of king-size Kools,' Hoke said.

The man reached behind him and put the pack on the counter. He slid the piece of wood to one side. 'Dollar seventy-five.'

'In Miami they're a buck and a quarter.'

The man put the cigarettes back and pointed east with his meaty arm. 'Miami's that way.'

'Give me a sack of Golden Grain and some white papers.'

'No Golden Grain.'

'A can of Prince Albert, then, and a pack of Zig Zag. White.'

765

Hoke paid for the tobacco and papers and rolled a thick ciga-rette. He lighted it and inhaled deeply. He hadn't rolled a cigarette in several years, and he had forgotten how good Prince Albert tobacco smelled and tasted. He would be able to roll at least forty cigarettes out of a can of tobacco, too.

'Does Mr Bock ever trade here with you?' Hoke asked.

'Is a bear Catholic?'

'I heard he was hiring.'

'My hearing's bad. But you can hear almost anything down at the Cafeteria.'

'What's the name of it, the cafeteria?'

'The Cafeteria. I just told you. Cross the road and down two blocks. You'll see the Dumpster in the parking lot.'

'Thanks.'

'What for?' The proprietor moved the block of wood back into place.

There were at least a dozen men in the parking lot, most of them in the near vicinity of an overflowing Dumpster, and a few cars were parked on the perimeter. Some of the men were hunkered down, Texas-style, squatting on their heels. Others were in small groups, and a few sat on wooden boxes. There were no Mexicans. Three bearded white men, middle-aged or older, were sharing a bottle of peach Riunite. The front glass window of the cafeteria, lettered THE CAFETERIA in black capitals and painted on the inside of the glass, had a handwritten menu taped to it beside the entrance. Hoke examined the menu, checking the prices.

With one meat, either roast pork or roast beef, a diner could have all the vegetables he could eat for $3.95. Soup was fifty cents a bowl, or a person could order a bowl of vegetables for thirty-five cents. Bread pudding, with white sauce, was fifty cents. Coffee or iced tea was a quarter. Corn bread was eight cents a slab, and margarine was two cents a pat. At these prices most of the tables inside were filled with customers. Tables were shared, and none of the chairs matched; but the diners were eating ser-iously. Little talk was going on, and they were going and coming from the line, serving themselves from large square pans at the steam table.

There was a heavy-set black woman working the stoves and refilling pans at the steam table. Several large pots simmered on the stove. A brown-skinned man with a hooked nose, mottled skin, and glittering black eyes worked the cash register at the end of the line. He also checked the tickets on all of the diners who came back for refills. A person with a $3.95 check could have more vegetables – all he wanted – but the man had to make sure that someone with a thirty-five-cent check didn't get another refill without paying another thirty-five cents.

Hoke got a tray, a bowl of thick lentil soup, and two slabs of corn bread, without the margarine. He paid and sat at a small table for two against the wall. Hoke thought this was the best lentil soup he had ever tasted. The soup was flavored with fatback, diced carrots, onions, barley, summer squash, beef stock, garlic, pepper-corns, and just the right amount of salt. Condiments were in a tin rack on the table. Hoke shook a few squirts of Tabasco sauce into his soup and began to spoon it into his mouth. A meal like this in Miami, he thought, if a man could find one like it, would cost at least five bucks. Little wonder the place was so crowded.

An Oriental woman nodded and bobbed her head and then slid silently into the empty chair across from Hoke. She had a large bowl of stewed okra and tomatoes and a piece of corn bread on her tray. Hoke stopped eating for a moment, to see if she was going to attack her gooey bowl with chopsticks, but she began to eat with a soup spoon.

The bank digital temperature gauge down the street had regis-tered ninety degrees. Hoke knew that Florida bank clocks were correct, but they always set their temperature gauges lower to avoid upsetting passing tourists, so it was at least ten degrees higher inside the unair-conditioned cafeteria. All the burners on the kitchen stove were lit, the oven was baking more corn bread, and the body heat from the sweaty diners added to the humidity. By the time Hoke finished his hot lentil soup, he was perspiring freely from every pore. He wiped his forehead and eyes with a paper napkin and returned to the line for a glass of iced tea. For a quarter he received a vase-size glass of overly sweetened tea, filled to the brim with chopped ice. He returned to his table, rolled a cigarette, and sipped his tea. Between sips he nibbled on chips of ice and inhaled deeply, savoring the taste of the aromatic tobacco.

The woman across from him giggled. 'Smoking no good for you.'

'Tell me about it.'

'You make me one. Smoking no good for me, too.' She giggled again.

Hoke rolled a cigarette, licked the paper, and handed it over. He lit her cigarette with his lighter. As soon as she had it going, she reversed the cigarette and put the fire side inside her mouth, holding it between her lips, and allowing the smoke to escape through her broad, flat nose. She removed the cigarette and smiled. 'My way, Filipino way, no waste smoke.'

'Don't you burn your tongue?'

She shrugged. 'Sometimes.' She replaced the fire side inside her mouth and puffed away.

'D'you live around here?' Hoke asked.

'Why? You want to fuck?' She removed the cigarette from her lips and spooned up the last of her tomato and okra stew. Chewing slowly, she looked into Hoke's eyes.

Hoke looked at her a little differently now. He didn't know whether she was a good-looking woman or not, nor could he guess her age. It had always seemed to Hoke that Oriental women looked about eighteen for many years, then suddenly turned forty overnight. There were a few crow's-feet around her slightly slanted eyes, but her thick hair was so black it had tints of blue in it when the light caught it. Her skin, the color of used sandpaper, was smooth, however, and she wasn't wearing makeup, not even lipstick. She wore a pale blue elastic tube top, and her breasts were barely discernible beneath the stretchy material. Her arms were as thin as a British rock musician's but were more wiry than skinny. On the ring finger of her left hand she wore an aluminum skull-and-crossbones ring, with tiny red glass eyes. Hoke remembered having had one just like it in junior high school. All the guys wore them then; they sold these rings in Kress's for a quarter. The teachers had hated the rings for some reason, making them even more popular.

'To answer your invitation, miss, that's just about the last thing I have on my mind right now. D'you know what *peristalsis* means?'

'You show me. I try it.'

'No, it's something I have to do all by myself. After this load of lentils I have to go down to the pepper tree to take a crap.'

'Pepper tree's for Mexicans.' She pursed her lips and lifted her chin, pointing to the cash register. The proprietor was examining a dwarf's check before allowing him to fill up his bowl again with collards. 'You are white man. He'll let you use his john.'

'Okay,' Hoke said, getting to his feet, 'I'll ask him.'

'You ask Mr Sileo. I wait. I save table for us.'

'You don't have to wait for me.'

'I wait.'

'I'd like to use your john, Mr Sileo,' Hoke said when he reached the register.

'It's for employees only.'

'And the pepper tree's for Mexicans, right? Where do white men go? I don't have a car, so I can't use the gas station.'

'You want a job?'

'Sure. I'm looking for work.'

'Okay, then.' Sileo took a key out of his front pocket and handed it to Hoke. 'The door next to the storeroom back there. Wash your hands when you get through, and start on the pots and pans. Marilyn'll need more pans soon, and then get going on the dishes.'

When Hoke came out of the john, there were a half-dozen dirty pots and pans in the sink. He turned on the hot water and went to work. His cuffs got wet, and he removed his shirt, which was already soaked through with perspiration. He hung it on a nail beside the storeroom door. When he finished a pan and dried it, he placed it on the counter. Marilyn, the fat black cook, would immediately start chopping vegetables into it. She chopped zucchinis, summer squash, onions, and potatoes with equal rapidity. The potatoes, Hoke noted, weren't peeled, nor were they entirely clean. But Marilyn knew exactly what she was doing, and she had several pots working on the stove. Hoke began on the dishes. He washed them in soapy water, rinsed them in clear hot water, and then carried the still-damp stacks of dishes to the counter beside the steam table. His job reminded him of the KPs he had pulled during basic training at Fort Hood, back in the Vietnam War, except that he was the only kitchen policeman here and soon found out that he was the dining-room orderly as well. When he got caught up on the dishes, Mr Sileo sent him out to clear and wipe the tables. The diners were supposed to bring their own trays and plates to the pass-through to the sink. Most of them did; but some didn't, and those who didn't left the messiest tables. Hoke got into the rhythm of the work and forgot all about the Filipino woman. Later, when he was mopping the kitchen floor, he remembered her, but by that time she was gone.

The cafeteria was open from six to six, but at five-thirty Mr Sileo locked the front door. He let the diners inside finish but didn't allow any more in.

Marilyn took all of the leftover vegetables from the steam table (but not the meat) and poured them all – mixed as they were – into a twenty-gallon pot. She held open the back door for him, and Hoke carried the heavy pot out to a tree stump that had been cut across the top to form a flat surface. The men in the lot were already lined up at the stump and were more orderly than he would have expected them to be. They came by with coffee cans, tin cups, and other receptacles (one guy had a cardboard box, lined with Reynolds Wrap foil), to dip out of the pot. When the pot was empty, Hoke brought it inside and washed it. He swept and mopped the dining-room floor and carried out two cans full of garbage to the Dumpster. The lot was empty. After eating, the al fresco diners had disappeared.

Mr Sileo handed Hoke a five-dollar bill. 'Want to work tomorrow?'

'Not for only five bucks I don't, no.'

'You only worked a half-day. All day you get ten, plus you eat free.'

'Hell, that isn't even a buck an hour.'

'Sure it is, if you count what you eat.'

'I don't know, Mr Sileo. I'll have to sleep on it. What kind of retirement plan have you got?'

Marilyn laughed, throwing her head back. Her body, including her massive buttocks, shook all over.

'What's so funny?' Sileo turned on Marilyn. 'No man ever stays more'n three or four days! I'd be crazy to set up any kind of retirement plan.' He turned back to Hoke, a little calmer. 'You want to work tomorrow, old-timer, be here at five-thirty. Otherwise, forget it.'

Marilyn had eight slices of bread on the worktable, and she made four roast beef sandwiches. She sliced the beef into quarter-inch slices, and each sandwich had two layers of sliced meat. She put two sandwiches into a brown paper bag for Hoke and wrapped her two in waxed paper. She had a vinyl shopping bag, and it was half-filled with canned goods, mostly pork and beans and canned pineapple slices. She added her wrapped sandwiches to the bag.

'I got carryin' privileges,' she said, smiling at Hoke. 'But I been here for almos' six months now.'

'I noticed,' Hoke said.

Mr Sileo padlocked the walk-in freezer, the refrigerator, and the storeroom. He hit the No Sale key on the antique cash register, placed a twenty-dollar bill in the till, and left the drawer open. There was no other money in the till, but Hoke hadn't seen him remove it. Either it was in his pockets, or he had locked it away in the freezer while Hoke watched Marilyn make the sandwiches.

Sileo frowned at Hoke. 'Somebody breaks in and don't find any money, he gets mad and breaks things up. So I always leave a twenty, just in case. It's cheaper'n buying new tables and equipment.'

'Have you had many break-ins?'

Sileo shook his head. 'Not since I been feedin' the homeless any leftovers. They kind of watch out for me now.'

'I heard down at the pepper tree that Mr Bock's been looking for a crew chief. That's what I do, you know. I haven't worked in a kitchen for years.'

'You did a good job here. Mr Bock's always lookin' for help, but you'll have a much easier life workin' here for me.'

'I need at least forty bucks a day, Mr Sileo. I've got a sick wife up in Lake City to support.'

'You'll make that much with Bock, but you'll earn it – that is, if you've got the belly for it.'

'What d'you mean by that?'

'He works Haitians, that's why. And he specks to get as much out of them as Mexicans. So his crew chiefs have to produce, that's all I mean. I don't hold nothin' against Mr Bock. He eats in here sometimes. You're big enough to run a crew, but I didn't figure you for a hard man.'

'How do I get to his farm?'

'You don't want to go out there tonight. He'll be down at the farmers' market in the morning around five. I'll be there too, buying produce, and I'll point him out. I think once you talk to him or his foreman you'll come back here with me.'

'I'll be there.'

Marilyn and Hoke went out the back door, and Sileo barred it from the inside. Sileo left by the front door and double-locked it. Hoke said good-bye to Marilyn in the parking lot. She squeezed her body into a fenderless whale-shaped VW Beetle with oversize tires and drove away. The sun was down, but there would be at least another hour of daylight. The western sky was a mass of purple clouds, each of them edged in gold, and there was a slight breeze from the 'Glades.

The Filipino woman Hoke had eaten lunch with rose from a wooden crate beside the Dumpster. She came over and plucked at Hoke's arm.

'You come home with me now?'

'Sure. In fact, if you've got a beer at home, I'll even share my sandwiches with you.'

Chapter Ten

Mrs Elena Osborne, née Elena Espenida, lived in the Lucky Star Trailer Park with her son, Warren, about nine sparsely settled blocks away from the cafeteria. As they walked together, Elena told Hoke a few things about her life. She was from San Fernando, Luzon, in the Philippine Islands, and had married a retired army staff sergeant. One of her friends in San Fernando had obtained a copy of a magazine called *Asian Roses*. The magazine was published and edited in Portland, Oregon. The subscribers were Americans, Australians, and New Zealanders who wanted to marry Asian women. Girls and women from Hong Kong, the Philippines, Japan, and Hawaii sent in their photographs, short biographies, and five dollars and were listed in the magazine. She and her girlfriend both had sent in snapshots, biographies, and five-dollar money orders. Her girlfriend had received three letters, and Elena had received only two. Her girlfriend was too timid to answer her letters, but Elena had answered one of hers. She hadn't answered the other because it came from a seventy-one-year-old man who had recently lost his wife, and he had merely wanted a young woman to keep him warm at night. But the other letter, from Sergeant Warren Osborne, was very persuasive. He was a very handsome man who wanted a mother for his children and a companion to share his life in Immokalee, Florida. He had been retired from the army for two years, owned his own mobile home in the Lucky Star Trailer Park, and worked as a checker for Sunshine Packers. He also owned a Toyota pickup, only two years old, and he had never been married before. His mother had lived with him in the mobile home, but she had been dead for more than a year, and he was very lonely. He also felt, now that he was forty, that it was time to get married and have a son to carry on his name. He had told the truth about Immokalee, explaining that the town was in a rural area, with the same climate as the Philippines and that there were cities nearby – Naples and Fort Myers – where they could go and shop on weekends and see first-run movies and major-league baseball games during spring training.

They had corresponded, and after a few airmail letters back and forth, and discussions with her mother, Elena had agreed to marry him. She was twenty-one years old, and although she had an eighth-grade diploma and could read and write English very well, her opportunities to find a husband in San Fernando as well-off as Sergeant Osborne were nonexistent. When she agreed, he made all the arrangements for her visa through a lawyer in Fort Myers and sent her two hundred dollars and her airplane ticket from Manila to Fort Myers, Florida. She had given her mother one hundred dollars of the two, packed a suitcase, and made the long flight, changing planes in San Francisco. He met the plane in Fort Myers, and they were married three days later in Immokalee. Her son, Warren Junior, was born ten months later. Her husband began to drink then, after her son was born, and, after three or four months, was fired from his job at Sunshine Packers. After he lost his job, he drank even more than he had before, and when he got drunk, he would sit at the little table in their trailer and cry.

One morning he went to the bank, drew out all his savings, and gave her five hundred dollars. He was going to drive upstate, he told her, and look for work. When he found a job, he would come back for her, Warren Junior, and the trailer. No one in Immokalee, he told her, would hire him now, so they had to move away. That was almost three years ago, and she hadn't heard from him since. His army retirement checks were no longer deposited electronically in the bank, and the teller at the bank didn't know his new address.

When her money was exhausted, she had applied for welfare, and she got an extra allowance because of Warren Junior. She also got food stamps, but there was very little cash left to live on after she paid her mobile home space rent and utilities. To make extra money, which she needed for Warren Junior, she occasionally turned a trick.

Hoke was puzzled mildly by her story. But not for long.

There were twelve trailer homes in the dusty park. A barbed-wire fence surrounded the lot, which had a single entrance gate.

Only residents had a key to the gate, and those residents who owned cars parked them outside the fence in a graveled lot. The manager lived in the first trailer beside the gate, and when Elena opened the gate with her key, he poked his grizzled head out of his front door to see who it was and then slammed his door again when he recognized Elena.

Elena's trailer was small, with one bedroom and a double bed, a combination living room and galley, and a short corridor to the bedroom. There was a bathroom off one side of the corridor and an alcove closet across from the bathroom door. The furniture was mobile home standard, with an eating nook and cushioned seats. A window air conditioner labored away above the table. A thirteen-inch black-and-white TV set was bolted to the wall beside the entrance door, and Elena switched it off when she ushered Hoke inside. There was a nose-tingling odor of urine and feces, but the trailer was clean. A framed black-and-white photo of Warren Osborne in his uniform was on the wall. The man was handsome enough, Hoke noted, but the photo of the soldier had been taken when he was nineteen or twenty years old.

Warren Junior was in a quilted box in the closet alcove, and Elena pulled the box out so Hoke could take a good look at him. The boy was wearing a Pamper, but nothing else. He moved his thin arms feebly within the box. His tiny legs had atrophied. He had thick, curly red hair, bulging green eyes, and a protruding forehead. The head was much too large for his short body, and he was obviously retarded. His mouth was full of overlapping teeth, and the harsh sounds he made in his throat resembled the caw of an aging crow. The retarded child, Hoke figured, undoubtedly explained the serious drinking and the disappearance of Sergeant Osborne. As Hoke looked at the boy, he wanted a drink himself.

Elena took a two-liter bottle of Diet Coke out of her refrigerator, filled a baby bottle, added a nipple to it, and gave the bottle to Warren Junior. She poured two glasses of Diet Coke and joined Hoke at the table. Hoke gave her one of his roast beef sandwiches, and she brought two plates to the table from the rack beside the sink. She cut her sandwich in half and then cut up one of the halves into small squares. She fed the bite-size pieces to Warren, who chewed greedily and sucked at the nippled bottle between bites. Hoke took her knife and cut his sandwich into bite-size chunks as well, and gummed them as well as he could before swallowing. When Elena finished feeding Warren, she sat across from Hoke and began to eat her own half-sandwich. Hoke got up from the table. With his foot, he pushed the box containing Warren back into the alcove out of sight. He was no longer hungry, and looking at this deformed kid gave him a sick feeling in the pit of his stomach.

'How long will he live? Warren, I mean?'

Elena shrugged. 'I don't know. We are all children of God, and God decides how long we will live.'

'That's one way of looking at it. If I don't get a job with Mr Bock tomorrow, I'll be going back to Miami. If you want me to, I can find out where your husband went. I don't think he'll come back to you, but there're ways to make him send you child support.'

'No.' She shook her head and smiled. 'When Warren finds a job, he will send for me.' She crossed herself. 'But sometimes, I think, maybe he is dead.'

'He isn't dead, Elena. When he dies, you'll be told, and the government'll give you a VA pension and an American flag to hang on the wall beside his picture. I can find him easily enough, if you want me to.'

'You are a good man, I think. I change Warren's Pamper, then we fuck, okay?'

Hoke went outside to roll and smoke another cigarette while Elena changed the helpless boy. He had never changed the diapers on his daughters (there had been no Pampers then) and had always gone out into the yard when his wife changed them. He didn't mind changing Pepe, however, so he thought he had gotten over this hang-up. He could not understand why, but he knew he wouldn't be able to watch Elena change her three-year-old without getting sick.

Hoke's initial problem had been solved, however. If Tiny Bock asked him how he knew about the job opening for crew chief, he could tell him that a Mexican at the pepper tree had told him about it, and also Mr Sileo. He would talk to Bock at the farmers' market, and then, when he was turned down, as he would surely be, he could return to Miami. On the other hand, if Bock and his foreman came to the market every morning, it might be possible to visit Bock's farm and look around while they were at the market. That would mean staying over another day or two, but then he could at least tell Brownley that he had nosed around and found nothing.

Elena opened the door, and Hoke took one more drag before stripping his cigarette and going back inside. Elena had taken off her elastic top and denim skirt and was removing her panties and bra when Hoke sat at the little table to finish his Diet Coke. Without her high heels she was much shorter – about four-nine – and despite her small breasts, she had long dark brown nipples. Her short legs were noticeably bowed. She had an abundance of pubic hair; but it hung straight down, like a lamp fringe, and there wasn't a single kinky hair. Hoke had never seen straight pubic hair before, and he found it exotic but not erotic. That was all he needed, he thought, a case of AIDS to take back to Miami with him.

Hoke took out Adam Jinks's wallet, removed the five-dollar bill Mr Sileo had given him and put it on the table. He weighted it with the catsup bottle so the breeze from the air conditioner wouldn't blow it away.

'I'd like to fuck you, Elena,' Hoke said, 'but I'm a married man. I've got a sick wife up in Lake City. Are you a Catholic?'

She nodded.

'Then you understand why I can't make love to you. But I'll give you this five if you let me take a shower in your bathroom and sleep here tonight. This table pushes up and the cushions make into a bed, right?'

She nodded again. 'But bed is too short for you. You take back bed, and I'll sleep here.' She went to the alcove closet and pulled out a gray-and-white seersucker wrapper. 'You go ahead. Shower. I'll stay up and watch TV.' She slipped into the wrapper and tied the sash into a bow. 'No hot water in shower, but it's not too cold.'

Hoke took off his shirt and went into the bathroom. The zinc-lined bathroom was cramped, and so was the narrow shower, and the water came out in a drizzling trickle. There was a brown bar of Fels Naptha soap in the dish, and he soaped his body and his hair. Elena opened the door and came in.

'You want a slow hand job in shower? Hand job not the same as adultery.'

'No, thanks, Elena. If I wanted a hand job, I could do it myself. Women don't know how to do it right anyway.'

'I know how. You like?'

'No, but thanks anyway.'

The lukewarm water felt good on his body, and Hoke took his time rinsing away the thick suds. After drying with Elena's clean pink bath towel, Hoke took his clothes to the bedroom and lay down on top of the bed. There was a sheet on the bed but no covers. None was needed. The chilly air from the air conditioner didn't reach this far back in the trailer, and he was soon perspiring again. Hoke set his mental alarm for 4:00 A.M. and fell asleep immediately on the rubber mattress.

Hoke awoke with a start in the dark, feeling uneasy, not knowing where he was for a moment, and then he sat up and dressed. As he pulled on his white socks, he regretted not washing them when he showered. The toes were sticky, and they were still stiff with sweat. The living room-kitchen overhead light was on, and Elena got up from the couch when she heard Hoke open the sliding door to the bathroom. When Hoke came out of the bathroom, she was stirring a pot of oatmeal on the tiny two-burner stove. She put two slices of white bread into the toaster.

'What time is it?'

'Four-fifteen,' she said. 'It's too early to get up.'

'I've got to find the farmers' market, and I'm not sure where it is.'

'In the big lot behind Golden Packinghouse. You'll see all the lights.'

Hoke rearranged the seats in the eating nook, pulled down the Samsonite tabletop, and locked it in place. He had slept well, but he was still sleepy. He rolled a cigarette. 'Aren't you going to make coffee?'

'No coffee.' She poured a glass of Diet Coke and brought it to the table. She then served Hoke a bowl of oatmeal and handed him a spoon. Apparently she was out of milk as well. Hoke crumbled his toast into the hot oatmeal. Cawing sounds came from the closet, and Elena gave Warren a nippled bottle of Diet Coke. The caws stopped, and she filled a smaller bowl with oatmeal for Warren and placed it on the counter to cool. She sat across from Hoke and watched him eat.

'You want to shave? I'll boil some hot water for you.'

'No. Yes, I want to shave, but I'm trying to see how I'll look with a beard. Aren't you going to eat anything?'

'Too early for me. I'm going back to bed.'

'I'm sorry I took your bed, but there was room enough if you wanted to sleep with me.'

'You said you no like me.'

'I didn't say that. I said I didn't want to fuck you, that's all, and I explained why.'

She shrugged and made a face.

'Have you got a social worker? D'you take Warren to a clinic for check-ups?'

'Sometimes. You want more oatmeal? Toast?'

'No, but thanks for breakfast.'

Elena got up from the table and picked up the small bowl of oatmeal and a teaspoon. Hoke didn't want to watch Elena feed Warren or even take a final look at the kid in his box. He patted Elena on the head, said good-bye, and left the trailer. There was a buzzer on a post that opened the gate from inside. Hoke pressed it and walked down the street. The city was dark, except for a brightly lighted area down by the tracks. Hoke headed for the lighted area.

The farmers' market was well lighted, and there was a great deal of activity in the large lot. Stalls were set up, and there were overhead strings of light bulbs crisscrossing the area. The larger hotels and restaurants from Naples, Fort Myers, and Marco Island sent cooks to buy produce in the market, and small farmers had regular booths. The buyers prodded and squeezed produce, and there were excellent bargains. Cantaloupes that sold for $1.39 apiece in supermarkets could be purchased here for thirty-five cents apiece. There were lugs of lettuce, tomatoes, turnips, and other vegetables that sold for only a fraction of the prices they sold for in supermarkets, Hoke noticed. Eight cents' worth of broccoli could be transformed by a Naples *nouvelle* chef into a $5.95 side dish. An old lady was selling doughnuts and coffee in a booth, and Hoke bought a twenty-five-cent Styrofoam cup of coffee. Carrying his cup, he strolled slowly through the lot, looking for Mr Sileo. He found him in the parking lot. Mr Sileo was hefting a fifty-pound sack of potatoes into the back of his Impala station wagon. The back was already loaded with vegetables. There was a dead naked child on the passenger side of the front seat. Startled, Hoke took a closer look and recognized that the body was the carcass of a dressed lamb.

'Good morning, Mr Sileo.'

'You ready for a good day's work?'

'I'm always ready to work, Mr Sileo. But I haven't had a chance to talk to Mr Bock yet. You told me you'd point him out.'

'Anyone here could do that.'

'There's a lot of people here. I didn't expect to see so many.'

'If you get here early, you get the best shit. And if you come late, you get what's left a hell of a lot cheaper. See that fucker sleeping in the back of the Ford pickup?' Sileo pointed. 'He drives all the way down here from Sarasota once a week, waits until nine or ten, and then loads up on what's left at rock-bottom prices. He has his own little grocery store up there in Sarasota, and he cleans up. I could buy the same way, 'cause I'm right here in town, but I'd rather be successful selling good food at reasonable prices.'

'Sure,' Hoke said, remembering that he had worked for less than a dollar an hour for this cheap Levantine bastard. 'How do I find Mr Bock?'

'He's in a tent on the other side near the coffee stall. He'll have a half-dozen Haitians with him probably. I'll wait here for you, and you can ride back to the cafeteria with me.'

'Don't wait. If Bock doesn't hire me, I'll work for someone else. I can't work for ten bucks a day.'

'I'll pay you twelve.'

'Give Marilyn my love.'

Hoke got another cup of coffee before he went to the tent that the coffee lady pointed out as Mr Bock's. Hoke realized that he was acting much too arrogantly for a man who was supposed to be a mendicant fruit tramp. He looked the part, but he still didn't feel like a migrant worker. After all, he was a detective-sergeant earning thirty-six thousand dollars a year. The farmers here were living marginally, and except, perhaps, for a few chefs from the better hotels in Naples and Marco Island, who were buying produce, Hoke probably had a higher annual income than anyone else in Immokalee.

The tent was a pyramidal army surplus top. All four sides were rolled up to waist level. Tiny Bock sat inside at a card table on a folding metal chair. He had a clipboard and a stack of vouchers on the table, the latter weighted down with a small chunk of brain coral. Bock wore a Red Man gimme cap, a blue work shirt with the sleeves cut off at the shoulders, creaseless corduroy trousers, and lace-up work shoes. His bare arms were muscular, and there was a blue rose tattooed on his left wrist. The forefinger of his left hand was missing down to the second knuckle. His thick eyebrows were gray and black and formed an almost straight line above his dark brown eyes. His tanned face was crisscrossed with hundreds of tiny fine lines. There was a sun cancer the size of a half-dollar on his right cheek, bordered by a quarter-inch hedge of gray stubble. He had a slight paunch, but it looked hard. He was probably a few years older than he looked, but he could pass for fifty-five.

Hoke rapped the doorway post but didn't enter the tent. 'Mr Bock?'

'The load's been sold,' Bock said, without looking up.

'I'm not buying, sir. I'm looking for work, and I was told you needed a crew chief.'

'Who told you that?' Bock looked at Hoke but raised his eyes without lifting his head.

'Mr Sileo told me, down at the Cafeteria. I was a crew chief down in the Redland, working tomatoes.'

'Why'd you leave? There's plenty of tomatoes left down there in South Dade.'

'I was fired. I got into a little fight in Florida City.'

'What happened to your teeth?'

'I had a set, but they were lost during the fight. When I got out of jail, I went back to the bar, but nobody'd seen them. Somebody probably found and pawned 'em, I guess.'

'Follow me.'

When he got to his feet, Bock was a much bigger man than Hoke had thought he was when he had been sitting. His thighs were so large they stretched his corduroys tightly, and Hoke figured that he was at least two hundred and forty pounds. Hoke followed Bock to the far edge of the lot, where five black men were unloading a semitrailer of watermelons and loading them onto another trailer. The two trailers were about fifteen or twenty feet apart. There was a man on each truck, and three men were on the ground passing the melons. The men were talking in Creole, and one man was laughing. But as Bock and Hoke approached, they fell silent. The pace of the work did not speed up, however.

'What's wrong with this picture?' Bock said, looking at Hoke with narrowed eyes.

Hoke scratched his neck. A rash had developed at the bottom of his beard, and scratching and perspiration had made his neck a little raw.

'The three men on the ground are all facing us,' Hoke said. 'If the guy in the middle turned around the other way, it would be easier to pass the melons. But that's not all that's wrong. If the trailers were backed up bed to bed, you wouldn't need anyone on the ground. Two men could transfer the melons instead of five.'

'Then what would you do with the other three men? Have them stand around with their fingers up their ass?'

'I'd give 'em some other work to do.'

'You're talking logic, but what we're dealing with here is Haitians. Two Mexicans could do it your way, but two Haitians would take all day to do it. If I made the man in the middle turn around, the other two would think he had an easier job than they did, and they'd squabble about taking turns in the middle. That would add at least another half-hour to unloading the truck. D'you see what I mean?'

'Not exactly.'

'Neither does the State Agricultural Commission. Two white men, or two Mexicans, can outwork five Haitians. And that's why

I pay these five bastards only as much as I would pay two Mexicans. Besides that, Mexicans wouldn't break melons accidentally on purpose so they could eat one.'

'What's the right answer then?' Hoke said.

'There isn't any right answer, and there ain't gonna be. Things are gonna get worse, not better. With the new immigration law, the supply of illegal Mexicans will dry up to a trickle. These Haitians will become legal residents, and they'll demand a minimum wage. If I don't pay it, the Labor Board'll fine my ass. If I hire the few illegal Mexicans who sneak through the net, I'll be fined or sent to jail. So next year my watermelons'll probably rot in the fields. Over in Miami fine restaurants put a three-inch slice of watermelon on a plate with a hamburger, and then they can charge six ninety-five for a dollar-and-a-half burger. But I can't get three bucks for a thirty-pound melon. I need a man who knows how to work Haitians. You ever hear of Emperor Henri Christophe?'

'In Haiti? Yes, sir, I've heard the name, but I don't know much of anything about him.'

'He's the man who built the citadel on the mountaintop above Cap Haitien. Big square stones weighing hundreds of pounds were pushed by hand up the mountain trail. When fifty men couldn't move one of them big stones, Christophe would remove ten men and kill them. The remaining forty then found out that they could push the stone with no trouble at all. See what I mean?'

'Yes, sir. I see what you mean. But Florida ain't Haiti.'

'That's right, and that's too fucking bad. My foreman does the hiring, not me. If you want to talk to him, you can ride back to my farm when the truck's unloaded. You can either help 'em unload now or stand around and watch 'em. I don't give a shit what you do.'

Tiny Bock returned to his tent. Hoke watched the Haitians work, not knowing what else to do. The man in the middle dropped a melon, and it broke into three large pieces. The two men in the trailers jumped down. The Haitians divided the broken melon. One of them offered Hoke a small piece.

'*Guette mama!*' Hoke said, grinning.

All five of the men laughed, and they ate their pieces of water-melon. When the melon was gone, they tossed the rinds aside and went back to work. Hoke found that it was boring to stand there and watch, so he went back to the coffee stall for another cup of coffee. He sat on an overturned crate where he could see the two trailers. When the job was finished, about forty-five minutes later, the sun was coming up across the Everglades, and the cloudless sky was the color of steel.

When Bock left the tent, Hoke joined him at the truck.

'Get in the back,' Bock said.

Hoke climbed into the back of the trailer with the five Haitians, and Bock drove away from the market.

Bock's farm was about ten miles away. After Bock crossed the wooden bridge over the canal, he drove down a twisting gravel road for almost a mile before he pulled into the farmyard. A sagging barbed-wire fence surrounded the vast yard. Beyond the fence, a field of skeletons, with little round knobs on the ends of the stems, stretched out for a hundred yards or more to the 'Glades. Brussels sprouts – as ugly in their natural state as they were in a bowl, Hoke thought.

There was a one-story concrete brick house with a wooden veranda in front, a barn, three rusting trailer homes behind the barn, and a dented yellow school bus. A few oaks, twenty feet tall, shaded the bus and trailers. A black Ford pickup was parked on the right side of the house. Instead of a license plate, a piece of cardboard, with 'Lost Tag' written on it in black ink, was Scotch-taped to the rear window. This was an old trick. In Miami, unless a man got stopped for a violation, he could drive around with a homemade 'Lost Tag' sign for years without buying a license tag.

Two pit dogs, with clipped ears and tails, were chained to a column of the veranda. Their chains were long enough to reach the porch and the doorway. The dogs stared stupidly at the semi, but they didn't bark. There were three loose goats in the yard. A black-and-white nanny bleated as she came over to Tiny Bock and rubbed against his leg when he climbed down from the cab of the truck. The Haitians jumped down, went over to the trailers behind the barn, and entered the one in the middle. Hoke dismounted and rolled a cigarette. He lighted it and joined Bock. Bock patted the nanny goat on the head. She bleated again and then trotted over to a wooden box and climbed on top of it. Her udder was full, and she wanted to be milked, Hoke thought; but he didn't see any kids around the yard.

A man came out of the house and crossed toward them. He said something to the dogs, and they both went under the veranda and crouched on their bellies in the dirt. The man was almost as big as Bock, with long black hair, that reached his shoulders. He wore a yellow bandanna headband, a white Orioles baseball shirt, low-slung jeans, and pointed cowboy boots. His hand-tooled leather belt had a silver buckle in the shape of a horseshoe. There was a wide scar on the left side of his face that went through his eyebrow and ended at his chin. His left eye was missing, and the skin had been gathered and sewn over the socket, leaving a star-shaped scar. His face was slightly darker than his brown arms, but he looked more like an Indian than he did a Mexican, Hoke thought.

'Chico,' Bock said, 'this fucker here told me he wanted to be a crew chief. If you look at his hands, you can see he's never worked a day in his life. He was willing to ride in back with the niggers instead of joinin' me in the cab. Find out who he is and what he wants.'

The Mexican nodded and hit Hoke in the solar plexus with a right jab that didn't travel more than eight inches. Hoke doubled over and fell to his knees. The cigarette flew from his lips, and Tiny Bock stepped on the cigarette before he crossed the yard to the house without looking back.

Hoke clutched his stomach with both hands and tried to regain his breath. The griping pain went all the way through to his spine. The Mexican kicked Hoke in the right side, and Hoke heard his ribs crack. A sharp, searing jab inside his gut made him yelp – just as his breath returned – and he felt as if his side had been pierced with a spear as the Mexican kicked him a second time in the same place. Hoke vomited then and his breakfast came up – coffee, Diet Coke, oatmeal, and bread chunks. Hoke was kneeling, with both hands on the ground supporting his upper body, and trying not to breathe. Even a shallow breath increased the pain in his side. The Mexican went behind Hoke and kicked him in the buttocks. Hoke's arms gave way, and he sprawled in the dirt, his face in the pool of vomit. The Mexican then picked up Hoke's feet and dragged him, face down, arms trailing, across the yard and into the barn.

On the near verge of passing out, Hoke thought: This son of a bitch is in trouble now, because I'm going to kill him!

Chapter Eleven

The Mexican Bock had called Chico – not Cicatrix – threw Hoke face down on a musty bale of alfalfa. The alfalfa was black with rot. It had been rained on, dried, rained on, and dried again and was so black and crumbly it looked as if it had been charred. The moldy dust made Hoke sneeze, and he felt as if knives were being jabbed into his side. Hoke rolled to his left to relieve the pressure on his right side. He couldn't think clearly; everything had happened too fast. He knew that his ribs were either cracked or broken, and if they were broken, a jagged splinter could pierce his lungs. His arms dangled helplessly over the bale, and he was afraid to move. Hoke suppressed his desire to cough and took shallow breaths through his open mouth.

Chico removed Hoke's belt and pulled his pants and Jockey shorts down to his ankles. Then he fastened the belt around Hoke's ankles and made a couple of tight loops to hold it in place. He took Hoke's wallet out of his trousers and went over to the dusty window a few feet away to examine the contents. In addition to the window, the barn had stabs of sunlight coming through cracks and holes in the roof.

Out of the corner of his left eye Hoke watched the Mexican read the letter from the wallet. His thick lips moved as he read.

'What's your name?'

For a long moment Hoke couldn't remember his assumed name. Before he could recall and say it, Chico, using his right fist as a club, brought his clenched fist down on the back of Hoke's neck. A loose rusty wire on the bale of alfalfa pierced Hoke's chin, and he began to bleed.

'Adam Jinks!' Hoke said, bracing for another rabbit punch. The pain from his bruised neck extended to his eyes, as if there were needles inside his head.

Chico dropped the wallet on the dirt floor, circled behind Hoke, bent down, and spread the cheeks of Hoke's buttocks. 'Jesus Marie!' Chico said. 'You got the ugliest asshole I ever seen! I'll have to pump it to get hard enough to fuck you.' He laughed and unbuckled his belt.

Hoke's sphincter tightened, and he groaned. His scrotum tight-ened, and his balls became as hard as a classical Greek statue's. The knowledge that this Mexican intended to cornhole him sent a surge of adrenaline through his body. With his right hand, Hoke broke off the piece of wire that had pierced his chin. It was about six inches in length. He bent it into the shape of a long U and placed it on his right middle finger with the prongs sticking out. He closed his fist. He had nothing else to work with, and he would have only one chance. Hoke pushed himself up from the bale and got shakily to his feet. He tottered, but he didn't fall. He jumped up, with both feet together and turned in the air. Chico had unbuckled his belt and had pushed his jeans down well past his hips. He wasn't wearing any underwear, and his dangling flaccid penis was much darker than the rest of his body. Chico held his waistband with his left hand and raised his right fist to club Hoke down again with a sidearm blow. When Chico was within striking range, Hoke jabbed the Mexican in his good eye with the stiff prongs of the wire and dodged the sidearm blow. In dodging, Hoke fell again. As fluid squirted onto his knuckles, Hoke knew that he had got him. Hoke got to his feet. The Mexican was screaming in a high, almost feminine voice and cupped his blinded eye with both hands. Hoke hopped to the opposite wall of the barn before bending down to unloosen the belt from his ankles. He kicked free of his pants and Jockey shorts.

Chico was moaning now, a harsh, strangling sound, and was staggering about in tight circles. His jeans had slipped below his knees or the circles would have been wider. The animal noises the Mexican was making would soon bring Tiny Bock out to the barn, Hoke thought, but then he thought differently. Tiny Bock – that son of a bitch – would think the sounds of pain were coming from him, not Chico.

The barn hadn't been used as a barn for some time. There were four stalls on one side, but no horses or mules. Dusty harnesses, which hadn't been used in years, hung from wooden racks on the wall beside the stalls. There was no wagon inside the barn, and Hoke hadn't seen a wagon in the yard. There was a stack of loose boards near the barn door. The wide double doors were open. Hoke couldn't let Chico stumble outside, where Bock might see him from the house. Hoke selected a two-by-four to use as a club and circled behind the Mexican. He didn't want to get too close to Chico. If the man got his big hands on him, or even one hand, he knew it would be all over. Holding his breath, Hoke hit the Mexican on his right kneecap, swinging the two-by-four as hard as he could. The knee snapped, and Chico fell over sideways. He didn't remove his hands from his face but screamed again as he fell. Hoke hit him squarely on the head, and the scream stopped abruptly. There was a whooshing sound as the breath left his throat. Hoke pounded the man's head again, and the two-by-four splintered and broke. Hoke's hands were punctured with tiny splinters from the piece of wood. Blood and gray matter oozed from the dead Mexican's head. Blood poured from his nose and ears, and the dislodged yellow headband was saturated.

Hoke's arms were weary, and he gasped with pain. The pain in his side had increased with the effort he had put into clubbing the man to death, and Hoke bent over double to obtain some relief as he limped back to the bale of alfalfa and sat down. His tailbone hurt from being kicked. Bending forward helped him breathe, a little, but not much. When he regained his breath, gradually, Hoke crossed to the other wall again and retrieved his pants and belt. He folded his jeans into a square pad, placed the pad against his injured ribs, and pulled the belt tight around his waist to hold the pad in place. He removed a nail from one of the loose boards and made a small puncture in his belt and fastened the buckle. He could breathe a little more easily now, so long as he took shallow breaths, and the pain was not as severe. His ribs, Hoke concluded, were only cracked, not broken. He hocked and spit into the palm of his hand. It hurt to cough, but there was no blood in the spit. If his ribs had been broken, after all his activity, he would be spewing blood by now. Blood from his cut chin had dribbled onto the front of his shirt, and both sleeves were ripped at the shoulder. Hoke removed his shirt and dabbed at the blood on his chin. The puncture was deep; it went through the fleshy part of his chin all the way to the bone.

It would only be a matter of time before Bock called for the Mexican to come to the house or came over to the barn himself to investigate the silence. Bock would have a gun. He would have several guns in the house, in all probability – a pistol or two, a rifle, and perhaps a shotgun. If the man owned three thousand acres of land in two counties, he would hunt them as well as farm them. When he found the dead Mexican, he would either shoot Hoke or call the sheriff, but Hoke didn't believe Bock would call the law. Obviously Bock didn't want any lawmen prowling around his property.

Hoke picked up his wallet, where it had fallen by the window, refolded the letter, and placed it inside. He wedged the wallet under his belt. With his thumb Hoke scraped a small circle in the dusty, cobwebby window and looked toward the veranda. Both pit dogs were on their feet, looking toward the barn. The moaning and the screams had made them curious, and the silence even more so. Hoke cupped his hands to his mouth and moaned. The bitch didn't move, but the smaller dog, a male, and probably her son, wagged his stump of a tail and strained at the end of his chain. The nanny goat came into the barn, bleated several times, and leaped up onto the bale of alfalfa.

Hoke had never milked a goat or a cow, but he had seen animals milked in movies. He grabbed both teats and began to strip them, letting the milk squirt onto the bale. Milking was slow work, and he didn't have the time for this, but he milked her long enough to give her some relief before he stopped. Milking the goat had not stopped him from thinking about what to do next.

Why hadn't the Haitians come out of their trailer when they heard the screaming? Perhaps they were used to the idea of the Mexican using the barn as a place to discipline workers? Maybe they weren't allowed to leave their trailer until they were told they could? At any rate, none of them had come to his rescue, even though he had been sent to see what had been happening to them or to their fellow countrymen. But then, they didn't know that; besides, Hoke didn't know how their minds worked. If a few of them, or a lot of them, had disappeared, why did the rest stay? Weren't they suspicious? Didn't they suspect that they might disappear as well?

He would have to get some answers from Tiny Bock.

Hoke selected a fresh two-by-four from the lumber pile and went to the back of the barn. There was a normal-size door, but it had been boarded over and nailed shut. Hoke pried the boards away and opened the door. Two gamecocks were staked out behind the barn, well separated from each other, of course, and three gamehens scratched listlessly in the yard. If he could get as far as the semi, about twenty yards away, without being seen from the house, he would be screened. Then he could circle around the back, giving the pit dogs a wide berth. There might be – in all probability there would be – a woman in the kitchen. Hoke doubted that Bock and the Mexican would do their own cooking, although they might. He would soon find out. Crouching low, he made a lumbering run to the side of the parked truck and trailer. The hot sunlight on his naked body was a shock, and his exposed genitalia made him feel, somehow, more vulnerable. Even though he had pissed his shorts when he had been thrown across the alfalfa bale, he wished now that he had put them on again.

The toolbox on the fender was closed, and a wire instead of a lock had been twisted through the hasp. Hoke untwisted the wire and raised the lid. There weren't many tools in the box. Except for a well-oiled jack, the other tools were rusty. Hoke took a monkey wrench out of the box and hefted it. It was fourteen inches long and had a good weight to it. It wouldn't be as effective as the two-by-four had been, but he could throw the wrench if he had to, and that was an advantage. Well screened from the front door of the house, Hoke crouched and duck walked to a small utility shed about thirty yards away. It hurt too much to run. The venetian blinds on this side of the house were closed. The dogs could still see him, and they looked at him without barking. If Bock turned them loose and sicced them on him, his situation could change radically. The only time a pit dog lets go is to get a better bite.

From the utility shed Hoke walked directly to the side of the house. To see him now, crushing the geranium and fern beds that surrounded the house, Bock would have to raise a window and look straight down at him. Hoke edged along the wall to the back and looked through the screened porch that led into the kitchen. There was a masonite-topped table and four padded aluminum-legged chairs on the porch. A deal table was flush against the wall, and it held a small hibachi for barbecuing. There was also an aged Kelvinator refrigerator against the wall, and it was dotted with rust. There was probably a new refrigerator in the kitchen, and this old one was used for extra storage for ice and drinks. The screen door was unlatched, and Hoke went inside. The Cuban tile floor was streaked with dried mop marks. The old refrigerator ticked away with a double beat, like two overheated engines after the ignition had been turned off, and Hoke's heartbeats were not in sync with either beat. There were two open doors. One led into the kitchen; the other, into a long hallway to the living room. Two doors on the right side of the hallway were closed. Hoke could also get to the living room through the kitchen and then through the dining room. There was no woman in the kitchen, and from the mess no woman had been near the kitchen in weeks. The sink and counter were filled with dirty dishes, pots, and pans, and two brown grocery bags in the corner were overflowing with garbage. An aluminum coffeepot was on the stove. Hoke touched it, and it was still warm. Crouching to minimize the pain in his ribs, Hoke inched down the hallway instead of going through the kitchen. Before he reached the end of the hallway, he recognized Donahue's voice. Jesus! *Donahue* was on the tube from 9:00 until 10:00. It seemed as if he had been up forever, and it was only a little after 9:00 A.M.! The living room was comfortably furnished. There was a long davenport covered with black leather and several brightly cushioned Monterey chairs. The hide of a ten-foot alligator had been nailed to one wall above a four-drawer highboy, and an over-head fan whirled in the ceiling. The Prussian-blue nylon carpet looked new, but several blue dust balls bounced about below the fan. The dining table, which Bock was obviously using as a desk, was piled high with ledgers, folders, and papers. There was a pen and pencil set with an onyx base and a file box covered with green leather. Four cushioned ladder-backed dining chairs were pushed up to the table. Tiny Bock, sitting in a deep pigskin chair, with his back toward Hoke, was watching Donahue on the tube. A white ceramic mug, with TINY baked into it in bold script, was on the glass-topped coffee table in front of him.

Hoke crossed the carpeted floor slowly, making no noise, and almost made it to the chair before Donahue said, 'We'll be right back.' A commercial for Colgate's toothpaste replaced him. Several workmen in hard hats were plastering plaque on the inside of a set of giant teeth. Bock got to his feet, stretched out his arms, and yawned audibly. He must have sensed Hoke's presence. He couldn't have heard him over the noisy commercial, but he turned around. His jaw dropped slightly as he saw Hoke, naked except for his high-topped shoes and belted makeshift pad, only three feet away from him. Bock's arms were still in the air as Hoke stepped forward and brought the business end of the heavy wrench down across the big man's nose. The nose cracked, and blood spurted from it. But Bock turned immediately toward the front door.

'I've got a gun!' Hoke said. 'Open the door and you're dead!'

Bock paused in midstep, raising his hands level with his shoulders. He then put his right hand to his bleeding nose. Hoke moved in swiftly, clipped Bock behind his right ear with the wrench, and the man toppled over. Bock was down, but not out. Hoke hit him again, aiming for the same spot, and then Bock was unconscious, with bright red blood staining his blue carpet.

Donahue returned, and Hoke switched off the set. He wanted to sit down. He wanted to lie down, but there was no time for that. Except for his broken nose, Bock wasn't hurt too badly, and he would come around soon. There was a Mercer 12-gauge shotgun, an over-and-under, together with a Winchester 30-30 rifle, in a gun rack on the wall beside the front door. Two canes and a blue-and-white golf umbrella were in a large brass stand beneath the rack. Hoke selected the shotgun and broke it open. It wasn't loaded. Hoke crossed to the sideboard that was half in and half out of the dining room and opened four drawers before he found a box of double-aught shells. He loaded the shotgun, closed and cocked it. Before sitting down, Hoke took a long swig from an opened bottle of Jack Daniel's black label that was on top of the sideboard. The whiskey helped. Hoke didn't want to get up from the comfortable chair, but he forced himself to get to his feet. Bock was already making sounds deep in his throat. Hoke took the cable box from the top of the TV set, jerked the long cord loose from the back of the set, and wrapped the cord around Bock's ankles. There was plenty of cord. After encircling the ankles and making square knots, he wrapped the extra cable around Bock's legs to the knees, and then wedged the box with its twelve push bars under Bock's belt at the back. That would give Hoke a few more minutes to look around. Even if Bock regained consciousness, he wouldn't be able to run.

Hoke went back down the hallway and entered the first door on his left. This was a bedroom. The double bed was unmade, but the sheets were clean. Hoke got a clean, long-sleeved sport shirt and a pair of blue serge suit pants from the closet. The pants were much too large for him at the waist; Bock outweighed him by at least fifty pounds, so Hoke didn't try on any of Bock's underwear. He slipped into the trousers, removed his belt, dropped his jeans-pad to the floor, and threaded his belt through the loops. He rolled the trousers up a turn at the cuffs and slipped his wallet into the right rear pocket. The shirt was an extra large, with square shirttails, and Hoke had to turn the cuffs back two inches.

Hoke entered the bathroom and opened the opposite door, which led to a smaller bedroom. Both bedrooms, then, had hall doors. The smaller room, Hoke supposed, was Chico's. There was a single metal cot, and the bed was neatly made, with hospital corners on the tucked-in Navaho blanket. Hoke returned to the bathroom and looked through the medicine chest and found a partially used roll of adhesive tape. He lifted his shirt and wrapped the tape around his waist as tightly as he could. He used all of the tape. He would have preferred to have the tape tighter than it was, but that was the best he could do, and it relieved the pain in his side much better than the improvised belt pad had.

Hoke returned to the living room. As he reached the end of the hallway, he heard the report and felt shards of plaster sting the back of his neck at the same time that Bock pulled the trigger on a .38-caliber pistol. Bock was sitting by the doorway, holding the pistol in front of his body with both hands. Hoke dropped flat to the floor and fired his shotgun as Bock shot a second time. Once again Bock's slug entered the wall instead of Hoke, and it went into the wall at least four feet above his prone body. Bock was trying to lower the pistol awkwardly as Hoke fired the second time. Bock dropped the pistol and fell over. At this distance, less than fifteen feet, almost all the shotgun pellets of Hoke's second shot had gone into Bock's upper chest. Hoke crawled toward the man on his knees and brushed the pistol away. He felt Bock's pulse. There was no pulse. Bock was dead, and there was no one left to answer his questions.

Hoke picked up the .38 pistol and shoved it behind the waistband of his trousers in the back. The pistol hadn't been in the sideboard, and Bock hadn't been armed when Hoke wrapped his legs with the cord. Bock had probably kept the pistol hidden in the bottom of the umbrella stand near the door. Hoke had another drink from the bottle of Jack Daniel's and then took the bottle over to the dining table and sat down. Both these deaths could have been avoided, Hoke reflected, if Brownley had let him keep his pistol. If he had only had his weapon, both these men – bastards that they were – would still be alive. Both deaths were justified, of course. He had had to kill the Mexican after he blinded him; blind, the man wouldn't have been able to find any work. The Mexican hadn't learned anything from the loss of his first eye, apparently, or he wouldn't have attacked Hoke in the first place. And Bock, of course, had fired at Hoke first. Twice, in fact. Hoke shuddered. He was lucky to be alive.

Hoke took another drink from the bottle, a shorter one this time. He put the cap back on the bottle. He couldn't feel the drinks, but it would be best to stop before he did. He went to the front window and peered through the venetian blinds. The door to the middle trailer was still closed. Hoke couldn't understand it. The five Haitians were still inside, or perhaps they all had fled when the shooting began. He decided to go through Bock's papers first and check on the Haitians later. If they had run away (American blacks would have started running at the sound of the first shot and would have disappeared forever, but he didn't know how Haitians would react), fine. If they were gone, they were gone; if not, he would decide what to do with them, but at the moment he wanted to sit down and rest. Hoke wasn't in bad physical shape, but he wasn't in good shape either. He spent too much time sitting at a desk writing reports. When he got back to Miami, he would talk Bill Henderson into playing a little handball a couple of times a week the way they used to when they were partners. Hoke hadn't been to the gym in more than six months, but a couple of years back he and Henderson had managed to squeeze in some handball once or twice a week.

Hoke looked through the papers and the ledgers on the table. There was a check for $1,700 made out to Bock Enterprises on top of the pile. It was signed by the treasurer of Gaitlin Bros., Ft. Myers, Florida. This was probably the check for this morning's truckload of watermelons. Most of the papers were bills, many of them second and third notices of overdue bills. Hoke went through the ledger, beginning with the first page. Not only was Bock broke, but he was heavily in debt, and there was a second mortgage on his farmhouse and on another four hundred acres of land he held in Collier County. The man had been land-poor, and during the last four years he had purchased more land than he could either farm or pay for; and on top of all that, he hadn't paid out any wages to anyone. Not a dime. If he had, there was no evidence in the ledger. Perhaps he had paid off his labor in cash. Even so, there should have been a record of the payouts somewhere.

Hoke went over to the body and took Bock's wallet out of the hip pocket. It contained $103, a VISA card, three gas credit cards, and the registration for the Ford half-ton truck. There were some business cards in the wallet as well. The keys to the Ford and the keys to the semi were in Bock's right front pocket. Hoke pocketed the money, the registration slip, and the keys and dropped the wallet on the floor.

Hoke reloaded the shotgun, stepped over Bock's body, and

opened the front door. The two pit dogs were whining and sniffing, smelling the blood, and they were at the ends of their chains. Both dogs were only two feet away from him. Hoke killed them both with the shotgun, stepped over their bodies, and crossed the yard to the trailers beneath the trees. The first trailer was empty, and so was the third, although there were signs that they had been occupied in the recent past. When Hoke looked at the closed door of the middle trailer, he solved the mystery. When the door had closed from inside, a flat metal bar on the outside, fixed with a spring at the top, dropped into a welded metal slot on the outside, and locked the men in. The bar could be raised and would stay put in its original position from the outside, but there was no way to lift it from inside the trailer.

Hoke raised the bar and opened the door. There was a brick on the floor to wedge the door open, and Hoke kicked it into place. The trailer was the same size as Elena's had been, but there was no furniture. Without moving away from the door, Hoke surveyed the interior. There was a stove and a counter, and a goat stew was cooking on the stove. The other half of a dressed kid was on the counter. The five men slept on the floor apparently. The stench from the overflowing toilet in the tiny bathroom was overpowering, and the bathroom door was missing. Four Haitians sat on the floor, their backs to the wall, and the fifth man was at the stove, holding a long-handled metal ladle. The five men looked at Hoke without moving; their eyes were wide, but their faces were expressionless. There was a stack of metal pie pans on the counter. The man with the ladle dropped his hands to his sides. The man sitting closest to the stove quivered like an Australian pine in a heavy wind and stared at Hoke's leveled shotgun. His bare black heels beat a tattoo on the metal floor.

'Who speaks English?'

'I speak a little,' the man at the stove said.

'You ever hear of Delray Beach?'

He nodded. 'I know Delray Beach.'

Hoke took out the bills he had taken from Bock's wallet and handed each man twenty dollars. He put the remaining three dollars into his pocket. He gave the man at the stove the keys to the Ford pickup and the folded yellow registration slip.

'There're about ten thousand Haitians in Delray Beach,' Hoke said. 'Go to Delray, and join them. There's no more work for you here, or in Immokalee either. So take the black truck and drive to Delray Beach. You got a driver's license?'

'No, sir.'

'A green card?'

'No, sir.'

'D'you know how to drive?'

'I drove a taxi in Port-au-Prince.'

'If you're stopped, this registration won't do you any good, but maybe one of the Haitians in Delray will know what to do with it. Don't take the Tamiami Trail into Miami. Take Alligator Alley instead and then the Sunshine Parkway to Delray. Do you understand me?'

The man nodded and put the keys into his pocket. 'I know Delray Beach.'

'The smart thing to do is to abandon – I mean, just *leave* the truck on the street somewhere after you get to Delray. And forget that you ever worked here for Mr Bock. Understand?'

'Yes, sir.' He nodded and licked his lips.

'All right. Tell the others.'

The man said something to the others in Creole. Hoke watched them as they nodded their heads. They all had broken into smiles when he had given them money, but their faces were solemn again now. Hoke left the trailer and its stench and waited in the yard until the men came out. They all had small bundles and blankets; one man had a faded quilt. The tall man also brought the pot of steaming goat stew, and they had their tin plates and spoons. The short, quivering man carried the other half of the dressed kid and had an OD army blanket rolled up and over one shoulder. Helping each other, they climbed into the pickup, two in front and three in back. Hoke waited until the truck was well down the graveled road before he returned to the house.

If they didn't speed, the chances were fairly good that the pickup would make it safely to Delray, with its huge Haitian colony alongside the railroad tracks. Trucks and old buses filled with laborers were plentiful on the Alligator Alley route to the Sunshine Parkway, and if a trooper did stop them, he would turn them over to the INS. The INS would, in turn, take them to the Krome Detention Center, but all the illegal Haitians knew by now to say that they came to America to escape political persecution. Now that Duvalier had been deposed, the persecution gambit didn't work any longer, but there were still enough immigration shysters in Miami to keep them in the States for months, sometimes years. And if they could contact a relative of any kind here in the U.S. who had somehow obtained a green card, a lawyer could get them paroled. Once paroled, they disappeared again, either to New York or to New Jersey. They wouldn't be able to explain how they got the truck if they were stopped, but Bock would never report the truck stolen.

There were additional papers and letters in the sideboard and in the highboy as well. From these, Hoke discovered that Bock had a married daughter living in Fitzgerald, Georgia. He also found the death certificate for Bock's wife in a drawer.

The Mexican hadn't owned much of anything. He had a yellow linen suit in his closet, fresh from the cleaners and encased in plastic, and a pair of polished cordovan loafers. But there was no correspondence from anyone, either in Spanish or English, or any personal papers. There was a coiled leather whip and a P-38 in a bottom dresser drawer, and Hoke left them there. The other drawers held underwear, T-shirts, and a half-dozen pairs of argyle socks – none of them worn.

Hoke left the house and looked inside the utility shed outside the house. There was a generator in the shed, to be used for emergency power, Hoke surmised. It was an old Sears generator and hadn't been used for some time. There were four five-gallon jerricans in the shed, and two of them were filled with gasoline. There were two aluminum tanks in one corner. DANGER! VIKANE was stenciled in red paint on both tanks. Hoke took the two filled cans of gas back to the house. He put them down in the kitchen and went into the bathroom to take a leak. When he looked at his face in the mirror, he shuddered. His face was haggard, and his eyes were red. Bits of oatmeal were lodged in his beard. He looked at least ten years older than he should look, even without his teeth. He swallowed three aspirin with water and then shaved off his beard, using a new Bic razor he found in the medicine cabinet. He put a Band-Aid over the puncture wound in his chin. He felt better, even if he didn't look a lot better.

Hoke poured a half-can of gasoline over Bock's body and then splashed the rest of the gas throughout the living room. With the last of the gas, he made a wide line to the doorway and out onto the veranda. He lit the gas with his lighter, and the fire snaked across the porch. It blazed fiercely when it reached Bock's body.

Taking the second can with him, Hoke got into the semicab, made a wide turn in the yard, and drove it into the barn as far as it would go. He poured half the can over the Mexican, more on the pile of loose boards, and splashed the remainder on the engine of the truck. He found his straw hat and put it on. He lit the gas from outside the barn and walked down the gravel road toward the highway. He looked over his shoulder but kept walking. The house and the barn both were on fire. In the middle of the yard the nanny goat, bleating, stood on her milking box.

When Hoke reached the highway, almost a mile away from the farm, he could still see black smoke from the two fires. No one driving down the highway, either way, would pay any attention to the smoke, and the farm itself was shielded by the palmetto trees on both sides of the gravel road. Farmers set fire to their fields to clear them all year round.

No one stopped to give Hoke a ride, and it took him almost four hours to walk the nine and a half miles back to Immokalee.

Chapter Twelve

There were a good many things to think about on his walk back to Immokalee, and Hoke had to sit down frequently to rest. During his rest periods he picked out most of the splinters embedded in his hands. His tailbone hurt with every jarring step, especially when he stumbled slightly, and his arms felt heavy and sore. Swinging that two-by-four had been like two hours of batting practice, and his muscles weren't used to being stretched.

Hoke hadn't spent any time looking around the farm for any buried bodies. Beyond the farm and the field of Brussels sprouts, the Everglades began, stretching to the horizon. If Bock and Chico had buried any bodies, they would have driven them to the sea of grass and dumped them into some deep water-filled sinkhole where the alligators would eat them. There was no way to prove it now, but Hoke had no doubt that Tiny Bock had killed his Haitian workers when they finished their jobs instead of paying them. All Bock had to do, when it came to payoff time, was to lock the men in their trailers, attach the Vikane gas tanks to the copper tubes that were used for propane cooking gas for the stove, and turn them on. Bock and Chico could then throw the bodies into the truck and drive through the fields to the water-soaked 'Glades and dump them. That still didn't account for the dead Haitian found behind the billboard on the road to Bonita Springs. With a hundred square miles of swamp in his backyard to dump bodies, why would Bock and Chico bury a dead Haitian behind a billboard on a fairly busy state road? It didn't make sense, because the body was bound to be found. Someday, perhaps, an illegal hunter might find a skull out in the middle of the 'Glades, but an illegal hunter wouldn't report a find like that; he would take it home and put it on his mantel as a *memento mori*. Someone else, other than Bock, must have buried the dead Haitian behind the billboard. After all, Bock wasn't the only grower going broke in Immokalee or in the so-called green belt surrounding Lake Okeechobee. In recent years many farmers had given up agriculture altogether and started catfish farming instead. And they were prospering. Five years ago catfish were hard to find in Miami, but now a man could get fried catfish in every seafood restaurant in South Florida, and it didn't have the muddy taste of wild catfish either.

By the time Hoke reached the outskirts of Immokalee he was depressed. Part of his depression was caused, he knew, by the unnecessary killing of Bock and Chico, but mandatory under the circumstances. If Bock hadn't been groggy from the blows to his head, he certainly would have killed Hoke with his first shot. He must have had double vision to miss at such short range.

There weren't many people on the dusty streets. A few Mexicans lingered beneath the pepper tree, and there was the same mix of homeless white winos and blacks in the parking lot of the Cafeteria, but the other townspeople – those with shelter – stayed inside during the middle of the day. Immokalee did not as yet have an enclosed air-conditioned mall, so many townspeople – those with cars, anyway – were probably shopping in Naples or Fort Myers. Local shop owners stayed inside their air-conditioned stores. There were workers in the row of packinghouses, of course, and huge sixteen-wheelers, both loaded and unloaded, rumbled through the streets; but there was a dead, lethargic feel to the town.

Hoke passed Myrtle's discount drugstore, stopped, and then went back to the store. He bought a roll of three-inch adhesive tape, the widest she had on hand, and a small box of extra-strength Tylenol, but decided against cigarettes. It hurt his side every time he took a shallow breath, so he would have to give up smoking for a few days whether he wanted to or not. He went past the 66 gas station on the next corner. Noseworthy's Guesthouse sign was on the following corner, as Mel Peoples had told him. The guesthouse was two blocks east, right next to an empty lot that had been used as a dump. The lot was littered with piles of bottles and tin cans and the burned-out wreck of an automobile. The twisted mass of metal was so black Hoke couldn't determine the make of the car.

The guesthouse, however, a two-story wooden structure with a sloping cedar-shingled roof, had been painted recently – a shiny off-gray, with white trim on the windows. All the windows, upstairs and down, had slanting wooden Bahama blinds on the outside. The house would be dark inside, but the slotted blinds would make it cooler. The small front yard was covered with gravel instead of grass and was surrounded by a low rock wall about two feet high. Such walls were common in the Bahamas, where homeowners always marked their boundaries with rock walls, but they were rare in Florida. There were some hanging plants on the porch, and three wicker rockers painted a glaring white. The guesthouse sign,

NOSEWORTHY'S
GUESTHOUSE

(EST. 1983)

in black lettering on a white board, had been tacked above the front door. The upper half of the front door was glass but was curtained with white draperies, so Hoke couldn't see inside. A smaller sign beside the bell read 'Ring and Enter.' Hoke rang the bell and opened the door. There was a maple costumer and an elephant-foot umbrella stand in the foyer. Straight ahead, to the left of the stairs, were a table and a chair. There was a sign-in book and a silver bowl containing jelly beans on the table. The living room, on Hoke's right, was crowded with mid-Victorian chairs and spindly-legged walnut tables, short and tall, either beside or in front of each chair. There was a brick fireplace containing a large bowl of daisies and a tall glass-fronted bookcase beside it. The walls were covered with old and faded pink wall-paper and cluttered with watercolors, photos, mirrors, mounted birds and small animals. Beyond the living room, a step up, was the dining area – a bare buffet table against the wall. A long mirror on the wall behind the table reflected the living room and made the crowded interior appear larger. There was a swinging door with a beveled glass window that opened to the kitchen beyond the dining area.

A tall black man came swiftly through the swinging door, and he crossed the room, dodging the chairs and wine tables, swiveling his hips like a broken-field runner. He wore a wide white smile and a black linen suit with a white shirt and a pearl-gray necktie. There was a hand-painted picture of a dog's head on the tie, either a collie or a wolfhound. Hoke wasn't sure. The man held out his hand, so Hoke shook it.

'Welcome to our guesthouse, sir.'

'You must be Mr Noseworthy.'

'At your service, sir.' The smile didn't leave his dark face, but his eyes took in Hoke's drooping shirttails and baggage – a small brown paper sack from Myrtle's discount drugstore.

'Can anyone overhear us?' Hoke pointed toward the kitchen door.

'Mrs Noseworthy's out back, but she's ironing on the back porch.'

'Any other guests?'

'Do I have a room, d'you mean? I have rooms, yes, but you must pay in advance. Usually reservations are requested well ahead of arrival, and I always require the first day's rent in advance on mail reservations –'

'Are there any other guests?' Hoke repeated.

'Yes. A Mrs Peterson. But she's not here at present. She was going to visit the Corkscrew Swamp Sanctuary today, she said. Where did you park your car, Mr –?'

'Let's cut the shit, Noseworthy. Mel Peoples told me to contact you. My name's Adam Jinks. Or did Mel give you a different name?'

'Jinks is correct, yes, sir, but I didn't expect you so soon. What happened to your chin?'

'A shaving nick. Can you contact Mel for me?'

Noseworthy shook his head. 'Not right away. Mr Peoples called me from the airport – Fort Myers – yesterday. He had to fly up to a conference in Tallahassee for three days. Of course, if he calls from Tallahassee, I can put you on the phone, but I don't know his number up there or where he's staying. I'll just have to give you a room, and you'll have to wait till he gets back or phones.'

'Terrific. Give me a room with a tub bath, if you've got one.'

'Our rates are sixty dollars a day, and that's with breakfast, of course. We have wine and cheese in the living room every evening between five and six –'

'I don't care what it costs. It all goes on Mel Peoples's tab, so give me the best room you've got.'

'He didn't say anything about that.' Noseworthy licked his lips.

'He didn't tell me he was going to Tallahassee either. What part of the Bahamas are you from?'

'Abaco. You may not know where that is –'

'But I do. We have something in common. That's the island my ancestors came from. They sat out the Revolutionary War in Abaco and moved back to Florida when the war was over. They were Loyalists, you see.'

'Have you ever been there? To Abaco?'

'No, I plan to fly over sometime, just to see it, but I've been busy. I also need a bath. Perhaps you can show me my room now, and we can talk about the islands later.'

'Sign in, please.' Noseworthy went behind the table, and handed Hoke a ballpoint. Hoke signed the register, 'Adam Jinks, Abaco, Bahamas,' and returned the pen to the innkeeper.

'I'm sorry you had to sign in.' Noseworthy shrugged. 'But they check on me sometimes, because of the tax, you know.'

'I understand. You aren't doing too well, are you?'

'Not yet, but word is getting around. I really don't understand it. There are many interesting places to sightsee, all within easy driving distance of Immokalee, as I was telling Mrs Peterson this morning.'

'Maybe you ought to put in a pool. It's ninety degrees out there, and eighty degrees in here.'

'We don't cater to that kind of clientele. Tourists who want a pool can stay at the Day's Inn or a Howard Johnson's. A guesthouse is for people who want a quiet atmosphere with homelike surroundings.'

'Yeah. Most people have stuffed squirrels and owls in their living rooms, so they'll feel right at home here.'

'It's upstairs. Follow me.'

Hoke's room was in the front of the house upstairs, and it had a large bathroom. The Bahama blinds shielded the window to the street, so there was no view, but there was nothing he wanted to see in Immokalee anyway. Noseworthy handed him the key. There was a brass tag on it with the name LeRoy Collins intaglioed onto the tag.

'The downstairs door is locked at ten, but your room key fits the front door as well, in case you go out.'

'Did Governor Collins ever stay in this room?'

'No, sir, but all the rooms are named for former Florida governors. Mrs Peterson is down the hall, in Governor Kirk's room.'

'A good idea, Mr Noseworthy. And educational, too. If Mel phones, come and get me right away – even if I'm still in the tub.'

'Don't worry, Mr Jinks, I will.' He closed the door behind him as he left.

There was a full-length mirror on a wooden wardrobe next to the double bed, and Hoke caught a glimpse of himself. No wonder Noseworthy had given him such a cool greeting. His serge suit pants, rolled up at the cuffs, were dusty, and the sport shirt was far too big for him. Hoke had rolled up the sleeves and had left the long square tails out to cover the pistol stuffed behind his waistband. Hoke turned on the hot water in the tub and undressed. A bruise the size of an orange was on his stomach, where Chico had hit him with his fist. It looked very dark against his white hairy stomach. The tub had claws for feet, and each claw clutched a large round marble ball. There was a framed sepia-toned photo of Queen Victoria on the wall, which was hardly appropriate for LeRoy Collins's room, Florida's former liberal and best governor ever. Hoke turned off the hot water and then ran enough cold to cool it so he could barely stand it. He eased his aching body into the steaming water. He soaked for about an hour, running the hot water again as the tub cooled, before he soaped himself and rinsed off.

He removed the wet tape and almost fell asleep before he decided to get out. He washed his white socks in the tub before he pulled the plug. He dried off and put fresh tape around his cracked ribs. He dressed again, putting his shoes on without socks. He felt refreshed, but his neck was still sore and tender to the touch. He was also hungry.

Hoke put the pistol under his pillow and went downstairs, leaving his room key in the door. Noseworthy wasn't in the living room, so Hoke pushed through the door and went into the kitchen. A woman, about thirty-eight or forty, with curly lion-colored hair, was sitting on a stool at the worktable, snapping pole beans into a green bowl. She was a handsome woman, even without makeup, and she looked at Hoke with cool blue eyes.

'May I help you? Mr Noseworthy went to the post office.'

'Are you Mrs Noseworthy?'

'I'm Mrs Noseworthy, yes,' she said, lifting her chin.

'Yes, ma'am. I'd like to get something to eat.'

She shook her head. 'We don't serve meals except for breakfast, and that's from seven-thirty till ten. Eleven is checkout time, you see. But we serve wine and cheese from five to six.'

Hoke nodded. 'Mr Noseworthy told me, but I missed breakfast.'

'I can give you a half-off coupon for the Cafeteria downtown.'

'I guess your husband hasn't told you anything about me. You'd better talk to him. I'm also expecting an important call.'

'He told me.'

'So I can't leave the house. If I have to wait till five for a piece of cheese, I'll starve.'

'I guess I could scramble you an egg.'

'If you're too busy, I can do it myself.'

'I'll bring a tray up to your room.' She bent over her bowl again, dismissing him.

'Thanks. By the way, Mrs Noseworthy, there's no Gideon Bible in my room. I checked.'

She lifted her head and stared for a moment. 'There's a bookcase in the living room for guests. But I don't think you'll find one there either.'

Hoke grinned as he climbed the stairs to his room. Mrs Noseworthy, whether she was actually married to the innkeeper or not, explained a few things that had bothered him. Here in Immokalee, on an unpaved side street, was the worst location possible for a guesthouse. The room, without a phone, radio, or television, was way overpriced, and there wasn't even a pool. But it was a safe place for a white woman married to a black man.

807

No one would bother the couple here, and the social stigma, in a backwater like Immokalee, would be minimal at best. There would always be some guests for their seven rooms. Even one guest at sixty bucks a day would provide a living for two people. The guesthouse would also serve as a safe house, a secure hideout for someone who wanted to cool off for a couple of weeks. Because of the recent drug wars in the Bahamas, particularly in Nassau, on New Providence, there was a real need for a quiet hideout like this one. And for his hot guests, Noseworthy would charge a lot more than sixty a day. Hoke looked forward to meeting Mrs Peterson, wondering how she happened to be staying here. He shook his head. He still had his own problems to solve. Instead of being curious about the Noseworthys and Mrs Peterson, he should be making up some kind of story to tell Mel Peoples.

On the long walk from the farm to town he had decided to tell Peoples the truth about what had happened. But after reflection, now that he had relaxed a little and was feeling better, he suspected that the truth would terrify a bureaucrat like Mel Peoples. If he told Peoples and Major Brownley the truth, he could get into a little trouble, perhaps a lot of trouble – There was a knock at the door.

Hoke got up from the bed, where he had been lying and staring at the photograph of Booker T. Washington on the wall. It hurt to move, and he groaned when he got to his feet. He crossed the room and opened the door. Mrs Noseworthy had put the tray on the floor outside the door and gone back downstairs.

There was a one-egg omelet on the large white plate, and a piece of white bread, skimpily spread with margarine. A small dish contained three prunes, and there was a six-ounce glass of skimmed milk – the kind his father called 'blue john.' As he put the tray on the bedside table, he regretted making the comment about the Gideon Bible. Hoke ate slowly, taking his time to make the meager meal last. Except for wine and cheese later, this would be the last meal he would get until breakfast. He would have to stay put in the house until he heard from Peoples.

There was a battery-powered digital alarm clock on the bedside table, but no phone. He could call Brownley in Miami on the downstairs phone and ask Brownley to come and get him, but that wasn't a good idea. When the fire at the farm was discovered, if it hadn't been already, there would be a sheriff's investigation, and Brownley should avoid this area altogether. He would just have to wait.

At five Hoke took his tray downstairs to the kitchen and put it on the counter by the sink before going into the living room. There were wrapped singles of Velveeta cheese food on a large platter arranged in an overlapping pattern. The center of the plate held an unwrapped waxed-paper square of unsalted soda crackers. There was also an opened half-gallon jug of burgundy on the buffet table. Hoke poured a plastic glass with wine but skipped the cheese and crackers.

He was on his third glass of wine when Mrs Peterson came downstairs. She introduced herself, and told him she was a retired history teacher from Rome, Georgia. She was driving around the state by herself, sightseeing, and staying at guesthouses. She loved out-of-the-way places, she said, and met very interesting people at the guesthouses. At first, she said, when she left Rome, she had stayed at motels. But they all were alike, and she hadn't met anyone. Then she got a list of Florida guesthouses from a travel agent in St Augustine, and it became a different trip altogether. She was in her early sixties, Hoke figured, wearing khaki culottes and a short-sleeved blouse, and she seemed to be a nice, pleasant woman. When she left Immokalee, she said, she was going to skip Miami and drive directly to Key West, where she had reservations for a week at the Cabin Boy Inn. Hoke knew that the Cabin Boy Inn catered primarily to gay couples on vacation from New York and New Jersey.

'You'll meet some interesting people there, I'm sure,' he told her.

She didn't ask Hoke a single question but rambled on about her afternoon at the Corkscrew Swamp Sanctuary. Mr Noseworthy had poked his head through the swinging door a couple of times, but neither he nor his wife joined them in the parlor. Mrs Peterson told him in some detail about the birds she had seen and ate a half-dozen slices of cheese. Hoke finally excused himself, poured another glass of wine, and took it upstairs to his room to get away from her.

Hoke undressed and went to bed and was asleep by seven-thirty. The house was quiet, and he didn't awaken until seven the next morning. He was still stiff and sore. He took a short tub bath before going downstairs for breakfast. He drank two cups of coffee from the Mr Coffee machine and ate a bowl of Cheerios, pouring them from the opened box on the buffet table. There was milk in a glass pitcher. There were only two slices of cantaloupe on a plate, so Hoke only ate one slice, figuring that the second slice was Mrs Peterson's. Mrs Peterson, on her retirement vacation, was still asleep.

After his frugal breakfast Hoke looked in the bookcase. Most of the books were paperbacks or *Reader's Digest* condensed books in hard cover, but there were a few interesting hardbacks, with dust jackets missing. Hoke took a copy of Sabatini's *Scaramouche* out of the bookcase and opened it to the first page. 'He was born with the gift of laughter, and the knowledge that the world was mad.'

Hooked, Hoke took the book back upstairs to his room and read until noon.

Chapter Thirteen

The following day at 1:00 P.M. Noseworthy came up to Hoke's room and got him. Mel Peoples was on the line from Tallahassee. Noseworthy went into the kitchen, and Hoke picked up the phone.

'Moseley, here.'

'What in the hell happened out there, Sergeant?' Peoples began, and his voice was higher than Hoke had remembered. 'I just talked to Sheriff Boggis a while ago on the phone, and he said the house and barn were burned down.'

'I imagine they are, because they were burning when I saw them. I spent my first night here in town and hitchhiked out to the farm the next morning. An old couple driving to Miami picked me up and dropped me by the gate. It was almost a mile out to the farm itself, but I didn't go all the way. As soon as I saw that the house and the barn were on fire, I walked back here to Immokalee. And I had to walk all the way, too. You should've left a number here for me to call you. I wasn't about to call Boggis or anyone else about the fire.'

'I realize that now, and I'm sorry. But I wasn't sure where I'd be staying. I guess I should've called Noseworthy last night to let you know. But what do you s'pose happened out there? There were no aliens on the farm, and Bock's half-ton is missing, Boggis said.'

'I have no idea what happened. As I told you, as soon as I saw the fire, I took off. With no official ID, I couldn't've explained what I was doing out there. You and Brownley already said you couldn't cover me. Did you tell the sheriff anything about me?'

'Of course not! He'd go through the roof if he knew a Miami cop was working in his county.'

'Well, don't let him find out, or both of our asses will be in trouble.'

'What've you been doing since?'

'Sleeping, reading, and eating skimpy meals here at the guest-house. How do I get back to Miami?'

'Let me think a minute.'

Hoke waited, although he could have suggested several methods.

'Hello? Are you still there?'

'Still here.'

'Tell Noseworthy to drive you to Four Corners in Bonita Springs. Trailways stops there, and you can catch the bus back to Miami. He can advance you the money, and I'll pay him back later.'

'I'll call him to the phone, and you tell him, Mel. Coming from you, he'll feel better about it. He's already worried about my tab here, even though I told him you'd take care of it.'

'Don't worry about the tab –'

'I don't. But Noseworthy does, I suspect.'

'Okay, put him on then. And thanks for your efforts, Sergeant. Tell Willie, when you get back, that we're "kits" now.'

'It was nothing, Mel. I got there too late to check into anything. How's your meeting going in Tallahassee?'

'It's a mess so far. Advance planning for the new immigration law. Mostly appointing new committees for studying the possible effects. It's too soon to actually write any state regs, and there are all sorts of loopholes in the law. For example, they're only going to fine an employer who knowingly hires more than twenty illegal aliens, which doesn't make good sense. How do you interpret something like that if he only hires nineteen at a time?'

'I'm sure you'll work something out, Mel. I'll get Noseworthy.'

Hoke went into the kitchen and got the innkeeper. Noseworthy was whispering something to his wife. As Noseworthy left to talk to Peoples, she looked at Hoke with her bold blue eyes and pushed a strand of hair away from her forehead. 'Is that the call you've been expecting, Mr Jinks?'

'Yes, ma'am. I'm afraid I'm going to have to leave now. But I've enjoyed my stay, especially the little trays you fixed for me. Be sure you add the meals to my tab.'

'I intend to, although, as I told you, we aren't set up for meals other than breakfast. To run a restaurant or a boardinghouse, another license is required. We aren't used to having people stay in their rooms all day either.'

'Well, I don't have a car.' Hoke shrugged. 'And it's too hot to walk around town in the sun.'

'So now you're leaving.'

'Yes, ma'am. And thanks again. And add a fifteen percent tip on my bill – for the meals, I mean.'

'I don't accept tips.' Her cheeks colored.

'Why not? My friend will be happy to pay for the extra service.' Hoke left the kitchen.

Noseworthy was sitting at the check-in table; his fingers were still touching the phone when Hoke joined him.

'Melvin said I was to drive you to Bonita Springs and buy you a bus ticket to Miami.'

'No, Mr Noseworthy.' Hoke shook his head. 'He didn't say that. What he said was that you're to drive me to Bonita Springs and advance me money for my trip. I'll buy my own ticket, and I'll need another twenty bucks for essentials.'

'What kind of essentials d'you need for a bus ride?'

'Several things, and perhaps a pint of bourbon. I'll get my stuff.' Hoke started for the stairs.

'What stuff?'

'Didn't your wife tell you? She cleaned my room. I've got some adhesive tape and a few Tylenols left. And my pistol, of course. I'll be right down.'

Noseworthy had a three-year-old Chevy station wagon. It was in excellent condition, with only twenty-five thousand miles on the odometer. He didn't turn on the radio, but he occasionally rolled his eyes toward Hoke and looked as if he wanted to ask some questions.

'How much,' Hoke said, 'did Mel Peoples tell you about me?'

'He didn't tell me anything. He just asked me to take care of you if you showed up at the house. But the way he said it, I didn't think you'd come. At least that was my impression at the time. If you called instead of coming to the guesthouse, he said to phone him right away and get your number.'

'Is that all?'

'That's all. But I can't say I'm not curious.'

'What do you want to know?'

'I've known Mel Peoples for three years. He's never mentioned you before, and I don't see how a man like you and Mel Peoples ever became friends. No offense, but –'

'None taken, Mr Noseworthy. But that's easy. I knew Mel up in Tallahassee. He was going to A and M and I was in FSU. I used to get student tickets to the FSU football games, and he scalped them for me. We split the profits sixty–forty. Those were halcyon days, Mr Noseworthy. We were young, carefree, and we both had brilliant futures. Ask Mel to tell you about his ticket-scalping days sometime.'

'He did tell me about that. What do you do now?'

'I'm a retired teacher from Rome, Georgia. I just travel around the state, visiting guesthouses and seeing the sights.'

Noseworthy frowned. 'If you don't want to tell me, don't tell me.'

While Noseworthy sulked, Hoke looked incuriously at the gray-green flatlands of Lee County. A lot of the land near the state road had been cleared for cultivation, and they occasionally passed small herds of Black Angus cattle in fenced fields. There were also developers' billboards as they got closer to Four Corners, advertising low pre-construction prices for new condo complexes that were still in the planning stages. When they passed the billboard advertising the Bonita Springs dog track, the sign where the dead Haitian's body was purportedly discovered, Hoke shook his head with sudden insight. The mystery of the 'dead' Haitian behind the billboard was now explained to his satisfaction, but he still didn't know why Mel Peoples and Willie Brownley had lied to him about it. He would find out, however, when he got back to Miami and talked to Willie, even if he had to twist Willie's arm.

There was no bus station at Four Corners, but there was a fifteen-minute rest stop for passengers at the restaurant, and Hoke could buy his ticket from the cashier. Noseworthy gave him money for the fare and an extra twenty dollars, but he handed the money over reluctantly. He shook hands with Hoke, however, and wished him luck before heading back to Immokalee.

Hoke ordered a breakfast of poached eggs, grits, and milk toast and drank three cups of coffee. He had to wait four hours before the bus for Miami pulled into the lot. He could smoke again, if he didn't inhale too deeply, and he smoked ten Kools while he waited for the bus. He was puzzled by Mel Peoples's sudden departure for Tallahassee and Noseworthy's intuitive feeling that he didn't think that any man named Adam Jinks would show up at his guesthouse. It looked as if Mel had been covering for himself, in case anything happened at Bock's farm, by being four hundred miles away from the area.

Hoke called his house from a pay phone in the Miami bus station. He let the phone ring ten times before he hung up. It was after 9:00 P.M., so someone should have been home. Hoke dialed again, thinking he had inadvertently dialed the wrong number. But no one answered the second time either. No one was home. Not one of the three females in his house would be able to let the phone ring ten times without answering it. As a general rule, one of the girls picked up the receiver by the second or third ring.

Hoke walked to the police station, a dozen blocks away. He took the elevator up to the Homicide Division; but his office was locked, and he didn't have his keys. Captain Slater was night duty officer in charge. Slater wore a black silk suit, a navy-blue shirt, and a striped blue-and-white necktie. His pale, pockmarked face, because of his dark clothes, made him look as if he were recovering from a serious illness, but he always looked this way. Slater looked Hoke up and down, and gave him a lipless smile.

'Back from vacation already? Where'd you go, anyway?' Hoke's right sleeve was scorched slightly, his oversize rolled-up trousers were baggy at the knees, and he needed a shave again.

'Just working around the house, Captain. Is González around?'

'He's still on days. I haven't seen him for a week or so. Half the time I don't even know what you cold-case people are working on.'

'That's up to Major Brownley. I report directly to him, as you know, but I'll get permission from him to fill you in if you want me to.'

'Never mind. I don't want to know. I've got enough on my plate already. You hear about Rodrigues and Quintero?'

'What about 'em?'

'Arrested. Both of them. They're both in jail on a hundred-and-fifty-thousand-dollar bond. It should be in the papers tomorrow.'

'What happened? They're on your night shift, aren't they?'

Slater nodded. 'They held up a crack house in Liberty City. It wasn't the first time, either, but this time IA undercovers were planted and arrested them with their hands out.'

'That's hard to believe.' Hoke shook his head. 'These guys've been in plain clothes for five or six years, and they're both married, with families.'

'It's a fucking shame, Hoke. But the money's too easy to get, and there's too much of it out there. And these are Homicide cops. God only knows what the Vice cops are stealing.'

'I blame Internal Affairs, Captain. Lieutenant Norbert sits on his ass over there, and he doesn't know half the things that are going on in the department. They should send Norbert back to Traffic, where he belongs.'

Slater pulled his thin lips back again. 'He managed to get Rodriguez and Quintero. They've been suspended, of course, and that leaves me four detectives short on my night shift. Smitty resigned yesterday, without being asked, and Reynaldo's on a six-month psychiatric leave. He'll never return to duty either. He was cleared at the hearing, but both those boys he shot were under sixteen, and the new chief won't take him back.'

'He can fight that with the PBA.' Hoke shrugged. 'Both those boys he killed had pistols.'

'Oh, I don't blame Reynaldo, Sergeant. I would've shot them myself in the same situation, but that makes six he's killed in five years. Six, as you know, is beyond chance. They'll give him a psychiatric disability pension, and he'll be fixed for life. What the hell, Hoke, Reynaldo's got sixteen years in. You take his pension fund money for sixteen years, and add a disability on top of that, and he'll make more retirement money than he would if he stayed for twenty.'

'I guess you're right, Captain.'

'I know damned well I'm right. I worked out the figures on my calculator.'

Hoke shrugged and took out his cigarettes. 'Reynaldo's always been a little flaky, if you ask me, but –'

'You can't smoke out here in the bullpen.'

Hoke put his pack away. 'But Quintero and Rodriguez were good cops.'

'"Were" is the word. Can I help you with anything, Hoke?'

'No, sir. I was just looking for González, is all. I'm still on vacation. I'll just leave a message in his box and tell him to call me at home tomorrow.'

'Okay. I happen to see him, I'll tell him to call you.'

Before going downstairs, Hoke put a message in González's box. He checked an unmarked Plymouth out of the motor pool and drove home to Green Lakes. He turned on the radio. Miles Davis was playing 'In a Silent Way.' Miles Davis hated white people so much he always played with his back to his audiences. But he took their money; he let them buy his records. Hoke switched to a Spanish station. An unhappy baritone was singing about his *corazón*. The Latins all had heart trouble, Hoke thought. He switched off the radio and drove the rest of the way home in silence.

No one was home, the house was dark, and Hoke didn't have his keys. Hoke's Pontiac Le Mans was parked behind Ellita's Honda Civic, and Sue Ellen's motorcycle was chained to the carport support column. He rang the bell several times, but no one answered.

Hoke went next door to Mr Sussman's house. Hoke hadn't talked to Mr Sussman for more than a month and wasn't eager to see him now; but Hoke kept an extra set of house keys at the Sussmans', and Sussman had left a set of his at Hoke's for emergency purposes. Mr Sussman was religious and wore a crocheted yarmulke at all times, even when he was inside his house. The old man had berated Sue Ellen one afternoon for revving up her motorcycle in the yard, and she had told him to go fuck himself. Hoke had talked to him about it and then had to persuade Sue Ellen to apologize. The two families weren't close; but Mrs Sussman was a nice old lady who made over Pepe whenever she saw the baby with Ellita, and Hoke didn't want to have a feud going with his neighbors.

Mr Sussman, wearing his skullcap, answered the door when Hoke knocked and peered at him with watery blue eyes. He had a pointed chin, and his cropped gray beard made him look like a billy goat. He took off his reading glasses but didn't invite Hoke inside.

'I don't have my keys with me, Mr Sussman, and no one seems to be home.'

'They all left, that's why. I'll see if I can find your keys.' He closed the door, and Hoke waited on the porch. Hoke lighted a cigarette and smoked while he waited. Sussman came back with the keys, unlocked the screen door, and handed them to the detective.

'What do you mean they all left? Both cars are still there.'

'They left with that man who moved in across the street. About ten this morning. They were all dressed up, and they had suitcases and the baby, too. They got into this stretch limousine – a big blue Lincoln – and drove away.'

'The man across the street, too?'

'That's what I said. There was a man driving the limo, and he was wearing a dark suit, but if he was a chauffeur, he didn't wear a cap. Sarah and me both watched 'em leave from the yard. I'd been on the phone for an hour or so, lining up volunteers for Super Sunday – that's for Federation, you see – and Sarah'd just got back from the store with Bumble Bee.'

'Bumble Bee?'

'That's white tuna. That's what Sarah always calls it. When she sends me to the store for tuna, she always writes down "Bumble Bee" so I don't get a different kind by mistake. Anyway, as I was saying, most people on the block, those that were home, came out to take a look at that stretch Lincoln. You could almost put my little Escort in the back seat.'

'They didn't say where they were going?'

'It only took 'em a minute. They seemed to be in a big rush, although I thought your daughter, Sue Ellen, said something or other to me when she got into the car. I don't know what it was, but I can make a pretty good guess.'

'That's all over with, Mr Sussman. Sue Ellen apologized to you for the last time, and she told me she was sorry, too. I won't bother you again this evening, Mr Sussman. I'll just hang on to these keys for now and bring 'em back to you tomorrow sometime.'

'Suit yourself.'

Hoke let himself in to the house and looked on the refrigerator door for a note from Ellita. There was no note under the pizza magnet or anywhere else in the house. His car and house keys were on top of his dresser, however, and that would have been a logical place to leave a message. But he couldn't find any notes, and he looked in the girls' room as well. Clothes were scattered about in Ellita's bedroom and the girls' room, but then, they always were – most of the time anyway. Both of Ellita's suitcases, the big bag and her expensive camelskin airplane carry-on, were missing. Pepe's blue nylon diaper bag was missing, too, but Ellita would need that if she were going to be away for only a couple of hours. Still, it was past ten now, and if they had left at ten this morning, they had been gone for twelve hours!

Hoke called the Sánchez house, hoping he would get the old lady instead of Ellita's father. Her English was better than the old man's, and when she had lived with Hoke for a month right after Ellita came home from the hospital with the baby, the two of them had got along fairly well. She was a good cook, and Hoke had praised her meals. She had certainly been a big help to Ellita during her postpartum periods of depression. For a couple of weeks, when she first came home with Pepe, Ellita had cried a lot for no apparent reason, and Hoke didn't know what was the matter with her. 'Don't worry,' Mrs Sánchez had said, raising her gray eyebrows. 'We all do that. She'll quit after two or three more weeks. She'd cry even more if she'd had a girl.'

On the fourth ring Mrs Sánchez answered the phone.

'It's me, Hoke,' Hoke said quickly. 'Sergeant Moseley. Don't hang up.'

'I didn't see you leave the party.'

Hoke had already forgotten about the party. 'I thought I said good-bye to you, Mrs Sánchez. I had to go to work. An emergency. I know I said good-bye to Uncle Arnoldo. How is Tío Arnoldo, by the way?'

'He has cancer. There's a tumor in his bowels.'

'I'm sorry to hear that.'

'He bleeds down there. He has to wear a pad. Like a woman.'

'That's too bad.'

'He's at Jackson now, but they're sending him home from the hospital to die in two days.'

'Back to Cuba?'

'No, here, at my house. He will die here in America, a free man, as soon as we get the Medicaid papers signed.'

'I'm sure you'll keep him comfortable, Mrs Sánchez. Is Ellita there? At your house?'

'No. I haven't seen her since the party. If she doesn't want to talk to her mother, she should at least call her father.'

'You don't know where she is then?'

'She hasn't called me since the party. If she doesn't want to talk to me, tell her to call her father. He is very sad about Tío Arnoldo.'

'Of course. Tell Tío Arnoldo I'll come by and visit him after he gets home. I don't like to bother people when they're still in the hospital.'

'I'll tell him. He will be pleased. And tell Ellita to call her father.'

'I'll tell her.'

After he put the phone down, Hoke undressed and went into the bathroom to shave and shower. He pulled off the Band-Aid preparatory to shaving, and found that the puncture wound in his chin was festering. He cleaned out the yellow pus with a Q-tip dipped in iodine and shaved carefully with a new Bic throwaway razor. He plastered another Band-Aid over the wound before he took his shower. He slipped into a pair of khaki slacks, a light blue sport shirt, clean white socks, and the Nikes he wore when he went to the gym to play handball. His black, high-topped shoes were dirty, and damp inside, so he put them outside the door to the girls' room so Aileen could clean and polish them when she came home. When she came home? Where in the hell would Aileen, Sue Ellen, and Ellita go with a creep like Donald Hutton? That is, if they'd gone willingly. Mr Sussman said that Sue Ellen had said something or other he couldn't hear when she climbed into the limo. Were they being kidnapped? That seemed unlikely, but on the other hand, if Hutton had a weapon, they would do what he told them, including packing their bags. One way or another Hutton would get his revenge, and a good way to do it was by doing something evil to Ellita and the girls. But Hoke couldn't entertain this thought seriously. If Hutton were going to kidnap Ellita and the girls, he would do it surreptitiously, not in broad daylight with a chauffeured limo.

There was plenty of food in the refrigerator. Hoke made a tomato and cream cheese sandwich on white bread and drank an Old Style with it. He had to make his report to Major Brownley, and he couldn't decide how much or how little to tell him. Brownley still had his badge, weapon, and teeth. Despite the hour, Hoke decided to drive to the major's house instead of phoning.

He threw the .38 pistol he had taken from Bock's house into the bottom drawer of his dresser and covered it with T-shirts. It might be useful as a throw-down weapon someday. He drove the unmarked police car he had checked out instead of taking his Pontiac. Brownley lived in the middle-class section of Liberty City, but to get there, Hoke had to drive through some mean black streets where kids often threw rocks at cars with white drivers. If rocks were thrown, let them throw at a department car instead of his Le Mans.

Hoke hadn't been to the major's house in more than two years. He had forgotten the address but knew where it was and how to get there. On Hoke's last visit Brownley, when he had been promoted to major, had thrown a backyard barbecue for all the off-duty detectives in the Homicide Division. Only five of them, including Hoke and Bill Henderson, had shown up. Ellita had been there, too, but the other detectives hadn't brought their wives. Mrs Henderson came along, of course, because Bill made her. It would have looked bad for him as the executive officer if he hadn't brought his wife. There was a full keg of draft beer and enough pork barbecue and baked beans for at least forty people. Brownley's three sons wore white shirts, red bow ties, and white pants, and his two daughters wore white party dresses with red sashes. It had been an embarrassing evening for the Brownleys, and Hoke thought at the time those kids would be eating barbecue for a week afterward. After that the major hadn't given any more parties for the detectives in his division.

Brownley had a four-bedroom ranch-style house, and it was surrounded by an eight-foot unpainted board fence. There was a kidney-shaped pool in the backyard. Three cars were parked on the circular asphalt driveway in front of the house. Hoke parked in the street and pushed through the gate, ignoring the Bad Dog sign. Brownley's dog, a fifteen-year-old poodle bitch named Mary, was half blind and too feeble to bark.

One of Brownley's sons, a boy of fifteen or so, let Hoke into the house and asked him to sit in the living room. This was a room rarely used, except for company, and it smelled strongly of Lemon Pledge. Hoke could hear talking and the sounds of the television coming from the Florida room in the back of the house. Willie Brownley, wearing plaid Bermudas, slippers, and a striped Saint Laurent shaving robe, joined Hoke within minutes. Hoke stood up. Brownley waved him back down and sat in a tapestry-cushioned straight chair across from him.

'I know it's late –' Hoke said.

'When did you get back?'

'This evening. I rode the bus from Bonita and checked a car out of the motor pool at the station.'

'Mel's pretty upset, Hoke. He's called me twice now, both times with new information. He's sorry as hell now, he said, that he asked me for help, and he's afraid I'll tell somebody. Apparently he's up for a big civil service promotion, and he doesn't want any word of your investigation to get out.'

'There's no investigation to talk about, Willie. Mel told me to tell you that you were "kits" now – I guess he meant "quits" – but all I can tell you is what I told him. I went out there all right, but when I saw the house and barn on fire, I took off in a hurry.'

'Did you see any Haitians out there?'

'I didn't see anyone, and no one saw me. The farm's almost a mile from the highway, and I couldn't see the fire till I walked down the gravel road to the farm. I could see smoke, but I thought at first they were just burning a field. There's a heavily wooded hammock between the highway and the farm, and the highway along there's bordered by palmettos.'

'The sheriff found two dead bodies, Hoke. Mr Bock was inside the house, and his foreman was in the barn. Bock's chest cavity was filled with shotgun pellets, and the Mexican's skull had been crushed with a blunt instrument.'

'No shit?'

'That's right. What do you suppose happened?'

Hoke shrugged. 'What about the workers?'

'He had some Haitians working out there, but no one seems to know how many there were. But they've all disappeared, and his truck's gone, too.'

Hoke nodded reflectively and touched his sore chin.

'What happened to your chin?'

'Cut it shaving, and it's infected, I think. Maybe his workers revolted, killed Bock and the foreman, and then took off. Perhaps they got word or found out that he's been killing Haitians instead of paying them, so they beat him to the punch.'

'I don't think so. Haitians are a pretty docile lot, and the illegals are afraid of getting picked up and deported back to Haiti. They're the most law-abiding non-citizens we have in Miami.'

'Ordinarily, yes. But maybe Bock threatened to turn them in to the INS. Besides, Haitians aren't all that docile. Their ancestors were warriors back in Africa, and they beat the French Army to get their independence.'

'I know a few things about Haiti, Hoke. We studied some about Haiti in my black history courses. They fought the French in the early eighteen-hundreds, but since then they've been kept down by one tyrant after another. Haitians don't have much fight left in them by now.'

'That's a generality, Willie. A few men, afraid for their lives, might act differently.'

A skinny black girl, about twelve or thirteen, with her hair in tight cornrows and wearing jeans, sneakers, and a Miami Dolphins T-shirt, brought in a tray holding two frosted steins of beer. She offered one to Hoke before taking the other to her father.

'Thanks,' Hoke said. 'What's your name?'

'Lily.'

'Her name's Lillith,' Brownley said, 'but we call her Lily for short.'

'That's a nice name, Lily,' Hoke said, taking a sip of beer.

The girl looked at her father. He tilted his head, and she left the room.

'What did you tell Ellita about me? To explain my absence?'

'Well ...' Brownley took a long swig of beer, swallowed. 'I didn't talk to her personally, Hoke. I had a patrolman drive your car over to your house, and I told him to tell Elitta you'd be out of town on a special assignment for a few days. Because of the nature of the assignment, you couldn't contact her, and she shouldn't try to get in touch with you. I left it at that. I figured if she got worried after a couple of days and called me, I'd make up something else to tell her. But she never called.'

'And she swallowed all that? Without any questions?'

'Why wouldn't she? She used to be a police officer, and it isn't unusual for a detective to go undercover. But you're holding something back, Hoke. What really happened over there?'

'Nothing. I've been on a vacation for a few days, that's all. I was on unofficial business, private business, and I didn't have my badge, weapon, or even my teeth. So whatever happened over there is none of your fucking business!'

'There's no need to –'

'That's right. There's no need for you to know anything. What you don't know can't hurt you. As you told me in the first place, if I got into any trouble, you couldn't back me up.'

'Mel said the two pit dogs were killed, too. Shot.'

'That couldn't have been me, Willie. You had my pistol. When I saw the fire, I also thought about the dogs. A fire like that can make dogs crazy, so they're another reason I left in a hurry. I know you told me how to catch 'em by the front legs and break them off, but without any practice I didn't want to try it. So I left before they could sniff me out.'

'Okay, let's forget about it. I'll get your stuff.'

Hoke finished his beer. He looked around but couldn't see a place to put down the stein without leaving a ring on the polished tables. He took the empty mug into the foyer and put it on the floor. Brownley returned and handed Hoke a brown grocery sack. Hoke shoved his holstered weapon beneath his belt at the back and pocketed his badge case and wallet. He looked at the floor for a moment.

'Ellita and the girls aren't home, Willie. Do you know where they are?'

'What d'you mean, aren't home? They might be at a movie.'

Hoke shook his head. 'I stopped at the house before driving over here, Willie. They're gone, and they left with packed bags. According to my next-door neighbor, they left in a stretch Lincoln with Donald Hutton. There was no note, but if you told Ellita not to contact me, that explains why she didn't leave one. That is, if she was able to write one. I can't think of anyplace Ellita and the girls would go with Donald Hutton. But my neighbor said they left the house at ten this morning.'

'That's strange, but I don't know anything about it. She didn't call me.'

'Hutton promised he'd get revenge on me, Willie. So if Ellita told him I'd be away for a few days, maybe he decided to kidnap them.'

'Not at ten, in broad daylight. There's probably some simple explanation.'

'They took their clothes along. They're on a trip of some kind, Willie.'

'In that case you haven't got anything to worry about. School's out, so maybe he took 'em down to the Keys. Why not call Ellita's mother? She'd know.'

'I did. She hasn't heard from Ellita since the party for her uncle.'

'Maybe she'll send you a postcard. I wouldn't worry about it if I were you.'

'Thanks, Willie. But if you were me, you'd worry about it.'

Brownley shook his head and smiled. 'If it was someone else other than Ellita, I might worry. But she's a match for any man, in my opinion.'

'I guess you're right. She still carries her pistol, and there's probably a simple explanation.'

'See what I mean? Hutton's got lots of money. Maybe he took them for a drive – up to Palm Beach or maybe on a boat ride.'

'Sure. Can you let me have Mel Peoples's phone number?'

'No. He doesn't want to talk to you again, Hoke. He wants all this shit to blow over.'

'Okay. Can you call him for me?'

'I guess so.'

'There's a woman in Immokalee, living in the Lucky Star Trailer Park. Her name's Elena Osborne, and she's got a retarded son about three years old. Tell Mel to get that kid away from her and put it in a state institution somewhere.'

'He's on the State Agricultural Commission, Hoke. He doesn't have any authority for something like that.'

'I didn't have any authority in Immokalee either. He owes me a favor for my investigation, and he knows the people over there who can do something.'

'What's your interest in this woman, Hoke?'

'Elena Osborne. Mrs Elena Osborne. None at all. The kid is ruining the woman's life, that's all. So tell Mel to get the welfare people to commit that kid. If he doesn't, I'm going to phone Boggis and tell him the whole story.'

'You'd be in trouble, not Mel.'

'I don't give a shit. If Mel's up for a promotion, he'll do it. If Bock and his foreman are dead, Mel can't afford to get his name in the papers, even though he meant well.'

'All right. I'll call him tonight. What's the woman's name again?'

'Osborne. Mrs Elena Osborne. The Lucky Star Trailer Park. And when you call him, tell him I'm going to check on this matter later, after things have cooled down over there in Immokalee.'

'I believe I can persuade him, Hoke.'

'Thanks, Willie, this is important to me. I'd like to see something positive come out of this fiasco.'

'I wouldn't call it that.'

'You wouldn't? What are my chances of getting a look at the autopsy report?' Hoke got to his feet and felt for a cigarette. He lit a Kool and put his lighter away. 'The dead Haitian. The one you said was buried behind the billboard.'

'Not a chance.' Brownley shook his head.

'That's what I figured. There isn't any dead Haitian, and there never was, right?'

'The dead Haitian was Mel's idea, Hoke, not mine. There are Haitians missing, that's true enough, but we haven't found any of them yet. But Mel thought that if we told you we had a dead one, it would be easier to get you to check out Bock's farm. How'd you find out?'

Hoke shrugged. 'The innkeeper in Immokalee drove me to Four Corners in Bonita Springs. Along the way we passed the billboard advertising the dog track. The billboard's in Lee County, not Collier County, so if you found a dead man buried behind it, the Lee County sheriff would've been called, not Sheriff Boggis. What the hell is going on, Major?'

'I can't tell you, Hoke. I'd like to, but I can't.'

'Okay. I'll accept that. But you owe me a big debt, Willie.'

'And you will be paid, Sergeant. That's a promise.'

Hoke drove home and went to bed. He was too exhausted to think about the matter. Just before he fell asleep, he decided that he would call the limousine services first thing in the morning and go on from there. That is, if Ellita didn't call him or return home by morning.

Chapter Fourteen

The next morning Hoke parked the unmarked Plymouth in the police lot. As he got out of the car, he flipped his cigarette on the ground and stepped on it. Three cars away, Captain Slater was just getting into his Lincoln Continental. He held up a hand and walked toward Hoke. His shoulders were straight, and his back was stiff, as if someone held a gun to his spine.

'Were you smoking in the car, Sergeant Moseley?'

Hoke nodded.

'That's a twenty-five-dollar fine.'

'Jesus, Captain Slater, I was alone in the car. My smoke didn't bother anyone.'

'It bothers the new chief. The rule's been posted, D-T-one-oh-seven, and that means unmarked cars as well as patrol vehicles. I'll have to put you down for a fine. Commander Henderson will have it deducted from your next paycheck. You're a sergeant, and you're supposed to set an example for the younger officers.'

'I forgot about the damned rule.'

'That's tough shit. Next time the fine'll make you remember it.'

Slater walked toward his car without looking back. Hoke checked the Plymouth in with the dispatcher, signing his name and time on the clipboard. From now on, he thought, when he smoked in an unmarked car, he would have to remember to sneak it.

Teodoro González, wearing a white linen jacket with the sleeves rolled up to the elbows, was already in the office.

'I called you at home,' he said, 'soon's I got your note, but no one answered so I figured you'd already left.'

Hoke nodded and pulled the two telephone books over to his side of the desk. He was going to look up limousines. The books were bulky, and this year the phone company had divided them so that half of the Yellow Pages were in A–K and the other half were in L–Z. This made it equally inconvenient to look up private numbers and commercial Yellow Page numbers.

González clasped his hands together and smiled expectantly across the desk. As Hoke looked at González's young, vacant face, freshly shaved and stinking of Brut, he wondered what would have happened to the young detective if Brownley had sent him to Immokalee. He would be one dead Cuban-American. For the first time since they had been working together, Hoke felt sorry for González.

'Report,' Hoke said, without opening the L–Z book.

'Report?'

'Report.'

'Oh, sure, now I know what you mean. I swallowed that peanut butter ball, just like Major Brownley told me to do, but I really didn't need to. I wasn't X-rayed, so it didn't make any difference. I made the appointment with Dr Schwartz, and I spent the first hour in his reception room filling in a medical history form before he saw me. By the way, what's enuresis? I didn't know what it was, so I put down I never had it.'

'I'm willing to bet good money you did. It means wetting the bed.'

'Oh, sure, I had that, until I was eleven or twelve. How'd you know?'

'Basic deduction, Teddy. What happened with Dr Schwartz?'

'He took my blood pressure, listened to my chest and back with his stethoscope, and asked me if I ever coughed up any blood. I said no, and then he asked me if I had a stressful job. I started to say yes, but I'd already put down on my form that I was a tennis instructor, so I had to say no again.'

'Tennis instructor? When did you start playing tennis?'

'I don't, but I had to put down an occupation that would let me get away for two hours in the morning to see a doctor. There aren't many jobs where they'll let you off to sit in a doctor's office.'

'Okay. Was he wearing the ring?'

González nodded, and plucked at his lower lip. 'He was wearing an onyx ring with a diamond in it. But I can't say for sure it was the same ring Dr Russell was wearing. Those rings are seen a lot around town, especially at the dog tracks. He was wearing a gold Rolex, too. But that may not have been Dr Russell's watch either.'

'What makes you say that?'

'On my way out of the office I saw Dr Schwartz's partner, Dr Farris. He was talking to the nurse, and he was wearing a gold Rolex. Once you start looking, you see 'em everywhere. Even Captain Slater's got one.'

'Captain Slater's a prick, Teddy, but he isn't a suspect. And neither are the one hundred and one drug dealers and lawyers who wear gold Rolexes. I'm glad you spotted the watch on Dr Farris, but now we have two suspects instead of one.'

González shook his head. 'Max Farris operated for Dr Russell that morning. After Sergeant Quevedo called the clinic, the nurse called Dr Schwartz first and then Dr Farris to perform the operation. Isn't that right?'

'Farris had enough time, and so did Schwartz. Russell was dead for about fifteen minutes when the deliveryman found him. That's the estimate, but it could've been longer. He had to go to a neighbor's to call nine-one-one. Then it took the police car about five or six minutes to get there after that. That's at least twenty-five. So Dr Farris had plenty of time to shoot Dr Russell and get back home before anybody called.'

'These are all approximate times.'

'But underestimated, not overestimated. Besides, it seems unlikely to me that either one of these doctors would do the actual shooting himself. I mean improbable, not unlikely. They both profited by Russell's death. The only reason Dr Schwartz is the prime suspect is that he profited most. He got Russell's house and wife, in addition to half the clinic. We're going to have to flush these fuckers out. One or the other or both.'

'What about my money?'

'What money?'

'I couldn't use my insurance because I had to use an assumed name when I saw the doctor. José Smith. The nurse gave me a little lecture, too, about not having any medical insurance. Then I had to pay one hundred bucks in cash. I had the money, knowing I'd have to pay something, but I didn't think I'd have to pay a hundred bucks just to be told to take Maalox. I talked to Commander Henderson afterward about getting my refund, and he said I couldn't get any refund without a legitimate bill from the doctor. My receipt, you see, was made out to José Smith.'

'How about department funds?'

'The undercover wasn't authorized in advance, Henderson said.'

'Jesus Christ. The undercover was tacitly authorized by Major Brownley when he explained the peanut butter ball to you. Did you tell Bill that?'

'I tried to, but I didn't have anything on *paper* in advance. So he said he couldn't do anything for me.'

'You still got your receipt from Dr Schwartz?'

'From his nurse, yes. Right here.'

'Okay, give it to me. I'll type a backdated okay of one hundred bucks in undercover expenditures and get Major Brownley to sign it. Then I'll give it to Bill and get your money for you. This is something you should've done yourself, Teddy. Paperwork isn't just a part of this job, it's ninety percent of it.'

González handed over the receipt. 'I'm sorry. But I really can't afford to lose that much dough, Sergeant.'

'Can you afford coffee and doughnuts?'

González grinned and got to his feet. 'Glazed?'

'One glazed and one burnt coconut.'

Hoke put the receipt into his in-box, as González left, and then walked his fingers through the Yellow Pages to limousines. There were more than fifty limousine services listed, to his surprise, not counting the large display ads that repeated some of the same numbers in larger type. Hoke chose the numbers from the display ads that advertised stretch Lincolns first and narrowed his search down to a half-dozen. He wrote the numbers on a legal pad and started from the top. On the fifth call he got lucky. The dispatcher said that a Mr Hutton and party had been picked up the day before in Green Lakes and had been driven to the Port of Miami. They were dropped off at Slip Three, for the *Caribbean Princess*. This ship visited Nassau, in the Bahamas, and the limousine was scheduled to pick up Mr Hutton and his party again when the boat docked at 10:00 A.M. on Sunday. 'Actually,' the dispatcher said, 'the boat's there by nine, but it takes customs about an hour on the boat to check out the crew and aliens first. Passengers start to disembark around ten. Then they get their luggage on the dock and go through a customs check. It all goes pretty fast, once it gets started, but it's usually eleven by the time they're ready to leave. But our man'll be there at ten because that's the official disembarking time.'

'How much do you charge an hour?'

'It all depends, Sergeant. Usually it's seventy-five an hour for a stretch Lincoln, but if you want the car and driver for three or four days, we work out a much lower rate.'

'But if your driver's at the dock by ten, you gain an extra hour, don't you?'

'Well, I guess so, but it's our experience that it's better to be early than late. People who rent limos don't like to wait.'

'Is the driver there?'

'No, sir, he isn't. He's home today.'

'Can you have him call me here at the police station?'

'If he's home, I'll tell him.'

Hoke gave the dispatcher his extension, thanked him, and racked the phone. He felt relieved but angered as well. He was relieved to know that Ellita and the girls hadn't been kidnapped or made to go with Hutton against their will, but he was angry because they had gone with Hutton and made him worry about them.

González came in with the coffee and two doughnuts and put the Styrofoam cup on the desk. The doughnuts were on a paper plate and covered with waxed paper. Hoke wadded the waxed paper into a ball and threw it at González, missing by two feet.

'What took you so long?'

'While I was down there, I decided to have a little breakfast. I thought – you know – while I was in the cafeteria, I might as well. It saved two trips, bring you the doughnuts and coffee, and then go back down again –'

'You thought wrong. Take the Russell file, and find the home addresses of Dr Schwartz and Dr Farris, and then go downstairs and find out from the desk sergeant who patrols the neighborhoods where they live. I want to see if they're patrolled in the daytime as well as at night.'

'What's this for, Sergeant Moseley?'

'I'll explain when you get back.'

Hoke ate his doughnuts and finished his coffee before he left his office to talk to Bill Henderson. Henderson was on the phone, and Hoke waited out of earshot until he finished talking and racked the receiver.

'Bill,' he said, handing him the receipt from Dr Schwartz's bill, 'González needs his hundred bucks back.'

'Not a chance.' Henderson shook his head. 'I already talked to him about it.'

'I know you did, but there's a way around it. Put his name on the insurance form, and then type "José Smith" in parentheses after his name. That'll make it a legitimate bill, and the insurance will pay eighty percent. González'll lose twenty bucks, but at least he won't be out the entire amount.'

'I don't know if that'll work, Hoke.'

'Sure it will. They do this over in Vice all the time when they check out doctor suspects, to see who's writing phony scripts for H. You can't expect undercovers to pay phony doctor bills, but most doctors want cash in advance before they'll even talk to a patient. I know they do it this way because Marcia in Vice told me so.'

'Okay, I'll send it in, but González'll still be stuck for twenty bucks. If you backdated a request for department funds and could get Major Brownley to sign it, he could get the entire amount.'

'I was going to do it that way, but I changed my mind. If González loses twenty bucks, next time he'll fill out his request in advance. I wasn't here to hold his hand, or this wouldn't've happened.'

'Okay. Have a good time on vacation?'

'Terrific.'

When González came back with the patrol schedules, Hoke went downstairs to Traffic and talked to Lieutenant Vitale, explaining what he wanted the patrol cars to do. 'The people who live at these addresses are witnesses in a cold case, Lieutenant. All I want the night patrolmen to do is stop for three or four minutes outside the house, put the spot on the address numbers or a front window, and then drive away. If they drive by two or three times a night and do this, they might look for any signs of departure. I mean, they can see if the occupants are getting ready to leave.'

'Won't this make the occupants suspicious?'

'Yes, sir. That's the idea. On the day patrols, when the officers take their breaks, I'd like to have them park in front of these houses for ten minutes or so. If anyone comes out of the house to ask what they're doing, just tell 'em to drive away without answering.'

'What are they looking for?'

'A U-Haul trailer, suitcases, whatever.'

Vitale frowned. 'This is all aboveboard, isn't it, Sergeant?'

'Yes, sir. I don't know about you, but I'm always happy to see a patrol car in my neighborhood. I like to know they're out there. Of course, if I was running a crack house, I wouldn't like to see one.'

'Are these suspected crack houses?'

'No, sir. The important thing is, I want the cars and the uniforms seen, but I don't want the officers to talk to the occupants.'

'Who lives here? In these houses?'

'You don't need to know. If you did, I'd tell you. But if the guy we're looking for is hiding out in either place, seeing blue-and-whites might flush him out.'

'I see. Now I see what you're after.' Vitale nodded. 'Why didn't you say so? How long should my men do this?'

'Two or three days and two or three nights. I appreciate this, Lieutenant.'

'No problem.' Vitale grinned, clasped his hands behind his head, and sat back in his swivel chair. 'I thought you came down to bitch about the fine you got for smoking in an unmarked car.'

Hoke went back to his office. 'Do you still have Farris's and Schwartz's addresses in your notebook?' he asked González.

'Sure.'

'Here's what I want you to do. First, go to Dr Farris's house. If the maid answers the door, flash your badge, tell her you're from Homicide, and ask her how long she's been working for Dr Farris. Just that, and nothing more. When you get the information, leave. Don't answer any of her questions. Just leave. If Mrs Farris, instead of the maid, answers the door, ask her if you can talk to her maid. Show Mrs Farris your badge, and be polite, but don't answer any of her questions either – if she has any. She'll get you the maid. Ask her then how long she's been working there, and write down her answer in your notebook. Then leave. Think you can do that?'

González nodded. 'Sure.'

'Then drive to Dr Schwartz's house and do the same thing. Ask the maid the same question, and then come back here to the station. If I'm not here, wait for me. I want you to drive me home tonight.'

González nodded. 'I heard you got caught by Captain Slater smoking in an unmarked car this morning.'

'Who told you that?'

'A guy from the motor pool, while I was having breakfast.'

'I did. Sometimes the rumors you pick up in the building are true. Do you understand what I want you to do?'

'Sure, but we don't need this information. It's all in the file, I'm sure.'

'Three years is a long time. They both may have new maids. And maids, sometimes, overhear a lot of conversations, whether they want to or not.'

'But if they're new, the information won't help our case any.'

'These doctors don't know that. Just do what I tell you to do.'

'I was showing some initiative. You're always telling me I don't show any initiative.'

'Okay, you've shown it. Now you can go.'

After González left, Hoke studied the Russell file for about ten minutes before the phone rang. It was the limousine driver, a man named Raúl Goya y Goya. 'I've had my chauffeur's license two years now,' Goya y Goya said, after identifying himself, 'and I've never had a ticket.'

'I'm not interested in your driving record, Raúl. You aren't in any trouble with the police. I just wanted to ask you a few questions about the passengers you picked up yesterday in Green Lakes.'

'Mr Hutton and party?'

'That's right. Did you overhear them saying anything that seemed a little funny or strange?'

'I don't listen in to passengers' conversation, Sergeant. I just go where they tell me, that's all. If I started listening in to what was being said in the back, I wouldn't've lasted this long. I've seen some weird stuff going on back there, but I've never been asked to do nothing wrong, like make an illegal U-turn or –'

'I realize you're a good driver, Raúl. I just wondered if you overheard them talking about the purpose of the cruise – why they were going, anything like that?'

'The two teenagers were excited, that's all. They'd never been on a cruise before, and they were asking Mr Hutton if they could play the slot machines, and like that. He also explained roulette to them, I believe, but as I say, I wasn't listening. The only thing that struck me funny was the lady. She was nursing the baby, and you don't see things like that much anymore. Not in the car, I mean. The windows are tinted some, but not real dark, and people can still see in at stoplights, you know. So when she started nursing the baby, I hung back a little so I wouldn't get stopped at the lights, and I concentrated on my driving.'

'Okay then. And you'll pick them up again Sunday morning?'

'I hope so. I asked for the run, but I may not get it. Mr Hutton tipped me a twenty. What's this all about, Sergeant? This was just a happy family, going on a cruise. I don't know what else I can tell you.'

'You've been very helpful, Raúl. And incidentally, you speak English very well.'

'I should hope so. I was born and raised in Springfield, Ohio.'

'Is that right? Well, if it'll help you any, tell the dispatcher I'd like you to do the pickup Sunday.'

'It'll help a lot. Thanks, Sergeant.'

Hoke hung up, satisfied, now that he had talked with the driver and knew that his daughters were okay. In the last few months Sue Ellen had saved a good deal of her money. He hoped that she hadn't taken all of it along to gamble away on the cruise ship. He knew she shot craps with the boys at the car wash, and she had been lucky a few times. But she wouldn't have a chance, shooting craps on the ship or at the Paradise Beach Casino in Nassau. What if she did lose it all? She had worked for it, so he hoped Sue Ellen and Aileen were having a good time. If Hutton thought he was getting even with him by taking his daughters on a free cruise, he

836

was nuts. Let the bastard spend his money on Ellita and the girls. Why should he care?

Hoke signed out, took the same unmarked Plymouth out of the police lot, and stopped for lunch at the Saigon Café in the Bayside Shopping Center. He liked the lemon grass soup served there, and the sole with hot chiles. The manager knew Hoke was a cop, and when he was there, he tore up Hoke's check, and all Hoke had to leave was a tip for the waitress. Hoke enjoyed the meal; it was nice to have his teeth again. After eating, he drank two bottles of Corona beer and smoked three Kools. The clinic was closed between twelve-thirty and one-thirty for lunch, and he had to wait for it to open. The café manager wasn't in, so Hoke paid his tab with his VISA card.

Hoke parked in the clinic's lot at one thirty-five. Three elderly patients were waiting in the reception room. One old man was reading *Modern Maturity*, and two old women were staring at two parrot fish swimming around in the saltwater aquarium. There was an aluminum toy diver in the bottom of the tank, with bubbles coming out of the top of his helmet. Someone had painted 'Mel Fisher' in white paint across the diver's chest. Hoke pushed the bell, and the glass window slid back.

'Mrs Burger?' Hoke said, showing the nurse his badge. 'I'm Sergeant Moseley, Miami Homicide.'

Mrs Burger was in her late fifties, with razor-blue hair in tight curls, and she wore gold-rimmed aviation glasses. She wore a pink nurse's uniform, but no cap, and she became flustered when she saw Hoke's badge. Her lipstick almost matched her uniform, and her two prominent upper front teeth had made little dents in her full lower lip.

'Did you have an appointment?' She looked at her clipboard.

'No, ma'am.' Hoke lowered his voice to a stage whisper. 'I'd like to talk to you, Mrs Burger, for a few minutes. Outside, if you don't mind.'

'I don't know. We just opened – and –'

'It'll only take a few minutes. Get someone to take over for you. I'll be outside.'

Hoke left the waiting room and waited on the brick sidewalk. He lighted a cigarette, and a minute later Mrs Burger came through the door. She was carrying her purse, a brown alligator bag with several gold buckles. Not all the buckles were functional, Hoke noted. Women always brought their handbags, Hoke reflected, even if they were only going to the bathroom.

Hoke took her arm. 'It's pretty hot out here in the sun. Let's sit in my car, and I'll turn on the air conditioning.'

'This isn't going to take very long, is it? I've got –'

'Just a few minutes.'

They got into the car, and Hoke turned on the engine and then the air conditioning. He took out his pack of Kools.

'Would you like a cigarette?'

'I'd love one. We can't smoke in the office, you know. I've got my own.' She opened her bag and took a long black More out of her pack. Hoke lit it for her and put his lighter away. He took out his notebook and ballpoint.

'What's this all about, Sergeant …?'

'Moseley. Dr Russell. You remember Dr Russell's murder?'

'Of course. I've been with the clinic for more than ten years. But I thought that investigation was closed.'

Hoke smiled. 'A murder case is never closed, Mrs Burger. The sergeant you talked to three years ago is no longer on the case, but it's never been closed. What I'm doing, I'm rechecking a few things. How well did you know Dr Russell?'

'Well, I knew him in the office, but not socially or anything like that. And I was shocked by the way he was killed. He didn't have any enemies, and I don't see how he could have. He worked all the time.'

'Did you like him? As a person, I mean.'

'Yes, I did. He was a little brisk sometimes, but I respected him and liked him. When he thought about it, he could be very kind. He wasn't very religious, and neither is Dr Schwartz. What I mean is, neither one of them took Yom Kippur off. But I wanted it off, and Dr Farris didn't want me to have it. He's a Methodist, you see, and because we close on Christmas Day, he thought I was trying to sneak in an extra holiday. Dr Russell stood up for me on that. There are eleven Jewish holidays altogether, but all I ever asked for was Yom Kippur, and Dr Farris didn't even want me to have that. I told him – Dr Farris – that he could dock me a day's pay if he wanted to, but I still wanted the day off. Dr Russell let me have it, and he didn't dock my pay either.'

'They can't dock your pay for a religious holiday, Mrs Burger. Have you had any trouble about that since Dr Russell was killed?'

'No, but I lost Christmas. I have to come in Christmas Day and answer the phone, even though the clinic's closed.'

'You don't care much for Dr Farris, do you?'

'I didn't say that. I work for both doctors, and I get along well with both of them. This is a good job, Sergeant. I used to be in OR, and I don't want to go back to that again, ever.'

'OR?'

'Operating room. I was in OR at St Catherine's for three years, and then Dr Russell offered me a job here. We're open on Saturdays, but we close Wednesday afternoons, and the hours are regular.'

'I see.' Hoke made some notes in his book.

'I told the other detective the same things. I don't have anything new to tell you.'

'When you learned that Dr Russell was shot, aren't you the nurse who phoned Dr Schwartz to take over Russell's scheduled operation?'

'Yes, sir.' She butted her cigarette and took out another. Hoke lit it for her.

'He wasn't here at the clinic? He was at home?'

'He was still in bed, he said. But he was very upset about the news and said he'd call Dr Farris to do the operation. We have an answering service when we're closed.'

'Well, thank you very much, Mrs Burger. You've helped me a lot.'

'I told all this before. Why are you asking me these same things again?'

'You want Dr Russell's killer caught, don't you?'

'Of course, but it all happened so long ago I thought you gave up on it.'

'D'you know how to keep a secret, Mrs Burger?'

'I certainly do. But I don't have any secrets if that's what you mean.'

'I don't mean that. I'll tell you something in confidence then, but I don't want it to go any further. If I tell you, can you keep it to yourself? After all, Dr Russell was your friend, and I'd like to tell you.'

'I won't say anything.'

'All right then. We know who killed Dr Russell, and we've known for some time now. An arrest is imminent. I can't tell you who did it, of course, but you'll be surprised when you learn who killed him.'

'Who did it?'

'I can't tell you any more than I have, and I shouldn't have told you that much. But keep what I told you to yourself. Don't tell anyone.'

'I will. My husband's been dead for six years.'

'In that case, you have no one else to tell. And thanks again for your help.'

'This is very good news, Sergeant Moseley.' Mrs Burger butted her cigarette in the ashtray. She took a mint out of her purse and offered one to Hoke. He shook his head, got out of the car, and then circled the car to open the passenger door. He winked, placed a forefinger to his lips, and she smiled and waggled her fingers as she started back to the clinic.

As Hoke backed out of the parking lot, he wondered how long Mrs Burger would be able to keep the 'secret'. One hour? Two? On the other hand, maybe she would keep it. Most nurses were privy to confidential information, and if they didn't tell their friends about their prominent patients who had doses of clap, maybe they wouldn't talk about murders either. But Hoke had dated nurses, and they had often talked about their patients to him. What else did nurses have to talk about?

Hoke drove to Dr Schwartz's house on Poinciana and parked in the driveway. It was a large two-story house, and the brick façade had been painted white. Four Corinthian columns on the concrete front porch supported nothing. They were there just for decorative purposes. Mrs Schwartz opened the door to his ring, and Hoke showed her his badge.

'Mrs Schwartz? I'm Sergeant Moseley. Homicide.'

Mrs Schwartz, a matronly woman in her late forties, was wearing dark green poplin Bermudas and a lettuce-green silk boat-necked top. Her pinkish hair, in a modified Afro, was obviously dyed. Her brown eyes were almost as dark as Hoke's, and her arched eyebrows were blackened half-circles. Her upper lip was thin, but she had made it fuller by adding a rim of lipstick above the lip.

'Would you like to come in?'

'If I may,' Hoke said, following her into the living room. 'I won't be long.' She sat on one end of the leather couch and indicated the other end for Hoke. He shook his head and remained standing.

'I've got some good news for you, Mrs Schwartz. It'll only be a few more days, but we know who killed your husband – Dr Russell. I wanted to prepare you for this because as soon as we announce the arrest, you'll have reporters coming around to see you, asking questions.'

'I don't understand.' She seemed genuinely puzzled. 'What's this all about? Another detective was here this morning, and he talked to my maid. Right after he left, she told me she had to visit her aunt in Mexico City. I thought he was here to talk to her about her aunt –'

'Has she left yet?'

'About an hour ago.'

'It doesn't matter. That must've been Detective González. He's also working on this case, and he wanted to see her to clarify a few things. How long was your maid with you, Mrs Schwartz?'

'It's been almost five years now. She doesn't live in, but we treat her very well, and I thought I knew her – but I didn't even know she had an aunt in Mexico City. She was more like family than a maid, if you know what I mean.'

Hoke shrugged. 'It's a cultural thing, Mrs Schwartz. I work with Latins in the department, but we rarely socialize after hours because we don't think alike. There's one more thing I'd like to ask you about, though. When your husband was shot, you were up in Orlando visiting your sister –'

'My half-sister, Becky Freeman. My maiden name was Goldberg, but when my father died, my mother married a man named David Freeman. So Becky's my half-sister.'

'Does she ever come down here to visit you?'

Mrs Schwartz shook her head. 'We're not very close. I invited her to the wedding when Leo and I got married, but she couldn't come, she said.'

'According to my notes in the file, you visited your sister – half-sister – for the first time when Dr Russell was killed. If you weren't close, as you say, what was the purpose of the visit?'

'I wasn't asked that by the first detective.'

'I know. That's why I'm asking you now.'

Mrs Schwartz tried to smile, but the corners of her lips turned down. 'Do you have to know?'

'Yes, I do. The man who shot your husband had to know you'd be out of town, you see.'

'All right. I can tell you, and you can check it out easily enough. Becky was mixed up with a married man and got pregnant. She got an abortion, and she asked me to come and stay with her for a few days. Our parents are dead, and I'm the only family she has left. So I went up there. You can check the records at the Fernandez Planned Parenthood Clinic in Orlando if you like. But that's behind her now, and I'd rather let it be. I don't see how it can have any bearing on this case. I don't know why Paul was shot. Who did it, Sergeant?'

'I'll have to withhold that information for a few days, but you'll know soon enough, I promise. And I don't think there's any need to bother your half-sister. If I do make inquiries, I'll be discreet. In a right-wing city like Orlando a schoolteacher could lose her job if the school board found out she had an abortion.'

'They don't know. The only ones who know are you, Becky and me, and the staff of the clinic.'

Hoke nodded. 'Don't worry.' Hoke grinned. 'But I did think I should prepare you for the announcement of the arrest. I know how women are. When TV cameras are involved, women want to look their best, and you might want to make a beauty shop appointment, buy some new clothes, or something. Not that you don't look lovely now, of course.'

'I see. Well, thank you. Could I get you something? A drink? Coffee?'

'No, thanks. I'm just glad I could finally bring you some good news. No need to get up. I can find my way out.'

Mrs Schwartz got up anyway and trailed Hoke to the door.

'It is good news,' she said, taking his hand after he had opened the door. 'But I don't know what else to say. It's been so long now I thought the police had given up and closed the case.'

Hoke shook his head. 'A murder case is never closed until the killer is tried and put away. For the time being, Mrs Schwartz, at least for a few days, please keep this information to yourself. Don't even tell your husband.'

'I will. How long will it be? Before you make your arrest, I mean.'

'Not long. Just a few more days, and that's a promise, Mrs Schwartz.'

Hoke got into his car, and the woman lingered in the doorway, watching him as he drove away.

Hoke was well pleased by the interrogation. It had gone more smoothly than he had thought it would. Before returning to the station, Hoke stopped at Larry's Hideaway for a shot of Early Times and a beer. Sergeant Armando Quevedo was sitting at the bar, and staring glumly into a seventeen-ounce strawberry margarita. A large strawberry floated on top of the drink. Hoke sat on the stool next to him and ordered a shot of Early Times and a Michelob draft.

'When did you start drinking that shit, Armando?' Hoke said.

Quevedo turned and grimaced. 'It's pretty awful, but the doc said I'd have to give up boilermakers. So I figured if I stuck to this belly wash, I wouldn't overdo it. It's sweeter than hell. Are you off today?'

'No, I'm working. I just stopped for a quickie. Have you come up with any ideas for our Homicide Crack Committee Report?'

'Yeah, one.' Quevedo laughed. 'It came to me the other night. What we should do, you see, is take all of the confiscated crack, all we've got, and all the DEA's got in storage, and then stage a big smoke-in in the Orange Bowl. We invite all the crack abusers and tell 'em they can smoke all they want free. Inasmuch as they'll smoke it until they die, we should be able to kill them all off, or at least the two or three hundred who show up. We can have TV cameras there, Channels Four, Seven, and Ten, and they can shoot the whole scene live. Maybe we can get Geraldo Rivera to emcee the event, and it'll show what crack does to the abusers. We can have black body bags stacked up, too, you see, and the medical examiner. As the ME pronounces each person dead, we can put the body in the bag, and then stack the bags on trucks. What do you think?'

'Sounds like a good idea to me, Armando. You type up the report tonight, and I'll sign it.'

'You talk as if you mean it, Hoke. I was only kidding.'

'Why not? At least it's an idea. I haven't been able to think of anything, and it'll give Brownley something on paper to turn over to the new chief.'

'If you really mean it, I'll type it up tonight when I go on shift. But you'll have to sign it. I sure as hell won't.'

'I'll sign it. Hell, I'd like to watch something like that on TV myself. Bartender!' Hoke beckoned to the man behind the bar. 'Give this gentleman a shot of Early Times and a beer, and dump this pink stuff in the sink.'

Quevedo sighed. 'I guess one shot won't hurt me.' He pushed the strawberry margarita to one side.

'The key to drinking is moderation,' Hoke said. He finished his beer, paid for the drinks, and drove toward the station. A block before he reached the station, Hoke stopped at the curb, emptied the car ashtray into the street, and then drove to the lot to turn in his unmarked car. Mrs Burger's black More cigarette butts, if found in the ashtray, would have netted him another twenty-five-dollar fine.

Chapter Fifteen

While Hoke was watching *Saturday Night Live* on the tube, the phone rang. Hoke cursed and turned the sound down before answering the phone in the kitchen.

'I'm sorry to disturb you this time of night at home, Sergeant Moseley, but I couldn't get ahold of Lieutenant Vitale. I'm Officer Clyde Brown, and my badge number, in case –'

'Never mind, Brown. You didn't wake me. What's up?'

'I'm on a one-man patrol, alone in the car, you see – out here at the airport. There's a redcap watching my car at departures, and I'm phoning here at Eastern from a pay phone. My instructions were to stop at Forty-one thirty-five Poinciana two or three times on my patrol and put the spot on the house number for a minute or so. I asked Vitale why, and he said the instructions came from you, and that was all I needed to know. I was only there, he said, to look for signs of departure.'

'Did you see any?'

'That's why I'm calling, Sergeant. On my second pass the house was dark. I didn't see anything unusual, but I noticed the white Mercedes in the driveway. I turned off the spot, and drove down to the next corner, and parked. I wanted a smoke, and you have to get out of the car to smoke. There's this new rule, you know about –'

'I know about the rule.'

'Okay. Anyway, I lit a cigarette. My car lights were out, and then I saw this white Mercedes drive by and recognized the number. I got back in the car and tailed it out here to the airport. He parked in the Eastern garage, up on the third floor. The man had a suitcase, and when he headed for the elevator, I drove around here to the Eastern loading zone and parked. I told the redcap to watch my car and waited inside the terminal. The man bought a ticket at the Eastern counter and then left for the concourse. After he left, I asked the ticket seller about the ticket, and she said the man's name was L. Black, and he bought a one-way ticket to Seattle. Flight Eight Thirty-two. The plane doesn't leave till twelve forty-five, and I can still pick him up. But I don't have any orders for that or any probable cause. So when I couldn't get ahold of Lieutenant Vitale, I thought I'd better call you. Captain Slater in Homicide gave me your home number.'

'How come you're in a one-man car, Brown?'

'It's part of the new austerity program, I guess. In quiet districts like mine a one-man car is all you need anyway. I can always call for backup. But I'm way the hell out of my district now, and I'm gonna have to get back. Unless you tell me to pick this guy up.'

'No, let him go. You did the right thing by calling me. When you write your report, send a copy to me, and I'll write a commendation for your file. The man's a murder suspect, but I don't have enough evidence to get a warrant. The best thing I could hope for was to have him run. You'd better get back to your car before someone steals it – unless you tipped the redcap in advance. And thanks again for calling me. If you get any flak for leaving your district, I'll cover for you with Lieutentant Vitale.'

Hoke turned off the TV set altogether, sat back in his recliner, and savored the report. There was no doubt in his mind now that Dr Schwartz was the killer. If the frightened bastard had used his own name to fly out to Seattle, the doctor could have said later on that he was on a vacation or visiting a friend. But 'L. Black,' an unimaginative pseudonym for Leo Schwartz, was a dead giveaway.

Before dressing again, Hoke called González at home, and told him to meet him at Dr Schwartz's house.

'Tonight?'

'That's what I said. If you get there before me, don't knock on the door. Just wait for me. We'll talk to Mrs Schwartz together. Bring your notebook, and take down everything that's said.'

'It'll take me about fifteen minutes or so to get there.'

'I may be a little longer, but wait for me out front.'

González's shiny black Mercury Lynx was parked in front of the house at the curb when Hoke arrived. Hoke pulled into the empty driveway, and González joined him on the lawn. He was wearing a white shawl-collared tuxedo jacket, with a red-and-blue bow tie and cummerbund, black tuxedo trousers, and black patent leather shoes.

'Why the semiformal?'

'I had a date,' González said. 'I'd just got home when you called. If things had worked out the way I planned, I wouldn't've been home to answer the damned phone.'

'You have your notebook?'

'Right here. I've also got a minirecorder in my jacket pocket, but I haven't turned it on yet.'

'That's even better. Turn it on now. You're beginning to show initiative after all.'

'It's mine, not the department's.'

'That doesn't matter, if it works.'

The porch light was on, and there was a light in the back of the house. Hoke pressed the bell ring, holding his finger on the button, and listened as chimes clanged softly behind the heavy metal door. Lights came on in the living room, and a square of light appeared on the lawn as the window whitened behind lace curtains. Louise Schwartz opened the door. Her eyelids were red and sore-looking, as if she had been crying. She wore a rose-colored negligee over her white satin nightgown, and her slippers were pink rabbits, upside-down rabbits, including furry heads, bright button eyes, and floppy ears. Hoke had seen slippers like these on sale in department stores but thought that only teenage girls bought them. The long rabbit ears flipped up and down as she invited them in and retreated to the living room.

'If you've come to arrest my husband, Sergeant Moseley, you're too late. He's gone.'

'I know that,' Hoke said. 'He's on his way to Seattle, but the sheriff'll meet the plane. We want to ask you a few questions, however –'

'I didn't know Leo did it – not until tonight, when he told me.'

'That was one of my questions.'

'When Leo came home this evening, he was irritable. Something was bothering him, and he could hardly eat dinner. Mrs Burger, his nurse at the clinic, told him in confidence this afternoon that the police knew who the killer was and would soon be making an arrest. I told him the same thing, what you told me. I know you told me not to, but he knew already, so I went ahead and told him. All he said at dinner was that he wondered who it was. But then he had three drinks after dinner. Brandy. He sometimes has one brandy, but when he poured the third one, I knew that he was worried about something. When I pointed out to him that this was his third drink, he got mad and said he didn't need a woman around to count his drinks for him. He went into his den and closed the door. I thought he'd be out in a few minutes to apologize, but then, when he didn't come out, I went upstairs and got ready for bed –'

She smiled at González. 'You look very nice, Lieutenant.'

González smiled, looking up from his notebook. 'I'm not a lieutenant. I'm just an investigator. Sergeant Moseley here is in charge.'

'You still look very nice.'

'Perhaps if we sat down ...' Hoke suggested.

'I have coffee in the kitchen,' Mrs Schwartz said. 'I could bring it out here, or we could go back to the breakfast room.'

'Sure.'

They followed her down the hallway to the kitchen, and she seated them in the breakfast room. One wall was open to the kitchen, and the other three walls, mostly glass jalousies, were surrounded by a patio. She switched on the lights outside. Hoke looked out and saw a leering stone gnome with a wooden wheelbarrow in the bushes encircling the patio. There was a large green metal frog inside the wheelbarrow. She brought cups and saucers to the table and poured the coffee before seating herself. Hoke put a half-spoon of sugar into his coffee, and noticed that the creamer held real cream, not milk or half-and-half. He also realized that Mrs Schwartz had used some delaying tactics, just as she had been about to tell all. But perhaps she was merely trying to organize her thoughts.

'How long have you known that Dr Schwartz killed your husband?'

She studied the tablecloth for a moment and nibbled her thin lower lip. There was a triangle of flesh-colored adhesive tape plastered between her eyes. This patch was supposed to minimize or reduce frown lines between the twin arches of her eyebrows, but the frown lines were under the tape all the same, Hoke thought.

'Not till tonight,' she said finally, with a shake of her head. 'I'm still trying to take it all in, what Leo told me, and it seems unreal.'

'Perhaps I can help you, Mrs Schwartz. Were you and Leo having an affair before Dr Russell was killed, or did it begin afterward?'

'Afterward. And it wasn't any *affair*, as you put it, because I was a widow then. I don't like the word *affair*. The implication in that word is that something sordid was going on, and that wasn't the case at all.'

'I'm not implying anything. I need information. I'm trying to determine what Dr Schwartz's motivation was, that's all. In their partnership arrangement Dr Farris and Dr Schwartz, after Dr Russell's death, had a fifty-fifty split of the clinic, so it wasn't necessary for Leo Schwartz to marry you in order to profit.'

'I also share in the profits, Sergeant. Not as much, but I still get a five percent profit until the clinic is sold or their partnership is dissolved. The thing is, as Leo told me, my husband was bringing in most of the money. He had the most patients, and he brought in more than half the money, and they were barely making up the second half. My husband, you see, had threatened to leave, to sell out his third interest to another doctor. If he'd done that, they would've been in trouble. That was Leo's motivation. It wasn't for me. I didn't know anything about the business side of the clinic. I got my insurance, of course, but then I turned to Leo for help. I didn't know how to invest my money or run my affairs, and he was very helpful. We saw a lot of each other, and then one thing led to another. It wasn't a mad love affair, and there was no triangle – I want you to understand that. We're mature people, and it seemed like a sensible arrangement to get married. It was easier for me, and it seemed foolish for Leo to keep a separate apartment when he was spending most of his nights here anyway.' She sipped her coffee but held the cup with both hands. 'But I didn't know that Leo had killed my husband. The idea never occurred to me. And I still can't believe it, even though he told me so tonight before he left. Taking lives is not something doctors do. They *save* lives, not take them, and Leo and Max Farris would still have made lots of money, even if my husband had sold out his third of the practice.'

'Some people never have enough money, Mrs Schwartz. Look at Ivan Boesky. Greed was Leo's motivation. This is not a community property state, so Dr Schwartz also got you, your house, the white Mercedes, and Dr Russell's ring. He also made a handsome profit, I suppose, when he sold his condo and moved in here with you. You'd better see a lawyer sometime tomorrow, Mrs Schwartz, even though it's Sunday. Salvage as much as you can before we bring Dr Schwartz back here for trial. Otherwise, he'll try to spend all your money, as well as his, for lawyer's fees. So get a good lawyer, and close your joint accounts.'

'I still can't believe that Leo would do such a thing.'

'He did it, all right. Detective González will be over here in the morning with a statement for you to sign. Try to get some sleep, and if you remember any pertinent details, give them to Detective González. The state's attorney will contact you by Monday or Tuesday.'

'Will I have to testify against Leo in court? I thought a wife wasn't allowed to testify against her husband.'

Hoke laughed. 'That isn't true, although a lot of people think it is. In your case your testimony will be necessary for you to avoid being considered an accomplice, you see. You'll have to clear yourself, which will be easy enough because you were out of town at the time of the murder. You see what I mean?'

She nodded. 'I guess so. Leo has a lawyer on retainer. Should I contact him or get another?'

'Get another. You can't ask Leo's lawyer to help you hide money and assets now, can you? I'm not allowed to recommend anyone, but call some of your women friends – preferably a woman who got a decent divorce settlement – and use her lawyer.'

Hoke got to his feet, and so did González. Hoke took his cup and saucer over to the sink, but González didn't.

'I have one more question, Mrs Schwartz,' Hoke said as he turned at the sink. 'How do you get your garage door open?'

'I – I just unlock it and lift it with one hand. Why?'

'You don't have electronic garage openers then?'

She nodded. 'We have two. Leo keeps one in his car, but I leave the other one here in the house. I had to order replacements when you kept Paul's opener as evidence, but the new ones don't work very well at times. Is this important?'

Hoke shrugged. 'Not any longer. Just a loose end. Let's go, González.'

'Thanks for the coffee, Mrs Schwartz,' González said.

She led the way to the front door to let them out. She opened the front door but blocked it with her body. 'One more thing, Sergeant. Leo took his pistol with him. In his suitcase. I'm afraid he might do something foolish with it. He was very distraught when he left.'

'Thanks for telling me this.'

After she closed the door, Hoke told González to meet him back at the office.

'This is Sunday morning already,' González protested. 'I'm supposed to take my mom to the nine o'clock mass.'

'If you get the statement typed, and then I edit it, and then you retype it without any mistakes, and then you get Mrs Schwartz to sign it before nine, then you can go to mass. Otherwise, phone your mother and tell her to make other plans. Our work is just beginning on this case. Now get moving.'

When he got back to the station, Hoke called the sheriff in Seattle and arranged for him to pick up Leo Schwartz, traveling under the name L. Black, when the plane landed at the airport.

'He'll have the murder weapon in his baggage, so it'll have to be returned as well. Even though he's a murder suspect, Schwartz isn't a dangerous man, and he likes high living. So if you can, Sheriff, make jail uncomfortable for him. Don't isolate him, but shove him into the drunk tank. I want him to suffer enough discomfort so he won't fight extradition.'

'I know what you mean, Sergeant. Two deputies will meet him at the airport.'

'It'll probably be Monday before I can wire you a confirmation order, but the weapon alone will be enough to hold him without bail till we get the extradition order.'

'No problem. How's the weather down there in Miami?'

'It was about eighty-five today – maybe a little higher than that.'

'It's cold and wet here. I've never been to Miami, but I'd like to come down there on a vacation sometime.'

'If you ever do, call me, and I'll show you a few high spots.'

'I might just take you up on that someday. How far's Miami from Disney World?'

'Hell, you don't want to go there, Sheriff. Orlando's a high-crime area, but if you come to Miami, I'll get you a permit to carry your weapon while you're here.'

The sheriff laughed. 'Okay, Sergeant Moseley. Leo Schwartz traveling as L. Black.'

'Right.'

It was almost 7:00 A.M. before González had a statement typed well enough to satisfy Hoke. Hoke made three photocopies and gave all four copies to González to take to Mrs Schwartz to sign.

'She'll probably be asleep now,' González said. 'Perhaps if I went over after the nine o'clock mass, she'd be awake.'

'You'll go now, before she changes her mind and before she talks to a lawyer who'll advise her not to sign anything. Then come back and put the statements in the safe. I'll probably still be here because I've got to write my notes for the file and a memo to Major Brownley. I want you to type up your notes, too, but you can come back and do it after you go to mass. I'll want to talk to Brownley first thing tomorrow to see how we should handle this thing with the state attorney. Here we are, with a solved case handed to us on a silver fucking platter, and all you can think about is taking your mother to mass.'

After González left the office, Hoke typed a redline memo to Major Brownley and put it in his box. He tried to phone Lieutenant Vitale in Traffic but couldn't get a line on his whereabouts. He then typed another redline to Vitale, telling him to call off the surveillance and commending Officer Brown for his alertness and initiative. Then he drove home.

Hoke wanted to be awake when Ellita and the girls got home, so he didn't undress and go to bed. He removed his shoes and sat back in his recliner, so he would awaken when they came through the door. As soon as he levered the seat back, his mind began to race, thinking of all the things he still had to do. Then, with an effort, and using a trick that had worked for him before, he imagined a heavy black blind in his mind. His fingers grasped the pull cord, and he slowly lowered the black mental blind. When it was down, all the way down, and completely dark, he fell into a heavy sleep.

Chapter Sixteen

Hoke awoke with a groan at ten-thirty. His neck, still bruised and sore, had developed a crick in it from his position in the chair. Shooting pains pulsed tiny darts into the backs of his eyes. Hoke showered and shaved, scrubbed his teeth, and rinsed his dentures in Listerine before adjusting them in his mouth. He made coffee, took three Tylenol, and was on his third cup of coffee when the phone rang. It was Major Brownley.

'Did I wake you?' Brownley asked.

'No, I was awake. Did you read my redliner?'

'Yes, I'm in my office now. That's one of the things I want to talk about. I'm taking you off the Dr Russell homicide. I gave it to Sergeant Quevedo to finish up.'

'There's still a lot to do, Willie,' Hoke protested. 'I've got to interview Dr Max Farris, and I want to talk to Mrs Burger again at some length. I told her something in confidence, and she could hardly wait to pass it on to Schwartz. The nurse knows a lot more than she ever let on when I first talked to her. Then I –'

'Never mind, Hoke. Quevedo's taken over. I've already given him the file, and González can fill him in on any other stuff he needs to know.'

'González doesn't know everything, Willie. He doesn't know about the garage door.'

'What garage door?'

'Mrs Schwartz's garage door. Sometimes it opens with the electronic opener, and sometimes it doesn't.'

'Hell, they're all like that at times, Hoke. Mine doesn't always work either. I think it's the humidity. Why is it so important?'

Hoke thought for a moment and then laughed. 'It isn't important, not any longer. It's just a loose end I wanted to tie up. If Dr Schwartz still has the murder weapon, it won't be an issue.'

'He's in jail now in Seattle, and the weapon – or *a* weapon – was recovered. I've already had word on that. Later on, Quevedo has a few questions, he can talk to you, but I don't think you'll have much time for him.'

'Even if you take me off the case, I'll have to testify at the trial.'

'That'll be two or three months from now. I'll say it slow: You are officially off the case.'

'I don't understand this, Willie. What –'

'I'm trying to tell you. Do you know where Molly's Coffee Shop is, on the Trail?'

'Not exactly. Although I remember passing by it.'

'It's at Eighth Street and Third Avenue. At the end of a new little shopping center there. Molly's the new chief's sister-in-law, so he likes to eat breakfast there two or three times a week. Anyway, you're to meet the new chief there tomorrow morning at eight o'clock.'

'What about? This isn't another weird undercover job like that Immokalee fiasco, is it? If it is, forget it. I'd rather go back into uniform and turn with the signals on Flagler.'

'I can't tell you what it's about, Hoke. The new chief will do that. Just be at Molly's at eight. That's all I can tell you.'

'Will you be there, Willie?'

'No. It'll just be you and the new chief.'

'I'm not going to do any more undercover work, Willie.'

'I wish I could tell you about it, Hoke, but I can't. I'll just say you'll be surprised. Pleasantly surprised. Okay?'

'I'll be there. One more thing, while we're on the phone. Let's do the division a favor and transfer González the hell out of Homicide. Ordinarily, when a man loses his ignorance, he doesn't regain it, but that doesn't hold true for González.'

'We're short seven detectives already, Hoke, counting three on suspension.'

'We can get a mutual. Do you know Murdock, over in Robbery?'

'I think so. What about Murdock?'

'I talked to him about a month ago, and he wants to get out of Robbery and into Homicide. He's been in plain clothes for about six years or so, and maybe we could make a mutual transfer between him and González.'

'No, we can't do that, Hoke, even if Robbery was willing to let Murdock go. It would throw off the ethnic balance. On a mutual transfer we'd have to have another Hispanic. But I'll check around, and if I can trade González for another Hispanic somewhere, I'll see what I can do.'

'That doesn't make sense, Willie. Murdock's an experienced investigator, and González is good with figures and statistics. He'd fit in well over in Robbery. They could let him handle inventories and simple things like that.'

'I know you're right, but Murdock's a WASP, and we can only make a mutual for another Hispanic.'

'Forget it then. Anything else, Willie?'

'No … I don't think so. What've you heard from Ellita?'

'She's just fine. I'll tell her you sent your regards.' Hoke hung up quickly before Brownley could ask any more questions.

A long blue stretch Lincoln pulled up in front of the house at eleven-thirty. As Hoke watched from behind the screen door, Sue Ellen and Aileen got out, and the driver opened the trunk to get their luggage. The driver, a squat dark-faced man with short muscular arms, was probably Goya y Goya, Hoke thought. Hoke retreated to his bedroom instead of going outside to help the girls with their luggage and to avoid giving the chauffeur a tip. Ellita and Hutton – 'Donnie' – were not in the car. When Hoke heard the girls talking in the living room, he walked back down the hall to greet them. Both girls were wearing straw hats, purchased from straw market vendors in Nassau, and their faces were bright with sunburn. Aileen ran to Hoke, hugged and kissed him. Sue Ellen, showing more restraint, kissed him on the cheek.

'How was Nassau, and where's Ellita?' Hoke said.

The two girls exchanged glances.

'I've got a present for you, Daddy,' Sue Ellen said, opening her bag on the couch.

'Me, too,' Aileen said, getting her bag.

Something is wrong, Hoke thought. So far neither one of the girls had looked him in the eye. Sue Ellen hadn't redyed her hair blue; it was now brown and curly, and she was wearing a new powder-blue sundress. The skirt barely reached her bony knees.

She handed him a gray T-shirt with dark red printing: MY DAUGHTER WENT TO THE BAHAMAS AND ALL I GOT WAS THIS LOUSY T-SHIRT.

'Thanks,' Hoke said, checking the collar to see if it was extra large. It was. 'I appreciate the sentiment. When I came home, I didn't know where you were. There was no note, and I had a problem finding out where you'd gone.'

'We wanted to leave a note, Daddy,' Aileen said, 'but Ellita wouldn't let us.'

'Why not? It's customary in this house, isn't it, to say where you're going and when you'll be back? I was worried, for Christ's sake.'

Aileen handed Hoke a small blue box, tied with a piece of red string. 'Open it, Daddy. Go ahead.'

Hoke untied the string and took off the lid. It was a ceramic salt and pepper set, covered with tiny coquina shells. One cellar read 'Salt' and 'Nassau'; the other read 'Pepper' and 'New Providence.' A few shells had become unglued and were loose in the bottom of the box.

'Thanks, honey,' Hoke said, putting the lid back on the box. 'This is very nice and something we can all use. Where's Ellita?'

Sue Ellen sat on the couch and placed her knees together. She clasped her hands and looked at her father, widening her eyes. 'You're going to find out sooner or later, Daddy, but I'm sorry you're hearing it from me instead of Ellita. Ellita and Donnie got married. That's why they didn't come back with us. They're going to stay another week for their honeymoon at the Paradise Island Hotel and then come back on the boat next Sunday.'

'Is that why you didn't leave a note? Were you afraid I'd fly over to the wedding? This doesn't sound like Ellita.'

'You don't understand, Daddy. She was afraid. She thought you might do something or other to stop them from getting married.'

'Hutton's on parole. Did he have permission to leave the country?'

'I don't think so, but you see what I mean? Ellita was sure you'd try to stop them some way.'

'It's none of my business what Ellita does. Why should I care if she gets married – even to a convicted killer like Hutton? What the hell, she's thirty-three years old. Who's taking care of Pepe?'

'The hotel got them a nurse for the baby. There's no problem getting women as maids in Nassau. Me and Aileen didn't go to the wedding, but –'

'Aileen and I.'

'Aileen and I. But we had a little party afterward, in their stateroom on the boat. Just the four of us, with wine and a plate of canapés the steward brought in. And Donnie gave both of us fifty dollars apiece to gamble with. I won eighty dollars playing blackjack –'

'They let you gamble? You're underage.'

Sue Ellen shrugged. 'I had my fake ID, but no one asked to see it. Besides, when I've got makeup on, I look eighteen.'

'When did they decide to get married?'

'Before we left, I guess, because they shared a cabin. But they didn't tell us about it till we got on the ship. Ellita, like I said, was afraid you'd find out and stop them some way.'

'I wonder why she'd think something like that. I'm happy for them, for Christ's sake. He's got plenty of money, and without the crying baby we can have a little peace and quiet around here. You're the oldest, Sue Ellen, so you can have Ellita's big bedroom. It's about time you girls had your own rooms anyway.'

To Hoke's surprise, the girls didn't argue about his hasty decision. Instead, they told him about their trip, the meals on the ship, playing the slot machines, and riding around Nassau on the wrong side of the road on rented motorbikes. They didn't want to talk about the marriage, and because Hoke knew that telling about a cruise afterward was the best part of it, he let them ramble on. They weren't hungry, having eaten a large breakfast on the ship, but he made sandwiches anyway. They ate them and went to bed. The girls had stayed up in the ship's casino until two-thirty the night before and then had to get up early because they were on the first sitting for breakfast. Aileen had lost the fifty dollars Hutton had given her on the slot machines, but she didn't mind because it wasn't her money in the first place. She had won at first, but it had all gone back into the machines.

While the girls napped, Hoke went into Ellita's room and put a sheet on the floor. He placed all her clothes from the closet on the sheet and pulled it together into a huge bundle. He needed another sheet to hold all her things from her dresser drawers. He took the two bundles out to the living room and placed them by the door. There were a lot of Ellita's and Pepe's possessions and furniture in the house, but she could sort them out later, after she got back. He knocked down her double bed, however, and put the carved head- and footboard and mattress in the Florida room, so Sue Ellen could have room for her bed when she woke up.

Hoke then drove to the Green Lakes Shopping Center and got a haircut. He bought a white button-down oxford cloth shirt at K-mart, and a green-and-white-striped necktie, so he would look presentable when he met the new chief in the morning. He drank two draft beers at the Green Grotto before driving home. The girls were up, and he helped Sue Ellen move into the master bedroom.

Hoke cooked spaghetti for dinner and made three lettuce and tomato salads and a pitcher of iced tea. There was ice cream in the freezer, but no one wanted any. Both girls were pleased to have their own rooms, but they were subdued at dinner. Reduced to three people, the family seemed very small, and the girls had run out of things to say about the cruise.

While the girls did the dishes, Hoke watched 60 Minutes on television. There was a rerun of The Burning Bed on Channel 33, and they all watched it together. Farrah Fawcett was beaten and battered by her drunken husband for an hour and a half, and then she set fire to him when he fell asleep and drove away in the car with her kids.

'What I don't understand,' Sue Ellen said when the movie ended, 'is why Farrah ever married a creep like that in the first place.'

'Probably because he asked her,' Hoke said. 'Women are like that, even mature women. Sometimes that's all it takes.'

'I don't think I'll ever get married,' Sue Ellen said.

'Me neither,' Aileen said.

'Good,' Hoke said. 'You can stay home and take care of me. That's my life's ambition: to grow old and be a burden on someone. Thanks, girls, you've made me a very happy father.'

'I don't mean I won't live with someone someday,' Sue Ellen said. 'That's natural. A woman's entitled to a sex life. But if you

859

get married and have kids like Farrah did, the man thinks he owns you.'

'It's just a movie, Sue Ellen. Who wants some ice cream?'

'I don't think so, Daddy. I'm going to bed.'

'I can hardly hold my eyes open,' Aileen said.

They kissed him good night and went off to their respective rooms and closed the doors.

Hoke stayed up and drank a couple of beers while he watched the tube. But he couldn't get interested in anything and soon turned off the set. He wondered what the new chief wanted to see him about. The new chief of the Miami Police Department was always called the new chief because he was always a new chief. The average tenure for a new chief was about eighteen months. The average tenure for a city manager (who hired and fired the police chiefs) was also eighteen months. So every time the city commission fired a city manager and hired a new one, the new one soon found a reason to fire the new chief and put in a new chief of his own. Then the new new chief shook things up in the department, transferring and promoting people he thought would be loyal to him. The three assistant chiefs, all colonels, had all been demoted and promoted several times apiece. Survival at or near the top was a tough proposition, no doubt about it. And the three assistant chiefs had to be the right ethnic balance – one black, one Hispanic, and one white man (but the white man couldn't be a Catholic because the Hispanic was a Catholic).

The new new chief was moving cautiously so far – Hoke had to give him credit for that – although he had vowed, when he was sworn in, that he intended to modernize the department, whatever that meant. The city manager was new, and his new chief was new, so there probably wouldn't be any radical changes for at least another year or so, Hoke thought.

Hoke popped the top on another can of Old Style and went outside on the front lawn to drink it. The house across the street was dark, and most of the lights in the other houses on the block were turned out. Tomorrow was a Monday, and people had to go to work again. They went to bed early in the Green Lakes sub-division on Sunday nights. Hoke returned to the kitchen, got an ice pick out of the utility drawer, and then crossed the street. He jabbed the point of the pick into the left front tire of Donald Hutton's Henry J. As the air hissed out, the sound seemed to direct him around the little car, and he punched through the other three tires. As the air hissed out, the little car sank perceptibly.

'There's a wedding present for you, you bastard,' Hoke said softly. Then, feeling a little sheepish but happier, he returned to his house and put the ice pick back into the drawer. Hoke undressed and finished his beer while sitting on the edge of his army cot. His muscles were sore, his cracked ribs ached, and his head buzzed from the beers. He fell asleep as soon as his head hit the pillow.

Chapter Seventeen

Molly's coffee shop didn't have much of a breakfast crowd, Hoke thought, but when he examined the menu, he could see why. There was no pass-through coffee bar, and this was an anomaly for Little Havana. Most of the Cuban restaurants on Eighth Street served a *desayuno especial* – two fried eggs, ham or bacon, long slices of margarined Cuban toast, and *café con leche* – for $1.49. Molly's breakfast was standard American – two eggs (your way), bacon, ham, or sausage, with grits or home-fried potatoes and white bread toast for $2.79. Coffee, at fifty cents, was extra, and there were no free refills. Molly probably made her money, if she made her nut at all, he thought, with the white-collar lunch crowd, workers from the office buildings over on Brickell Avenue. There were several salads on the lunch menu and a few light lunch items that would appeal to legal secretaries.

Hoke got a table by the window and ordered coffee. He was early, and he had brought the sports section from the *Miami Herald* along to read while he waited for the new chief. He read a long interview with Vinny Testaverde, the Miami Hurricanes' hotshot quarterback, and then folded the paper and tossed it onto the empty table behind him. In another five years, Testaverde would be a multimillionaire, Hoke thought, and he'd be trying to make ends meet on a pension of $734 a month, unless, of course, he stayed on the force and tried for thirty years. He shuddered at the prospect.

Hoke signaled the waiter, a sullen-faced Iranian, and asked for another cup of coffee. The new chief came in and joined Hoke at the window table at eight-fifteen. Hoke had talked to the new chief only a couple of times, but then the man had had his job for only three months and hadn't settled in. Hoke hadn't made up his mind about him yet. The old new chief had always worn his uniform, one he had designed himself, complete with four stars on each collar and four more on each epaulet. His cap bill was loaded with gold scrambled eggs. He had been a reserve major in the U.S. Marines, and by giving himself four stars to wear, he had achieved his lifetime ambition to become a general. And like most generals in the army and marines, he had delegated everything, including some important decisions he should have made himself. When a few scandals broke, he didn't know whom to blame, so he had been fired.

The new chief never wore a uniform and probably didn't have one. He wore tailored tropical suits, complete with vests – even when the temperature soared into the nineties. And when he left the station in his Lincoln town car, he wore a white panama hat with a one-inch black silk hatband. He had had a few years' experience as a police chief in Lawrence, Kansas, but he had spent most of his adult life in college classrooms, lecturing students on sociology and juvenile delinquency. He was purportedly an authority on juvenile delinquency and had written two books on the subject that were used as texts in a dozen colleges. At least he wrote clearly, compared with the old new chief's memos and written directives. The ex-marine new chief had been semiliterate, and Bill Henderson used to circle all his sentence fragments and misspelled words with a red grease pencil before posting his memos on the bulletin board.

The new chief placed his panama carefully on an empty chair, smiled at Hoke, and said: 'It's nice of you to join me here, Sergeant Moseley, and I appreciate it.' The new chief was in his early forties, and the pale skin beneath his blue eyes was puffy. His black hair was quite full, with a widow's peak, and two locks were curled on each side of his forehead like commas. Either his wife cut his hair, Hoke thought, or he paid at least thirty bucks for his haircuts.

'I didn't have a hell of a lot of choice.'

'Did you order yet?'

'No, sir, I was waiting for you.'

'I'm sorry I held you up, but I had a phone call just as I was leaving my apartment. My sister-in-law owns this place, and I hope she can make a go of it. She and my brother were divorced three years ago, and if she can make a decent living here, he'll be able to ease up on some of his alimony payments.'

'I know what you mean, Chief, but it doesn't work out that way. My ex-wife married a ballplayer who makes three hundred and twenty-five thousand a year, and I still have to pay alimony. It was in the settlement, you see, when we got our no-fault, and I was dumb enough at the time to sign it.'

'Perhaps if you petitioned the judge?'

Hoke shrugged. 'I could do that, I suppose. The kids live with me now, as you probably know, and they didn't when we got our divorce. What I do now is send her a check when I have some money left over and skip it when I don't. And about two weeks after a skipped check I get a nasty call from her bitchy lawyer.'

The Iranian came over and took their order. The new chief ordered two three-minute eggs in a cup, one slice of dry toast, and a small glass of orange juice. Hoke ordered a Belgian waffle with sausage links and told the waiter to have the cook heat the syrup.

'I always try to eat a light breakfast,' the new chief explained. 'I drink coffee all day long in the office, and Mrs Sincavage, my secretary, always has a box of Dunkin' Donuts on her desk. About ten or ten-thirty I usually succumb and take one.'

'My father does that,' Hoke said, smiling. 'He loves jelly doughnuts.'

'How is your father?'

'He's in fine shape for his age. He plans on living forever, and I think he'll make it, too.' Hoke lighted a Kool, and the new chief frowned.

'You're still smoking?'

'Yes, sir. It's an acquired habit.'

'Have you tried to quit yet?'

'I'm not ready to quit yet.'

'You can do it if you want to badly enough. I smoked two packs a day, and I managed to quit.'

'Is that why we met this morning, sir, to discuss my smoking?'

The new chief exposed a row of tiny blackened lower teeth. 'I'm sorry. Ex-smokers, like ex-drinkers, have a tendency to preach the good word. No, that isn't why I asked you here. Ahh – here's breakfast.'

The waiter placed the plates on the table. Hoke tested the syrup in the small white porcelain pitcher with his forefinger. 'It isn't heated. Take it back to the chef and have him warm it up.' The waiter shrugged and left with the little pitcher.

The new chief crumbled his slice of toast into his runny eggs and stirred the mess with his spoon. Hoke buttered his waffle, cut it into bite-size pieces, and then cut up his three link sausages. The waiter returned with a steaming little pitcher of syrup.

Hoke dribbled some of the syrup onto his chopped-up waffle and dug into his breakfast. They ate silently. The new chief shot quick glances at Hoke occasionally, but he didn't say anything until he finished eating his eggs and drained the four-ounce juice glass.

'We've got some problems in the department, Moseley, as you are well aware.' He took out a round tin of Copenhagen snuff and removed the lid. The lid was of silver, made to fit the regular container of Copenhagen, and an eagle was engraved on it. He put a small pinch of snuff behind his lower lip, replaced the lid, and put the can back into his jacket pocket. 'Eight cops are now waiting trial for murder, and three cops are in jail waiting trial on home invasion charges. It's bad enough to invade a home, terrorize the residents, and rob them, as these men did. On the murders the men killed were all drug dealers, so there's no loss there, but they weren't killed in a legitimate raid   they were killed during a drug rip-off. At least three of these cops'll be exonerated, but it looks bad for the department when you have that many cops being tried for murder. And when it looks bad for the department, it makes me look bad.'

'It not only looks bad, it is bad, Chief, but it's the money. When a patrolman's only making twenty thousand a year or so and can make ten in only two hours on a drug deal, it's hard for him to turn down. Especially if he's married and has a family.'

'Would you risk your career and take a chance on going to prison for ten thousand bucks?'

'Not a chance, Chief. But my background's different from these younger cops'. Besides, my father's rich and in his late seventies.

When he dies, I'll get a good chunk of cash, even though his new wife'll get most of it. In addition to that, I have only five years to go for retirement.'

'I know this, Moseley. Major Brownley and I have gone over your jacket and records, and we know more about you than you do because you've forgotten a lot of it. Major Brownley recommended you for promotion, and I concurred. In two more days, Wednesday at ten, I'll swear you in as a lieutenant in your new office.'

'Can't I think this over, Chief? I like working on the cold cases, and so far I've been doing a fair job. I know I took the exam and all, but that's because I didn't think I'd get promoted.'

'No, you don't have a choice. You're going to head Internal Affairs. What you'll have to do, and you'll report directly to me, is get rid of our bad cops before they've had a chance to become bad cops. I want you to begin with the new graduating class at the academy. Check their jackets, interview each man personally, and if you have any doubts about any one of them, check his name off the graduation list. They've all been tested for drug use and had a battery of psychological tests, but that isn't good enough. If you don't want a man to graduate, you don't have to give a reason. Just scratch his name off the list. There are also some pending suspensions to investigate, but you'll know how to handle these without any trouble. Later on, maybe by next Friday, we'll get together in my office and discuss further probes. I'll have Mrs Sincavage call you and set up a time.'

'This is a big responsibility, Chief. What about Lieutenant Norbert? I don't respect him, and I don't think I can work with an asshole like him.'

'You're Norbert's replacement. He's retiring. He's got twenty-four years in, and I persuaded him to put in his papers. He retires Wednesday, and you'll take over the office. There'll be a little ceremony for both of you in the office when he retires and you're sworn in. The press'll be there because I want the change to be known by everyone as soon as possible.'

'I'd still like some time to think this over, Chief.'

'There's nothing to think over. The decision's been made, Lieutenant. Incidently, Moseley, Sheriff Boggis, over in Collier

County, was mighty grateful about the way you took care of the little problem he had. And that's good for us, too, to have a friend of the department over in Collier County. Don't look so surprised. I had Brownley set this up to see how well you could work on a secret assignment, and you came through beautifully, just as Brownley told me you would.'

The new chief got to his feet and waved to the waiter. 'Put these breakfasts on my tab, son,' he said when the waiter came over, 'and add a fifteen percent tip for yourself. And be sure to tell Molly, when she comes in this morning, that I was here for breakfast.'

The waiter nodded, picked up two empty plates, and turned away.

Hoke started to rise, but the new chief put a restraining hand on his shoulder. 'Stay and finish your coffee, Lieutenant. Take some time off, and I'll see you Wednesday morning at ten. Till then clear out your desk, do some shopping. Buy a new suit perhaps.'

The new chief left abruptly, departing through the front door without looking back.

Hoke sat still for a moment, benumbed, and then leaped up from the table. He stumbled slightly as he rushed through the empty tables to the men's room at the end of the short hallway. When he started to remove his teeth in the men's room, he noticed he was still clutching his coffee cup. He put the cup into the sink, removed his teeth, and then vomited into the toilet bowl. It all came up: sausage, waffle, warm syrup, coffee. Hoke flushed the toilet. He washed his face at the sink, let the cold water flow over his wrists, and then put his teeth back in.

Major Brownley and the new chief, with an assist from Mel Peoples, had set him up. Hoke had suspected something that morning at Monroe Station, when he had asked the major if this was a test of some kind, but he hadn't suspected anything so deviously Byzantine. The new chief had come up with this weird plan to make sure that he would have something on him; it was a way to ensure that Hoke would be his man. But it wasn't blackmail; it was a stalemate, a Mexican standoff. There was no way that the new chief could use this knowledge without implicating himself,

Brownley, and Mel Peoples. If Hoke didn't like it, he could resign from the department, and they wouldn't do anything to prevent that. But if he did resign, he would lose everything – his occupation and his pension. A man is defined by his job, by his work, and if he weren't a detective, he would be nothing. Nothing.

Hoke rinsed his cup at the sink, returned to his table, and ordered fresh coffee. He was calmer now and could think a little more clearly. Deep down he had wanted to be promoted to lieutenant, but it had seemed so far away in the future he hadn't let himself think about it. Looking for dirty cops was a rotten job, and even the straight cops – the majority of the department – resented the men in IA. But a good man was needed for the job, and he knew that he could handle it. Norbert, ever since he got his twenty years in, had been coasting, and there was a lot of work to be done to clean up the department. Now that he thought it over, he realized that the new chief, with Brownley's recommendation, had picked the best man for the appointment. Not only did he know where a lot of bodies were buried, but he now had the shovel to dig them up. He had no intention of confining himself to investigating cadets.

He was feeling better about his new promotion and appointment already. But first things first. He'd order a new tailored uniform, and buy two new black suits like the ones Captain Slater usually wore, black silk, with a little shine to the material. The new chief had wanted his own man in the office, but he would learn, in time, that Hoke Moseley was nobody's man but his own.

Hoke finished his coffee, dropped a crumpled dollar bill on the table, drove home, and phoned his father in Riviera Beach to tell him about his promotion to lieutenant.

Chapter Eighteen

Three weeks later, on a Sunday afternoon, Hoke was fixing sandwiches in the dining room. He had a plate of assorted cold cuts, a loaf of rye bread, and some freshly picked beefsteak tomatoes he had purchased that afternoon from a stand on Krome Avenue. Aileen sat across the table from him, watching, and Sue Ellen was making potato salad in the kitchen.

Evening meals were rather casual now that Ellita had gone away. They rarely ate together in the evenings, except on Sunday, although Hoke had taken the girls out to dinner at Burger King a few times.

The Huttons, Donald, Ellita and Pepe, lived in a new two-bedroom condominium apartment Hutton had bought in Hallandale. Hutton wanted to be near the track, he told Ellita, but Hoke knew that Hutton hadn't liked the girls coming across the street all the time to see Ellita and the baby. Hutton had also sold his Henry J by putting a classified ad in both daily papers. Before they had moved out of the house across the street, a man had come by for it with a tow truck. Ellita still had her little Honda Civic, but Hutton had bought a new Mercury Lynx station wagon to haul the baby's stuff around with them when they went out together.

Except for wishing Ellita good luck, when she returned from Nassau with a gold band on her ring finger, Hoke hadn't spoken to her again. When Hutton came over for her furniture and other belongings, Hoke had gone to Larry's Hideaway and stayed there until everything was moved.

'What do you want on your sandwich? Mustard or mayonnaise?'

'Mayonnaise,' Aileen said.

Sue Ellen came in from the kitchen with a bowl of potato salad and placed it on the table. 'Help yourself to potato salad. I still have to sugar the tea.'

'D'you want mustard or mayonnaise on your sandwich?'

'Both.' Sue Ellen returned to the kitchen.

'Daddy,' Aileen said, 'don't you ever miss Ellita?'

Hoke shook his head. 'Did you ever watch Ellita eat a Cuban sandwich? First, she'd nibble the bread all the way around, and then she'd take off the top slice. She'd eat all the ham with her fingers, and then she'd put the top slice back on the cheese and pork. After the ham was gone, she no longer had a Cuban sandwich, for Christ's sake, she had a pork and cheese sandwich. If she wanted a pork and cheese sandwich, why didn't she order one in the first place instead of asking for a Cuban sandwich? Hell, why would I miss a woman who ate a sandwich like that?'

Suddenly, Aileen began to cry. Tears, unchecked, streamed down her cheeks.

'What's the matter? Why are you crying?'

'Be-because,' she said, finally, still sobbing, 'because you can't!'